The Dawning
Trilogy

BRIAN RATHBONE

Copyright © 2008-2016 Brian Rathbone

All rights reserved.

ISBN: 1530643058
ISBN-13: 978-1530643059

CALL OF THE HERALD

Prologue

Within his cabin, General Dempsy adjusted his uniform, making certain every medal was straight and every button oriented properly. Moving automatically to counter the movements of the ship was normally as natural to him as breathing, but he felt unsteady on his feet, as if his years of sailing had suddenly been forgotten. It was not a feeling he was accustomed to. At sea or just about anywhere on Godsland, his power was undeniable, his orders obeyed without question. There was one place, however, where his power was surpassed, and even a man of his accomplishments must exercise great caution: Adderhold, seat of the Zjhon empire. It was from there that Archmaster Belegra ruled with an unforgiving will, and it was to there that General Dempsy was destined.

He had no reason to expect anything but a warm welcome, given his success, but there was an uneasy feeling in his gut. Again, automatically, he adjusted his uniform, as if a single stitch out of place could decide his fate. The general cursed himself for such weakness, yet he jumped when there came a knock at his cabin door. After cursing himself again, he answered in his usual commanding tone: "Come."

Mate Pibbs presented himself and saluted. "Adderhold is within sight, sir. We've been cleared by the sentry ships, and there is a slip reserved for us. Do you wish to be on deck when we land, sir?"

General Dempsy nodded, and Mate Pibbs saluted again before turning on his heel. To some the salute is a source of great pride and a feeling of power, and most times General Dempsy felt much the same, but on this day it felt like mockery. After a final check of his uniform, he made his way to the prow. From there, he watched Adderhold grow larger and more intimidating with every passing moment. It was a feeling that should have passed long before, but the builders of Adderhold had done their job well. The place looked as if it could swallow his entire fleet in a single strike.

When they reached the docks, General Dempsy was unsure of what to think. There was no fanfare; no throng awaited the returning army, and there was not so much as a victory dinner to celebrate their conquest of an entire continent. The Greatland was theirs to rule, yet Adderhold bustled with preparations for war. Barges surrounded the island, and they sat low in the water, piled high with grain and supplies, ready to transport the goods to the waiting armada. These were not the usual preparations for an assault on a coastal province. The scale of their provisions foretold a lengthy sea voyage, and the taste of victory turned to bile.

General Dempsy knew, long before the page arrived with his new orders, that the Church had declared holy war. He tried to convince himself otherwise, but what he saw could only mean an invasion of the Godfist, a preemptive strike intended to stave off the prophecy. He thought it was sheer madness. Archmaster Belegra would ruin everything by sending them on a fool's quest. This was a hunt for some fantasized adversary, one not only destined to destroy the entire Zjhon nation, but also one that might herald the return of a goddess Archmaster Belegra and the devotees of the Zjhon Church had both dreamed of and feared. The devout believed that Istra would imbue them with miraculous gifts but that her presence would also mark the return of their greatest adversary.

In the face of such fanaticism, General Dempsy struggled to maintain his equilibrium. To him, the Zjhon beliefs made little sense. Though he had played his role in many ceremonies, he believed none of it; he simply did what the Church asked of him because it furthered his own goals. His military genius had only served to strengthen the Zjhon and their beliefs, and though it had granted him the power he desired, he suddenly wondered if it had been a mistake--a grave and deadly mistake. To say his army was unprepared for an assault on the Godfist was a gross understatement. Two-thirds of his men came from lands that had only recently been conquered; few were well trained, and fewer still were loyal. With his experienced and trusted men spread throughout the regiments, he was barely able to maintain control. He knew it was a suicide mission and that it would be years before they were ready to undertake a long-distance campaign.

Orders to get his army ready for the invasion confirmed the insanity, and when he saw them, he requested an immediate audience with Archmaster Belegra under the pretense of misunderstanding the mission. It was highly unusual for any member of the armies to meet with the archmaster in person, but General Dempsy felt he was entitled. He and his men had offered up their lives for the empire, and they deserved to know why they were being thrown away.

Days passed before he was granted the audience, and that gave him time to ponder every word he might use to implore the archmaster to change his mind. When a page finally arrived with his summons, the uncertainty was festering in his belly. Archmaster Belegra was the only person with enough power to have him executed, and his every instinct warned that the wrong choice of words could send him to the headsman's block.

A slight figure in dark robes greeted General Dempsy with little more than a slight bow. Though his features were concealed within a deep hood, the general knew of him. He was the nameless boy whose insolence had cost him his tongue. As he led General Dempsy to a private hall, he served as a silent warning. This had the potential to be a very dangerous encounter.

When he entered the hall, General Dempsy saw Archmaster Belegra swathed in thick robes and huddled in an ornate chair that was pulled up close to the fire. Though the years had barely grayed his hair, he looked like a feeble old man. As austere as ever, he did not acknowledge General Dempsy in any way, as if he were oblivious to his presence.

"A humble servant of the Zjhon requests the consideration of the Church," General Dempsy said in a polite tone, trying to sound unassuming, but he feared it came out sounding forced and insincere. Archmaster Belegra did not look at him, nor did he speak; he simply extended his right hand and waited. The general did not hesitate in moving to the archmaster's side, taking his hand, and kissing the signet ring, wishing to dispense with protocol as quickly as possible.

"The Church recognizes her child and will suffer you to speak."

"With all due respect, Your Eminence, I must ask you to reconsider this course of action. Launching an attack on such a distant nation, when we've barely secured the lands surrounding us, will put everything we've achieved at risk." General Dempsy was more direct than was advisable, but he was determined and pushed on. "It's not that I don't believe the prophecies, but sending two-thirds of our strength on a--" Archmaster Belegra raised an eyebrow, and Dempsy stopped. He knew he was treading in dangerous waters, and he preferred to keep his head.

"The prophecies are quite clear on this matter, General, but I will refresh your memory if I must. Vestra, God of the Sun, has ruled Godsland's skies for nearly three thousand years, but he will not always reign alone. Istra, Goddess of the Night, shall return to preside over the night skies. A harbinger shall be born of her hand and will be revealed by the power they wield. Thus, the advent of Istra shall be heralded. Faithful of the Church, beware, for the Herald of Istra shall desire your destruction and will endeavor to undo all you have wrought."

General Dempsy despaired. The prophecies were impossible to argue since no proof could be offered to discredit them. They were sacred and above reproach.

"It is your responsibility to protect this nation and all the inhabitants of the Greatland. The Herald of Istra poses an imminent threat to the Church and the entire Zjhon empire. The holy documents have rewarded us with clues regarding the timing of Istra's return, and we must use these divine gifts to our full advantage. To do otherwise would be sacrilege and blasphemy. Is that clear?"

General Dempsy nodded, mute. He struggled to find words that would drive away the madness, but they remained beyond his grasp.

"You have your orders, General. You know your duty; the army is to set sail for the Godfist by the new moon and is not to return without the Herald of Istra. Go forth with the blessings of the Zjhon Church."

Chapter 1

Life is the greatest of all mysteries, and though I seek to solve its many riddles, my deepest fear is that I will succeed.
--CiCi Bajur, philosopher

* * *

Immersed in its primordial glow, a comet soared through space with incredible speed. Three thousand years had passed since it last shed its light upon the tiny blue planet known to its inhabitants as Godsland, and the effects had been cataclysmic. A mighty host of comets followed the same elliptical orbit as the first as they returned from the farthest reaches of the solar system. Their light had already charged the atmosphere of Godsland, and the comets themselves would soon be visible to the naked eye.

The cycle of power would begin anew. Radiant energy, though still faint, raced toward Godsland, bearing the power of change.

As the force angled over the natural harbor where the fishing vessels were moored for the night, it soared beyond them over the Pinook Valley, and nothing barred its path. Beyond a small town, amid foothills dotted with farmsteads, it raced toward a barn where a young woman dutifully swept the floor. A slight tingle and a brief twitch of her eyebrows caused Catrin to stop a moment, just as a chance wind cast the pile of dirt and straw back across the floor. It was not the first thing to go wrong that morning, and she doubted it would be the last.

She was late for school. Again.

Education was not a birthright; it was a privilege--something Master Edling repeatedly made more than clear. Those of station and power attended his lessons to gain refinement and polish, but for those from the countryside, the purpose was only to stave off the epidemic of ignorance.

His sentiments had always rankled, and Catrin wondered if the education was worth the degradation she had to endure. She had already mastered reading and writing, and she was more adept at mathematics than most, but those were skills taught to the younger students by Master Jarvis, who was a kind, personable teacher. Catrin missed his lessons. Those approaching maturity were subjected to Master Edling's oppressive views and bland historical teachings. It seemed to her that she learned things of far more relevance when she worked on the farm, and the school lessons seemed a waste of time.

Master Edling detested tardiness, and Catrin was in no mood to endure another of his lectures. His anger was only a small part of her worries on that day, though. The day was important, different. Something was going to happen--something big; she could feel it.

The townies, as Catrin and her friends called those who placed themselves above everyone else, seemed to feed on the teacher's disdainful attitude. They adopted his derogatory manner, which often deteriorated into pranks and, lately, violence. Though she was rarely a target, Catrin hated to see her friends treated so poorly. They deserved better.

Peten Ross was the primary source of their problems; it was his lead the others followed. He seemed to take pleasure in creating misery for others, as if their hardships somehow made him more powerful. Perhaps he acted that way to impress Roset and the other pretty girls from town, with their flowing dresses and lace-bound hair. Either way, the friction was intensifying, and Catrin feared it would escalate beyond control.

Anyone from the countryside was a target, but it was her friend Osbourne Macano, son of a pig farmer, who bore the brunt of their abuses. The low regard in which his family profession was held and his unassuming manner made him an easy target. He had never fought back, and still the attacks continued. Chase, Catrin's beloved cousin, felt they should stand up for themselves since passive resistance had proven fruitless. What choice did they have?

Catrin understood his motives, but to her, the problem seemed unsolvable. Surely retaliation would not end the struggle, but neither had inaction, which left her in a quandary. Chase seemed to think they needed only to scare the townies once to make them realize such treatment would not be tolerated. That, he said, was the only way to gain their respect, if not their friendship. She could see his logic, but she also saw other, less appealing possibilities, such as a swift and violent response or even expulsion from the school lessons. Too many things could go wrong.

Chase was determined, though, and she would support him and Osbourne in their fight, if that was their choice. But she did not have to like it.

From bribing a woman who had once worked as Peten's nursemaid, Chase learned that Peten had a terrible fear of snakes--any snake, not just the venomous varieties. Chase planned to catch a snake and sneak it into the hall during lessons, though he admitted he had no plan for getting it near Peten without being seen. Just thinking about it, Catrin began to feel queasy, and she concentrated even more on her work. As she slid the heavy barn door closed to keep out the wind, she was submerged in darkness and had to resweep the floor by the light of her lantern.

Her father and Benjin, his close friend, were returning from the pastures with a pair of weanlings just as she lugged her saddle into Salty's stall. She watched the skittish colt and filly enter the barn wide eyed, but they gave the experienced men little trouble and would soon become accustomed to frequent handling. The lamplight cast a glow on Benjin's dark features. Bits of gray showed in his neatly trimmed beard, and his ebon hair was pulled back in a braid, giving him the look of a wise but formidable man.

Salty, Catrin's six-year-old chestnut gelding, must have sensed she was in a rush, for he chose to make her life even more difficult. He danced away from her as she tossed the saddle over his back, and when she grabbed him by the halter and looked him in the eye, he just snorted and stepped on her toes. After pushing him off her foot, she prepared to tighten the girth, and Salty drew in a deep breath, making himself as big as possible. Catrin knew his tricks and had no desire to find herself in a loose saddle. Kneeing him in the ribs just enough to make him exhale, she cinched the strap to the wear marks. Salty nipped her on the shoulder, letting her know he didn't appreciate her spoiling his joke.

Dawn backlit the mountains, and heavy cloud cover rode in with the wind. A light spray was falling as Catrin walked Salty from the low-ceilinged barn into the barnyard. Salty danced and spun as she mounted, but she got one foot in the stirrup and a hand on the saddle horn, which was enough to pull herself up even as he pranced. His antics were harmless, but Catrin had no time for them, and she drove her heels into his flanks with a chirrup to urge him forward.

In that, at least, he did not disappoint as he leaped to a fast trot. She would have given him his head and let him gallop, but the wagon trail was growing muddy and slick in the steady rain. Cattleman Gerard appeared in the haze ahead, his oxcart leaving churned mud in its wake. Trees lined the narrow trail, and Catrin had to slow Salty to a walk until they cleared the woods. When they reached a clearing, she passed Gerard at a trot, waving as she rode by, and he gave her a quick wave in return.

Fierce gusts drove stinging rain into her eyes, and she could barely see the Masterhouse huddled against the mountains; in the distance, only its massive outline was visible. Harborton materialized from the deluge, and as she approached, the rain dwindled. The cobbled streets were barely damp, and the townsfolk who milled about were not even wet. In contrast, Catrin was bespattered and soaked, looking as if she had been wallowing in mud, and she received many disapproving looks as she trotted Salty through town.

The aroma of fresh-baked bread wafting from the bakery made her stomach grumble, and the smell of bacon from the Watering Hole was alluring. In her rush, she had forgotten to eat, and she hoped her stomach would not be talkative during the lessons, a sure way to irritate Master Edling.

She passed the watchtower and the large iron ring that served as a fire bell, and she spotted her uncle, Jensen, as he dropped off Chase on his way to the sawmill. He waved and smiled as she approached, and she blew him a kiss. Chase climbed from the wagon, looking impish, and Catrin's appetite fled. She had hoped he would fail in his snake hunt, but his demeanor indicated that he had not, and when the leather bag on his belt moved, any doubts she had left her. How he had concealed the snake from her uncle was a mystery, but that was Chase, the boy who could do what no one else would dare attempt.

His mother and hers had died fifteen years before on the same day and under mysterious circumstances; no one understood what killed them. Since then, Chase seemed determined to prove that he wasn't afraid of anything or anyone.

Catrin pulled Salty up alongside him, and they entered the stables together. Once clear of the gate, she turned to the right, hoping to slip into her usual stall unnoticed, but instead she saw another insult. All the stalls were taken, despite there being plenty for those students who rode. Many of the townies, including Peten, rode to the lessons even though they were within walking distance. In a parade of wealth and arrogance, they flaunted their finely made saddles with gilded trim. It seemed they now felt they needed pages to attend to their mounts, and they, too, must ride. It was the pages' horses that had caused the shortage of stalls. Catrin stopped Salty and just stared, trying to decide what to do.

"What's going on, Cat?" Chase bellowed. "Have the townies gotten so fat they need two horses to carry each of them?"

"Hush, I don't want any trouble," she said with a pointed glance at his writhing bag. "I'll stable Salty at the Watering Hole."

"Strom may let you stable him there, but certainly not for free. Where does it stop, Cat? How much abuse do they think we'll tolerate?" he asked, sounding more incensed with each word.

"I don't have time for this now. I'll see you at the lesson," she said, turning Salty. Chirruping, she gave him a bit of her heels, trotted him around the block, and slowed only when she neared Baker Hollis, who was busy sweeping the walk. He gave her a sidelong glance and shuffled into the bakery. Inside, Catrin saw his daughter, Trinda, who stared with haunted eyes. She rarely left the bakery, and it was said she spoke even less often. Most thought she was daft, but Catrin suspected something entirely different, something much more sinister.

As she turned into the alley behind the Watering Hole, she whistled for Strom, who emerged from the stable looking tired and irritable.

"Cripes, it's early, Cat. What brings you here?" he asked, rubbing his eyes. He had once attended the lessons and had been friends with Catrin and Chase. After his father died, though, he had gone to work as a stable boy for Miss Mariss to help support his mother. He was shunned by most.

His humble circumstances and departure from the lessons marked him as undesirable in the eyes of many, but Catrin enjoyed his company and considered him a good friend.

"I'm sorry to wake you, but I really need to stable Salty here today. The stable at the academy is full, and I'm already late. Please let me keep him here--just for today," she asked with her most appealing look.

"If Miss Mariss finds out, she'll have my hide for a carpet. I can only stable a horse if the owner patronizes the inn and pays a copper for the stall," he said.

Digging into her coin purse, Catrin pulled out a worn silver half she'd been saving for an emergency. She tossed it to Strom. "Buy yourself something to eat and take good care of Salty for me. I have to go," she said as she grabbed her wax pad from her saddlebags.

Strom rolled the coin across his knuckles as she sprinted away. "I hate to take your money, Cat, but I assure you it won't go to waste!" he shouted.

Catrin raced back to the academy, turning toward the lesson hall at a full run. Master Beron shouted for her to slow down, but she was nearly there. She reached the door and opened it as quietly as she could, but the hinge betrayed her, squeaking loudly. Everyone in the room turned to see who would be the target of Master Edling's ire, and Catrin felt her face flush.

She entered with mumbled apologies and quickly sought a vacant desk. The townies gave her nasty looks and placed their wax tablets on the empty chairs near them, clearly indicating she was not welcome. In her rush to reach the desk next to Chase, her wet boots slipped on the polished floor, leaving her suspended in air for an instant before she hit with a crash. The air rushed from her lungs with a whoosh, and the room erupted in laughter.

As soon as she regained her breath, she immediately held it, seeing Chase take advantage of the distraction. He slinked behind Peten and slid the leather pouch under his chair. The drawstrings were untied and the top lay open, but nothing emerged. Catrin stood and quickly took the seat between Chase and Osbourne, still blushing furiously.

"This isn't going to go well for you, Cat. Edling looks boiled," Osbourne whispered, but Master Edling interrupted in a loud voice.

"Now that Miss Volker has seen fit to join us, perhaps she will allow us to commence. What say you, Miss Volker? Shall we begin, or do you need more leisure time?" he asked, looking down his nose, and several of the townies sniggered, casting her knowing glances. Catrin just mumbled and nodded. She was grateful when Master Edling began his lecture on the holy war; at least he was no longer adding to her embarrassment by making a bigger fool of her.

"When Istra last graced the skies," he began, "the Zjhon and Varic nations waged a holy war that lasted hundreds of years. They fought over conflicting interpretations of religious documents, none of which could be proved or disproved. Meanwhile, the Elsic nation remained neutral, often acting as a mediator during peace talks. Many times peace was made only to be broken again upon the first provocation.

"Then there came a new Elsic leader, Von of the Elsics. He ascended the throne after killing his uncle, King Venes. Von had been clever and murdered his uncle during the harvest festival, when there were hundreds of people in attendance who might have wanted the king dead. No one could identify the killer, and a veil of suspicion hung over the court. Elaborate conspiracy theories were rampant, and Von encouraged them since they served his purposes well. Those who believed treachery was afoot were much less likely to speak out for fear of being the next mysterious death."

The teacher droned on. "Von believed his nation's historical neutrality in the war was folly and that it would be better to conquer both nations while they were weakened by the prolonged war. The Elsics did not condone the use of Istra's powers, claiming it was blasphemous, and none of their scholars were skilled in arcana. Von had no large army at his disposal either, so he concluded that Istra's power was the only way he could defeat both nations. He would use the very powers that were flaunted by the Zjhon and the Varics as the agents of their destruction.

"He staged clandestine raids against each nation, disguising his men as soldiers from the opposing nation. His instructions were clear: he wanted people captured, not killed, because he wanted slaves. Those captured were transported in secret to the Knell Downs, which we believe to be high in the Pinook Mountains. Camps were built, and the slaves were forced to experiment with creating powerful weapons using Istra's power.

"There were many failures, as most of those captured had no experience in such things, but after countless attempts, a slave named Imeteri made a deadly discovery. Weakened from working in stuffy quarters, he convinced his captors to let him work outside whenever the sun shone. His efforts were fruitless for many weeks, and many of his experiments lay about in disarray, unfinished or forgotten completely, except for the details in his copious notes. Most of them consisted of various compounds of elements he placed in clay mugs, which he sealed with mud. One day, while working on his experiments, an explosion knocked him off his feet, and he knew one of his concoctions had worked. It took many more efforts for him to duplicate his success.

"One major problem was that his explosive needed to charge in the light of both Istra and Vestra before it would detonate. As it became saturated with energy, it would begin to glow, gradually getting brighter and brighter until it would eventually explode.

"Von was pleased by Imeteri's discovery, and after several refinements and small-scale demonstrations, he declared it the success he had been looking for. Imeteri was raised to the highest status of slave, barely less than a free man. Von ordered the other slaves to build enormous statues in the likeness of Istra and Vestra sharing a loving embrace. These great behemoths became known as the Statues of Terhilian, and packed with the new explosive, they were sent to the various Zjhon and Varic cities. Appearing to be tokens of peace, they were readily accepted and revered. The wars had drained the Zjhon and Varic nations, and lacking the resources to fight, they were relieved to receive the gifts.

"It was an abominable tactic and one I hope is never eclipsed. Drawn to the statues like moths to a flame, the faithful and war-weary congregated in enormous numbers around the likenesses of their gods. All but a few of the statues detonated, resulting in cataclysmic explosions that leveled entire cities, killing countless souls. The toxic aftermath debilitated those not killed by the initial blasts, and most died soon thereafter. And so began mankind's darkest age, a time known as the Purge," Master Edling continued, his unvarying cadence threatening to put Catrin, and most of the other students, into a deep sleep.

The snake, which Catrin now saw was an olive-green tree snake, was lured from Chase's pouch by the stillness, its slender head and neck poked from the pouch, looking like a bean pod with eyes. Catrin held her breath as it slithered forward and coiled itself around the chair leg. Peten noticed Catrin's sideways glances and gave her a snide look, tossing his long, blond hair over his shoulders.

With his muscular build, strong jaw, and piercing blue eyes, he cast a striking figure, but his attitude and ego made him the least attractive person Catrin had ever met. She felt little pity for him as the snake continued to follow its instinct, which was to climb. Peten was oblivious to its presence and continued to look bored, casting his own glances to get the attention of Roset Gildsmith.

The snake slithered up the slats on the back of his chair; it brushed against his curls, and still he remained unaware. He shifted in his seat, as if sensing the stares of Catrin, Chase, and Osbourne, and turned his head to glare at them. As he did, his eyes met those of the snake, and he shrieked. His high-pitched scream and sudden movement alarmed the snake, and it struck, biting him on his nose. Catrin knew the snake was not venomous, but Peten obviously knew nothing of the sort.

He leaped from his chair, sending his desk and the snake flying. Charging from the hall, he knocked Roset and another girl from their chairs. He showed no concern for anyone in the hall, and it was obvious his only care was for his own safety.

Master Edling stormed to the back of the hall, fuming, and snatched the agitated snake from the ruins of Peten's chair. After releasing it at the base of a tree in the courtyard, he returned, pushing Peten before him, forcing the shaken young man to return the desks to order.

Chase's eyes danced with glee, and Osbourne let a giggle slip. The townies and Master Edling glared at them with eyes like daggers. Catrin sat quietly, hoping the situation would somehow improve, but instead it worsened.

"Peten Ross, you are a coward and a boor," Roset said with a haughty look. "Do not aspire to speak to me again." She turned smugly away, her jaw stuck out in defiance.

Chase seemed to think things were going very well, but Catrin could see Peten's fury rising, his embarrassment fueling his desire for retribution. How Chase could not see mounting danger was a mystery to Catrin. Perhaps he was simply caught up in his own thirst for revenge.

Master Edling concluded his lecture and dismissed the class curtly. Catrin was just glad to have the lesson over and tried to flow out with the rest of the crowd, but Master Edling barred her path.

"Miss Volker, I would have a word with you," he said, and he clearly did not wish to compliment her.

"Yes sir, Master Edling, sir," Catrin replied softly. "I'm sorry I was late, sir."

"I'll have no excuses from you. It is your responsibility to arrive before the appointed time. If you cannot do so, then I recommend you do not attend at all. Since you wasted my time at the beginning of class, it is only fair I waste your time now. Be seated," he said, and Catrin slumped into the chair nearest the door, anxiously waiting for her punishment to be concluded.

* * *

Outside the lesson hall, Chase ducked into a darkened recess and waited for Osbourne. Roset came first, and she cast him a haughty glance, but he was grateful that she said nothing. Using the darkness for cover, he held his breath as Peten stormed by, followed by a mob of agitated townies. Minda and Celise walked by, and Osbourne seemed to be trying to hide behind them. Hoping no one noticed, Chase grabbed Osbourne by the shirt and dragged him into the alcove. Osbourne let out a small yelp before he realized it was Chase who had grabbed him, and he looked over his shoulder more than once.

"Looks like Edling held Catrin after class," Chase said.

"I told you he looked boiled," Osbourne said, but there was a tremble in his voice, and he looked nervously over his shoulder. "Are you going to wait around for Cat?"

"I can't. I promised my dad I'd help with the afternoon deliveries."

"I can't either," Osbourne said. "I've chores to do, and I should probably study for the test we have coming up."

"Bah, who needs to study?" Chase asked with a grin. "Just remember everything Edling says; that's all."

Osbourne shook his head. "That may work for you, but my father'll tan my hide if I bring home bad marks. I'd better get Patches saddled and get going, or I'm going to run out of light."

Chase peeked around the corner before walking back into the light, half expecting to find Peten and the rest of the townies waiting for him, but the stables were eerily quiet. Only Patches remained in her stall, and Chase stayed with Osbourne while he got her saddled.

"Never seen everyone clear out so quickly," Chase said.

"I'm starting to think the snake was a bad idea," Osbourne said as he tightened the girth. "Feels like I've got squirrels in my guts. You don't think they'll do anything to Cat, do you?"

"You worry too much," Chase said, but he secretly wondered if Osbourne was right. It seemed strange that Peten and the others had left so quickly, and letting Osbourne and Catrin travel home alone suddenly seemed like a very bad idea. There was nothing he could do about it, though, no way to take back what was already done, and he tried to drive the worry from his mind. "I'm sure everything will be fine."

"I hope you're right," Osbourne said as he mounted. Patches, who was a well-mannered mare, must have sensed Osbourne's nervousness, for she danced around the stable, her ears twitching as she spun. Osbourne soothed her with a hand on her neck, and she trotted away with her tail tucked. "I'll see you tomorrow," Osbourne said with a wave.

"Be careful," Chase said, betraying his own fears, and Osbourne rode away looking more nervous than ever.

Checking around every corner as he went, Chase made his way to the mill. At each turn he expected to find the townies waiting, and their absence only increased his anxiety. "I wish they would just get on with it," he mumbled to himself as he passed the market.

When he saw his father waiting with the wagon already loaded, though, he forgot his fears. They had enough work to keep them until nightfall, and he would have time to think of little else.

* * *

After sitting far longer than needed to make up the time she had missed, Catrin began to wonder if Master Edling had forgotten she was there. He was completely engrossed in his text, and she was hesitant to interrupt. She tried to be patient, but she desperately wanted to talk to Chase, and she shifted in her seat constantly.

"You are dismissed," he said suddenly without looking up.

"Thank you, Master Edling; it won't happen again, sir," Catrin said as she rose to leave.

"It had better not. And do not think for a moment that I'm unaware of your involvement in today's disruption; you can pass that along to your cousin as well," he said, and Catrin did not bother to deny it, knowing it would do no good.

She walked quickly to the Watering Hole, arriving to find Strom busy with the mounts of two nobles. She waited in the shadows, not wanting the nobles to complain about riffraff hanging around the stables; it had happened before, and she didn't want to impose on Strom. Once the nobles made their instructions abundantly clear, they strolled into the Watering Hole, and Catrin emerged from her hiding place.

"Thanks for keeping out of sight," Strom said. "Salty's in the last stall. You can saddle him yourself, can't you?" he asked with a smirk.

"I think I can manage, though the task is beneath me," Catrin replied, and her sarcasm brought a chuckle from Strom. Her tack had been cleaned and hung neatly outside the stall; he had treated her horse and gear as if they were his own, and she appreciated the gesture. Salty gave her no trouble, being aware he was on his way home, where his feed bucket waited. Strom was still attending to the nobles' horses and tack when she mounted.

"Thank you, Strom. I appreciate your help," she said, waving as she left.

"Don't mention it, Cat; just try not to make a habit of it," he replied with a wink and returned to his work.

Salty needed little prompting, and he broke into a trot as soon as they left town. Catrin turned him onto the wagon trail that meandered toward her home, hoping Chase would meet her there. She had expected to find him waiting at the Watering Hole, and his absence concerned her. She was tempted to push Salty to a gallop but resisted the urge. The trail was muddy and slick, and speed would only put her and Salty at risk. Her father and Benjin had warned her about such behavior, and she heeded their advice.

Engrossed in her thoughts, she let Salty cover the familiar distance without her input, but as she approached the woods, she heard someone cry out. Urging Salty forward, she scanned the trees for signs of trouble. Through the foliage, she saw flashes of movement in a clearing, and harsh laughter echoed around her. When she saw Patches, Osbourne's mare, wandering through the trees, still saddled and bridled, she nearly panicked. Osbourne would never leave his horse in such a state, and she knew he was in trouble.

After jumping from the saddle, she tied Salty to a nearby tree and approached Patches, who recognized her and cooperated as Catrin tied her to another tree. Meanwhile, she heard more muffled cries. Running as fast as she could toward the nearby sound, she burst into the clearing. Osbourne was near the center on his hands and knees. Blood flowed freely from his nose and mouth, and he clutched his side. Peten Ross, Carter Bessin, and Chad Macub were on horseback and appeared to have be taking turns riding past Osbourne, beating him with their wooden staves.

"Stop this madness!" Catrin shouted as she ran to Osbourne's side. She crouched over his body, hoping to protect him yet knowing she could not; she was overmatched. He whimpered beneath her, spitting blood through his ruptured lips.

"Out of the way, farm girl, or you'll share this one's fate. He needs a lesson in showing respect to his betters," Peten said as he spurred his horse. As he swept past, he swung his staff in a powerful arc, landing a solid blow on Catrin's shoulder. She barely had time to recover from his attack before Carter approached. His mount was blowing hard from the workout, sweat frothing around saddle and bridle alike.

His staff swung wide, striking her on her hip, but she barely felt the pain. As Peten wheeled his horse and dug in his heels, his eyes were those of a madman. He seemed intent on killing her and Osbourne, and Catrin became convinced her death approached. Peten was a well-muscled athlete who had trained in the jousts for as long as he could ride. He would not miss his target again, and her defiance clearly enraged him, leaving little chance of mercy.

Time slowed, and as she cried out in fear, her voice sounded hollow and strange in her ears. Still Peten came, aiming his mount so close that she feared they would be trampled. He did not run them down, though; instead he brought his horse just close enough to provide a clear shot at Catrin. She watched in horror as his staff swung directly at her head, and she saw her own terrified reflection in its highly polished surface as it blocked out the rest of the world. Intense sadness overwhelmed her as she prepared to die. Though she hoped Osbourne would survive the encounter, it seemed unlikely.

In the next instant, Catrin's world was forever changed. Her body shuddered, and a sound louder than thunder ripped through the clearing. She tried to make sense of what she saw as the world seemed to fly away from her. Everything took on a yellowish tint, which faded to blackness as she crumbled to the ground.

* * *

Nat Dersinger turned his nose to the wind and inhaled deeply. The wind carried the smell of misfortune, and he had learned better than to ignore his instincts. Despite the fact that he'd caught no fish, he pulled in his nets. Looking out at the clear skies, broken by only fluffy white clouds that seemed frozen in time, he wondered if he was just being silly, but the ill feeling persisted and grew more intense with every passing moment.

With a sense of urgency, he raised his sails and guided his small craft back to the harbor. Along the way he passed other fishing vessels, but no one waved or shouted out in greeting, as they did with other fishermen. Most just cast Nat suspicious glances, others glared at him until they were lost from sight. Nat tried not to let any of it bother him, but he soon realized he was grinding his teeth and his hands were clenched into fists. Too many times he'd been treated as an outcast, as if he were not even human. With a long sigh, he released his frustration and concentrated on avoiding the scores of hidden rock formations that flanked the harbor entrance.

At the docks, he received more strange looks--partly because he was back long before most of the other fishermen would return, and partly because he brought no fish to the cleaning tables, but mostly it was because he was Nat Dersinger, son of a madman. Most would rather see him dead or exiled; others simply tolerated him. There were few people he trusted and fewer still who trusted him. It was a lonely and unforgiving existence, but he had to believe it was all for a purpose, some grand design beyond his ability to perceive or understand. He let his mind be consumed by the possibilities, and he entered an almost dreamlike state; nothing around him seemed real, as if he walked in a place somewhere between this life and the great unknowable that lay beyond.

Unaware of where he was going, he let his feet follow a path of their own choosing, permitting his unconscious mind--rather than his conscious mind--to guide the way. It was one of the few lessons his father had taught him: sometimes the spirit knows things the mind cannot; never ignore the urgings of your spirit.

When he reached the woods outside of town, he barely recalled the walk. His feet continued to carry him into the countryside, and he wondered--as he often did--if he was simply fooling himself, assigning himself otherworldly powers rather than admitting he shared his father's illness. In truth, that was the crux of his life. Most seek answers to a myriad of questions, but Nat was consumed by one question alone: Had his father been a true prophet or a madman? As he found himself suddenly climbing over a hedge of bramble, he was inclined to believe the latter, but then the ground trembled and the air was split by a mighty thunderclap. Leaping over the hedge, Nat moved with confidence and purpose, suddenly trusting his instincts more than his senses. For the first time in a very long time, he believed not only in his father, but also in himself.

* * *

As the sun was sinking behind the mountains, casting long shadows across the land, Catrin woke. She sat up slowly, dizzy and disoriented, and put one hand out toward the ground to steady herself; it found Osbourne's chest. He was unconscious, his breathing shallow, but at least he looked no worse than he had when she'd arrived. She hoped he was not seriously injured. Her body ached as she moved, and she closed her eyes. Drawing a deep breath, she tried to calm herself.

Moans broke the eerie silence, and Catrin heard someone behind her gasp. She turned to see who it was, and only then did she behold the devastation that surrounded her. The clearing was a good bit larger than when she'd entered it; every blade of grass, bush, and tree within a hundred paces had been leveled. She stood, unsteadily, at the center of a nearly perfect circle of destruction. All the debris pointed away from her, as if she had felled it with a giant sickle.

Turning around slowly, she took in the awful details. Supple stalks of grass had been so violently struck that they were broken cleanly in half. In all her seventeen summers, Catrin had never witnessed such a terrifying sight. Behind her stood Nat Dersinger, a local fisherman who was thought to be mentally unstable. He leaned on his ever-present staff, his jaw slack, and made no move. The staff was taller than he was, half its length shod in iron, which formed a sharp point. His wild, graying hair stuck out in all directions, and his eyes were wide, making him look every bit the madman some thought him to be. Though he was of an age with Catrin's father, the lines on his face made him appear much older.

Peten's horse lay, unmoving, in a tangle of downed trees. Horrified, Catrin saw Peten's boots sticking out from under the animal, and she feared him dead, but she could not make herself move.

"Help, my leg is broken!" she heard Carter shout, and she turned to see him struggling to get out from under his own dead horse. Chad wandered aimlessly, followed by his faithful mount, which limped badly.

"Gods have mercy. I bear witness to the coming of the Herald. The prophecy has been fulfilled, and Istra shall return to the world of men." The words poured out of Nat and struck fear into those who heard them.

Townsfolk and farmers had begun to arrive, having heard the blast and been guided by the shouting. They tended the wounded, and word was sent to the Masters as well as the parents of the students involved. People scrambled to help Peten and the others, and many cast frightened glances at Catrin as they passed. Osbourne regained consciousness, and a kindly old man helped him to the edge of the clearing to await the Masters.

Few folk had the courage to speak to Catrin, but those who did all asked the same question: "What happened?"

"I don't know," was the only honest answer Catrin could give, but no one seemed to believe her. When her father arrived, he ran to where she stood, tears filling his eyes. Overwhelmed, she collapsed into his embrace. He hugged her and tried to comfort her, but he seemed unable to find the right words. Instead, he tied Salty to his saddle and pulled Catrin atop his roan mare, and they rode home in cautious silence.

* * *

A pool of molten wax and a dwindling wick were all that remained of Wendel Volker's candle, and he let it burn. His eyes, swollen with tears, were focused beyond the blank wall he faced. Raising Catrin alone had never been in his plans. He had done the best he could without Elsa, but in Wendel's mind it never seemed enough. If not for Benjin, he wasn't sure they would have survived. All along, they had struggled, but now they faced a danger far too great. The chill of fear crept up his neck--fear, not for himself, but for his beloved daughter.

Remembering the damage in the clearing, Wendel felt goose bumps rise on his skin. More disturbing than the damage was the look in Catrin's eyes. She felt responsible and guilty; that much was clear. Wendel tried to figure out what might have happened, but he found no answers. Instead, he accepted the fact that he might never know. What mattered was that people would be angry, confused, and afraid; all of which put Catrin in danger. Stronger and deeper than his greatest personal desire was the need to protect his daughter. So powerful was this urge that he went to where she slept and stood over her, watching her breathe.

"Help me be strong for her, my dearest Elsa," he said under his breath. He wept quietly. "If ever you've heard me, hear me now. I can't do this alone. I need you. Catrin needs you." Then he stiffened his jaw and firmed his resolve. "Watch over her, my love, and keep her safe."

* * *

As darkness claimed the sky, Nat Dersinger stood at the center of the clearing. All the others had long since gone to their homes and were probably discussing the day's events over their evening meals, but Nat tried to push that vision from his mind. Such thoughts brought him only pain and misery, and this was not a time he needed to be reminded of his loss. What he needed was guidance on what to do next. The prophecies warned of disastrous events, but they gave no indication of anything that could be done to prevent the foretold dangers. There must be something he could do, Nat thought, but he came to the same realization he had come to in the past: It would take more than just him. Somehow, he would have to convince those who had enough power to make a difference. Given his past failures, he found it difficult to be optimistic. Bending down, he pulled a blade of grass from the ground and marveled at how cleanly it had been broken. He let his mind wander for a time until something tugged at his awareness and demanded his attention. A familiar yet indefinable smell drifted on the breeze, and Nat's eyes were drawn to the heavens. As a sailor, he knew the stars as friends and followed their guidance, but on this night, they seemed almost insignificant, as if their power were about to be usurped, their beauty eclipsed. Nat had nothing more than his feelings to guide him, and his thoughts ran in a familiar pattern. So many times his instincts and gut feelings had caused him nothing but trouble. He would spill his heart to save those who showed him only hostility. "Why?" he asked himself for what seemed the thousandth time. But then his familiar pattern changed, irrevocably, as he looked at the blade of grass and the tangled mass of downed trees that lined the clearing. It was proof. No one could argue it or claim that it was a creation of his deranged mind. This was real and undeniable. For the first time in more than a decade, he did not question himself.

When he looked back to the sky, he believed completely. His father had been right all along. There was little consolation in this knowledge, for it foretold a difficult and perilous future for all, but it was vindicating for Nat nonetheless. As his thoughts wandered, he felt himself drifting into a different state of awareness, his eyes fixed on the sky yet focused on nothing. He felt himself being drawn upward, lifted to the heavens. His eyes felt as if they would be pulled from their sockets, so strongly did the sky seem to reach for them, longingly and insistent. The vision began more as a feeling than images in his mind; he felt small and afraid in the face of a coming storm. Lightning flashed across his consciousness, and thunder rattled his soul. From the skies came a rain of fire and blood, and the land was rent beneath his feet. A single, silhouetted figure stood between him and the approaching inferno. Nat reached out, his hands clawing toward salvation, but his only hope faded along with the vision.

Lying faceup at the center of the grove, just as Catrin had found herself, Nat drew a ragged breath. Sweat ran into his eyes, and his heart beat so fast and hard that he thought it might burst. He realized then that it might be better if he were truly mad.

Chapter 2

If peace cannot be made, then peace shall be seized.
--Von of the Elsics

* * *

As daylight streamed in through the open window, Catrin woke from a restless sleep, and she struggled to bring herself fully awake. Nightmarish visions plagued her slumber. Twisted dreams were so vivid that she had trouble distinguishing which events were real and which were nightmares. She pulled herself from her sweat-soaked linens, hoping the attack on Osbourne had been nothing but a dream. Sleep still filled her eyes and muddled her thoughts as she padded into the small common room she shared with her father.

He had left water in the washbasin for her, but that had been some time ago, and the water was no longer warm. Catrin tried to wash away the sweat from her fevered dreams, wishing that she could scrub away the horrors she felt closing around her, waiting to strike. The cold water helped clear the haze from her mind, allowing her to separate fantasy from reality. Her aching body brought her to a chilling realization.

It was real. The attack, the explosion, the strange way she was treated were all real!

On shaking legs, she dressed in her leathers and homespun, tears welling in her eyes as she imagined the consequences. Her life would be forever changed, and depression overwhelmed her. In an effort to feel normal, she got ready to do her chores. She donned her heavy boots and worn leather jacket, which had been left by the fire to dry. The jacket was covered in creosote stains and had a host of minor rips and tears, but she insisted on wearing it until it fell apart completely. Like a cherished companion, it had been with her on many an adventure, and she was loath to abandon it.

After she strapped on her belt knife, she gathered her laundry, a washboard, and some bits of soap. If she wished to have something comfortable to sleep in, she would need to get her things hung to dry. Not even raising her head as she stepped from the cottage into the barnyard, she let her feet carry her across the familiar distance. It was a short walk to the river, and she had a well-worn path to follow.

Turbulent thoughts rattled her mind, and when she reached the river's edge, she did not recall most of the walk. Kneeling on the shore, she dipped her nightclothes into the clear, frigid water, which numbed her fingers. She applied a bit of soap to the garments and scrubbed them vigorously on the washboard, but then she heard shouts coming from the barn. Throwing her garments into the dirt, she sprinted to the barn, fearing someone was hurt. The sound of several voices shouting carried across the distance, which alarmed her even more since her father and Benjin were normally the only ones about.

She stopped short when a familiar-looking man backed out of the barn, waving his arms in front of him, and he came close to falling over backward. Two more men followed, both in similar states of retreat, and Catrin was shocked to the core of her being when her father charged out next, looking like a man in a murderous rage. Benjin swarmed out at his side, his pitchfork leveled at the retreating men.

"You expect us to live with that abomination in our midst?" one man shouted as he backpedaled. "That hussy damn near killed m'boy. He might die yet from what she did to 'im."

"You've no proof of that, Petram, nor do you, Burl, nor you, Rolph. You'll take yourselves off my property this instant, or so help me . . ." he said through clenched teeth; then he actually growled at them. A threatening step forward sent the other men scrambling back. Benjin had not said a word, but the look in his eyes made it clear he would not hesitate to stick them with his pitchfork if they persisted, and it appeared as though the men might leave before any blood was shed.

Massive waves of fear, embarrassment, and guilt washed over Catrin, freezing her in place. She wanted to flee or scream but could do neither. Instead she stood still as a stone and watched the events unfold, hoping to remain unseen, but it was not to be. The men spotted her and glared.

"What are you staring at, you boiling little witch?" one man shouted, and Catrin recognized him as Peten's father, Petram. She also recognized the fathers of the other boys. As they scowled at her, she quailed; the hatred in their eyes made her feel small and dirty.

"You will burn for this, Catrin Volker!" Burl shouted over his shoulder, but his speech was cut short when Benjin swung the pitchfork handle at his head, and the three men fled.

"The council will hear of this!" Petram shouted.

Then they were gone, leaving Catrin to consider their words. Her father turned to her, and the look on his face softened. She stood silent, tears streaming down her cheeks, unchecked, and her lip quivered as she struggled to maintain her composure.

"Ah, Cat. I wish none of this were happening. You've certainly done nothing to deserve what those sons of jackals just said. Don't take their words into your heart, dear one. They are just scared, confused, and looking for someone to blame. I'll take care of them; don't you worry. Come along now. We've horses to tend, and I need to make a trip to the cold caves this afternoon," he said as he guided her into the barn.

Catrin's father had inherited the cold caves from his father, Marix. A popular barroom tale said her grandfather had won the caves in a wager with Headmaster Edem. They said Edem had been drinking with Marix at the Watering Hole after the Summer Games. Edem's son had won the cross-country horse race, and he celebrated with Marix, who had trained the horse, and they both got too far into their drink. Edem bet Marix he could not get the innkeeper, Miss Olsa, to show them her wares. Miss Olsa was an older woman at the time, though not unattractive, and she had a reputation for being a shrewd businesswoman.

Marix called her to his table and whispered into her ear for a long time. When he pulled his cupped hand away, Miss Olsa turned to the drunken headmaster, pulled up her blouse, and boldly revealed herself. Then she ran into the kitchen, giggling like a young girl. No one knew what Marix said, but the locals swore no one ever duplicated the feat, which made her grandfather a bit of a town hero. Catrin suspected he said something regarding the free cold cave storage still enjoyed by Olsa's daughter, Miss Mariss, long after Olsa's passing.

Benjin had followed the men off the property to make sure they caused no more trouble, and he returned just as Catrin entered the barn.

"Don't let those fools bother you, li'l miss. They haven't got the sense the gods gave 'em," he said, hefting his pitchfork in mock combat. On his way back to the stall he'd been cleaning, he stopped and patted Catrin on the shoulder with his over-large, calloused hand. His simple act of kindness shattered Catrin's fragile composure, and with each step, more tears flowed down her cheeks. Sobs wracked her, and she stood before her father, trembling, her shoulders hunched forward. She could not bring herself to look him in the eye, and she stared at the ground instead.

Her father never let the tribulations of the day disturb his routine, which gave Catrin comfort. He brought Charger, his roan mare, from her stall and put her on cross-ties. He ran a currycomb over her muddy coat with one hand and smoothed the freshly brushed coat with his other. Charger was accustomed to his ministrations and promptly fell asleep, letting the cross-ties hold up her head.

"What happened in the woods yesterday?" her father asked without looking up from his task.

"Peten was angry at Chase and Osbourne for playing a trick on him, and the townies attacked Osbourne on his way home. I tried to protect him, and they attacked me. I thought I was going to die, but right before Peten hit me, the world exploded. It's hard to explain; it was so strange and so very horrible," she said, and she tried to continue, but her sobs would not be suppressed.

She hugged herself in an effort to maintain control while her father deftly unhooked the cross-ties and returned Charger to her stall. After closing the stall gate, he went to Catrin and awkwardly put his arms around her. It was a rare gesture, which neither of them was truly comfortable with, but it meant a lot to her nonetheless.

"You certainly have your mother's knack for turning the world on its side, my little Cat. It'd be easier if she were here; I'm sure she would know what to do, but we'll get through this together, you and I. Don't you worry yourself sick. It's not so bad as it seems," he said with a forced laugh as he tousled her hair. "Now you run along and take the rest of the day for yourself. You've more than earned it with all of the hard work and long days you put in this winter," he continued. Catrin tried to argue, but he insisted. "Benjin and I can handle things around here."

"Off you go now, li'l miss. Maybe you could catch us some nice bass for dinner, eh?" Benjin said with a wink, and her father shot him a good-natured scowl.

"I give my daughter the day off, and you want her to catch your dinner?" Wendel said, shaking his head.

Laughter released some of Catrin's anxiety, and she left to fetch the laundry she had abandoned by the river. After she finished the washing, she took it to the cottage to hang it up to dry. When she was done, she took a piece of waxed cheese, some dried fruit, and a few strips of smoked beef for her breakfast. On her way back out of the cottage, she grabbed her bow, two fishing arrows, and her fishing pole. There was more than one way to catch a fish, and she was determined to bring back dinner.

Following the path back down to the riverbank, she turned north onto the trail that ran alongside the river, feeling as if every step took her farther from society and away from the source of her fears. She climbed past the shoals and falls, where the path was often steep and rocky. Along the way, she turned over rocks and collected the bloodworms that had been hiding in the darkness. By the time she reached the lake at the top of the falls, she had an ample supply of bait. Along the shores the water was shallow and slow, and the fishing was generally quite good. When she reached one of her favorite places, she laid out her gear.

Dark red blood oozed over her delicate fingers as she slid a bloodworm onto her hook, and she wiped it on her jacket, adding yet another stain. Her fishing line was far too coarse for her liking, but good fishing wire was expensive; she would have to make do with what she had. After checking the knot that held her lightwood bobber in place, she cast her line near a downed tree, which was partially submerged in the dark water, forming a perfect hiding place for the fish.

A towering elm gave her shade, and its moss-covered trunk provided a comfortable seat. She leaned against the tree and waited for the fish to bite.

The stillness of the lake stood out in stark contrast to the maelstrom of thoughts that cluttered her mind. She attempted to review the events of the previous day, but she could not focus; when she tried to concentrate on one thought, another would demand her attention then another and another. Frustrated, she tried to put it all from her mind.

Her pole jerked in her hands, and the lightwood bobber jumped back to the surface. With a hurried yank, she set the hook and pulled the fish in, relieved it had not gotten away with her bait. The large-mouth bass put up a good fight, and when it emerged from the water, she was pleased to see it was longer than her forearm--not enough to feed three but a good start.

After baiting her hook again, she cast it near where she'd caught the first fish, but she got no more bites for the rest of the afternoon. The dark shadows of large fish moved below the surface, taunting her, and as the sun began to sink, she decided to try her luck with the bow. Normally, fishing arrows were used only when the carp were spawning since they made easy targets as they congregated in the shallows. Bass would be much harder to hit, but she had been practicing her archery skills, and she hoped the effort would pay off.

After securing her long string to the fishing arrow, she tied the other end off on an elm branch. Not wanting to lose her arrow, she double-checked her knots. Confident they were secure, she located a likely target and took aim. Ripples in the lake surface distorted her depth perception, and her first few shots missed their marks. Determined, she did her best to compensate for the distortion, and her next shot was true, catching another bass in the tail and pinning it to the bottom.

"Nice shot," Chase shouted from behind her, and she nearly leaped from her skin.

"Don't you know it's not nice to sneak up on people?" she said, truly glad to see him. He just grinned in response. She gave a tug on her string, but her arrow was firmly wedged, and she removed her boots, preparing to go in after it.

"Let me get that for you," Chase offered.

"I can get it; I'm not crippled," she retorted angrily and instantly regretted it. She had no reason to be angry with Chase, but she felt helpless--a feeling she despised--and she needed to lash out at someone. Chase took it in stride, though, and simply sat on the shore while she waded out to the flailing fish. She freed the arrow quickly and grabbed the fish by the tail; it was slightly smaller than the first, but it would be enough.

The bruises on her hip and shoulder ached as she climbed from the water, her muscles stiff from the time spent sitting beneath the tree. Chase grabbed the other fish and Catrin's bow while she retrieved her pole and her other fishing arrow. She was grateful for his help; without it, she would have had a difficult time carrying it all home. Chase was quiet for the first part of their walk, and Catrin allowed the silence to hang between them.

"I visited the infirmary this morning," he said after a while, and when Catrin made no reply, he continued. "Osbourne is doing much better and should recover quickly. He has a broken nose, a couple of badly bruised ribs, and a score of bumps and bruises, but he was awake this morning. He told everyone that you saved his life." Catrin grunted but said nothing.

"Carter has a broken leg, but otherwise he's fine. Chad has a head wound and can't remember much of anything; heck, he didn't even know who I was. The Masters said his memory should return in a few days, but his mother is hysterical. She just keeps shouting that her baby has been mortally wounded. Peten's hurt bad. The Masters won't say if he will live or die, but he did wake up for a while this morning. I think he'll recover myself; he didn't look nearly as bad as most were making him out to be." He stopped, and Catrin turned to look him in the eye. Her lip quivered, but otherwise she maintained her composure.

"I didn't do anything, Chase. I don't know what happened," she said, and Chase remained silent. "The last thing I remember was Peten bearing down on us and swinging his staff at my head. I saw my reflection in his staff, Chase. It was coming right at my face. How could I not have a mark on my head?" she asked, not anticipating a response. "At the very moment I expected his staff to crush my skull, there was a loud bang--like thunder but without the lightning. Just before I passed out, it looked like the world was flying away from me, and when I woke, it was like being in a nightmare."

"I believe you, Cat. Besides, even if it was something you did, you were just saving Osbourne from those boiling townies," he said.

She didn't like the insinuation that it could have been something she did, but she couldn't blame him. What evidence was there to prove otherwise? She began to doubt herself, but for the moment, she clung to what she knew to be true.

"They were going to kill poor Osbourne; I just know it. They probably would've gotten away with it too. I'm sure they would have just made up some story about him trying to rob them or some other rubbish, and that is just the kind of thing the Masters would believe of us farm folk," she said.

"They'll believe worse than that. The main reason I came was to warn you: rumors are spreading. Some say you are a witch or monster, and others have even claimed you are a Sleepless One. There have been some who have spoken up for you, but several suffered beatings as a result. I don't think it's safe for you to go into town right now; too many people have lost their senses, and they are starting to believe some of the crazy things people are making up," he said sadly.

Catrin sniffed and wiped her eyes but made no other sound.

"I'm truly sorry, Cat. I feel like this is my fault; if I hadn't brought that snake in, none of this would've happened. I'll do anything I can to help you, and I'll always stand up for you--"

"No," Catrin interrupted. "I don't want you getting hurt because of me. Keep your thoughts private. You'll be more help to me if you just listen and let me know what people are saying. Perhaps you could bring me my lessons," she said, but her voice cracked, and she could not get the rest out.

"Don't worry. I'll bring your lessons to you, and I won't do anything stupid, but I'm not going to let them get away with telling lies about you either."

"Thank you," was all she could manage to say without sobbing, and they walked back to the farm in silence.

As they approached, her father and Benjin waved, and they held up the bass in silent greeting. Benjin let out a whoop of glee on seeing the fish, and her father just shook his head. Benjin met them halfway.

"Nice catch ya got there, li'l miss. Here, let me take those. I'll get started on the cleaning," he said with a smile. Catrin started to object, but Benjin grabbed the fish and looked quite happy carrying them off to be cleaned and filleted.

"You go get washed up for dinner!" he shouted over his shoulder, and Catrin was happy to oblige; she was wet, dirty, and in need of a good scrubbing. After she and Chase washed up, they joined Benjin and her father in the cottage and were greeted by the smell of vegetable stew.

"I knew you wouldn't come home empty handed, li'l miss. I'll just boil the fish and add it to the stew; we'll eat like kings," Benjin said as he stoked the fire.

* * *

Chase pulled the rough but warm blanket around his shoulders as he curled up in front of the fire. Everyone else slept, but he could not. His thoughts would not allow it. He had been ready to face the repercussions of his actions, but he had not been prepared for Osbourne and Catrin to pay the price in his stead. He decided he didn't like the taste of guilt and remorse.

Catrin was gentle and fragile, and he was supposed to protect her. He had promised Uncle Wendel that he would always look after her, but when she and Osbourne had needed him most, he had failed them. Running his thumb over the locket that hung around his neck, he vowed to do better. Somehow he would shield her from the harshness of this world.

* * *

Wendel sat upright as he woke with a start. Darkness covered the land, and the wind made the rafters creak. But he was accustomed to hearing those noises; something else had disturbed his sleep, but he no idea what. Straining his hearing, he listened for anything out of the ordinary but heard nothing distinct, only brief hints that someone was moving outside the cottage. Creeping through the darkness, with the precision of intimate familiarity, he dressed and reached beneath his bed to retrieve Elsa's sword. Touching it normally brought tears to his eyes, but this was the first time in more than a decade that he unsheathed it with the intent of using it, and he moved with purpose.

Using skills he had long since abandoned, Wendel crept without a sound to where Catrin slept. Her chest rose and fell, and her eyelids twitched as they do only when one dreams. Seeing her safe relieved much of his anxiety, but Wendel was not yet satisfied. Perhaps the noises he'd heard were made solely by the wind, but he knew he would never be able to sleep without checking.

The predawn air carried a chill, and dense fog hovered above the ground. As Wendel emerged, the air grew still, as if he had somehow intruded on the wind and chased it away. The world seemed more like the place of dreams, and Wendel wondered if he could still be asleep. The snap of a branch in the distance startled him, but he could see nothing from where the noise had come. Could it have been a deer?

After checking around the cottage, he checked the barns, careful not to let the horses hear him, lest they give him away. Shadows shifted and moved, and the fog constantly changed the landscape, but Wendel found no signs of anyone about. Still his anxiety persisted, and he waited for what seemed an eternity for the coming of the false dawn. Across the barnyard, a shadow moved, and Wendel froze. Shifting himself from a sitting position to a more aggressive stance, he watched and waited. Again he saw movement, and he moved in to intercept. Out of the night came a blade to match his own, but before the blades met, he knew whom he faced. "Was that you I heard sneaking around the cottage?" he asked.

"You woke me while you were out here stomping around," Benjin said with a lopsided smile.

"We're getting old," Wendel said.

"I may be fat, lazy, and out of practice," Benjin said, "but watch who you're calling old."

"Catrin will be up soon. I don't want her to know we were both out here like a couple of worried hens."

"She won't hear it from me," Benjin said, and with a wave over his shoulder, he wandered back to his cabin.

Catrin was still asleep when Wendel returned to his bed, but it seemed only moments later that she began to stir.

Chapter 3

Anything worth having is worth working for. Anything you love is worth fighting for.
--Jed Willis, turkey farmer

* * *

Catrin woke, feeling oddly refreshed, happy to have slept well, and ready to face the day with more optimism than she would have thought possible. After dressing, she stirred the stew, which hung over the banked coals of the fire. More flavorful than it was the night before, it made for a good morning meal.

She stoked the fire and hung a pot of water over the flames, warming it for her father, who said washing with cold water made his bones ache. Benjin wandered in from outside, looking barely awake but smiling appreciatively as Catrin handed him a mug of stew. While he ate his breakfast, Catrin ladled a mug for her father, who had begun to stir. She knew he would be hungry when he emerged. He grunted in acknowledgment as he accepted the food, and she left them to their meal.

Lighting her lantern, Catrin left the warmth of the cottage and walked into the damp coolness of the early morning air. Millie, a gray and white tabby cat, greeted her at the door, weaving in and out of her legs. By the time she reached the feed stall, a mob of cats surrounded her, demanding attention and, more emphatically, food. Catrin kept a supply of dried meat scrap and grain in an old basin, and she used a bowl to scoop out enough for all of them.

A parade of scampering felines following in her wake, Catrin put the food outside the barn. The cats fell on it, each wanting their share and more, and they were soon begging again. Catrin stopped and looked at the cats trailing her. "Now listen to me. If I feed you any more, you'll get fat and lazy and not catch any mice," she said, shaking her finger and smiling. The cats looked at her and dispersed to various hay bales and horse blankets, content to preen or nap for the moment.

Catrin mixed oats and sweet grain into neatly organized buckets. Some horses required special herb mixtures in their feed, and Catrin took great care to be certain the mixtures went into the correct buckets. Giving an animal the wrong herbs could have dire consequences, and it was not a mistake she wished to repeat. A week of cleaning Salty's stall after giving him oil of the posetta by mistake had left a lasting impression on her.

Growing impatient, the horses banged their water buckets and pawed the floor to let her know they wanted their food immediately. Benjin came into the barn and started dumping the small buckets into the larger buckets that hung in the stalls. He knew the order; this was a dance they had performed many times.

"How much wikkits root did you put in Salty's feed, li'l miss?"

"Two small spoons of wikkits and a large spoon of molasses," Catrin replied, and Benjin chuckled.

"You did good; looks like you mixed it in fine. Never thought I'd see a horse eat around a powder, but he'll eat the grain and leave a pile of powder in the bucket. I'm telling ya, he does it just to spite me," he said, walking into Salty's stall. He gave the gelding a light pinch on the belly. Salty squealed and stomped and grabbed Benjin's jacket in his teeth, giving it a good shake. Without missing a beat, Benjin emptied the feed into the bucket and patted Salty on the forehead.

"Nice horsy," he said, and Catrin had to laugh. "Ah, there is that smile, li'l miss. It's good to see it again," he said with a wink.

She made no reply, unsure of what to say, and returned to her work. As she opened a bale of hay, mold dust clouded the air. They had lost too much hay to mold this year, and she knew not to feed the horses moldy hay. There was not much more they could have done to prevent the problem, though. The weather had turned bad at harvest time, and they had not been able to get the hay fully dry before bailing it. Forced to store the hay damp, they salted it to reduce moisture, stave off mold, and help prevent fire. Mold claimed much of the hay nonetheless, but at least it had not caught fire.

Her grandfather had lost a barn to a fire caused by wet hay. When hay dries, it goes through a process called a sweat, where it sheds water and produces heat. If packed too tightly, intense heat can build up and cause spontaneous combustion. The lesson had been passed to her father then down to Catrin. It was something she planned to teach her own children someday.

The moldy bale of hay she threw to the steer, which could eat just about anything, and she grabbed another bale for the horses. After giving each horse two slices of hay, she collected the water buckets, carrying them to the well her father and Benjin had dug long ago. It was something the men took great pride in, and Catrin was glad to have it. Her father often said it was not deep enough for his liking, and he feared it would run dry during droughts, but it had yet to fail them.

He once explained to Catrin that they were at the upper edge of an artesian basin. Water became trapped between layers of rock and was subjected to immense pressure. If you were to penetrate the rock anywhere along the basin, water would rise on its own, possibly forming a small fountain. Some places in Harborton had such wells, which had been allowing water to escape for hundreds of years.

After dumping out the dirty water, she gave the buckets a good scrubbing before refilling them; then she and Benjin hung them in the stalls. Afterward, they took hay and water to the horses that were out to pasture. The routine soothed Catrin; the rhythm of life on the farm was predictable and comforting. The tasks were familiar, and she could perform them skillfully, which gave her great pride. She liked nothing better than to do something well; doing a mediocre job was one of her greatest fears.

Finding herself thirsty, she walked over to the well for a drink and was disturbed to see a shiny black carriage under the trees. A squire tended a fine black mare, and Catrin was dumbfounded to see Master Edling speaking with her father. He was garbed in formal black robes, the blue embroidery as bright as a bluebird. He seemed out of place on the farm, a place of sweat and dirt, far from the pristine halls of the Masterhouse. Her father did not look happy, but neither did he appear to be angry, at least not with Master Edling.

Frozen in anxious suspense, Catrin stood very still, hoping no one would notice her and fighting the urge to flee. Benjin came to her side, carrying a spare water bucket.

"Don't let them get the best of you, li'l miss. They are no better than the rest of us, no matter how prettily they dress or how clean they keep their fingernails," he said, filling the bucket. He pushed her toward her father as he carried the bucket to the squire. Her father shot her a steely glance and pointed to the cottage, an unspoken command. Catrin followed the two men into the cottage, cowed.

Her father offered Master Edling a seat and served summerwine and cheese. After a respectful interval, he turned to Catrin.

"Master Edling has come for two reasons. First, he is here to represent the Council of Masters. They've decided, due to the serious nature of the 'incident,' it would be best if you did not attend the public lessons--at least until this has all been sorted out," he said.

Catrin heard his words, and she understood what the council meant. *We don't think you should appear in public again--ever,* she thought, shrinking in on herself.

"Second, Master Edling has volunteered to act as your tutor. He must still instruct the public lesson days, but he will come here on the off days to give you lessons. Quite kind of him, I'd say," he said with a nod to Master Edling. "I should be getting back to work, so I'll leave you to your lesson. If you'll excuse me, Master Edling."

"Yes, yes, indeed," Master Edling said, absently waving him from the room.

Catrin felt trapped, forced into isolation. Master Edling's visit was just the beginning. Keeping her away from town would only make her appear guilty of some crime. People would start to believe the crazy stories about her. She would be shunned for the rest of her life. Master Edling was not there to tutor her, she thought; he'd come only to see if she had grown horns or sprouted wings. Her mood dropped from fear into anger then to frustration. Her rage was building, seeking release, and it took great effort not to lash out. She had committed no crime. She had only tried to save her friend. As thanks, they would ruin her life, and it made her want to scream.

"Miss Volker?" Master Edling said, interrupting her mental torment. "I think that will do for today," he said, giving her one of his most disgusted looks. "I do not believe you heard a single word I said, did you? I could give you the same lesson on the morrow, and you would know no difference," he added in disgust. Catrin could not argue with him; she had not even realized he had begun his lecture, but his attitude only fueled her anger.

Master Edling stood and left without another word, his robes billowing around him. Catrin doubted he would return; he had seen what he had come to see. She was no monster or evil murderer, just a rude farm girl who had ignored and insulted him. His departure was bittersweet; while Catrin was not sorry to see him go, his leaving was like the death knell for her friendships. She wondered if she were destined to live as a hermit because of one freak incident.

Her father came back into the cottage, looking concerned. "Is your lesson over so quickly?" he asked. "Master Edling barely spoke a word as he left." His movements made it clear he was not pleased.

Catrin could not look him in the eye. She stared at the floor, stifling her tears. "I'm so sorry, Father. I was angry and confused, and I was thinking about everything and what it all meant and--" Her voice cracked, and she knew she was going to cry.

"Slow down, Cat. Don't get too upset on me. Let's just talk about this," he said gently, and Catrin did her best to steel herself and try to keep her emotions under control.

"I don't think Master Edling believes I am a worthy student."

"Are you?"

"No, sir, I don't think I am," she replied sadly.

"Now, Cat, you must stop this. Master Edling came here to help you, and you ignored him. He may never return. I can't send you back to the public lessons. Even if I could convince the council, it would be asking for trouble. Talk in town has grown a bit wild of late. Nat Dersinger has convinced some people that you are the Herald and that Istra will return to the skies of Godsland soon," he said then stopped, fearing he had gone too far and frightened his daughter.

"Now most sane people don't believe a word of it, Cat. Everyone that knows you loves you. They know you as the spirited young athlete who competes in the Summer Games and as the hardworking girl that doesn't hesitate to help at a barn building. Your friends and family won't give up on you just because something unexplainable happened," he said, pulling up a chair. "I'm disappointed in you for insulting Master Edling today, but I can understand your distraction. I'll have a word with him on your behalf. Your best hope is that he has it in him to forgive you."

"Yes, sir," Catrin replied, looking downcast.

"There's no sense dwelling on it; we'll just have to see what tomorrow brings. For now, I want you to look after a few more things around the farm."

* * *

In the darkness of the bakery attic, where the heat was more than most could bear, Trinda watched, just as she always did. Always careful to remain undetected, she watched and waited, looking for anything that might please the dark men. It seemed all her life had been lived in fear of the strange men who came in the night, and here every waking hour was devoted to keeping them pleased. As long as she gave them what they wanted, they would never hurt her again. The memories still seared and burned as if they were new. The dark men were coming again; she could feel them getting closer.

When Miss Mariss walked out of the Watering Hole, Trinda jumped and then chastised herself for her carelessness. Of all the people she did not want to know about her spying, it was Miss Mariss. The dark men always asked questions about her; they always wanted to know whom she talked to and what they talked about. Trinda had only some of the answers they wanted, and it was all she could do to come up with enough information to satisfy them.

Holding her breath, Trinda froze until Miss Mariss was lost from view. She was, no doubt, coming to place her order. Without the breads her father baked or the dough she used to make her famous sausage breads, Miss Mariss would surely suffer. The relationship between her and Trinda's father had always been tense and strained, but they were both professionals, and they did not let personal feelings stand in the way of business.

As Trinda stood, ready to climb down and make an appearance by the ovens, she stopped. Someone she didn't recognize was approaching the Watering Hole, and he went neither to the front entrance nor to the stables; instead he walked into the shade provided by an old maple. It seemed a strange thing to do, considering there were no doors on that side of the inn. Knowing her father would scold her for not appearing while Miss Mariss was in the bakery, Trinda stayed, intrigued by this unknown man's mysterious behavior.

For what seemed a long time, he stood in the shadows, only the toes of his boots visible from Trinda's vantage. Then, when the streets were empty, he squatted down and wiggled a loose piece of the inn's wood siding. After sliding what looked like a rolled piece of parchment into the space behind the siding, he quickly adjusted the wood until it looked as it had. Then he melted into the shadows and disappeared.

* * *

"Where is Trinda today?" Miss Mariss asked, trying to make the question sound entirely casual, as she always did, and Baker Hollis looked nervous and fidgety, as he always did.

"Must know there's work to be done," he said. "Any time there's somethin' needin' done, she turns invisible."

"Those her age can be like that," Miss Mariss said, despite not believing any of what he said. "I'll be making double the usual amount of sausage breads, and I'll need triple the usual baked loaves for the Challenges. That won't be a problem will it?"

"No problem at all," Baker Hollis said, and he looked over his shoulder as if expecting to see Trinda. Miss Mariss was as surprised as he that she had not shown herself. It seemed whenever Miss Mariss came to the bakery, Trinda would make a point of making herself seen. "Everyone's sayin' this year'll be better than any before. I suppose we'll have to rise to the challenge," he said.

"I'll send Strom over in the morning for the daily order," Miss Mariss said as she turned to leave. Before she reached the door, though, a small, sweat-soaked head peeked around the corner and briefly met her eyes. Miss Mariss could read nothing from Trinda's expression; it was the same bland and sullen look as always. With a sigh, she left the bakery behind and soon forgot about Trinda as the responsibilities of running her inn once again consumed the majority of her thoughts and time.

* * *

Sitting on a bale of hay with his knees pulled to his chest, Chase kept to the shadows, not wanting to cause any trouble for Strom, who was busy saddling a pair of horses. So many things had changed in such a short period of time that Chase could hardly believe it. He no longer felt safe in places where he'd once felt quite at home. People he had considered friends no longer met his eyes, yet he could feel the stares that lingered on his back as he walked away.

"Sorry about that," Strom said once the customers had ridden around the corner.

Chase just handed him the jug of huckles juice they were sharing. "Do you remember when things used to be normal?"

"I remember," Strom said. "I remember things were sometimes good and sometimes bad, but it always seemed like things would get better. Now . . ."

"I know what you mean," Chase said. "I really made a mess of things."

Strom laughed. "You're still blaming yourself for all of this? You sure do think a great deal of yourself. Are you so powerful that you can control everyone else? I don't think so. You need to face the fact that you're just as helpless as the rest of us. Whatever happens just *happens*, and there's not a thing you can do about it."

"Thanks for the uplifting speech," Chase said. "I feel much better now."

"Don't come to me if you want sunshine and roses. That's not how I see the world. You could go talk to Roset. She still lives in a land of buttercups and faeries; maybe she could make you feel better."

"She won't even talk to me," Chase said, his mood continuing to be dour in the face of Strom's humor.

"You see? You're utterly powerless. Therefore you can't possibly be at fault. Doesn't that make you feel better?"

"If I said yes, would you stop talking about it?" Chase asked.

"Probably not."

* * *

Catrin spent the next few weeks throwing herself into every task her father assigned. Master Edling did not return, despite her father's many requests. Benjin and her father did what they could to teach her, but what they remembered of their own lessons was fragmented and disjointed. Catrin learned other things from the extra time she was spending on the farm. Benjin taught her the basics of shoeing horses along with other farrier skills. She was an apt student and excelled with little practice. It interested her because she loved horses, and they had always been part of her daily life. She had seen it done a hundred times, which helped her to quickly master even the most difficult techniques.

Forge and anvil became outlets for her frustration. She coerced the hot bars into the desired form, shaping them with her will. The song of the hammer and anvil soothed her, and she quickly replenished their supply of horseshoes. Benjin also taught her to make shoeing nails, whose shape was critical. Wide heads prevented the shoe from slipping over the nails, while the tapered edges prevented injuries by forcing the nail to turn outward to the edge of the hoof against the taper.

As long as a farrier is careful not to drive one backward, the nail will always poke back out of the hoof, a finger's width above the shoe. The farrier would clip most of the tip of the nail then crimp the remains against the hoof. The technique provided a secure fit and better protection from sprung shoes.

"A horse will always spring a shoe at the worst possible moment, and it's good to know how to handle it," Benjin said. "You seem to handle the hammer well. Would you like to make a farrier's kit?" he asked. Catrin was delighted with the idea.

The hours she spent at the forge with Benjin were the only times she forgot her worries. Using tools to create new tools enthralled her, and she was immensely proud of her new implements. In a way, they brought her freedom. There were always coppers to be made shoeing horses and trimming hooves at local farms, and the knowledge that she could earn her own way was comforting. She would take pride in whatever work she did with them. Smiling, she tucked them into her saddlebags with care.

The weather was becoming unusually volatile, and intense storms confined Catrin to the barn or the cottage much of the time. Clear skies could quickly turn dark and foreboding, and fierce winds drove the rain. One afternoon, the sky was an eerie shade of green, like nothing she had ever seen before. Hail made her run for cover, each stone growing in size as she ran, some even larger than her fist. Benjin and her father sprinted into the barn just behind her.

Wind howled so fiercely through the valley that it lifted a hay wagon into the air and over a fence, depositing it, unharmed, in a pasture. When the storm passed, they checked for damage. Catrin helped her father and Benjin repair the roofs on the cottage and barn. The chicken coop had also suffered damage, but Benjin mended it quickly.

Abe Waldac, a local cattleman, drove his wagon behind a team of mules to the front of the barn. "Anyone hurt?"

"Luck was with us, Abe. We're fine. Thank you for checking on us, though. It's much appreciated," her father replied.

"You've always been good neighbors. I'm glad to see you all well. A funnel cloud ripped through the lowlands; looks like it made a boiling mess of things. I'm going to see if anyone needs help."

"We'll go with you. I'm sure they could use some extra hands down there. Catrin, you stay here and mind the farm. We'll be back late. Gunder may come for his mare. She's in the second stall," her father said, and the men rode off in Abe's wagon, leaving her alone. She knew someone had to watch the farm, but Catrin could not help feeling ashamed. Her father did not want to be seen in public with her.

* * *

Depression drove Nat back into seclusion. No one wanted to face the truth, even with the proof visible to all. It sickened him. They would rather die than admit he might have been right all along. In the end, he gave up trying to convince anyone else of the danger they faced. There seemed no point in even trying. Miss Mariss, at least, had listened politely, but even she refused to see the truth.

Returning to his normal life seemed almost surreal at first, but the feeling grew faint over time until he no longer noticed it. After days of blue skies and good fishing, he had almost been able to forget about his visions and feelings of impending doom; his life had been almost normal, even tranquil. The storm changed all that. Sudden winds had forced him north, well beyond the waters he normally fished, out to where dangerous currents had been known to carry away craft as small as his boat and pull them into open water.

Despite his efforts, he was pushed farther and farther from shore, and with every passing moment, the chances of his survival diminished. His only hope lay with a change in the wind. Occasionally he felt a shift in the air, as if a crosswind fought against the storm, and Nat prayed it would win.

Lightning splayed across the clouds, illuminating them from within and revealing the intricate structures and formations. Taller than mountains, yet flowing like rivers, the clouds seemed to reach from the sky and attack the sea itself, and Nat shivered. Though he hated the life of a fisherman, longing instead for the life of a scholar, the seas were the giver of life, and he quailed at the sight of waterspouts, which thrashed the waves, tore them asunder, and tossed them into the sky.

As the storm finally passed, the sun began to set. The failing of the light was like a slow death knell for Nat, who was near despair when he saw a sight that chilled his soul. Silhouetted against the orange and purple sky along the edges of the storm was a multimasted warship. Like the image that haunted his dreams, it came to life and gave him reason to fear. Only the sudden shift in the wind gave him any hope.

* * *

Osbourne recovered from his wounds and came with Chase to visit Catrin on several occasions. The boys seemed to feel it was their duty to keep her informed of the happenings in town. Much of the news they brought seemed to have lost all significance in her life. She no longer cared what girls the boys were fighting over or whose father had been thrown into the lockup for being drunk. There were other times, though, when she wished she could achieve the same level of detachment.

"Nat Dersinger came back from fishing the northern coast, and he claims to have seen long ships on the horizon," Chase said. It was not the first time Nat claimed to have seen long ships, only to have them disappear before another ship could verify the sighting. Nat was not the only fisherman to have seen strange ships in the distance, but he was certainly the most vocal about it.

"He said our ancient enemies, the Zjhon, were planning an attack. Waving his staff over his head while he ranted, he really went overboard. He said the Herald would destroy the Zjhon, according to some prophecy. He even said the Zjhon would kill all the inhabitants of the Godfist--just to be sure they kill the Herald. Most folks pay him no heed, but some fools actually believe him."

Osbourne said rumors of unusual occurrences were increasing. A shepherd reported losing half of his flock in a single night without ever hearing a sound, and a western village claimed the community well had run dry for the first time in recorded history. Fishermen complained of dangerous shifts in the currents; fishing was poor for the most part, though some returned with bizarre and unknown fish. They said the strange creatures were caught in warm water currents, unusual for so close to the Godfist because they normally stayed much farther out to sea.

Unsure if the exotic fish were safe to touch or eat, most fishermen threw them back into the sea. Some claimed to have been stung by poisonous fish, and others grew fearful of anything not easily identified. Most simply cut the lines when they brought up something they did not recognize.

"This year's Spring Challenges are going to be the grandest ever," Osbourne said, seemingly trying to lighten the mood. "You should see the new game fields, Cat, and the rows of benches for spectators." Catrin was lost in her own thoughts and barely heard him. Chase elbowed him in the ribs to make him stop.

Catrin had participated in the Challenges since she was old enough to ride, and most years she qualified for the Summer Games, but this year would be different. She knew she would not be allowed to compete, and she had no need to ask because it was understood. The townspeople did not want her. She was unwelcome.

"I was thinking about going on an outing, maybe a hike into the highlands," Chase said. "Telling stories around a campfire would be more fun than the Challenges and a lot less work. Wouldn't you agree, Osbourne?" Chase asked, elbowing him again. He had known Catrin her whole life, and he knew how crushed she must be.

"I can't attend the Challenges, but that doesn't mean the rest of you shouldn't. I know how much both of you like to compete, and I was looking forward to hearing of your victories," she said with a slight catch in her voice, which she had tried to control.

They stood, and Chase announced, "I'm going camping," crossing his arms and inflating his chest.

"So am I," Osbourne said, mimicking Chase, though he didn't look quite as imposing.

"But--" Catrin began. Her words were cut short when Chase tackled her. He and Osbourne coerced her into submission by means of the dreaded tickle torture. It was the first time Catrin had truly laughed in a long while, and she felt better for the release.

Despite her acquiescence, she still needed her father's approval, and she feared he would deny the request. She found him sitting at the table, working his way through a stack of parchment. Catrin sat across from him, waiting for him to finish what he was working on. After a few moments, he looked up from his work and acknowledged her with a strained smile.

"What's on your mind?" he asked in his usual straightforward manner.

"I don't think I should compete in the Challenges this year," she said, and he nodded in silent agreement. "Chase and Osbourne are boycotting the Challenges; they want to spend the time with me instead," she continued, and he raised an eyebrow but remained silent. "I was wondering if we could camp at the lake those days," Catrin asked, finally getting to her point. She was always amazed at how much information her father could get out of her without ever saying a word.

"I tried to talk them out of boycotting, Father, really I did, but the harder I argued, the more they argued back," she said with a smile and actually giggled. "They made me agree by means of tickle torture."

Her father chuckled and smiled briefly. "Tickle torture, you say? That does sound serious. I guess I could let you go for a few days. I wouldn't camp near the lake at this time of year, though. The mosquitoes will suck you dry. It'd be better if you climbed past the lake and continued to the highlands. There is a natural stair near the falls, and a grove of ancient greatoaks is due west of there. It's a fine place to camp, and the land is too rocky and dry for mosquitoes to be much of a problem. It's half a day of walking and climbing, but it would be well worth the effort," he said.

Her father had told her stories of the place, but he had always forbidden her to go that far. The closest she had ever ventured was to the very end of the lake, where a large set of falls drained from the river above. There she had climbed the tallest tree and gazed in all directions but was unable to see the grove. She was genuinely excited about the trip and hugged her father and kissed him on the forehead.

"Thank you," she said, smiling broadly. He patted her on the shoulder and told her to run along. She retired to her bed and dreamed of ancient trees dancing in the light of a campfire.

* * *

Jensen piled the last of the lumber near old man Dedrick's barn and gave a wave as he climbed back into his wagon. With all the deliveries done, he had enough time to stop at the Watering Hole. A mug of ale might help the world look better, and Chase always loved it when he brought home some of Miss Mariss's sausage breads. This time of day was a busy time at the Watering Hole, and the tie-offs were all taken. Jensen guided Shama to the back of the inn.

"G'afternoon to ya, Mr. Volker," Strom said as he walked from the stables, but there was an odd look of fear in his eyes, and his voice trembled slightly. "We're just about full up. You might want to come back another day."

"Just the same," Jensen said, looking Strom in the eye. "Mind if I tie Shama off back here."

"Of course, sir," Strom said.

"Give her a bit of water," Jensen said while removing Shama's bridle. He hooked a lead line to her halter and tied her off to a nearby post.

Strom approached with a bucket of water. "Some of those inside are looking for a fight," he whispered without looking at Jensen. "There's been a lot of talk about Catrin. I'm sorry, sir. I don't believe any of it, and I couldn't let you walk into trouble not knowin' it."

"You're a good man," Jensen said, but he failed to keep the anger from his voice, and Strom backed away. "Unhook the wagon and saddle Shama for me," he added, handing Strom three coppers. "I may need to leave in a hurry."

Strom looked as if he would be sick, but at Jensen's nod, he began unhooking Shama. Jensen walked to the kitchen door and slowly pulled it open. Miss Mariss, ever in control of her inn, noticed him immediately and moved in his direction without actually looking at him. "You ought not be here right now," she said. "Petram is acting like the fool he is, and there's a parade of fools ready to follow 'im. I won't have you all settling this in my common room. You understand me?"

"I understand," Jensen said, but he was undeterred. When he stepped inside, Miss Mariss threw her hands in the air. "I promise you there will be no fighting," he said.

"Men," she said. "Stubborn mules refuse to listen to anyone else." Though her irritation was clear, she did not stand in his way.

As he entered the common room from behind the bar, only those at the bar noticed him, and none of them seemed interested at what Petram Ross was shouting to anyone who'd listen. Jensen nodded to the men at the bar then slipped into the crowd. Some turned and glared at him as he pushed his way closer to Petram, but when they saw who it was and the look on his face, they moved aside without a word. Eventually, Jensen found himself standing in front of Petram, and everyone else seemed to be taking a step backward. Enthralled by the sound of his own voice, it took Petram a moment to notice the change in his audience. At first, he seemed annoyed, but then his eyes landed on Jensen, and he instantly took a step back, only to find himself trapped by the hearth he'd chosen to use as a backdrop.

Jensen stepped forward but said nothing. Instead, he glared at Petram with a look that conveyed a host of threats, most of which came from Petram's imagination, which was just as Jensen wanted it. He wanted this man to fear him more than death. Again he moved forward, and Petram looked as if he wanted to climb up the chimney despite the fire burning in the hearth.

"If you even look at my niece the wrong way," Jensen said softly, all the while raising his hand, which was held like a claw and moving toward Petram's throat. Just a hand's breadth away, he stopped and slowly closed his fingers. Petram's eyes bulged as if he were truly being choked. When Jensen finally lowered his hand to his side, Petram ran from the room, leaving a stunned silence hanging over the common room. All eyes were trained on Jensen, and he searched for words, suddenly unprepared. He thought a moment about the little girl who brightened his life and those of everyone around her. "She's a good girl," was all that he could say through his sudden tears. Those who had been gathered now lowered their heads and dispersed.

"I guess you might as well eat since you chased off all my customers," Miss Mariss said as she brought him a platter of cured meats and cheese. "Fools they may be, but a fool's gold is as good as any other."

* * *

Crouched in the darkness, Benjin listened. Only the sounds of frogs and the barking of a distant dog broke the stillness. Creeping into Wendel's cottage, he checked on Catrin and Wendel. Both slept soundly and neither woke. He left as stealthily as he had come.

Feeling silly, he walked back to his cottage. Only moments before, he had been sleeping soundly, but dreams of terror and loss drove him from his bed, demanding he check on those he loved. Assured of their safety, he returned to his bed, but the dreams returned.

When morning finally came, the harsh sunlight seemed to mock the warnings of his dreams. Still he could not shake the sense of foreboding that pressed in on him, suffocating him. With a deep breath, he stood and prepared himself to face the day.

Chapter 4

The mind can travel farther in a single day than the fastest horse could traverse in a lifetime.

--Trevan Dalls, Master of the Arts

* * *

Dense fog hung over the land, holding Catrin's world in its damp embrace. Days like this never seemed real to her, as if, on rare occasions, she left her usual world and stepped into the world of dreams. Even the calls of the birds and the noises of the farm sounded different, almost magical. Catrin suspected she was not the only one who had such feelings, as her father and Benjin also seemed changed in this other world.

"G'morning, li'l miss," Benjin said.

Her father stood behind him with a lopsided grin. "Go in and get Charger harnessed and bring her out to the wagon," he said. "We're going to make a trip to the cold caves."

Catrin nodded and went into the barn, a feeling of anger and shame building in her gut. Going to the cold caves had always been an adventure for her and Chase. Some of her fondest memories were of them playing there as children. It had been like a world of their own, a place where adventure and magic were real and where they could explore the depths of the underworld. The rooms filled with blocks of ice had always drawn them, despite the lectures her father and uncle had given about avoiding those very places. She and Chase had climbed on top of them and slid across their slick surfaces, which were always wet, as the ice melted slowly yet inexorably. As they grew older, much of their time was spent moving stores in or out of the caves, but there were special times, in the winter, when they would gather fresh snowfall to be stored in the caves. Catrin and Chase had spent wonderful days packing the snow into all kinds of shapes and storing them within the caves.

As she harnessed Charger, tears gathered in her eyes, but she refused to let them fall. By the force of her will, she held them in check, determined to be strong. It was something she had learned from Chase, and it seemed that now it was a skill she would need to master. Only the tremble of her chin escaped her control, and she hoped her father and Benjin didn't notice.

Outside they waited in the preternatural light that gave the world an almost greenish hue. Heavy clouds threatened rain, and it seemed unlikely that the fog would burn off as it did on most days. Catrin held Charger's head as Benjin and her father slid the shafts of the wagon through the loops on the harness. While they secured the breast-collar to the shafts, the power of her will began to fade; tears streamed down her cheeks, and her lip quivered noticeably. She hoped the men would simply climb into the wagon and leave without the need for her to speak, but she doubted it, and she chastised herself for showing such weakness. Staying to mind the farm was not so terrible.

"She's all hooked up," her father said as he climbed into the wagon's passenger seat beside Benjin, leaving room for another. "Get the barn door closed and check the gates. We need to get going."

Catrin wiped her tears and ran to the barn, a smile forming on her face. Perhaps it was the fog. Perhaps her father figured no one would see her through the mist, but she did not care. Not only did he plan to let her go, the driver's seat was still vacant, and Catrin eyed it unsurely.

"Are you going to drive us there or not?" her father asked, his grin like a ray of sunshine.

"Yes, sir," she said as she climbed up. He handed her the lines, and Catrin smacked Charger lightly on the rump with them while making a clucking noise with her tongue. Charger knew her business and moved out at a moderate pace. In the mist, Catrin had to use landmarks to guide her around obstacles, but she knew the path well and had little trouble steering Charger along a clear path where she was not likely to trip.

When they reached the place where the Harborton trail met the upland trail, she turned Charger slowly and deliberately. The upland trail was narrow, and Catrin had never driven a wagon on it before. Parts of the trail were treacherous, and there were places she was hesitant to even ride Salty; driving the wagon was much more challenging.

"Move a little to the right," her father said. "There's an old tree stump on the bend, and you don't want to hit it with the wheels."

Charger never faltered and, in truth, knew the way better than any of them. There were times that she corrected the path for Catrin before her father or Benjin could even warn her of an upcoming obstacle. When they reached Viewline Pass, her father asked her to stop. Catrin pulled back on the lines until Charger stopped then maintained moderate tension on the lines to keep her stopped. Charger was not accustomed to stopping here, and she fidgeted constantly.

When she turned to her father, Catrin's gaze passed over the view that gave the pass its name. Below her, looking like an elaborate child's toy from the heights, was her homeland. The fog continued to blanket the land, making it look like an ocean of white with emerald islands, sailed by buildings that floated like ships. The illusion was difficult to break, but her father demanded her attention.

"When driving through the pass, you must be extra careful. Rocks often fall here, and we have no way to know if there is anything beneath this fog that could injure Charger. You must hold the lines with confidence and authority here. Charger fears the rocks and formations that will flank her through the pass, and she often jumps sideways for reasons only she knows. Let her know that you are in control, and she will follow you instead of her fear. Understand?"

"Yes, sir."

"You can do this, li'l miss," Benjin added. "You just have to know you can do it."

With a strange mixture of pride and trepidation, Catrin urged Charger slowly forward. Small rocks caught under the wagon wheels, but Charger showed her worth and pulled the wagon over the obstacles. It made for a bumpy ride, but there was little to be done about it. As Charger reached the place where rocky peaks flanked her, her ears began to flip forward and back, and when she turned her head, Catrin could see the whites around her eyes.

"Make her follow you. Let her know you're in control."

Her father's words bolstered her confidence, and she held the lines firmly but without fear. Charger still sidestepped and pranced, but Catrin maintained control. Soon they were beyond the pass, and the way became easier again.

"You've done well," Benjin said, and Wendel nodded his agreement. From the two of them, it was high praise and Catrin beamed.

When they reached the cold caves, they found it was among the few places not still mired in fog. The main entrance was invisible until one reached the rock face where it hid. Between two mighty slabs of stone stood a chasm just wide enough for a horse--but nothing larger--to fit through. Benjin tied Charger to a stake they had driven in the stone many years before.

"Benjin and I will load the wagon," Wendel said. "Most of what we're after today is heavy. Go back to our personal stores and get what you would like to have for your camping trip."

Catrin wasted no time. Without another thought, she was bounding through caves, passing through the network of corridors that were like old friends. There were some of the deeper tunnels that Catrin had never really liked, but she had most of the place memorized. When she reached the area her father reserved for their storage, she sifted through and grabbed what she thought the others would enjoy as well.

After loading her supplies in the wagon, she did her best to help her father and Benjin. Despite the hard work and the sweat that ran into her eyes, it was the most fun she'd had in quite some time. Only the strange looks from those to whom they made deliveries threatened to spoil her mood, but most of the people they saw were friends of her father's and none treated her with anything but kindness--albeit awkward kindness. For Catrin, it was good enough. Only at the end of the day, as darkness began to creep back over the land, did her fears return. The hairs on the back of her neck stood as she passed by a thicket of trees bathed in shadows; the feeling of being watched was almost overwhelming. Catrin was barely able to resist the urge to push Charger for more speed, but she knew the horse had put in a full day's work, and it would be unfair to ask more of her. The ill feelings persisted, and Catrin hoped that Benjin and her father did not sense her fear.

* * *

Miss Mariss heard all the gossip; she knew where in her inn to be if she wanted to hear the conversation at a specific table. Much of the inn had been designed around this purpose, though most would never have guessed it. Simple things, such as a knothole in the common room floor that continued through a bored-out log all the way to the cellar, made her task a great deal easier. Her exceptional hearing gave her the advantage of being able to attend to the work of running her inn, all the while collecting valuable information.

Whether Catrin was the Herald of Istra or not remained to be proven in Miss Mariss's mind, but either way there would be much work to do. Everyone in Harborton was tense and afraid, and that alone had far-reaching effects. If it turned out that incident in the clearing was simply a freak occurrence, she would be just as happy, though she knew Catrin would never escape the stigma. Still, that seemed far better than the alternative--far better indeed.

* * *

Anticipation drove Catrin from her sleep earlier than usual. She had been looking forward to this day, and it was finally upon her. She dressed while reviewing her mental list, making sure she had not overlooked some important detail. Her tinderbox and extra clothes were already packed, and she added some dried fruit, smoked beef, and salted fish to her backpack. A trip to the cold cellar yielded a bottle of springwine and waxed cheese she had brought back from the cold caves. Her bedroll wrapped in her leather ground cloth and secured atop her backpack, she wondered what it was she was forgetting; there had to be something.

Her morning chores needed to be finished before she left, and she had asked the boys to give her until daylight. Still, she was not completely surprised when she heard laughter that sounded like a couple of halfwits trying to be quiet and failing. When she opened the door, she found Chase and Osbourne side by side, grinning like fools, and her father walked up behind her at the same moment.

"Good morning, boys. You're here early," he said over her shoulder while she grinned back at the boys.

"G'morning, Mr. Volker," Osbourne replied.

"Good morning, Uncle Wendel. Sorry we're early, but we thought we could help get Catrin's chores done faster, and then we could get an early start," Chase said, but then he jumped as if someone had pinched him. "Oh, yeah, I almost forgot," he twitched again and laughed, squirming. "We have a surprise for you, Cat. Guess who is coming with us?" he asked as he and Osbourne stepped aside with a dramatic flourish. Strom entered the cottage smiling and bowing.

"I'd wager you weren't expecting to see me here," he said. "G'mornin' to you, Mr. Volker."

"Good morning to you, Strom. It's good to see you again. Now, you grinning scoundrels, get out there. Clean and fill those water buckets. Catrin, you get the horses fed and take care of your cats, and then you can go," Wendel said with a smile. He seemed as excited about their big trip as they were.

The group of exuberant young people gave Wendel a mock salute and, almost in unison, said, "Yes, sir."

They made quick work of the buckets and feeding. Benjin wished them a safe trip and told the boys to behave themselves or he would hunt them down like rabid dogs. He said it with a smile, but the boys nodded seriously and said again in unison, "Yes, sir." Benjin laughed, shook his head, and walked into a stall with his pitchfork.

The excited campers waved good-bye as they shouldered their packs and started their walk down the river trail. The false dawn had not yet shown on the horizon, but the moon was bright enough to light the way. They had little trouble getting to the river; once there, they turned and climbed past the shoals and falls. They had covered half the length of the lake by the time the sun cleared the mountains.

They laughed and talked while they hiked, having a generally good time of things, and Catrin began to feel the distance between her and her troubles. A small clearing, shaded by tall pines, seemed like a good place to rest, and they flopped onto the bed of needles. Catrin dug in her pack for the dried fruit and cheese, but it was Strom who got a whoop of delight from the others when he produced four of Miss Mariss's sausage breads. Each one was twice the size of his fist and wrapped in waxed paper.

Strom cleared his throat and said, in his best imitation of Miss Mariss's voice, "Miss Mariss sends these with her best wishes to some of her favorite patrons. She looks forward to your next visit. Her words, not mine," he added, just to make sure Catrin understood the message was intended for her. The subtle message surprised Catrin, as did the support from Miss Mariss, who had always been stern with her, but she decided she would process that information later. Today she was on a grand adventure, and she wanted nothing more than to enjoy the sausage bread.

Her bottle of springwine was drained all too quickly, and she realized she should have brought more.

"No fears. I came prepared for just such an occasion," Strom said, seeing the concern flicker across Catrin's face, and he produced a bottle of springwine and a bottle of huckles juice from his pack.

"I knew we brought you along for some reason," Chase said, patting him on the back. Strom elbowed him in the ribs as he shouldered his pack.

"Sorry about that, m'friend. I didn't see you there," he said, laughing and pushing his way past Chase and Osbourne.

Catrin watched as the boys jostled and roughhoused along the trail, meandering in the direction of their intended campsite, but as the valley narrowed, they walked single file. The sound of the rushing falls grew as they approached the end of the lake, and when they reached the clearing, Catrin smiled in recognition. There was the tree she had climbed so long ago in hopes of catching a glimpse of the enchanted grove. She needn't wonder any longer; now the grove was her destination.

* * *

In search of the natural stair Catrin's father had mentioned, they approached the base of the falls, the mist rolling over them in clouds. Sunlight danced in the moisture, casting rainbows across the clearing, and they moved quickly, hoping to avoid a thorough soaking.

"There it is," Chase said, and Catrin followed his gaze. Rounded lumps, blanketed with moss and soaked with accumulated moisture, formed the crude base of the stair. The rest of the formation created an illusion, appearing flush with the rock face until the spell broke, and Catrin could see the form plainly. A narrow shelf angled up the rock face, its slope irregular.

Heights had never been a problem for Catrin, but the stair was daunting. There was no room for error; any slip could send her over the sheer drop with nothing to break her fall. As they climbed higher, the stair became dry and, in some places, distinct and well formed. Catrin found them a wonder, as if fate had carved a path for them, and she was thankful for the gift.

The mental image did not last long, though, as they soon came on a crumbled section of stair, which was barely passable. Perhaps fate did not wish to speed her trip after all, Catrin thought, laughing at herself. They managed to negotiate the treacherous section of the stair with a bit of help from each other, but none of them looked forward to climbing back down. The remainder of the climb proved to be fairly easy, and they reached the top of the cliff unscathed.

Moving west, they searched for the trail Catrin's father said they would find. Seeing no obvious breaks in the tree line, they moved along it, peering through the branches. Ahead of them, a buck emerged from the forest, his ears flicking forward and back, as if he sensed them. With a snort, he bounded back into the woods, disappearing from view but aiding them nonetheless. As they neared the spot where he had been, a trail materialized within the outer barrier of leaves.

Catrin led them into the forest, following the narrow trail. The canopy of leaves blocked much of the sunlight, and they moved within a shady world that was filled with life. Deer moved almost silently through the woods, while smaller animals ran through the leaves with wild abandon. Squirrels at play sounded like a herd of beasts crashing through the undergrowth. Colorful birds flitted from branch to branch, their varied warbles filling the air.

Menacing spiders had built elaborate webs that spanned open areas between trees. When Catrin walked into one of the clinging webs, she thought she felt its occupant land in her hair, and she gave the boys a good laugh while she tried to shed the imagined spider. Afterward she armed herself with a long stick, which she waved in front of her like a wand, clearing the webs as she walked.

The sound of the waterfall faded into the distance, and Catrin picked up the hint of a noisy brook. She knew a stream ran near the grove, and she wondered if it was the same one. The incline grew steep, and sweat soaked them as they hiked, their legs aching. Soon, though, they emerged from the forest onto a large plateau, which was carpeted with thick, green grass broken occasionally by weathered outcroppings of obsidian rock. Emerald moss clung to the megaliths, marbling their surface, as the land slowly reclaimed the masses of stone.

Ancient and immense, the greatoaks were unmistakable in the distance, towering above the tallest elm. Unlike any trees they had ever seen, the greatoaks soared into the sky, their tops obscured by low-lying clouds. As the group drew closer, the sheer magnitude of the trees became even more evident. Twenty-four in all, they were evenly spaced and formed a nearly perfect circle, but each one was a force unto itself. The trunks were so massive that twenty people could stand around one, with arms outstretched, and still their hands would not meet. Awed by the magnificence of the place, none of them made a sound, afraid to break the spell.

Magical in its beauty, the grove lured them, but Catrin was drawn by more than just the aesthetics. She could feel the power of the grove, a place in which the very air seemed alive with energy. They walked in slow reverence, as if entering a holy place. Much of the grove was blanketed with lush grasses, but an irregular circle of bare stone dominated the heart of it. There were no writings or symbols, nothing beyond its sheer might to indicate it was sacred, but it felt that way. The black stone was smooth and level with the grass, and Catrin found it strange that no moss or grass had encroached on it. It seemed almost as if the plants kept their distance out of respect for the mighty stone.

"I don't think we should camp in here," Osbourne said into the eerie silence, and yet the spell remained unbroken. "I feel like we're welcome, but I don't want to disturb the beauty of this place."

In quiet agreement, they walked toward the far side of the grove in search of a suitable campsite. The western clearing was much the same as the one in the east, and at about the same distance, the forest began again. Only the area between the two sections of forest was clear of underbrush. As Catrin searched for a place to camp, she concentrated on the sound of running water and moved toward it.

An almost imperceptible waterfall glistened down the valley wall. The water flow was slight, but it fed a small stream that lay hidden in the folds of the land. The stream was narrow but its water cool and clear. Not far from the base of the fall, Catrin spotted a large shelf of rock protruding from the cliff face and knew it would provide some shelter. On further inspection, it was obvious that others had camped there before, though it appeared to have been some time ago. A bare spot looked to have been used as a fire pit, and a few rocks still lay in a circle around it.

Catrin and the others knew without saying a word that they had found their campsite. They dropped their packs and stretched sore muscles. Catrin went in search of stones to complete the fire circle.

"Would you boys gather some wood?" she asked, and they set off for the western forest since no dead trees or branches were to be found in the grove. By the time they returned, Catrin had finished constructing the fire circle and gathered dried grass for kindling. Chase and Osbourne dumped their armloads of wood directly into the circle of stones, and Strom started a woodpile off to one side.

They left Catrin to start the fire while they ventured out for more wood. The wood they left was damp, and she knew she would have a hard time getting it to burn. Strom had left some sticks and leaves along with the larger pieces of wood, and Catrin gathered what was dry, placing it at the center of the fire circle. She retrieved her tinderbox from her pack and pulled out some dry shavings and her flint. She piled the dry shavings neatly at the base of her kindling pile and grabbed some larger pieces of wood, leaning them against one another so they formed a cone above her kindling.

Sparks flew as she struck her stones against one another, but few actually made it to the shavings. After several sparks hit the shavings, going out almost immediately, one took hold, a small flame blooming around it. She cupped her hands and blew gently, and though the tiny flame went out, the shavings glowed red. The flames returned, double their size, and quickly consumed the kindling but barely even dried the damp branches. Piling even the damp kindling atop her small blaze, she sent a cloud of smoke into the air. With a few puffs, though, the flames returned, licking eagerly at the branches.

"Is that little fire the best you could do? I was expecting you to have dinner cooked by now," Chase said, dumping his armload of wood, and he jumped back as Catrin took a swipe at him. He laughed and went to lay out his bedroll. He chose a spot that was near the fire yet still shaded by the rock overhang; Osbourne and Strom threw their bedrolls down near his. By the time they were comfortable, Catrin had a nice fire going. The air above it shimmered, and the light danced over them.

She retrieved her bedroll, only to find all the sheltered spots taken, and the boys pretended not to notice her irritation. She stood with her hands on her hips, glaring at each of them. Chase could no longer keep up the ruse and was the first to start laughing.

He and Osbourne moved their bedrolls closer together, and Strom moved his to the other side, making a spot in the middle for Catrin. She curtsied and pounced on the newly cleared spot, leaving them no chance for reconsideration. Something about being in a strange place together and sitting around a fire made everything seem right with the world.

They rummaged through their packs in search of various goodies, and they feasted on sausage breads, cheeses, and dried fruit. They made sure to leave themselves enough supplies for a few more meals, but what they ate was delicious--it was adventure food, free of restraint and responsibility. There was nothing to clean up when they were done, and they could relax with full bellies. They had no reason to wake in the morning, no chores awaiting them; it was a glorious feeling, only slightly dampened by the knowledge that it was temporary.

Catrin just watched the flames, but Chase seemed obsessed with tending the fire, constantly shifting the coals and poking them with a stick. She excused herself, suddenly stifled by the heat of the fire. Wandering into the deepening shadows, she drank in the fresh air and savored it. Stopping for a moment to take another deep breath, she looked up at the skies. Cloud cover was slowly breaking up, and a few stars were visible through the gaps.

Leaning her head back, she closed her eyes. She felt her mind expanding and perceived an almost audible click, as if a doorway in her mind suddenly opened. Her body felt intensely alive, every sensation magnified. With her arms wide, she stood, basking in the light breeze as it tousled her hair.

Chase yelled from the campsite, "Catrin, are you going to sleep out there?"

"It's such a pretty night," she said. "I think I'm going to take a walk. Would anyone care to join me?"

"Nah, we'll just stay here and eat all the food," he replied, laughing, but the boys roused themselves and joined her.

The night drew them on, pulling them into the ring of mighty trees. Beams of moonlight shone through the parting clouds, lighting Catrin's way. She let her body go where it wished, her path leading straight toward the center of the grove. The others followed in silence, as if entranced by her rhythmic movements.

Cold stone caressed her feet, soothing them as she strode upon it. Feeling as if she could ride the wind, Catrin whirled in a rhythmic dance. Around her pulsed the beat of life, and she danced to its lilting cadence. Life energy was everywhere, but it was more focused in the grove, almost tangible. Spinning on the wind, she closed her eyes and raised her hands to the heavens. Energy from above bathed her in its warmth, and she grabbed onto it with her mind, tasting its sweetness, smelling its fragrance, caressing its texture. Its beauty overwhelmed her.

She clung to the energy, letting it suspend and hold her. Overcome with joy, tears coursed down her cheeks. The boys' talking shook Catrin from her revelry. She opened her eyes to see the night sky and two bright sources of light. It took a moment for her eyes to focus; then she clearly saw the moon and another bright object. The second was like nothing she had ever seen. Elliptical, with a long trail of light in its wake, it sparkled with life and called to her. It was so beautiful, she could not look away.

"By the gods, do you see that?" Chase shouted, and Catrin returned to herself somewhat again.

Another, closer source of light stole the brightness from the doubly lit night sky. Lightning danced along her fingers in powerful arcs, and twin beams of liquid energy extended from the palms of her hands into the sky, twining themselves into a single thread of energy. Colors raced along it, constantly shifting and changing, each moment bringing something new.

Catrin heaved, her mind finally reconciling what her eyes reported. She yanked her hands down violently, feeling an awful tearing sensation as she pulled herself away from the massive energy flow. In that moment, she realized her feet were not touching anything, and she had no time to brace herself before they struck the black stone beneath her. Even in her confused state, she realized she must have been high above the ground, judging by her impact, which buckled her knees and tossed her onto her back.

She remained supine for a moment, staring at the sky, and she caught another brief glimpse of the comet before fast-moving clouds once again obscured it. The clouds, Catrin realized, were moving far too fast; a storm was upon them. Lightning ripped across the sky in a vast web of light, and the wind howled as bands of horizontal rain assaulted them.

"Run for cover!" Catrin shrieked above the wind, and they fled to the relative shelter of their campsite. Hail pelted them as they ran. The stones were small at first but steadily grew larger and more dangerous. The light of their windblown fire illuminated their belongings as they were scattered around the campsite, sent tumbling by the wind. After scrambling to collect their things, they huddled under their packs, watching helplessly as gale-force winds snuffed their fire.

The darkness was nearly complete, broken only by monstrous bolts of lightning as they set fire to the thunderheads. The wind howled and intensified, screaming at them, sucking their belongings into the night. Thunderous cracks and booms mixed with the wailing call of the wind and battered Catrin's senses, making her think she was about to go mad. Dirt and debris, carried by fierce gusts, stung her exposed skin.

Catrin screamed as lightning illuminated the plateau long enough for her to see a mass of branches and leaves hurtling toward them. It struck the ground in front of them with incredible force, driving the air from her lungs. Startled but uninjured, Catrin and her friends huddled under the massive limb, hoping nothing else would fly from the darkness.

* * *

From the deck of his flagship, *Rebellion's End*, General Dempsy stared at the skies in disbelief. It was not the storm that came as such a surprise; it was the comet. Archmaster Belegra had told him it would come, but he had not believed; instead he had chosen to deny the truth, to go into the greatest of peril unprepared because of his own blindness. It took some time for him to accept this new reality, since it seemed everything in his world had suddenly changed.

Next came his anger. What did Archmaster Belegra expect him to do against the ultimate adversary? How could he ever be expected to achieve victory? His father had taught him that joining a battle where there is no chance for victory was to die a noble fool, but General Dempsy could see no honorable way out. No matter what his father had said, honor was a thing worth dying for, and he would not back away from his responsibilities because of fear.

In his mind, a plan began to form, and his face settled into a look of determination. Whether his plan would achieve victory or utter defeat, General Dempsy would use every trick he had ever learned. May the Herald beware.

Chapter 5

In our darkest moments, we come to know the true measure of our souls.
--Ain Giest, Sleepless One

* * *

As dawn illuminated the valley, turning it into a rippling palette of light and shadow, Catrin and her friends could see the full extent of the storm damage. The majestic grove that had drawn them was no more. Not even one of the greatoaks remained standing. They were strewn about the plateau as if felled by a mighty hand. Some were almost whole but had been torn from the soil and apparently flung about. Others had been twisted then sheared off, leaving fingers of wood sticking out from stumps like splinters of bone protruding from grisly wounds. It was the lightning-struck trees, though, that disturbed Catrin most. The bark was blasted off in many places, and the exposed wood was so warped, it resembled partially melted candle wax.

Catrin surveyed the damage, walking ahead of the dispirited group toward the place that had once been the center of the grove. Her heart was hurt at the sight of the ruination, but some morbid sense drew her on, forcing her to commit the images to memory. Since passage was hard to find among the fallen leviathans, their progress was slow, but no one spoke a word of protest. Catrin ran her hands along the fallen trunks as she passed them, bidding them a silent farewell.

It took her a moment to recognize the center of the grove when she reached it. Tears filled her eyes, and her body trembled as she gazed upon the black stone. None of it had escaped damage. That which was not crushed under the fallen giants had been blasted by lightning and pounded by massive hail. All that remained was a mass of rubble and gray powder that crunched under their boots. Grapefruit-sized hailstones still littered the area, serving as poignant reminders of nature's power. Catrin turned wordlessly back to her friends, who remained downcast and silent; they had tears in their eyes, and she could see the fear in them.

"It was so beautiful," Osbourne said in a low whisper.

His words stung Catrin like a physical blow, and she moved away from the place quickly, trying to escape the oppressive weight settling on her shoulders. She wanted to believe the destruction of the grove was not her fault, but she found no comfort . . . only tremendous shame and grief. Her father had finally trusted her enough to share the knowledge of how to find his special place, and she had destroyed it. Her depression deepened when she realized it had not really been her father's place at all. Someone planted the greatoaks, by her guess, many generations ago. She had entered a sacred place and, by some unconscious action, had brought about its desecration. She felt as if she had betrayed her ancestors, and she could almost sense their accusing stares on her, denouncing her. Tears clouded her vision as she stumbled through the maze of debris.

When she reached what remained of the campsite, she began to gather what she could find of her gear. Chase reached her side but remained silent for a time.

"You can't blame yourself for the weather, Cat. This wasn't your fault. This was just like the storm we had three weeks ago. That funnel cloud did a lot of damage too, and you had nothing to do with it either," he said.

Catrin wanted to agree with him. She was no goddess or sorceress with influence on the weather. To believe she was would be silly. But she still needed a reasonable explanation for the strange occurrences that seemed to center on her. She supposed her dance above the stone could have been a hallucination, but such rationalizations did not ring of truth. When she considered the appearance of the comet, the odds against it all being coincidental were staggering. Perhaps, she thought, she had just been in the wrong places at the wrong times, but things were too similar for those events to have been purely accidental.

Once she and the others finished packing what they had left, Catrin shouldered her pack and looked at her companions. They looked away, and she understood their fear because she, too, was terrified. They probably believed she was somehow responsible for the devastation of the grove, and she feared they could be right.

"What happened last night, Cat?" Osbourne asked. "What happened to you?"

"I don't know," she said, her voice shaking. "I'm so sorry. Let's go home."

The others nodded and followed her wordlessly. They picked through the storm-tossed foliage but had to backtrack several times before finding clear passage. When they emerged in the eastern clearing, they found that it, too, was littered with debris and slowly melting hailstones. The forest trail was blocked in many places, and they had to shoulder through the brambles and thorns that abounded alongside the trail.

When the forest eventually thinned, they emerged into a bright and sunny afternoon. The valley ahead appeared largely untouched by the storm, and it seemed as if they were drifting out of a nightmare and back into a pleasant reality. Catrin relaxed when she saw a part of her world unblemished, but the images of the grove were still vivid.

Travel was easier when they were clear of the forest, and they soon approached the stairs. They descended carefully, aware that the slightest misstep could send them tumbling. Strom lost his footing once and slipped, frightening them, but he caught himself, and only loose chips of rock dropped over the edge. It took a few moments for them to calm themselves before continuing at a slower pace, and they were relieved when they finally reached the bottom.

The misty air surrounding the falls drove them onward. Once clear of the spray, they found themselves at the shady spot where they had eaten lunch the day before. They stopped and ate the last of their provisions in silence.

Familiar sights and smells brought Catrin some comfort, and as the group neared her home, she began to feel almost safe again, but the illusion was shattered when Benjin seemed to materialize from the shadows. He placed a finger to his lips, motioned for them to follow, and led them into a dense stand of pines. Catrin grew even more concerned when she spotted leather bags and packs stacked in an orderly pile, filled nearly to overflowing. The boys followed her gaze and seemed to come to the same cold realization: something else had gone very wrong.

"Don't have much time to talk, but I'm so glad you're here. Wendel and I guessed the storm might bring you home early. Couldn't be certain, but it saved me coming to find you," Benjin said just above a whisper. "Yesterday afternoon, y'see, there was a huge crowd at the Spring Challenges, even though it looked like bad weather. The games were over before the storm hit, but it was dark when everyone started to leave. Then a swift wind parted the clouds. Don't know who saw it first, but people shouted and cried when the comet appeared and didn't know what to do with themselves. They just stood and gawked and carried on about it until Nat Dersinger climbed up onto the reviewing stand.

"He started out rambling on that Istra had returned to the skies of Godsland, and Catrin's power meant she was the Herald of Istra. Yes, li'l miss, he called you by name. And now, this morning, over a dozen fishing boats came back early, each saying they had seen foreign ships. The details varied from ship to ship, but they agreed on one thing: a large host of ships is approaching the Godfist.

"When they heard this, people panicked and started shouting. A bunch of angry citizens went to the farm looking for you," he said, nodding at Catrin. "Your father and I had anticipated trouble, and I was already packed when they got there. I hid until they left. Your father knows how to deal with people, and he managed to convince them he'd sent you to the cold caves. He said you were retrieving supplies and would return on the morrow.

"He told 'em he'd let them know as soon as you came back, li'l miss. He need not have bothered with that, for I'm betting the townsfolk are now watching every road and trail that enters Harborton. I'm just glad they didn't post a sentry here at the mountain paths, or we'd have been hard pressed. Your father wanted to be here, but he knows he's being watched. He sends his love and will join us when he feels it's safe for him to escape."

"Where are we going?" Catrin asked, her voice wavering.

"High in the mountains, there's a spot Wendel and I found years ago. It's a good hiding place, and it has most of what we'll need to survive. Now we need to get going. We don't want to meet up with the townsfolk, and they could send sentries here at any time.

"Strom, Osbourne, come with us if you wish, but if you decide to stay, you must not tell where we are going. Chase, your father asked me to take you along, and I hope you want to come. He fears for your safety and thinks you'll be a help to us."

"I'll go with you," Chase said.

"Sounds like a long camping trip. I want to go," Osbourne added a moment later.

Strom seemed to struggle with some inner turmoil, and they watched as they saw him thinking. "I hate to leave Miss Mariss without a stable boy, and my mother will be without the extra income, but I'm a terrible liar, and I'd surely give you away if someone asked me. I think I should come too," he said.

With that settled, Benjin repacked the provisions and distributed the bags. Each of them was carrying a great deal when they set off, their burdens heavier than just the weight of the packs. Benjin led them through the trees, staying as far from the open trail as possible and keeping to the shadows, even though it slowed their pace.

They had covered very little distance when the fire bells began ringing. Even from a distance, the cacophony was startling and disconcerting. Benjin motioned for them to stop, dropped his pack and bag, and climbed a nearby tree. It took him a few moments to gain a clear view of the harbor. Once there, he scanned the horizon. Cursing, he scrambled back to the anxiously waiting group and tried to catch his breath.

"What did you see? What's happening?" Chase asked, fear in his voice.

"The warning fires are lit," Benjin said.

"Which fires? Is the one near the Watering Hole lit?" Strom asked anxiously.

"All of them are lit. The Godfist is under attack." His words seemed to linger in the air, and a feeling of impending doom crept across the group. Benjin cocked his head to one side as if listening intently. "We need to go. Now."

"But my father . . ." Catrin protested.

"Your father can take care of himself, li'l miss. He'd wring my neck if I let you go back there after 'im. You know he would. You're in far more danger than he is. Now go!" he said firmly, his tone leaving no room for argument. He led them on a meandering trek from shadow to shadow. They moved as quietly as they could, but every noise seemed to echo across the valley. They heard no sounds of pursuit, but they would have had to struggle to hear anything over the pounding of their hearts and their labored breathing.

Rather than head for the falls, Benjin angled north and east, and when they reached the eastern ridgeline, he started up the incline. It was a difficult climb, but it would take them into the neighboring valley, Chinawpa. It was narrower than the fertile Pinook River Valley. Bramble and thorn bushes grew thick, and few ventured there.

After having been hidden by the shadows, Catrin felt as if the whole world could see her on the face of the mountain. They climbed in anxious silence, occasionally disturbing loose rocks, which bounced down the steep incline with what sounded like a terrible clatter. Benjin occasionally stopped to scan the valley for signs of pursuit, but he saw none.

Sweaty and tired, they crested the ridgeline and stared into the valley below. The descent into the Chinawpa Valley was not as steep as their climb had been. Benjin continued to lead, moving carefully down the ridgeline at an angle to make the descent more gradual. Daylight was failing them, and he cautioned them to beware of loose rock and scree. A few tenacious trees growing out of the rock face steadied them in treacherous places.

It was early twilight when they finally reached the valley floor, tired, sore, and in need of rest.

"I know you would all like to stop, but we have to get as far away as possible before we camp for the night," Benjin said, although it was unnecessary to tell them what they already knew.

Catrin trudged along behind him, not really paying attention to where she was going, just following the body in front of her and concentrating on staying upright. She was exhausted, her muscles cramped, and she clutched her side as she walked to try to ease the aching. Staying near the ridgeline, where the vegetation was sparse, Benjin seemed to be searching for something.

"Are we looking for something specific?" Catrin asked in an irritated tone. She knew she sounded childish and contrary even as the words left her lips.

"There's a place up ahead where your father and I once made camp; it provides some shelter, but it is primarily defensible should the need arise. I don't think we'll be found tonight, but it's better to be prepared for the improbable--and sometimes the impossible. You'll have to trust me that it's the best place for us to stop," he said, continuing to walk.

Darkness settled over them and slowed their progress. The skies were overcast, and Catrin could barely make out the moon and comet behind the clouds. She could feel the energy enveloping her, but it was strange and frightening, and she closed herself to it. Still, it pulled at the edges of her mind, promising warmth, security, and power.

"Are you all right, li'l miss?" Benjin asked, concern clearly audible in his voice.

"I'm just tired and not feeling well," she replied, feeling guilty for telling only part of the truth, but she wasn't going to tell them about her strange yearnings for power. She wouldn't blame any of them for thinking she was a witch, and at this point, she was decidedly unsure of herself.

"We're just about there. We'll be resting soon, I promise. Just a little farther," Benjin said, and soon they approached a huge split in the rock face. An enormous slab of stone leaned against the valley wall, leaving a gap several paces wide. It was open on both ends, providing two routes of escape. They filed into the gap and dropped their packs. Chase began to set up a fire circle, but Benjin waved him from the task.

"No fire tonight, I'm afraid. It's just too risky."

The others knew he was right, but that did little to improve the atmosphere. They ate a cold meal in relative silence; then Benjin urged them to get some sleep, saying he would take the first watch. Deep breathing and occasional snores soon surrounded Catrin, but she could not sleep. Despite her weariness, she lay awake, wondering if she would ever feel safe again.

* * *

From high on a hill, Wendel watched the Zjhon come, frozen in morbid fascination as what looked like a wave of fire and destruction rolled through Harborton and the lowlands. He'd come here to survey the situation, to reassure himself that his friends, neighbors, and countrymen would be fine and that going after Catrin would jeopardize no one. Watching the horror unfold before him, he was faced with a new question: Would staying to defend his homeland make any difference?

His awareness was flooded with a vision of Catrin, hunted by the Zjhon, vulnerable and calling out for him. Never before had Wendel ever been so conflicted, he felt as if his spirit were being torn apart, ripped into pieces by a decision no one should ever have to make. He felt Elsa looking down on him, and he wept as he shamed her and shamed himself. His feet had taken him to the barn, where he had already, subconsciously and automatically, started saddling Charger. From beneath a pile of hay, he pulled his portion of the supplies he and Benjin had stashed away. From one of the bags protruded a painful reminder, a physical representation of his guilt and weakness. Elsa's sword reminded him of all the things he was not, of all his failings and shortcomings. It challenged him to save his countrymen *and* find Catrin--Elsa would have saved them all.

Wendel found himself in the saddle, ready to ride away from his farm, his friends--his entire life. Just as he gave Charger his heels, he caught movement from the corner of his vision. Turning his mount with his knees, he saw a mounted soldier closing on a single-horse cart. Driving the cart was Elianna Grisk, a woman of more than eighty summers. She was as sharp as a sword and took no guff from anyone, but she was more than overmatched. Her horse was little more than a pony, and he was weary with age; he labored to pull her at little more than a walk, and the soldier's horse showed only the beginnings of a sweat.

Wendel cried out in dismay. His mind had been made up, his course set, but now he found himself swayed. Reaching back, he grabbed Elsa's sword and released a battle cry that had not been heard in many seasons. As he charged toward the approaching soldier, he saw the look of relief on Elianna's face; she believed he would save her. Life had given Wendel no other choice; there was only one way he could ever live with himself: he had to save them all.

* * *

In the darkness, all of Benjin's fears came to life and stalked him from every direction, waiting for him to let down his guard for even a moment. He was soft and slow with age, and he was unprepared for what lay ahead. Too long had he lived an easy life, forgetting the lessons his father and grandfather had taught him. He had always thought there would be time to prepare, time to train his children to face the coming storm, but now the storm had come early, and his work was not even begun.

Things most people thought of as legend were now here as flesh and blood, wood and iron, pain and fire. The Masters had always said it would only cause a panic if the truth was known to all, and thus they kept their knowledge hidden. The citizens of the Godfist would pay for the Masters' folly . . . and his.

Chapter 6

Men are fickle creatures, capable of kindness and compassion yet fascinated by the basest atrocities.
--Argus Kind, Zjhon executioner

* * *

When Catrin pulled herself from her bedroll, all but Benjin still slept. Their shelter blocked much of the morning light, and the air was still cool in the shadows. Benjin stood at the southern opening of the crevasse, his silhouette standing out in stark contrast to the bright landscape beyond. Catrin padded silently to his side and put her arms around him. He gave a start at her touch, and she knew he must have been in deep thought since he was usually impossible to sneak up on.

"Sorry," she said.

"It's all right, li'l miss. You just startled me."

"Not just that. I'm sorry about all of this. I never meant to cause so much trouble. I'm not even sure what I did, but now I've dragged all of you into my mess," she said, and she leaned her head against his shoulder for comfort.

He patted her on the head and guided her into the sunlight. "None of this is your doing, Catrin."

She looked up at him, surprised he would call her by name. She was so accustomed to "li'l miss" that her name sounded odd on his lips.

"We live in times of change, and all of us will be affected whether we wish it or not," he continued.

"But it seems, everywhere I go, trouble follows. It doesn't seem safe to be near me," she said, wanting to tell Benjin about the destruction of the grove, but she could not bring herself to speak of it.

"You can look at it that way if you wish, but I suggest you concentrate on what you can do to make the situation better. You cannot change what has already happened, but you can prepare yourself for the future. I can't say what this day will bring, but I vow to face it with my head high and my wits about me. I suggest you do the same. You can wallow in self-pity if you like, but it'll only bring you misery. There's a greatness in you that you don't realize yet, Catrin, so you must not lose hope. We'll get through this together and be stronger for it."

"I know you're right. I'm sorry."

"And no more 'sorrys' from you," he said, shaking his finger at her. "I'll strike a bargain with you: If you promise not to intentionally hurt me, and I promise not to intentionally hurt you, then there will be no more need for another 'I'm sorry' between us. Do I have your word?"

"You have my word," she said with a small smile.

"And I give mine," he replied with a flourish and a bow. He smiled and touched her shoulder. "C'mon, let's go make the best of things."

Catrin felt a great deal of comfort from their talk. He'd forgiven whatever mistakes she might have made, and now maybe she could forgive herself. She made a conscious effort to tell herself she was forgiven and was surprised at how much it eased her guilt and anxiety.

She acknowledged that most people never intended to hurt her; her pain had been an unintentional by-product of their actions. A great weight seemed to lift from her soul, and she decided to focus on positive things. Taking a deep breath, she released her anger in a long sigh. A renewed Catrin strode back into the crevasse with confidence.

After they broke camp, Catrin helped the others stow their bedrolls and check their packs. Benjin led them by memory, and they often had to backtrack when the way was blocked. Numerous game trails crossed the valley floor, and he seemed to have trouble finding distinguishable landmarks. By noon, it seemed they had covered very little distance.

Chase, Strom, and Osbourne talked quietly among themselves. They were worried about their families and the other people they had left behind. They speculated about the invaders: who they might be and why they would attack.

Catrin listened in silence. She ached to know her father was safe, and she tried to have faith. Her mental image of him was one of strength and unbending integrity, and bringing that image to mind soothed her. She could not picture a man of such goodness and fortitude ever being in danger, and she clung to that illusion.

"I heard said some of the ships bore a symbol of a man and woman in an embrace. Sounds like the mark of a Zjhon warship to me. As much as I hate to speculate, I fear invaders have come from the Greatland," Benjin said.

"The Greatland!" Strom snorted. "I thought that existed only in fairy tales and legends. There's been no contact with other civilizations for thousands of years. Only the old texts mention the Greatland and the Firstland, so what reason do you have to believe they even exist?"

"I assure you the Greatland does indeed exist, and the danger presented by the Zjhon empire is all too real," Benjin stated flatly.

"You talk like you've been there," said Strom.

"That's because I have been there, but that's a story for another time. What's important now is that you know the Zjhon empire has not forgotten about us. They believe the Herald of Istra will be born on the Godfist and will be revealed through great acts of power. The Zjhon prophecies say the Herald will betray them and destroy their nation . . . or something like that. It's hard to tell just what they mean.

"I believe they'll go to great lengths to capture and kill anyone they believe could be the Herald. As much as I hate to admit it, I think Nat Dersinger was right: they've come to destroy us in a desperate attempt to save themselves. They will not find the Godfist an easy place to conquer, though; the Masters and a few select families have been making preparations for decades."

"You knew they were coming?" Osbourne asked, incredulous.

"In a sense we *knew*, but our information was thousands of years old, and it was nearly impossible to tell truth from fairy tale. Huge amounts of information were lost during the great wars and the Purge, and no one knew if the prophecies were anything more than legend, but we did know the Zjhon believed them to be sacred and quite real. We did our best to prepare for an invasion, and seeing their ships over the years kept us vigilant, but we thought we'd have much more time before it would happen. I guess our calculations were wrong," he said, stopping to untangle himself from a thorn bush.

"I don't understand," Chase interjected. "How could you *calculate* when they would attack?"

"It's a long story and rather complicated, but I'll try to explain. About twenty years ago, we heard the Zjhon Church had started quoting certain scriptures again, the ones that tell the Zjhon their duty is to fight in the name of Istra. The scriptures also say Istra's return will be the divine signal to embark on their holy war. We know they calculate the Vestran cycle to be about 3,017 years, but by our reckoning, it has only been 2,983 years since Istra departed."

"I *still* don't understand," Chase persisted. "I thought Istra was a goddess. What do you mean she has returned to the skies? All I've seen in the sky is a comet."

"A long time ago, people made up stories to explain things they couldn't understand. When a comet storm lasted over a hundred years and seemed to grant otherworldly powers, they glorified it and named it 'Istra, Goddess of the Night.' The comet we saw was most likely the first of many to come.

"It's said that during the Istran Noon, some seventy-five years into the storm, there can be as many as a thousand comets visible in the sky on any night. Some of the old tales refer to the first comet as the Herald of Istra, but others say it will be a person born here on the Godfist. I'm not really certain what I believe," Benjin added.

He called for a quick break, and while the young people rested, he walked a short distance in each direction. He was pushing his way into some heavy underbrush when he exclaimed, "Aha! I knew we were going in the right direction." He emerged from the underbrush with a gleam in his eyes.

"What did you find?" Catrin asked, and he beamed at her.

"When your father and I came this way, we left a few markings in case we ever wanted to find our way back. Beneath the underbrush and a thick layer of moss, I just found one of them. We carved it deep, and, luckily, it survived the passage of time. Our destination is due east, about a day's walk from here."

They were encouraged that they were on the right path and glad they would not have to carry their packs much farther. Benjin's excitement urged him to move on, this time leading them on a much straighter path. "Try to leave the forest undisturbed," he said. "Any sign we were here will help trackers."

Now there were fewer times they had to double back, and as they ascended a sloping hill, the forest became less dense, allowing them to move with greater speed. Just before nightfall, they crested a large rise. Tall trees provided cover, and there were a few open spaces for camping. They made no fire, for fear of being seen, but the mood was cheerier than it had been the night before. The evening air was cool and not uncomfortable. They snacked on their provisions and drank springwine, but Benjin cautioned them not to overindulge.

"Your packs may seem heavy now, but soon you may wish we could've carried more."

Chase and Strom both volunteered to take the first watch to let Benjin get some rest. "Thanks, boys. I'll fare better if I can get some sleep. Sentry duty is no pleasure, and it requires concentration. Your first duty is to remain awake. Sleep has claimed many sentries, and their groups have perished. I suggest you try to achieve a restful but alert state. Quiet your minds and concentrate on your breathing. The trick is to keep part of your mind focused on sight, hearing, and smell. It takes practice, but once you master it, you'll be able to achieve it at will.

"Don't shout or make any loud noises if you spot someone, as that might draw them to us. Wake the sleepers quietly, and sleepers should try to remember to wake quietly. Our sentry's stealth may go for naught if one of us wakes in a panic," he lectured. "I trust you will do your best to remain alert during your watch, but I think it'd be best if you double up for now. Chase and Catrin, take the first watch, Strom and Osbourne, the second, and I'll take the third.

"Periodically report to each other during your watch. Walk to where the other one is posted to check. Plan to alternate which sentry goes to the other. Changes will help keep you from getting sluggish."

The night was quiet, and Catrin dozed off during her watch. She flushed with shame when Chase woke her from a deep sleep, and she stood for the rest of her watch. When morning came, Strom and Osbourne admitted they had also fallen asleep, and they vowed to do better.

When they began their hike the next day, Benjin told them to be watchful for game trails, likely watering holes, and streams or ponds where the fishing might be good. "The land we're crossing now should be within our hunting range. There's a lot of game, but it's crafty because it's had to learn to avoid wolves and mountain cats. Animals are large out here, and they can be dangerous. Keep your wits about you."

* * *

Deep in the heart of the Masterhouse, within the mountain rock that held the most sacred halls, far from the stench of refugees, Master Edling paced. Here, fresh air vents allowed him to breathe freely for the first time since he awoke. Like so many vermin chased upward by floodwater, they had come to the Masterhouse, expecting to be fed and protected, and like the great soft-hearted fool he was, Headmaster Grodin let them in. It was suicide. With the emergency provisions stored deep in the mountain, those who dwelt in the Masterhouse could have easily lasted several winters, but with the boiling refugees, they would be lucky to last until spring. Even with strict rationing, they would most likely starve.

"We should send them to the cold caves with the Volkers," Master Beron said. "They've got plenty of food."

"Grodin would never allow it, the boiling fool. He doesn't deserve to be Headmaster. That position is reserved for someone with a strong enough will to make tough decisions when they need to be made," Master Edling said. "There must be another way. The problem we have right now is that the refugees are everywhere, like lice. Thank the gods that Grodin has at least the decency to maintain the sanctity of the sacred halls. If we could get him to agree to isolate the refugees in the audience halls, we could collapse the entrances and be rid of them."

"And let them starve?" Master Beron asked, looking as if he might be sick.

"That's a big part of your problem, Beron; you've got no backbone. Would you prefer we offer them up to the Zjhon as slaves? Would you rather be a slave or die free?"

Master Beron sat for a moment before responding, but Master Edling's glare demanded he say something. "I suppose I'd rather die free," he said with uncertainty.

"You're boiling right you would. Now act like a man. These are terrible times, and if we're to survive, then terrible things must be done."

* * *

By midday, they reached an area where the vegetation thinned, giving way to mature trees that were widely spaced. Benjin scanned the valley walls, looking for another landmark.

"There was an ancient landslide--huge boulders in an enormous mound of rubble that was grown over with moss. It looked like a sleeping giant leaning against a cliff," he said as he searched, growing anxious as they traveled with no further sign of a landmark. "Wendel and I carried lighter packs, and maybe we were able to cover more ground. It was a long time ago, and my memory is not what it once was." They continued their hike for what seemed like ages, and still they found no signs of the sleeping giant. Benjin called a halt and looked for a place he could climb the valley wall.

"Maybe from a height I'll be able to see it," he said.

"I'll go with you," Chase said, following him. Catrin, Strom, and Osbourne settled into the shade to rest while they climbed.

"We've gone too far," Benjin announced when they returned. "Chase spotted some trees growing high and at odd angles, and I think they are growing out of the mound."

"Great job, you two. We must be getting close now. I trust your instincts," Catrin said.

After a short hike, Benjin smiled widely. "I think we're almost there!"

He walked closer to the cliff and found another set of marked stones, and they soon saw signs of the ancient rockslide.

"Chase and I will climb up first to locate the entrance. The rest of you stay here and remain alert. You'll want to back off a ways because we could loosen some stones," he warned. Using trees and bushes for support, they climbed the rocks, nearly slipping on places slick with moss.

In a loud whisper, Benjin said, "The entrance is blocked. We're going to have to clear it, and some debris may fall."

Chase and Benjin stacked the stones they removed to the side of the entrance, trying to keep them from falling, but a few still tumbled down the slope and crashed through the trees. The shadows were long by the time they cleared an opening large enough for Benjin to squeeze himself through to take a look.

"The place looks about the same as when I last saw it. Let's finish getting this opening cleared," he said. From inside the entrance, he was able to dislodge large sections of rock. They took two ropes and tied them to a remaining boulder and tied small stones to the other ends. Chase and Benjin tossed down the ropes, and although the stones helped to propel them through the foliage, only one reached the ground; the other caught high in the branches. Chase pulled it back up and tossed it again; this time the rope got low enough for Strom to reach it.

"Secure the packs, one at a time, and we'll haul 'em up," Benjin said. "Gather wood and kindling, preferably dry," Benjin called down after they began pulling the packs up. "Tie it off in bundles, and we'll haul them up."

Catrin and Osbourne scrambled to find wood in the failing light while Strom tied the bundles and guided them as they rose. Benjin's request for wood meant they would have a fire, which was reassuring because it meant he felt they were safely away from any pursuers. When darkness threatened to make scrounging impossible, they made the climb while they could still see, a relatively easy task when unencumbered.

No one spoke as they passed through the entrance and stared at the sight before them. The narrow opening emptied into a spacious hallway, which sloped downward at an angle. Perfectly rectangular, the hall was clearly not a natural formation, which was further evidenced by the worn scrollwork that decorated the lichen-covered walls. A short distance ahead, the hall gave way to a cavernous chamber. Its floor was littered with debris and the bones of small animals, and despite its relatively smooth appearance, it was pocked with small holes.

A narrow opening in the ceiling let in moonlight, which was reflected by the still waters of a subterranean lake. As they crossed the area that stood between them and the lake, the massive size of the cavern became apparent, and the scale of it dwarfed them. The vaulted ceiling was almost invisible in the growing darkness, and the dark waters of the lake seemed to stretch on forever in the distance.

"What *is* this place?" Catrin asked.

Benjin stood up from the bags he had been unpacking and joined the others. "Your father and I found this place by accident when looking for shelter from a storm. We couldn't figure out much about it other than the fact that this chamber had once been inhabited, possibly before the Purge. Other passages once led to this chamber, but they had all been blocked or the ceilings had collapsed. We investigated a bit, even built a small raft we used to explore. I bet it's still here." His eyes took on a faraway look as he remembered the time long past, but he pulled himself from his memories and returned to the present. "Let's get a fire started, shall we? I'm hungry and I'd really like some hot food. We can explore later."

Catrin got the tinderbox from her pack and started a fire. "Don't make the fire very large, li'l miss," Benjin warned. "We haven't put anything across the entrance yet, and the light could give us away. The cavern's big enough that it'll take up the smoke before it escapes through that hole up there, but we'll still need to be careful.

"The lake water should be safe to drink," he continued, "but I think it'd be best to boil it first. There's a kettle in one of the bags. After the water is boiled, you can put the kettle in a shallow part of the lake to cool it quickly.

Let's fill our flasks too."

Catrin and Strom set about boiling water and getting ingredients together for a stew. She was glad to see Benjin pull recurve bows, strings, and several quivers of arrows from one of the long bags, along with a couple of short fishing poles.

Long before the stew was really done, they decided it had cooked long enough and fell to it. Full stomachs made them sleepy, and they were soon curling up in their bedding, letting Benjin take the first watch.

* * *

On trembling legs, Nat approached the ruins of the greatoak grove. Tears filled his eyes as he beheld what had once been a sacred and beautiful place. Now it looked more like a battlefield of epic scale, like a vision of what was yet to come.

Catrin.

This was where she and her friends had come to camp. They were here when the storm struck. She had to be connected to the destruction. This place had been undisturbed for thousands of years, and after only one night in her presence, it was destroyed. The evidence around him only served to strengthen his convictions. He had to do something, but he lacked the resources and connections. There was only one person who could do what needed to be done: Miss Mariss. Only she was powerful enough within the Vestrana to make such a decision.

As he crept back to town, sliding from shadow to shadow, his mind was consumed, trying to find the words to convince Miss Mariss that he was right. It would not be easy, but he had to succeed. To fail again would mean certain disaster.

Chapter 7

With dogma and aspiration, one can spin sand into gold.
--Icar the glassmaker

* * *

In the late morning, Catrin awoke and saw Benjin looking exhausted. As soon as she stood, he stumbled to his bedding.

"Don't leave the cavern," he mumbled then flopped down heavily and fell asleep.

Catrin used a stick to stir the remnants of the fire, and she added twigs to the glowing coals beneath the ash. She soon had a fire large enough to boil water. Kettle in hand, she approached the lake, and it shimmered in the light breeze, its surface rippling like the scales of a snake. Concentric rings added to the impression of a giant serpent curled around itself. She wondered at its beauty, amazed that something so massive and alluring could lie hidden inside a mountain for ages.

Was something beautiful if no one saw it? Her life had been that of a farm girl, and she hadn't entertained such philosophical thoughts that she could recall, but she had changed lately. Perhaps it was the bizarre events she had experienced recently, or maybe she was growing up; either way, she knew she would never be the same. It occurred to her that she and the rest of the group, with the exception of Benjin, would be growing up fast.

Curiosity gnawed at her, and she decided to wet her feet in the lake, if only to conquer her fear of something grabbing her and pulling her in. She let the water cover her ankles, finding it curious that little sand or mud covered the lake floor. The black stone was smooth and cool under her toes, almost too slick to stand upon. With the kettle filled, she pulled herself away from the mysterious serpent lake. The entire place intrigued her and sent her awareness into motion. So much of the cavern was obscured by darkness; her imagination bridged the gaps with grand images. Some of her mind's creations filled her with an almost irresistible desire to explore; others urged her back to the relative safety of camp.

Walking toward the fire, she looked up at the distant ceiling, which appeared to be a natural stone formation, in contrast to the man-made entrance hall. Stalactites reached inexorably toward the water below. When she looked ahead again, she saw Chase about to walk into her, his head craned upward. He, too, was caught up in the majesty of their hideaway, and a fair amount of water sloshed from her kettle onto his feet when Catrin stopped short to avoid the collision.

"Sorry," she said.

"No problem. I should've seen you coming. It's just that this place is so mystifying. It's not that it scares me or anything, but there's a strange feeling in the air--or something."

"I know what you're saying, and I feel like that too. I like it, and yet it frightens me a bit. Let's just sit by the fire while you dry out."

Strom and Osbourne came over to join them by the remains of the fire, bringing their mixture of nuts and dried fruit and hard, dark bread. As their eyes adjusted to the relative darkness of the cavern, they found they could see quite well despite the low light. Revitalized by the snack, Chase suggested they have a look around, and Osbourne agreed to stand guard.

As they skirted the lake, the walls began to close in, and the rock shoreline tapered to a narrow point, beyond which the water lapped directly against the nearly vertical walls of the dome. They couldn't quite make out the far side of the cavern, but they could make a fair guess at the distance. It was farther than any of them thought they could swim, not that they wanted to swim in that ominous-looking water.

The place had a powerful energy, and the black water brought to mind visions of giant serpents lurking just below the surface, lying in wait for unsuspecting swimmers. They had seen no indication of fish or any other creatures in the lake, but that seemed logical considering the lack of sunlight. They continued on along the shoreline, which was relatively smooth and free of debris.

Along the opposite shoreline, Catrin spotted an irregular shadow against the cavern wall. Moving in for a better look, they found the remains of the raft Benjin and Wendel had made years before. It looked as if they had pulled the raft to shore, stood it up, and propped it against the cavern wall. The logs were crumbling, and the rope had long since deteriorated, falling away when Chase gave it a tug. They left it where it was so Benjin could see it. Perhaps, Catrin thought, it might spark some good memories.

When they returned to camp, Benjin was pulling the kettle from the smoldering coals. He strode to the lake, kettle in hand, and it hissed as he placed it in the cold water. He dropped the handle and hastily pulled his hand away then waved to the returning group with a smile.

"Well, did you find anything exciting?" he asked.

"We found your raft," Chase announced with pleasure. "It definitely needs some new rope to hold it together, but I think it could still float."

"There really isn't much to see from what I recall, but if we find the time, we could lash it back together just for old time's sake," Benjin said then paused a moment before addressing them in a more serious tone. "We may need to stay here far longer than we are prepared for, and we need to get ready so we have food during the winter," he said as he walked over to where he had unpacked the bows and fishing rods.

"Catrin, you and Chase are both experienced hunters, and I'd like you to see if you can bring down any game. We can't afford to be picky. We're going to need as much meat as we can get. I believe there's a stream to the north and east of here. If you find it, look for a good fishing hole. I don't think there are any fish in this lake, but you never know. On a rainy day, we could try dropping a line." He handed Chase and Catrin each a bow, string, and a quiver of arrows.

"Try to retrieve any arrows you loose. My fletching skills are not what they used to be, and I was never very good to begin with," he said.

Catrin and Chase strung their bows, and Catrin was glad to have her familiar hunting tool in hand. After drawing her belt knife, she cut off a length of rope and coiled it around her belt. Chase seemed satisfied with Benjin's bow, and he got some dried beef strips from their provisions so they would have something to eat while they hunted.

"I want Strom and Osbourne to help me gather wood so we can build a small smoke room inside the cavern. We can also work on getting more water boiled, cooled, and into the flasks," he continued. With the responsibilities assigned, they got their gear and set off.

"Be back before dark," Benjin instructed. "Stay quiet and always remain alert. If you need help, howl like wolves."

Catrin and Chase made short work of their descent and headed east. They saw a few game trails, and Chase spotted a couple of buck rubs on the trunks of some nearby trees, but they found no other signs of wildlife.

"We need to find water. If we find water, we'll find game," Chase said.

They stood quietly, listening for the sound of moving water, but they heard only leaves rustling in the light breeze. Catrin checked the air for the scent of apples or berries, knowing that those, too, would attract animals, but she didn't detect anything. They turned toward the east since Benjin had mentioned a stream somewhere in that direction. Walking in stealthy silence, they were alert for any movements, large or small.

Chase stopped to wipe the sweat from his eyes. "It may be hot now, but there's a storm coming. I can smell it."

"I smell it too," Catrin said. "Let's hope it waits till after nightfall to rain. We better get moving."

A moment later, though, Chase stopped and stared, open mouthed, at a large eagle, which swooped in for a kill just a short distance ahead. Catrin watched in awe as the magnificent bird smashed into the ground and just as suddenly propelled itself back into the air with a huge black snake in its claws. The eagle had to work hard to gain the air, the weight of the snake holding it down, but it pumped its powerful wings and flew back into the treetops. They soon heard the screams of the eaglets demanding their turn to be fed.

Catrin and Chase pressed on, hugging the valley wall to keep from getting turned around in the cover of the trees. Catrin froze when she heard a branch snap off to her right. She and Chase nocked their arrows and took up positions behind nearby trees, but nothing emerged from the woods. Catrin was about to give up when Chase tapped her on the shoulder and pointed.

A little farther north from where the noise had come, a medium-sized spike buck was following a pair of does into a narrow clearing. Catrin took aim at the buck, the largest of the three. Her arm trembled as she held the bowstring taut, waiting for a clean shot. The buck suddenly flicked both ears forward and snorted, and all three deer turned and fled, their fluffy white tails standing up straight.

Taking hasty aim, Catrin loosed her arrow. Her shot flew over the buck's head, but it didn't miss by much. The sound of the arrow frightened him, and he turned aside, giving Chase the broadside shot he'd been waiting for. Chase's arrow hit just behind the buck's shoulder, and he reached the deer almost before it hit the ground. Catrin held back a moment and allowed him time to grant the animal a quick death. She understood the need to hunt, but she didn't like to kill or see anything die. Chase would take care of that part, and she was grateful. She tossed him a length of rope with a sad smile, and he tied the buck's ankles.

"Nice shot," she said.

"Couldn't have done it without ya, Cat. If you hadn't panicked and taken the bad shot, I might never have gotten a good one. Your shot wasn't even close, you know," he said, grinning.

"It was close enough to make him hesitate and change his course, which gave you a sleeping bull for a target," she scolded and set off in the direction her arrow had gone. She pushed her way farther into the underbrush, and caught a sudden movement from the corner of her vision.

Stumbling backward, she found herself staring down at a large boar. She let out a yelp as she met the boar's eyes and knew immediately she had made a big mistake. The threatened boar interpreted her direct eye contact as a challenge and dropped its head as it charged. Catrin backpedaled as quickly as she could, and she could hear Chase scrambling behind her, trying to come to her aid. In a split second, she realized she could not possibly outrun the boar and knew her best chance was to shoot it before it gored her.

She spun gracefully, pulling an arrow from her quiver as she turned. With practiced precision, she nocked the arrow and drew, but in mid-draw she realized that she was not going to be fast enough. The boar was going to reach her within an instant of her firing. She leaped into the air as she loosed her arrow, and she heard the air whistle as Chase's arrow whizzed by. Both arrows struck the beast in the chest, but the boar's momentum carried its enormous weight forward and sent it crashing into Catrin's legs while she was still in midair. She felt a tusk stab her in the shin as she was tossed higher into the air by the impact.

Face-first, she landed on the flailing hooves of the mortally wounded boar. Her landing knocked the wind out of her, and she was kicked in the face several times before she could get her breath and roll free. Fortunately, the boar was in its death throes, and the kicks had little force behind them. Chase quickly finished off the boar and turned to Catrin, who sat dazed and winded.

Her vision clouded as her eye started to swell shut, and blood poured freely from her nose and lips. The boar's tusk hadn't penetrated her leather pants, but her leg felt as if it were bruised to the bone. She sucked air through her teeth as she pulled her pant leg up to expose the wound. Her leg was swelling, and she soon had a large lump on her shin.

"I'll go back for help," Chase said just as a light rain began to fall.

"I can walk," she said, but she winced when she put weight on her wounded leg.

"Our kills weigh more than the two of us combined. I'm going for help," Chase said firmly. He turned and jogged back toward the cavern, occasionally howling like a wolf. He and the others returned more quickly than Catrin would have thought possible. She stood to greet them, and Benjin's face paled when he saw her. Her wounds were not as bad as they appeared, but she made a ghastly sight. The rain had streaked the dirt and blood on her face, and the swelling was getting worse.

"Cripes, Cat. You were supposed to shoot the game, not tackle it," Strom said. "It looks like he put up a pretty good fight."

Benjin gave her a thorough looking over and shook his head. "You got mighty lucky, li'l miss. Not many survive facing a boar that size. I'd say you fared pretty good by the looks of things. D'ya think you can walk?"

"Yes. It hurts a bit, but I don't think anything is broken," she said through gritted teeth. She put some weight on her leg and it held, but it throbbed painfully.

Benjin looked for a fallen branch but found none that suited him. He cut down a nearby sapling, stripped it of branches, and cut it to be as long as Catrin was tall. He handed her the makeshift walking stick. "We all need a little help sometimes. Lean on this."

Chase and Strom hacked at a couple of saplings with their belt knives and stripped them of branches. Benjin tied the animals' ankles then inspected the saplings. They slid the smaller sapling under the ropes that tied the buck's ankles and took the larger sapling to the boar.

Benjin helped them get the boar on the pole then stood and wiped his hands on his pants. "Strom and I will take the boar. Chase and Osbourne can carry the deer. Are you sure you want to walk, li'l miss? We could come back for you."

"I can make it," she said, wiping blood from her nose, but she leaned heavily on the walking stick. Benjin and Strom each put a shoulder under the sapling and struggled to get the boar off the ground.

"I know I said we couldn't afford to be picky, but in the future, let's stick to game smaller than a horse," he said between clenched teeth. With that, they began lurching back toward the cavern.

Chase and Osbourne moved in behind them, struggling a bit with the weight of the buck. Catrin limped along, lost in thought as she struggled to keep up.

They reached the base of the rock pile where the cavern was located, dropped the boar and buck to the ground, and flopped down beside them. They lay there, exhausted. Catrin leaned against a tree and tried to ignore the pain in her face and leg.

"With these kills, you and Chase should be able to sit back and relax. My stomach thanks you," Strom said with a smirk and a quick bow. Benjin had rigged a harness to lift the kills up to the cavern while Chase and Catrin had been out hunting. After they raised the deer and the boar, Benjin gave her his shoulder to lean on as she carefully put her injured leg into one side of the harness he had crafted. She leaned heavily on him as she gingerly lifted her other leg into the apparatus. "We'll take it real slow. Just let us know if you need help or if you feel you are in trouble," Benjin said.

As soon as her feet left the boulders, she started spinning, and she had to catch herself on a nearby branch. Chase did what he could to steady the rope from his perch in a tree above her, but his movements shook the tree, showering her with rainwater. He pushed the rope out away from a large branch, and she passed well clear of it. When she finally cleared the ledge, they looked at the boar then at the deer and finally at their small smoke room.

"We're going to need a bigger smokehouse," Osbourne said.

Benjin attended to Catrin's wounds while the others dressed the carcasses. She winced as he wiped the dried blood from her face and nose. Her eye was nearly shut, and her nose was sore, but those were barely noticeable compared with the throbbing pain in her shin. She pulled back with a sharp intake of breath when he lightly ran the damp cloth over it. He got his wax-sealed herbal kit and another flask of clean water and told Catrin to tilt her head back and open her mouth. She did so reluctantly, knowing what was coming. He sprinkled a fair amount of ground humrus root into her mouth and handed her the flask. She gulped, and water splashed down the sides of her face as she hurried to wash down the bitter-tasting herb. She took several more large gulps before she would let Benjin take the flask from her.

He put a bit more of the powder in his palm and poured a small amount of water on it. He mixed it into a paste and told Catrin to lie back and relax. She sprawled on her back but could not relax; her leg was still throbbing, and she tensed in anticipation of his touch on her swollen shin. He did it as quickly and gently as he could, but she cried out in pain, and tears flowed down her cheeks.

"It'll take a little while for the humrus root to dull the pain, but it should help you sleep tonight," he said. Soon, mercifully, the potion began to take effect. Her pain was mostly dulled, and exhaustion overtook her. The herbs and the rhythmic sound of the falling rain soon lulled her into a deep sleep.

* * *

Though he had met with General Dempsy in the past, Kern felt an ache in his stomach and his knees trembled. This mission was different from all that had come before it, and the general's mood had been ranging from seething to bitter. The men had come to fear him more than ever as he lashed out in anger. His judgments over disputes became increasingly harsh, often punishing both the accused and the accuser. Most disputes were now handled between the individuals for fear of General Dempsy's decisions.

Biting his lip, Kern rapped on the general's cabin door.

"Come."

"Good afternoon, General Dempsy, sir."

"Overseer Kern. Report."

"We've covered the farmlands, sir. She's not there. I've sent men into the mountains, but I've received no reports yet. We'll find her, sir. You can depend on that."

"You'd better. Your men are supposed to be the best. I suggest you prove it, or your next medal could be posthumous."

"Yes, sir."

Chapter 8

The righteous are bound by duty to enlighten the heathens and emancipate the souls of those beyond reform.
--Archmaster Belegra

* * *

The next few days passed more quickly than Catrin had thought they would. Her wounds were healing well, and she spent most of her time dressing, butchering, salting, and smoking the game Benjin and Chase brought back. Strom had had some luck with a fishing hole, and there were fish to be filleted then cooked, salted, or smoked. Racks made of fresh-hewn saplings now lined one of the cavern walls, and a few were already laden with cured venison, pork, and fish. Strom had been elected to find fruits and nuts, and he brought in apples, berries, and sacks of black walnuts.

As the provisions mounted, Benjin said, "I'm pleased with your work, but we still need at least three times what we have if we're to survive the winter."

"I'd rather not live here, but if I must, I don't want to go hungry." That was the mantra that kept the young people working. No one was happy with the prospect of a prolonged stay, but they tried not to dwell on it; their lives depended on the work they had to do, which meant less idle time to speculate about the future and the fates of their loved ones.

Despite Catrin's rapid recovery, Benjin continued to apply humrus paste to her shin, though he used it sparingly to conserve his supply of herbs. Catrin gladly retired her walking stick when she could put weight on her leg without any pain.

Benjin described a few herbs he thought might grow in the area and asked them to harvest only half of any plants they found, making sure to leave enough for repopulation. "If you only find one or two plants, just pick a few leaves. Some will be better than none," he said.

Within a few weeks, they had food to last until spring with strict rationing. They had to use the last of their salt supply, however, and their herb-gathering efforts had produced little. "There's no help for it, I suppose," Benjin said when he shook the last of the salt from the bag, too little even to cover a perch fillet. "We can't smoke too much meat without giving away our location. We'll need to eat as much fresh meat and fish as possible until we can no longer hunt. Any food that'll keep is off limits. We'll need it before spring arrives, no doubt. I want Strom and Catrin to gather more black walnuts, since they seem to be plentiful, and any other nuts or fruits you find.

"I know I've been pushing you all hard, but I've little choice in the matter. The storms can be intense this high in the mountains, and the snow doesn't melt till spring. Once the snows start, we could be trapped in here until spring. We need to gather more food so we can eat comfortably this winter, and we're going to need a much larger supply of firewood. I want you to spend half of each day hunting and foraging and the other half collecting wood. If you can do both at once, then you'll certainly impress me. I'm going to look for herbs. Our supply is far too small for my liking, and I know the places they like to hide," he said with a wink as he shouldered his pack.

When Benjin returned that evening, he was laden with plants and roots, and he entered the cavern with a big smile. "I feel a bit better now, I should have enough medicinal herbs to deal with most ailments, but try not to fall off any cliffs and watch out for snakes," he said. Along with the herbs, he produced turnips, asparagus, and even some wild garlic, which he used to make a delicious soup.

* * *

"I hope we don't have to eat all of these walnuts to survive," Strom said while he and Catrin were returning from one of their many nut-gathering outings, and she admitted that she was dreading the winter as much as he.

Tension grew as the weeks passed, and even Benjin began to show signs of worry. One night he sat them all down around the fire. "Wendel and I made an agreement. If he hadn't joined us within forty days, then I was to sneak back as close to Harborton as I could to see what's going on. I'm going to leave tomorrow before dawn, but I only plan to be gone for four or five days. You all know to remain quiet and stay hidden, keep the fires small, and try not to leave obvious signs of your passage when you're out hunting and gathering," he lectured.

"Maybe I should go with you," Chase offered.

"It'll be a very dangerous task, and I'm more experienced at this kind of thing. I want you all to stay here and continue on as you have been, but be extra careful; you must protect one another."

"What if you don't come back in five or six days?" Osbourne asked, concern written clearly on his face.

"The best thing you can do is keep yourselves safe and carry on as you have been. If you think you've been spotted, or if you need to escape, try to go east. About a half a day's walk from here, there's a large river. Follow the river north. When you reach the waterfall, climb to the top if you can and then follow the valley north by northeast," Benjin said, pausing a moment to look into the troubled faces in front of him to gauge their concern.

"I don't think you'll have any trouble; you're well hidden here. Just remember to stay inside as much as possible and keep quiet. You'll have enough provisions to last through the winter if you use good judgment. Strom, take the first watch and wake Chase for the second. I'm going to need my sleep tonight," he said before retiring to his bedroll.

Catrin and the others exchanged worried glances but didn't speak. They wanted to know what was going on outside their hideaway, but they feared for Benjin's safety. The tension in the cavern was palpable.

Catrin woke in the dead of night to find Benjin already gone. Chase sat near the fire and waved when he saw her sit up, and she joined him by the fire.

"How long ago did he leave?" she asked quietly.

"It's been quite a while. His idea of morning is more like the middle of the night," he replied. He declined her offer to take the rest of the watch, and instead they talked until dawn.

* * *

Though most of his wounds had healed, Peten Ross still walked with a limp, and not a moment passed that he did not feel pain. Yet no one showed him the slightest bit of favor or kindness--he was just another refugee, lumped in with commoners and men he wouldn't let shine his boots. The stench alone was enough to make him want to escape, but it was the chance to prove his bravery and worth to Roset and everyone else that was too alluring to resist.

She and the others had shunned him ever since the snake incident. Even knowing the snake was harmless, Peten recoiled from the thought of its touching him. He would prove Roset and the others wrong. While most chose to spend their time wallowing in self-pity, Peten had been looking for a way out. There were too many people confined in the Masterhouse, and he was convinced that Wendel Volker and those who followed him to the cold caves were getting fat on the Ross family's meat. For generations his family had been storing sides of beef in the cold caves, but only now did that practice seem a liability. It infuriated Peten that he should have to endure a strict ration when those who didn't deserve it dined on his food.

Things had seemed hopeless until Peten met a dirty little man whose name he did not remember nor care to know. All that was important was that this man was willing to reveal some of the Masterhouse's secrets for nothing more than a few silvers.

When everyone else was asleep, Peten walked on the tips of his toes over the still bodies that seemed to carpet the cold flagstones. One man cursed him when he stepped on a finger, but no one else seemed to notice or care.

At the entrance to the hall that led to the sacred chambers, those denied to the refugees, a bored-looking guard seemed to be having trouble keeping his eyes open. It seemed an eternity that Peten waited, but then the moment came: the guard let his eyes droop closed. After waiting for a few more anxious moments, Peten moved as quietly as he could past the guard, his limp making the act of being silent even more difficult. His right foot seemed to want to drag across the stone with every step, and he gritted his teeth against the pain.

Voices carried through the halls, and Peten flattened himself against the corridor wall, feeling exposed and vulnerable.

" . . . can smell the boiling vermin from here."

"Won't be much longer before that problem is . . ."

The voices faded and Peten hastily resumed his quest, suddenly panicking, worried he had forgotten what the man told him. Was it left at the fifth hall then right at the third? Or was it the other way around? Sweat dripped into his eyes as he concentrated. Part of him wanted to give up, to go back and hide with his family and friends, but another part seemed to have awakened. He could make a difference. His actions could save countless lives. In his mind he played through the drama and pageantry that he imagined would follow his great victory. His people needed a leader, a person who would take action in the face of death, and he was that leader. All he had to do was prove that to everyone.

With determination, he strode forward as fast as his limp would allow. Following his gut instinct, he turned left when he reached the fifth hall and right at the third. No more voices broke the silence, and finding the room the man had told him about sent Peten's confidence soaring. If only his confidence could defeat the smell, which was worse than the smell of the refugees. The thought of climbing through a sewer made Peten want to wretch, but it was the path to his salvation. Driven by his need for power and a deeper, almost unrecognizable, feeling of responsibility for those he cared about, he entered the sewer.

The journey was something he hoped he could erase from his memory for all time, but he doubted it. At least the man had been true to his word about leaving a torch. Obtaining flint from a fellow refugee had cost him another silver, but it was coin well spent. Without the torch, he would have been lost. When he rounded a corner and saw a splash of dim light illuminating the way ahead, though, he quickly tossed the torch into the fetid water.

When he reached the grate, he nearly wept. Grasping at the bars that blocked his way, he cursed the dirty little scoundrel who had sent him on a fool's quest. Anger boiled in his belly, and he growled in fury. It took every scrap of will he possessed to refrain from crying out, from venting his rage on the heavens. In his anger, his muscles contracted and he could feel the bars digging into his flesh, but then something amazing happened: One of the bars began to move. It was only the slightest movement, but it was enough. Increasing the pressure, Peten began to push and pull on the bar as hard as he could. Mortar fell away in large chunks, and with a suddenness that sent Peten stumbling backward, the bar gave way.

Again Peten had to refrain from crying out as he pushed his way past the remaining bars. Rock and metal bit into his skin and left him with a dozen minor cuts, but he gained the fresh air and his freedom.

The drainage ditch that ran from the mouth of the sewer ended at a small cove so fouled and stagnant that no one would stay near it for long, and Peten decided that it could be no worse than the sewers had been, and it was his best chance to slip into the water undetected.

Beyond the cove he bathed in the crashing waves, letting them blast the foulness from him, but the smell seemed to follow him no matter how hard he scrubbed. In the end, he gave up washing and concentrated on swimming and, at times, wading his way along the coast. The sun began to rise, as if Vestra wished to expose him to the Zjhon.

Peten cursed his luck and looked for a good place to leave the water and gain the shore. He had seen no shadows and heard no voices for quite some time, and he knew he needed to cover a lot of distance in a hurry. When he reached the shore, he climbed a pair of massive stones that cradled an ancient tree between them. Using a branch to pull himself up, he had no time to react and not the slightest chance of avoiding the boot heel that was hurtling toward his face. In an instant, the world went dark.

* * *

A broken twig and a plant that stood at an angle, its leaves crumpled and broken, were Benjin's first warning, and it was far too close to their hideaway for his comfort. There were more signs as he moved closer to the populated lands. Years of training became fresh in his mind once again, as the need for stealth became paramount. When he neared the farm, his fears grew. It seemed the Zjhon were everywhere at once. Their numbers were difficult to believe, and he considered abandoning his quest, but the need for information drew him on. It was all too clear to him now that they would not be able to remain in the cavern until spring, the Zjhon would tear down the forest and pick the mountains clean if that was what it took.

When he reached the tree line that bordered the farm, he crouched behind a tree and waited. Soldiers milled around the area, and he thought he might have to wait until after dark. In the distance, a bell rang, and many of the soldiers stopped what they were doing and headed back toward Harborton; a few remained. "Not perfect," Benjin said to himself, "but it's an improvement."

One man went to the well, and two others walked toward the cottages. No one else could be seen. Benjin made his move and charged up to the back of the barn. Looking through a knothole in the barn door, he checked for Zjhon but saw none. Doing his best to be quiet, he slid the door partly open and slipped in. First he went to the feed stall, and was pleased to find that the Zjhon had not taken everything. A salt block sat in the corner, and there were still some oats in one of the barrels. Being as quiet as possible, he broke up the salt block and put it into a couple of sacks that had been hanging from a wooden peg. He put some of the oats in a sack as well, but he did not take too much, knowing he could carry only so much and still maintain his stealth.

It took time to carry each sack into the loft, but he figured this was the safest place to hide them until he came back. The loft was also where he'd hidden his sword, and he pulled it from behind some bales of moldy hay. He had considered taking it with him when they first left for the mountains, but he hadn't been able to bear the thought of talking to Catrin about her mother. He could not lie to her, and if she saw the sword, she would surely have questions. Any answers he gave to those questions would certainly have led to questions about Elsa. The memories were still painful for him, and he could see no good that would come from revealing things to Catrin that would only confuse and hurt her. Now, though, his need outweighed his desire to spare Catrin the pain of knowing.

Even as the thought occurred to him, he heard the barn's front door open and the sound of horses walking into the barn. In the next moment, he heard something that chilled his bones and made him curse his own stupidity: "Why is the back door open?" someone asked in Zjhonlander. Benjin hadn't heard it spoken in many years, but he recognized the peril of his situation immediately. After making sure the sacks of salt and grain were well hidden, he climbed over the bales of straw that were stacked almost to the angled roofline. Squeezing himself through the cobwebs, he ducked under the rafters that gave him barely enough room to pass. When he finally reached the other side, he quietly slid down into the small open area between the straw pile and the back door of the loft.

From what he could hear, the soldiers below had not called out or raised the alarm, but he heard them climb to the loft. As quietly as he could, Benjin opened the loft door just enough to see if anyone was outside. When the way looked clear, he opened the door and climbed out onto the narrow ledge that ran along the top of the barn doors. With his back to the barn, Benjin closed the door and scooted himself sideways until he reached the makeshift ladder he'd built many years ago. It had taken a only few scraps of barn board cut into short strips and nailed to the side of the barn to create a nearly invisible ladder. As he climbed down it, he was thankful for his own ingenuity.

When he reached the bottom, he saw the soldiers coming back down from the loft, and he raced to the fence. Using his momentum and a hand on the top rail, he launched himself over the fence. In truth, he was lucky his grip did not miss the top rail since the entire fence was overgrown with honeysuckle and blackberry bushes. It was the growth that gave him cover while he fled. Running while crouched is not an easy thing to do, and his knees ached terribly when he finally reached the tree line. From there, he watched and rested.

The Zjhon seemed quite relaxed. They had taken Harborton and the highlands, and now those who remained to hold these seemed content to get fat on what had been left behind by the people of the Godfist. Anger and resentment burned in Benjin's belly, and when a sentry came too close, he moved without hesitation. Silently he approached the bored-looking soldier and caught him completely by surprise. Using his momentum and leverage to focus the power of his muscles, Benjin landed a devastating punch that dropped the soldier without a sound. After dragging the man back to the tree line, Benjin took his uniform and left him there.

Knowing it was only a matter of time before someone noticed the sentry was missing or found his body, Benjin hurried through the trees, looking for the game trail he used to hunt. When he found it, he took a moment to change into the soldier's uniform, and he stashed his clothes near the trail. He tucked his hair beneath the jacket collar and hoped his disguise would be sufficient, though he knew it was thin.

Getting to Harborton was as easy as following a series of trails through the woods that dominated the foothills, but when he reached the edge of town, his task became a great deal more difficult--the darkness his only boon. After sifting through a garbage heap on the outskirts, Benjin found some things that might help him get to the Watering Hole without having to answer any questions. He cut the top off an old leather flask and filled it with a noxious mixture of rotting vegetables and stale wine, and he hid the flask within his coat.

When the moon was high, Benjin walked the streets, doing his best to look as if he belonged there. Careful planning took him along a route that he guessed would have the least traffic. One street ran along a narrow canal whose smell kept most people at a distance, and another was little more than a dirty alley between two rows of buildings. The refuse that had accumulated there over many years made getting through difficult, but Benjin was grateful for it.

At the end of the alley, he could see his destination. The faded and chipped sign above the inn had always been a welcoming sight, but now

Benjin knew better. The Zjhon religion declared churches and libraries sacred and decreed that they must not be destroyed during the conquest of a city, but it was the soldiers who declared inns sacred. It was a longstanding practice that those the Zjhon conquered were allowed to continue a limited and heavily taxed business, and it appeared this was still the case, for the sounds coming from the Watering Hole indicated the inn was still operating. Benjin could only hope that Miss Mariss was well and still running the inn.

Taking a deep breath, he prepared himself for what would likely be the most dangerous part of his journey. A patrol of soldiers walked the streets looking half asleep and utterly disinterested, and Benjin waited for them to pass. As soon as they were out of sight, he left the safety of the shadows and walked into the moonlight, hoping no one chose this moment to leave the inn. As he crossed the street, a loud outburst of laughter emanated from inside, and Benjin nearly leaped from his skin, but no one emerged.

With an ill-advised burst of speed, he covered the last bit of distance between himself and the shadows alongside the inn. Just as he rounded the corner, he encountered a soldier who'd been relieving himself in the bushes.

"Who's there?" the man asked in Zjhonlander, and Benjin nearly stumbled as he was taken by surprise. Quickly he turned and leaned over, making vomiting sounds and pouring some of his foul mixture on the ground. "If you can't hold your drink, you shouldn't indulge," the man said as he came closer. "What's your name, soldier? Whom do you serve under?"

Benjin felt a hand on his shoulder, and he prayed for good luck. As he turned toward the soldier, he never raised his head, and he made more retching noises, and then he poured the rest of his mixture on the man's boots. The soldier stepped back, and Benjin waited to see if his plan had worked or if it would be the end of him. The soldier must have gotten a whiff of the foul mixture and Benjin heard his stomach heave. Without another word, the man turned and left, probably hoping to keep the contents of his stomach where they were.

As soon as the man turned the corner, Benjin stumbled around the back of the inn and was pleasantly surprised the find the back door unguarded. Miss Mariss's kitchen looked much as it always had, save there were fewer people and a lot less food to be seen, and now there was an oppressive pall of desperation that hung in the air.

When the kitchen door suddenly swung inward, Benjin crouched down, but Miss Mariss saw him instantly. Her face registered no surprise or fear; she simply held a finger to her lips, grabbed half a loaf of bread, and walked back to the common room. Admiring her strength, Benjin moved to a darkened corner and waited. It took some time for Miss Mariss to convince her unwelcome guests that the inn was closing for the evening, but she eventually came back to find Benjin. Again she held a finger to her lips and led him to the cellar, which, like most cellars, was damp, cold, and had a smell like moldy soil.

"It's good to see you, Benjin," she said after leading him to a place between the stacks of crates and barrels, most of which appeared to be empty. "There's been much worry over the safety of you and those in your care."

"We've worried about you as well."

"I've got it good compared to most. I have to put up with the scoundrels in my inn, but I have most of my freedom. As for the rest, things could be a great deal better."

Benjin nodded his agreement, and they settled down to discuss their plans.

* * *

When five days had passed and Catrin and the others still had seen no sign of Benjin, they were worried, but they tried to be optimistic.

"I'm sure he's just being extra careful, and all the rain we've been having is probably slowing him down as well," Chase said.

"Knowing Benjin, he's probably so overloaded with salt and cheese that he'll barely make it back before the first snow." Strom laughed.

After ten days, the group was anxious and restless. Catrin had so much pent-up energy, she thought she could probably sprint all the way to the ocean. She was fretful and paced constantly.

"I'm going fishing," Strom announced, clearly wishing to escape the oppressive atmosphere, even if it was only to sit in the rain. Chase seemed to share his desire.

"I think I'll go hunting in the high reaches today," he said nonchalantly.

"The high reaches?" Catrin asked. "What kind of game do you expect to find up there? Goat?"

"Perhaps no game at all. I want to find a high place with a good view of the valley. I have a bad feeling about Benjin."

No one disagreed, and Strom offered to go with him, but they jointly decided one person stood less of a chance of being spotted than two. They were going against Benjin's orders, but they all felt compelled to do something--anything. Catrin and Osbourne felt helpless, left without much to do.

"I think we should keep watch while they're gone," Osbourne said, looking pale and shaken. "I'll take first watch."

"I'm going to look again for another exit from the cavern in case we need it," Catrin said.

She retrieved a coil of rope and a couple of torches that Benjin had fashioned and made her way back to the old raft. She lowered the logs to the ground and lashed them together. It was a hot job, and her eyes burned with sweat by the time she finished, but the raft looked strong. She grunted with effort as she pushed off into the dark water. The raft seemed to float well, and she hoped it would be stable. She pulled it back to shore.

Searching through the woodpile, she found a branch she could use to push herself across the water. It still had leaves on one end, and she hoped it would work like an oar if the water got too deep for poling. When she returned to the fire to light one of her torches, Osbourne looked concerned.

"I don't think it's a good idea for you to go off on that raft. It's not safe."

"Nothing we do these days is safe. But don't worry; I'll be fine."

Catrin put her spare torch on the raft along with the rope and her makeshift oar and climbed tentatively aboard the awkward craft, holding her lit torch aloft. Her weight caused the raft to sink lower into the water, and at times it was almost completely submerged; only her quick reactions kept the second torch from getting saturated. The sudden movements threatened to overturn the raft. It was precarious, but she was determined.

Poling and holding the torch up at the same time was hard, but she managed to move along the shoreline, still staying close to the cavern wall. There was no real shoreline this far out, but she did occasionally come across what appeared to have been other passageways leading into the cavern. They were all blocked with fallen rock and debris, and none appeared passable.

As she became more adept at poling, she moved more quickly toward the far end of the cavern. The water grew deeper, and she had to put her entire arm in the water to reach the bottom with her pole. Eventually the water was too deep to reach the bottom, and she pushed off the cavern walls when she could. Occasionally she pushed herself out too far and had to paddle back. Her branch made a poor paddle, and at times she made more progress by setting the branch on the raft and paddling with her free hand.

When she reached the back of the cavern, she came on a collapsed corridor that was larger than all the others. Fallen stone blocked this one too, but the size of the arch intrigued her. As she began to wonder if someone hadn't blocked the tunnels intentionally, a small breeze caressed her cheek. She sniffed the air--a bit dank but not foul.

After pushing the raft closer to the doorway, she latched onto some of the rocks that blocked it. She wedged her torch into a nearby crevice and pulled herself onto the top of a protruding rock, hoping the raft would not drift off. There wasn't much room for her on the small shelf of rock, but she managed to balance as she reached out to the raft. She had to stretch to grasp her rope, which she used to secure the raft to one of the jagged rocks at the bottom of the doorway.

Cooler air continued to seep through the rocks, and Catrin loosened some of the top pieces. It was slow work, but she cleared a hole about the size of her head. She poked her torch into it to see what lay beyond. She could see very little, but it did appear that the corridor was mostly clear beyond the initial blockage. When she pulled her torch back, she noticed a narrow rectangular slit in the stone above the doorway and shivered as she recalled the lessons that spoke of old castles having arrow slits above the entrances, often referred to as death holes. The sight of it was unsettling.

She needed a much larger opening to crawl through, but several large stones were wedged tightly just below the hole she had created. She finally got one of the large rocks to wiggle and rocked it back and forth, moving it a little more with every sweep. She gave it a hard yank and nearly fell from her perch when it jerked free, the stone hitting the water with a loud splash. Catrin leaned back against the rocks and took a couple of deep breaths.

"Are you all right?" Osbourne shouted across the water, and his words echoed loudly in the cavern.

"I'm fine. I've found another passage, and I'm going to see where it goes."

"Don't be gone too long, Cat," he said in a quieter voice. "I don't want to be here alone."

"I'll be back as soon as I can."

The hollow left by the large stone gave her more room to work and made the removal of the next one a bit easier. She soon had a hole she thought she could squeeze through. With her torch held through the hole, she saw the rubble pile sloping down and away on the other side. Dropping the torch onto the rocks on the other side--carefully so as not to extinguish it--she wriggled her way through the hole, getting slightly stuck when her belt knife caught on the stones. After freeing the knife, she slid farther through the hole. A rock broke away and moved out from under her hand, and she began to slide. She landed noisily, her face just inches from the burning torch she had tossed into the space. She wasn't bleeding, but she was a sore in several places.

After gathering her gear, she moved past the rest of the debris. The ceiling and walls were unbroken, and Catrin was convinced these halls had been sealed intentionally. It also occurred to her that whoever had done it had most likely done it in a hurry. Otherwise, the barrier would have been much more substantial. She recalled the arrow slits above the doorway and thought perhaps they had not needed much more of an obstruction.

When she moved her torch closer, she could see how cleanly the stone had been cut. There were no visible seams in the smooth walls, which seemed to be one continuous surface. The floor was also smooth, though covered with a thick layer of dust and dirt.

Walking slowly down the corridor, Catrin felt like an intruder in a place long lost to the living. Ahead she saw a doorway, but there were no tracks in the dust on the floor, so she didn't think she would encounter any wildlife. Still, she crept ahead slowly, half expecting a specter to jump out at her. Instead, she found a short hall with several doorways on either side. She looked into one of the rooms and saw some crumbled pieces of pottery and rotted wood that may have once been a bed frame. In the other rooms, she found similar hints that these had once been sleeping chambers, but the rooms were rather small. She doubted they had been rooms for the wealthy, and she wondered if they had been servants' quarters.

In another she found a washbowl behind the ruins of another bed frame. The bowl was almost perfectly preserved, with the exception of one sizable chip out of the rim. It was unlike anything she had ever seen before. She bent down and wiped her finger across the surface to find under the dust that the bowl was shiny with elaborate designs below the glaze.

As she bent down to inspect it more closely, a clump of reddish clay caught her attention. It was wedged inside one of the bed frame's wooden joints, as if it had been hidden there when the bed was still whole. Drawn to the clump by some mysterious desire, she pried it away from the disintegrating wood, and a small shape revealed itself.

In the dwindling light of her torch, it appeared to be a carving of a fish, made from some kind of milky crystal, its surface porous and rough. She placed the little carving in her pocket and in that moment saw her torch was not far from burning out. She had been gone a while, and she figured Osbourne was probably worried. She turned back, eager to tell him what she had found.

Though she hoped not to use it, her spare torch was tucked into her belt. When the first torch sputtered out, she had to quickly decide if she wanted to light the spare while the first was still hot enough to ignite it. She decided to save it since she was not far from the opening, and her vision would eventually adjust to the darkness.

Shuffling along the smooth wall, she worked her way back to the pile of stone and poked her head through the hole. The raft waited below, and she was grateful it had not gotten loose. Looking across the water, she saw Osbourne's silhouette leaning against the wall near the cavern entrance. Sliding forward carefully, she was in a very awkward position when shuffling noises and deep voices shouting words she did not understand suddenly echoed in the cavern.

Twisting her neck and body so she could see across the water again, she saw three shadowy forms outlined against the light of the no-longer-shaded entrance. Helplessly, she watched as two large men tackled Osbourne and tied his hands and ankles behind his back. Two more forms entered the cavern, and she knew she needed to escape. Jerking herself back through the hole, she retreated into the dark corridor.

For a brief moment, she stopped to think; there was nothing she could do to help Osbourne, but horrifying visions of Osbourne as a captive tormented her. She was no match for two grown men, let alone four, especially not men as large as those, and she had no idea what her next move would be.

* * *

With four redfish in his sack, Strom stood and stretched his legs. A light rain fell, thoroughly soaking him, but at least he was outside. He had never been afraid of confined spaces, but the cavern made him feel like the world was closing in on him. Breathing in the fresh air, he started back toward the cold and dark of the cavern.

His fears returned as he got closer, and he wondered what would happen to Catrin next. It was as if the gods were toying with her. Thoughts of the gods had always seemed distant to him, but now he was overwhelmed by nagging questions. The rules of his world had suddenly changed, and he was no longer certain what was real.

It was almost too much for him to absorb, and he turned his mind to the task of getting back safely. Not far from the cavern entrance, he encountered Chase.

"Did you see anything?" he asked.

"There's an army coming from the north, and I thought I saw movements in the trees, so I came back to check on everyone."

"Did you hear that?" Strom asked. "That sounded like it came from the cavern."

Chase didn't bother to respond; instead, he took off at a run, Strom close on his heels.

* * *

When Benjin reached the farm, he sneaked back into the hayloft to retrieve the things he'd hidden there. Under the cover of darkness, he carried the sacks down from the loft and used a piece of rope to tie them together before he slung them over his shoulder. Then, knowing every moment he stayed only increased the danger, he made his way along the fence.

Morning would arrive soon, and Benjin knew the chances of his escaping were rapidly dwindling. Surely someone would find the man he'd stolen the uniform from, and it was obvious that men were searching the mountains for Catrin. Quickening his pace, he tried to cover as much ground as possible before sunrise.

When he reached the place where he'd first seen signs of soldiers in the mountains, he froze. Nearby the snap of a branch warned of imminent danger, but he couldn't pinpoint from what direction it had come. Not wanting to lead anyone to Catrin and the others, he began moving in the opposite direction. The sound of moving leather was all the warning Benjin received before a sword whistled by his ear. Reeling from his evasive maneuver, Benjin let go of the string that held the sacks over his shoulder and rolled away from them.

The soldier who stepped out from behind a nearby tree was a giant of a man with muscles like cords of thick rope. His face showed no fear or battle frenzy; instead what Benjin saw was the cautious confidence of a seasoned warrior. Benjin managed only a single swing of his sword. The ill-timed and out-of-practice attack proved to be a critical mistake. Even as he swung, Benjin saw the man raise his thick sword to meet his strike. On the bottom of the soldier's blade, just before the crosspiece, was a large notch. With the precision of a practiced movement, like a dancer spinning in time with the music, the soldier lodged Benjin's blade into that notch and used his strength, leverage, and a quick snap of his wrist to shatter Benjin's sword.

Left with only the handle and crosspiece of his sword, Benjin could only hope that a technique he'd learned long ago would allow him to use his opponent's size and strength against him.

Chapter 9

Mistakes are a necessary part of life, but they should never be repeated.
--Wendel Volker, horse farmer

* * *

Shrouded in darkness, Catrin continued along the wall. Her hand glided over the smooth stone, and she slid her boots across the floor, testing each step as she went. Her fingers found another doorway. She peered inside but could see nothing in the darkness. There were side passages and doorways at irregular intervals but nothing to indicate a way out. Each junction tested her will. Could it lead to daylight? Her gut told her to continue straight and let any pursuers explore the rest of the place.

In the darkness, tactile imagery gave her a sense of her surroundings, but she felt lost without her sight. In her fear, she moved with exaggerated caution, anticipating unseen obstacles. When she heard muffled shouts, though, she became desperate to move with greater speed, and she stumbled several times in her rush to put distance between herself and those behind her. Her instincts screamed for her to run as fast as she could, but she made herself take it slowly for the sake of safe passage, knowing that even a minor injury could lead to her death in these circumstances.

No more shouts broke the silence, but that did little to ease her anxiety. Only when she was far into the depths of the mountain, by her reckoning, did she begin to let down her guard. Beyond a steep incline, the hall grew level. A few steps beyond the plateau, her fingers encountered what felt like cloth that had been attached permanently to the stone, and it crumbled under her touch. Her imagination conjured up the image of an ancient tapestry, depicting heroic lords as they performed mighty deeds. Unwilling to damage whatever it might be, she used only the toe of her boot as a guide; beauty, even imagined, should not be destroyed.

Occasionally she tested the wall with a finger, but the tapestry stretched on for what seemed an impossible distance. Her mind could not conceive a work of art so massive, and she began to wonder if she were fooling herself. When her finger once again met bare stone, she was almost surprised. The stone felt cool under her hand, and she let her fingers glide along, feeling her way into the unknown.

Her thumb encountered a deep swirl carved in the wall, and that was all the warning she had before she walked into a stone column. The pain and shock left her shaken for a moment, but then she explored the column with her fingers: The top was tapered gracefully, and the bottom was broad. At the base, she found elaborate carvings, which felt like oddly shaped faces. Hopeful, she stepped to the center of the corridor and through an arched doorway, beyond which she discovered a cavernous hall. Towering pillars, so massive their scale was difficult to fathom, were illuminated in the pale light.

The distance separating her from the light source further revealed the enormity of the hall, and she almost doubted what she was seeing--this hall dwarfed any man-made structure she had ever heard of. Even the floor was a marvel, covered with an uncountable quantity of tiny tiles. Large sections of the design were missing, and the loose tiles made for lousy footing.

Distant rumblings of thunder warned of a storm, and in the stillness, Catrin thought she heard rain. Straining her eyes in the darkness, she headed in the direction of the diminishing light but was soon plunged back into near blackness, and she feared she would fall if she tried to go much farther.

Exhaustion drove her to the nearest column, and she settled near its base, her knees pulled to her chest. Anxiety burned in her belly, and fear iced her spine. She worried about Osbourne's safety and that of everyone else she knew and loved. Unable to sleep, she tried in vain to find her meditative state of awareness. Occasional flashes of lightning illuminated the great hall only long enough to produce quick and frightening glimpses, and the thunder and the rush of rain left distorted echoes lingering in the air. Images of demons and phantoms, lurking in the darkness, tormented her.

She didn't remember falling asleep, but when she woke, she saw the far end of the cavern bathed in a soft, pale glow. A jagged chasm, high in the wall, was the source of that blessed light. Her muscles protested when she stood, but she rolled her neck, stretched her legs, and started toward the light.

What appeared to be a throne of rough-hewn rock seemed to grow out of the far wall beneath a colossal bas-relief. The throne was grossly oversized--large enough to hold ten men--and was flanked by a pair of statues in the shape of men. Similar figures lined the walls, and they made Catrin's flesh crawl. She soon realized they were not statues, but suits of heavy armor, the likes of which had not been seen in recent history. Under her breath, she muttered, "Strange. Empty armor guarding an abandoned throne."

The magnificence of the hall left her awestruck, and she wondered what kind of person would sit on such a throne. How could anyone not have felt tiny and insignificant in this enormous display? She pictured herself in that high seat, and seeing herself sitting there in her leathers and homespun made her smile. Thoughts of Osbourne and the others, though, soon banished all humor.

The chasm bisected the wall above the relief like a gaping wound, and Catrin desperately wanted to reach it. She tried to gauge the distance from the ledge that ran along the top of the relief to the bottom of the gap. It was at least three times her height, and she knew she would never be able to jump that far. There didn't seem to be any other way out, so Catrin decided to inspect the wall above the great mantle.

Climbing onto the throne, she hoped the ghosts of whatever kings may have occupied it would not be offended by her trespassing. The relief was easy to climb, its worn image providing an easy grip. She hated to climb on that ancient beauty, but it was unavoidable. The wall above the ledge was rough hewn, like that of the throne, and it bore many scars and cracks. Running her fingers over it, searching for any notches she could use during her climb, she was disappointed to find no suitable handholds within her reach. She needed something to stand on.

The suit of armor on the far side of the throne was in fairly good condition, and she approached it apprehensively, halfway fearing it would come to life and attack her. It remained still, and she ran her hand along the breastplate; it was pocked and corroded, but it still had much of its tensile strength and mass.

Weight was a problem. She would be able to carry only so much while climbing. Knocking on the side of the helmet, she found it was quite solid and pulled it free from the rest of the armor, marveling at the craftsmanship. Even covered in dust and grime, she could see it was beautifully done, and she hated that she was going to use it as a stool.

Climbing the relief with one hand was out of the question. She considered tossing the helm onto the ledge but feared the noise. Finally, she decided to wear the helmet. After cleaning out the inside with her shirt, she gingerly pulled it over her ears. It was too big for her and flopped from side to side whenever she moved her head. Her vision was partially blocked, and the smell was most unpleasant, but she endured the discomfort and made her way to the top of the relief. She set the helmet in the most stable position possible, and after a deep breath, stepped onto it with one foot. Slowly, carefully, she put her weight on it and brought her other foot up to rest on the best toehold she could find.

The toehold was not so good, but it took some of her weight off of the helmet and allowed her to extend herself. At the top of her greatest reach, she felt a knob of rock. Hopeful, she climbed down and slid the helmet perilously close to the end of the ledge. When she stepped back up on it, the helmet shifted and nearly upset her balance, but she caught herself in time.

The protrusion above was wide but not well enough defined to provide a firm grip. Frustrated, she used her belt knife to chisel around the top. The tip of the knife snapped off, and she cursed her luck, promising herself that her next belt knife would be more like a pickaxe.

Using what was now the blunt point of her knife, she fell to work on the stone. What remained of the blade was not as sharp, but it was thicker and stronger, so it had become a better tool for the task. She worked in a precarious position, perched on the helmet and overextended, but she landed several solid blows on the rock. Chips of stone and sparks flew before her determined stabbing.

With her handhold more defined, she began the perilous climb in earnest. She had to expand a few chinks while she clung to the wall, and her energy was nearly spent by the time she reached the large crack, but getting to it gave her a burst of energy. Grappling her way to the base of the opening, she found it difficult to enter. The bottom was too narrow for her to fit through, and her feet scraped against the rock below, unable to find purchase.

With an effort born of desperation, she used her arms to heave herself into the crevice. Dangling in what was an extremely uncomfortable position, she rested her quivering arms. Breathing heavily, she remained there for a few moments before pulling herself the rest of the way in. Catrin knew how close she had come to falling, but her curiosity won out over fear and physical exhaustion, and she moved on.

The crevice continued for a short distance before it opened into fresh air. Catrin made her way to the opening, and she felt moist, chilly air on her face. The sight below terrified her: a sheer drop of several hundred feet was all that stood between her and the valley floor. She realized she was now on the opposite side of the mountain. Edging herself out of the opening, she craned her neck to see how far she was from the crest.

It looked as though she might be able to climb it, and she knew she could not descend the cliff face safely. Gathering her strength, she climbed to the top of the crevice. There were large foot- and handholds, and the opposite wall of the cleft gave her leverage. The ledge above the crevice provided a commanding view of the Pinook Valley, and Catrin saw the sun for the first time in many days.

Columns of smoke, far to the north, rose into the sky. It did not look like a forest fire, and the recent rains reduced that possibility even further. A cold feeling crept into her stomach as it occurred to her that she was seeing the smoke from hundreds of campfires. Her gut told her that an army approached from the north.

She felt naked and exposed on the side of the mountain, especially knowing the men who captured Osbourne might have been army scouts and they could still be looking for his companions. Though she didn't think Osbourne would tell them anything, the supplies and bedrolls in the cavern clearly indicated he had not been alone. She simply had to trust her luck and hope she would not be seen, but she was not optimistic.

From atop the crevice, she had a better view of her climb to the peak. It didn't look easy, but it was certain to be a great deal easier than her escape from the throne room. Having no desire to remain in the open, she began to climb. The incline was fairly gradual, and she walked much of the way. Occasionally she had to get on her hands and knees to make it through a tough spot, and in several places, she had to climb over large rock formations that stuck out of the mountain. From her higher vantage point, the rock face below resembled the edge of a huge crater, as if some god had taken a bite out of the mountainside.

When she gained the crest, she flattened herself down against the rock and crept along to look into the Chinawpa Valley. Trying to take advantage of the excellent view, she searched for the cavern entrance, but she had lost her bearings and was unsure how it would look from above. A small ridge sloped gently down the mountain face, and she decided to follow it to the base. About to stand, she caught movement in her periphery. Flattening herself further, she turned to look.

Nothing stirred, but she remained as still as stone. Fear paralyzed her when two figures emerged from behind a rock outcropping. They were south of her but near the top of the ridgeline, concealed by the shadows, and they seemed to be trying to stay in the darkness. Catrin froze and tried to become invisible. When the forms stopped and turned in her direction, tears came to her eyes and her lip began to quiver. She saw one motion to the other then point in her direction. Escape was unlikely, and she decided she would rather throw herself from the cliff face than be captured.

Standing quickly, she turned to make her desperate retreat. She had taken only three steps when some instinct made her look behind to see if she was being pursued, and she nearly shouted out for joy.

Benjin and Chase emerged from the shadows, waving their arms at her.

Stopping in midstride, she nearly fell. Rushing to meet them halfway, she hugged each of them and asked, her voice trembling, "Osbourne?" She was shocked to see both of them smile.

"He's fine," Chase blurted, unable to control his excitement. "Strom and I saw the soldiers approaching the cavern, and we sneaked in behind them. They were busy tying up Osbourne, and we caught 'em by surprise. We used the rocks we had by the entrance to kill one and knocked the other one out," he said matter-of-factly. "Benjin got back late last night," he added.

"We'll talk about this later," Benjin said. "Right now there's an army approaching, and they have two scouts who haven't returned. They look to have been a few days ahead of the army, but they'll soon be missed. Let's get back to the cavern."

Catrin swayed on her feet when she realized the second set of shadowy forms she had seen had not been soldiers at all; it had been Strom and Chase. Had she stayed a moment longer, she would have seen them rescue Osbourne. All the fear and pain she experienced in the past day had been for nothing. She began to cry as she realized she could have just climbed back onto the raft and poled herself safely back to camp.

"Are you all right, li'l miss?" Benjin asked, looking her over for any signs of injury.

"I'm fine," she replied, but the tears of mixed joy and frustration kept flowing.

Chapter 10

Security is the blindfold worn by those who cannot accept the uncertainty of the future.
--Mundin Barr, speculator

* * *

One of the soldiers lay supine near the fire, still unconscious, and Benjin seemed to think there was little chance he would ever wake. They hoped he would regain consciousness soon so they could squeeze some information out of him. For the moment, though, he would give no more information than his deceased companion. Catrin did not want to know what they had done with the body of the other man, so she didn't ask. The thought of Chase killing someone, even to defend himself or a friend, seemed so out of character with his gentle nature that she blocked any image of that from her mind.

Not far from the lake lay a new raft made of many saplings that had been hastily bound together with rope and vines. When Strom saw her looking at it, he walked to her side. "I was coming to look for you," he said. Catrin felt tears filling her eyes, and in a rare moment, Strom put his hand on her shoulder. "Come on. Let's get something to eat."

Seeing their provisions, still intact, brought a wave of relief; she had feared it all lost to the attackers. It was odd that she had gone a relatively short time without food, yet she felt as if she had not eaten in weeks. It was as if the time she'd spent thinking about starvation had had a physical effect on her. Though she was able to eat only half of what she took, she kept the rest nearby for when her appetite returned; its very presence brought her comfort.

Benjin filled her in about his journey. "Let me first say that I believe your father is well and is adequately defended in the cold caves. Miss Mariss is also faring well, given the circumstances. I was unable to get information regarding Osbourne's family, and the only information I got about Chase's father was that he was last seen with Wendel. I'm guessing he's in the cold caves as well.

"Miss Mariss said Wendel led many people to the cold caves, and once inside, they blocked the entrances with rocks and hastily laid mortar. As far as she knew, they are continuing to build up the blockade even as the Zjhon remove it, but that process is slowly forcing them farther back into the caves. Others fled to the protection of the Masterhouse--far too many to be comfortably housed there. Riots broke out when the Masters began strictly rationing food and water since their supplies were not plentiful enough to support such numbers," he said and stopped to consider his next words.

"There is a bit of good news and more bad news. First the bad news: Peten Ross was captured and forced to talk. Peten told them he thought Catrin was the Herald and about the day Osbourne was attacked. He also described each of us, as well as a few others, in great detail. He told them that Strom, Chase, and I had mysteriously disappeared, and he thought we had run to hide in the mountains with Catrin," he continued.

"The good news is also bad news. I guess I failed to mention that. The Zjhon know who you are, what you look like, and that you are most likely not in the Masterhouse or the cold caves. Because of this, they have changed their strategy. Now they only wish to contain the people who are trapped and use their numbers to scour the rest of the Godfist looking for you. This'll take much of the pressure off of those who are under siege, and there should be less loss of life. The bad part, of course, is that they'll be combing the mountains looking for us."

Catrin shivered and pulled her knees to her chest as the weight of his words settled into her consciousness. The Zjhon wanted only her. Maybe if she gave herself up to them, they would leave the people of the Godfist alone.

"There is another part of this story I've not told you yet," Benjin said. "I must stress how very important this is. You are being entrusted with sacred information that you must never reveal. Can you all promise me that you will never reveal any of what I tell you to another living soul?"

They all nodded solemnly.

"Miss Mariss told me things she was strictly forbidden to tell anyone not of the Vestrana." He paused and looked at each of them solemnly. Catrin tried to remember where she had heard the word *Vestrana* before, but all she could recall was some talk about a secret society that was shrouded in mystery.

"In order for me to tell you these secrets, you have to swear the Vestrana oath, but first I must explain some things so you'll know what you're swearing to. You don't have to swear the oath, but if you don't, I'll not be able to tell you some things, and neither will anyone who has sworn." The young people looked at each other, wondering if any would refuse to swear.

"At the end of the last Istran phase, the Varics were nearly destroyed, and they went into hiding to survive. They knew their knowledge and beliefs were important and needed to be passed on, so they formed a secret society known as the Vestrana, and my family has been a part since its inception. My grandfather swore me in when I was still a boy," he confided.

"The Vestrana opposed the Zjhon and their practice of conquering lands and then forcing the conquered peoples to convert to their religion. The penalty for refusal was death. Our secret exile has gone on for thousands of years, and we have replenished our numbers. We'll not dictate religious beliefs to others, as we wish every person to choose his or her beliefs freely and not be persecuted for them. We strictly oppose any religion that mandates killing people simply because their beliefs are different. Do you all understand?" he asked.

"I'm no good at lying," Strom admitted for the second time. "Every time I try to lie to Miss Mariss, she calls me on it--on the spot. I'm just not good at keeping secrets, so I don't know if I should take the oath."

"The choice is yours; I'll not force you to take an oath you feel you cannot keep. I will tell you, however, that you won't have to lie. You just cannot say certain things. You can be completely honest with someone without revealing any of the things you must keep safe," Benjin said.

"I *can* be quiet, and if I don't have to lie, well, then, I think I can do it," he said, looking a bit more confident. Benjin gave him a moment to reconsider before he continued.

"Before I can tell you any more, I'll tell you the oath, and if you feel it is right, you should swear it.

"Here it is: 'I swear to uphold the values of the Vestrana. I will not divulge any information considered within confidence of the Vestrana. I will seek to free the oppressed and vanquish the oppressor. I will give my life before I will betray myself or the Vestrana,'" he intoned.

It was simple enough, but Benjin made them explain it back to him in their own words to be sure they understood its meaning. "I must ask you to understand that people generally prepare for several seasons before they are allowed to take the oath. There are many things you do not know, so you must not say anything at all about *any* of this to *anyone* for *any* reason. Ever! Is that clearly understood?"

They all nodded soberly.

Once he was satisfied they understood the gravity of the situation, he asked if any of them wished to swear the oath. All of them wanted to, and each recited it individually. Benjin made them repeat it until they could speak it from memory, and he formally welcomed each of them to the Vestrana and kissed them on their foreheads.

"I've never sworn anyone in before," he admitted and seemed much more relaxed when he spoke again. "Many innkeepers across the world are members of the Vestrana and serve as part of a huge information network. Miss Mariss is one of those innkeepers, and she has access to information few else on the Godfist are privy to. The Vestrana have many allies, some of whom may make a living in shady dealings, but they honor the Vestrana. Miss Mariss suggested we seek out one particular ally. In doing so, she had to reveal one of her most trusted secrets to me.

"There is a harbor on the east coast of the Godfist; it's along a rough section of coast that offers very little safe anchorage because of the many surrounding islands and reefs that'll sink an unwary ship. The only ships known to safely dock there are pirate ships, and even those are somewhat rare events.

"The Godfist is pretty far outside established trade routes, and pirate ships only dock here to avoid pursuit, though sometimes they trade goods and information with the Vestrana. There are now two ships docked at the cove, as far as we know. They sought refuge from the Zjhon fleet, fearing the ships had been sent after them. The last Miss Mariss had heard, they were still there. She's going to try to get word to them and arrange passage for us. Though they are not here with us, agents of the Vestrana are doing all they can to help. I know the Zjhon are going to scour the Godfist in search of Catrin, so I propose we travel to the cove and leave the Godfist with the pirates. Even if Miss Mariss is not able to contact them, we may be able to work something out, and to be completely honest, I don't have any better ideas."

His words were met with utter silence, and Catrin struggled to make sense of all of it. She could not imagine leaving the Godfist, her home, and had never thought about going any other place. The others seemed to be having similar problems assimilating the information. Chase was the first to find his voice.

"Where would we go?" he asked.

"We should go to the last place they would expect us to go, to the Greatland--into the heart of their empire."

"Do you really think that's the best thing to do?" Catrin asked, incredulous.

"The Greatland is the largest and most heavily populated landmass on Godsland. We can disguise ourselves and hide much more easily among so many people, not to mention the huge area they would have to search to look for us. It may also be that getting you to the Greatland is the best way to help fulfill the prophecy."

"You really believe I'm the Herald?" Catrin asked, fearing his answer.

"I'm not sure what I believe," he said, "but I know you have important tasks ahead of you, and no matter what you or I believe, you have already done some important work. There's no going back, I'm afraid. From now on, you'll be the one who was declared the Herald, whether you are or not. Truth can be a difficult thing to find."

Catrin had never heard Benjin speak so profoundly, and she wondered what else she didn't know about the man she had worked beside for so many years.

"I'm sorry I don't have all of the answers. I wish I did," he said, shaking his head. "In many ways, I'm just as confused as you are. To follow our hearts and hope we make the right decisions is the best we can do. Do we agree we should make for the cove?"

He knew their answer and told them what to pack and what to leave behind. During this activity, he pulled Catrin aside but seemed to have trouble choosing his words.

"I've sworn the Vestrana oath," he began. "A message given into my trust must be delivered, unopened, to the intended recipient unless it cannot be done. There is a strict protocol on this, and I must honor it, even when I don't want to. I considered breaking my oath when Miss Mariss gave me this message. I thought about reading it before I gave it to you. I even considered destroying it without reading it. I'm ashamed to admit I was tempted, but I will keep my oath. This unopened message is for you. You don't have to tell me what it says. I'm just the messenger," he said as he handed her a tightly rolled parchment closed with wax. The seal impressed in the wax belonged to Nat Dersinger.

After moving off to a quiet place by the fire, Catrin stared at the parchment. She did not want to open it, afraid of what it might say. Nat was a pariah, his outlandish ranting about the coming of Istra and the dawning of a new age too disturbing for most people to give any credence to. Some said he was mad; others claimed he was afflicted with some disease, but most agreed his public sermons were the ravings of a deranged mind. Catrin had to wonder, now that many of his prophecies were actually coming true, whether Nat was mad or everyone else was.

An uneasy feeling gnawed at the pit of her stomach as her beliefs began to crumble beneath her. Fear crept in where her fallen truths no longer held sway, and yet she felt liberated to pursue limitless possibilities that would open to her. She tore the wax seal away and unrolled the parchment.

My dearest Catrin,
My fondest wish is that you will walk in peace and light and that your mind will always remain free.
Some say I'm deranged, but I leave that for you to judge. What I am sure of is that you must embrace your role as the Herald. I implore you to use the divine gift you have been given and that you do not squander it.
I have studied all scriptures and holy books available to me, and I want to help you learn to use the power of Istra's light. You have experienced its improper use, even though you did not intend to exploit it, so you are aware of its power.
If you choose to pursue the divine gifts you have been given, I beg you to seek knowledge. I hope to bring knowledge of these to you, but if I cannot make my way to you in time, seek out the Cathuran monks; they may be able to help you.

Before your journey takes you beyond the Godfist, you will be besieged. Remember these words when you fear you have made the wrong choices:

Vestra's light warms Godsland.
Water ascends upon the wings of his warmth, and the skies disperse it at will.
Rain shapes the land and gives life to the fishes, and the fishes sparkle in Istra's light.
May Istra and Vestra guide and bless you,
Nat

Catrin sat back, confounded by what she had read. Nat was right about the disastrous results of her tapping the strange energies, but his words of warning were unclear to her. That he would make this effort to get a message to her only to leave her with a riddle seemed ludicrous. Frustrated, she tucked the parchment into her pocket, hoping to make sense of it at some later time.

When she rejoined the others, Benjin's eyes met hers. When she had no comment, he simply nodded and finished checking his pack. He then stood and pulled several pieces of rolled parchment from his pack.

Addressing all of them, he said, "You've been sworn, and this information is in the Vestrana confidence. You must not divulge it to anyone, and you must destroy this if you believe it could fall into anyone else's hands," he said, handing a copy to each of them. "The journey we're about to undertake will be perilous. I wish I could offer you the chance to walk away, but our situation is too dire; you are in peril if you stay or if you go. I think we should stick together, but I want each of you to have a map in case we get separated.

"This is a highly unusual practice. It's dangerous in the extreme to have so many copies of anything in the Vestrana confidence, but this is a highly unusual case, and I've made an exception. Be certain no one else gets these maps," he reiterated firmly. "We leave before dawn, and I want a double watch tonight."

* * *

The snap of a branch in the distance behind Nat increased his level of panic. For weeks, he'd been hiding in the hills. Miss Mariss had urged him to find Catrin, but he had no idea how to do that. Only his visions and dreams provided any guidance, but those proved difficult to interpret and decipher. The only things he knew for certain were that Catrin must survive and that she was in terrible danger. In the end, he was left to wander in the wilderness, battling his own despair as he searched for someone who did not want to be found. He could have passed her and her companions a dozen times and he would never know. He was a fisherman, not a tracker.

Finding Catrin was now the least of his problems, though. The Zjhon were searching for her as well, and they were close behind him. If they found him . . . He tried not to think about the horrors he might face. Even with his staff, he was no match for a trained swordsman. Instead he concentrated on moving into the thickest and most forbidding undergrowth he could find. When he could no longer make forward progress, he curled into a ball beneath a veil of thorn and briar, hoping those who pursued him would simply pass by.

Eventually the light began to fade, and the beat of Nat's heart slowed. Weariness more complete than any he'd ever known began to wash over him, coaxing him to sleep, luring him into the land of dreams.

Somewhere between sleep and wakefulness, the scene before him changed, no longer did he see a canopy of twisted vines and curved thorns bathed in moonlight; instead he watched as Catrin was surrounded by the shadows of death. Moving like the wind, the darkness closed in on her, blocking out the light and her life. Just as he thought her flame would be extinguished, Catrin fought back. To Nat's horror, she did not attack the darkness directly; instead she tore the land asunder and hurled it at her foes. Her every step rent the land, leaving cavernous gouges and craters wherever she trod, and still the darkness came, unthwarted and undaunted.

Clawing his way through the darkness, Nat clenched his jaws as the thorns bit deep. He could not stop, though, no matter how great the pain-- he had to find her.

Chapter 11

One man's offal is another man's harvest.
--Icari Jundin, mushroom farmer

* * *

Benjin woke them early. When he checked on the health of the unconscious soldier, he seemed almost relieved the man had died in the night. He and Chase dragged the dead man from the cavern and hid the body with the other.

When they returned, Benjin examined the pile of armor and weapons the soldiers had carried. He took a short sword, belt sheath, and bracers for himself. The sword had a black leather handle and a decent edge--not a fine blade but good to have. He motioned the others over and began to distribute the dead soldiers' belongings to the rest of them. He gave Chase the other short sword, belt sheath, and bracers. The boots went to Strom and Osbourne to replace their lighter shoes.

Catrin asked for one of the belt knives left in the pile, and Benjin handed her one still in the sheath. She was hesitant to discard her old knife and decided to wear both, not wanting to abandon the old one with the broken tip.

Osbourne pulled the other soldier's knife from its sheath; Catrin expected some sort of noise when he unsheathed it, but it slid free without a sound. The wicked-looking blade curved slightly before the tip. Its upper edge was serrated, and it had a straight edge on the bottom. He pronounced it perfect for him.

"The plan is simple," Benjin said. "We travel north and go straight at the approaching army, but we stay high in the mountains. Once we sneak past them, we will turn east, toward the desert. Perhaps we'll get lucky and have foul weather to hide us, perhaps not; either way, we'll need to be ready to take cover at all times. Keep your eyes open for places to hide as you may only get a moment's notice. We could go due east from here, but I fear those passes are heavily guarded. As outrageous as it may sound, sneaking past the army is probably our safest choice.

"I doubt the patrols will be this far out by first light. We need to get to the next plateau soon if we are to avoid them," Benjin said, and he set out at a breakneck pace.

When they crested a rise, Benjin paused and strained to see into the distance. "We should be able to see the falls from here, but I can't make them out," he said. Catrin and the others squinted in the predawn light, but visibility was low.

"I think they are still a long way off," Chase said.

Benjin nodded. "Let's go. We've no time to waste," he said, heading off at a brisk walk.

As they drew closer, Catrin saw the falls. They did not seem as grand as Benjin had described them, barely visible in the distance. Perhaps they had been larger when Benjin last saw them, but she wondered how that could be possible when this was the rainiest spring any of them had ever seen.

They froze when Benjin hunched down and signaled them to do the same. "I thought I saw something moving in the trees," he said after a few moments. "I think it's clear, so let's move."

As they neared the base of the falls, the banks of the river came into view. "Above the falls there is no eastern shore. The river runs along the rock face. We'll need to stay on the west side for now," Benjin said.

As they came closer to the river, they were surprised by what they saw: the water level was extremely low, the flow muddy and sluggish. The water was well below the normal watermarks, and they estimated it was less than half what it should be.

By the time they reached the base of the falls, the sun was high in the sky, and Benjin said he planned to use the sun for cover. They would climb the jagged cliff wall while the sun was high, which would make it harder for soldiers to spot them with the sunlight in their eyes. He found a place far enough away from the falls for them to remain dry, and there were many irregularities in the rock face, which would make for an easier climb.

Their ascent was slow and tenuous, irregular rocks providing some handholds and footholds, but in many places they were widely spaced. In some instances they had to scale the nearly sheer face with little, if anything, to grab onto. When they finally reached the plateau, they did not find the river they had been expecting and instead saw a muddy lake that covered almost the entire plateau. Chase spotted the cause of the flooding near the top of the falls. The recent storms had downed a large number of trees. At least a dozen had been swept away by the river and were creating a dam just before the falls, where the river narrowed. Only a fraction of the water flowed past the debris; the rest continued to flood the plateau.

A narrow ribbon of land separated the newly formed lake from the cliff, but it was clearly saturated. The valley beyond the plateau was completely swamped by the backed-up river, effectively cutting off their escape.

"Cripes," Benjin said, "we're going to need to find a way around this. Stay alert." An enormous rock finger jutted into the air above the valley. Skirting the lake, they plodded through the mud, which threatened to remove their boots with every step. At times they walked through ankle-deep water. Around the rock finger, the soil border was less than a pace wide. The promontory was slender and appeared fragile, warped and twisted by eons of windborne sand.

"Stay back. I'm going out for a look," Benjin said.

"You aren't really thinking of walking out on that rock, are you?" Strom asked, incredulous. "That thing looks like it could fall at any moment, even without your weight on it."

"It's been here for thousands of years, and I'm betting it'll be here for thousands more; its frailty is only an illusion."

Benjin crept onto the rock; the winds whipped around him, and he was nearly blown off. He caught himself, but the movement sent rocks bouncing into the valley below.

"I think we've been spotted," he said. "There are soldiers below, and they are climbing toward us. We need to retreat as fast as we can; we must go back the way we came. I don't think we'll be able to get through the flooded valley without ruining our food supply or drowning."

Catrin sat to one side, absorbed in her thoughts, and with every moment her anger grew. The Zjhon threatened everything she held dear. Struggling to think of a way to stop the approaching army, or at least hamper its progress, she stewed, biting her lip. Benjin interrupted her thoughts.

"C'mon, li'l miss, we need to get out of here."

Catrin wondered if she was making a mistake; then she recalled the words Nat had written: "Embrace your role as the Herald. I implore you to use the divine gift you have been given." She considered those words, and they urged her to act.

"No," she said in a firm voice. "I will not run from this challenge, and I will no longer tolerate these invaders of my homeland."

"What would you have us do, Catrin? I am yours to command," Benjin said, shocking everyone. He knelt in the sodden soil and bowed to her. Chase, Strom, and Osbourne stood silently.

Catrin considered her next words carefully, not knowing what she was going to say or do. She looked around her, and the muddy water brought back a part of Nat's message, one line in particular, and she said, "The water shapes the land."

"I want you to dig. From here," she said, pointing to the soil around the base of the finger of rock, "to here. We need a trough from the dry to the wet, and it should be as deep as possible."

"What are you talking about, Cat? We don't have time for this; we need to get out of here," Chase said.

"We cannot run anymore, Chase; there is nowhere safe to hide. I choose to fight," she said, and she began to dig with her bare hands as Benjin loosened the soil with his sword. All but Chase began to dig, but he soon crouched down along with the rest. The trench grew quickly, the sodden soil making their work easier.

"Stay on the north side of the trench," Catrin warned.

"But we need to go south to escape," Chase argued, looking at a massive fist of rock that blocked their path and would not budge.

"Just dig around it," Catrin said, following Chase's gaze. "The trench need not be straight." As they dug their way closer to the water, the ditch began to flood, and they continued to dig from higher ground. As water began pouring over the cliff's edge, Catrin and Benjin looked over to see what was happening below.

A few soldiers watched from the valley floor, but most were scaling the cliff face in an effort to reach them. Catrin and the others watched the water move through the ditch, eroding the soil around it. Deeper and wider the trough grew, gradually sending larger amounts of water into the valley, but it was not enough; it was happening far too slowly to make any difference. It mocked their meager effort, and helplessness washed over Catrin.

She watched the flow intently, seeing tremendous potential energy latent in the calm water, and she knew there must be a way to unleash it. Without realizing it, she opened her mind to Istra's energy and attempted to ply it with her will. She started by trying to push the water over the edge, hoping to make it go faster, but the water repelled her.

Any force she exerted on the water became fragmented, scattered in a hundred directions, and her efforts had no visible effect. Her frustration flared into anger, and she turned to the rest of the group. "Go north. I'll catch up with you soon."

"But, Cat--" Chase began, but she cut him short.

"If you value your lives, go north. Now!" she said in a commanding voice, despite her fear. Her legs trembled; her face flushed and nostrils flared; her heart pounded in her ears. Chase and the others headed north, frequently looking over their shoulders. A strange feeling came over her as she watched Chase walk away. So many times she had followed him on his adventures, but now she knew she must stand alone. As she embraced the energy around her, she prayed she would not unwittingly create another disaster. The lives of her friends now rested in her hands, and she was determined to save them.

With confidence born of every lesson her father and Benjin and Chase had ever taught her, Catrin moved to the finger of rock. Its base had been exposed by the modest flow of water that rushed by, but she strode to the end of the finger, seemingly oblivious to the winds tearing at her. Doing her best to keep from trembling, she spoke in a voice that carried across the Pinook Valley.

"Armies of the Zjhon! You are not welcome here," she began. In the next moment, though, she panicked. No more words would come; her throat was closing. She was no hero; she felt like just a little girl. Old fears constricted her heart, and she nearly fled, but then, in her mind, she saw the faces of Benjin and Chase and her friends. With a fire burning in her belly, she renewed her commitment and tried to find words befitting a great hero. "I am the keeper of this land, and I forbid you passage. Retreat now, or feel the weight of my wrath!" she said, and her statement carried on the air to the soldiers below.

They laughed at such threats coming from a girl, and Catrin turned without another word. She strode back to the edge of the widening trough, gazing at it a moment more before moving north. Some fifty paces away, she stopped, hoping Chase wasn't right. Maybe she had lost her senses, but it was far too late to turn back. She would have to endure the consequences of her decisions and actions.

Facing the cliff, she felt the heat of her anger toward the invaders, and it purged her fears. Her body quivered with energy as she gathered it and pulled it to her, reveling in its glory. She could smell its fragrance and taste its sweetness, but a searing pain in her left thigh distracted her for a moment, feeling as if her limb were on fire. She ignored it and drew in a deep breath, letting the soldiers' laughter feed her rage.

"You bear witness to the Call of the Herald," she announced. "I have warned you, and you have mocked me, and you will suffer for that." She clasped her hands high above her head, energy swirling through her fingers and dancing over her palms. It pulsed around her. She brought her hands down in a powerful arc as she shouted, "You will not pass!"

When her fists struck the soil, a huge shockwave sent ripples of power through the plateau with a massive, echoing boom, and the land pulsed as if it were liquid. Waves of energy rolled away from her. The floodwaters transferred the energy as waves crashed against the irregularity of the far cliffs and returned to punish the saturated shoreline. Unable to withstand the power of the water, large sections of rock and soil were dislodged and pushed into the Pinook Valley.

As tremors shook the ground beneath her feet, Catrin ran toward her companions. The massive chain reaction gained momentum, and the thunderous roar became nearly unbearable, but even in her retreat, Catrin was compelled to witness what she had wrought. Water crashed around the finger of rock, carrying gobbets of dirt and rock away with it, and with an ear-shattering crack, the rock slumped forward and leaned into the valley. Water rushed in eagerly to fill the gap, and a tremendous roar reverberated through the valley; Catrin watched in disbelief as the finger of rock tumbled away in the deluge.

In a massive release of potential energy, water assailed rock and soil, and the cliffs parted. Gravity pulled the water into the valley, and the din of a massive rockslide accompanied the rush of the fall.

Rock and debris clogged the valley, and a towering wall of water rushed to greet the main body of the advancing army. Cries of man and horse rose above the din, but Catrin had no time to consider what her senses told her as more of the plateau began to collapse. She fled the devastation and tried to catch up to the rest of the group, already moving swiftly north. The Upper Chinawpa Valley, which lay ahead, drained quickly, and muddy shores rose from the depths; there Catrin's friends stopped to wait for her.

Unsure of what to say, she approached them tentatively, half expecting them to tell her she was crazy or leave her behind, but they welcomed her silently.

Chase grabbed her in a bear hug. "I'm sorry I doubted you," he whispered.

Benjin held up his hand to speak. "You have followed me, but I can no longer lead you," he said. "I've heard the Call of the Herald, and I will go wherever she leads me, I will do what she asks of me, and I will lay down my life to save hers," he finished, bowing to Catrin.

The others made similar vows, and Catrin was left to stand in wonder. She'd had no preparation for this, and she did not know what was expected of her. She knew that she was leaving one reality and stepping into a new existence, and she was unsure of the consequences of this new power.

Finally, Strom broke the uncomfortable silence. "I'm just glad Catrin's on our side."

* * *

Sweat dripped into Nat's eyes as he scrambled down a craggy face. He climbed with a mixture of haste and care. His experience urged him to exercise caution, but his instincts told him he must flee. The Zjhon were close--closer than ever before. Already he had been near enough to see their eyes. Using his staff to steady himself, he climbed past an awkward outcropping.

When he reached the narrow band of greenery that stood between the base of the mountain and the sand, Nat cursed. He was starving and exhausted. After giving up on finding Catrin, all he had wanted was to get back to town, to find some way to get to Miss Mariss and food. The need for food and water was sapping his strength and his sanity. Several times he had found himself wandering without any idea of where he was going or where he had been; all he could remember was that he needed to keep moving.

Suddenly stopping, he realized he'd done it again. Ankle deep in sand, he turned and only the mountains behind him gave him a sense of where he was. What he saw when he lowered his gaze made his location seem irrelevant: half a dozen mounted men were heading straight for him, and there was little Nat could do but wait for them to arrive. Maybe they would give him food, he thought, but what was left of his reason suggested it was unlikely. Turning away from the Zjhon, back the way his subconscious had been leading him, he walked. When he raised his eyes again, certain the Zjhon would overtake him at any moment, he was confused to find that he must have gotten turned around again, for before him came riders in a cloud of dust.

Chapter 12

If you wish to find yourself, you must first admit you are lost.
--anonymous philosopher

* * *

Catrin left the crumbling plateau behind, her body throbbing with energy, her senses heightened. As the breeze caressed her skin, the hairs on her arms and neck stood up. The roar of the mudslide pounded against her overly sensitive hearing, and she retreated from the din. Followed by Benjin and the others, she headed toward the northern end of the valley. There the mountains turned east and the valley grew wider. With little dry ground, they had to slog through a foul morass. Clinging mud made loud sucking noises as it hung on to their boots, weighing them down.

As the valley widened farther on, small sections of dry land appeared more often, like giant turtles in a sea of murky water. The valley floor was made up of rolling hills, and when they found dry spots at the tops of hills, it was only before they descended into valleys of muck. Puddles harbored fish stranded by the rapidly receding water.

Catrin wanted to take the fish back to the river, but she knew it would require too much time to do it right. She and Benjin had spent hours once catching fish in buckets after they were stranded by the Pinook River, which had overflowed its banks. Because the fish would die if they were quickly moved from warm water and put into frigid river water, they put the buckets into the river at the shallows until the water temperature gradually dropped. Then they tipped the buckets over so the fish could swim out. She had enjoyed seeing the fish disappear into the river, safe, and wished she could save these fish too, but there was no time.

The mountains threw long shadows as the waning sun set fire to the skies; bold strokes of crimson and ocher made for a breathtaking display. Patches of dry land gradually became larger, and some were almost suitable campsites. "I think that hill up ahead looks like a good place to camp," Catrin announced.

"There's not much cover there. I think we should try to find a better hiding place," Benjin advised.

"No," she said quietly, determined to embrace her new role, despite her insecurities. "I'm not going to hide anymore. I have to show the Zjhon I don't fear them. Instead, I will strike fear into them. Let them find us in the open, sitting by our fire, and let them see we are not hiding. Let us invite them to take us if they will. They will feel my wrath if they do."

No one but Benjin seemed to know what to make of the change in Catrin. He had accepted her as the Herald and let her be in complete control of their destinies. The others had known Catrin most of her life--and theirs--and seemed to have a difficult time accepting her now as the figure of legend from the prophecies. But they had seen too much of her power to deny it, and slowly they came to believe.

"As you wish," Benjin said with a short bow. He walked ahead to look for dry wood; Chase matched his stride. Strom and Osbourne remained alongside Catrin as she headed toward the campsite.

"Is there anything you need us to do, Miss Catrin?" Osbourne asked, looking uncertain.

Catrin sighed. "Please don't call me 'Miss Catrin' . . . not you or Strom or Chase. You're my friends, and I need you. I'm sorry I bossed everyone around and was so mean," she said, sounding much more like herself.

"Oh, that's all right, *Miss Catrin*," Strom said with an impish grin. "We know you have the whole 'Herald of Istra' thing to contend with. We could probably forgive you for being weird."

"I want you to dig," Osbourne said in a high-pitched voice, "from here"--he posed and pointed--"to here," he finished with a flourish.

"You best be careful, Osbo. You don't want risk the wrath of Miss Catrin. Fear the wrath, boy. Fear the wrath," Strom said as he ducked away from Catrin's playful jab.

While she was relieved to know she had not lost her friends, Benjin's behavior concerned her. His sudden change in personality was as bizarre as her own, and she needed to talk to him soon, but she feared she would insult him. She had looked up to him for so many years, and he had always been the first one to help her with her unusual ideas. She would never hurt him on purpose, but she did need to understand some things about him.

When they reached the top of the hill, Chase and Benjin were setting up a fire circle beside a small supply of firewood already stacked to one side.

"You're absolutely certain about the campsite and the fire, Catrin?" Benjin asked.

His use of her name annoyed her for reasons unknown, and she suppressed her irritation. "Yes, this will be fine. Strom, Osbourne, you asked if there was anything you could do, and now there is. Would you gather fish from the puddles please?"

Strom and Osbourne both nodded, and they left seeking fish.

Catrin turned to Chase. "Can we talk for a moment, please? I really need to know your opinion on something."

Chase raised an eyebrow and nodded before following her. A nearby tree grew around a large bolder, cradling it in its massive trunk, like a great claw clutching a mystical orb. Catrin climbed atop the bolder and sat cross-legged.

"Do you believe I'm truly the Herald of Istra?" she asked. Chase had always been her closest confidant, and they trusted one another. Before their tragic deaths, their mothers had been quite close, and Chase and Catrin had spent most of their childhoods together. Chase had the same pain she had, and she knew he would be honest with her.

"I think . . ." He paused a moment, thoughtful. "I think I do, Cat. I mean, all the signs are there, and you have shown your power." He pondered for a moment then returned the question. "Do *you* believe you are truly the Herald of Istra?"

"Yes, I do," she replied. "I didn't want to believe at first. I tried to tell myself it was all coincidence, but things just kept happening, no matter what I believed."

"What is the Herald supposed to do?"

"I have no idea," she admitted. "I wish I did know; it would certainly make things easier. I guess I'm supposed to destroy the Zjhon, but I'll be boiled if I know how or why."

They sat quietly for a while. Strom and Osbourne returned with an abundance of fish, and Catrin watched them while her thoughts drifted.

"What did you do on the plateau today? I mean, how did you hit the ground so hard? I've never seen anything like that."

"It's hard to explain," she began. "It's like trying to describe an eagle's call to someone born deaf or a sunset to someone born blind. I guess in this sense, *I* was born blind, but something opened my eyes. I'm still uncertain about a great many things, but I'll give you my best guess. I think the comet flooded our world with energy, and somehow I can gather that energy, focus it, and release it. I'm not exactly sure how I do it; that's just how it feels when it happens."

"I think I understand. What opened your eyes?"

"It could have been a number of things, I suppose, but I think it was Peten's staff." She paused. "Something inside me snapped. I can't tell you exactly what happened, but I'll tell you what I remember. When I saw my reflection in the wood of his staff, I knew I saw my own death approaching. I think my conscious mind accepted my fate and waited for the killing blow. Perhaps it was my unconscious mind that reacted instinctively." She realized how strange her words sounded, but they were the closest thing she had to an explanation.

"Well, Cat, this is how I see things: You're the Herald and you have great power, but you don't know how to control it. Your instincts seem to tell you things the rest of us cannot hear. I don't think you're any different from the rest of us, except that you've had some experiences that expanded your mind. The prophecies say you'll destroy the Zjhon nation, so I guess we should concentrate on doing that first."

Catrin saw thousands of complexities, and Chase had reduced them to a few simple statements. She shook her head and laughed. "I'll get right on that nation-destroying thing."

The pain in her left thigh got her attention as she got down from the boulder. Most of her body was sore, but her thigh felt different; it felt as if she had a small spot of sunburn. Then she recalled having pain in her thigh while she was engulfed in power. She reached for the tiny carved fish still in her pocket, precisely over where she felt the sting.

The carving looked worse than she remembered, now dull and chalky. It retained its shape, and even in its current state, it was oddly beautiful, and she was surprised it hadn't been broken or crushed during her misadventures. She guessed it must have bruised her leg during the climb, and when she could find no other reasonable explanation, she accepted that.

"What've you got there?" Chase asked.

"I found this while I was exploring the passage beyond the cavern; I had completely forgotten about it. It looks like a carving of a fish, don't you think?"

"It's pretty crude, but yes, I'd say it resembles a fish. I don't think you want to keep it in your pocket if you want it to stay whole. Here, I have something for you." He reached into his shirt and pulled out a plain and simply made silver locket, its worn surface dented and scratched. Catrin had seen the locket many times but had never seen what was in it. It hung from a necklace made of thin leather strips braided together and tied in a knot.

He deftly separated the strips and removed one. He retied the two remaining strips and slipped his necklace back on. "You never know when these thongs will come in handy," he said with a wink. She watched him form a tiny noose from the leather thong. He extended his open palm, and she placed the small carving in his hand. He looped the little noose around the tail of the fish, and created a necklace that firmly secured her carving.

"May you wear it in good health," he said, placing it in her hand. She admired his handiwork, holding it up and studying it for a moment before slipping it around her neck. She let it hang outside her shirt, so it could be seen.

"It's beautiful in its own way. Don't you agree?"

"It's a lot like you, Cat. If you look hard enough, it's kinda pretty," he said with a smirk. "Perhaps you're both jewels in the rough."

He ran ahead of her back to the campfire, drawn by the smell of cooking fish. Benjin and the others were eating fish and drinking the last bottle of springwine. More fish roasted over the fire, with a plate of fillets waiting to be roasted.

"I give thanks to the mighty fishermen who have provided so well for us. My compliments to your skills," Catrin said with a smile.

The day had left them tired and hungry, and the fish were satisfying. The springwine disappeared, and they wished that bottle were not the last. Despite their exhaustion, restlessness set in. Benjin kept a watchful eye on the surrounding land, alert for any movements, but the night remained peaceful and still.

Catrin longed for something sweet and, thinking she smelled apples, stood and said she was going to look around. Clear skies and a full moon illuminated the night, and she searched the sky for the comet. It was smaller and farther across the sky, but when she spotted it, her thoughts focused on it, and she was drawn to it. It mesmerized her and drew her closer, but she became frightened and turned aside when arcs of power leaped between her fingertips. Shaken, she walked on, following a trail defined by smell alone. She was nearly at the base of the hill when she spotted the trees, mere paces above the mud line.

They were few and stunted, but they were heavily laden with fruit. Catrin scanned the branches for ripe apples and picked those within her reach, but she wanted a few more. As she stood on the tips of her toes and stretched toward an apple, hands grabbed her waist. She gasped when they lifted her into the air but was reassured when she heard Benjin chuckle. She snatched four beauties from the highest branches, and Benjin lowered her gently.

"It looked like you needed a lift."

"Except for the fact that you frightened me out of my wits for a moment, I thank you. I'm glad you're here too. I need to talk to you." He nodded, and she went on. "Do you believe I'm the Herald of Istra?"

"Yes, I do believe you are," he replied slowly and deliberately. "I believed it the instant you said you were. I was undecided until that moment. When I returned from Harborton and found out you were gone, I was worried beyond reason. Chase and the others were just as distraught, and we reviewed everything we knew. They told me about the night in the greatoak grove. I'm truly sorry about that, Catrin."

"Why do you keep calling me that? You've called me 'li'l miss' for as long as I can remember. Why don't you still call me that?"

"I'm sorry, Cat--uh, li'l miss," he fumbled. "You've changed in the last year . . . and for the better; you're becoming a strong young woman. It's not the changes in you that caused me to use your name, though," he said, and Catrin glanced up in surprise. "I've been remiss, you see. I have failed to properly perform the duties of a position passed to me by my grandfather.

"When I was a boy, he said he had a very important job for me. He said we were Guardians of the Vestrana, though I knew very little of what that meant at the time. I had already been sworn to secrecy, and he knew I could keep a secret. I guess he was right about that, at least, because you are only the third person I've ever told.

"He said our job was difficult but had a single aim: we were to protect the Herald and their line and swear our lives to them. Since I didn't understand at first, he explained it. 'A time will come when the Herald will need protection, and our family will answer the call; that is our destiny and our duty,' he said to me. He told me to train myself both as weapon and shield, and so I became a soldier." Fascinated, Catrin nodded for him to continue.

"That's why I started calling you by name; it is my duty to show you proper respect." Catrin needed time to absorb what she had heard. Her perceptions of events and people kept shifting.

Benjin had always lived at the farm with her and her father and had been a part of her world. She'd never before wondered why he lived there and had no wife or children of his own, and she began to see him in a new light.

"Well, the Herald is telling you to stop it," she said, smiling and waving her finger in his face. "You can call me by name if you like but not solely because I'm the Herald."

Benjin smiled. "Li'l miss, consider it done."

"What do we do from here?" she asked.

"I think we should do what you think is best. I'll give you my best advice if you want it, and I'm sure Chase and the others will as well, but my first duty is to protect you. I hope you consider our advice, compare it to your senses and your gut, and then make your decisions based on those things. I'll do my best to help--no matter what you decide."

She felt inadequate and small, yet it was up to her to decide what actions to take, what course to follow. The responsibility was a little frightening. What if she made the wrong choices?

"I don't want you to stay with me because your family was sworn to protect the Herald. I want you to stay because you want to stay," she managed through tears she hadn't realized she was crying.

Benjin pulled her into his arms, hugging her close. "There, there, li'l miss. Don't you cry. I'm here because I want to be here, and no one could tear me away. My duty to the Herald is just a fortunate coincidence that tells me to do what I would have done anyway."

Catrin cried and hugged him back; then she wiped her eyes and gathered the apples, while he picked several that were not yet ripe, saying they would make a nice treat in a few days. When Catrin stood, he noticed her carved fish.

"I like your necklace."

"Thank you. So do I. I found it while I was exploring the cavern, and I just remembered it when I was talking to Chase. He made the necklace for me," she said.

"He did a nice job; it compliments you."

* * *

Premon Dalls shuffled along the halls with the rest of the refugees as they were moved to their new homes within the audience halls. As the seemingly endless line of humanity poured into the halls, pushing, shoving, and vying for any scrap of space they could claim as their own, Premon faked a coughing fit. Standing in the arched entranceway, flanked by the strange carvings that adorned the archway and pretending to catch his breath, he examined the mechanism Master Edling had told him about.

The entranceways were narrow, yet long, and they served more than one purpose. Though the ceiling was decorated and appeared to be of solid rock, it was a ruse. The designers of the Masterhouse had foreseen the possibility of a siege, and they had built defense mechanisms into their fortress. Above these corridors lay a mountain of rubble and rock supported by joists that could hold its weight but little more. Above that stood a massive shaft, and at the top, an enormous weight was suspended by a chain. All Premon had to do was retrieve the special rod that Master Edling had told him how to find, insert it into the mouth of either carving, twist, and yank. That was all there was to it, at least that was what Master Edling had said. How Premon was supposed to trigger all three collapses before anyone emerged was something of a mystery, but Premon didn't care. He had nothing to lose.

The thought of killing all those people, sentencing them to starvation, would have made most men sick, but Premon considered himself a practical man. The loss of the refugees would mean many more months before those in the Masterhouse would either starve or be forced to surrender themselves into slavery. When he had revealed to Peten Ross that he could escape through the sewers, Premon had known he was sending the boy to his death, but he had also known that it would mean one less mouth to feed. Now he would achieve the same result, only on a much larger scale.

Chapter 13

Even the greatest catastrophes bring new opportunities for life.
--Brother Ramirez, Cathuran monk

* * *

Eager to put the plateau behind them, Catrin set a brisk pace. The sodden valley reeked of rotted vegetation and dead fish. "This valley runs all the way to the coastline, but the mountains on our right turn south and open into this area, the Arghast Desert," she said aloud while glancing at her map. She remembered the Arghast Desert from school: a vast wasteland. Nomadic tribes were said to wander the area, but no one had reported seeing them in generations.

The ragged northern coastline bordered the desert and was lined with mountains, which dwindled in the east. The southern coast was flat and lined with long stretches of sandy beach. It would be a long hike south, but Catrin thought it might be easier going than the mountains. She thought of how nice it would be to walk along the ocean with the sounds of crashing waves to soothe them. "Do you think we should go north or south when we reach the desert?"

"North," Benjin replied immediately. "The southern coast would be a more pleasant journey, but there's no cover there, and those lands can easily be patrolled by ships. We'd be inviting the entire Zjhon fleet to intercept us. The northern coast is much less accessible to enemies. There is very little safe anchorage, and most of the shoreline is made up of steep cliffs and mountains. If we stay close to the mountains, we should only have to skirt around the edges of the desert, which is not only uncomfortable, but often deadly. However, it is our best route."

"How many days would it take us to walk straight across the desert?"

"It's hard to say," he said after a moment. "I'd say six days at the least and as long as ten in the event of sandstorms. The days are hot and the nights cold, and there's almost no water. Venomous snakes, lizards, and scorpions are almost impossible to avoid." Before Benjin could continue, Catrin cut him short.

"I agree we should avoid the desert, and I agree the southern coast is too dangerous, so let's discuss the northern coast. What kind of difficulties do you expect on that route?"

"There are venomous snakes in that area as well--but fewer. We must be watchful for glass vipers. They're deadly, and because of their ability to take on the color of their immediate surroundings, they can be almost impossible to see. Beyond that, there are predator cats, roaming packs of wolves, and possibly bears, but they should not pose too great a threat. We'll just need to be cautious. The foothills are partially forested, which should provide additional cover should we need it."

"How many days will it take us to go north around the desert? Do we have enough provisions?"

"I'd say fourteen days until we reach the east coast, and then another two south to the cove. We have enough food to last ten days comfortably, the full fourteen if we stretch it. Of course, we may find game along the way, but I wouldn't count on it. We've got enough water for three or four days, and we'll need to replenish our supply as we travel."

Catrin nodded, scanning her map for indications of water features, but they were few. "Are there other sources of water to the east? I don't see many marked on the map."

"We'll need to be watchful. I'm sure there are streams and creeks that aren't on the map, but we'll have to find them. Once we reach the desert and turn north, we'll be entering territory I've never traveled, and I'll know little more than what the map shows us."

The sun rose higher, and so did the temperature. As they were trying to get some relief from the heat, Benjin snapped his head to the left, squinting in the bright light. Chase saw it too.

"I saw something moving in those trees."

"I did too," Benjin said, "but I didn't get a good look." They all watched the trees for a long while, but nothing moved; if someone lurked there, he remained hidden.

"Probably just a deer," Chase said.

Anxieties ran high, and they often looked over their shoulders for signs of pursuit. The tension and uncertainty gnawed at Catrin like an itch she could not scratch. Distant noises and glimpses of movement were the only indications of pursuit, but each occurrence renewed their apprehension. Catrin tried to convince herself it was her vivid imagination that each distorted echo was an approaching battle cry and that within every shadow lurked men intent on killing them. Though she had vowed to show the Zjhon no fear, she hadn't promised not to feel any.

As the valley widened into a broad plain, trees became more numerous and thickets more dense, and they had to use game trails or clear paths of their own. The shade provided respite from the glaring sun, but the underbrush slowed their journey. On a steep slope covered with thorny bushes, brambles, and vines, they found a patch of berry bushes, but the fruit lay beyond a thick screen of the plants. Working with great care, they cleared a narrow pathway to the berries. Benjin knew which ones had poisonous berries and others whose fruit was edible. Soon they had ample raspberries, blackberries, and even huckles. In a brief moment of levity, they filled themselves with the fruit.

Once beyond the wall of thorns, the land became more hospitable; underbrush gave way to tall grasses, and trees were sparse. Ahead lay marshy lowland, and already dark clouds of gnats buzzed around them. Emerald biting-flies darted around their heads, and walnut-sized mosquitoes attacked in legions.

"When I last passed this way, a strip of dry land bordered this marsh on either side. Now it appears we'll have to wade through it," Benjin said, scowling with squinting eyes over the saturated lowland, which now stretched across the entire valley. Narrow islands appeared throughout the marsh, creating a disjointed maze of land almost entirely immersed in stagnant water, and the search for a dry path became paramount.

As they moved deeper into the marsh, the stretches of water separating the islands became longer and deeper. Osbourne was the first to notice the leeches, which had attached themselves to his legs. He yanked his pant legs up and pulled the leeches off, throwing them. The rest discovered the same effect, and Benjin suggested they tuck their pants into their boots.

Slogging through the mucky quagmire was difficult and unpleasant, and Catrin was relieved when the marsh began to give way to some patches of high ground. Then a nearby scream and a series of splashes broke the silence.

"I saw something flailing around behind those weeds, but I'm not sure what it was," Chase said. "Shouldn't we go back to check?"

"I think we should take a look," said Benjin. "That sounded like a man shouting, and it sounded like he was hurt. If someone is following us, I want to know for certain. Let's go, Chase."

When they returned, Benjin said grimly, "A soldier was tracking us. We don't know if he was alone, but he'll follow us no more; he was bitten by a poisonous snake, and he took his own life before we arrived. We didn't go very close, since the snake was coiled in our path, but I could tell the man was no ordinary foot soldier. He was a member of an elite unit; at least that's what I gather from his attire. Unlike the other soldiers, he was equipped to move quickly; his armor was light and his weapons advanced. We'll have to remain more alert. I suspect more soldiers are tracking us."

"Let's move on, then," Catrin said. "I'd like to put as much ground between us and this marsh as possible. I don't want to camp anywhere near here."

* * *

By the light of one of the precious few candles that remained, Wendel

Volker packed his gear. Elsa's sword lay across the blanket-covered crates he'd been using as a bed. He took no food, and in no way, other than burning the candle, depleted the provisions that would be needed by all those who remained in the cold caves. A twinge of guilt made Wendel pause and reconsider; these people needed him, or at least so they thought. An equally painful guilt hovered over him for abandoning Catrin, and his duty as a father had finally won out over his duty to his people. Those he had gathered in the cold caves were now as safe as they were going to be; there was nothing more he could do to ensure their well-being. In a moment of self-justification, he asserted that by leaving, he would consume less of the rations; therefore, he was doing everyone who remained a favor.

Like all others, that moment passed, and he was left to deal with guilt over leaving Jensen behind. He and his brother simply saw things differently. Jensen had as much anxiety over Chase's fate as Wendel did over Catrin's, but he steadfastly refused to go after them, and he had done everything within his power to persuade Wendel to do the same. When he was honest with himself, Wendel realized that Jensen was the only reason he had stayed as long as he had. With a deep breath, he firmed his resolve and shouldered his pack. The journey ahead would be difficult and fraught with danger, but the hardest part was behind him; as he stepped out of the chamber that had been his temporary home, the journey was begun. He would find Catrin.

His candle was not overly bright, but he shielded it as best he could while allowing enough light to guide his way. To those who were immersed in darkness, even the dimmest light can shine like a beacon, and Wendel had no desire to alert anyone of his departure. Fortunately, most avoided the deepest tunnels, where the air was the coldest and the feeling of the land pressing down the greatest. Wendel had grown accustomed to the feeling long ago, and he walked without fear, though not without anxiety. He should have left a note for Jensen, something to explain his motives and reasoning, but he could not turn back now, and there was no time to waste. Jensen would wake soon, and another day would be lost, and Catrin would be another day farther from him. In the back of his mind, a voice warned that she was already too far away, that he would never reach her in time. Ignoring that voice, Wendel moved as quickly and quietly as he could.

Deep within the network of tunnels and caves, the scent of fresh air drifted. Only in a few places did shafts penetrate the rock and allow air and, in some cases, light into the caves, but Wendel now stood below one of these shafts. He had never found one of the shafts from above, mostly due to the fact that this part of the cold caves lay directly below a series of steep and formidable peaks. Not knowing what he would face when he emerged gave him pause, and he took a moment to plan this critical part of his escape.

First he tied a length of rope around his waist and secured the other end to his pack. The knife on his belt was all that he would carry, and all that he could use to defend himself should the outlet of the shaft be guarded. Though he thought it unlikely, Wendel made himself consider the possibility. Chastising himself for allowing fear to stall him, he moved to the crates of cheese that were stacked nearby, and he placed them on top of one another beneath the air shaft, giving himself just enough of a boost to gain his first handhold. Once inside the shaft, the climbing would be easier since he could use both sides of the shaft to support himself. The fear of getting stuck in a section where the shaft was too narrow nearly made him abandon this course, but his decision was made.

"Only cowards and thieves sneak away beneath a shroud of darkness," came Jensen's voice from below. "I never believed you to be either of those things, yet here we are."

Nearly howling in frustration, Wendel cursed himself for whatever carelessness allowed Jensen to find him here.

"I could see it in your eyes, and I could hear it in your voice when we discussed the plans today. I knew from the way you held yourself that you had no intention of being here when those plans were put in place. You cannot hide things from me--never could. Thought you would know that by now. So . . . if you are determined to leave, at least come down here and face me like a man."

With a final glance toward the sky--though he saw little in the darkness--Wendel lowered himself back to the crates, wondering if he would ever see Catrin, Chase, or Benjin again. The thoughts were nearly as painful as seeing the disappointment in his brother's eyes.

* * *

As the trees grew thicker, the group moved slowly along a narrow game trail. The air vibrated with the percussive cadence of hammer-locusts, and Catrin could feel their call thrumming through her. A mass of downed trees suddenly loomed before them, deteriorating beneath a bed of moss and lichen. Thorn bushes around the rotting mass created a formidable barrier.

"These trees are crumbling, so you'd better watch your footing," Benjin said. Catrin made the climb easily, stepping lightly across the slick limbs. Just as she gained solid ground, she saw the trunk beneath Osbourne's boot collapse, and his leg was immersed in a writhing, humming, black mass. Playing harmony to the hammer-locusts, a growing cloud of angry hornets defended their nest.

Engulfed by the storm, Osbourne let out a cry and ran past Catrin, who sprinted after him. Burning stings on her neck and head spurred her to reckless speed, and she pumped her legs as fast as they would go. Each new pain drove her forward; unable to distinguish hornet stings from the bites of thorns, she fled. Dark shapes darted around her, striking without mercy. Her head throbbed in time with the pounding of her pulse, and her vision deteriorated as her eyebrow swelled.

A loud splash was the only warning she received before she hurtled through open air. Her brief flight ended as she struck water, which was deep enough to break her fall. She plunged under for an instant, but then her feet found bottom, and she propelled herself back up.

When she broke the surface, coughing and gasping, she was thankful no hornets awaited her. Her left eye was nearly closed, and the swelling in her neck made it difficult to turn her head. Osbourne was thrashing on the far shore in obvious agony, his entire head swelling. A moment later, Benjin and the others plunged into the water.

Catrin ran to Osbourne, who had gone still. His eyes were mere slits trapped between exaggerated folds of puffy flesh, and the flushed skin of his lips curled outward to contain it. His skin deepened from mottled red to purple, and his body occasionally twitched.

"Cut his shirt away from his throat," Benjin barked, approaching with his herbal kit. "Pull his lips open and depress his tongue." Catrin pried open Osbourne's slack jaws and pressed his tongue down firmly with her fingers. Benjin pinched a generous portion of Celia's root, which he blew into Osbourne's open mouth; then he puffed the fine powder into Osbourne's lungs, using his hands to seal the opening of their mouths. A fine cloud of powder escaped when Benjin pressed on Osbourne's chest with his hands, causing Osbourne to exhale. Then Benjin blew into Osbourne's mouth again.

When Osbourne went into spasm and coughed, Catrin let out her breath, only then realizing she had been holding it. The boy was wracked with violent fits of coughing, which left him gasping, and each new breath tickled his throat, causing him to cough harder. Only wheezing and vomiting separated his fits, but he was breathing.

Chase had stings on his neck and arms, but the swelling was minor. Strom had been behind them and was untouched by the angry mass of hornets that had pursued the others. With Osbourne out of immediate danger, Benjin mixed a large batch of sting remedy from several of his powders and some clean water. When he looked up from his work, Catrin saw that his bottom lip had been stung several times and was twice its normal size. She realized then how painful it must have been for him to blow into Osbourne's mouth, and she marveled at his strength.

Osbourne's breathing gradually eased, but his eyes remained shut. Benjin told him to take shallow breaths until the tickle left his throat and leaned him against a tree. In time, the herbs took effect. His body relaxed, and though the swelling was not gone, it no longer seemed to be getting worse.

Benjin prepared another mixture, which he said would help with the swelling, but they would have to swallow it. It was bitter and left a vile aftertaste. Osbourne drank the mixture diluted with water, but he choked on it and suffered another coughing fit.

Benjin's lip grew huge, but he kept working despite his obvious discomfort. When he checked their packs, he sighed. The others watched as he removed the smoked and salted goods that had gotten wet, and the pile of food he discarded was distressing to see after the work they had put into preparing it. They sat for a while and watched Osbourne recover. He seemed to be having less trouble breathing, but his eyes were still shut. Catrin wanted to make for higher ground before they camped for the night, and she was trying to decide what to do when Benjin drew her aside.

"I don't think Osbourne should walk any farther today. I should go ahead and scout out a suitable campsite while the rest of you wait here. You all can rig a litter and attend to Osbourne's needs while I'm gone. Agreed?" She nodded. "Good." He got his bow and a quiver of arrows, set off at a rapid pace, and was soon lost from sight.

Chase and Strom found saplings, while Catrin unpacked her leather ground cloth and made a hole near each corner and several more along each side. She took a length of rope and unbraided it so she would have the six smaller lines she needed. She then lashed the ground cloth to the saplings to form a litter for Osbourne.

"Sorry I took so long," Benjin said when he returned. "I found a decent campsite and a fairly clear path there." After lifting Osbourne gently onto the litter, trying not to aggravate any of his injuries, they set off at a steady pace. Benjin and Catrin pushed bushes and saplings aside in narrow places, allowing room for the stretcher Chase and Strom were carrying.

The land finally began to slope upward, and Benjin led them to the top of a hill shaded by an enormous tree. Under the tree waited a pile of firewood, pears, and a brace of rabbits, which explained why Benjin had been so long in returning.

Catrin removed her ground cloth from the makeshift litter while Strom lit a fire and Benjin dressed the rabbits. They made soup for Osbourne because he was quite ill and might not tolerate solid food. The campsite was a good choice: the area shaded by the tree was soft and covered with spongy moss, making it far more comfortable than rough ground.

Strom, the only one unscathed by the attack of hornets, looked around the fire and shook his head. Benjin had a very fat lip, Catrin's eye was swollen nearly shut, Chase had large lumps on the back of his neck, and Osbourne was puffed up as if he were filled with water.

"You're a sorry-looking group, I have to tell ya," he said, grinning, but within moments he began to shift where he sat. He grumbled as he stood and vigorously scratched the seat of his pants, apparently wishing he'd been more careful selecting leaves after relieving himself. Benjin shook his head and retrieved his ever-diminishing supply of herbs. He made a suitable mixture, poured it into Strom's hand, and gave him a water flask.

"You'll have to apply that yourself, m'friend," he said, casting him a sidelong glance. "You're on your own."

* * *

Master Jarvis hurried along the inner corridors, his mouth and nose still covered with a scented kerchief to mask the smell. No one was immune to the effects of the siege, though he no longer even considered this a siege; it was more like containment. The Zjhon were not trying to get in anymore, they just didn't want anyone to get out. Master Jarvis could not decide which was worse.

The thought of Catrin in the hands of the Zjhon nearly made him sick; he'd taught her since she was a little girl, and she'd always been one of his favored students. The only thing that sickened him more was the thought of what Master Edling was trying to achieve. Some would say that Jarvis was seeing things that were not there, but he knew better; he'd known Edling for too long. Master Grodin had been swayed into moving the refugees into the audience halls based on the premise that the people would feel more secure surrounded by their peers than if kept apart. It was a ruse, and Jarvis knew it. Though some people had expressed feelings of loneliness and a sense of being disconnected, he doubted any of them would consider being crammed into the audience halls an improvement. The fact that one of the special release bars used to trigger the cave-in mechanism was missing only solidified the reality in Master Jarvis's mind.

When he finally reached Master Grodin's quarters, he was pleased to see the old man awake and alone. "May I trouble you?"

"Who's there? Is that you, young Jarvis?" Master Grodin asked. "There are some candied cherries in the dish there. Help yourself. I know how you like them. Then run along and be a good boy."

"Thank you, sir," Master Jarvis said, knowing that sometimes Master Grodin seemed to drift into the past, remembering a time when Jarvis was but a student of his. "The refugees have been moved into the audience halls."

"Yes, I know. They can all be together with their family and friends now. I wish I could do more for them. Maybe you could take them some candied cherries?"

"Perhaps I will," Master Jarvis said. "I'm concerned about Master Edling's motivation. I suspect he had another reason for wanting the people moved."

"You and Edling must end this rivalry between you," Master Grodin said as he wagged his finger. "Wasn't it just last week I caught the two of you fighting in the store room?"

In truth, that had been nearly thirty years ago, but Jarvis knew better than to tell Master Grodin he was mistaken; instead he tried to nudge his aging mentor back into the present. "I'd feel more comfortable with the refugees in the audience halls if all of the cave-in release keys were accounted for. One is missing."

Master Grodin turned sharply and chewed on his beard a moment before he responded. "I suppose that leaves me only one course of action," he said, his eyes clearer than Jarvis had seen them in some time. "Since Edling feels compelled to represent the refugees, then that is how it shall be. Let it be known that he and his must remain in the audience halls at all times, so that he can personally ensure the safety and well-being of his charges."

Jarvis left with a smile on his face, wondering how much of Master Grodin's condition was an act, and how much was the guise of a clever old man.

Chapter 14

The bitter taste of betrayal can be purged only by fire.
--Imeteri, slave

* * *

The next few days were long and miserable while they waited at the campsite to heal, taking time when they could to gather supplies. They were not in very good shape for hunting, so they settled for gathering fruits and nuts.

The weather was clear and warm, and light breezes carried the many scents of summer. The comet was no longer visible in the night sky, and no new comets showed themselves. Catrin wondered if it had all been just a cosmic joke, the first comet really being the only comet. She could still feel a charge in the air, but she wondered if it was just a lingering effect from the first comet.

"Do you think there'll be more comets?" she asked Benjin.

"Can't be certain, but I assume so. Legends say thousands of them crowd the night skies during the Istran Noon, which should occur some seventy-five years from now. I'm guessing we'll see a gradual increase over time."

They had seen no further signs of soldiers, for which they were grateful, but the fact seemed to disturb Benjin. He was nervous, edgy, and constantly looking for signs of the Zjhon.

"I know there're more soldiers following us. I'm almost certain the man who died in the marsh wasn't alone, but I can't understand why they don't attack. They're more heavily armed than we are, and they have to know that. They know where we are, and they've had time to bring a larger force here," he said.

"They may be heavily armed, but I bet none of them has ever changed the course of a river or knocked down the side of a mountain like I saw Catrin do," Strom said. His words sounded strange to Catrin--like something from a fireside story.

"But they knew they were coming here to face the Herald," Benjin replied. "They must have known she would have great power. I don't think they're totally reacting out of fear, although I do agree they have good reason to be cautious. I still think they must have some other reason for following us but not attacking."

"Perhaps they are bringing more troops here to confront us," Chase said. "Maybe the terrain has just delayed them. We should remain watchful."

"Maybe they don't need to attack us now because they already know where we're going," Osbourne observed. "They're probably just waiting for us to walk into an ambush."

Benjin nodded and hesitated before he said, "You may be right, but I'm not sure. They may have other plans for us. Still, we'll need to be alert for signs of either ambush or pursuit."

* * *

Catrin spent a long day looking for fruits, nuts, and the herbs and spices they needed to replenish Benjin's medicinal supplies. When she returned to camp, her companions seemed to be better, a great relief after days of misery. There was a strange look in their eyes as she approached.

Strom stared at her so intently that she finally couldn't stand it any longer. "What are you looking at?" she asked Strom more sharply than she'd intended.

"I'm looking at your necklace, Cat. It didn't look like that when you first showed it to us. It was all milky and dull, and now it's . . ."

Chase finished the sentence for him. "It's just beautiful."

Catrin lifted the leather thong over her head and examined the carving, amazed by what she saw. The carved fish was now clear and almost lustrous. It caught the light and sent small prisms dancing around her. She ran her finger across it and found the surface smooth where it had seemed rough and porous before. Trying to find a reasonable explanation for the transformation of the small carving, she wondered if it had just been dirty and in need of cleaning. She tried to remember exactly how it had looked when she had first found it. It had seemed almost as if it were dried out rather than dirty.

"Maybe your swim cleaned it off," Chase said, which made better sense than anything else she had come up with, but Catrin wasn't so sure. She tried to put it from her mind, but in its place came anxious thoughts of Istra.

Somehow, the light of a comet, or a goddess--depending on how she chose to perceive it--gave Catrin access to powers of which she had no knowledge or aptitude. Through some unknown process, she knew she could gather the comet's energy and release it in devastating ways, but she didn't know how to control it. Only when her life was in danger did she even seem to have full access to it; most of the time it was a distant dream, tickling her senses then receding too fast to pursue.

She needed to know how to use the energy without hurting anyone. If she did not learn to control her outbursts, it might kill her and everyone around her. It was an uncomfortable feeling, and it put Catrin on edge. Her mind whirled with questions and only a handful of answers, and those answers only spawned more questions.

Trying to her calm herself, she sat down and closed her eyes. Fears and anxieties cluttered her mind and prevented coherent thought.

"Are you all right, li'l miss?" Benjin asked.

"I have too many thoughts in my head to concentrate on anything because other thoughts keep pushing themselves into my mind. It's frustrating, and I don't like it at all."

"I understand," he said with a slight nod of his head. "Let me try to help. There are many techniques you can use to quiet your mind and get a clearer view. Would you like me to teach you some of what I know?"

"Yes, please. Would you?"

Benjin told them to all sit in a circle around the fire, directing Catrin to sit directly across from him. Sitting with his legs crossed and his arms relaxed, he put his hands on his knees, palms facing up. The others followed his example.

"Close your eyes and concentrate on slow, steady breaths to the count of seven. Breathe in through your nose and out through your mouth. Keep your eyes closed, and relax your muscles," he said, watching them. "You need to relax a bit more, li'l miss; you're as rigid as stone. On every exhale, concentrate on your muscles becoming looser."

Catrin tried to calm herself, but the harder she tried, the more tense she became, and she grew angry with herself for not being able even to relax properly. How could she ever hope to control her power if she could not even control her own state of mind? Realizing her fists were tightly clenched, she opened her eyes with a frustrated sigh. The others still had their eyes closed and looked relaxed. Benjin's eyes met hers.

"Perhaps we should try another technique that can be useful when your mind refuses to be quiet. When our heads are full of thoughts, it can be nearly impossible to suppress them. It's often better to deal with each thought individually as they come to you. Not all of them are pleasant, but we have to learn to accept them; they are a part of us. We should deal with them and try to understand them, but at the very least, we should accept them.

"I want to teach you an ancient exercise. First, close your eyes and begin your breathing again. When a thought comes to you, grab on to it and accept it. Recognize it as your own, and try to understand why you are thinking it. Picture it as a small ball of energy; hold your hands out and cup that energy in your palms. Examine the energy and analyze it until you come to know it. When you are comfortable thinking about it, take a deep breath, and when you exhale, release that energy into the universe.

"Your thoughts are your own, but your pain and suffering can be eased when you let the universe help, and your joy and happiness can be shared with the whole of existence. Your hope can go to every part of creation. By sending out your thoughts, you will feel less alone with your feelings. You can help others find their happiness, and you will receive help dealing with your troubles."

Catrin was surprised by his philosophical words; she had never heard him speak that way, even in his previous lessons about meditation. She tried to concentrate on taking his advice rather than analyzing it, but concentrating was a challenge. Breathing deeply, searching for calm within the violent storm of her thoughts and emotions, she became detached from the world, transported to a place of her own making that was comforting yet unfamiliar. Letting the thoughts swirl around her for a moment, she tried to find her center and braced herself for the onslaught.

A feeling of anger and betrayal flashed into her consciousness: it was hot and painful, and further images of anguish and pain came to the fore. She remembered the townies' abuse of her and her friends; visions of the attack on Osbourne played through her mind. Then her dreamlike vision moved on to another scene: the townspeople challenging her father and accusing her of being a witch. Images of the invading army hammered her until she almost lost her focus.

After a deep breath, she accepted the anger that was part of her. Releasing the thought as she exhaled, she blew it away from her.

While floating between thoughts for a moment, she was surprised by the lull in the maelstrom of her consciousness. She felt a great release from the thoughts she had accepted; she chose to persist, believing she was ready for her next thought. It did not take long before it drifted in from somewhere in the back of her mind. This was a warm, comforting image, however, and it felt secure and safe. She realized that thought was Benjin.

She envisioned him with his salt-and-pepper beard, his long black hair with streaks of gray pulled back with a leather thong. She saw his strong features and muscular build. Pouring herself into the meditation, she concentrated on that thought, building it up for a huge release. She felt great gratitude to Benjin for protecting her, for being her friend and mentor, and for caring so much for her. She let the thought expand to include all those around her then to all those she had left behind. To all who had ever been kind to her, she sent out this thought as a gift of thanks. With her next exhale, she let it pour from her.

Catrin floated blissfully above her consciousness, having experienced a massive, gratifying, and unexplainably beautiful release of tension.

"Your minds have become very quiet now," Benjin said in a low and rhythmic voice, hardly more than a whisper. "Focus your consciousness. I want you to picture a strawberry. Focus on the details rather than the whole. Envision the colors and textures; picture the seeds and leaves until every detail is complete."

Catrin heard his words somewhere in her mind, and she tried to comply. She began to visualize the strawberry, and soon she tasted the sweetness of the freshly picked fruit, strawberry jam, and strawberry-rhubarb pie. All her memories of strawberries permeated the thought, but she was brought out of her meditation by the sound of Chase laughing and talking excitedly.

"That was great, I'm telling ya. I could actually taste strawberries."

"And strawberry jam," Osbourne added.

"I tasted pie," Strom said with a grin.

"Hey, Cat. Do you remember the time you tried to shove strawberries up my nose?" Chase asked, and Catrin laughed; she'd been thinking about the same thing.

"Did any of you experience anything else?" Benjin asked.

"When we first started, I felt angry," Osbourne said. "I remembered the way I was attacked and the way Catrin was treated."

"I felt a lot like that too," Chase said, "but then I got to thinking about how Benjin has protected us and kept us safe. And then I felt like I was a protector too."

"Me too," Strom added, and Osbourne nodded.

Catrin sat back, wondering if it was all coincidence. Could they all have been thinking the exact same things? Benjin met her eyes.

"I didn't want to say anything without some confirmation, but Catrin's powers are beginning to manifest in different ways," he said. "During your meditation, I could actually see the energy above Catrin's palms. It's difficult to describe. It shifted and moved, but I got a general sense of what she was thinking. It seems she was able to influence our thoughts."

"She can control people's minds?" Osbourne asked, his face pale.

"I don't think she has any control over our thoughts or any way to read them. It does seem, however, that she can project her emotions to those around her," Benjin said.

"I didn't try to make you think those things," Catrin objected. "Those were the things I was thinking about, but I just concentrated real hard on them; that's all. I wasn't trying to influence your thoughts. Honest." Her voice was practically pleading now. "And I'd never try to read your minds. Sometimes I can sense people's emotions, but I don't even do that intentionally."

"We know you wouldn't do anything like that on purpose," Chase said. "You should guard your thoughts more closely from now on, though. Try not to concentrate that hard on anything you want kept secret."

"Well said," Benjin said.

"I need to see this for myself," Catrin said. "I'm going to try to do it again."

Benjin did not discourage her, and the others looked as if they wanted to see it, so she took a deep breath and centered herself. The excitement made the meditation as difficult as her previous frustration had, but she closed her eyes and concentrated.

This was important. This was an opportunity to learn something about her powers, a chance to take control of her life. Hope, excitement, and curiosity were predominant in her thoughts, and she focused on them.

"Look now," Chase whispered.

It nearly cost Catrin her concentration, and she kept her eyes closed until she regained her focus. Slowly she opened them. The light was almost blinding, but soon she could see a ball of energy floating above her cupped palms. Like a shimmering jewel with countless facets, it was exquisite. It spun and danced in her hands, constantly changing.

The more excited and fascinated she became, the larger and brighter it grew. When she could no longer contain it, she tossed it into the night sky, where it burst into a cloud of twinkling lights no larger than grains of sand. They dimmed and disappeared before reaching the ground, but the air was charged with excitement.

"That was amazing," Chase said.

"I'd have to agree," Benjin added.

Catrin's mind raced with possibilities and questions. What else could she do with her powers? What other abilities might she stumble on? The thoughts were as terrifying as they were exhilarating. Even after she retired to her bedroll, she lay staring up at the stars, hoping whatever power she found next would not destroy anything or kill anyone.

Chapter 15

Bonds of blood are sacred and immutable.
--King Venes of the Elsics

* * *

Catrin woke during the night and decided to relieve Benjin from his watch. She figured it would be best if he were the one rested for the next part of their journey. Pulling her coverlet around her shoulders, she wandered past the glowing coals of the fire. She found Chase in Benjin's stead. He smiled at her.

"Couldn't sleep?"

"I slept great, actually. I just woke up for some reason . . . not sure why. How long ago did you relieve Benjin?"

"Not long ago. I'm awake and alert. I'll take the rest of the watch. Get some more sleep; you'll probably need it," he said. Catrin was glad to take him up on this advice. Her sleeping spot had gone cold and she shivered, but soon she slept again.

Chase woke them during the false dawn. Catrin felt she had closed her eyes only moments before, and they were still clouded with sleep. Their routine well practiced, they broke camp in record time, and Catrin slowly recovered from her disorientation.

Wanting to cover as much ground as possible while the air was still cool, they set off without delay. Catrin set a moderate pace for Osbourne's sake since he was still experiencing headaches and shortness of breath. His condition troubled her, but they had to keep moving. Benjin did what he could to ease Osbourne's afflictions using the few medicinal herbs he still had left, and Catrin hoped it would be enough.

The broad valley morphed into rolling hills, and as they crested a steep rise, Catrin caught sight of what lay ahead. The rising sun cast a myriad of colors across the sky and the desert below. The horizon was a lush canvas of texture and color, pastels and blush highlighted with hues of violet. Waves of sand appeared almost fluid, lapping against a meandering shoreline. The relative flatness stretched into the distance, the horizon broken only by distant, shadowy mountains. The sheer size and deceptive beauty of the desert cast an intimidating pall on those who viewed it.

Catrin had never been away from the mountains before. Realizing the feeling of security they had always given her, she was glad they would follow the mountains for much of their journey.

"Do not let its beauty fool you," Benjin said. "The desert is deadly. We'll be skirting it for some time, and though the mountains will give us some cover and possible storm shelter, we won't be immune to its dangers. Keep watch on the horizons and be alert for storms or large clouds of dust."

At the mouth of the valley, they turned north, following the narrow band of lightly forested grasslands that huddled between stone and sand like an emerald river. The air above the desert shimmered in the heat of the morning sun, and they moved along in relative silence to conserve their energy. They drank sparingly from their flasks, knowing they could run out before they escaped this arid landscape.

Catrin let Benjin lead and found herself walking in a trance, part of her mind watching where she was going, but another part deep in thought. She tried the technique of clearing her mind that Benjin taught her, but she could not focus, and she wandered from thought to thought, seemingly at random. The deluge of thoughts flowed past her consciousness, and she let them skirt her awareness, creating an odd, transitional state of mind. She became aware of a curious hum, like background noise in her head, a buzzing that seemed to be just behind her ears. She tried to focus on it, but it stayed at the edge of her senses, elusive and indefinable.

Taking a different approach, she tried to specifically not think about it and concentrate on something else. No matter how hard she tried to ignore it, though, the humming crept along the edges of her senses, tickling her awareness. She tried to evoke powerful memories and the emotions they brought, hoping to overpower the distraction. She called up the vivid memory of her first kiss, and the buzzing pounded into her thoughts. Grasping it with her mind, she latched on to it with all the focus she could muster.

Her body thrummed in the powerful chorus, a lilting melody that ebbed to a mere whisper only to resound again insistently. Concentrating on hearing alone seemed insufficient to perceive the energy, and she split her focus to include the vibrations she felt. At this point, she began to experience it in a completely new way. The energy took shape and form, though its form continuously shifted like the surface of a lake. Fragrances overlaid her other senses, and even the taste of the air colored her mental imagery.

After tripping on a gnarled tree root, Catrin caught herself on the trunk. Her palms slammed into the bark, and she was overwhelmed by her impression of the tree: Vitality and strength flowed through the physical bond like a torrent of life. The tree exuded ancient wisdom and lack of cares. It existed simply and simply existed. It did no right or wrong, made no mistakes, had no opinions. It was beyond reproach and indifferent to criticism. Catrin was comforted by its energy and felt a gentle calm wash over her. Chase stumbled into her back, jarring her from her mental state.

"Sorry, Cat. I didn't realize you stopped."

"My fault. I wasn't watching where I was going," she explained, not wanting to discuss her experience until she understood it better.

After her shocking contact with the tree, Catrin had a better idea of what to expect and how to interpret what she felt, and she began to sort through her perceptions of the various energies around her. Everything she saw had its own pattern, its own unique energy: her companions, the trees, grass, mountains, and especially the desert. She was surprised to find so much life energy within the desolation of the desert. Her senses skated along the sands. She didn't know what all the energies were, but she knew they existed.

The auras surrounding her companions were storms of emotional energy, which gave her a strong sense of their moods. She had always been sensitive to people's feelings and tried always to ascertain people's mental states in order to understand them. Posture, stance, and movements were all indicators, but none had ever given her such clear insight as she had now. Oddly, her new sense felt completely natural, as if it had always been a part of her, latent, waiting to be recognized and used. But it was also a burden. It made the fear and anxiety surrounding her companions almost palpable and impossible to ignore. Devoid of any means to assuage their fears, she simply accepted them and let them be.

A vibrant burst of energy off to her right caught her attention. It burned with life. She used her eyes to identify the source and saw an emerald hummingbird visiting the flowers of a trumpet vine. As if sensing her scrutiny, it flew in front of her face and hovered there. After a brief moment, it chirped, backed up, and darted into the azure sky. Catrin's impression of the hummingbird--vibrant and alive--stayed with her, its bold curiosity refreshing.

The more she used her new life sense, the easier and more natural it became. She found that, after a while, she could sense it without focusing on it, though it was most intense when she concentrated, just as she could hear without consciously listening.

New sensations invigorated her, as if feeling a cool breeze on her face for the first time, and she was exuberant. Another small life force moved nearby, and she was surprised to see a honeybee. It did not seem angry or aggressive, as she had always perceived stinging insects; it was just going about the business of being a honeybee.

There was an abundance of life in the soil itself, including things too small to be seen. Catrin saw the ways death served to feed life. Deciduous trees shed leaves, which fell to the ground and decomposed. Organisms that used the decaying leaves as food aided the decomposition. Their waste and the decayed matter become soil, which, in turn, nourished the trees and plants. Catrin had never recognized the chain of life as a varying cycle of composition and decomposition before, and such realizations were rapidly changing her perception of the world around her.

Nature, in all its majesty and glory, was beginning to be revealed to Catrin through senses she had not been aware of before. For the first time, she saw the ecosystem as a unit and saw how each part of the system contributed to the whole; without any one component, life could fail. Predators could not exist without prey, and herbivores would die without plants, and plants would shrivel without materials provided by the death and defecation of animals. When she considered how many factors had to be in place for life to endure, she was amazed it existed at all, and yet it flourished, even in the harshest of environments--simply astounding.

Involved in her thoughts, Catrin was surprised when Benjin selected a place to camp. Most of the day's hike was a blur to her, and she had to reorient herself with the landscape. The mountains cast long shadows over the grassland as the sun set; the air cooled quickly, and it was almost chilly by twilight. The campsite Benjin selected backed up against the rock face. Although a few trees dotted the area, they were weathered and twisted. It was not much cover, but it was certainly better than the open desert.

"I've been thinking about what Osbourne said about an ambush," Benjin said as they ate. "If there's a trap, I think it would be best to spring it without Catrin with us," he continued. "There shouldn't be many places for the Zjhon to hide near the cove, and if I make it that far without seeing anyone--"

Catrin cut in. "So your plan is to go into an ambush . . . alone? Without me?"

"Now, Catrin, please understand, it's to protect you," he began, but Catrin silenced him with a look. He clamped his mouth shut, his eyes down, and waited silently. Catrin knew she was being unreasonable, but the thought of him walking into an ambush was horrifying. Some other option must exist, one without Benjin as bait. No one spoke until Benjin drew a breath, but Catrin cut him short again.

"You'll think of another plan," she said with a sharp nod. "Our only recourse cannot be a suicide mission for any of us. I will not accept that."

"Why, yes, of course. There must be a better way," Benjin replied without looking at her.

Catrin looked out into the night, terrified by the thought of being without Benjin. He made her feel safe. Without looking at the others, she went to her bedroll. She knew her anger was driven by fear, and that was the only way she could hide it.

* * *

"Now what do we do?" Chase asked once it appeared Catrin was truly asleep.

"For now we just have to keep moving toward the cove," Benjin said. "We have few other options."

"Maybe you and I should leave now and scout the way," Chase said.

"I don't like that idea at all," Strom said.

"There has to be something we can do," Chase insisted, his own desperation driven by fear. Survival almost seemed too much to hope for given the circumstances.

"When we get closer," Benjin said, "we can sneak away to spring the trap. We'll speak of it no more until then. Catrin won't like it, but it's what's best for her."

"And what then?" Strom asked, anger clear in his voice. "You go off and spring the trap and die, and what happens then? Catrin, Osbourne, and I go off and fight the world? Cat's right; you're both being idiots. Should we run through the desert to see if it's hot? No." He paused a moment to return the stares currently aimed at him. "When we get close, we watch and we wait. If we're clever enough, we'll see some sign of activity before they see us. I'm not sure what we do from there, but that's a far cry better than running in there and jumping around like a couple of idiots with torches and getting yourselves skewered."

There was a long moment of silence when Strom finished speaking. He crossed his arms and dared anyone to challenge him.

"Nobody said we were going to go running in there," Chase said, slightly downcast. Strom glared at him.

"Especially not jumping around with torches," Benjin added.

Chapter 16

This life is but a brief tenure, one of many perspectives a spirit must experience in the quest for eternity.
--Sadi Ja, philosopher

* * *

The clear skies and cool air would have been perfect for hiking, but they were accompanied by gusting winds. Funneled closer to the sands by the narrowing grassland, Catrin and her companions were relentlessly pelted with stinging sand. They held pieces of clothing over their faces, but their eyes still suffered.

"Be watchful for water. We need to replenish our supply as often as we can," Benjin said. They saw troughs left by a previous deluge but no water. Catrin mentally explored the landscape as they traveled, hoping to find a spring, but the only water she sensed was deep beneath the sand.

"Do you see that dark column of rock? Is that a waterfall?" Strom asked.

"If it is, it's awfully small," Chase said.

Catrin cast her senses toward where Strom indicated, hoping she would detect water. She tried not to be upset when she found nothing, but she realized she had truly expected to be successful. Determined to make a thorough examination, she tried running her senses across the distant soil from another angle. Her spirit soared when she felt the slightest pressure of resistance.

Focusing on that place, she sensed a very small amount of water, but water it was. "You are both correct. It is a small waterfall," Catrin said, and despite some sideways glances, they began walking toward the waterfall. As they approached, the land rose at odd angles and was difficult to traverse; loose rock and scree made matters worse.

A small flow of water trickled down the rock face, a shallow pool at its base. The water was cool and clean, and they refilled their empty flasks. They tried to wash themselves in the small basin, but their results were only cursory. The murmuring water gave an air of tranquility; a tall tree provided shade, and moss grew thick over the rocks surrounding the basin. It would have been idyllic to stay there, but they knew they had to move on. Despite efforts to find anything edible, they had not found a morsel since leaving the valley. They were running out, thanks to the dunking most of their food had taken, and needed to find something soon.

As they departed, the wind died down, making the rest of the day's hike bearable. The northern coast loomed in the distance like the edge of the world. Trees and vegetation became sparse, and gouts of dust rose from their boots with each step. They continued on, well after sunset, despite their weariness. The nearly full moon in a clear sky provided ample light, and the air became cooler, almost comfortable. Catrin was still wary of seeing more comets. She yearned for the exhilaration of their energy yet feared the consequences.

An abrupt turn in the mountains and the rush of the pounding surf signaled their destination, and the exhausted group made camp in a stupor. In the morning they would turn east, marking another milestone in Catrin's mind. Another step completed and another step closer to safety--at least that was their goal. They ate a little that night, trying to conserve what they had.

The next few days were long and uncomfortable. They found no game and no water, though Benjin did find some edible roots and a couple of rare herbs.

"Beware the cactuses," he warned as the plants became so numerous, they were nearly unavoidable. "Those with fine, hairlike spines can be worse than those that look more intimidating. Stay alert and avoid them if possible."

The next day they picked their way along the coastline, and the mountains dwindled to hills. In a few places, as the terrain allowed, deep blue waters could be seen in the distance. Those waters were surrounded by a barrier reef and were said to be littered with rock outcroppings and extensions of the reef just beneath the surface.

Strom stopped abruptly, startling the rest of the group. "I saw a bright flash of light--over there," he said, pointing into the distance behind them. They watched for a few moments but saw no more flashes or signs of movement.

"You most likely saw one of two things: a soldier's gear reflecting light, or a mirror being used to send a message," Benjin said.

"Do you see that cloud of dust?" Chase asked, pointing into the desert. It appeared out of place. It did not look like a funnel cloud and seemed too narrow and isolated to be caused by wind.

Benjin shaded his eyes and gazed into the distance. "Take cover! Now!" he ordered.

"There is no cover," Strom observed darkly, but his voice shook with panic. All that dotted the landscape were small bushes and a few straggly trees, and a mass of riders was thundering straight for them, leaving little doubt they had already been seen.

"Boil them!" Benjin swore. "Draw your weapons and guard each other's backs. If we must die this day, then let's go down with a fight."

Belt knives and short swords seemed like a pitiful defense, but Catrin committed herself. She considered stringing her bow, but she knew it would do her little good in close quarters. Her hands shook and her heart pounded. She had never been so terrified. The roiling dust cloud grew closer, and she imagined hundreds of soldiers bearing down on them, intent on her destruction.

"Let them come," Strom said through gritted teeth. "I'm tired of running and hiding. Let this be done now."

They stood grimly, determined to face this enemy. Catrin's instincts shouted that they should find some hole to hide in, but she knew they would be found.

The shimmering air obscured the riders even as they came into full view, and they slowed gradually as they approached. They used no reins, which was foreign to Catrin. She saw, though, it was so each rider could carry spears, crossbows, and slings.

The horsemen were at ease in the desert environment. They expressed no hostile action, but neither did they appear overtly friendly. They just moved forward with the confidence of those who know their land and their horses. Lean and muscular, their mounts' coats were lustrous, and their manes thick. Even their fetlocks bore long, thick hair that draped over their hooves.

"The tribes of Arghast approach," Benjin said. "Sheathe your weapons and hold your ground. Don't do or say anything unless I tell you. It's said they'll generally only attack if you insist upon crossing the desert." The riders slowed their horses some fifty paces away.

Catrin estimated more than a hundred horsemen spread before her, and she studied them, needing to understand this new adversary. There were several distinct variations in their clothing and saddles. The differences were subtle, almost imperceptible. One group had thin, dark sashes across their chests. Another group was distinguished by the braided manes and tails of their horses and yet another by tattoos branded on their horses' withers.

Only the occasional rattle of a harness broke the silence, and the riders made no attempt to communicate, seeming content to wait. Catrin glanced at Benjin, who stood patiently. She could see no sign of emotion on his face, but she could feel the anxiety of his energy and marveled that he could hide his emotions so well.

Seven horsemen broke free of the line and walked their horses forward at a measured and deliberate pace. Six of them wore the same styles she had noticed, but the seventh rider was different. He rode clumsily and bore only a tall, iron-shod staff. His horse was tethered to the horse of the leading rider, and he appeared to be struggling to remove his headgear. They were close when he finally got the headgear off, exposing his frayed hair and wide, blinking eyes. Catrin drew a sharp breath when she saw Nat. He smiled sadly and waved as he approached.

When the horsemen stopped, they dismounted gracefully, except for Nat, who nearly fell out of the strange saddle. The Arghast gave a signal, and their horses backed away. An equally subtle command sent the horses to their knees.

"What do we do?" Catrin whispered to Benjin.

"You and I will approach them. The rest of you, stay here," he said.

Catrin felt her face flush, and her anxiety rose to a new level, but she would show no fear. She and Benjin approached the Arghast but remained silent. The still-hooded man next to Nat stepped forward and spoke in halting words.

"We leaders of Arghast tribes. I, Vertook of Viper tribe, speak for all tribes. This man say you Herald of Istra," he said, nodding toward Nat, who looked terrified. "True?"

Benjin nodded his head slightly.

"Yes, it is true," Catrin answered. Nat seemed relieved but said nothing. The tribesmen considered her answer and spoke harshly among themselves.

As Catrin turned her head to check on the others, her eyes swept along the horizon, and she saw a light flashing in what appeared to be a pattern.

"The Zjhon," she whispered to Benjin, and he nodded again. She turned her attention back to the tribal leaders. Their conversation had grown more animated, and hushed tones gave way to angry shouts.

Knowing the Zjhon's arrival could lead to a bloodbath, Benjin stepped forward. "Gracious tribal leaders, I beg your pardon, but I fear dire happenings."

"Who you?" Vertook asked.

"Benjin, Guardian of the Herald."

"Speak," Vertook said after a moment.

"Enemy soldiers follow us. They are signaling each other. We will all be attacked if we stay here," Benjin said with a slight bow.

Vertook turned to the others, and his words led to more shouting. He turned back to Benjin. "Soldiers follow this one too," he said, nodding to Nat, "but we take care of them. We no fear soldiers but will take you to safe place." He placed two fingers in his mouth and whistled a long, high-pitched note. Several horsemen broke away from the line and brought five riderless horses forward. Vertook pointed to Chase and the others and waved for them to come forward.

The approaching horsemen dismounted and presented headgear to each of them. A major difference between these headgears and the ones worn by the tribesmen were that they bore no eye slits, and they would not be able to see where they were led. Each of her party was paired with a tribal leader, their horses tethered to those of their custodians. The tribesmen waited for the others to put on their headgears then helped them onto the horses.

The headgear was suffocating, and being unable to see left Catrin disoriented and queasy. A sudden cry broke the air, and the horses whipped around, moving off at a fast trot. Holding on to the horse's mane, she tried to synchronize her movements with his, but it was difficult without her sight and what seemed an erratic path, but she let her other senses guide her. Through their physical bond, she made contact with the horse. She felt an overwhelming sense of power and endurance but mostly loyalty. When she dug deeper, though, she could not help but sense the overwhelming sadness. This horse would carry her to the end of the world if he was asked, but the one to whom his loyalty belonged was gone. A feeling of separation and loss washed over Catrin, as her mount projected his mourning. Tears soaked her cheeks and the inside of her headgear; her nose became congested and breathing became even more difficult.

By the time they finally stopped, Catrin was exhausted mentally, physically, and emotionally. A muffled voice told them to remove their headgears, and she wrestled it from her head. Her sweat-soaked hair clung to her scalp, and even the warm breeze felt cool on her face. She gulped air as if she had been suffocating. Leaning against her mount, she felt as if he were leaning equally on her, as if bearing her here had brought some purpose to his life. It shocked her to sense his gratitude, and she was trying to let the noble animal know she felt the same when she noticed Vertook watching her. He approached, pulled his flask from his belt, and handed it to Catrin. She nodded her thanks and drank. The liquid had a tingling sweetness that was warm going down even though the liquid was relatively cool. She wondered for a brief moment how he kept it so cool then handed the flask back to him.

"You feel better now," he said roughly.

She thanked him and realized her eyes had adjusted to the fading light. She was surprised to find herself in the mountains, but these were not like the mountains of her home. They looked more like enormous piles of clay that soared high into the sky, taller than any she had seen before. They formed an almost complete ring around the small valley, and it was cool in their shade.

The tribesmen attended their horses, removing saddles and scraping sweat. They used large leather bags to water the horses. It took Catrin a moment to locate Benjin and the others, and she was relieved to see them unharmed. When she found Nat, he was limping toward her, leaning heavily on his staff. The ride had been rough on him as well.

As Catrin strode forward to meet him, no one moved to stop her. She walked past many tribesmen, who paid her little mind, seeming to be utterly consumed with tending to their mounts. The leaders, though, were gathered in a tight circle, obviously involved in another heated argument. When she reached Nat, he spoke out of the side of his mouth.

"We have much to discuss, but I can't speak freely," he said just above a whisper, and at the same moment, the tribal leaders separated. Vertook glared at Nat, and he moved away quickly.

"Calm and confident, li'l miss," Benjin whispered as the leaders approached. Catrin tried to appear composed, despite her anxiety.

Vertook swaggered up to them. "You, Catrin Volker, claim to be Herald of Istra, yes?"

"Yes," Catrin replied, wondering why they would ask her again.

"Prove it," he said simply.

Chapter 17

That which is not broken can be made better.
--Ivan Jharveski, inventor

* * *

Frozen in place, Catrin was terrified that trying to prove her powers and failing would mean their deaths. Even success would be fraught with danger.

"Do your thought-isolation meditation, *now*," Benjin said to her even as Vertook's glare demanded his silence.

She wasn't certain she could do it, but she had no better ideas. She sat on the ground, cupped her hands, and closed her eyes. Her mind was hammered with intense thoughts too fleeting to grab on to. She focused on her frustration, squeezed her eyes shut, and ignored everything else.

The gasp from a tribesman distracted her, and she channeled it into annoyance, letting it feed her anger. She forced her mind to be consumed by a raging tirade that included a litany of irritants and annoyances. Each grievance was slammed into that thought. While some part of her cautioned against such anger in a meditative state, she slammed that thought inside too and let it feed the rest. She had no choice but to give this effort all she had.

When her energy reached its apex, Catrin could find only an angry haze of emotions. She raised her cupped hands slightly and threw them out wide. Concentrating on a second, more positive thought, she slammed her hands together, smashing the accumulated mass of negative energy with the positive charge. A blast of hot air rolled away from her, and booming echoes resounded.

Catrin opened her eyes to see what she had wrought. Benjin had sat down heavily, looking as if he had been assaulted. The others looked as if they had been struck by an enormous hand, so dumbstruck were their expressions.

The leaders once again convened in a circle, and the meeting almost instantly transformed into a brawl. Men quickly separated those who fought, and soon they were back to their heated argument. Several more scuffles erupted, and Catrin waited in silence for the madness to play itself out. No one said anything, lest the enraged group turn on them.

The fighting reached a crescendo, and it seemed all of the tribal leaders were involved. An elderly man advanced toward the writhing mass, shouting, waving his arms, and pointing at the men. Catrin did not know what he said, but his words seemed to demand order.

The brawlers removed their headgears and began to treat their wounds. Vertook's nose was bloodied, and he began to stuff small bits of cloth up his nose to stanch the bleeding. The old man lectured the leaders while they dressed their wounds, and it was plain that he shamed them. When the meeting reconvened, it did so in a much more subdued fashion. After what seemed an interminable time, they appeared to come to some conclusion, and they turned to face Catrin. Vertook stepped forward.

"We not believe you. Proof not enough," he said, having difficulty speaking with his nose plugged. Catrin heard his words and felt a cold, sinking feeling in her stomach. This was not going well at all, she thought, and Nat's stricken look confirmed her fear.

"One more chance; you show *big* power"--he waved his arms out wide-- "or all die for trying to fool Arghast," Vertook said.

Catrin moved in front of each tribal leader and looked each one in the eyes. She measured them individually, and many became offended and enraged. One man had to be restrained by his tribesmen, but Catrin did not flinch. These men were threatening to kill her and her companions, and she had nothing to lose. She strode slowly back to the center of the group and addressed everyone in the valley.

"The tribes of Arghast have assaulted the Herald of Istra and her Guardians. They have asked for proof of the Herald's power, and they have found her demonstration insufficient. Now I will show the tribes of Arghast the true power of the Herald at their own peril. Power is a dangerous thing, and to see it is to be threatened by it. Once unleashed, fate will choose its targets. I have tried to spare you, but you leave me no choice; I must put us all at risk. You have made your decision. So be it."

Her words echoed and hung ominously over the valley. Not waiting for a response, she strode straight to Nat and looked him in the eye. His fear was showing.

"May I have your staff?"

"I can deny you nothing, Lady Catrin," he said loudly and bowed, presenting his staff. She accepted it, and it felt good in her hands, lighter than it appeared. The iron-shod tip somehow balanced the strange staff, and she could feel its strength, as if it had power of its own. The wood was smooth and highly polished but was not slippery or oily. She hefted it with a determined smile and turned to her companions.

"Guardians of the Herald, I call you to duty. Please assist me while I satisfy the curiosity of the mighty Arghast tribes."

Benjin winced as a few men reacted to her comment. He and her friends stood before her, awaiting her command. She was not surprised that Nat joined the group, but when Vertook stepped up, it gave her heart.

While the tribes had been fighting, Catrin had been scanning her surroundings for energy. The mountains revealed nothing to aid her--except a small clue: water. She guessed heavy rains fell there occasionally, and when they did, the runoff would have to go somewhere.

She looked at the sand, sensing the surface then delving beneath it. The sand was not very deep in the valley, and in some places it was only a couple of feet deep. Under the loose sand, a layer of compressed sand formed brittle sandstone. Not far beneath the sandstone, she sensed a layer of bedrock. When she cast her senses deeper, through the bedrock, she found water.

Her father had taught her about artesian basins, and she remembered her lessons well. This valley had all the criteria. Rainwater drained from the mountains and into the basin, where it fed an underground aquifer. Layers of rock that rose higher into the mountains also collected and held runoff. Water was trapped below an impermeable layer of bedrock and, subsequently, was under intense pressure.

Trusting her instincts, she scanned the bedrock for thin spots and found her target at the back of the valley, a short walk from where she stood. Asking her Guardians to follow her, she strode confidently toward that spot.

The valley floor sloped downward, and the sand was a shade darker in the area Catrin selected. She stood atop the spot, closed her eyes, and reached into the sand with her senses, trying to be fully focused. Her mind pierced the bedrock and felt the intense repulsion of the water. Moments passed while she considered her options. The lives of many depended on her decision, and she did not want to make it in haste.

"What do you want us to do, Catrin?" Chase asked. "I think they're losing patience."

"I want you to dig."

"Oh for the love of everything good and right in this world, not the digging thing again," Strom said, and Chase smacked him on the back of the head.

"We'll do what you say, Catrin," Chase said. "Just tell us."

"Dig a hole here, please. Make it as deep as you can," she replied, leaning on Nat's staff while the others dug. She needed to conserve her energy for the task ahead, although she was not certain she could do anything. The energy the comet had spilled into her world was fading like a scent on a breeze, and it was becoming increasingly difficult to detect its energy, let alone harness it.

Her senses seem to have dulled in the time since the comet was last seen in the sky, and she wondered if she could get those sensations back, but she put the thought from her mind and concentrated on what she must do. Her

Guardians made good progress, and the hole was already quite deep. Chase stood in the hole, and only his head and shoulders were above ground level.

The initial dig had been relatively easy, allowing them to use their hands as shovels, but when they reached the layer of sandstone, they had trouble going deeper. They used everything they had to break up the brittle sandstone, and they removed it in large chunks. Catrin desperately hoped the tribesmen would have enough patience to let them finish, and as the last of the sandstone layer was cleared from a small area, she saw the bedrock.

Running her senses over it, looking for the thinnest point, she found a likely spot, but it was close to the edge of their hole. "Clear that area, please," she said, and they quickly removed the sandstone. "I need to finish this," she said. Benjin helped her into the hole and handed Nat's staff to her.

With a deep breath, she gathered all the energy she could pull from the night air. The moon was bright above the mountains, but she felt little energy from it. She mustered what she could and drove the staff into the bedrock with all her strength. The staff struck stone and rang a sharp discord through the valley. Sparks flew and a few small chips broke away, but her blow had done little damage. Her next blow struck with such force she felt the staff flex in her grasp, and she feared it might snap in two. She paused to catch her breath and looked up at the concern in her Guardians' faces.

The crushing weight of responsibility threatened to smother her, and she could almost feel the walls of the hole closing in around her. Struggling to stay calm, she reached into the rock, looking for any imperfection, any flaw she could exploit. Close to the surface, she found an almost imperceptible hairline crack, and her hopes soared.

She concentrated on the crack and focused on her target point. She hefted the staff and struck the bedrock hard, large chunks of stone shattering among the sparks. There was a long way to go, but she had made some progress.

"You'd best hurry, Catrin. The tribes are growing hostile," Benjin said.

As she leaned down to look closely at the rock, her fish carving fell from her shirt and hung just below her face. She pulled the leather thong over her head and held the carved fish in one of her palms, wondering if she could draw energy from it. She remembered how the carving had grown hot enough to burn her leg when she slammed the ground with power, and she wondered if she hadn't been drawing from it then. The carving had appeared to recharge itself when kept in the light, and her gut said she had just stumbled onto its secret.

Grasping the staff in both hands, she held it aloft, the carving wedged between the staff and her palm. She centered herself as the carving grew warm, and she felt energy begin to flow into her. Her senses heightened as the power coursed through her veins, and as it entered her, she sensed it leaving the carving. Knowing she had no time to waste, she used all her strength and all her emotion to drive the staff into the bedrock, striking it with such force that the blow sent shockwaves echoing through the valley.

The bedrock gave way as she reached the bottom of her massive swing, and she fell forward for an instant as a large section collapsed downward. Almost instantly, the force of the trapped water sent the broken rock soaring into the air. Catrin fell back as the staff was ripped from her grasp by a huge column of water, which shot high into the night sky.

Catrin scrambled backward out of the hole, the powerful spray buffeting her as she clawed her way to safety. She retreated from the water's fury, and the Arghast backed away before her in fear and reverence. Vertook stared at the fountain, dumbstruck.

Chaos ensued as the enormous shockwave sent loose rocks and stone tumbling down into the valley. Several people were struck, the horses panicked, and men scrambled to reach them to prevent the frightened animals from injuring themselves.

They all stared at the towering fountain with amazement and disbelief. When the height of the fountain did not dwindle, they slowly began to believe that they were in the presence of the Herald.

Catrin watched as the water fell from the sky and seeped into the sand. The sand became saturated, and soon water would fill this end of the valley.

Benjin, Chase, Osbourne, and Strom moved to her side, overjoyed. They speculated on how long the fountain would last. Catrin was physically drained, mentally exhausted, and wanted nothing more than sleep. The carved fish still in the palm of her hand looked terrible; it was chalky to the touch, and its surface was again dull.

She leaned over and placed it back around her neck. When she looked up, she found herself surrounded by kneeling tribal leaders and tribesmen; even her Guardians knelt. Vertook was in the front and center of the mass, and she realized that he alone belonged to all three groups.

Nat retrieved his staff from the sand. Then he stood before Catrin, facing those assembled. "Behold the Herald of Istra! She calls you to your duty. Will the tribes of Arghast answer her call?"

Catrin was startled by the ululating cry that rose from the throats of the Arghast and was overwhelmed when she saw that the horses, too, had gone to their knees. And her mentor and strength, Benjin, was prostrate on the ground.

Her power and accomplishment would have exhilarated her at any other time, but the day's events had been exhausting and she was lightheaded. Her vision fading, she grew dizzy and fell to the sand.

* * *

Standing before the fountain, where before had been nothing more than sand and rock, Vertook was in awe. No power could have been more moving to him than to bring water to the desert, no feat more seemingly unachievable. All his life he had waited for this moment, waited for some event to prove his life had meaning. Now that he had witnessed that event, he realized his entire life had been wasted, wandering from one dried up hole to another. For him, nothing would ever be the same. The things that had meant the most to him in life, besides his wife and his horse, suddenly were meaningless. All that mattered now was to serve Catrin, to protect her so that she might bring water to all the world.

He made in a moment a decision that should have been agonizing, yet it was surprisingly simple. "Harat!" he said without taking his gaze from the water. Only a moment later, he felt Harat by his side, sensed the calm determination and sense of honor that had always marked him as a leader. Without saying a word, Vertook untied the sash that looped over his left shoulder--passing directly over his heart. He'd taken reassurance from it many times, knowing that the sash of the leader would protect his valiant yet frail heart. Now he no longer needed it, but even more, he could no longer uphold the responsibilities that came along with the sash. Remaining silent, he handed the sash to Harat, who hesitated to take it. Vertook thrust the sash into Harat's hand, his final command as tribal leader. Harat took a step back, placed his hand over his heart, and when he bowed down, tears fell from his eyes.

As Harat walked away, Vertook pulled his gaze from the fountain long enough to watch the man who would now protect and guide those he loved. Tears fell from his own cheeks as he released the responsibilities he had worked so hard to obtain. Harat placed the sash underneath his garment, as of yet unwilling to reveal Vertook's wishes. He walked quietly through the crowd as if nothing out of the ordinary had occurred, and Vertook breathed a mighty sigh of relief; he had chosen well.

* * *

Not far from where Vertook stood, Chase, Strom, and Osbourne gathered.

"When she said to dig, I wasn't expecting . . . I mean . . ." Strom began, but he just trailed off and shrugged.

"I know," Chase said. "I can't believe it either."

"How did she know?" Osbourne asked, looking at the fountain. "How does she do these things?"

"I don't know," Chase said. "I don't understand any of it, and I really want to. This whole thing just keeps getting bigger, and I don't know where it'll stop." He knew he should try to be more positive for the sake of the others, but he couldn't help but speak what was on his mind. "I just don't want to see Cat get hurt. You know how she is."

"The first time I ever met her," Osbourne said, "she was all dirty and scraped up from catching one of our pigs that got loose. The pig was nearly as big as she was, but she carried him all the way across the field to bring him to us. Looked like she took a tumble or two on her way too. She cried 'cause she thought he was hurt."

"I met her at Master Jarvis's lessons," Strom said. "She always looked sad and fragile after her mom died." His words were met with silence heavy with emotion.

"I know I've said this before," Osbourne said without looking up, "but I'm really sorry about your mom and Catrin's mom and Strom's dad. I wish they didn't die."

Chase kicked the sand in front of him. He chastised himself for letting a tear gather in his eye. The pain should be forgotten, he thought, those wounds long since healed, but they were not. When he noticed Strom struggling with pain of his own, it made him feel no better.

Osbourne shifted his weight from foot to foot in the uncomfortable silence. "What do we do now?" He asked, his voice betraying his anxiety.

Chase put a hand over his growling stomach, "I think we should try to track down some food."

Chapter 18

Of all the varied life forms on the planet Godsland, the pyre-orchid is the most curious, only blooming in the wake of forest fires.
--Sister Munion, Cathuran monk

* * *

Catrin opened her eyes for a moment, adjusted the pillow beneath her head, and pulled soft blankets over her shoulders. The morning air was cool, and she closed her eyes to drift back to sleep when voices awakened her. When she became fully aware, she noticed her surroundings. She lay on a light, fluffy bed with a similarly made pillow, which she guessed were both stuffed with down.

A small tent, made of sheer material, shaded her. The breeze passed through the fabric, but bugs could not. It was artfully made and was doubtless the finest the Arghast had to offer. Still dressed in the clothes she'd lived in for days, she was in desperate need of a good bath. Pushing back the tent flap, she walked out into a bright glare that momentarily blinded her, and she heard the sudden murmur of many hushed voices. When her vision cleared, she found all of the Arghast watching her intently. She was not sure what they expected, but their stares were intense and disconcerting. It took some time for her to decide what to say to the assembled crowd, and what came from her mouth was the plain truth.

"If I could trouble someone to help me, I am quite hungry. Is there any food left from the morning meal?" she asked almost timidly. The activity resulting from her request was astounding, and it seemed they all felt compelled to try to help. Some men scrambled to set up a small table; others made a comfortable seat for her from several large cushions, and still others erected a makeshift sunshade made of the same material as her tent.

She sat at the table and waited. People began to approach her with a lavish array of foods. Women were now part of the group, some in typical female clothing and others dressed like the men. Catrin had seen no women the day before and was surprised to see them now. The crowd was now nearly double the number she recalled. Men and women offered fruits, meats, breads, and one elderly man brought her more of the drink she remembered Vertook had given her. Catrin recognized him from his castigation of the tribal leaders, but he gave her a kindly smile.

"What is this drink?"

"Desert mist," he responded with a wink. "How to make is secret, something only spoke in private. We speak alone soon, yes?"

"Yes, of course, and thank you." She paused to take a sip of the desert mist. "What are you called, sir?" she asked.

"Called Aged Goat by most," he said with a toothless grin, "but true name is Mika. You call me Mika. Yes?"

"Indeed, Mika, I will," she responded warmly, and Mika retreated through the masses. Catrin had never been served in such a way, and she found it disquieting; it felt wrong to accept their generosity, to be selfish and indulgent, but it seemed just as wrong to refuse their gifts.

Her hunger sated, she wanted a nap, but more than that she desperately wanted to get clean. As if someone were reading her mind, several women approached Catrin with soft towels and scented soaps. One motioned for her to follow and walked toward the towering fountain Catrin had created. She was delighted to see a pond forming outward from the fountain, and she hoped it would continue to grow. She envisioned a lush oasis nestled in the valley, full of life and vigor--a jewel in the desert.

Two women unfolded a large, thick cloth, which they held up for privacy. Catrin took soap that smelled of peppermint then undressed and dipped her toes into the water. It was bitterly cold, and the frigid spray made her shiver, but she was thankful for the opportunity to get clean. The shallow water at the edge was not quite as cold, and she used it to wash herself. The soap created a rich, aromatic lather, and Catrin lavished in the fragrance as she washed off the grime of many days.

When she emerged from the pool, the same woman who had led her to the pond brought her a soft towel. She dried herself and looked for her clothes, but they were not where she had left them. Another woman approached with clothes similar to Catrin's. She knew that it had taken them much thought and effort to find these for her, and she felt almost unworthy. She put on the borrowed clothes, and they were a fair fit. The shirtsleeves were a little long, but she rolled them up, insisting that it was just the way she liked her sleeves.

There was more food and drink when she returned from her bathing, and Benjin and the boys were there too. In the flurry of the morning, she had not thought of them, and she was relieved to see they were fine--just dirty. The women offered the towels and soap to them, and they wasted no time in getting to the fountain.

The leaders had congregated nearby, looking subdued and clearly waiting for her to speak first. With her hunger satiated and her friends attended to, Catrin turned her attention to them.

"Leaders of the Arghast tribes, will you sit with me?" Slowly the men began to come forward and seat themselves on the ground around her. As Catrin lowered herself to the ground, several rushed to get her a cushion, but she declined with a smile. "I've not come here to rule you or to be worshipped by you. I'm a simple girl, not a goddess or a queen. I don't place myself above you. Speak freely and know your worth."

There was confusion in the crowd, and Vertook approached Catrin. He repeated what she said in his own words and she nodded. With Vertook translating, Catrin continued, trying to find simple words to express complex things. "I praise your leaders for their devotion to truth, for they did not blindly accept my claims or the words of Nat Dersinger. They chose to make me prove myself, just as I would have done. I've now proven my power to you, and we need to reach an understanding. We must put aside any mistakes we've made and forgive others for hurting us," she said, pausing. Murmurs passed through the crowd as Vertook translated. When she addressed them again, she spoke louder.

"Will the tribes of Arghast protect the Herald of Istra?" she asked. The people raised their voices in a high, ululating cry and shook their fists above their heads before Vertook even spoke. Catrin raised her hands to them, requesting silence. She spoke again.

"Tribes of Arghast! Embrace your duty and take pride in what you have already done. You answered the Call of the Herald, and your valor will not be forgotten. You have pledged yourselves to the Herald, and she calls you to battle. How do you answer?" Their cries echoed off the mountains and reverberated along the peaks.

"The Godfist is under attack. Invaders have come to destroy us. The Godfist needs a defender, and the Herald of Istra calls on the tribes of Arghast because they are strong, they are fierce, and they will prevail!" she said, the words spilling forth from her heart. Vertook translated her words with as much emotion as she had expressed, and then he started the crowd shouting "Catrin" in unison. The chanting grew louder and louder. She raised her arms, and the crowd hushed.

"I thank you for your bravery and honor. Take great pride in yourselves and your mighty nation. I will meet with your leaders, and we will make our plans. Many blessings to you all!" As the crowd dispersed, Catrin returned to her seat.

"You very gracious, Lady Catrin. We honor and support you. We have many gifts to give upon you, and we have sorrow for doubting of you," Vertook said then took a deep breath. He continued hesitantly. "I been asked again to speak for all Arghast. Others not understand your talk as much."

"Please speak how you feel, Vertook, and so will I," she said, smiling. Turning to the men closest to her, she said, "Please tell me your names and the names of your people."

The leaders smiled and nodded, and each introduced himself: Harat introduced himself as the chief of the Viper clan. Catrin cast a confused glance at Vertook, who had previously claimed to be chief of the Viper clan, but he said nothing. Halmsa was chief of the Wind clan, Irvil of the Sun clan, Malluke of the Horse clan, Spenwar of the Scorpion clan, and Cheslo of the Cactus clan.

"I am honored to know the names of the revered leaders of the Arghast. As you have received me, I pledge to protect you with all of my strength. But now I have to ask for your help. I must leave the Godfist on a boat, and the enemy soldiers will try to stop me." She knew she could be risking the entire Arghast nation by involving them in a war, but she did not know what to do but follow her instincts and hope they were right.

"I need some time with my Guardians," she said, and as Vertook started to stand, she asked, "Vertook, would you please stay here and plan our escape? We can meet again later."

"Vertook is glad to do that," was his reply, and he turned to the group and began to talk with the leaders.

"Greetings, Lady Catrin," Nat said as he walked toward her. He wore clean clothes, and his hair was not as wild as usual.

"Hello, Nat, and please call me Catrin, like you always have."

"As you wish, Catrin. I'm sorry I couldn't deliver this dire news sooner, but it wasn't possible with what's been going on," he said. "I'm afraid that by some deception, your destination is known to the Zjhon. I don't know how they found out, but we'll need to be extra careful about who we talk to about our plans."

"How did you come to know the Zjhon knew where I was going?"

"It wasn't just one thing, you see. Much of the Zjhon fleet left the harbor, sailing east toward the cove, but ships were also reported off the northern coast. Before I escaped Harborton, Miss Mariss got news the cove had been raided and one of the pirate ships captured. It was enough. The news came from the ship that escaped, and those on board suggested a new place to meet you. We need to get you there as soon as possible. Every day they remain in hiding is risky." It seemed like a thin hope to Catrin, surrounded by the Zjhon, and she felt trapped.

"Before I leave, there is a most unpleasant task I am obligated to perform," he said and took an object from within his robe unlike anything Catrin had ever seen before. An ivory tube, it was about as long as her forearm and decorated with fanciful carvings that were enhanced with gold and gemstones. The ends were topped with gold caps in the shape of a man and woman embracing--the symbol of the Zjhon empire. Catrin reached out slowly, unsure she wanted to accept it.

"This is the other reason I think we've been betrayed. This contains a message and was delivered to Miss Mariss through the channels of the Vestrana. Somehow the Zjhon have infiltrated the Vestrana, and we have no idea whom to trust. I'll leave you so you can read the message, but we must speak again soon. There are many things we should discuss," he said as he walked away.

Catrin felt a new burden on her shoulders. She feared what was written inside, afraid the words might find some way to hurt her and those around her. She walked to where Benjin stood. He looked refreshed after his bath and was pulling his hair into a braid as she approached.

"A storm is coming," he said, rubbing his shoulder, but when he saw the look on Catrin's face, he waited for the bad news. She handed him the tube and told him how it had been delivered. Benjin was stunned and hesitated to take it--perhaps for the same reasons Catrin was loath to hold it, both fearing what it might contain.

"Please, read it for me. I don't have the courage."

"Perhaps that would be wise. They could have rigged it with a trap," Benjin said. He carefully removed the golden cap. It fell away, and nothing leaped from the tube. He pulled the rolled parchment from the tube, placed it on the ground, and examined it closely before picking it up. He unrolled it and read aloud.

Salutations to the Herald of Istra from His Eminence, Archmaster Emsin Kelsig Belegra, spiritual leader and chief evangelist of the Holy Church of Zjhon.

The Zjhon nation has extended its warmest greetings, and you have evaded my emissaries and ignored our requests for talks of peace. You must not care that lives will be lost.

I do not know why you wish ill toward the Zjhon nation, but we only seek your salvation. Our request for talks of peace still stands, despite your refusals. If you present yourself to any of my emissaries, they will bring you directly to me, unharmed. Your companions are also welcome.

If you persist in your attempted flight from the Godfist, we will interpret it as a hostile action against the Zjhon nation. For your own sake, do not seek to flee or to invade the Greatland. My emissaries will remain on the Godfist until you have presented yourself to me personally. This matter must be settled between you and me. It would be a pity if your countrymen and mine suffered needlessly as a result of your selfishness. I beg you to put away your ego and do what you know is right.

I trust you will choose your path wisely.
Most gracious regards,
Archmaster Belegra, humble servant of the Gods

"I don't know which part is the most offensive," Catrin began. "I've never heard so many thinly veiled threats and insults. Why would they wish to provoke me in such a way? What does he mean, I have refused their offers for talks of peace? No one has made any such offer. He makes it sound as if their invasion is my fault!"

"Please stay calm, li'l miss. They wrote those things to provoke you, hoping you would do something hasty and foolish. It's a common tactic in warfare: taunt your opponent and instill doubt and fear in him whenever possible. There's not much in that letter we didn't already know. Try not to fret over it."

But she could not put the message out of her mind. "I'm going to take some time to meditate. Perhaps I'll find some inspiration," she said as she went into her tent. Her own clothes were by her bed, cleaned and folded. The solitude of the tent and the feeling of changing back into her old clothes comforted her, as if they helped her hold onto that which was Catrin. Her thoughts were scattered, and she tried to focus and meditate on each one. She pondered the archmaster's words and Benjin's reaction to them, but she thought there had to be some undercurrent she was not seeing. She found no answers.

The sound of many people shouting yanked her from her thoughts. Shadows ran past her tent, and the commotion continued to grow louder. Benjin reached her as she was emerging from her tent.

"What's going on?" she yelled above the noise.

"I don't know. When I heard all the commotion, I came here to make sure you were safe. Let's find Vertook." They scanned the sea of confusion for Vertook, but it was difficult to identify anyone in the morass, and it took a while to locate him. Benjin spotted him wading through the mob and heading for Catrin. He shouted and waved his arms, but they could not hear his words, and they waited anxiously for him to get clear of the throng. He rushed toward them, and the chaos he left behind seemed to take on a purpose as horses were saddled. That meant the Arghast were preparing to ride, and Catrin's anxiety was intense when she heard Vertook's words.

"Many soldiers coming from all around us."

Chapter 19

Belief systems are fragile things. How will you react when your reality suddenly ceases to exist?

--Ain Giest, Sleepless One

* * *

"You ride with me," Vertook said, giving Catrin no choice but to follow him to his horse. They would all ride on horses with the other men, whose saddles contained a second set of passenger flaps that held soft leather stirrups. The flaps provided little cushion, but they had a large ridge around the back that would help keep them in place when they were riding at speed.

Before Catrin could get her boots into the stirrups firmly, Vertook issued a battle cry and the horse leaped into a full gallop. Catrin grabbed at the leather straps that hung from the sides of the saddle and held on with white knuckles, struggling to get her boots in the stirrups. Once her boots were firmly planted, she settled into the rhythm of the horse's powerful stride. Vertook's eyes showed his pleasure that the Herald had such fine riding skills.

The riders sent clouds of dust into the wind, and Catrin squinted to keep sand from her eyes. Vertook reached into his saddlebag and produced a headgear for Catrin--this time one with eye slits. She felt a little unsteady as they rode, but it was much better than sand in her eyes.

Cheslo and the others rode in tight formation with Vertook, and Catrin saw her companions donning headgears as well. Like a flash flood, they rolled toward the valley entrance in a headlong rush, lest they become trapped.

The mouth of the valley was narrow, and the horsemen funneled together, close enough for Catrin to touch the rider beside her, and as they passed through the narrow opening, they smashed together, nearly unhorsing her.

Clear of the valley, tribesmen surrounded their leaders in a tight, diamond-shaped formation. Vertook directed them straight toward the line of Zjhon soldiers approaching from the north. The wind whipped, and visibility dropped to near zero. The Zjhon were obscured by a veil of dust and were barely visible along the horizon. Despite greater numbers, the Zjhon attack seemed ill advised; they were still distant and spread thin, but

Catrin supposed their hands had been forced when the Arghast intercepted their prey. Had the Arghast been less vigilant, she would have been trapped.

She turned her head to see who was behind her, but she could see little through the headgear and the dust that roiled up behind them. As she gazed higher, she could still see the top of the towering fountain, and she was amazed to see a pair of eagles floating on the thermals in the mist surrounding it. They swooped and dived through the water, and Catrin felt a moment of vindication and joy.

The Arghast remained true to the straight path they had chosen, and the enemy forces seemed to be gauging their purpose. As the Zjhon formed into a more dense and organized force, Catrin shouted to Vertook, telling him to take evasive action, but he continued on his direct course.

Looking at the dense formation of Arghast surrounding her, she wondered if Vertook planned to ride straight through the gathering Zjhon. The closer they came to the Zjhon, the more prepared the enemy appeared, looking ready to stand fast against the approaching onslaught. Many soldiers dismounted and held long pikes to protect against the charge, but by concentrating in one area, they committed themselves to holding that ground.

Vertook raised a reverberating cry, and riders charged in every direction, forcing the Zjhon to abandon the ground they held. Catrin held on tight as Vertook turned his mount sharply and headed east. The Arghast horses were winded, but so were those carrying the Zjhon. The Zjhon horses had not been desert bred and were on unfamiliar turf.

Catrin looked around desperately for her Guardians, but the headgears and the dust made it nearly impossible to identify anyone. Vertook's gambit provided a temporary advantage, but hordes of Zjhon reinforcements began to flood the desert, swarming around isolated pockets of the Arghast. One of the tribal leaders rode in close, and Catrin heard Nat shouting and pointing northeast.

"To the cliffs! Must get Catrin to the cliffs!"

Vertook nodded and angled them in the direction Nat indicated. No matter which direction they chose, they would have to break through the Zjhon at some point, and Vertook veered for the largest gap in their lines. In the same instant, Nat cried out in warning. Catrin snapped her gaze to where he pointed, and Vertook cursed when he spotted a formation of soldiers closing in from the north.

These men and their horses wore protective gear, making them much better prepared for desert fighting. The horses showed a bit of lather but did not appear as winded as the horse beneath Catrin. Vertook shouted and turned east, pushing their mount to the limit. Catrin was humbled by the dedication and courage of the Arghast horses, who gave all they had. Feeling such affection and gratitude for the mount that was so valiantly bearing her and Vertook, she placed her hand on the horse's croup behind the saddle, and unaware, her emotions--love, peace, and energy--flowed from her hand into the horse. As she touched him, her hand grew hot, and a tingling pulsated in her palm. The horse seemed to respond to her gentle touch and was rejuvenated. It leaped ahead of the horses surrounding it.

Vertook slowed his mount to let the others make up the ground he had gained. The approaching Zjhon formed into a tight wedge and closed at great speed, making Catrin wonder if this was where the fighting would truly begin. It was terrifying and she could not envision it.

The tension in the air was palpable, and she could hear little above the muted thunder of hooves pounding the sand. No one spoke, shouted, or cried out. It was eerie and unnerving, and Catrin could feel the hair on her arms and neck stand on end. The approaching Zjhon were mostly armed with swords, but a few carried bows. The Arghast were armed with wooden spears, and they looked puny beside the cold iron.

Vertook desperately sought to evade the menacing wedge, but it continued to grow closer. The low din was shattered when the Zjhon overtook them, cries of man and horse ringing above the muted thunder, accompanied by metal striking hardened wood. Catrin ducked under a sword as it whistled by her head and was still off balance when a soldier slammed his mount into hers. She was nearly knocked from the saddle by the impact and leaned out perilously to one side as Vertook smashed the soldier across the face with the butt of his spear.

As she straightened in the saddle, Catrin caught a glimpse of Cheslo and Benjin. She screamed as she saw them collide, at full speed, with a Zjhon soldier. She watched in horror as all three went down, and she was unable to distinguish anything in the chaos. The Zjhon were trying to divide the Arghast to deal with them individually, and they were doing an alarmingly good job of it. Vertook and Catrin were forced away from the others and found themselves surrounded by Zjhon.

* * *

Riding behind a man whose name he did not know and whose dialect he did not seem to speak, Chase watched Benjin go down. He thought he saw Catrin nearby. A Zjhon soldier was bearing down on Benjin, and at the same time, at least a dozen were going after Catrin. Time seemed to slow as Chase was torn by a decision that must be made in an instant; there was no time for debate or second thoughts. He yanked on the shoulder of the man in front of him, pointing and screaming, and by the mercy of the gods, the tribal leader turned his horse toward where Benjin had fallen. Chase cursed and climbed to one side of the horse. Putting his right leg in the left stirrup, he coiled his muscles like a snake about to strike. An instant before a Zjhon blade would take Benjin's life, Chase jumped.

* * *

Osbourne cried out as one of his boots slipped from the stirrup, only Spenwar's firm grip kept him from tumbling to the sand. Riders came from all directions, and it was difficult to tell friend from foe, but when a horse materialized from the dust bearing two riders, he knew it was one of his friends. Strom roared as they passed, throwing what looked like a pear at an oncoming Zjhon horse. The fruit struck the horse in the forehead, startling the animal while it was at a full gallop. The horse and its helpless rider veered sideways and crashed into another Zjhon soldier.

Osbourne would have cheered the victory, but more riders came, and he followed Strom's lead. He opened one of the pouches along the saddle and found soft cheeses wrapped in broad, supple leaves. Knowing they would have no need for food if they did not first escape, he took half of them and began throwing them at approaching Zjhon riders. Though he was aiming for the horses' eyes, he often missed, but one bundle of cheese struck a Zjhon soldier in the face and exploded on impact.

The blinded soldier dropped his reins and tried to clear the cheese from his eyes, but the cheese clung to his skin and lashes, and sand began to collect on it, making matters worse. Unprepared when his horse suddenly veered around a fallen rider, the soldier flew from the saddle and plowed face-first into the sand. Osbourne let out a brief cheer just before a Zjhon horse struck them broadside and at full speed. As the world tumbled around him, Osbourne gave thanks for all that life had given him.

* * *

Activity to Catrin's right caught her attention, and she turned to see what was happening. The Arghast had adapted quickly and were using the Zjhon's ramming technique against them. She watched, horrified, as the Arghast crashed recklessly into the Zjhon. One horse caught her attention as it bowled over an unsuspecting Zjhon soldier, its second passenger taking down the Zjhon with his staff. Nat howled, wide eyed, like a man possessed as he searched for a new foe.

Catrin recognized Irvil of the Sun clan, who rode before Nat. Irvil attacked with a fury, driving his horse into the Zjhon, thrashing them with his spears, and yelling exultantly whenever Nat landed a blow. They cleared a hole in the Zjhon line just large enough for them to break free. Vertook and Irvil urged their horses on, and somehow the marvelous beasts found their wind. They surged ahead of the pursuing Zjhon and thundered toward the rocky borderland where a sparse forest skirted the cliffs.

Vertook let Irvil and Nat lead since only Nat knew their destination. Catrin could see several Zjhon closing in from behind. She feared their swords, but the men armed with bows terrified her more. Her back exposed, she felt naked and vulnerable and continued to watch for arrows, but the archers were out of bow range and had loosed none, which only increased her terror. Skilled archers would not waste arrows on bad shots, and these men seemed prepared to wait.

As the land sloped upward, stunted trees grew thick, stinging with their branches, and loose rock shifted under hooves. The trail became as much an adversary as the Zjhon, and the nearly spent horses struggled with the terrain.

A sharp crack sounded from behind, followed by sickening thud, and as Catrin spun around, she saw a horse go down, its leg shattered. The flailing animal tumbled down the rocks, taking two others and their riders with it. Irvil struggled to outrun the remaining Zjhon, following a winding path that was barely more than a game trail. Low-hanging branches assaulted them, and brambles clung, biting deep. Catrin counted four Zjhon remaining, and she shouted to Irvil, urging him on, but he was hard pressed, and despite his best efforts, the Zjhon were making better time. All they could do was press on as relentlessly as they could.

Irvil barked a warning, and Vertook veered away from a hornets' nest so large it covered the tree that hosted it. Catrin watched as the Zjhon grew closer to the nest; then, in one fluid motion, she drew her knives and launched them at the nest.

Her old belt knife with the broken tip flew wide, striking only bark, but in the next instant, her Zjhon blade struck home, exploding the nest into a cloud of paper and enraged hornets. Moving like an angry specter with a shared life, the mass descended on the Zjhon with unmitigated fury.

Cries of man and horse split the air, and Catrin watched, awed but horrified by what she had done. Two horses went down and the rest panicked. Some of the hornets overtook Catrin and Vertook, and their horses surged ahead with renewed energy born of pain. Vertook had to duck under many branches, and Catrin was nearly unhorsed by leaves that raked her face and a branch that struck her in the forehead.

The Zjhon fell farther and farther behind, and Irvil took full advantage of the situation. He pushed his mount through brush and brambles, and the noble animal lowered his head and pressed on, ignoring his scrapes and many bleeding cuts. Catrin kept a watchful eye on the woods behind them, seeing soldiers moving between the trees, but they were still a good distance back and moving more slowly.

The forest thinned and gave way to a rocky incline, beyond which loomed the bluffs--the absolute edge of Catrin's world. Sorely winded, the horses were clearly in no condition to carry them across such terrain.

Vertook and Irvil spoke quietly and, in a moment, seemed to agree on a difficult decision. First, they dismounted; then they helped their passengers to the ground.

Vertook and Irvil then did what would have seemed unthinkable in other circumstances: they commanded their horses to go on without them, but it was entirely contrary to the animals' nature, and they stood their ground, confused and agitated. The men persisted, and Catrin watched in anguish as Vertook chased his horse away with a flick of a switch. The bond shared by the Arghast and their horses was like mated souls, and it grieved Catrin to witness the scene. The image of these animals, going against their very natures, retreating through the trees--their ears pinned back and their tails tucked--was burned into her senses, and she knew she would never forget it.

Nat took the lead and scrambled up the rocks to look over the edge. He scanned the water, pulled a piece of polished metal from his robe, and signaled wildly. Sounds of pursuit grew closer, and Nat searched the water desperately. Then Irvil grabbed him and spun him to the right. A bright signal, not far east of where they stood, was coming from small boats secluded under the shadow of the cliff. Elated, Nat rushed east along the cliffs. Catrin still feared the soldiers would catch them, and Vertook and Irvil stayed as far from the edge as they could.

Suddenly soldiers emerged from the trees, and Catrin saw one of them nock an arrow. Nat ran to a large rock that jutted out over the water. Catrin and Vertook rushed to join him. When they looked down at the small boats below, the height terrified Catrin, and she turned to retreat. Before she could take a step, however, Irvil cried out and rushed toward the approaching soldiers. He held his ground against a man wielding a sword, but Catrin saw the archer draw and loose his arrow in one smooth motion. She knew where it would strike even as the archer's fingertips slid from the bowstring. Tears filled her eyes as she turned back to the cliff. Vertook stood at her side, looking grim and determined. As one, they prepared to meet their deaths, but as they turned to make their final stand, Nat spoke softly.

"I'm very sorry to have to do this," he said, and Catrin knew what was about to happen as she felt his hand on the small of her back. She screamed as he pushed her over the edge.

* * *

Dust and the smell of blood choked Strom as he pulled himself from under the horse that had given its life to save his. Luck had been with him, and he was uninjured. The same could not be said for Malluke, who was under the horse, dead. As Strom stood, his head spun, and the world around him was a blur. After a moment of shock, he recalled the danger and took a sword from the nearby body of a soldier. Before he could even test his swing, a shadowy rider materialized within a cloud of dust and bore down on him with speed.

Stepping back and bracing himself, Strom prepared to take a desperate swing, but then he saw it was Chase. Leaning down from his saddle, Chase reached out and grabbed Strom as he passed, barely slowing. Strom grabbed on and leaped up in the saddle behind Chase, and he was glad to see that Chase had stolen a Zjhon horse. At least it had a bridle and reins.

"Where are the others?" Strom shouted.

"I don't know. Let's go find them," Chase replied as he drove their mount to greater speed.

Chapter 20

There is no greater act of faith than to put your life in the hands of a stranger.
--Guntar Berga, soldier

* * *

The wind buffeted Catrin about mercilessly as she fell after Nat pushed her off the cliff. The air was sucked from her lungs, and she was unable to control her limbs. She flailed wildly to right herself then tucked herself into a ball, preparing to absorb the impact.

The waves rushed toward her with impossible speed, and she struck the water feet first. The impact forced the last of the air from her lungs, and her momentum drove her far beneath the waves. Terrified, she fought to reach the distant surface. Hampered by her clothing, she didn't think she would make it. Her lungs burned for air, and only willpower kept her from parting her lips to inhale water.

Above her, light reflected off the surface, dancing, taunting her, just out of reach. Her body demanded breath, and she gulped, repulsed by the salty taste and burning in her throat. Her body went into spasm and thrashed with little effect. Something hard struck her, but she barely felt it. Darkness was settling on her as rough hands yanked her from the water.

When the darkness faded, she found herself in the belly of a small boat. A man was beating on her chest and blowing air into her lungs with his mouth. Her body convulsed, and he turned her onto her side so she could empty her lungs and stomach. The small boat tossed violently, compounding her disorientation.

As she tried to right herself, the men in the boat continued to row vigorously. Her stomach betrayed her again, and she clung to the gunwale, feeling sea spray on her face. The wind was cold, and noticing her shivering, one of the men draped a blanket across her back. She wrapped herself tightly, but still she shivered violently and her teeth chattered.

As she regained control of herself, she saw there were four men huddled in the small craft, rowing as if their lives depended on it. Several other boats floated nearby, and they all struggled against the current. The men were oddly garbed and had darkly tanned skin. Catrin had never seen men adorn themselves with jewelry, but these wore rings on their fingers and some had earrings. She had seen tattoos, but none like the complex patterns that ran up one man's arms, looking like a live painting.

None spoke, though, not even to one another, and Catrin huddled in silence, not trusting her voice to speak. Cold rock jutted from the water, looming over them, and Catrin feared the waves would batter them against the imposing cliffs. As she watched, the men turned the boat sideways to the bluffs and rowed into the shadows. As they entered the gloom, an opening materialized before them, previously hidden in the darkness. Cool, musty air barely stirred, and as they rounded a bend, they were bathed in soft torchlight. The violence of the thrashing waters subsided completely.

Their rowing was now confined to keeping the craft in the center of a natural channel that flowed into a large cave. It was lined with jagged rock, and firelight danced on the water ahead. Around a bend floated a ship in a cavern just barely large enough to contain it. The ship didn't look quite right, and Catrin realized it was missing its mainmast.

Above them, on a rock shelf, a fire burned and at least a dozen people milled about, but when they saw the boats return, they ran up the gangplank of the ship, tossed down lines, and secured them to large iron rings on the boat's rails. The men above used a windlass and a series of large pulleys to haul the heavy boats up to the point where they were level with the deck. It was only then she realized there were three boats in addition to her own that must have been waiting for her and her companions below the cliffs. When each boat was empty of people, they hauled it onto the deck and turned it on its side. It took a dozen men to lift the boat to the hooks where it normally hung, but they quickly secured it and dropped the lines down for the next boat.

In relatively short order, all the men were aboard, and the boats were stowed. Catrin found Nat and was amazed to see he still held his staff. It took her longer to locate Vertook, but she eventually saw him huddled in a corner, his head cradled in his hands.

"Are you hurt?"

"No," he said, shaking his head slowly and slightly. "I did not know there could be so much water, or that it could be so"--he struggled for the word--"tall."

She nodded her understanding, touched him on the shoulder, and walked back to the railing. This ship did not move as violently as the small boat had, but it still moved constantly, and Catrin found it disquieting. As she leaned on the railing, trying to move with the movement of the boat and compose herself, a young man presented himself. A skinny lad with bright red hair and freckles, he was the only sailor she had seen without a dark tan.

"Hullo, miss, I'm Bryn. Cap'n wants to see you right away. I can take you to 'im if you'll just follow me."

Catrin nodded and followed him to one of the doorways leading into the deckhouse. As she stepped through the hatch, she immediately felt confined and closed in. She bumped into the walls as she stumbled and had to catch herself to keep from falling. The ship's motions were subtle, but they wreaked havoc on her sense of balance.

Bryn led her down the corridor to a door with no identifying marks. He tapped lightly, opened the door, and motioned for her to enter. The floor of the cabin was lower than the deck, and Catrin looked down as she stepped inside, a motion that proved to be a mistake. As soon as she lowered her head, dizziness overwhelmed her and her stomach heaved.

Desperate to escape the cabin before she lost control, she shoved Bryn aside and ran headlong to the railing where she expelled the remains of her stomach contents; she didn't think there'd be any more after her revival in the small boat, but there was. Bryn came to her side and offered her water and a towel.

"Thank you," Catrin said after a tentative drink. "I'm sorry I pushed you."

"Not to worry. I understand. I was sick for days when I first boarded the *Slippery Eel*," he said with a wink. The cool air soothed her, and she slowly began to feel better. She breathed in deeply then realized Nat and another man had joined them. When she turned toward them, both men stepped forward.

The man next to Nat looked different from the others. His hair was light brown, and he was slight of build. His nose hooked oddly, as if it had been broken more than once. He wore no jewelry, had no tattoos, and his age was difficult to gauge, but Catrin guessed he was in his middle years. Had she been asked, she would have thought him to be a farmer or fishermen, but certainly not a pirate.

"Lady Catrin, I'm Kenward Trell, captain of the *Slippery Eel*, and I welcome you aboard," he said, going to one knee. "Please accept my apologies for not recognizing your discomfort. I've brought you a bit of herb to calm your stomach, and it should also help with the headaches." The herb mixture tasted vile and nearly made her retch, but she had confidence in folk medicine and she focused on keeping it down as she waited for relief.

"You should feel better in a little while," the captain said. "For now, we can talk where you are comfortable."

"Thank you, Captain Trell. Your men saved our lives, and we will be forever grateful."

"Please, Lady Catrin, call me Kenward. Captain Trell was my father's name, and I've never answered to it," he said with a grin.

"Thank you, Kenward, and I am just Catrin."

"I'm disappointed Benjin is not with us yet, but a man as stubborn as he is could never come to harm. I'm sure he'll be along soon," Kenward said. "Your passage fees have been paid by Miss Mariss, though I'd have done it for free had she only asked," he said, winking. "I'll only be taking you part of the way; the *Eel* is stout, but the journey across the Dark Sea is best made in a larger ship. I'll get you as far as the Falcon Isles, where you'll board a larger ship."

"I've never heard of the Falcon Isles."

"Most haven't. It's a string of little islands inhabited mostly by primitive tribes, but they also serve as trading ports and hideouts for pirates, mercenaries, and other misfits--like me." He winked again.

"How do we know there will be a ship there for us?"

"Have no worries. My family has a large ship at port there right now, and they are waiting for the *Eel* to deliver goods before they sail for the Greatland. Your passage has been arranged for on that ship. You've probably heard the folklore about pirates, but we're just free sailors who bow to no government, and we trade goods with other, like-minded groups and individuals. They call us pirates, and we use it to our advantage; it makes us seem more frightening." He chuckled. "That label helps us in many ways. We're in a tight spot now, no arguing that--the cliffs on one side and the reef on the other, not to mention the obstacles in between. We'll need half a day to reach a sizable gap in the reef, but when we're clear, we have open seas to the Falcon Isles.

"Our biggest problem is that the Zjhon know we're trying to escape, even if they don't know for sure where we are. They've probably guessed we're within the reefs and will most likely have the gaps guarded. I doubt they'll bring tall ships inside the ring, for their drafts are much too deep. And let me tell ya that we had quite a time getting the *Eel* in here ourselves, but she's a sneaky wench. The *Eel*'s faster and more maneuverable than the Zjhon ships, so we'll just have to weave our way through them.

"The cabin past mine is reserved for you, and there are dry clothes in the chest. If your gut is still sour, feel free to sleep on the deck," he said. Their conversation had taken her mind from her upset stomach, which, now that she thought about it, was feeling much better. Her body seemed to have adjusted to the movements of the ship. Getting dry seemed like a good idea. She thanked him and excused herself. As she walked toward her quarters, Vertook approached Kenward.

"How can such a big thing stay on top water when a man falls under?" he asked Kenward.

"It's all about buoyancy, my friend. Let me show you . . ."

Their voices faded as she walked past the captain's quarters to her own and stepped inside. It was just large enough to hold a hammock, chair, and a small chest. A narrow shelf was built into one wall, and on it was a small lamp, burning low.

Catrin took off her damp clothes and sifted through the chest for something near her size. She found pants that were close enough. She had to pull the belt strings tight to keep them up, but they were comfortable, and she found a baggy shirt made of light material.

A knock at her door interrupted her thinking about how to get into the sleeping hammock.

"Who is it?" Catrin asked.

"Nat," came the response.

"Come in."

"I'm so sorry I pushed you off the cliff, Catrin. It was the only way to save you. I wanted us to go farther east where we could have climbed down slowly. But the soldiers were too close behind us; we would have made easy targets. The bowmen would have done us all in, and I didn't want Irvil's sacrifice to be for naught. I did what I had to do, as much as I didn't want to do it," he said.

"You really frightened me, and you terrified Vertook!"

"I know it. Vertook is quite wroth with me, and I fear he will not be so forgiving. He hasn't spoken to me since we boarded the ship, and he has been shooting me some nasty looks. Would you explain things to him for me, please?"

In that moment, Catrin realized Vertook, who was from a different culture, might want to take revenge to protect her as well as his honor. Although being pushed over the cliff may have been the only way to save her life, Vertook might not see it that way.

"Certainly. I'll talk to Vertook, but right now, I'm simply exhausted and really need to sleep." Another knock came at the door, and Nat slipped out as Bryn stepped in, carrying a mug of soup.

"Hullo again. I thought you might like something to eat," he said. "It's compliments of Grubb, our cook. He says that'll cure what ails ya."

"You are all very kind."

"It's still hot," he warned before she tasted it. It was a hearty broth with chunks of vegetable, and Catrin knew it was the kind of sustenance she needed.

"Would you like me to get your clothes laundered for you?" he asked pointing to the pile of clothing she had dropped on the floor.

"That would be kind of you. Are you sure you have the time?"

"You're my main responsibility for most of this trip," he said. "Cap'n wants me to make sure you're comfortable and that you have everything you need."

She watched him as he folded her dirty clothes over his arm and backed out of the cabin door.

"G'night, miss. If you need anything, be sure to holler out. There's always someone on watch. Right now, you'd best get some sleep. Tomorrow'll be a long day," he said as he closed the door.

Their journey would begin at first light, and Catrin was too exhausted to stay awake and worry, but her dreams were visions of blood and fire.

Chapter 21

Stars are the souls of old sailors. They plot the skies and guide the wayward home.
--Aerestes, Captain of the *Landfinder*

* * *

Dawn found the *Slippery Eel* deserving of her name. The crew scrambled, and the passengers huddled in the deckhouse, trying to stay out of the way. Maneuvering the ship with incredible skill, the crew prepared to guide the *Eel* through the cavern entrance, which was just barely wide enough for the ship to pass, and wood occasionally strained against rock. Using oars and poles, they worked in concert to guide the ship around the many obstacles, but some were unavoidable, and the ship listed and jerked underfoot.

"Have no worries; the *Eel* can withstand those little bumps and a lot more. We've taken no damage," Kenward assured them as they rounded the last bend, the horizon beyond. Waves battered the coastline; swirling vortices formed around unseen rock formations, and Catrin feared they would be crushed on the rocks. Kenward barked orders, and the crew responded with alacrity, but the men seemed stretched to their limits, and there was frenzied activity on the weather deck.

The ship rolled and turned sharply as they cleared the entrance, caught in a dangerous current, and the waves drove the ship dangerously close to the rocks. Kenward orchestrated the movements of his crew decisively with instincts born of many years.

As the *Eel* glided into deeper water, there was an audible, collective sigh of relief, but the mood and tension on the ship did not lighten completely. There were still obstacles in the narrow channel, and they could not afford to take damage.

Sailors began their practiced routine of unlashing long sections of mast from racks along the deckhouse, while others retrieved massive iron sleeves. They used rope, pulleys, and a windlass to raise the broad bottom section into place and guided it into a huge iron ring amidships. It slid nearly half of its length into the hull. Once the base was settled in its mounting hardware, the crew secured it with spikes, iron bars, and threaded bolts of Kenward's design.

The crew continued to raise sections of the mast, joining them with the sleeves. When the sails and rigging were assembled and ready to be raised,

Bryn climbed the bowsprit to attach several lines, and Catrin admired his bravery. Before long, the ship was moving under a small amount of sail.

With her homeland sliding by, Catrin's thoughts turned to all those she had lost and left behind. Tears filled her eyes as she thought of her father and Benjin. Equally distressing were worries over the safety of Chase, Strom, and Osbourne, her faithful companions. They had stayed by her side and risked their lives for her, and now she was abandoning them. Unable to bear the pain, she wiped her tears and concentrated on what lay ahead.

As they sailed into deeper waters, the wind gusted, churning the water to a choppy froth, and the western horizon was lost to view, despite the rising sun. Kenward surveyed the skies and the seas.

"I'd hoped for wind to give us speed, but this weather may be too much for us. We cannot turn back now, though. The water will only get rougher, and we would be hard pressed to enter the cavern again. I'm afraid we must face the weather and the Zjhon on this day. May the gods shine their light upon us," he said solemnly. "We've a strong ship and a seasoned crew, and we've been through tighter spots than this."

All on board kept a watchful eye on the horizon, looking for signs of enemy ships and gauging the weather. Catrin wondered if anyone else felt the intensity of the energy, as if the air were charged. Her carved fish sparkled in the light as she drew it from her shirt, and it looked nearly flawless. She left it out, exposed directly to the light. Breathing in the energy, she felt it flow through her, tingling and vibrating. Her head leaned back, she inhaled deeply, relishing the power as it pulsed around her. Part of her mind warned her against indulgence, but the ecstasy overwhelmed her. Never before had she felt the energy so strongly. It washed over her in massive waves, much the same as the waves' relentless assault on the cliffs.

The energy made her body feel intensely alive, and she wanted desperately to use it. The warning voice in the back of her mind would no longer be denied, and she suddenly realized she heard little besides the wind, water, and rigging. She opened her eyes slowly, returning to the here and now and feeling the loss as she let the energy out of herself. When she focused on her surroundings again, she felt an uncomfortable silence, but it was broken when someone urgently announced enemy ships in sight. The crew sprang into action. Kenward commanded them by hand signals and guided the ship close to the cliffs to hide in the shadows. Everyone remained silent, and the tension grew exponentially as time passed.

Zjhon ships were still visible in the distance, but they neither closed the gap nor appeared to be getting any farther away. Catrin felt in her gut that they had already been seen and were heading into another trap. The feeling persisted, and soon the Zjhon ships moved closer.

"Break ahead!" the lookout called from the crow's nest, and they all looked in the direction he was pointing, knowing they needed to get free of the confining reef and reach the open seas. "Enemy ships charging the break, sir! They're going to beat us there!" he rang out a moment later.

"Prepare for contact!" Kenward commanded. The crew moved with the swiftness of experience. They armed themselves, secured lines, and erected a protective enclosure around the helm. The captain climbed the rigging and joined the lookout, and when he climbed down, he was issuing a steady stream of curses.

"You'd best get to your cabin, Catrin. We may be boarded, and there'll most likely be fighting on deck. Please remove yourself from harm," he pleaded.

"While those around me risk their lives, I will not run and hide, Kenward. I am neither weak nor afraid."

"Do you know how to use one of these?" he asked, drawing his sword.

"I'm better with a bow, but I can wield a sword when I must."

Kenward nodded and sent Bryn after a short sword and a bow. Bryn handed Catrin the sword in its leather scabbard. She drew it out to inspect it. The heavy blade was awkward in her hand, and she sheathed it, hoping she wouldn't have to use it. The bow was larger than she was accustomed to, but she could draw it. Slinging the quiver over her shoulder, she turned her attention to the Zjhon.

As they drew closer to the gap in the reef, Catrin noticed an unusual apparatus on the bow of a Zjhon ship, but she didn't know what it was. The Zjhon ships stayed back, away from the breach, but they were close enough to close the distance quickly, especially with the high winds to drive them.

"Bloody mother of a ballista! Those common som'bits," Kenward ranted.

Catrin had never heard of a ballista, but when she looked again at the ship, she was appalled. The ballista resembled a crossbow, only much larger--far larger than any weapon she had ever imagined. A supply of huge bolts, which were the trunks of small trees, lay beside it. She didn't know if the *Slippery Eel* could survive any hits from such a massive weapon, and she dreaded the impact and aftermath if any struck their mark.

"We're going to have to rush 'em and get the other ships between us and the ballista. We'll be vulnerable for a time, but I'm going to try to make that time as short as possible. That thing'll make a loud noise when they fire it, so be ready to take cover when you hear it," Kenward said. "We're going to shoot the gap at full speed, and then we'll head straight for those two ships. Be ready to repel boarding attempts; you all know the drill. For you newcomers: If it comes from the other ship, kill it. If it attacks you, kill it. And remember to cover my back."

"I will be proud to fight beside skilled and honorable men," Vertook shouted, and a cheer rose up from everyone on deck.

Though the break looked plenty wide enough from afar, it sloped down gradually on each side, leaving only a narrow channel. Going through it at full speed seemed folly, and the crew and passengers shared a nearly palpable anxiety. The gap rushed toward them, faster than seemed possible.

The way looked clear, but still they braced themselves as the ship entered the channel. Dark water closed around them, and the *Eel* slowed and spun, scraping along the reef. The vessel creaked and groaned, struggling to break free, but the impact left it perpendicular to the reef, the waves threatening to drive the ship atop it. Kenward was busy shouting commands, but he stopped suddenly at the sound of an awesome thrum.

"Take cover!" he shouted. The ballista bolt arched across the sky and struck the mainsail with a dreadful tearing sound. Kenward shouted more orders, and the crew rushed back into action. Bryn sprinted by with a long needle between his teeth and a ball of heavy string in hand. He scrambled up the rigging to the tear, which was steadily growing larger, but he got ahead of the ripping and continued to mend it, at times holding onto nothing but the sail itself.

Again the ballista thrummed, and Bryn stopped stitching just in time to brace himself. This bolt struck the sail higher, tearing another large hole, but after piercing the sail, it glanced off the mast and whipped around violently. Bryn didn't see the blow coming and was struck in the back of the head. He went limp, and Kenward yelled for a net to catch him.

Tangled in the stitching, Bryn's arm was all that kept him from falling. When he opened his eyes, he gasped as he realized his predicament. His movements were sluggish and awkward as he regained his grip on the rigging.

"I'll be fine," he said, but then he braced himself as the ballista fired again. The ship dipped low amid the growing waves, and the shot flew harmlessly over the bow, the rough seas and high winds saving them from being struck. Despite his injury, Bryn persisted, and he slowly and deliberately climbed to the other tear and began stitching.

While the attention of the crew had been focused on the ballista ship, the Zjhon had taken full advantage. Another ship was headed toward them on the starboard side at ramming speed. The *Eel* spun slowly away from the approaching ship.

As the Zjhon ship came within bow range, Catrin nocked an arrow and drew. Looking down her shaft, she located a target. He was young and wore a look of determination and fear. There was no hatred in his eyes, only duty. She hesitated and closed her eyes, but in her mind's eye, she saw a Zjhon shaft strike down Irvil of the Sun clan. As quick as thought, she rotated and found a new target: the man giving orders. Her fingers slipped from the string and the arrow sped through the air.

The man Catrin assumed was the captain of the Zjhon ship shouted one last order before he dropped over the side, her shaft protruding from his chest. Still the ship came and struck a glancing blow that sent the ships careening away from one another.

The Zjhon ship was much larger than the *Slippery Eel*, and it rode higher in the water. Sailors leaped from the height to the decks of the *Eel*. Many landed without injury, but some were knocked unconscious when they hit the deck, and others missed the ship completely and plunged into the raging depths.

One sailor landed not far from where Catrin stood, and she drew her short sword. The man smirked, seeing an easy victim, and he waved his sword menacingly. He approached slowly at first then suddenly sprung at her. Catrin was ready for his attack. She dropped to the deck, kicked him hard in the groin, and prepared to swing at his ankles. As he reeled from her kick, though, the anger on his face changed to utter surprise when Bryn swung down from the rigging and kicked him squarely in the chest. The sailor dropped over the railing without another sound, but Bryn lost his grip while fully extended and fell, faceup, landing hard. He looked up at Catrin, moaned, then passed out.

When he did not wake, Catrin dragged him to the deckhouse and into the first cabin. She tried to comfort him before leaving, feeling that she should stay by his side but not knowing what else to do for him. When she returned to the deck, most of the fighting was over. Nat and a crewman forced a final tenacious sailor over the railing and looked for anyone else left to fight. Kenward issued roll call, and eight men failed to report, including Bryn.

"Bryn was hurt in the fight. He banged his head twice and was knocked out. I took him to the first cabin." Kenward was overjoyed to learn Bryn was still with them, and he hugged her, kissed her on the forehead, and rushed to the deckhouse. Catrin joined the cheers when a crewman was pulled from the water. Six men lost were far too many, but it was much better than seven or eight.

The man at the helm earned his keep, swiftly putting distance between them and the Zjhon ships, all the while keeping a Zjhon ship between them and the ballista ship. As they sped northwest, aiming for open seas, they trimmed the sails to take full advantage of the wind while the Zjhon ships lumbered in sluggish pursuit. The gap steadily grew, and the crew became less tense, but as the northwestern tip of the Godfist came into view, their spirits dropped.

"Sails ahead, sir! I count a dozen northwest and three northeast! Zjhon outpost to the northeast and more ships on the horizon, sir!" called the lookout. The Zjhon had constructed a huge lift system for raising men and supplies to the mountain valley high above the sea. Luckily, it appeared mostly abandoned, and only three ships were moored in the harbor. Catrin began to feel much as she had when escaping from the desert--trapped--and the noose was tightening.

Kenward changed course, angling between the ships approaching from the makeshift docks and those still out to sea. Ominous storm clouds darkened the western horizon, casting a depressing pall over the crew. Webs of lightning illuminated the clouds, and as the sound of thunder grew closer to the lightning, the wind intensified.

The crew of the *Slippery Eel* pushed her to her limits, using more sail than was advisable in high winds, and the ship groaned in protest as it tore through the massive waves. Even with the speed advantage, it became obvious they would not be able to evade all the Zjhon ships. Whether the ships were part of a massive trap or were simply returning to harbor to wait out the storm didn't matter. It looked as if the *Slippery Eel* would be trapped between the Zjhon ships and the Godfist.

Huge, growing swells crashed over the rails and forced everyone on deck to hold on to something. Many fled for the deckhouse, but Catrin fought her way to where Kenward had rooted himself near the helm.

"I don't know which I fear the most," he admitted. "The storm alone could put an end to us, and there are far too many Zjhon ships to avoid. Every option appears to be suicide, and I cannot decide which death I prefer."

Catrin knew in that moment that it was time for her to test her powers again. "Make for the center of the Pinook harbor," she said. Kenward raised an eyebrow and considered her a moment, seemingly trying to decide if she knew what she was talking about.

"The center of the harbor? Are you certain about that?" he asked.

"I am as certain as I've ever been about anything. There is no path that would not likely lead to our deaths except this one. Is there anyone with another plan?" she asked. "Make for the center of the harbor," she repeated after an uncomfortable silence. "When we arrive, drop anchor and prepare to ride out the storm."

Kenward seemed convinced by the force of her convictions, gave a simple nod, and the crew did what they knew to do without another order.

Darkness fell earlier than usual as storm clouds blotted out much of the remaining light and bands of horizontal rain pelted the crew. The winds forced them to lower part of their sails, and yet they still managed to maintain their speed. The seas were impossibly high. When in the troughs, Catrin could see nothing but walls of water on either side of the ship, and it looked as though they would be engulfed and sunk at any moment.

The *Slippery Eel* entered the Pinook harbor in relative darkness and made for the deeps. Many Zjhon ships were already in the harbor, though most had dropped anchor in preparation for the approaching storm. Many were still making for the harbor and could effectively block their only route of escape. Catrin knew they had reached the point of no return, and as she looked at the crew, all eyes were on her. Holding her amulet tightly, she prayed . . .

* * *

Staring at the familiar knots in the richly grained wood of his cabin walls, Kenward wondered if this was the last day he would spend on the *Slippery Eel*. Memories of his first ship, the *Kraken's Claw*, flooded his mind with every sight and sound of her sinking. Wringing his hands, he prayed this was not another mistake.

Catrin seemed sincere in her convictions, but escape from the harbor would be nearly impossible. Only the intervention of the gods could save him this time, and he could only hope they had not lost patience with him. Though he was not usually a religious or superstitious man, he found himself walking to the rails and tossing a gold coin into the dark waters, an offering to the sea.

Having done what he could do, Kenward returned to his cabin, hoping it was enough.

Chapter 22

The most awesome powers are those not wielded.
--Enoch Giest, the First One

* * *

The journey to the center of the harbor ahead appeared endless to the crew of the *Slippery Eel*. The Zjhon ships already in port were secured for the storm, and they remained where they were anchored. It seemed no one noticed the smaller pirate ship, and nothing barred their path. Even if they had seen her, it would have taken hours for the large ships to pull up their many anchors and raise and set their sails. The Zjhon ships following them into the harbor were so busy contending with the storm that they had to concentrate on survival rather than pursuit.

Catrin, alone for a moment, let her mind turn to a myriad of thoughts and emotions that she attempted to process. She didn't know if her friends were safe, and she felt a pang of loneliness and loss when she thought of them. When she thought of her father and her uncle Jensen, her heart nearly broke.

Her thoughts flashed to memories of the animals on the farm: the horses, cats, and all her cherished companions. She hoped Salty and the other horses were in green pastures, and that Millie and the other cats had found good hunting. Tears slid down her cheeks, but she stifled her grieving, knowing she would need to focus her energy on survival.

She did not want to destroy the Zjhon or their nation, but she could not allow them to continue their siege on the Godfist, and it was clear they would take over her homeland even if she escaped. No words would deter them; they would persist until forced to leave. She wanted to end the siege without the slaughter of men she realized were only doing their duty. That thought struck Catrin like a hammer blow: these men were not evil or her enemy; they were acting on orders. Archmaster Belegra was not evil either. He truly believed that what he did was good and right and protected his nation. Even if he was wrong, he was simply as fallible and flawed as any other person. The actions of the Zjhon were precipitated by prophecies and religious beliefs that spanned thousands of years. It was as if what they did was foreordained and inescapable.

The Zjhon believed the Herald of Istra would descend on them and attempt to destroy them. When she tried to look at things from their perspective, Catrin realized they perceived her as the embodiment of some ancient evil, as the reincarnation of a legendary adversary, and that it was their duty to protect their families and their nation from imminent destruction.

She figured most of the Zjhon would seek high ground once they secured their ships. Rage burned in her belly when she imagined soldiers waiting out the storm at her family's farm. She felt an intense sense of personal violation but pushed it aside. Such self-indulgence would have to wait.

In a universe filled with possibilities, she knew some solution must exist. Battle with the Zjhon seemed inevitable, but she could see no way to defeat such a superior force even with all the people of the Godfist. The Zjhon ships provided them food and mobility, and those things would allow them to starve out those trapped in the cold caves and the Masterhouse. The ships were the key; without them, the Zjhon would be stranded and lucky to survive the winter.

Food was limited on the Godfist, the land barely supporting the current population, and the fields were untended due to the siege. The Masterhouse and the cold caves each had large stores of food and water, and though their food supplies were limited, they had proportionally more than the Zjhon would if deprived of their ships.

Destroying a fleet was not something Catrin would have ever thought herself capable of, but she had to consider the events that led to this moment: She thought of the explosion that saved her from Peten's staff and the storm that ravaged the greatoaks. She remembered her actions on the plateau and the staggering effects of her power. Her abilities were undeniable. The striking of the artesian well proved her ability to accomplish previously unthinkable things when she used Istra's power.

The storm, bearing down on the harbor, drove enormous swells toward land, and ships strained against their anchors. Catrin considered the storm, which was the biggest threat and possibly her greatest source of power. Whenever she reached for the comet, the energy seemed to form a spinning vortex, and she had the same sense of spiraling energy from the massive storm.

Stepping back, she tried to look at her world objectively and to shed her preconceptions. The comet and other heavenly bodies gave evidence of unimaginable size and distance. The shapes in the sky had one common factor: they were all spherical. The Godsland was a sphere, Catrin realized, and it, too, was spinning. She reveled in her intuitive realizations as if shedding overly tight skin.

The sphere, she realized, was the primal shape of the universe. As she extended her senses toward the storm, she felt the atmosphere spinning. It was a vertical column of air, sheared by the rotation of the planet itself, just as her tendrils of energy had been sheared. Insight and understanding, albeit limited, gave Catrin an added measure of confidence. She realized the mechanics of this universe could be used to her advantage.

Waves continued to batter the *Slippery Eel*, the winds making it difficult for the crew to work. The motion of the ship became increasingly violent, threatening to send Catrin over the railing. Nearly everyone else had gone belowdecks, and they were taking turns cranking the bilge pumps. Massive swells forced the bow under water, and the ship took on water as fast as the crew could pump it out.

Catrin had to stay on deck to carry out her plan, and she would need to remain standing. Grabbing a coil of rope from near the helm, she looped it around herself and the mainmast, creating a crude harness that she hoped would keep her in place.

Alarmed shouts from the crew interrupted her thoughts, those remaining on deck pointing wildly out to sea. Catrin saw only a wall of water at first, but when they crested the next wave, she saw two Zjhon ships headed straight for them. She guessed they were among the ships that had been pursuing them, and they seemed intent on finishing the job they had started. The two ships were dangerously close to one another, and Catrin was shocked to realize they were actually chained together.

Men leaped from one ship to the other; some made the jump, but many fell to their deaths. Other men scrambled across the massive chain that hung between the ships, but the chain would suddenly go slack then, just as suddenly, snap taut again as the ships moved closer together and farther apart on the waves. Catrin watched in horror as men were thrown into the air.

Their actions made no sense to her at first, but then she came to a harsh realization: they were evacuating one ship because it was on a suicide mission. She guessed they would leave a few men onboard to control it to make sure it rammed the *Eel*. A direct hit at their current speed could very well sink both ships, but the Zjhon had ships to spare.

Activity on the deck of the *Eel* became intense as men scrambled to mobilize the ship. They might not be able to evade the approaching ship, but they wanted to get the anchors raised so the other ship might only push them out of the way.

No more men attempted to abandon the suicide ship, and the chain was released during a brief slackening. The mostly unmanned ship continued to bear down on the *Slippery Eel* while the other turned aside sharply.

As the *Eel*'s crew hastily secured the anchors and ran for cover, Catrin braced herself and reconsidered the wisdom of tying herself to the mast, but there was no time left to escape. The Zjhon ship rode atop a huge wave, towering above the *Slippery Eel*, and it appeared to Catrin as if the ship suddenly dropped from the sky. The initial impact rocked the *Eel*, and

Catrin's head smacked against the mast, leaving her stunned.

Seemingly unstoppable, the Zjhon ship slammed into the aft side of the deckhouse, easily pushing it out of the way. The supple wood flexed and groaned, barely withstanding the incredible force. The *Slippery Eel* rolled under the massive weight, and Catrin heard wood snapping just before she struck the frigid water.

Struggling against the ropes she herself had tied, she grew frantic, having been under water for what seemed a very long time. The ship rose suddenly and righted itself, tossed by another wave. Catrin hung limply against the ropes and tried to get her breath. Above the sounds of the storm, she could clearly hear Vertook praying as he worked the bilge pump like a man possessed.

Shrieking winds left no doubt that the massive storm had arrived and was engulfing the harbor. Catrin knew she had missed her chance to act before the full force of the storm struck, even as she knew she was drawing energy from it. Tied to the mast, she had to endure the high winds and brutal, stinging rain.

The crewmen were all focused on their tasks of trying to drop the anchors again, but they were hampered by the buffeting wind and waves. They looked as though they had suffered injuries--probably from the violent motions of the ship--and they moved slowly and deliberately. Some were bleeding heavily and appeared to be in pain but persisted in trying to do their jobs.

The ship rose high into the wind, which pushed a huge swell toward shore. The massive wall of water rushed on, inexorably, with an awful roaring sound accompanied by deafening cracks and snaps. Many of the Zjhon ships were torn from their moorings, and as Catrin watched, they began to float aimlessly, some crushed against the rocks, others smashed to bits against other ships.

The anchors of the *Slippery Eel* dug into the harbor floor once again, and the ship groaned as it faced the storm. The swells grew so massive that the ship was nearly pulled under by the weight of her own anchors as she crested the tallest waves. A huge piece of sail and rigging hit Catrin, and she couldn't tell which ship it had come from. She was uninjured, except for a gash across her forehead. Blood began to run into her eyes, clouding her vision, and she used the tail of her shirt to wipe the blood away.

Hours passed, but the storm continued, unabated. Then the winds suddenly died and the sky cleared. A surreal calm set in as the eye of the cyclone moved over the harbor. Catrin looked up into the night sky and was astonished to see five comets amid the stars, three of which were little more than small dots with tails, but the other two were large and bright.

The crewmen moved around the deck quietly, trying to take advantage of the brief respite. They all knew the way these storms behaved and that the other side of the storm was yet to come and would likely be worse. Using large hunks of rope, soaked in tar, they temporarily patched the holes in the damaged hull.

"Catrin, please come belowdecks. You could be killed out here," Kenward said as he passed her.

"I'll be fine here. Are there any clean bandages?" she asked. Kenward retrieved one for her and applied it to her wound.

"How is the crew holding up?" she asked.

He sighed. "They've taken some pretty hard licks, but they have to keep working despite their injuries. They are good, strong men, and they'll heal quickly. Bryn's awake and complaining a lot, so I'd say he'll be fine as well."

"Thank you, Kenward. I have to tell you that what I am about to try will be risky, but I must try to save us," she said.

"I have faith in you," he said simply.

As she turned to face the harbor, she saw men scrambling to take advantage of the short lull to try to prevent further damage to their ships. She drew a deep breath and opened herself to the intense energy surrounding her.

"Armies of the Zjhon nation, behold!" she said in her most powerful voice, which was amplified by the power running through her. "You bear witness to the Call of the Herald, and she calls you not to war, but to peace."

She paused then continued. "You came here to defend yourselves against one who had no intentions of destroying you, and by your very actions, you have brought about your own fears. I bear no ill will toward any of you, but I cannot allow you to lay siege to my homeland." She paused again as her words hung in the air. "Without your ships, you will have no food. You will have to choose between peace and death. You'll not survive a winter on the Godfist without the help of her inhabitants.

"I declare the armies of the Zjhon disbanded. All of you are now citizens of the Godfist, whether you wish it or not, and I'll not wage war with you," she said, pausing again for her final statement. "The Zjhon ships, however, are forfeited, and I will destroy them. If you wish to see the dawn, abandon your ships now." Her words hung in the air, echoing in the distance.

Without another word, she reached toward the largest and brightest comet in the sky. The cyclone's eye wall was rapidly approaching, and she had to act. Power and pleasure washed over her as energy flowed through her tingling body. Tendrils of energy reached toward the comet, the spinning of the planet causing them to shear and spin. A massive vortex of energy and swirling colors formed in the air above her.

Wind thrashed and churned the water around the ship, and Catrin expanded her vortex to envelop the ship and keep it within the relative calm

CALL OF THE HERALD

of the center. Her senses heightened, she could feel the immense energy pent up in the storm. The clouds were highly charged and seemed to be searching for a place to release their abundant energy. When she cast her senses over the ship, she perceived a massive negative charge, and the result was as if the clouds and the ship reached toward one another, seeking balance. She could almost see a strand of negative energy reaching from the mast to the sky, and she shuddered as she realized one was also extending from her own head.

Casting about the harbor, she found a web of negative filaments rising from the Zjhon ships as well. Targeting the closest one, she reached out to its largest thread of negative energy, which rose from the mainmast. Her connection to the ship created an almost visible link between them, a thread of gossamer stretching into the night. She fed negative energy to the Zjhon ship, and the tendril grew more distinct and extended higher into the sky. The clouds reached down with their positive charge, yearning for ground.

A bolt of lightning suddenly completed the arc with a furious discharge. Up close, it resembled a plummeting fireball with a life of its own, and it struck the Zjhon ship with a fury, engulfing it in flames. The lightning was not spent, though, and it leaped along Catrin's thread of energy, racing toward her. She broke her link with the ship, and the lightning split apart, dissipating. Balls of fire cast waves of intense heat over her, only to fizzle and disappear before they reached her. All of this occurred within a fraction of an instant.

Her energy vortex raged on, unabated, and the eye wall was nearly on them. As the winds pounded against her power, they were forced aside and sheared off, causing them to spin wildly. The intense rotation spawned monstrous waterspouts that thrashed violently through the harbor, tossing ships about like children's toys. Several waterspouts became tornadoes as they left the water and moved over dry land.

Catrin sought more Zjhon ships, but the high winds and rain had returned with the other side of the cyclone's wall and obscured her vision. Determined, she reached out to them with her power alone, casting her energy over the water, feeling her way to the ships as if her power were an extension of her fingers. When she sensed the wooden sides, she knew she had found a target.

Her energy cast about the ship and located the mainmast. She attached a thread and fed it negative energy. Within a short time, lightning pounded her target and illuminated the spectacle for all to see. She released the link more quickly this time, but the bolt of lightning still came perilously close to reaching her, daring her to try again. Massive hail fell from the skies, pounding the ships mercilessly, and Catrin tried to target ships that were less damaged. Soon, the entire harbor appeared to be afire, and despite the driving rain, the fires spread and intensified.

Catrin noticed a nearby ship, which was largely undamaged, and reached out to it, calling the lightning to do her will. Too late she realized the *Slippery Eel* had also built up a massive negative charge. Looking up she saw a fireball racing along a jagged course. It slammed into the mainmast, and she was helpless to protect herself as it descended on her. It struck with a force greater than anything she had ever imagined, and the ropes securing her were vaporized, along with much of her hair and clothing. She fell to the deck, stunned and smoking, her energy vortex collapsing. Darkness overwhelmed her.

* * *

When Catrin opened her eyes, she was lying faceup on the heaving deck. Disoriented, she had difficulty focusing her thoughts. She was about to pull herself back to the mast when a bizarre phenomenon occurred: hundreds of fish, large and small, rained from the sky. It was a dangerous spectacle, and Catrin was struck in the leg by an enormous jellyfish. The gelatinous creature exploded on impact, and its stinging tentacles caused intense pain. Reaching the mast, she wrapped her arms and legs around its base and held on. Flames danced amid the rigging, but the fire was quickly extinguished.

Exhaustion overcame Catrin, her mind and body screamed for rest, but if she relented, she knew all aboard the *Slippery Eel* would surely perish in the powerful storm. Forcing herself to concentrate, she worked to reestablish her protective energy vortex. When she reached for the comet, though, the exertion was just too much in her weakened state. Struggling to hang on to the mast and remain conscious, she closed her eyes and squeezed herself tight around the mast.

The carved fish dug into her chest where it still hung on its leather thong. She had forgotten about it, and it gave her enough hope to try again. She pulled the carving from her shirt and lifted the thong over her head. Placing the small fish in her palm, she wrapped the thong around her fingers. With the carving firmly secured, she tried again to create a vortex.

The carving grew warm in her hand as she drew on it, and she reached into the night sky. Heavy water vapor in the air thrashed her vortex wildly as it tried to form. Catrin poured herself into the vortex. Straining with everything within her, she fed the vortex with every emotion she contained. Fear, anger, resentment, joy, and love all went into the shimmering funnel. It fluctuated and wobbled around her, liquid veins of color dancing across its surface, but it finally established itself and became organized.

As the vortex grew, chaos ensued throughout the harbor as more waterspouts were spawned, and lightning picked its own targets. The vortex provided some protection from the storm, but not all dangers would be so easily held at bay. Catrin was nearly knocked loose from the mast when another ship crashed into them. It had broken loose from its moorings and was now being tossed around the harbor. It rammed against the *Eel* several times before finally breaking free, sent spinning toward shore by the driving winds.

The carved fish had grown hot in her hand, but she continued to draw on the energy reserves it provided, determined to protect the ship and its men from further damage. It was obvious the ship was wounded because she had begun to list to one side, but Catrin could hear the crew still working the bilges, and she prayed the *Eel* would remain afloat.

The relentless storm pounded them for what seemed an eternity, putting Catrin's endurance to the test. She lost feeling in her limbs, and her mind grew fuzzy; she could no longer remember why she needed the vortex so badly, but some part of her held on tenaciously. Only when she felt a hand settle on her shoulder did she become aware of her surroundings again. The dawn had come, the storm passed, and still she held on to the dwindling vortex.

Once fully convinced she no longer needed it, she released the energy and slumped forward. Her body was leaden, and her heart seemed weary of beating. The hand was still on her shoulder, and she looked up to find Nat looking at her with extreme concern. He had risked himself by reaching through her vortex to touch her.

"Are you well?" he asked as he wrapped her in a thick blanket.

"I don't think so."

"What did this to you," he asked.

"Lightning," she responded, unable to elaborate.

As her senses returned, she felt intense pain in her right hand, and she opened it slowly. The leather thong was still twined around her fingers, but as her hand opened, the fish carving crumbled into dust. Instinctively she knew she had lost something far more important than a simple carving or even a mighty tool. She'd destroyed something precious and irreplaceable. The flesh of her palm was covered with tiny blisters, and when she concentrated on it, the pain was overwhelming. She would have collapsed on the spot, but she saw the rest of the crew hurriedly preparing for their departure. The crew repaired what damage they could, and the *Slippery Eel* soon began limping toward the open seas.

"I want to go back. I want to go home," Catrin said.

"Do you think they will welcome you? Do you think peace can so easily be achieved?" Nat asked, shaking his head. "I think not. Your countrymen have already declared you a witch and were ready to turn you over to the Zjhon. And what of the Zjhon? You may have declared them citizens of the Godfist, but you also sentenced them to a hard winter here. You stole from them their only way home." He placed his hand on her shoulder to soften the blow of his words.

"No, Catrin. You cannot go home now. I see dark days ahead on the Godfist, and I fully expect there to be unrest, if not civil war. But even if none of this were true, I would still urge you to seek out knowledge that cannot be found here. I know little of your power, but I know one thing for certain: if you do not find a way to better control your gifts, then they will be the instruments of your destruction."

In the silence that followed, Kenward shifted uncomfortably and waited for Catrin to respond, but she did not. "Do you want me to take you home?" he asked, earning a glare from Nat.

"I do," she responded softly, her eyes downcast. "But I cannot go back. Nat is right. I must go to the Greatland and seek out the Cathurans. I must learn to control my power. It's what Benjin wanted. It's what my father would want."

Kenward nodded and returned to his work. Nat put his hands on Catrin's shoulders and turned her to face him. "I know this is hard for you, and I know it's not what you desire, but you do what is right."

Catrin walked to the bow of the ship in silence. She took one last look at her homeland, knowing she might never see it again. Only when the Godfist had dwindled in the distance did she pull herself from the heart-wrenching sight and shuffle to her cabin.

Just as she was entering the deckhouse, one of the crew shouted in alarm. In the distance, the *Slippery Eel*'s sister ship appeared on the horizon. The Zjhon had captured the *Stealthy Shark* during the raid on the pirate's cove, and no doubt they now planned to use her to their advantage. The *Shark* appeared to have less damage than the *Eel* and was moving swiftly toward them.

Catrin's will and energy were spent. She climbed into the hammock and tried to think of a way to evade the ship, but her muddled thoughts were indistinct, and she fell exhausted into a deep sleep.

Epilogue

Premon Dalls crouched in the drainage ditch, waiting for the Zjhon patrol to pass. Acrid smoke still hung heavy in the air, stinging his eyes and irritating his throat, making him fear he would soon be coughing. Debris from the storm littered the ditch, and he pulled as much as he could over him, trying to make himself invisible.

He assumed these men were still loyal to General Dempsy since they still marched in formation and there was no one he recognized in the group. The defectors were with the followers of Wendel Volker since the Masters refused to accept any of them. With tensions rising between the Masters and the rebels, as Wendel's followers were called, the mysterious presence of the tribes of Arghast only increased the uncertainty of the situation. How they had come to be allied with the rebels was still a mystery.

Spying on the rebels had yielded little new information, but Premon was determined to use every morsel to his advantage. His plain looks had been a handicap when he was an ambitious young man struggling to gain status, but now his appearance was a benefit. Few took notice of him, and even fewer knew his name.

Getting back to the Masterhouse was proving to be more difficult than ever before, as the Zjhon patrolled constantly, seemingly intent on maintaining control over the docks and shipyards. This was not an entirely bad thing, for when the Zjhon repaired their ships and left the Godfist, he would be free.

For the moment, though, he was content to wait.

* * *

While it was still dark, Premon hauled himself out from the mud and trash and crept to the foul-smelling sewer grate he'd told Peten Ross about. Looking around to make sure no one was nearby, he removed the broken bar from the grate and set it inside. Even with the bar removed, he had to squeeze through, and he was bruised and scratched by the time he got down into the sewer. He replaced the broken bar and picked up the torches and flint he'd stashed there several days before. The stench was overwhelming, and he struggled to breathe.

By the time he reached the drain that led to the upper halls of the Masterhouse, his sense of smell was gone, and the powerful odor no longer bothered him. The steep climb to the upper halls was an even worse part of the journey, but he suffered through it, thinking of the future. A place of power awaited him, and it would all be worth it.

Using one of the many service tunnels to gain access to the Masterhouse, Premon made his way to the appointed place without being seen. Once within the darkened room, which was little more than a closet, he waited.

He was sleeping when Master Edling finally arrived, and Premon struggled to pull himself from his stupor.

"Don't you ever bathe?" Master Edling asked, covering his nose and mouth with his hand.

"Stealth has its price," Premon said, shrugging.

"What have you found out?"

Premon thought for a moment before he replied. "The rebels plan to take back the farmlands and the highlands and leave Harborton to you."

"How very kind of them."

"I've heard talk of settling the Zjhon defectors in the upper Pinook and Chinawpa valleys. It seems they're willing to give away our lands to the enemy," Premon continued.

Master Edling appeared lost in his own ruminations, and Premon pressed on, hoping to gain any advantage he could. "General Dempsy's men have already repaired one warship, and they are scavenging materials to repair more. From what I've heard, they plan to pursue the Volker girl once they have three seaworthy ships. The deserters will be left behind."

Master Edling watched Premon but showed no reaction.

"There is one other thing," Premon continued, his lips curling into a sneer. "Wendel Volker sleeps in an unguarded room near one of the shafts that allow fresh air into the cold caves."

"Does he now?" Master Edling said, raising his eyes to meet Premon's. "It would be a pity if he were to die in his sleep, especially with no one to inherit his lands."

Premon could not keep the smile from his lips. "Indeed," he said, a plan already forming in his mind. Acres of farmland were far from enough to satisfy him, but it was a beginning.

The Greatland

INHERITED DANGER

Prologue

Impenetrable darkness shrouded the cold caves, and Wendel Volker shivered as the freezing dampness crept into his bones. His persistent cough rattled in his chest. Though he had gone to his bedroll hours ago, his mind refused to quiet. His troubles demanded attention, demanded he find some way to act, some way to set things right. He had thought of little else for days, but no answers were revealed to him, only feelings of guilt, anger, and despair.

Catrin was gone, and he would probably never see her again. For all his strength and devotion, he had failed to protect her, just as he had failed to protect Elsa, and now they were both lost to him. Like a coward, he'd hidden in the cold caves when Catrin had needed him most. He had relied on Benjin to stand in his place. He'd been a fool. Perhaps Elsa had been wrong all those years ago; perhaps she should have chosen Benjin instead.

Balling his hands into fists, Wendel tried to drive the thoughts from his mind, but memories of Catrin would not relent; they flooded him with guilt and remorse.

When he turned his thoughts to his present situation, there was no relief. Catrin had left behind a troubled land. Though he knew she had done the best she could and was immensely proud of her, her actions had not been enough. To achieve peace under these circumstances was more than any individual could accomplish, and Wendel wondered how the Godfist would ever overcome the turmoil threatening to consume them all. General Dempsy's men still held the harbor, and no one could know what they planned to do next. Headmaster Grodin was succumbing to age, and he ruled over those within the Masterhouse only in name. It was Master Edling and his followers who truly held sway, and their stubborn arrogance only exacerbated the problems. By refusing to grant amnesty to the Zjhon soldiers who defected, they had divided the citizens of the Godfist.

Though the tribes of Arghast had helped defend those in the cold caves, their presence had only served to confuse matters. Once it seemed the Zjhon no longer presented an immediate threat, they claimed to have fulfilled their oath to Catrin but left a force of thirty mounted men behind to guard the cold caves. It was difficult to believe they had come in the first place, especially since they claimed to be bound to Catrin.

Perhaps he just couldn't accept it, Wendel thought. Even after witnessing some of the events in the harbor, he could not convince himself that Catrin was the Herald of Istra. It just seemed too surreal. She was his little girl, not a harbinger of doom. He made himself believe it was all a coincidence, that Catrin had nothing to do with the bizarre occurrences. Either way, it mattered little now. The Godfist was caught up in a three-sided war, and he doubted he would ever see his daughter again.

The thought of leading a revolution had no appeal for Wendel, yet he found himself caught in that position. His attempts to relinquish power had been fruitless; no one was willing to take his place. Even when he threatened to step down and leave them leaderless, no one volunteered.

Exhausted and ill prepared, he struggled to find a solution. If he surrendered to the will of the Masters, then the Zjhon defectors would be cast out with nowhere to go, and the bloodletting would begin again. Wendel could not accept that.

Jensen insisted they retake the farmlands and highlands, but Wendel was loath to leave the protection of the cold caves. Here, at least, they had the benefit of natural fortifications. If they retook the countryside, then they would be spread too thin to adequately defend themselves. It seemed a puzzle with no solution, and his thoughts ran in circles.

Their supplies were dwindling, and soon they would have no choice but to leave their shelter despite the danger. Sighing, he tried once again to put the problems from his mind. Hoping some revelation would come to him in the morning, he rolled onto his side and continued sweating despite the prevailing cold.

Shades of darkness shifted in his room, moving as if specters lurked in every corner. Chiding himself for letting the stress affect him in such a way, Wendel rolled to face the cave wall and squeezed his eyes shut.

When a foul smell reached his nose, it was already too late to escape. Even as he cried out, a cold blade parted his flesh.

Chapter 1

Hope can be foolish or in vain, but without it, all is lost.
--Ebron Rall, healer

* * *

The seas behind the *Slippery Eel* churned in her wake and left a visible wash of turbulent water. The ephemeral trail gradually dissipated in the distance, where, once again, the waves became nearly indistinguishable before another ship churned them anew. The *Stealthy Shark* remained within sight and kept pace with the *Slippery Eel*, but she did not close the gap. The two ships were evenly matched when in top condition, but the *Eel* was heavily damaged and wallowed sluggishly. She had been taking on water since before leaving the harbor, and the crew had been unable to stop all the leaks. The bilge pumps were the only things keeping them afloat.

The loss of men during their flight from the Godfist left Kenward severely shorthanded, but clear skies, fair winds, and calm seas were a boon to the crew and made their work a bit easier. Catrin, her hair cut short, stood alongside Kenward at the stern, both watching the ship that trailed them.

"I don't understand it," Kenward said. "The *Shark* is in much better condition than the *Eel*; she should've overtaken us long before now. Fasha and her crew are definitely not aboard. The *Shark* is being sailed by boilin' *amateurs*," he continued, knowing his sister and her crew were either dead or stranded on the Godfist.

"I'm sorry," Catrin said, touching his arm.

"Fasha's the most stubborn and tenacious person I've ever known," he said with fierce pride. "She'll swim her way back to the *Shark* if that's what it takes."

His obvious pride in her made Catrin smile, and she thought again, as she had so many times before, of what it would be like to have a brother or sister. Chase was the closest thing she had, and she shared Kenward's loss. That thought led to her wondering again how her father, Benjin, and the others had fared. Wanting desperately to see them or at least know they were well, Catrin despaired. That knowledge was beyond her reach, taunting her. She had no illusions about the journey ahead of her, and she accepted the possibility that she might never see any of them again.

"There, you see?" Kenward said suddenly. "The rigging's all wrong. They're already blowing off course. If these fools catch us, it'll be no one's fault but mine." He walked away, a sour look on his face. Catrin matched his stride, following him to the helm.

"What can I do to help?"

"You've done enough already. Without your magic, I don't think any of us would've escaped the Godfist. Those of us who live owe our lives to you."

"And I owe my life to you and your crew. You risked yourselves to save us, and I'll always be grateful." His mention of magic sent a chill up her spine. She had never considered her powers to be *magic*, and the image disturbed her.

"Well, I hadn't thought of it in that way," Kenward said. "And we could certainly use you. Bryn has been promoted, since Jimini, the bosun, was lost in the storm. Jimini was a good man--the best, but Bryn is deserving of the post. Ask him to show you what you can do."

After searching much of the ship, Catrin located Bryn, who was high above her head, methodically examining every part of the rigging. He checked line, pulley, and sail for damage. Glancing down for a moment, he noticed her, and she waved.

"Can we talk when you have a free moment?" she called up to him.

"No more free moments for me. I'm 'fraid," he shouted in response. "I'm comin' down." His movements were slow and methodical compared to his previous acrobatics. "M'head still hurts; my balance is off. I feel like a bumbling fool."

"It'll pass, and then you'll be back to yourself. I know you're busy and short of hands. What can I do to help?"

He looked dubious for a moment then winked as she put her hands on her hips. "The first thing you must learn is how to tie knots. All of them."

"Is that all?"

Bryn chuckled and retrieved a small canvas and a length of supple line. He handed them to her. "Come back when you have them all mastered," he said, and Catrin accepted his challenge.

Spreading the canvas out on the deck, she held it in place with a couple of spare pulleys. Painted with fine illustrations, depicting each knot and its name, the canvas was intimidating. She hadn't known so many different types of knots existed. This was indeed a test.

Determined, she began with an easy knot. It was a simple pattern, but the line twisted in her hands and seemed to resist forming even the simple bowline loop. Still she persisted and was proudly admiring her first knot when Nat approached.

"I think we should talk."

"I suppose we should," Catrin replied, not liking the look in his eyes or his tone.

"I'm sure Benjin planned to tell you certain things," he said. "I hope he has already discussed this with you. Do you remember your mother?"

Catrin turned sharply and stared at him. She had not expected such a personal question, and in response, she nodded sadly. Memories of her mother were faded, more like gauzy images, but when Catrin thought of her, she felt warm and safe and often smelled roses. Her mother had loved roses.

"Did your father ever tell you about your mother's family?"

"No. He doesn't like to talk about it, and I never wanted to make him unhappy, so I never asked," Catrin replied.

"Did Benjin tell you about his relationship with her?" he asked, looking somewhat disgusted.

"Benjin and I have never discussed my mother for the same reasons," she answered.

Nat sighed. "They should've told you, but since they did not, I will. I'm sorry. It would be better if this came from Benjin or your father."

Catrin grew anxious, uncertain she wanted to hear what he had to say. "I think... I don't... I don't think I want to know," she said, but her imagination was already conjuring frightening images that continually grew worse.

"I'm sorry, Catrin, but your destination is the Greatland, and your life may depend on this information," he said firmly, and she nodded. "You've probably heard that my father was deranged, and people say I inherited his disease. My father had visions. He saw things that urged him to take one course of action over another. They were not always specific things. They were more like overpowering intuition." He watched for her reaction.

She had heard the rumors, but she judged Nat for herself. After all, he had given her information that had been instrumental in her escape from the Godfist. Without his help, she might never have gotten away. She owed him her life. Thinking of what Kenward had said, she realized they all owed their lives to each other. None of them could have survived alone.

"How did you know what to write in your letter?" she asked suddenly. "Where did those words come from, the part about land and water? How could you see the future?"

It was Nat's turn to be dumbstruck. "See the future? I can't see the future. Those words just occurred to me as I wrote. Now that I think about it, I'm not even sure what they mean." He looked thoughtful for a moment. "Were they somehow prophetic?"

His words had seemed strange when she read them because they had made no sense. Yet when she needed inspiration, they rang in her mind.

Water shapes the land.

His strange poetry had changed the course of history. As she recounted what happened on the plateau, his eyes grew wider with every detail.

When she finished, he sat, staring at his hands. "My letter changed the face of the Godfist and killed hundreds of men."

"I'm not proud of it," Catrin said a bit defensively.

"A thousand apologies. I know you did your best. I was just taken aback by the effect of my spontaneous words. You were protecting your homeland, and you are a true hero."

Catrin didn't consider herself a hero. She was a scared little girl, unprepared to face the challenges ahead. Kenward and Bryn, who'd been watching the *Stealthy Shark* wander farther off course, approached before she had a chance to sort out her feelings.

"I don't think they have the skill to catch us, sir," Bryn said. "They've made up no time during our repairs, and now that we can make more speed, we could lose 'em."

"We need food, and now's the time to fish," Kenward said. "If we fill our hold, we'll not starve crossing the barren seas, but it'll slow us down. If those fools ever figure out what they're doing, they could catch us."

"We could jettison the fish if'n they catch a miracle wind, and I, for one, would rather not starve," Bryn said.

Kenward smiled. "Drop the lines, men. Let's fish."

Large trawl tubs were prepared with multiple lines, hooks, and bait. Catrin gasped as an emerald green carpet began to cover the waters around the ship except for the trail of dark water in her wake.

"It's from the storm," Kenward said. "We call it a storm oasis. The force of the storm dredges up nutrients from the seafloor, and large amounts of plankton flourish in the normally barren waters. The plankton fields lure fish, and they draw more fish and birds." He pointed off the starboard side, and Catrin strained to see. An enormous creature suddenly rose up to the surface, and she jumped back in fear.

"Whales. There'll be more. Keep your eyes to the seas, and you'll see things you've never imagined."

Catrin watched the whales, afraid they would attack the ship. Kenward assured her they posed no threat, but she was still anxious around such massive creatures. Porpoises played in the ship's wake. They chittered at Catrin and the crew, entertaining with their antics. Some jumped high into the air, while others walked across the water on their tails, and the natural beauty took Catrin's mind from all that was troubling her.

Later, when the crew hauled in the first of the trawl tubs, they were energized as they strained to work the windlass, and they let out a cheer when three massive tuna were pulled onto the deck.

Large coffers of salt and pine boxes were brought from the hold. Cleaned fish were placed in the boxes and packed with dried sea salt. The salt would draw the moisture from the fish and prevent spoilage. Catrin and Nat helped as much as they could. After seeing Nat filet fish with efficient and skillful strokes, the crew seemed to look at him with newfound respect. Soon they were laughing with him and patting him on the back while exchanging tales and techniques.

Catrin had no skill for gutting fish and little desire to learn, so she settled for packing salt around the fish. The salt supply dwindled rapidly, but the crew was already boiling off large pots of seawater in an effort to replenish their supply. It was a slow and tedious process.

Kenward watched intently as Catrin and the others worked alongside his crew. "I'd like to welcome the new members of the crew. They may not yet know bow from stern, but they work as if their lives depend on it," he said, smiling broadly, and Catrin thought it an odd compliment, but the crew hooted and stomped their feet. Catrin flushed but was glad to have earned their respect. She was also thrilled to see Nat working as part of the crew. Never before had he seemed so happy.

The seas yielded a bounty, and at the end of the day, nearly half the hold was filled with salted tuna, round eye, and shark. Grubb, the ship's cook, prepared a feast of fresh fish for the evening meal, and the aroma from the cookhouse had mouths watering.

Catrin felt good for her efforts. Hard work had always helped keep her from worrying over things she couldn't change.

After stowing the rope and canvas in her cabin, she sought out Nat. Their conversation was unfinished, and she needed to know what else he planned to tell her. His cabin door was closed, but she could hear him moving within. She knocked lightly and waited.

Nat opened the door and sighed when he saw her. "Come in. I suppose you want to hear the rest," he said while pulling himself into his hammock. He stared at the ceiling as he spoke.

"When your father, Benjin, and I were about your age, my father had a vision. He was convinced the Zjhon would attack the Godfist. I did not believe him then. As far as I knew, our people hadn't encountered any others in hundreds, if not thousands, of years. I'd begun to see truth in what others said about him. I thought he was stricken by madness.

"He tried to convince me to go to the Greatland to search for information. I refused. I wanted only to court Julet and convince her to marry me. He said terrible things would happen if I did not go, but I was young, stubborn, and foolish," he said, his voice overlaid by the waves of anxiety that poured from him like a wellspring.

"He gave up on me and approached your father. Wendel was proud and brash and would do just about anything to prove his bravery. When my father challenged him, your father took the bait, hook and line. There was nothing anyone could do to dissuade him, not that many knew of the situation." He drew a deep breath before continuing. "Benjin thought the quest was a delusion, and he argued with your father, but somehow Wendel convinced him to go."

Nat's tone had gradually changed until he seemed to be talking to himself, having forgotten she was there, consumed as he was in his own memories. "Father made the arrangements. Benjin and Wendel boarded a small pirate ship along the southern shores of the Godfist. They were supposed to travel to the Falcon Isles but somehow managed to travel all the way to the Greatland aboard that small vessel. It's a wonder they did not perish." Nat grew quiet, his hands balled into fists, and Catrin thought she heard a growl escape his throat. He started to speak several times but had to stop to regain his composure.

"I tried to forget about them and my father's warnings. I pretended none of it was real, telling myself they were all mad, but then sweet Julet died." He sucked in an unsteady breath before he went on. "She was bitten by a glass viper, which are extremely venomous and usually only found in the desert. How it came to be in her bedding is still a mystery, but it cost me everything. All my hopes and dreams died with Julet, may her soul be free."

No words could adequately express Catrin's condolences, and she could think of nothing to say that wouldn't sound trite. Instead, she chose to put her hand on his and give it a gentle squeeze. She gave him a few moments to grieve. When he had composed himself, he continued.

"My father blamed me," he said haltingly. "He said I had affronted fate, and fate had treated me in kind. In a desperate attempt to convince fate to return my Julet, I tried to set things right. I knew it would never work, but that didn't stop me from trying. I could no longer stand the sight of my homeland. Everything reminded me of my failure, of how my actions had killed Julet," he said, smashing his fists against his thighs. "I left the Godfist in a small fishing boat, hoping to find Wendel and Benjin. It was a terrible journey, and it took me over a year to find them. When I did, I met your mother.

"It was a difficult time," he said, looking her in the eye for the first time since he had begun speaking. "I'm sorry to have to tell you this," he said, and he paused as if he were unsure he should continue.

"Your mother captured both Wendel's and Benjin's hearts. She seemed truly unaware of their feelings, and the tension grew. Wendel and Benjin became bitter toward each other and were both miserable. One day they told Elsa she would have to choose between them, but she cared for them both and refused. Eventually the tension was too great, and Benjin challenged Wendel. They argued at first, but it escalated, and they fought like madmen, nearly killing each other. Elsa and I pulled them apart, and we were both injured in the process. They fought us blindly and did not thank us for our interference.

"After the fight, Elsa tended Wendel's wounds. I'm not sure if it was the loss of his friend or Elsa's silent choice that drove him, but Benjin left without a word. Your father was saddened by his departure but did not go after him."

Catrin could feel her heart breaking as she listened, unable to bear the thought of her father and Benjin fighting. "Why are you telling me this?"

"I'm telling you because there are many in the Greatland who will remember your parents and the events surrounding their departure from the Greatland. You see, your mother was the daughter of a very wealthy noble, a prominent member of society." He paused a moment to look at Catrin. "And you are her mirror image."

Tears blurring her vision, Catrin could bear no more and fled the cabin.

* * *

Nat wasn't proud of himself, but he'd begun to do what was right. Still, he dreaded what would come next and doubted any words would make Catrin understand. With a deep sigh, he tried to sleep. It would not come. A haunting but familiar sensation grew steadily, and he braced himself. The taste of blood filled his mouth as his muscles clenched and the vision overwhelmed his senses.

The land shivered under the weight of an ill, green light. A foul demon with eyes of ice sundered the air, and the skies caught fire. In the demon's path, Catrin stood, abandoned and alone, her arms cast wide and power flowing around her. Roaring as it came, the demon engulfed her in its flames, and she disappeared into the conflagration.

Nat sucked a deep breath as the seizure released him, and he felt himself being ripped apart, torn among the visions, duty, and the wrath of men long dead.

Chapter 2

The past is indelible, but our every action weaves the fabric of the future.
--Enoch Giest, the First One

* * *

Catrin avoided Nat for the next few days and kept herself busy practicing knots. Mastering all of them gave her great pride, and she sought out Bryn. He watched her demonstrate.

"Not bad," he said, "but on a ship, you have to be able to tie them without thinking or even watching what you are doing. Come back when you can do them all with your eyes closed."

Disappointment was overwhelmed by the need for success. Refusing to fail, Catrin squatted on the deck. Her eyes closed, she found her other senses heightened. Things that normally complemented her visual image were now her only source of awareness. When Nat walked across the deck, she knew him from the rhythmic click of his staff against the deck. The sound grew closer and stopped, and she was not surprised when he spoke.

"I'm sorry, Catrin. I didn't want to hurt you."

"Then why did you? You could have simply told me I looked like my mother and people might recognize me!" she said, realizing even as the words left her mouth that she was being unreasonable. Nat was not to blame for the pain his message stirred within her.

"I'm sorry," he said.

"No. I'm the one who owes you an apology. I reacted poorly and have been acting like a child. Please sit with me," she said, motioning to the spot next to her. Nat eased himself slowly to the deck, grunting as he settled himself.

"I'm gettin' old."

"I've been meaning to ask you something," Catrin said. "How did you manage to swim and hold on to your staff at the same time?" She remembered her own terrifying plunge into the sea.

Nat's back stiffened and his face grew stony. "I had to choose," he said. "I had to choose between my life and my father's last wishes. I knew I couldn't swim with the staff in my hands, at least not very well. But to drop the staff would have been to betray my father. I would not allow the consequences, not again--I couldn't." The venom that poured from him, as if she had lanced a festering wound, surprised Catrin. "They said I was crazy to hold on to the staff, that only a madman would try and swim with an iron-shod stick," he said with an angry, hurt look toward the crew.

"I see," Catrin said, looking him in the eye.

It was Nat's turn to feel foolish; he seemed to realize the crew could not have known how that would hurt him. He shook his head. "I must have seemed crazy to them, risking my life to save a piece of wood and metal. There was no way they could have understood. I would have died without their help."

He sighed. He looked down at the deck, breaking eye contact with Catrin. "It pains me to trouble you more, but I must. You left before I could tell you the rest. I cannot go with you to the Greatland," he blurted.

Catrin sat back so quickly that she smacked her head on the deckhouse. Unable to formulate a response, she just stared at him in shock.

"It's not that I don't want to go. Please understand. I know I swore to protect you, and I will for as long as I can. But I cannot go to the Greatland. It was forbidden to me. I have known this time would come and have dreaded it, but now it has arrived and I shall do my duty to my father," he said.

Catrin was not sure how much more she could take.

"On his deathbed, he made me swear I would never again set foot on the Greatland. He said that if I did, something far more dreadful than Julet's death would occur, and I cannot allow that to happen."

He looked directly at Catrin. "It seems I've taken too many vows, and now I must choose, for I cannot obey them all. Will you, Catrin Volker, Herald of Istra and my dear friend, please release me from my vow?" he asked, kneeling and placing his forehead on the deck before her.

"I cannot," she said forcefully, and his head jerked up from the deck. He could not contain his utter dismay, and his face went slack. He looked into Catrin's face and was confused when she smiled back. "You can keep *both* vows. There is no need to choose. I am flexible, you see. You don't need to come with me to protect me and my interests; I'll need someone to look after things on the Godfist."

Nat smiled when he realized she had cleverly solved his dilemma, allowing him to keep his word *and* his pride. Catrin, though, had an icy feeling in her stomach. She would go to the Greatland with only Vertook to guide her, and she was not yet certain how Vertook felt about the journey. She might have to face the Zjhon alone.

"Your passage from the Falcon Isles has been paid, and I have gold for you. Members of the Vestrana should be available to help you on your quest once you reach the Greatland."

"Thank you," Catrin said, nodding, but things had changed between them. Knowing he would not accompany her, their relationship felt thin and strained. Nat sat for a while in uncomfortable silence then excused himself. It was a strange parting, and Catrin was saddened by the tension. She tried to wish Nat well, but she kept seeing herself alone in a strange land where everyone wanted her dead.

A sudden wind threatened to blow away the canvas and line. Catrin quickly gathered them up and ran to her cabin. When she stepped inside, she heard muffled shouts from the deck and the sound of men running. Throwing the line and canvas aside, she rushed back to the deck. Several crewmen ran by her on their way to the stern. When Catrin arrived, most of the crew was already gathered there, trying to get a good view.

She could see nothing at first, but Bryn saw her dilemma and hoisted her onto his shoulders. Finally able to see above the other men, Catrin saw the *Stealthy Shark* on the horizon, listing badly and riding too low in the water.

"They're gonna sink her."

"It's a trick."

Kenward watched in tortured silence. Unable to stand still, he paced back and forth. The *Shark* listed sharply, driven by the growing wind. Part of her rigging struck the water and snapped off, and it became clear this was no ruse; the *Stealthy Shark* was foundering and beginning to sink.

"Turn this ship around!" Kenward shouted. "Set a course for the *Shark*. I'll not let her sink this day."

The crew sprung into action, arming themselves as they prepared the ship to come about. They all seemed to know that Kenward was doing this for his sister. He might not be able to save her, but he could save her ship. The *Eel* turned slowly, and Catrin urged it forward, as if her desire might somehow propel the ship. The *Stealthy Shark* had fallen far behind and looked as if it might sink before they arrived.

As the *Stealthy Shark* gradually grew larger on the horizon, her crew became visible. One man waved his arms frantically, and the others struggled to move about the deck, clinging to the rails. The ship was out of control, and the men seemed barely able to hang on. Catrin's knees buckled when they grew close enough to see the men's faces. It was Strom who waved.

"Strom!" she screamed, and everyone aboard the *Slippery Eel* looked at her. "Those are my friends. Help them!" All this time they had been right behind her, and now they were in mortal danger.

Kenward could not pull his ship alongside the *Shark* for fear of colliding with it. The seas were choppy, and unpredictable winds gusted at gale force, so they had to lower the small boats into the water. Men scrambled down, and Catrin saw Kenward begin his descent. Without another thought, she leaped over the railing and shimmied down one of the ropes. The boat below was overfull, and the waves tossed it as Catrin wedged herself between two men.

As they approached the sinking ship, men threw ropes onto the deck. Catrin spotted Benjin and called to him as he grabbed one of the ropes. He tied it to a pair of sturdy bollards on the deck and stopped just long enough to smile and wave to her. Within moments, they were all aboard the *Shark*, the crew scrambling to assess and repair the damage. Vertook climbed on deck, went straight to the bilge pump, and began to crank it.

"Kenward!" Benjin shouted. "Do you have any pyre-orchid?"

"Not in many years," Kenward replied.

"Dreadroot! Have you any dreadroot?"

"Bring back dreadroot on the next trip," Kenward yelled to a sailor.

"Now! The need is urgent," Benjin insisted, and Kenward ordered the man to hurry.

Catrin had never heard of pyre-orchid, but Benjin's request for dreadroot terrified her. The only use for dreadroot she knew of was to treat severe infections, and it was only used in cases where the infection was out of control and likely to cause death. Dreadroot could wipe out rampant infections, but it was so powerful, it also killed many of the people treated with it.

"The hole in the hull is far too large to be repaired with oakum alone, sir. We'll need to patch it and then seal it," a crewman reported.

"Get the shelves from the cabins and use those to patch it," Kenward ordered. "We'll need more oakum from the *Eel*."

Benjin appeared stricken as he realized the materials needed to repair the ship had been onboard all along. "Boil me, I wish I'd thought of that. I had hoped the oakum would hold long enough to catch you, but it blew out with no warning, and I knew we were in trouble. Thanks for coming back for us."

Trying to account for all of her Guardians, Catrin searched the ship. She had seen Strom already, but in the chaos, she could no longer locate him. Osbourne appeared for a moment but was then lost in a flurry of sailors. Men struggled to repair damage at the helm; Benjin and Kenward rushed to their aid before Catrin could ask who needed the dreadroot. Praying it wasn't Chase, she decided to have a look in the cabins and moved toward the deckhouse.

Checking each cabin, she found them all empty, and when she reached the last door, she wondered where else to look, but the smell told her she had found him. Covering her nose and mouth, she entered the cabin and sobbed when she saw Chase, pale and shivering, an open wound on his right shoulder. Angry flesh, mottled red and purple, surrounded the wound, and Catrin could feel the heat radiating from it without touching him.

He did not stir, even when she blotted the sweat from his forehead. His breathing was shallow and labored, and Catrin feared he was already lost, too far into sickness to ever recover. She cursed fate for its cruelty. All this time the herbs Chase needed had been just out of reach. If only she had known her friends were aboard the *Stealthy Shark*, then Chase would be safe.

The rough and unpredictable motions of the ship caused the hammock to sway wildly at times. Chase's body was dead weight, and Catrin winced as it soundly struck the cabin wall.

Benjin charged into the cabin, carrying a small vial and a flask of water. The dreadroot Kenward had provided was not in its usual powder form; instead it was concentrated oil. Benjin used extreme care in applying a single drop to Chase's tongue, knowing a larger dose would almost certainly kill him.

Chase did not react at first, but then his face wrinkled and he looked as if he wanted to spit. He shook his head back and forth wildly, trying to swallow. Benjin poured water over his lips, but Chase swallowed very little and sprayed most of it across the cabin as he coughed. After a moment, though, he drifted off, settling back into unconsciousness. His breaths were short, and Catrin encouraged him on each one, fearing it would be his last.

She was distracted when she noticed Benjin having trouble closing the vial with one hand, his left arm hanging limply at his side. Catrin moved to him and reached for his shirt, but he pulled away.

"I'm fine," he said. "Right now I need to help Kenward and the others attend to the ship. Stay here with Chase, please. Shout if his condition worsens." He rushed from the small cabin, not waiting for a response.

Holding Chase's hand, Catrin watched his chest rise and fall. Physical contact gave her the distinct impression of heat and corruption, and she could sense his life forces slipping away.

Uncertain of what to do but unwilling to do nothing, she placed one hand on his forehead and the other on his chest. After synchronizing her breathing with his, she began to concentrate on his getting well. Love and friendship poured through the physical bond, and her hands grew warm. A tingling sensation thrummed in her palms.

Energy swirled from her hands and into Chase, and she focused on the foulness raging within him. The infection gave her the impression of immense hunger and single-minded reproduction. It would consume him. She could not tell if the dreadroot was having any effect, for the infection seemed to remain strong, overcoming his body's weakened defenses.

Soon, though, his breathing became more regular, and Catrin decided to try something different. Holding both hands over his wound, she concentrated on the inflamed flesh. It repulsed her, but she refused to pull away. Energy poured into the diseased flesh.

A small trail of blood seeped from the wound, and Catrin grew alarmed, but the blood seemed to cleanse the area, carrying away foul contaminants. She sensed Chase's body beginning to fight the infection forcefully.

Kenward entered with a cloth and a basin of diluted wine. "Can you hold him in place while I do this?"

"I can do it," Catrin replied.

Kenward nodded and began to cleanse the area around the wound first. Chase moaned and thrashed, but Catrin held him fast. Kenward wiped the wound directly then applied pressure around it, forcing the foulness out. Chase shouted incoherently, but Catrin held him, speaking soothing words in his ear, her tears mixing with his sweat.

"That's all I can do for now," Kenward said after bandaging the wound. "Get him to drink water if you can," he added as he left.

Catrin helped Chase drink whenever he woke, and several times, she woke him just to give him more water. The ship's motion became more stable, and the listing subsided. In the hours before dawn, she leaned her head against the cabin wall for a moment of rest, and her eyes closed. She was asleep before she drew another breath.

Chapter 3

On the cusp of life and death stands a veil of gossamer, and those who behold it are forever changed.
--Merchill Valon, soldier

* * *

A terrified cry woke Catrin in the dawn hours, and she fell out of the chair she had been sleeping in. Pulling herself from the floor, she checked on Chase and drew a sharp breath. His body was covered in an angry rash. Every part of him was discolored and inflamed.

"I'm gonna die, Cat. I don't wanna die," he said through swollen lips as Kenward and Benjin arrived. Holding his breath, he endured while they inspected his wound, checked his temperature and pulse, and listened to his chest.

"I think you are going to make it," Kenward said with a smile. "The rash is not life threatening. It's one of the least deadly effects of dreadroot."

"Dreadroot? You gave me dreadroot? Are you mad? Were you trying to kill me?" Chase asked, incredulous. He tried to sit up quickly but immediately fell back to the hammock.

"You were near death, Chase. We had no choice," Catrin whispered, and he nodded slowly, asking with gestures for water. Once his thirst was quenched, he asked for food; the return of his appetite boded well for his recovery.

"Some great sorceress you are, Cat. We were behind you all that time, and you couldn't tell us from the enemy. What use are you anyway?" he said with a tired and forced smirk, which made her certain he would recover.

"Perhaps you should've thought of that before leaping on someone's sword," she said. He laughed a bit too hard and winced from the pain. "You relax." She kissed him on the forehead. "I'll get you something to eat."

"Are you having any trouble breathing?" she heard Benjin ask as she slipped out of the crowded cabin. She left the door open to freshen the air.

Approaching Farsy, one of the crewmen she recognized, she asked if they could get broth for Chase. Farsy winked and pulled a polished piece of metal from his pocket. He then began sending signals to the *Slippery Eel*. It took a moment before anyone responded, but when they did, the ensuing conversation of flashes was surprisingly short.

"The signal language is quite intricate," he said. "We can convey many things quickly, as long as both people are well trained. The skill has saved many lives."

Catrin watched as two men from the *Slippery Eel* scrambled into a boat and rowed toward the *Stealthy Shark*. When they arrived, Farsy threw down a line, and the men below secured a heavy basket. Once it was on deck, Farsy opened it and revealed a surprisingly large amount of food.

"You didn't think he was the only one hungry, did you?" he asked, seeing her look of surprise. "No sense making a trip for a mug of broth, I'd say. Besides, I knew Grubb would take care of us--he feeds us, and we keep him afloat. It's a fair bargain for all."

Catrin's stomach agreed with Farsy, and she thanked him. He nodded his reply, his mouth full of salted fish. Grabbing the covered mug of broth and some food for herself, she walked carefully back to Chase's cabin. The air in the cramped quarters was less foul when she returned, and a crewman had mopped the floor before throwing down some dried reeds.

Chase slept, but the rich aroma of the broth soon brought him from his stupor. He accepted it with shaking hands and sipped it, savoring the flavor. He thanked Catrin and she nodded, her mouth full of hard bread. Feeling much better after eating, she was thankful Farsy had thought to get enough for everyone.

Chase emptied the mug and handed it back to Catrin with mumbled thanks. He was asleep as soon as the hammock cradled his head. With Chase cared for and her fears for him diminishing, Catrin sought out Benjin. He stood near the helm with Kenward and Nat, and they seemed to be discussing plans for the rest of the voyage, but they fell silent when Catrin approached.

"Chase is doing better. He's had some broth and is sleeping again," she said, and the tension lessened slightly. She stood for a moment, watching Benjin, her emotions spanning the gamut. She could not decide if she was more glad, hurt, angry, or scared. The overwhelming circumstances made it difficult for her to maintain her focus, and when Benjin met her eyes, the words that left her lips surprised everyone.

"Why didn't you tell me you were in love with my mother?" she blurted, regretting the words as soon as she spoke them.

Benjin was dumbstruck, and Nat looked as if she had physically assaulted him. A dreadful silence hung in the air, broken when Benjin spun fluidly. His face contorted in rage, he struck Nat as quick as a snake. Catrin barely saw him swing, but a sharp crack echoed across the water, quickly followed by the thud of Nat's body against the deck.

Roaring in anger, Benjin spun away from Nat, and another crack resounded. Benjin's head snapped back, and Catrin stood, fists clenched, trying to decide if she needed to hit him again. Blood welled on his lip. The sight of it was too much for her, and she retreated to Chase's cabin. No one on deck uttered a word as she fled, and tension continued to hang heavy in the air.

Chase was awake when Catrin returned, and her distress must have been obvious.

"What's going on out there?" he asked without waiting for her to sit. She let out a sigh and shook her head. It took her a moment to compose herself before she could speak. Her voice wavered as she told the tale, and he listened in relative silence, though he let out a low whistle when she told him about her father and Benjin fighting over her mother. As she finished, she felt as if she had just poured her soul onto the cabin floor and left herself completely vulnerable.

"Things will be fine," Chase said optimistically, and his cheer in the face of his condition shamed Catrin; she had crumbled under the weight of much smaller problems. The things Nat said had brought her pain, but they also brought her a greater understanding of her circumstances. She realized her question must have been a shock to Benjin, and probably brought him enormous pain. Again, she regretted her insensitive words.

A brief meditation calmed her mind, and she considered seeking him out. Part of her wanted to avoid him, but she needed to make amends, knowing she would have no peace until she did. She found him at the bow of the ship, glowering out to sea and leaning heavily on the rail. Catrin read his posture: he wanted to be alone, but she decided not to honor his unspoken request for privacy. She approached him and placed her hand on his shoulder.

"I'm sorry," she said softly. He made no response for a few moments; he just continued to stare out at the endless waves. When he reached up and patted her hand, he left his hand covering hers, and she relaxed a bit.

"No more sorrys from you," he said, but his voice was husky with emotion. Catrin put her arms around him and laid her head against his back. They stood quietly for a while, neither of them willing to break the silence. They had unpleasant business ahead of them, but they silently and mutually decided to enjoy a few moments of peace together first. The stillness was broken when Bryn called for all hands on deck, and everyone aboard the *Stealthy Shark* gathered near the bow, where Kenward awaited them.

"Your efforts have paid off," he announced. "Both ships have been repaired sufficiently. We are ready to raise our sails and ride the wind." A cheer rose up from all those assembled, and the crew aboard the *Slippery Eel* answered in kind.

Kenward began the difficult process of dividing his crew and the inexperienced travelers between the two ships. They would be hard pressed to man both ships adequately, and everyone would have to work double shifts. Catrin and the others were assigned to experienced crewmen, to act as assistants and runners. Glad to be paired up with Bryn, Catrin would remain on the *Stealthy Shark*, where Benjin would serve as partner to Farsy.

Despite her repeated requests, Benjin refused to let her examine his wound. "It's healing well," he said. "I'll have no trouble performing my duties. Don't you worry any more about it. I'll be fine."

Strom, Nat, and Osbourne were assigned to the *Slippery Eel*. They exchanged quick hugs and farewells with Catrin. Even though they would be nearby, she missed them even before they departed. She hadn't yet had a single moment with them since they had been busy helping the crew. They left with promises of many tales when they could be together again. Catrin noticed Benjin talking with Nat and became alarmed, but she was immensely relieved and proud of them both when they shook hands.

The crews of both ships prepared to make full sail, and the new members of the crew were initiated in a frenzy of activity. Commands were issued, and admonitions abounded when mistakes were made. Praise was hard to come by, but when it was given, it meant a great deal more for its rarity. Catrin had helped a little during the first part of their journey, but now she was expected to act as a part of the team, and her actions could determine another crewman's fate.

Bryn did not tease or challenge her as he had with the knots; instead, he very seriously instructed her on which tasks were the most dangerous. She gave him her full attention and tried her best to complete each task, but many of the terms he used were unfamiliar to her, and he often had to do the work himself. Catrin watched closely, and she was proud that he never had to perform the same task twice. Once she had watched him do something, she was able to do it herself the next time. Even when struggling, she stubbornly insisted she needed no help.

The days and nights were exhausting, but the crews found a rhythm and began to operate almost efficiently. One day, Kenward returned from the *Slippery Eel* for a surprise inspection. After scrutinizing every part of the *Stealthy Shark*, he called for all hands on deck, and the crew gathered quickly. Bryn stood nearest to Kenward, waiting for the verdict. The ship had been under his command, and it appeared he would take this evaluation as a reflection on himself.

"The condition of this ship is surprising," Kenward said with obvious disappointment. Bryn did not hang his head, but the muscles in his jaw tightened, and Catrin knew he had hoped for better. Kenward smiled, no longer able to hold on to the lie. "Considering the circumstances and the shortage of hands, you've done an exceptional job, and you are all to be commended for your efforts. I can expect no more from you, but I will continue to expect no less," he continued, and the crew let out a cheer. "Catrin and Benjin will join me on the *Eel* for the rest of the day. I'll return them on the morrow."

Catrin was a bit surprised by the summons. She felt bad leaving Bryn, but he assured her that her efforts had already reduced the backlog of work, and he would manage until she returned. She was still trying to determine if he was being sarcastic as she climbed down to the boat waiting below.

On arrival, Kenward took them directly to the galley. Catrin was pleasantly surprised to see Strom, Osbourne, Nat, and Vertook already seated in the large room, which held them all comfortably. Kenward gave them some time to greet one another, and the room was soon filled with the buzz of several conversations, along with the delightful aroma of the special meal Grubb was creating.

Given their limited provisions, what Grubb provided was a feast. The honored guests were presented with a filet of tuna coated with herbs and spices and wrapped in a thin layer of seaweed. The filets were so large that they hung over the edges of the ship's largest wooden plates. Catrin noted with some interest that Benjin's filet was the largest by a significant margin, and she did not miss the sly wink Grubb gave him. The galley grew quiet except for the sounds of eating and groans of pleasure.

"As fine a meal as I've ever had," Kenward said. "A thousand compliments, Grubb."

"Will you eat with us?" Catrin asked, noticing that Grubb did not eat. "I have plenty to share if you would like some."

"I thank the lady for the invitation," he replied with a smile. "She is quite considerate, but I only eat when everyone else has been fed. Please, enjoy." He said it as if it were a simple fact and not a matter of preference, so Catrin let it drop. Still, it bothered her to have someone watch her dine, waiting for her to finish before he would eat. She wasn't sure she could consume such a large portion, but the meal disappeared more quickly than she would have imagined.

Grubb cleared the plates and brought bowls filled with dates, prunes, dried apples, and a few sugared lemons. Everyone tried a little of each kind of treat, and they all commented on the quality of their feast, knowing it had taxed their stores. Their stomachs full, most leaned back and found comfortable positions to relax in, while Grubb served a deep red wine in small wooden mugs.

"Friends," Kenward said after clearing his throat. "I've asked you here to discuss our common goals and dangers. I've known some of you for many years and others for a much shorter time, but we've already been through a lot together, and I consider us friends and allies. After all, we all owe each other our lives in some way or another. Now we must share what we know with one another. I fear we'll need all the knowledge we possess just to survive this struggle." Looks were exchanged as Kenward spoke, and Catrin noticed Benjin shifting in his seat. She respected and trusted Kenward, and she listened intently as he continued.

"I must begin by asking if anyone here has secrets they feel they must keep from the rest of the group. I want you to really think about this and be honest with yourselves. If you have any secrets you would not reveal to anyone in this room, even if their lives depended on it, then speak up now," he said and waited patiently to see if anyone would respond. Catrin mentally sorted her deepest and darkest secrets, including things she had trouble admitting--even to herself. It was not a pleasant process, but if it would keep her companions from harm, she would reveal them all without another thought.

Kenward let the silence hang while he refilled everyone's wine mugs. Catrin was surprised Grubb did not protest, but he was now happily eating his own meal, which made her feel much more comfortable.

"Good," Kenward said when no one responded. "So it is safe to say we all trust one another. I know it's not always wise to reveal everything you hold in confidence, but we need to divulge anything relevant to this conflict. I'll be the first to reveal information I hold in confidence, as a show of faith.

"There are Zjhon ships in the Falcon Isles, and my family has been trading with them openly. The last I knew, my mother's ship was commissioned to make supply runs for the intermediate forces stationed there. She bought time by claiming they needed to wait for the next cutting of herbs in order to satisfy the quantities required by Archmaster Belegra, which was a very convenient truth. I don't know if that relationship bought safety for my sister, but it is a possibility. I can only hope.

"The *Stealthy Shark* and *Slippery Eel* could not be seen in association with the legitimate trade fleet, and we departed as soon as the Zjhon arrived. We suspected the ships were chasing us, and we fled to the cove on the east coast of the Godfist. We've had no word since we left the Falcon Isles, and I don't know what has transpired there.

"We'll be approaching the isles soon, and we'll need to make the last part of our journey quickly and under cover of night if we wish to remain undetected. We'll be traveling to a cluster of remote islands, and there we should find a message from my mother. It'll tell us which anchorage is currently safe, and where to meet. Once we drop anchor, we'll take boats to the meeting place, and from there we can smuggle you aboard the *Trader's Wind*, my mother's ship.

"The journey to the Greatland is long and arduous under normal circumstances, but you will be confined to private chambers, where you can travel unbeknownst to the others aboard. The solitude and confinement will be a trial, but it is your best chance of making it to the Greatland undetected. Fortunately, the *Trader's Wind* will be well supplied and you should not have to fear starvation. Do you have any questions?" It took a few moments for them to digest the information.

"Where will we go once we get to the Greatland?" Strom asked, and Kenward gave others the chance to answer before he spoke.

"The *Trader's Wind* will be bound for New Moon Bay at Endland, that being the largest trade port on the east coast of the Greatland. There should be many merchant ships there from different parts of the Greatland; perhaps you could disappear into the crowds. It would be a perilous venture. If you decide on a different destination, though, you need not go all the way to port aboard the *Trader's Wind*. There are ships much like the *Slippery Eel* that work around that area. Once you are within the range of those smaller ships, we can arrange passage to just about anywhere on the coast and a few places where large rivers run inland," Kenward said, producing a large map of the Greatland, which he rolled out on the table.

Catrin studied the map and was dismayed by the size of the landmass so colorfully depicted. Gauging by the number of cities, rivers, and mountain ranges, the Greatland dwarfed the Godfist. The thought of such an enormous place intimidated her, and she wondered how they would decide on a suitable destination. Nat and Benjin had mentioned the Cathuran monks, but she had no idea where they would be found.

She considered asking, but then she realized Benjin had not uttered a word, and he did not look at the map. He remained where he was seated, occasionally rubbing his shoulder and looking grim. Catrin was puzzled by his manner until Kenward spoke again.

"I think your destination depends a great deal on what happened in Mundleboro seventeen summers ago, and there is only one person here who can give a firsthand account of those events. I hate to draw you out of your silence, my old friend, but I've waited many years to hear this tale, and the telling is long overdue," he said, looking at Benjin.

Cursing herself for not understanding sooner, Catrin sympathized with Benjin. Kenward had set a trap for him, and he walked into it, knowing it for what it was and allowing himself to be snared nonetheless. It was obvious he had no desire to relive those memories, but he must have decided it was indeed relevant, for he cleared his throat. Before he began, though, he walked to where Kenward stood.

"You may have a few gray hairs, but you've not changed a bit," he said in a low voice.

Chapter 4

Before we can truly understand our role in this life, we must first admit our reliance on every other life form.

--Hidakku the Druid

* * *

Benjin stood before the assemblage and spoke as if they did not exist. "Wendel and I spent most of our childhood trying to outdo each other, and when old man Dersinger started filling Wendel's ears with talk of the Greatland, there was no stopping him. Somehow, I knew his grand adventure would be dangerous and possibly fatal, but Wendel failed to see it. He was convinced we would take the Greatland by storm--just the two of us. We would save the world," he said in a rhythmic cadence. He seemed to have left the present, and the past poured from him.

"I didn't even know what we were supposed to be searching for. 'Clues about Istra' was all we had to go on, but Wendel seemed to think it was enough. Old man Dersinger sent us through the Chinawpa Valley to the Arghast Desert. We skirted the desert to the south and eventually arrived on the beaches, battered by storms all the way, and we feared we were too late. We saw no sign of the promised ship, and for nine days, we waited.

"When the ship finally arrived, though, Wendel became more determined than ever. When we met Kenward, I knew things were going to get worse." He paused as Kenward involuntarily choked, temporarily breaking the spell, and Benjin seemed to realize, once again, to whom he was speaking.

Catrin's sudden desire to smack Kenward must have shown on her face, for he nodded a silent apology to her.

"Kenward was on his first solo voyage with his new ship, the *Kraken's Claw*," Benjin continued. "He and Wendel seemed to fuel each other's fires. Kenward's mother, Nora, had given orders to deliver us to the Falcon Isles. Wendel challenged Kenward to disobey those orders and sail directly for the Greatland. Kenward knew it was too long a voyage for a ship as small as the *Claw*, but Wendel fed his ego, and it was more than he could resist," he said.

Kenward rolled his eyes, but when he noticed Catrin's glare, he assumed a neutral posture and tried to look innocent.

"I'm grateful that the crew proved themselves to be some of the craftiest and most resourceful sailors ever to set sail. It took every bit of their ingenuity and tenacity to survive the suicidal voyage. We almost starved and were nearly caught several times by patrolling military vessels, but Kenward and his crew found a way to escape each time," Benjin continued, and Kenward puffed his chest out.

"His seemingly endless luck drove Wendel to believe they were both invincible. When we reached the Greatland, Wendel walked in like he owned the place, and may the gods bless him, he pulled it off. He acted as if he truly belonged there, and no one questioned him.

"Somehow, he got us passage with a caravan and even got them to let us ride in one of the new carriages they were delivering. Wendel enjoyed the ride and played his part as if it were true. In contrast, I constantly feared someone would call his bluff, and then they would hang us both. We made the entire trip to Mundleboro without anyone giving us more than a second glance, but as the caravan waited in the tariff line, the trader rushed us out of the carriage. His customer had ridden out to meet him." He paused a moment and seemed to be reliving his memory.

"She sat atop her horse in leathers and a fur-lined coat, and her brow furrowed as Wendel and I climbed from the carriage that bore her family's crest on the doors--a pair of intertwined roses. Her eyes afire, she dismounted, moving like an angry cat. She demanded to know who we were and how dare we ride in her commission. The situation got worse when Wendel told her to mind her own affairs and added that her father would understand the needs of men. It was a stupid thing to say, and I'm still not sure exactly what he meant, but it enraged her.

"She grabbed him by the arm, swung him around, and demanded he explain himself and pay for a thorough cleaning of her carriage. He refused, of course, and brushed his hands over the seat cushions, as if that would satisfy her, or perhaps he did it because he knew it would infuriate her. I could never figure those two out. They argued until after dark. I finally told them I was leaving and would rejoin their argument in the morning." Benjin looked at Catrin, a silent apology in his eyes, and she knew before he continued that he would not coat the truth with honey.

"When Wendel said he had no more to say to 'Miss Self-Important' and would join me, she said her name was Elsa Mae Mangst, and he would do well to remember it. They started arguing all over again, and somehow he argued her into having dinner with him. They voiced their conflicting opinions over cold food for hours. As I said, I never understood those two.

"I tried to convince Wendel to move on quickly and escape the unwanted attention that his relationship with Elsa could only bring, but he insisted she was the key to our quest. She was highborn. She would have access to important information and would have contacts at her disposal. It didn't help matters that the Zjhon were waging war along the coasts, and the Mundleburins were building up forces along the border with Lankland. There had already been skirmishes, and the long-standing feud between the

Mangst and Kyte families had begun anew. No one could remember what caused the original feud, but times of peace never lasted long.

"On the day of her majority, Elsa claimed independence from her parents' rule and took command of a border-patrol unit. The event caused quite a stir, but no one attempted to stop her. She had been well trained, and she assembled a force of elite fighters and rangers, those who could be as stealthy as they were lethal. Somehow, Wendel convinced Elsa we should be part of her force, and I think she agreed only for the opportunity to humiliate him. We trained alongside the veterans and did our best not to look like rank amateurs. Wendel succeeded more so than I, but I completed all the exercises. When we set out on our first official mission, we left through a fanfare that lined the streets of Mundleboro's capital city, Ravenhold.

"I'd thought Kenward and Wendel were the worst possible combination, but that was before I saw Wendel and Elsa fight together. They were brazen and reckless, taking careless risks that were just not necessary. Several good men were wounded in the first sortie, and the veterans chastised Wendel and Elsa for their foolish behavior. The journey back to Ravenhold, the ancestral home of Elsa's family, was downcast and subdued. Word of the events spread fast. Elsa's mother promptly bribed each member of Elsa's patrol to seek reassignment. Most accepted eagerly, not wishing to die while Elsa proved something to herself.

"Wendel refused the bribe, and he urged me to do the same. In the end, though, Elsa abandoned her service in the patrols. She said she wanted to be an independent ranger, a one-woman elite force. What Wendel did then was one of the stupidest things I've ever witnessed: he told her everything-- our entire story. I thought she'd have us hung, but she surprised me and was lured by the danger and excitement, especially the possibility of reclaiming ancient knowledge. It wasn't long before the three of us began our journey across the wilderness in search of clues.

"We wandered aimlessly from hamlet to farmstead, listening to legends and fireside tales, but we found nothing that struck us as significant. They were pleasant days for the most part, with the exception of the incessant bickering between Elsa and Wendel. I often wondered why two people who irritated each other so much would choose to spend their time together.

"Elsa was kind to me and never let me feel left out of conversations, but Wendel seemed to forget I existed. Elsa was beautiful and strong and high-spirited. She was exciting, and I fell in love with her. It wasn't something I did intentionally. I even made myself find things I disliked about her, but even her flaws endeared her to me. I was hopelessly smitten, and neither of them saw it. They were blind, and so was I," he said.

Catrin was lost in his story. She felt as if she were there with them, living through Benjin's memory.

"One night we sat around our fire discussing the Zjhon and their recent conquests, and Elsa told us of their strict religious beliefs. As they conquered new lands, they quoted spiritual doctrine and forced the people to join their faith or face death. Wendel realized the Zjhon scriptures could hold a treasure trove of clues, if only we could get a copy.

"Elsa said the common folk didn't have complete copies. They had to write them down or commit them to memory as sermons were read. The only places that had pristine copies were churches and the Masters' homes. Not satisfied with getting just any copy, Wendel and Elsa decided to steal one from the cathedral at Adderhold. They were convinced such a prestigious site would have a very old copy of the scriptures and, hopefully, one that had not been transcribed too many times.

"When we reached the hills along the shores of the Inland Sea, Elsa asked me to stay at camp and guard the horses, but I knew they really just didn't want me along. I could not deny her request and watched helplessly as they walked away, intent on sneaking into the Zjhon center of power to steal holy documents. I didn't think we'd escape the Greatland once such a high crime had been committed, knowing the Zjhon would be relentless in their search." Benjin stopped speaking long enough to drink from his mug. People shifted in their seats, but they waited quietly for him to continue his tale. He took a deep breath and began speaking again in a soft voice that some strained to hear.

"The alarm bells woke me the next morning. I hid in the hills and waited. After seven days, I nearly left. Patrols had been scouring the countryside, and I had to keep moving to avoid them, but still I waited, hoping they would return. One afternoon, as I was hunting in the hills, I saw a man stumbling through the narrow valley. It was Nat. Not the most pleasant company, for either of us, I suppose, but we waited two more days together.

"When Wendel and Elsa finally returned, they were all smiles. They were triumphant and ready for a pleasant journey home, but when we approached the Lankland border, we found it heavily guarded and patrolled. Wendel's plan was to simply act like we belonged there and march straight through the border check. 'Just act like you belong here and we'll be fine,' he said. 'The guards look tired and bored, so we'll just blend in with the other merchants.'

"I thought it was a terrible plan, but Elsa sided with Wendel again. Nat and I had to either play along or stay behind. Everyone else played their parts well, and I did my best to hide my fear, but my nervous sweating nearly gave us away. Wendel convinced the border guards I was sick, and they rushed us along so they would not catch my illness. When we made camp within a secluded patch of forest, Wendel and Elsa celebrated their victory. He swept her up in his arms, and then he kissed her," he said, looking as if every muscle in his body were contracting. His hands were balled into fists, and his back was hunched. Catrin hated to see him relive such a painful memory, but she supposed it was necessary.

"I was young and foolish and in love," he said with tears in his eyes. "I confronted them and told them I was in love with Elsa. She said nothing. She just stood with her hand over her mouth in shock. Wendel laughed. It was the final insult. I could take no more. Something inside me snapped, and I attacked him. I took out all my fears and frustrations on him. I beat him mercilessly. He landed blows of his own, but neither of us would give up the fight. Nat and Elsa separated us, and we scorned them for it.

"When it was all over, Elsa ran to Wendel's side. I was left with the sympathies of Nat. I ran as far and as fast as I could and never looked back. Eventually, I found my way to Kenward and negotiated passage back to the Godfist. We sailed to the Falcon Isles, where I was to board a smaller ship. Elsa and Wendel arrived in the Falcon Isles not long after, having posed as traders and traveled in luxury on a larger ship. We traveled back to the Godfist on the same, smaller ship. I avoided them. Elsa sought me out once, but I pushed her away. She was hurt, I know, but no more than I was.

"I avoided them still when we returned to the Godfist, and the news of Elsa's pregnancy burned my soul. It was not until her death that I chose to go see their child, and I've not been the same since. I hid in the trees and watched Catrin and Chase play in the mud. Catrin was a tiny and perfect little replica of Elsa; she stole my heart away." He glanced at Catrin with pain in his eyes. "I made amends with Wendel, and over time, we became friends again. I stayed close to him and kept my eyes on Catrin and Chase. We knew Elsa and Willa's deaths weren't natural despite the lack of any proof, and we were constantly alert for danger," he said, his voice hoarse.

Catrin was captivated by his tale but felt a terrible weight of responsibility. She could not help the pain brought by her resemblance to her mother, but she felt guilty nonetheless.

"There. I've told you the story and revealed many of my secrets. I've no more to say this night," Benjin said as he stood to leave. Kenward did not try to deter him. Instead, he dismissed everyone, saying they would meet again after they had sufficient time to reflect. Catrin was grateful for the respite, unsure she could take any more revelations this day. She retired to the quarters of a man who was on duty and fell asleep almost as soon as she was in the hammock.

* * *

In the dim lamplight, Strom looked much older, and when he spoke, there was something new in his voice, something Osbourne couldn't yet define.

"Listen, Osbo, I gotta know what you think. How are we ever going to be able to help Cat? We're powerless in all this. I'm no soldier or guard; I know how to stable horses, and you're a pig farmer."

"Without pig farmers, there'd be no bacon."

"Yeah, Osbo. I know. I do," Strom said under Osbourne's glare. "Lighten up."

"I don't know how to help Cat either," Osbourne said, feeling small and insignificant. "I don't know how to help any of us. I'm scared."

"Don't you worry, Osbo. Just stay with me; we'll figure out a way to have some fun before this is done."

"Now you're really scaring me," Osbourne said, his grin finally returning. "Your idea of fun usually ends up getting someone hurt."

"You only get hurt if you don't do it right," Strom said with a wink, and Osbourne sighed. "I guess, as far as helping Cat goes, we just do the best we can. Agreed?"

"Agreed."

"We better get some sleep. I've a feeling we're going to need it."

* * *

In the morning, they ate a quiet breakfast in the galley before Catrin and Benjin departed for the *Stealthy Shark*. Kenward waved as they climbed down to the boat. Catrin halfheartedly returned his wave.

The next two weeks passed slowly. The mood aboard both ships was somber and strained, despite making headway. The time spent in barren waters taxed their food supply, and they were down to minimal rations. Tired and overworked, they performed their tasks as best they could. Catrin checked on Chase regularly, and his condition continued to improve. Once he was no longer confined to his hammock, his recovery became more rapid.

"When we reach the Falcon Isles, you can finish healing and then return home," Catrin said as they stared out to sea.

"And leave you to have all the fun? I wouldn't wager on it," he said.

She shook her head. "We both know this is probably not going to end well. This may be your last chance to save yourself. I wouldn't blame you. There's much that needs to be done on the Godfist, and I wouldn't keep you from it," she persisted.

"Leave it be, Cat. I'm coming with you, and you'll like it. End of discussion," he said with a firm nod, and she let him win the battle.

"Nat will be staying in the Falcon Isles," she said, unsure what reaction to expect.

"How d'ya feel about that?" Chase asked, giving no indication as to how he felt about it.

"I wish him well, but I'm glad I won't be going to the Greatland alone," she said, and he simply nodded, apparently unwilling to say any more. Strom and Osbourne also insisted on continuing on to the Greatland and would not be dissuaded.

"Nat is doing the right thing," Benjin had said when she had spoken with him earlier that day. "Staying behind was probably the harder path to choose, and I think he truly fears for you more than he does for himself."

Catrin didn't know how to feel. Nat had his own circumstances and reality, but he had proven himself both brave and honorable, and she decided to believe he was making a sacrifice instead of seeing him as a deserter. She was still trying to decide what she would do upon her arrival in the Greatland when the lookout called from the crow's nest: "Land ho!"

"These are not populated isles," Bryn said. "There're hundreds of islands that make up the chain, but only the larger ones are inhabited, and these are among the most remote."

As they approached a small cluster of rocks that jutted from the sea, Catrin noticed several objects floating in the water. Kenward saw them as well, and he set a course that would take the *Eel* dangerously close to the rocks. The floating objects were actually large pieces of lightwood attached to something below the waves with coarse rope.

"Crab pots," Bryn said. "The local fishermen use colorful markings to indicate ownership," he added with a wink, and Catrin realized this was the message from Kenward's mother. Her thoughts were confirmed when Kenward contemplated the markings for a few moments before declaring their plans.

"We'll remain here until dark and hide in the shadows. Hopefully no one will spot us. Once night falls, we'll make our way to safe harbor to meet my mother's men," he told his crew, and his words were conveyed to the *Stealthy Shark*. Both crews took advantage of the downtime, and most sought food and drink. Their supplies were low, but with land in sight, they worried less. Others sought their hammocks. Catrin took the opportunity to arrange a meeting with Nat. Bryn rowed her to the *Slippery Eel*, and she found Nat in his cabin.

"I've spoken with the others, and we'll all be continuing on to the Greatland. I'm sorry to leave you alone," she began, and he nodded silently. "I have no specific tasks for you. You're free to do as you wish. If you find any way to help my cause, however, I expect you to act. Agreed?"

"Agreed. I've been thinking about staying in the Falcon Isles for a while. Things on the Godfist will be what they will be whether I'm there or not. Perhaps I can learn more here. To be honest, I find the thought of living where no one knows my past quite appealing."

"I hope you find happiness. Farewell, Nat Dersinger. Thank you for all you've done and endured. May fate be kind to you," she said with a sad smile.

"Thank you, Catrin. You are kind and gracious, may the light of Istra and Vestra shine on you," he said formally and bowed deeply. "Before we part, I have a gift for you. My father said there'd come a time when someone would have greater need of this than I, and I believe that time has finally come. My family has guarded this staff for ages untold. The knowledge of its origins has been lost to time, and I can only hope our efforts have not been in vain. May it support you when you need it most." He held his staff out to her, and she accepted it hesitantly.

"Thank you, Nat. I'll take good care of it," she said, not knowing what to say. As she held the staff in her hands, she noticed for the first time that the metal heel bore a subtle engraving of a serpent head with empty sockets for eyes. It was disconcerting to look upon, as if it were yearning for something.

"I must say a few more farewells--if you'll excuse me. May we meet again someday," Nat said, and she was glad they were able to part without ill feelings.

Catrin thanked each crewman individually for risking his or her life to save her and her companions then returned to the *Stealthy Shark* to visit with those who'd been her shipmates. Those who share such experiences are never forgotten; even if the names fade with the years, the mental images remain indelible.

When they raised anchor again, the skies were clear and a nearly full moon shone among the stars. Catrin saw no comets and sighed; disappointment filled her whenever she looked and did not find them. Oddly, they brought her comfort, and she missed the feeling of security they gave her. A part of her worried there would be no more comets, no more energy for her to revel in, but she pushed her fears aside. What would be would be, and worrying over it would do nothing but sour her stomach.

The crews of both ships demonstrated their abilities as they navigated the many small islands, sailing generally north and west, and eventually a large landmass emerged from the night. Into a narrow channel they sailed with only lanterns to light the way, and they followed it to a small, natural harbor. Catrin could see no sign of anyone else about until lanterns opened aboard several small boats that drifted along the shoreline. No one made a sound, and Catrin kept her mouth shut. She waited for some instructions from the *Slippery Eel*, while she assisted Bryn and the crew in dropping anchor as silently as they could. Afterward, Benjin helped her strap Nat's staff to her back so she could carry it with both hands free.

Kenward signaled with a lantern, and Bryn quietly ordered one of the small boats dropped. He guided Catrin and Benjin to the rail and told them to climb down. He sent some men to help Chase, and he followed them. While Chase struggled to climb down with one arm, Catrin sat in the boat, wondering what life would throw at her next. She was about to embark on an extended voyage to a massive, foreign land whose inhabitants considered her the enemy. As they approached the small gathering of boats, she wondered if her life would ever be normal again.

* * *

Osbourne sat in the boat with his knees pulled to his chest, wondering at how quickly his life had changed. What had always seemed permanent and unchangeable was gone in an instant, and now he wandered through a new and frightening world, one where childhood friends wielded devastating powers.

Still unable to find calm within the chaos of his mind, he clung to the hope that Catrin would always be Catrin deep down and would never become one of the monsters that haunted his dreams.

Chapter 5

Expectations can be surpassed only by the unknown.
--Mariatchi Omo, philosopher

* * *

The boats that awaited them were far smaller than those from the ships, and the climb from one to another was treacherous. Vertook nearly panicked as he stepped into the small boat and lost his balance. One man steadied him while others countered his movements in order to keep the boat from capsizing. Once those bound for the Greatland were aboard the small boats, they rowed into the narrow channels that snaked through the coastal marshes. Like a natural maze, there were many dead ends, but the experienced men navigated them without difficulty.

As they glided across the still waters, no one spoke--the need for stealth understood. Mists swirled above the water, and clouds of biting insects appeared from nowhere. Kenward motioned them to stay down and be quiet. Soon after, distorted voices echoed across the water, and lights backlit the reeds and marsh grasses. The channel emptied into a large harbor, where several ships were moored. One of the ships was the largest vessel Catrin had ever seen. Dwarfing even the Zjhon warships, it made the *Slippery Eel* look like a rowboat.

It was to this ship the men steered while trying to remain hidden. Deep shadows on the seaward side of the ship swallowed them. The ship stretched high above them. Once alongside it, the men laid down their oars, and a rope ladder dropped from above. Kenward silently instructed them to climb one at a time, sending Catrin up first.

The rope ladder twisted and turned in her hands as if it had a life of its own, but she made the climb quickly. The ladder took her to a small access door on the side of the ship, and she was glad she didn't have to climb all the way to the deck. Hands reached out and guided her into a lavishly furnished apartment. Her staff caught on the opening, and she struggled a moment to free it. Two men helped her in then tugged on the ladder. While the others took their turns climbing, Catrin explored the spacious quarters, wondering to whom they belonged. It was certainly finer accommodations than she and her companions expected.

Thick carpet, stitched in delicate patterns of flowers and birds, covered the floors. Unwilling to soil something so beautiful, Catrin removed her boots and walked around the room with them in her arms. Rich, hardwood doors lined two walls, each with an ornate brass knob. Another, smaller door stood on the inner wall. Elaborately carved tables and chairs dominated the interior. The chairs looked comfortable, covered with embroidered cushions of varied design, but Catrin was drawn to a set of shelves recessed into one wall.

There she found a marvelous treasure: books of every description. Leather-bound volumes with gilded titles and designs on their spines stood beside books bound in colorful cloth. One especially intriguing tome appeared to be bound in some sort of tree bark. Afraid to even touch the precious volumes for fear of damaging them, Catrin just stared in awe; she'd never seen so many books in one place. She heard the others as they entered the room, but she was engrossed in the titles of the volumes, many of which were in foreign languages. When she stood from examining the bottom rows, Kenward stood beside her.

"I'm sorry. I didn't mean to pry," she said. "I'm fond of books, and this is a wonderful collection."

"Think nothing of it. Those're here for your enjoyment during the long voyage. I fear you'll find the collection insufficient before your journey ends. Incidentally, you can put your boots on the carpet; it's not a problem," he said.

Still self-conscious, she took off her jacket and laid it on the floor, placing her boots atop it.

Kenward just chuckled and shook his head. He asked everyone to gather around. "Welcome aboard the *Trader's Wind*. This ship was designed specifically for the long journey between the Greatland and the Falcon Isles, and she's well provisioned. She's still being loaded with the bales of dried herbs that are her main reason for being here, but she should set sail within two or three days. We were fortunate the rains delayed the harvest, or we'd have come too late.

"These rooms will be your quarters for the next half a year, and I'm sure you'll tire of them, but your attendant will try to make your stay as comfortable as possible. You must not leave these quarters for any reason. There are many merchants and their men aboard this ship, and we can't guarantee everyone's loyalties," Kenward said.

Catrin was shocked to realize these elaborate quarters were reserved for her and her party; the others appeared impressed and pleased as well.

"You'll need to double up in the sleeping quarters, but you should find them well appointed. It's not often the *Trader's Wind* has this many discreet travelers in the same group," Kenward continued with a smirk. "I'll meet with my mother and then return with your attendant. I'm sorry she won't be able to come herself, but we must maintain secrecy. The captain is rarely alone, and it can be difficult for her to explain sudden trips belowdecks. I'm sure she'll arrange for a meeting during your journey. In the meantime, I assure you that you're in good hands."

After lighting a lantern, he left by the door that stood opposite the hatch; it opened into a dark and cramped hallway. He closed it behind himself, and they were left to get acquainted with their surroundings. The sleeping rooms were relatively large; each held two hammocks and a feather bed along with two wooden chests. They quickly picked their rooms. Catrin chose a room to share with Chase, and Strom and Osbourne selected another, which left private rooms for Benjin and Vertook.

The arrangement suited them all, and they were still standing around when Kenward returned since none of them was comfortable sitting on the furniture in their dirty clothes. Kenward knocked before entering and was followed by a shy-looking young man who did not raise his eyes.

"This is Pelivor," Kenward said and introduced the young man to each individual. Pelivor's smile was warm and friendly. When he was introduced to Catrin, he shook her hand, only then raising his eyes to hers.

"Pelivor is fluent in High Common and Zjhonlander, as well as the Old Tongue and High Script. He'll help prepare you to blend in once you reach the Greatland. He'll be your only contact with the crew and will visit you periodically to assist with any needs you may have," Kenward continued, and Pelivor nodded.

"I must leave you now; my duties await, but before I leave, I have joyous news. We got word that Fasha and some of her crew have survived and escaped during the destruction of the Zjhon fleet. The *Slippery Eel* will leave for the Godfist with the dawn, and we look forward to reuniting the *Stealthy Shark* with her crew. Her missive mentioned something about a group of fools stealing the *Shark*, but I'm sure she'll forgive you," he said with a mischievous grin. "May the winds be fair and your journey swift, and I hope we meet again someday." He finished with a bow, and Catrin gave him a kiss on his cheek before he could escape through the hatch. He smiled and waved farewell.

Pelivor was nervous and unsure of himself. He was slight of build and seemed to shrink under their scrutiny, but then he noticed Catrin's boots sitting on her jacket, and he seemed braver for the sudden remembrance of his duties.

"I'll bring basins for washing. There are various articles of clothing in the chests. I'll be happy to care for your garments. Just leave them in a pile after you've changed," he said, nodding and walking backward toward the door. He slipped out without another sound.

Within the chests, they found neat stacks of garments. Other than size, they were all very similar, made with a light, soft material Catrin could not identify, whose color ranged from white to tan. She raided the other chests for garments in her size, and she soon had an ample wardrobe stored in her chest. The others had similar success, but the search had left their quarters in disarray--the pristine cabin suddenly looked as if a storm had struck.

Catrin was just about to start cleaning up when Pelivor returned.

He carried four clay water basins, a large wooden pitcher, and a stack of soft, white towels. He nodded to Catrin over the towels as he set them down. She was impressed he managed it all in one trip, but the mess also embarrassed her. Pelivor's face registered no surprise, though. He immediately began folding and stacking the piles of clean garments. Catrin rushed to help him, but he seemed shocked.

"Please enjoy yourself. I'll just tidy these up. No need for you to bother with it. Would you like me to bring a washbasin into your room?" He walked to the basins, filled one, and questioned Catrin with his eyes as to which room she had chosen. He placed the washbasin in the room she indicated, handed her three soft towels, and returned to folding clothes.

The others, except Chase, who waited for Catrin to finish, were pouring water for themselves as she closed her door. It felt wonderful to get clean, and the moment of privacy was a luxury in itself. She took longer than she should have, but she felt refreshed and renewed when she finally emerged. Comfortable in her snug-fitting trousers and lightweight shirt, she had no more qualms about using the furniture.

"Thanks for being quick about it," Chase said with a twinkle in his eyes and a playful swat at her shoulder. Wrinkling her nose, she kept him at a distance. He smirked and went off to get clean.

Pelivor made several more trips, bringing them platters of fresh fruit, cheeses, and hard bread. Another trip yielded a case of the deep red wines favored by Kenward and his family. The rest of the evening was the most pleasant time Catrin had spent in far too long: she was clean and comfortable, her stomach was full, and she was relatively safe. The possibility of being discovered gave her some anxiety, but it seemed unlikely, and she put it from her mind.

Loaded with empty platters, Pelivor excused himself for the night, saying he would be back in the morning. No one said much for a while. They were content to relax or nap on the comfortable cushions and feather beds, though Chase said he had grown accustomed to the hammock and retired to their room.

* * *

Soon the novelty of leisure wore off, and the group began to systematically read all the books written in High Common. Catrin had been confused at first, having never heard the language she spoke given a name.

"Most nations speak High Common," Benjin said. "In the past, it was only the Zjhon who spoke Zjhonlander, but their influence has spread, and most people of the Greatland now speak both languages. Very few people understand the Old Tongue or High Script. Pelivor is quite a rarity."

Pelivor would accept no credit for his accomplishments. He would only say he was fortunate to have received a fine education. His self-effacing attitude annoyed Catrin. She could not stand to see such a bright and talented person think so little of himself, and she was determined to convince him of his self-worth. He seemed to sense her desire and was unnerved by it. She asked him pointed, personal questions and watched as he squirmed uncomfortably while attempting to formulate suitably humble responses.

Benjin and the others almost seemed to have sympathy for Pelivor, and they gave him advice on how to handle women. Their advice, however, seemed to disturb him more than Catrin's constant probing, and he often appeared to be fleeing as he departed their company, which seemed to amuse the men.

Catrin enlisted Pelivor's help in getting herbs for Chase. His shoulder still pained him, and Pelivor happily accepted the task. The next day he arrived with a special tea for Chase. Catrin would have preferred the herbs themselves, but she decided to trust Pelivor's judgment. However, she kept a close watch on Chase's condition just as a precaution.

"We should set sail by nightfall," Pelivor said on his next visit, and excitement rippled through the cabin. The journey ahead would be long, and everyone was anxious to be under way.

Pelivor became slightly bolder over time, and he spent most of his days helping them learn different languages. He concentrated on Zjhonlander, which Catrin found quite easy to learn. She made a mental mapping of each word in High Common and its Zjhonlander equivalent. It was easier for her to learn proper sentence structure, verb conjugation, and other linguistic nuances when she already knew many of the words and their meanings. Still, Pelivor insisted she learn to speak in three different ways, depending on where she was.

"There are many dialects and accents," he said. "If you wish to fit in wherever you go, you must not speak like a Southlander when in northern Mundleboro."

Before long, Catrin could speak passably with each accent, but some of the others struggled. While Pelivor worked more with them, Catrin picked up a book written in Zjhonlander but found it depressing. The other Zjhonlander books had a similar effect on her. They seemed to be written with the intention of making her feel inadequate and unimportant. More like propaganda than stories, they told her she should be thankful her betters were in control of her life and destiny.

One, in particular, raised her ire; it was among the newest and most recently written. On the cover, an embossed image portrayed Istra and Vestra in their immortal embrace. The now familiar symbol of the Zjhon triggered her initial anxiety, but the words within infuriated her, defying everything she'd ever been taught. Descriptions of the Statues of Terhilian made them sound as if they would be the salvation of mankind, if only they could be found. Everything Catrin had been taught about the statues portrayed them as terrifying weapons disguised as gifts from the gods.

"What do you know of the Statues of Terhilian?" she asked Pelivor, but he seemed hesitant to answer.

"I know very little about them," he said after a long pause, "but I know a great deal about what other people believe to be true. The statues are the source of the greatest and deadliest debate our kind has ever known. It would be presumptuous of me to offer any information as fact. Some believe the statues will destroy the world; others believe just as strongly they will save it. I remain unconvinced by either argument."

"Another unanswerable question," Catrin said as she put the book aside.

Disgusted with Zjhonlander writings, she convinced Pelivor to help her learn High Script. "In ancient times," he said, "the spoken language was much different from written language, and even in those days, High Script was understood by only a very small part of the population. We will concentrate on the written." He taught her how to form each of the symbols, and the sheer number of them, many of which were only slight variations of others, discouraged her.

"You mustn't make the strokes in the wrong direction; it distorts the character," Pelivor said as he watched over her shoulder. Over time, she came to see that it did.

It took much longer for her to grasp the intricacies of the archaic language, and many of the concepts seemed foreign to her, but she persisted nonetheless. Once she gained a rudimentary understanding of the language, she attempted to read books written in High Script, but they were confusing. Most contained accounts of family bloodlines and little else. Often, when she asked Pelivor what specific words meant, they were names of places, people, or families.

The books written in High Common were a luxury; most were tales of adventure and intrigue with happy endings. Nothing in them would help her prepare for the Greatland, though, so she pressed on with her studies.

Strom and Osbourne both gained passable knowledge of Zjhonlander, but Vertook steadfastly refused. He had tried at first, but no one spoke his native dialect; thus, it was much more difficult for him to learn. Catrin doubted Vertook would ever be mistaken for a native of the Greatland, and it probably didn't matter anyway. If they kept him disguised, perhaps he could be convinced to remain mute.

Boredom plagued the men. They didn't share her passion for books and needed some other way to occupy themselves.

"Any chance you could find us some dice?" Benjin asked Pelivor one afternoon.

"I suppose there's a chance. I'll make some inquiries on your behalf."

In the meantime, he brought a new stack of books for their entertainment; most were in High Common, but a few were in High Script. Those in High Common were soon divided among the others, and Catrin supposed more ancient lineage wouldn't kill her. She picked up a badly faded and ancient-looking tome and was pleasantly surprised to find it actually told a story.

It was an impossibly difficult text to translate, and she often had to read a passage several times before she had even a cursory understanding of what it meant. Even when she thought she made sense of something, she wondered if she weren't misinterpreting it. Based on her best guesses, she surmised that there had been two warring factions: the Om and the Gholgi, and the Gholgi were very powerful. Some passages seemed to indicate that the Om were forced to live underground in order to avoid the Gholgi. This confused Catrin, and she was almost certain she was reading something incorrectly, but she continued, hoping to find something to confirm or deny her assumptions.

"What do these two words mean?" she asked Pelivor.

"I don't know what Gholgi means. I apologize for my ignorance. This book is from the captain's personal collection, and it is probably the oldest text I have ever seen. Based on the ancient form of High Script, I suspect this is a relatively recent transcription of a much older work. Some of the words it contains may have never been translated before or may have no translation. The other word you asked about, Om, could be similar to Ohma, which means men."

"That makes no sense either, unless the men were fighting women. Perhaps Gholgi is the word for woman," she said.

"I doubt that. Uma is the more modern form of woman. Perhaps the old form was Um," he speculated, and Catrin scanned the pages in hopes of confirming his guess. She was almost disappointed to find the word Um used later in the text since that bit of conjecture only made the rest of the puzzle appear more complex.

The further she read, the more confused she became, and she eventually set the book aside in frustration. Pacing the cabin relentlessly, she was like a caged animal. She needed answers, not guesses, but all she had were feelings and assumptions. Her confinement became like a tangible thing; it trapped her and prevented her from getting the answers she sought. She knew, deep inside, it wasn't true, but frustration overwhelmed her good sense. She stewed in her uncertainty and anxieties until she worked herself into a frenzied state. The men seemed to sense the rising storm, and they exchanged glances, as if wondering where she would strike.

Fears and concerns overwhelmed her, and she realized not all of the worry was hers. She could sense the others, and their moods were influencing hers. And she wondered if she could remain sane while trapped with so much emotion in what now seemed like small quarters.

Pelivor broke the tension when he brought dried fruits and walnuts soaked in maple syrup. Everyone gathered around him and sampled the unexpected treats. The mood lightened, and soon they laughed while licking their fingers. Chase and Strom told tall tales along with more than a few true tales, and Pelivor laughed so hard he nearly choked. Chase patted him on the back, and as soon as he was breathing again, they launched into a series of humorous anecdotes that nearly killed the young man.

Vertook surprised everyone when he told the tale of an adventure with his horse, Al Jhadir. He was somber at first, and Catrin could sense his pain, but she was also glad to know Al Jhadir's name; she would never forget him.

He said that he and Al Jhadir were once caught in a tremendous sandstorm, a storm so terrible, his love feared for his life. They limped back to camp barely alive and bearing a mighty thirst. The first thing they came upon to drink were jugs of whiskey. Laughing so hard that tears ran down his face, he had trouble finishing his tale. He finally managed to tell them that he and his horse nearly drank themselves to death, and his lover threatened to leave him after she found him passed out, his arms around Al Jhadir. Pelivor fell from his chair laughing.

The sight of Pelivor enjoying himself lightened Catrin's soul, as she felt somewhat responsible for his new confidence. It was Chase, though, who sent Pelivor over the edge. His rendition of their trip through the marshes sent Pelivor into fits. Even those who had endured those trials found Chase's comical reenactment too humorous to resist. When Chase got to the part about Strom realizing he had mistakenly used the leaves of a poison plant for personal purposes, Pelivor's eyes grew very large and he covered his mouth. He could not make a sound as he pointed and stared at Strom, tears streaming down his cheeks.

Claiming his stomach hurt from all the laughing, Pelivor excused himself, and they were all sorry to see him go. His mood had been infectious, and they all felt better for it. The silence he left behind seemed to lend itself to quiet reflection, and Catrin found herself reviewing many of the good times in her life. The silence held as if everyone in the room were enamored with it, and Catrin wondered who would finally break the spell.

All of them nearly jumped from their skins when there came a loud knock on the door just before it opened. A motherly looking woman gracefully entered the room and addressed them. "Greetings, friends. I'm Nora Trell, captain of the *Trader's Wind*. I welcome you aboard, even if it is a bit late," she said as she looked each of them over, and she smiled brightly when she got to Benjin. "Ah, so there's a storm cloud aboard one of my ships again. Benjin, you scoundrel, it's good to see you again."

Benjin approached her, and they exchanged a brief hug.

"This one nearly let my Kenward and your father get him killed," she said while pinching Benjin's cheek and arching her eyebrows at Catrin. "Kenward has said many a time that sailing with Benjin was like sailing with a thunderhead. I'm guessing it's still true," she said and laughed as Strom and Osbourne nodded vigorously in agreement. Benjin shot them a good-natured scowl, but Nora looked at Benjin seriously. "I still owe you a debt, Benjin Hawk, for helping to keep my fool son afloat. I would repay that debt now," she said, and she pulled a small bag from within her stout robe.

An assortment of brightly colored dice rolled out when she emptied it onto one of the tables. Benjin sucked in a breath, for these were not ordinary dice; each one was carved from a different type of gemstone, and they sparkled in the light. The faces of each die bore detailed designs, along with the etched value of that face. They ranged from four to eighteen sides, with several variations of each. Catrin didn't know the value of the stones themselves, but each of them was a work of art. Gauging by Benjin's reaction, she guessed they were very valuable indeed.

"It's too much, Captain Trell. I cannot accept such a generous gift, even if it is in the exact form I desired. I thank you, though."

"Nonsense," she replied. "I insist you take them, as they are not for you alone. Miss Catrin saved the *Slippery Eel* in rather spectacular fashion, I'm told. I hope to repay part of that debt this day and satisfy my curiosity. I'm not certain I wish to see anyone rip the clouds from the sky, as Kenward described your attack on the Zjhon, but the description creates a vivid image. He's an excitable boy, and he tends to exaggerate, but he seemed sincere in this?" she said, making the statement a question and looking at Catrin for confirmation.

"I wouldn't have used those words, but I cannot say his description is inaccurate," Catrin replied as humbly as she could. Benjin and the others nodded in agreement, and Nora was duly impressed.

"Truly powerful indeed," she said. "You have your mother's look about you. I hope you have a more conservative disposition than she did, given the power you wield." Captain Trell seemed to realize how harsh her words sounded. "I'm sorry, my dear; that was insensitive of me. Sometimes I forget when I'm not speaking to a member of my crew. Please forgive me. Your mother was a lovely young woman, and I was very sorry to hear of her passing."

Catrin nodded in silent acceptance of the apology.

Captain Trell broke the uncomfortable hush and changed the subject by asking Catrin if she had been able to read the books she sent with Pelivor. Catrin was downcast as she admitted she had grown frustrated with the old book, but Nora was sympathetic.

"Don't let it bother you. I've had several scholars examine that book, and they could tell me very little about it. Mostly they said the writings were so old, they were written in a language that preceded High Script. I cannot remember what they called it now," Nora said, and she looked thoughtful as she shuffled through her memories. "It was a long time ago, but I believe one scholar thought this book told of the discovery of the Greatland."

Catrin was unsure what good the information would do her, as she doubted she would ever be able to fully translate it, but she tucked the knowledge away.

* * *

In a tangle of vines, Nat's long knife became wedged. Sweat dripped into his eyes while he yanked on the handle, trying to pull the blade free. Frustrated and tired, he prepared for a final yank when a hand rested on his shoulder.

Neenya moved his hand from the handle and stepped in front of him. Taking the handle, she moved it up and down as she pulled, and it soon slid free.

"Thank you, Neenya," Nat said, letting her, once again, take the lead. Her long knife seemed to sail through the undergrowth, but when he had tried to lead, he found it impossible to do. Neenya was a gift from the gods.

Among the villagers, he was seen as something special. It was impossible to know what it was they really thought since he did not understand their language, and even worse, none would dare speak to him. Even the village elders would only nod, shake their heads, or point. When they pointed, they almost always pointed to the same place: a high peak on the far side of the island, which was often obscured by clouds. It was there Neenya would take him.

As soon as Nat had shown the slightest interest in reaching that mountain, Neenya had stepped forward and the elders rushed them to start their journey. Since then, Neenya had been leading him deeper into the jungle, and Nat began to wonder if he would leave it alive. Snakes, lizards, and even frogs were threats here. Whenever a threat was near, Neenya would make a sharp hissing sound and point.

Despite the danger, Nat did want to see what the villagers thought was so important about this mountain. Something was there, waiting for him. Whenever they gained a clear view of that narrow yet majestic spire, he would stand in awe, overwhelmed by a feeling of anticipation.

Nat found himself staring at the still distant mountain and realized he'd stopped again. Neenya had continued to clear a path through the underbrush, and he jumped at the sound of her sharp hiss.

Chapter 6

Wager your coin only when you know something the rest do not.
--Hidi Kukk, gambler

* * *

Captain Trell's gifts provided days of entertainment; Benjin taught them to play a game known as pickup. He drew a grid on the back of a piece of leather and drew a number in each square. Players put their bets on the squares they wanted, and the dice would be rolled. They used a combination of dice whose maximum was equal to the number of squares on the grid, which made every roll a potential winner. If the number you bet was rolled, then you got all the bets on the grid.

The group had very little in the way of coinage, which made it difficult for them to play, but Pelivor solved their problem. He brought them a long strip of rawhide that he said they could cut up and use as pretend coinage. The idea was an instant success, and Pelivor even joined them for a few games. Benjin was an experienced player, and he tried to teach them the nuances of the game. Each player could bet more than one square per roll, but no more than one coin per square. They took turns placing bets until everyone passed on their chance to bet or until the grid was full.

The game could be frustrating at times; especially when they could not remember who had placed bets on which squares, but they had fun learning.

"Many places in the Greatland have elaborate pickup tables with colored betting chips for each player that make it much easier to keep track of, but this is better than boredom by far," Benjin said, to which they all agreed.

Catrin played on occasion, but most of the time she returned to her book, which she now thought was entitled *Men Leave*. This at least made sense given what the captain knew of the book. Even with the additional knowledge, she had few revelations. The latter part of the book seemed to describe the shipbuilding process, but she was unsure, and there were no illustrations to help her. The information Captain Nora provided was inconclusive, and Catrin began to wonder if it was influencing her attempts at translation. Perhaps, she thought, she had been better off before finding out what someone else thought the book was about. At the times when she could no longer take the frustration, she talked with Pelivor or played pickup with the men.

Her games of pickup grew fewer as the intensity of the games began to increase. Benjin was no longer the most experienced player, and Vertook surprised them all by consistently winning. They asked him how he won so often, and he always gave them the same obtuse reply: "Patterns." This answer served only to infuriate the rest of them, as they sought to see these magical patterns Vertook used to beat them. Each time they played, they were more determined to win, and they demanded rematch after rematch, even after he had taken all their bits of rawhide numerous times.

"What do you mean by 'patterns'?" Catrin asked when she cornered him one day.

He just shrugged. "Patterns all around, but you must learn to see them. Some things more likely than others, and when one pattern happens, probably not happen again. Patterns not always right, but better than no patterns."

Catrin was not sure she understood his logic, but she began looking for patterns in everything, as Vertook suggested, and in many ways, she found confirmation of his words, not the least of which was his obscene winning streak. Despite her efforts to duplicate his feat, she was never able to see the patterns in relation to pickup, as Vertook did.

* * *

When they were near the end of their ocean journey, Pelivor brought them a large map of the Greatland that he rolled out onto one of the tables.

"Captain Trell wishes to know your desired destination, as she needs time to make the arrangements for the final leg of your journey. She does not recommend you land at New Moon Bay; the security will be tight, and you would stand a good chance of being discovered. It would not be the first time the *Trader's Wind* has been searched from top to bottom before being allowed to enter port."

The months aboard the ship had dulled the group's sense of urgency and allowed them to become complacent. Catrin had been able to forget some of her fears and anxieties, while the seclusion and comfort had fostered the illusion of security. With the map in front of them and the decision upon them, the thin veil of perceived safety vanished. Catrin trembled as a sense of foreboding weighed on her until she thought she would be crushed. Her eyes rested on the soft clothing she wore, and she felt the need to regain her edge and vigilance.

Determined to completely shatter the illusion, she excused herself, retreating to her quarters to don her leathers and homespun. Pelivor had cared for them well, and her garments were in considerably better condition than when she arrived. Her borrowed garments had been designed specifically for comfort, and Catrin found her utilitarian clothing rough and binding in comparison. The effect helped to remind her of the seriousness of her situation, and she visibly shifted her posture and attitude. The effect was not a complete regression to that which she had been before boarding the *Trader's Wind*, though; her new persona was better educated, more confident, and better mentally prepared.

When she returned to the common area, she found the atmosphere completely changed. Gone were the reclining figures garbed in white and tan; in their place, she found adventurers. The abrupt shift appeared to unnerve Pelivor, and he looked as if he were surrounded by predators. Catrin could understand his unease; she, too, was disquieted by those who paced the apartments like angry beasts, despite being one of them. Her attempt to reassure Pelivor came out as a shrill demand that he not look so meek. He seemed uncertain of how to respond and quickly excused himself.

Benjin was the first to speak. "We'd best prepare ourselves for the rigors that await us. This journey has provided respite and opportunity for recuperation, but it's also softened us. Let's approach our next decision with wisdom as well as caution. Let's discuss the best possible place to disembark the *Trader's Wind* as well as our ultimate destination. Let us consider our decisions well before we act," Benjin said, and his formal words struck their hearts.

Catrin nodded and joined the somber group around the map.

Benjin produced the bag of dice and poured a few into his hand. He placed them strategically on the map. The dice were a perfect metaphor for Catrin but one that struck too close to the truth for comfort. She imagined the dice rolling, her fate decided by patterns she failed to perceive. Benjin looked thoughtful and placed one last die on the map.

"I've marked these locations for a number of reasons. On the southeastern tip of the Greatland, we have Drascha Stone, one of the oldest Cathuran strongholds. We could land on the southern tip of Mundleboro and travel east to Drascha Stone. Far to the north, in the Northern Wastes, there is Ohmahold--thought to be the first stronghold on the Greatland. It's remote and surrounded by deep snow for much of the year.

"There are other, less significant Cathuran outposts in the remote parts of Sylva and the Westland," he said, motioning to the three smaller dice. "We'll be approaching the east coast, and traveling all the way to the west coast by ship would be risky. The Southland and Mundleboro have been occupied for only a few years, and the Zjhon influence has less hold there, but the southern coasts are brutally hot. Landing on the shores of the Southland would be difficult, as there are several key ports along the peninsula, and that area will likely be patrolled heavily."

"What about landing along the Northern Wastes or northern Endland? That would make for a relatively short journey to Ohmahold," Chase asked.

"Endland is densely populated, and the Northern Wastes are aptly named; they are barren and lifeless, and they can be deadly to cross.

Autumn is nearly upon us, and the winter snows will soon cover the Wastes. I think we'll be best served by going south to Drascha Stone," Benjin replied.

After much deliberation, it was agreed that Benjin's plan was the most sound. His knowledge of this foreign land was far greater than what Catrin and the others possessed. When Pelivor returned, Captain Trell accompanied him. She greeted them briefly before getting straight to the point. "Where will you go?"

Benjin looked as if he would speak, but Catrin beat him to it. "We'll travel to the southern coast of Mundleboro, presuming the arrangements can be made."

"Your choices are few, and all of them dangerous, but I assume you are well aware of that. My options are limited in these dire circumstances, and I'm afraid your accommodations will be much less comfortable from here. There's a ship that should do this deed for me since her captain owes me his skin, but he is not the most trustworthy fellow. You are certain of your course, are you not? I'll not be able to change these arrangements once they are set. Please consider your options wisely. I'll send Pelivor for your answer on the morrow," Captain Trell said before she left.

None of them came up with a better plan, despite hours of contemplation, and on the next day, they gave Pelivor confirmation of their desires. Catrin had hoped she would feel better once the decision was made, but instead she found her anxiety increasing. Life was about to start moving at full speed once again, and she was afraid she'd lost her stride--if she had ever truly had it.

The months spent in close quarters had taken their toll. It seemed the group had run out of things to say, and each moment seemed to drag on. Having been reminded of the dangers ahead, Catrin and the others dearly wished to just get on with it.

Three days later, Pelivor brought them a large meal and word to prepare to change ships. "Your passage was difficult to secure, but Captain Trell bribed a mercenary ship to carry you to Mundleboro. The *Nightfist* should arrive after midnight. I'll let you know when they are prepared to receive you," he said then excused himself. He returned a short while later laden with packs, bedrolls, and a rather large coin purse. "Compliments of Captain Trell. She sends you luck."

Benjin accepted the gifts and weighed the purse in his hand. He looked as if he wanted to return it, to say it was too much, but then he seemed to swallow his pride. Catrin was glad he mastered himself. They would need coin during their travels, and now she had one less worry.

"You may keep the clothes that fit you, and I'll be happy to pack them if you wish," Pelivor said.

"Thank you," Catrin replied. "That is a generous gift, and we'll gladly accept it, but we can pack them. It'll give us something to occupy our idle hands." Thinking about the journey ahead, she could not decide if she was more excited or terrified; the two emotions churned in her gut, and she began to feel ill. A big part of her wished to stay aboard the *Trader's Wind* and hide for the rest of her life, but she knew she could not.

Chase and Strom tried to appear confident, but they could not hide their trepidation from her; she could feel the anxiety radiating from them. Her senses had become more attuned to her companions during the long voyage, and she felt much closer to them all, if not too close. She could sense that Benjin was reliving old and painful memories, and Vertook was terrified of boarding a smaller ship again, but she could also sense his desire to reach dry land.

"Get some sleep while you still can," Benjin said. "We'll want to be well rested when we board the *Nightfist*."

While Catrin agreed, she found it impossible to sleep. Knowing she was not alone in her insomnia did nothing to console her. When Pelivor finally arrived, Catrin yawned and had trouble keeping her eyes open. The rush of excitement had worn off, and she was drained and exhausted. Cursing herself for not sleeping while she could, she pulled herself from the comfortable chair and watched as the others rose no more quickly.

"I want to thank you all for your kindness during this journey," Pelivor said. "Thank you for including me in your games and storytelling. I enjoyed it very much. Captain Trell sends her thanks as well." Pelivor presented each of them with a gift. His gifts were simple, but the thought behind them was without price. To Vertook he gave a carving of a horse; the mighty steed it depicted was in full stride with its mane and tail flying in the wind. Vertook marveled over it and shocked Pelivor by embracing him in a bear hug.

When Pelivor turned to Strom, he produced a small canvas painted with brightly colored depictions of several plants. "This canvas can be used safely in an emergency," he said with a straight face, "but the plants drawn on it should be avoided." Strom flushed, but when Pelivor cracked a smile, he laughed aloud.

Next, Pelivor made his way to Chase and presented him with a small herb kit, complete with notes on which herbs to use for various ailments. "I hope your shoulder heals well, but in the meantime, this should help," he said, and Chase thanked him for the generous gift, shaking his hand firmly.

Osbourne clearly didn't know what to expect, and Pelivor had a sly smile on his face as he approached. He handed Osbourne a small stone vial filled with clear liquid. "This perfume is guaranteed to win the affections of any woman who smells it," Pelivor said loudly. Osbourne flushed and looked extremely uncomfortable. Catrin asked for a sniff, and Osbourne quickly but carefully stashed the vial in his pocket. Catrin laughed, and Pelivor winked at her.

Benjin stood with his arms crossed and stared down his nose at Pelivor, managing to look somewhat imposing. Pelivor hesitated for a moment.

"You deserve whatever you get, Benjin Hawk," Catrin said, "especially after the way you teased him about women."

Benjin let a small smile play across his face but maintained a defensive posture. Pelivor presented him with a hand-painted pickup grid. The lines were precisely drawn and the text beautifully penned. "Thank you, Pelivor. You are kind," Benjin said, patting him on the back.

Catrin wondered what Pelivor could possibly have for her. His smile was bold and impish as he moved to stand before her. "There are three gifts for you," he said then walked to the bookshelves, where he located the books Captain Trell had sent for her. The last item he held was a satchel that consisted of wax-coated layers of leather. He placed the books in the water-resistant case and handed them to Catrin. "The captain insists you take these. She only asks that you inform her of anything you learn of them. The last gift is from me," he said, and his face flushed. He hesitated for a moment but then seemed to realize this was his last opportunity. He put his arm around Catrin's waist, dipped her back, and kissed her firmly on the lips.

The others had to suppress their laughter and hooting for fear of making too much noise at such a crucial time, but the moment would never be forgotten. Catrin was befuddled by Pelivor's kiss, and she was speechless when he stood her back up. He ran his hand across her lower back as he released her, and she felt a chill run down her spine. Weak-kneed, she waited to see what would happen next.

Pelivor walked away without another word, opened the exterior hatch, and secured and unrolled the rope ladder. Catrin dreaded climbing out of the hatch backward, especially with her staff slung across her back, but she set her jaw and prepared herself. Pelivor helped her climb out into the darkness, and she groped in the air with her toes, trying to locate the next rung. It was a frightening climb, but she reached the boat that waited below. Her eyes were slow to adjust to the darkness, and she could not make out any details of the men in the boat. No one spoke a word.

Each of her companions made their stealthy descent, and Catrin was pleased to note that Chase had little trouble with his climb, though he was out of breath when he reached the boat. He had healed well, and now he could regain his stamina.

The sound of the oars stroking the water gave an eerie quality to their mute departure, and it felt like a dream. Catrin gazed back at the *Trader's Wind* and would always recall the memories of their journey with fondness, but she feared what lay ahead. The path before her was perilous and filled with uncertainty. She tried to harden herself in preparation.

The *Nightfist* appeared, at first, as a shadowy silhouette that became more solid and distinguishable as they approached. It looked dark and oily, and it gave Catrin the shivers. The crew dropped a boarding net that Catrin and the others climbed easily. The rough and mean-looking men on deck were no friendlier than those in the boat. Most wore vicious sneers on their faces. Several of them eyed Catrin in a way that made her very uncomfortable, and she was relieved when a man stepped forward, grunted at them, and motioned for them to follow him. He led them to a room that resembled a cell more than it did a cabin.

Catrin entered the dark room with trepidation and was grateful when Benjin refused to allow the man to close the door behind him. They were left alone, cabin door slightly ajar. Two benches were the only items in the room, but she and the others made themselves as comfortable as they could. Chase, Strom, and Osbourne unrolled their bedrolls and rested on the floor. Benjin and Vertook sat, leaning against the walls, and Catrin reclined on one of the benches. Eventually Vertook moved to the other bench and slept.

"I don't trust these men," Benjin said. "I'll be much happier when we've parted company. I'll keep watch if you want to sleep."

Catrin tried to remain vigilant, but her eyes drooped with exhaustion as the subtle motions of the ship lulled her.

* * *

The ship's movements became abrupt, disrupting Catrin's sleep, and she nearly rolled off the bench as the ship executed a full turn. Benjin and the others felt it as well and were soon on their feet. Opening the door, which had slammed shut, Benjin peered into the darkness, and Catrin worked her way to his side, but all she saw were furtive shadows sliding in and out of the darkness. Whatever the crew was up to, they were doing it in utter silence.

Benjin tapped Catrin on the shoulder and pointed to the south. It took her a moment to spot the distant lights, but then she saw a great many as the ship crested a swell. Benjin closed the door and motioned for everyone to gather around.

"There are Zjhon ships to the south. I'm guessing the *Nightfist* will head to open water and try to skirt the patrols. Our current course argues against that logic, but I may be disoriented," he said, and they had to put their faith in the strange men who controlled their fate.

The hours passed in excruciatingly slow fashion; each moment seemed endless as they waited in silence. Catrin wanted to go out on deck to assess the situation, but the mercenaries had made it quite clear that she and her companions were not welcome there.

In the last hours before dawn, the man Catrin presumed was the captain entered the cabin and motioned for them to follow. When they reached the rails, a couple of the crewmen laughed, leering at Catrin, but she concentrated on their surroundings. A rocky shoreline, where waves pounded against jagged formations, was visible in the distance. She looked down, expecting to see a boat waiting below, but instead she saw only dark water lapping against the *Nightfist*. She screamed as hands grabbed her from behind, lifting her from the deck. They groped her everywhere at once, and she heard her companions shouting. Hands pulled at her staff, but it was held fast by the straps around it.

In a sudden panic, she tried to draw on her powers, but she was not quick enough. After a sudden thrust, she fell with a shrill scream, plunging into the water. Others hit the water as she regained the surface, and she wiped her eyes just in time to see Benjin land a solid blow on the captain's nose before he leaped over the railing.

Vertook was Catrin's first concern; he could not swim, and she feared he would panic. Her fears were confirmed by the loud splashing noises he made as he thrashed in the water. Hampered by the weight of the staff, she reached him shortly after Strom and Benjin did. Vertook landed several solid blows on his would-be rescuers before they could get him to stop flailing. Benjin assured him he would not let him drown, and Vertook went limp in his arms.

Chase swam ahead with an awkward stroke and looked for a safe place to gain the beach. Though he slipped several times on the algae-covered rocks, he found a relatively clear path. Vertook was overjoyed when they reached shallow water and he could feel the sand beneath his feet. Benjin appeared glad to have the large man supporting his own weight again. Slowly they made their way across the treacherous rocks.

When they reached the sand, Catrin sat down, trying to contain her anger. How dare those men just dump them in the water?

"I don't know about the rest of you, but I always feel refreshed after a good swim," Chase said in an effort to lighten the mood; Vertook threw sand at him.

Chapter 7

We appreciate most that which we have lived without.
--The Pauper King

* * *

Shivering as the wind chilled her wet clothes, Catrin walked along the rocky beach in miserable silence, still stewing over the way the mercenaries had dumped them in the water--and not even at their desired destination. They'd given no explanation and had afforded them no indication of where they actually were.

"I believe we're in northern Endland. Perhaps a day or two walk from the Wastes," Benjin said. "We've little choice now but to brave the snows and make for Ohmahold. The lands to the south are too heavily populated for us to cross safely."

Ohmahold was by far the closest Cathuran stronghold if he were correct about their current location, and no one could argue his logic. They trudged along the coastline, covering as much distance as they could before sunrise, knowing they needed to be away from inhabited lands before the sun rose or they would almost certainly be discovered. Catrin had known the comforts of the *Trader's Wind* would soon be behind them, but she hadn't expected such an abrupt return to the world of cold and wet.

The sun rose on the weary group, and the mountains of the Northern Wastes loomed in the distance. The land became progressively steeper as the rolling hills grew in size.

"We'll need to turn inland eventually, but I think we should go as far north as we can first," Benjin said, but then he stopped as if just remembering something. He patted his belt and jacket then began to curse. "Boil me. What a fool I am. Now I understand what all the fuss was about when we were thrown overboard. It was a distraction. The coin Captain Trell gave us is gone--thieving sons of jackals. Now we have only the small amount I kept in a separate purse."

Catrin's opinion of the mercenaries sank even lower, and she vowed to inform Captain Trell of their treacherous actions.

In the midafternoon Chase spotted sails on the horizon. Fearing they had been seen, Benjin urged them into the hills, but the ship continued along its course. They skirted the hills for the rest of the day, walking until it grew dark, and they were exhausted by the time they finally struck camp. They ate some salted fish, decided who would take each watch, and those not on watch fell quickly to sleep.

Late in the night, Benjin walked to where Chase and Catrin slept. He woke them gently for their watch, but as he stood, he froze. "Be alert," he whispered. "I see a fire through the trees. I'm going to check it out. You two stay here. If anything goes wrong, wake the others."

"Take Chase with you," Catrin said.

"It'll be better if I go alone. I won't be long. Stay here," Benjin said, and he disappeared into the night. Catrin and Chase took up posts at either end of their camp, and Vertook stood watch with them, apparently awakened by his instincts.

"I sleep when Benjin returns," he said.

Catrin jumped when she heard a sharp snap in the woods, but nothing emerged from the darkness, and other noises followed, leaving the sentries on edge. When Benjin did return, he did so silently, which startled Catrin as much as the noises had. It wasn't that she was surprised by his stealth; it was just that seeing a figure suddenly materialize from the darkness could give one quite a start.

"There're two monks camped a few hills over, but they're in a drunken stupor, and I didn't want to frighten them. Better to approach them in the morning. Perhaps they can help us on our journey to Ohmahold," he said in a whisper then retired to his bedroll.

Vertook seemed satisfied and went to his bedding as well, leaving Catrin and Chase to keep watch. The rest of the night was uneventful, but they were vigilant nonetheless. Benjin rose before the false dawn and woke those who slept.

"During the night we discovered two monks camped nearby, and I'm going to go speak with them. Chase, come with me; the rest of you, stay here. Remember that we're in hostile territory; remain alert. I don't know if anyone else frequents this area, but we can't be too careful."

"Hurry back," Catrin said, the suspense gnawing at her. She had spent her entire watch wondering if the monks would be friendly. Her recent luck caused her to fear the worst possible outcomes, and she envisioned a thousand different ways things could go wrong. Strom and Vertook paced with her, expressing their own helplessness with muttered curses.

As the sun rose, its warmth raised a heavy mist from the ground, which concealed the irregularities of the land and made the act of pacing difficult. Catrin nearly lost her footing a number of times, but she couldn't seem to stand still. The mist had dissipated by the time Benjin and Chase returned; they looked relieved but not ecstatic.

"They're friendly," Benjin said. "Their names are Gustad and Milo. I'd never met either of them before, but we have a common acquaintance. Many years ago, while searching for Kenward, I met a Cathuran monk named Gwendolin. She was gathering and researching some rare herbs that grow only in remote parts of the Southland, and I shared her interest in herb lore. She helped me a great deal, and I shared some of my knowledge with her. Gustad said Gwendolin is at Ohmahold, which should help our cause. He was reluctant to discuss her, which I suppose is natural; the Cathurans are a secretive lot.

"There's one other thing, though. The monks came here to gather materials for something they are working on. They've got far more than they can carry, and they seem to have lost their mule. They were going to make several trips, but they dallied too long, and the first winter storm could strike at any time. Since we just happened to be destined for Ohmahold as well, I, um, volunteered us to help carry the materials." He looked as if he were prepared for a negative reaction, but everyone agreed it would be worth the effort to have the aid of the monks. Catrin was just glad someone was willing show them the shortest way to Ohmahold.

After breaking camp, they hiked to the where the monks waited. The distance passed quickly in the daylight, and the camp soon came into sight. Catrin was shocked to see two of the dirtiest men she had ever encountered, surrounded by more than a dozen large, leather bags. Each man was completely covered in soot and ash, and their eyes stood out in stark contrast. The bags themselves were filthy with accumulated ash, and every step stirred small clouds. A bowl of land cradled the remains of an enormous fire, much of which still smoldered.

"We must put out the fire before we can leave," one said to the other as they approached.

"Yes, I suppose we must. Tiresome work, I say. Tiresome indeed. I'm grateful fate has afforded us some helpers."

"Brother Gustad, Brother Milo, allow me to introduce my companions," Benjin said, and he introduced each of them in turn. The monks placed both hands around the hand of each person they met. It was a show of honor, but the black stains left behind lessened the effect. It didn't take long, though, until those minor stains were of little consequence. Almost immediately, Gustad began issuing orders.

"Empty the bags of dried sand into a pile, refill the bags with sand or dirt and dump it on the fire. Repeat, until we can walk over this area. Don't empty the bags filled with ash, only those filled with sand," he barked, and Catrin was taken aback by his manner, but the monks were not lazy. They worked alongside the rest, dumping the dry sand in a tidy, cone-shaped pile. Armed with empty bags, they sought more sand, but the soil around the camp was covered with grass, and the beach was on the other side of a steep hill.

Dry sand was lighter than wet, but it was hard to find on the saturated coast, and damp was the best Catrin could find by her second trip. Gustad attempted to carry water back to the fire, but his bag leaked and he had only about a third of what he'd started with by the time he reached the fire.

Steam rose into the air as the coals hissed and snapped, but his efforts covered only a small area, and he went back for more sand.

"Maybe next time you could build your fire pit a little closer to the water," Strom said, his tone dripping with sarcasm, but he could not have known the debate it would spark.

"Would take longer to get the fire started out in the wind," Gustad said.

"Less cover in case of a storm," Milo said before Gustad even finished.

"We wouldn't have to sleep by the fire."

"The tide could put out the fire for us."

"Before we're done. What good is wet ash?"

"Might be better if we made ash bricks while it's wet."

"Sand would contaminate the ash."

The argument continued and transcended human understanding. The monks loudly and simultaneously expressed strong opinions on the merits and flaws of moving the fire pit. It wasn't that they ignored one another while they spoke; it was a barrage of verbal communication that only they appeared to fully understand. Feeding off one another, they spoke ever more rapidly. Each statement made by one influenced the next statement made by the other, and somehow they seemed to keep track of everything said. To Catrin, it was like someone beating her with a flower to show her how it smelled. Strom walked away, shaking his head in disbelief.

It took four trips each before Gustad could be convinced the fire was completely out. Even then he threw fistfuls of dirt to cover a few remaining coals. Satisfied, he instructed them to refill the bags with the dry sand. Catrin and the others did the best they could to reclaim it all, but it was an impossible task. Milo looked critically at the bags that held close to a third less than they had before, but he said it would suffice.

Gustad, Chase, and Benjin went off to find saplings, and they returned after a short time with a fresh-cut shaft for each of them. Catrin placed the sapling over her shoulders; then she asked Chase and Strom to place bags on each end. The bags were heavy, but balancing them made the load easier to carry. Still, her shoulders began to ache almost immediately, but she used her staff for extra support, and it lent her strength.

On a northwesterly course, they marched through the hills. No path or trail guided them, and this did not appear to be a trip the monks made with any frequency. Hiking with the bags balanced across her shoulders proved treacherous, and Catrin concentrated on the ground ahead of her. They stopped often to rest, but their urgency increased as banks of dark clouds crowded the horizon. A frigid wind descended upon them, and they feared they would be stuck in a snowstorm. Breaks grew shorter and less frequent as the air continually grew colder and the storm clouds nearer.

"We've a long walk ahead of us still," Gustad said during one break, his breath visible as he spoke.

Catrin thought she saw a snowflake fall from the sky. She had no desire to be stuck in the Northern Wastes in the middle of a blizzard, and she expressed her desire to keep marching. Gustad, Benjin, and Milo all agreed that waiting could be deadly, and they pressed on as fast as they could manage. Catrin counted the number of steps she took between seeing snowflakes. At first, it was ten or twelve, but then the snow began to fall in earnest. Bearing a biting chill, the wind picked up, and soft snow turned to stinging sleet and hail, only occasionally changing back to snow.

With darkness upon them and the storm raging, Catrin wondered if they were going to make it. Gustad and Milo suggested abandoning the bags of ash and sand, but Benjin and the others did not put them down, they just kept plodding along, not wanting to give up after having come so far. Sleet and snow clung to Catrin's face and hair, and she felt as if her head were encased in ice. She and the others were near exhaustion, and as they struggled up a steep incline, she considered just lying down and letting the snow cover her. But at the crest of the hill, she raised her head as she heard the others exclaim.

A massive sprawl of sporadic lights stood before them. The brightest and closest were torches that burned on either side of the natural crevice that led to Ohmahold and warmth. The ancients had chosen the location well. The crevice and surrounding mountains made for excellent defenses.

"Mighty Ohmahold has stood for over three thousand years, but there is speculation that it was inhabited long before then," Gustad said. "The natural defenses have been reinforced over the eons, but one of Ohmahold's best defenses is currently falling around us. It won't be long before the lands surrounding us will be completely impassable."

Cold and tired, they struggled to cover the last bit of distance between them and safety. The sight of their destination gave them heart and quickened their steps despite their exhaustion. The storm worsened steadily. Snow became so thick at times that it completely blocked the torches from view, and the footing was deadly slick in places. When they finally reached the winding crevice, they gained meager shelter from the wind and ice. As soon as they entered the crevice, Gustad motioned them to rest. He walked to where a large metal sheet hung and retrieved a mallet from a hook. The metal sheet rang a discordant note as the mallet struck it, and the echoes distorted its call even further. Three times he struck it; then he waited.

"Let me do the talking," Benjin said to Catrin and the others, and they nodded their agreement. "May I use your staff, li'l miss?"

Catrin wasn't sure what he wanted it for, but she didn't bother to ask. Instead she just handed it to him. As they waited, less than patiently, in the cold, they concentrated on keeping warm. Soon, though, a man appeared around the corner and nodded to Gustad and Milo. He regarded Catrin and the others with mild interest, but, after he spoke with Gustad for a moment, he ran back toward the fortress.

"It's safe now. We can enter the main gate," Gustad said, retrieving his load. He and Milo began another of their arguments, and Benjin led the others on.

The number of manned armaments they encountered higher along the narrow defiles alarmed Catrin, but she supposed these were dangerous times. The natural defenses combined with the man-made additions were seemingly insurmountable, and Catrin could not imagine a force mighty enough to conquer such a place.

As a small horse cart approached, Catrin and the others squeezed themselves against the crevice walls to let it pass. The cart was not moving at high speed, but the angry look on the driver's face inspired them to move, and they heard him shout as he approached Gustad and Milo.

"What happened to Penelope? You best not have lost my mule!"

". . . must have wandered off," was all of Milo's response they heard before the other man launched into a tirade.

Benjin took the lead as they rounded a corner, and another impressive sight waited. A single, massive gate, made of entire tree trunks, towered above them. A natural formation of stone jutted out on one side, and stonework fortifications secured an enormous hinge. The opposite side of the crevice was blocked by the largest man-made structure Catrin had ever seen. Huge stone blocks were stacked on top of one another to form an impenetrable wall that encased the locking structures. Standing at attention before the gates were three armed men, and the man in the center stepped forward as they approached.

"State your business."

"We are travelers from afar, and we seek refuge. I'd also like to renew my acquaintance with Sister Gwendolin, if she is indeed here," Benjin said, and Catrin noted how little information he revealed to the guard. She and Benjin were both surprised when the guard gave him a disapproving look.

"*Mother* Gwendolin is quite busy and does not have leisure to greet wayward travelers," he said, looking down his nose.

"A thousand apologies, sir. It has been a long time, and I was unaware of her appointment."

"What's your name, then?"

"Benjin Hawk."

"I'll alert Mother Gwendolin to your presence. Perhaps she'll send some correspondence, but I wouldn't hold out my hopes. I presume you'll be lodging at the First Inn?" he asked archly, and Benjin simply nodded in response. "You must leave all weapons here. You may not enter with swords, knives, bows, arrows, maces, pole arms, spears, or any other deadly implement. We'll return your belongings when you depart Ohmahold."

Catrin and the others created an alarmingly large pile of deadly implements in the crate he provided, and he looked at them with suspicion. He ran his hands lightly over each of them, checking for concealed weapons, but he found none. Benjin leaned on Catrin's staff and made no move to turn it over.

"Your staff, sir."

"You'd deprive a man of his walking stick?" Benjin asked. The guard was taken aback by the question and stood in confusion for a moment, but then he gave the command to open the gates, and Catrin wondered if Benjin's mention of Mother Gwendolin was what swayed him. He scowled at them as they passed through the gate, as if he knew Benjin's limp was contrived.

Hoofbeats echoed from behind, and Catrin stepped aside to let the horse cart pass. The man driving looked like a storm cloud, and he slapped the leather lines on the horse's rump to get more speed. The wagon bounced and shook as the driver seemingly aimed for every bump.

Gustad and Milo rode in the back of the wagon and were thrown several hand widths in the air with each jolt. The bags of ash and sand spewed their contents with every landing, and the two men calmly bounced along in a cloud of ash, all the while arguing over who had been responsible for watching the mule.

As soon as Catrin and the others were inside the gates, men used horses to pull on massive ropes that attached to the gate on the other side of equally large pulleys. The horses strained against their harnesses as they strove to move the tremendous weight, and the gate slowly began to swing closed. Catrin paused to look when she heard the command to hold the gate, and she watched in disbelief as a very angry and icy mule charged through the gate, braying the entire way. Catrin smiled, assuming Penelope had found her way home.

A small city huddled within stout walls, and beyond the walls lay the inner city and temples. Even in the distance and relative darkness, the architecture was spectacular. Wondering where the First Inn would be found, Catrin turned a questioning gaze to Benjin, who looked slightly embarrassed.

"I'm not really sure where the First Inn is. I just couldn't give that horse's rear the satisfaction of asking directions. My apologies," he said. Catrin laughed and patted him on the back.

Small buildings and shops crowded against one another in the limited space. The streets were little more than narrow strips of cobblestone, most not wide enough to walk three abreast. Almost all the buildings were dark and closed up tight. Finding the inn turned out to be as simple as looking for lit windows, and in truth, it was difficult to miss. Constructed entirely of whole tree trunks, it was one of the largest buildings in the outer city, and a rosy glow emanated from cracks around the doors and shutters. The massive size of the trunks indicated they had come from ancient, and most likely virgin, forest. Double doors, hewn from a single tree, made for an imposing entrance. A large sign hung above the doors, depicting a tree with doors in the base of the trunk, and black metal lettering read, *The First Inn.*

Benjin pulled one of the doors open against the force of the wind, and a blast of warm air rushed out. After ducking inside, Catrin basked in the warmth, and the others wasted little time joining her. Tables crowded the large common room, and a cavernous fireplace took up most of one wall. Evidence of a large fire remained in the form of glowing coals.

At a corner table, three men sat conversing in hushed tones, paying Catrin and the others little mind. A man sitting near the fire slept in his chair, his head lolled to one side and his hand still holding a mug of ale. In a darkened corner, another man sat silently, and Catrin thought his gaze a bit too direct. She noted his presence but refused to look directly at him again, and whenever she cast him a sidelong glance, he seemed to be appraising her.

A rotund woman emerged from the kitchens and made her own appraisal of Catrin and her companions. She wrinkled her nose at their filthy appearance, making Catrin self-conscious. The woman, who was obviously the keeper of the First Inn, simply shrugged. "The baths are out back. You'll have to clean up before you can eat or lodge, agreed?"

"Yes, baths will be most welcome. We found ourselves helping a couple of monks with some rather dirty business," Benjin replied, and the innkeeper seemed to warm to him a bit. She warmed even more when he paid her for the baths along with advance payment for a hot meal.

"I am Miss Chambril. Welcome to the First Inn. I'll send Wonk to the bathhouse with water and towels in a moment. You can leave your bags here if you wish," she said as she walked into the kitchen. Catrin sifted through her pack in search of the soft clothes she had packed from the *Trader's Wind,* looking forward to being warm, dry, and in comfortable clothes. She sighed, realizing the time aboard the *Wind* had completely ruined her. In days gone by, she would have judged clothes by how tough or water resistant they were; now comfort was a definite consideration.

Wanting to get clean and dry as quickly as possible, she and the others hurried to the baths. Wonk turned out to be a man in his middle years, and he seemed like a pleasant sort of fellow. He brought a stack of towels on his first trip and asked if any of them needed a robe. Catrin and the others declined the offer but appreciated it nonetheless, and they were grateful when he returned with a basin of lukewarm water. He said he would be back with more, but they descended on the washbasin with intent purpose.

Catrin filled her cupped hands and splashed her face repeatedly. Each time, gray water seeped into the corners of her eyes, stinging and burning. When Wonk returned with another basin, Catrin stuck her entire face in the warmer water even before he had settled it on the stone bench. Using one of the towels, she dried her face and frowned when she saw how dirty the cloth came away. It seemed she might never get clean, but Wonk tirelessly brought fresh basins of water.

Eventually, the cold drove Catrin and the others from the baths, and they sought that warm meal. Miss Chambril did not disappoint. Bowls of steaming stew emerged from the kitchen even as they seated themselves. Catrin noted that only the sleeping man remained in the common room; the rest had apparently gone to their beds. The stew smelled fantastic, and Catrin blew on a hot spoonful, waiting less than patiently for her first taste. It was worth the wait. She tasted salty beef and tomato with onion, garlic, and celery. Large pieces of carrot were a treat, and she ate the carrots from Osbourne's stew as well.

Miss Chambril brought soft bread still warm from the oven, and they used no restraint when spreading it thick with apple butter. Catrin thought it might be the most delightful thing she had ever tasted, and she told Miss Chambril so. The innkeeper took the compliment in stride and brought them more bread and apple butter.

"What is that aroma? It smells wonderful," Benjin asked, sniffing the air. "Is that a brisket?"

"You've a discerning nose for such a dirty little man."

"Could I beg a shaving or two? It'd be an honor to sample your work in progress," he said with sincerity.

Miss Chambril visibly reappraised him. "I suppose that would be acceptable," she said. "Wonk will show the rest of you to your rooms when you've finished your meal," she continued, motioning Benjin to follow her into the kitchen. "I don't normally let strange men into my kitchen."

"Not to fear. I try not to make a habit of being strange in the kitchens of beautiful women," Benjin replied.

Catrin shook her head and asked Wonk to show her to her room. He led her to a small but private room. Despite being the first one in her bed, she was awake long after the others found slumber, and somewhere between sleep and wakefulness, she thought she heard the sound of birds taking flight.

* * *

Sitting before the dwindling fire, as the shifting glow cast wandering shadows over the faces around him, Strom tried to drive the chill from his bones, but still he shivered. "I don't know if I'll ever be warm again," he said.

"At least we made it here," Chase said, rubbing his hands together. "We could still be out in the Wastes. I'm just glad to have a full belly and a dry place to sleep tonight."

"I know I should be grateful we're here," Osbourne said, his eyes downcast, "but this place gives me the crawls. I feel like an outsider. You saw how that guard looked at us. I'm not sure we're welcome here."

Benjin had been quiet for some time, seemingly content to let the others express their concerns, and he had a distant look in his eyes, as if he were reliving the past. "It'll be all right," he said. "The Cathurans are a suspicious lot, and they tend to be aloof, but rarely are they cruel. Get some sleep, and things will look brighter by the light of day."

"I hope so," Strom said, but as he looked around, the anxiety of his companions was palpable.

"I'm going to bed," Chase said with a wide yawn. Despite his exhaustion, Strom knew he could not sleep--not yet. Too many fears dominated his thoughts, and he stayed in front of the fire until the coals no longer provided their welcoming warmth. With little to light his way, he stumbled to his room. As he crept along the dark upper hall, he wondered at the candlelight that washed from under one of the closed doors. A chill ran down his spine as he passed the room, and he tried desperately to convince himself that his fears were unwarranted.

Chapter 8

A single act of kindness can change the world.
--Byrber Dra, philanthropist

* * *

A jolly sort of noise brought Catrin drifting to wakefulness, but it was her nose that drew her from the comfortable bedding. She smelled bacon--bacon! The alluring aroma drew everyone from their rooms, and she soon found herself seated in the common room with her companions. A young girl served other customers, but Miss Chambril arrived at their table and served them herself.

The innkeeper didn't ask what they wanted; she simply brought plates laden with some of everything, and Catrin could not fail to notice the large cut of brisket she served Benjin. Reveling in the tastes of bacon, sausage, and cheese, no one at their table spoke a word.

One of the doors flew open and a tired-looking guard entered the common room. Catrin recognized him as the man who had searched them the night before. When he saw Benjin, he approached and went to one knee.

"A thousand apologies, sir. Mother Gwendolin wishes to see you immediately. I sincerely apologize for my insolence. I was out of line." He stayed on one knee, his eyes downcast.

Benjin laughed and patted him on the shoulder. "Come now, let us begin again. I'm Benjin Hawk."

The man seemed shocked that Benjin would not use his advantage, and he accepted Benjin's hand with thinly veiled uncertainty. "Burrel Longarm, captain of the guard, sir," he said, seeming more sure of himself after Benjin's firm handshake.

"Please join us and sit a moment, Captain Longarm. I assume your orders are to escort us to Mother Gwendolin?" Benjin asked and Captain Longarm nodded. "I cannot offend Miss Chambril by leaving these platters full, and we sure could use your help cleaning them if you'd be willing." Benjin winked and motioned for him to take a seat. Captain Longarm was hesitant for a moment but then gave in to his hunger.

Benjin cut a large slice from his brisket and slid it onto the plate Catrin handed to Captain Longarm. Catrin spooned a bit of everything else onto his dish. He thanked them with his mouth full. Miss Chambril appeared impressed when she saw the empty plates, but then she noticed Captain Longarm.

"I suppose I'll need to bring a larger meal next time, I didn't realize you'd be feeding the guard as well," she said as she cleared the plates. Captain Longarm looked uncomfortable and seemed to be wondering if he had offended her, but Miss Chambril just laughed and brought him a basket of sweet rolls for the guards.

"Thank you, Miss Chambril. I'll make sure the men on duty get every one of these," he said, and she laughed, throwing another roll at him. He caught it deftly and smiled as he took a bite. "Many thanks, Miss Chambril. Many thanks," he said as he led Benjin and the others out of the First Inn. Within a few steps, he cast a sidelong glance at Benjin, who walked without limp or staff. "Your leg feeling better today?"

"Much," Benjin replied with a sly smile.

"I should get these to the men before they get cold," Captain Longarm said, a question in his voice.

"Yes, I agree. That gift would be wasted if delivered cold," Benjin replied.

Captain Longarm happily jogged toward the gates along the path that had been cleared through the knee-deep snow. He returned shortly after and led them on a different path, one that meandered toward a second set of massive gates. The gates opened as they approached, and no one questioned or searched them. The men manning the gates nodded in deference as they passed, and Catrin smiled in return. After passing through two smaller sets of gates, they reached an enormous temple. Built into the side of a mountain, the massive structure was covered with elaborate images of trees and animals meticulously carved into the rock face. So cleverly carved were some of the creatures that they seemed to move.

Craning her neck, Catrin tried to soak in the myriad of details while she walked. She nearly tripped a few times, but she got to see distant waterfalls, hanging gardens, and even small ponds filled with orange fish. If the monks Catrin saw noticed her and her party, they gave little indication. Some sat in quiet meditation; others read. Some had their heads and even their eyebrows completely shaved, and Catrin reflexively reached for her hair. It had grown long in the months since she had left her home. Even after it was singed, it grew back quickly, and she had come to like the feel of it on her neck; it made her feel womanly.

Engrossed in her thoughts, she didn't notice that the others had stopped, and she walked into Strom's back. He made no comment, but somehow he came to be standing on her toes. She pinched him, and he laughed as he stepped away. Before the entrance of the temple, Captain Longarm remained silent. One of the men standing guard simply nodded and disappeared into the temple. The other guard motioned them to follow him inside, and he led them to a small side chamber.

The entryway floor was of polished stone, and the walls were lined with shoes and boots. No one needed to tell them they should take off their boots, and the guard simply nodded when they started unlacing. Conscious of her pale and pickled-looking feet and her crooked toes, which had all been broken at least once, mostly under Salty's hooves, Catrin suddenly wished she did not have to go barefoot. The guard pointed to some washbasins, indicating they should wash their feet before entering the temple, and they respectfully complied.

As Catrin rinsed her feet, she caught movement from the corner of her eye. A petite woman walked gracefully toward them, her robes gliding evenly across the floor, as if she moved without walking. Distracted, Catrin lost her balance as she removed her foot from the basin. She hopped on one foot for a moment, took a bad hop, and slipped on the wet floor. Her feet were above her head when she struck the stone floor, and the air rushed from her lungs. With an angry bump forming on the back of her head, she could not have been more embarrassed and was grateful when someone helped her rise from the floor. When her vision focused, she found it was the dainty woman who assisted her. "Greetings, child. I'm Mother Gwendolin. Are you hurt?"

"Um, no, Mother. I'll be fine in a moment--just a bump on the head," Catrin replied. She did not resist as Mother Gwendolin guided her into another, smaller room with thick carpets and comfortable-looking cushions strewn about on the floor. Mother Gwendolin led her to a large cushion and helped ease her down to it. Catrin slumped onto the cushion and ran her fingers along the back of her skull. She felt no blood, but the lump was tender to the touch.

"Greetings, Mother Gwendolin," Benjin said. "The years have been kind to you."

"It's good to see you again, Benjin. It seems like only yesterday we searched for herbs and roots together," she replied, and Catrin looked up to see Benjin give her a brief hug. The others seated themselves, and Benjin began by making the introductions. He worked his way around the room until he came to Catrin, and she suddenly realized she had not given Mother Gwendolin her name.

"This is Catrin Volker, daughter of Wendel and Elsa Volker," Benjin said quietly enough to remain discreet.

"I'm sorry I didn't introduce myself, Mother," Catrin blurted involuntarily.

Mother Gwendolin just smiled. "You need not fret. I'm not easily offended, and you did suffer quite a fall. My position often seems to impose courtesies that my ego does not require and that I would much sooner forgo. There are those who feel I must maintain my aloofness as a requisite, but I find it tiresome. It creates a barrier between me and just about everyone else. Ah, but I did not come here to tell you my troubles. Please, tell me the tale of your journey," she said, but she noticed Benjin make an exaggerated glance toward the open doorway. "Perhaps this is a tale best told in a more accommodating location. If you'll follow me, I'll find us a more comfortable place to talk," she said, and Benjin nodded in agreement.

She led them through the large hall and down a wide, rounded flight of stairs that opened into another equally large hall. Fewer people were gathered in this part of the temple, and many of the doors that lined the hall were closed. Catrin saw people in rooms where doors were open or ajar, but they made very little noise; most appeared to be in various states of meditation.

Another flight of stairs took them into a smaller hall with fewer doors on either side. Mother Gwendolin selected a room that had empty rooms on either side, and when they were all inside, she closed the heavy door behind them.

"I apologize, Mother, but our tale must be kept in confidence. I fear anyone who learns of it will be in danger. I'm hesitant to place such a burden on you, and I'm prepared to tell you pleasant lies if you decide that is best. I would ask your preference," Benjin said.

Mother Gwendolin smiled, nodding in acknowledgment of his warning. "First, I must ask you to address me as Gwendolin while we're in a private setting. It will lighten my heart to enjoy your company as equals. Second, I wish to hear your tale, no matter how dangerous the information may be. I sense this is no minor matter, and I'll do what I can to assist you."

Everyone in the room seemed to relax once those things were understood, and Catrin let Benjin's voice pull her along as he told their tale. He left out no details, shocking everyone with the extent of his disclosure. He spoke of Catrin as the one who had been declared the Herald of Istra, and Mother Gwendolin gave her more than a few glances during the telling of her deeds. Catrin immersed herself in Benjin's telling, and she let herself experience the tale from his perspective.

He wove the story with skill, and his details painted vivid impressions in her mind. She liked the texture of his rendition and stored his memories alongside hers. Mother Gwendolin made not a single sound. She listened intently until Benjin reached the last part of his tale. When he described their journey with Milo and Gustad, she dropped her face into her hands and sighed; then she laughed. Benjin fell silent and Mother Gwendolin looked at each of them anew.

"You've endured many trials along your journey, and you've more challenges ahead. Benjin's words tell me you have acted wisely and bravely, and I honor your courageous deeds. He also alluded to Catrin's desire to learn from us. I would ask what it is you seek."

"I . . . uh . . . I came here hoping to learn about my magic," Catrin answered, caught off her guard.

"Pah! Magic? What do you need with magic? Do you wish to perform tricks at country fairs?" Mother Gwendolin asked, incredulous, and Catrin gaped. "What you possess is not magic, child. You have *power*. Not the perception of power like that which politicians wield, but real, tangible *power*. It would seem you were right to seek us out, for you have much to learn, but we will remedy that, shall we not?"

"Thank you," Catrin responded. "I don't want to be a burden, but any help and information you can offer will be greatly appreciated."

"You couldn't just come to visit, could you, Benjin?" Mother Gwendolin asked with a wink.

"I suppose not."

"I think Catrin and I should spend some time together," Mother Gwendolin said. "Perhaps she could rejoin you this evening at the First Inn?"

"Certainly. We can find our way out," Benjin said.

"You should pay a visit to Milo and Gustad. I'm sure they'd be glad to show you their experiments," she replied with a wave, and Benjin closed the door behind himself.

Nervous and self-conscious when left alone with Mother Gwendolin, Catrin quailed. The woman's grace and eloquence made her feel crude and ignorant, and she was somewhat cowed by Mother Gwendolin's reaction to the word *magic*.

"Well now, where shall we begin, hmm?" Mother Gwendolin said. "Perhaps you could describe your experiences with power. That would help me understand what you know."

Catrin sighed, took a deep breath, and prepared to verbalize the indescribable. She began by detailing the events surrounding the attack on Osbourne and how she had thought she would die. Then she tried unsuccessfully to relate the feeling of the world flying away from her.

"Hmm, yes, that explains a great deal," Mother Gwendolin said. "It is my belief that the human brain is capable of much more than most people realize. There are doorways in our minds, like portals to ancient knowledge, most of which are closed. Some doors can be opened gradually over generations. I believe those opened by a parent before the time of a child's conception are made easier for the child to open, and I have hypothesized that these doors can be blown apart by traumatic experiences. It is my unproven theory that the unconscious mind can sometimes override the conscious mind for the sake of self-preservation, but I digress.

"It would seem a major doorway fell before the threat on your life, and you instinctively triggered a chain reaction, unleashing a blast of energy. It is my belief that one cannot create energy. One can store energy, harness it, release it, but not create it. Again, I digress, please continue," she said.

Catrin went on with a bit of excitement. She hadn't known what to expect, but at least Mother Gwendolin had some answers for her, even if they were vague and unproven. She managed to tell the tale of the destruction of the greatoaks without crying, but Mother Gwendolin's astonished reaction made it difficult.

"By the land. The Grove of the Elders and the Heartstone destroyed."

"You know of the place?" Catrin choked.

"Only from legends and scripture, but you described it perfectly. It was a very sacred place where the land's energy was said to be almost palpable."

"It was. I felt it." Catrin sobbed, once again suffering the guilt of destroying the once beautiful place.

"You could not have known, dear. Now, now, don't cry," Mother Gwendolin said softly.

Catrin then told of her experiences on the plateau and how the water seemed to repel her. She described the emotions she had been experiencing when she slammed the ground, and Mother Gwendolin looked thoughtful but remained silent. She went on to tell about her trials among the Arghast, and about the striking of the well.

"Clever," Mother Gwendolin said.

Finally, Catrin described her attack on the Zjhon fleet. She tried to express in words her energy vortex spinning in a similar manner to the rotation of the storm, and how exhausted she had grown trying to maintain it. Only when she reached that part of her tale did she remember the fish carving, and she quickly filled Mother Gwendolin in on the overlooked details. Mother Gwendolin's eyes flew as wide as saucers, and Catrin grew quiet.

"Wait one moment before you say anything more," Mother Gwendolin said. She went to the door and summoned a nearby guard. After she whispered something in his ear, he left at a run. Catrin wanted desperately to ask what was going on, but she sensed Mother Gwendolin had good reason for her silence, and she also sensed an aura of excitement.

A sudden knock at the door startled them both, and Mother Gwendolin rose to meet the guard. The man was winded and said nothing as he handed her a leather-bound book. Mother Gwendolin turned back to Catrin and quickly flipped the pages, clearly not wishing to prolong Catrin's torment; then she held the open book out.

"Does it look like that?" she asked, no longer able to contain her excitement. Catrin's heart slammed into her throat, and she knew before she looked at the pages that she had found and destroyed some ancient relic. One glance at the page confirmed her fears, and she nodded with tears in her eyes. She didn't miss the caption written in bold letters above the drawing; it read, *Imeteri's Fish*. Mother Gwendolin looked at her with a mixture of horror and foolish hope. "Please tell me you lost it," she pleaded then sat down hard as Catrin shook her head.

"I didn't know," Catrin said through her grief. "No one told me. I swear I didn't know. I needed the strength to stay alive. I didn't know." She sobbed and curled into a ball, and Mother Gwendolin held her.

"I'm so sorry, dear Catrin. I'm a foolish old lady. I didn't realize the extent of your pain, and I've only served to make it worse. You are a remarkable young woman, and I'm proud to be known by you. I'll be more careful from now on. I promise," she said while Catrin cried on her shoulder.

"I destroyed Imeteri's Fish."

* * *

The aroma that came from Miss Chambril's kitchen was enough to drive away most of the group's fears, but Chase had no appetite. Since their arrival at Ohmahold, a nagging intuition kept him from ever truly relaxing, and he paced the common room, waiting for Catrin to return.

"She'll be fine," Benjin said as if reading his thoughts, and Vertook nodded firmly in agreement, but even their reassurances sounded thin and weak to Chase's ears, and he continued to fret.

"What do you think will happen next?" Osbourne asked, his voice quivering, betraying his own fears.

"The snows have begun," Benjin said. "The passes will soon be impassable, and I doubt anyone will arrive at Ohmahold or leave before the spring melt. We have little choice now but to settle in for the winter and make the best of the time we have."

"What will we do?" Strom asked.

"Perhaps a visit to Gustad and Milo, as Mother Gwendolin suggested, would be a good place to start. Learn all that you can, for you can never say what knowledge will mean the difference between life and death. Keep me apprised of all that you hear, and somehow we will piece together a plan."

"You go," Chase said to Strom and Osbourne as they stood to leave. "I'll wait here for Cat." Strom looked him in the eye, and they exchanged a silent vow: Somehow they would keep her safe--somehow. Icy wind tore through the common room as Strom and Osbourne pushed opened the doors and leaned into the wind.

When the doors slammed shut, Chase kicked a nearby chair, venting his frustration. Catrin needed him, and he had no idea what he was supposed to do. Anxious and frightened, his thoughts ran in circles, and still no path became clear. He could only hope that something would show him the way. Until then, he would pace.

Chapter 9

The world is but a pyre of timber waiting for the tiniest spark to unleash an inferno.
--Ain Giest, Sleepless One

* * *

Deep in the night, Catrin woke to find herself curled up on a cushion. Nearby, Mother Gwendolin snored softly. Catrin felt strange and scared in the silent darkness. Curling into a ball, she concentrated on positive thoughts and sought her center. As she drifted between sleep and wakefulness, she began to feel deep vibrations of power from within the stones of the temple. It was a comforting sort of energy, and it lulled her back to sleep.

When she woke again, she was alone; a tray of fruits waited in a corner. Rubbing the sleep from her eyes, she plopped down next to the tray and helped herself to some apple slices and a few grapes. The sweet taste refreshed her and helped chase away her morning lethargy. Suddenly remembering that Benjin and the others had expected her back and knowing they were probably worried about her, she scrambled to her feet and charged toward the door just as it opened inward.

"Good morning, Catrin. How are you feeling today?" Mother Gwendolin asked as she glided into the room.

"Much better, thank you. I'm sorry I was such a bother last night. I didn't mean to keep you from your bed. I must let Benjin know--" Catrin began, and she would have continued if Mother Gwendolin had not placed a finger on her lips.

"I sent word to Benjin last night, and you have nothing to worry about. Now that the snows have fallen and continue to fall, those within Ohmahold shall stay, and no more will arrive before the spring melt. For now, you may enjoy some respite," Mother Gwendolin said with a smile. "I've asked Benjin and the rest of your party to dine with us this evening, but there is something I wish to discuss with you before then. Would you like a little more time to greet the day?"

"Now is fine," Catrin said, barely able to stifle a yawn, and Mother Gwendolin shook her head in a good-natured way.

"It seems you have a great many questions, but few of them are clear in your mind. Perhaps it would help if you were able to achieve a clearer state of consciousness," Mother Gwendolin began, and Catrin gave her a perplexed look. "A common belief among the Cathurans is that every bit of food and drink you consume affects the functions of your body and mind.

Every substance you ingest alters your mental and physical state in some way. The only exception is clean water, the substance of life itself, which carries toxins from the body. I'm suggesting that you not only fast, but also undergo the purification ritual."

"What's that?"

"The ritual consists of a series of traditional ceremonies that help rid the body of stress and toxins. The ritual is also required of anyone who wishes to enter the Inner Sanctuary, which is where you may find some of your answers, though I make no promises. The ritual is not trivial. It lasts thirty days, during which time you will be unable to visit with anyone."

Catrin's anxiety must have been easy to see.

"Do not fear. I've undergone the ritual many times, and I find it helpful when I am undecided about something. I don't want to pressure you. The choice is yours. Would you like to walk in the gardens? Let us take in some beauty while we contemplate."

The thought of a relaxing walk appealed to Catrin, and the warm coat Mother Gwendolin provided would make it more comfortable. All the walkways had been completely cleared of the previous night's snowfall. The sun shone brightly but brought little warmth along with its light, and Catrin was thankful for the coat.

The gardens were breathtaking. Many plants still carried their fall shades of red and yellow, standing out in contrast to the pristine snow that partially covered them. Some of the colorful leaves were completely encased in sparkling ice. Droplets of water formed as the ice slowly melted, and rainbows danced across the gardens. A lone monk, his long gray hair flowing behind him, stood silently. He held what looked like two small bowls, one on top of the other. The top bowl appeared to be ringed with small holes that had flowers painted around them.

Unsure what the man could possibly be doing, Catrin was shocked to see a rather large hummingbird land on the rim of the bowl, chirrup happily, and drink. Its extended visit gave her ample time to observe its markings: deep purple, with a bluish belly and a bright red throat. When she commented on the exotic bird, Mother Gwendolin seemed surprised that she didn't recognize the species.

"My father taught me to identify most of the birds that live on the Godfist, including several types of hummingbird, but I've never seen one like that before," Catrin said.

When the avian wonder sprang into the air, it zoomed backward then buzzed past Catrin's ear, causing her to duck involuntarily.

The monk lowered the dish and turned to his audience with a smile. "I'm glad I got to see him before he made his winter journey. He'll need the energy from that sugar water to get to the Godfist. It gladdens me to help the gorgeous creatures," he said in warm greeting.

"Catrin, this is Brother Vaughn. He tends to our aviary and has a love affair with anything that soars on the wind. Brother Vaughn, this is Catrin Volker. She'll be visiting with us for the winter."

"Splendid," Brother Vaughn responded. "It'll be nice to have a new face around the halls."

Catrin knew Brother Vaughn would appreciate knowing the hummingbird was most likely not flying to the Godfist, but she was unsure how much information to reveal. Mother Gwendolin looked at her briefly and skillfully used her body language and facial expression to communicate her opinion. Catrin got the distinct impression that Mother Gwendolin trusted this man, but it was up to her to decide what she would reveal, and she decided to trust him as well.

"I've studied the birds of the Godfist, and I have no recollection of ever seeing a hummingbird that large or with that coloring," she said, and his eyes lit up.

"You've seen the birds of the Godfist, for yourself, in their natural habitat?" he asked, and Catrin nodded. "What a treasure you've brought for me, Mother! I hope you'll allow me some time with Catrin. I have so many questions she may be able to answer," he said, his excitement clearly gaining momentum. He began talking softly to himself, listing the many things he would ask, and he excused himself so he could write down his list. "I don't want to forget to ask something important," he said with a smile.

Catrin decided it was good that she would have time on her hands. Brother Vaughn could probably keep her busy answering questions for days. For this day, though, she decided to simply enjoy the peaceful surroundings and majestic views. She and Mother Gwendolin spent the rest of the day touring the Outer Sanctuary, specifically avoiding discussions of any real consequence. Catrin enjoyed the amiable companionship, and she appreciated Mother Gwendolin's not pushing her into any intense conversations.

As the sun began to fall, they walked to a private dining room. A small fire chased away the chill and provided a rosy glow. Catrin sat near the hearth, warming her hands. She heard Benjin and the others as they approached, and they soon joined her around the rectangular table, where the long benches made for cozy seating.

The monks serving their meal must have been watching for the honored guests to arrive because they entered almost immediately with bowls of steaming broth and vegetables. Catrin and the others laughed as they all blew on their soup, and made slurping noises as they tried not to burn their lips or tongues. Other monks served platters of cheese and fruit, and they carried the empty bowls away. Mother Gwendolin ate in relative silence, letting them exchange news.

"We visited Milo and Gustad at the forge," Strom said. "They used the sand and ash to make perfectly clear glass. You should see it, Cat."

Osbourne beamed. "It's fascinating. You should come see the forge and the lenses they are working on. Milo said he would teach me to work glass."

Catrin smiled at their obvious enthusiasm. She looked down the table at Vertook and asked him what he did with his day.

"I talked to Brunson, the man with mule. He is a good man. Just don't lose his animals," he said. "I will teach him to raise a horse in Arghast way. He will ride without silly bridles by spring."

Catrin mentally wished Brunson luck; she could not imagine riding without reins in her hands.

It seemed all but Benjin and Chase had found ways to pass their days. She sensed grim determination from each of them, and though it pained her, it made her feel safe. They could spend the whole winter drinking and playing pickup, but she doubted they would.

Considering all the ways she could spend the long winter, she asked herself if she were doing everything she could to prepare for what lay ahead. She was not. It was an unpleasant realization, but she accepted the truth of it. She needed knowledge, understanding--comprehension; without those, she would wander in the dark. Mother Gwendolin had implied that the Inner Sanctuary was the place to seek such clarity, but Catrin had an unexplainable fear of the purification ritual; it just seemed too bizarre.

Catrin knew that others underwent the process, but thinking about it gave her a cold feeling in her stomach. In some ways, she was afraid of what she might find once she achieved clarity, but much of her anxiety was centered on the ritual itself. The thought of fasting did not appeal to her. She could not imagine dealing with the hunger pangs. She tended to get cranky when she was hungry, and she wasn't certain she would be able to control herself.

Still, the possibility of learning something important was almost irresistible. Mother Gwendolin sat in silence, and Catrin met her eyes briefly. No words were exchanged, but Catrin clearly understood that the decision was hers alone.

"Mother Gwendolin says there is a purification ritual that I must perform in order to enter the Inner Sanctuary, but it takes thirty days and I'm afraid. I don't want to be away from all of you for so long."

"What kind of ritual takes thirty days?" Chase asked. "I'm not sure I like the sound of that."

"I cannot tell you much," Mother Gwendolin said, "except that many have undergone the ritual before Catrin, and none have come to harm."

"Still don't like it," Chase said.

"I'm certain Mother Gwendolin would not invite Catrin do something that was not in her best interest," Benjin said. "But I'll not push Catrin into doing it either. You must make that choice for yourself, li'l miss."

"If you're not back in thirty days," Strom said, "we'll come in after ya."

"Thanks, Strom, Benjin. I appreciate your words. I heard what Chase said as well, but I cannot let fear stop me from doing what I must. I came here in search of knowledge and understanding, and I must pursue those above all else. I want to undergo the purification ritual, so I can enter the Inner Sanctuary," she said before her commitment wavered, and a small smile played across Mother Gwendolin's face. Benjin also seemed to agree with her decision. Strom and Osbourne said they would miss her, but she had their full support, and she drew strength from their encouragement.

"I don't like it," Chase insisted.

"I'm sorry, Chase. I have to do this."

"Be safe," he said. Then he grew very quiet.

When the meal was finished, Mother Gwendolin led her from the dining room. Catrin took one last look over her shoulder at her friends sitting at the table. They all smiled encouragingly at her. They would be only a short distance away, yet she would not see them for weeks. She would miss them, but it was comforting to know they would be nearby.

Catrin and Mother Gwendolin moved deeper into the Outer Sanctuary. They reached a hallway with plain wooden doors lining each side. One door was open, and Mother Gwendolin stepped inside. Catrin followed her into the sparsely furnished room. It contained a sleeping pallet, a small wooden chest, and a lamp hung on the wall, but it was otherwise bare.

"I must leave you for now," Mother Gwendolin said. "I've some things I must attend to."

Though the room offered little in the way of amenities, it was comfortable to Catrin. To her, it symbolized the beginning of a new journey, and she was determined to get everything she could from this adventure. Uncertainties that had nagged her became gleaming possibilities. No longer concentrating on what might be embarrassing or uncomfortable, she chose instead to focus on the good that could come from the experience.

Benjin had attributed his knowledge of meditation to the Cathurans, and Catrin hoped she, too, would leave with lessons that would last the rest of her life. Settling herself into serenity, she practiced some meditation techniques. It made her feel closer to her friends, despite the walls and distance separating them.

* * *

When morning came, Catrin had no recollection of falling asleep and woke feeling refreshed and ready to start her new journey; at least she thought she was ready. A gentle knock on the door made her jump. She got another shock when she opened the door: a robed and hooded figure stood in the hallway, hidden within the shadows of the cloak. A strange feeling came over her, and she suddenly wondered how trusting she could be within the Outer Sanctuary. Perhaps the anonymity of her escort was a test of some sort to see if she were ready for the ritual.

The hooded figure did not move or speak, but Catrin sensed impatience, and she mumbled a muted apology as she stepped into the hall. The figure made no response and glided deeper into the Outer Sanctuary. Catrin followed in silence, taking in the strange and wondrous sights. Indoor fountains and rock gardens drew her eyes, and they passed through massive arches that were elaborately carved with scenes of forests and animals. Paintings hung on some walls, and mosaics decorated the floors. None of the artwork she'd seen within the sanctuary depicted people; all seemed to focus on the glory of nature.

Catrin followed and marveled at the gracefulness of her guide. The fluidity of movement and the way the robes flowed along the floor gave the impression that her guide was floating rather than walking. The illusion was temporarily broken when they reached a spiral staircase that descended into the heart of the mountain. The gliding movements shifted to rhythmic, and Catrin watched the body of her guide bob up and down in front of her as they descended. The graceful and measured movements now gave the impression that her guide was made of soft springs, but she forced herself to concentrate on not falling.

They climbed down for what seemed a long time, passing many landings and archways but no other people. The bottom of the stairwell was lost in the darkness, and the dim light provided by occasional lamps stopped several turns below where they currently stood. When they reached the last illuminated floor, her guide turned and floated through one of the four archways that opened onto the landing, taking one of the lamps from its sconce.

Catrin tried very hard to shake the illusions surrounding her guide, and she concentrated on sensing the being beneath the robe. She explored the energy and tried to envision the shape based upon the aura she sensed. Only a fuzzy impression was revealed to her. Concentrating harder, she nearly stumbled when she sensed a male aspect of his energy; the sudden rush of it was bizarre yet wonderful. Her heart leaped to her throat, though, when he stopped gliding and turned to face her. Mortified that he had somehow sensed her intrusion, she froze, and despite his face being hidden in darkness, the reprimand was palpable.

When he began walking again, the illusions surrounding him seemed to have been shattered. His grace was still obvious, but he no longer appeared to float. Vindicated by the victory over her senses, she took note of her surroundings again. The hallway ended a short distance ahead. The walls of the corridor were unadorned, and the floor was smooth but unpolished.

Cold emanated from the stone; it seeped into Catrin's bones, and she shivered as she walked.

As they approached the end of the hall, they came upon an opening in the left wall, and her guide walked into it. In this hall, the walls were carved with intricate patterns, and the floor was covered with many colored tiles. Unlike the mosaics she had seen, these tiles formed only varying patterns that seemed to follow no logic or reason. Her guide turned left where several corridors intersected; then he made an immediate right, his movements confident and sure. After a number of junctions and turns, Catrin could no longer recall the way back, and she guessed they were within a massive labyrinth.

The longer they walked, the more she came to think her guide was utterly lost. Watching the patterns on the floors, she was nearly certain they had passed the same spot several times, only to take a different passageway each time. She considered leaving some sort of marking on the floor or walls, but she didn't want to offend her guide again.

Her faith was tested again when they turned a corner and emerged into a small room. The center of the room was dominated by a massive stone table, and on either side of the slab stood a robed and hooded figure. The slab's resemblance to a sacrificial alter was disconcerting, and the effect was amplified by the gleaming knives held before the monks. Hesitating in the doorway, Catrin tried to convince herself it was safe. Instincts urged her to flee, but she knew she would only get lost within the maze.

If these people wanted to harm her, this was a perfect opportunity, yet no one rushed her or pressured her to move ahead. With renewed determination, Catrin stepped into the room and felt as if she had finally taken the first true step on her journey.

The man who guided her turned and walked gracefully from the room without a sound. Those who remained issued a wordless command for her to lie on the stone slab, and she did so with trepidation, wondering what she had gotten herself into. Lying on her back, she saw a large spiral, painted in purple, on the ceiling. As she stared, it began to spin and looked as if it would suck her in. Still on her guard, she closed her eyes before it put her in a trance.

Concentrating on the robed figures, she attempted to sense their gender. The hands holding the knives had looked decidedly female, but she ran her senses over them for confirmation. Now, knowing what to look for, she quickly confirmed her suspicion: both were female.

The confirmation brought her some comfort. She felt more at ease with her fate in the hands of women. Still, it startled her when the women moved to her sides and the tips of their blades descended toward her. It took every bit of restraint she possessed to remain on the table. As the blades hovered a mere finger's width above her eyes, she hoped and prayed that she had not been duped.

***

Rolling into a defensive posture, Chase squared off, planting his feet and flexing his knees. Quicker than he'd expected, Benjin charged in again and lunged, overextending himself. Seeing the opportunity to finally score a hit, Chase raised his sword for a mighty blow. Anticipating his move, Benjin spun in the air, landing his practice sword squarely on Chase's knuckles.

"Too slow," Benjin said as Chase writhed on the grass, holding his knuckles and cursing. "You had plenty of time to strike me, but you had to draw yourself up like a hero in a fireside tale. Trust me, real battles are nothing like that. If I leave you an opening, take it, but don't leave yourself exposed in doing so. Understand?"

In answer, Chase swung himself and kicked Benjin in the back of the knees. Benjin collapsed to the ground, and Chase approached with caution, ready for a surprise attack. Benjin groaned and held his knee.

"I suppose I deserved that, but try to take it easy on an old man's knees, will ya?"

Chase nodded, ashamed of himself for taking advantage of Benjin that way, and he offered his hand. Benjin clasped it and pulled Chase forward, planting his feet on Chase's chest and thrusting. Chase hurtled through the air and did a complete flip before landing in a not-so-forgiving bush. Two girls, not much older than Chase, watched from nearby, and they giggled as he climbed from the bush.

"Perhaps you should try walking," one of them said with a smirk. "You fly like a stone."

His face flushed, Chase returned to where Benjin waited.

"Don't let down your defenses," Benjin said.

Captain Longarm approached. "Takes time to learn such things, but you'll get it eventually. Those practice swords working well for you?"

"That they are," Benjin said. "It'd be better if we didn't need them, but these are dangerous times. Thanks again for your generosity."

"We do what we can," Captain Longarm said. "I fear you're right. I've got a bad feeling in my gut." His statement left tension in the air, and he coached Chase as Benjin squared off. Together they trained into the night.

***

"Too much you look at bone and muscle," Vertook said as Brunson stood from his examination of the weanling. "Look at eyes. Look at heart. Look at soul. There you see true measure of horse."

Trying not to offend Vertook, Brunson did as he said and was surprised by what he saw. Staring into the eyes of one weanling, he saw fear. In another, rebellion and pride. Off in a corner, though, was a weak-looking filly with short legs. Until then, Brunson had ignored the filly, figuring she was unsuitable for someone his size, but when he looked in her eyes, he saw love and loyalty and a yearning for someone to return those feelings. As he approached her, she trembled not with fear, but with what seemed like anticipation. Running his hands gently over her coat, she leaned into him.

"Now you see, yes?" Vertook asked.

"I think I do," Brunson said, surprised by his own heart's reaction to the filly. When Vertook had come to him, boasting of the Arghast way, Brunson had been skeptical, believing that his ways were the only ways to properly raise animals. Now he began to wonder if he'd been blind, for much of what Vertook said seemed to be true. Swallowing his pride, Brunson vowed to learn what he could from this stranger, and he felt a new journey was about to begin.

He watched with anticipation as Vertook approached each weanling, looking at their eyes only. When he settled on the colt that had seemed prideful and rebellious, Brunson failed to hide his surprise.

"Like me, this one is: stubborn but strong, willful and defiant. Farhallian is his name. What is filly's name?"

"I hadn't thought of a name yet. I suppose I'll have to think of something suitable."

"Think? No. She tell you her name. Look in eyes and ask; then you know."

Not certain Vertook was serious, Brunson knelt down before the filly, wondering if he were being made to look a fool. When he met her eyes and asked her name, though, he was shocked to have something immediately pop into his mind, and he knew it was right. It was not simply a name for the filly, it was *her* name: Shasheenia.

Vertook nodded and smiled when Brunson spoke the name. His voice an awe-filled whisper, he repeated it over and over, feeling its rightness.

Shasheenia.

Chapter 10

The stench of fear can be cleansed only by eliminating its source.
--Datmar Kahn, assassin

* * *

The feel of cold metal against her skin was the most frightening thing Catrin had ever experienced, but she was not cut or stabbed, and none of her blood was shed. She kept her eyes closed and her breaths shallow as the blades glided across her taught flesh. Starting with her eyebrows, they carefully and skillfully shaved her. Cool air brushed the newly exposed skin left in their wake. Bits of loose hair tickled her face, but she was afraid to flinch as her mind filled with visions of sharp knives biting deep.

Her hair fell away silently, without pain or struggle, but Catrin felt as if she were being assaulted. The robed women continued their ministrations until her head was completely shaved.

Upon completing their task, they helped Catrin stand. After helping her undress, they wrapped her in a warm, soft robe. When not bearing knives, the women seemed much less threatening. She sensed empathy and caring from them, and when they led her through a door in the opposite wall, she followed with a mixture of anticipation and wonder.

They emerged into a long corridor lined with doors on both sides, all of which were closed. Darkness shrouded the far end of the hall, hiding what lay beyond. The women approached the first door on her left, and it opened silently with the slightest push. The hallway beyond was dimly lit by the reddish glow of a small fire. Around a bend was what looked like a natural rock formation, though many of its features appeared to have been shaped by skillful hands.

Pools of clear water filled the room, a haze of steam shifting above them. Near the edge of the largest pool stood another stone table, but this one was topped with a soft pad. The women silently instructed her to disrobe and climb atop the table, and Catrin did so with less inhibition than she would have expected. Her embarrassment dissipated, and she found it liberating.

As she lay on the table, though, a chill tightened her flesh, and she wished for a blanket or something to cover her. Looking about, she saw the women use wooden tongs to remove a variety of smooth stones from the steaming water. They lined the stones along the pool's edge and, using their slender fingers, appeared to test the temperature of each. When they were satisfied with each stone, they placed them under and around her with care.

Catrin reveled in the heat emanating from the stones, which were now in her palms, under her feet, and behind her neck, and still more were coming.

Soon Catrin wished she were wearing some sort of clothing just so she could take something off. The heat permeated her skin and soaked into her body. Sweat poured from her, and she wondered if she would shrivel into a dried husk, but she continued to shed water, beads of sweat sliding down her face and the length of her body. As the stones cooled, the women replaced them with hot ones. The purge was intense, and Catrin licked her parched lips.

After they removed the stones and returned them to the hot pool, the women brought basins of water that had been soaking in the hot pools. They dipped soft cloths in the water and cleansed the sweat from Catrin's body. As they helped her up, she grew dizzy, but the spell soon passed. She donned her soft robe again and gratefully accepted a large of mug of water. It was cool and sweet and tasted delicious.

One of the women guided her back to the hall then walked straight to the opposite door. It led to a small room that contained only a sleeping pallet and chamber pot. The other woman arrived a moment later with a pitcher of water and a mug. Then they left, closing the door behind themselves. Left alone with her thoughts, Catrin spent the rest of the day in quiet reflection, trying to ignore pangs of hunger.

* * *

In the oppressive heat of the forge building, the cold and snow seemed a distant dream. Sweat rolled into Strom's eyes as they waited for the molten blob within the crucible to reach what Gustad considered the optimal consistency.

"Do you really think we can do this?" Osbourne asked.

"Don't know," Strom said. "Milo said we just need steady hands, and I suppose we have that."

"So much work has gone into making the glass; I don't want to ruin it."

"No worries, my boy," Milo said from across the room. "You boys are just what we need to achieve the perfect pour. Practice it may take, but you will succeed, of that I am confident."

"See," Strom said. "Milo believes in us."

"Yeah," Osbourne said, his voice barely above a whisper, "but that's coming from someone who sets himself on fire at least once a day."

"He hasn't gone up in flames today," Strom countered.

"The day is young yet."

Gustad bent down to peer into the small opening in the furnace, admiring the molten glass in the crucible. "I believe we are ready to pour," he said. "Remember, the key is slow and steady, and you must increase the rate of your pour as you reach the bottom of the crucible. Understand?" Strom and Osbourne nodded, though Strom wondered if his confidence were misplaced. He certainly had no reason to believe he and Osbourne were capable of a task that required such precision, but he was determined to try. "Steady now," Gustad said as they slowly eased the crucible out of the furnace, their arms hidden within long, thick, leather gloves.

Despite their efforts, hot coals clung to the crucible and fell to the floor. "Don't let any coals drop into the mold," Milo said, his eyes wide with excitement.

"Hurry now," Gustad said. "We must not let the glass cool. Begin the pour. Slow and steady, boys. Slow and steady."

Strom tried to keep his hands from trembling, but the pressure was on him. Osbourne's task was simply to balance the long pouring rod while Strom regulated the rate of the pour. Slowly he began to tip the crucible. Like heated tree sap, the molten glass oozed from the crucible, and Strom tried to ignore the sweat that was seeping into his eyes.

"Easy, now. Nice and slow," Milo said, moving closer to inspect the pour, his long robes gliding across the floor.

"Increase the flow," Gustad said after most of the glass had left the crucible; only a small amount remained. "Steady now. Steady."

Squinting, Strom tried his best, but his eyes burned, and the crucible wobbled slightly.

"Blast!" Gustad said. "So very close. You nearly had it. Put the pouring rod and crucible on the rack."

After replacing the rod, Strom turned and shook his head. "Milo," he said.

Milo ignored him as he examined the glass cooling in the mold. "Not bad," he said. "Almost as good as what we've accomplished on our own-- only a few bubbles. If only my hands did not shake with age, we could have had this done a dozen times."

"Milo," Strom said more forcefully while trying to catch up with the monk who now paced the floor.

"I wonder if we should change the shape of the crucible so we don't have to increase the rate of pour so dramatically--"

"Milo!"

"What is it, m'boy?" Milo asked, suddenly sniffing the air.

"You're on fire again."

* * *

The next morning brought two more robed figures, and Catrin sensed these were not the same women from the day before, but women they were. Acquainting herself with the aura of each robed figure, Catrin became more adept at the process. Using only her senses, she examined the robed figures with no apparent reaction from her subjects, but she kept her investigations brief and cursory, not wanting her exploration to be discovered again.

They led her down the hall, past several doors, and picked a door seemingly at random. It led to a man-made chamber that housed another large stone slab, but this slab differed from the others in that it had a large cavity hollowed out of its base, which was filled with glowing red embers. The women helped Catrin from her robe and motioned for her to climb atop the table. Catrin ran her hand across the slab. It was quite warm. She seated herself on the end of the table and lay back slowly.

The stone seemed too hot on her skin at first, but as she eased herself down, the intensity seemed to lessen. Both women sorted through a tray of small vials; then they anointed her with hot oils. Each drop brought its own unique sensation, and a variety of pungent smells assaulted her senses. The mixture was heady, and it nearly gave Catrin a headache, but as she relaxed, the pain subsided. As the women massaged the oils into her skin, she relaxed further. Kinks in her stiff muscles seemed to melt, and she was amazed by how many places were sore. She'd felt fine before she lay down, but the women worked knotted and sore muscles she had been completely unaware of.

They brought her water and gave her time to drink. When Catrin had had her fill, they motioned for her to lie back down, and she complied without complaint. The massage treatment had been wonderful, leaving her feeling limber and relaxed.

She wasn't certain what to expect when they returned to her side, each holding some sort of narrow cone that was as long as her arm and appeared to be made of waxed cloth. After inserting the small ends of the cones into Catrin's ears, they placed her hands around them, making it clear she was to hold them in place. Catrin had begun to expect unusual things during the ritual, but she could not imagine what would come next.

They returned, each holding a long piece of dried reed. They knelt down, and when they stood, the ends of the reeds were afire. Catrin nearly shrieked when the women lowered the flaming reeds toward the wax cones. Instinctively, she thought of her hair then realized she no longer had any. Tilting the cones forward, she saw flames dancing on the ends of the cones from the corner of her vision, but the waxed cloth burned slowly. A strange but not unpleasant sensation filled her ears, and she laughed. The hooded women just stood and watched the wax cones burn, but Catrin sensed their mirth.

"I know you're smiling under those hoods," she said, and she stuck her tongue out at them. While they showed no visible reaction, she could almost feel their mental laughter, which made her smile. She tried to relax and trust the women not to set her head on fire, but it was difficult, and she was glad when they removed the burning cones from her ears.

* * *

Within the halls of Adderhold he stood, the boy with no tongue. He watched as liveried servants prepared a banquet, but he knew it for what it was: a trap. Soon the nobles would arrive, dressed in finery and expecting to be treated as honored guests, and so some would be, but for others, there awaited a surprise.

Keeping to the shadows, the nameless boy watched and waited, knowing there was nothing he could do to stop it; there was nothing he could do to gain his freedom or to preserve the freedom of others. He was powerless, a slave, capable of little more than serving his master, and to this fate he resigned himself. There was no one who cared for him; no one would come to rescue him from this prison of flesh and bone. He was alone--now and for the rest of his days.

With a sigh, he moved through the dark corridors known to only a few and made his way to the banquet hall. Standing behind scarlet curtains with gilded trim, he hid, hoping no one would remember he existed. Once he had been brash and proud, but now all he wanted was to be left alone, to be forgotten.

As the guests began to arrive, he watched, waiting to see who would show the signs. His heart beating faster with every arriving noble, he almost dared to hope, almost convinced himself that none would have real power. When the nobles began to take their seats and servants served the first dishes, it seemed his wishes had been granted, but he knew better. Nothing he had ever wished for had really come true, and he had no reason to believe things would change now.

When servants rushed to escort a late arrival to the hall, he was not surprised to see a nimbus of power around the man they led. Dressed in lavish colors and bejeweled raiment, the man stood tall and proud. This was a man accustomed to power, both physical and political, but it was obvious he knew nothing of his real power, the very thing that made him, in this case, most vulnerable.

With a shuddering sigh, the nameless boy retreated, not needing to see any more. He knew what was to come, and he could only lament. He was powerless--a slave.

* * *

That night Catrin was led to a large room, most of which was taken up by a huge stone basin filled near to capacity with a colorful array of rounded and polished stones. Two pitchers of water and a jar for drinking were also present in the room, along with a few other amenities. On the edge of the rock basin was a single red rose. Her guides gave her no indication why it was there. Instead, as they left, they wordlessly instructed her to sleep in the stone basin.

Her thirst unquenchable, Catrin drained one of the jars before approaching the basin. The rose drew her closer, and she inhaled its fragrance, felt the texture of the petals with her lips, and marveled over the bead of moisture hidden within its folds. It was surprising how enamored she could become with a rose, something she had walked by a hundred times without really noticing, but here, in her isolation, taken out of its context, the rose was a magnificent work of art. Soft, red petals stood out in contrast to the emerald stem with its brownish thorns; it seemed a magical thing.

As she climbed into the strange basin, the stones were cool against her skin. The more she moved, the deeper she became submerged in the rainbow of spheres. She saw topaz, turquoise, black onyx, and a host of others she could not identify. The energy of the stones surrounded her, and she basked in it. Each type had its own unique energy, much in the same way that each type of living creature had its own signature.

Turning the basin into a game of sorts, Catrin wiggled her feet through the stones, grabbing at random with her toes. Then, using only her impression of the stone and her physical contact with it, she tried to identify what kind it was. For those types whose names she did not know, she made up names such as "Pretty Red" and "Purple Swirly." Within a short time, she could correctly identify four out of five stones without looking at them. As enjoyable as she found her little game, she paused and took time to simply bask in their energy. Within moments of quieting her mind, she slept.

* * *

"Please, Lord Jaharadin, do come in and sit with me," Archmaster Belegra said.

"Thank you, Archmaster. You honor me," Icari Jaharadin replied as he eased himself into one of the chairs near the fire. The upholstery was far too gaudy for his taste, but the deep cushions were softer than they appeared, and the chair seemed to suck him in, as if it were consuming him alive. It was a feeling that left him on edge.

While an audience with the archmaster was indeed an honor, Icari couldn't shake the feeling that he was in grave danger. Still, he could not resist the opportunity to bring greater standing and wealth to his family, not that declining was an option; to do so would be too great an insult. He had seen what happened to families that displeased the archmaster, and he had no wish to find himself working in the fields or rotting in a dungeon. "My mother sends her respects and asked that I extend an invitation to our humble--"

"Yes, of course she did," Archmaster Belegra said, his eyes narrowing and a feral grin crossing his face. "Your mother is a weathered hag, and I'd sooner wallow with the pigs than dine in your hall. You are here for a reason, Icari, and that reason is not to flatter me."

Icari could not have been more shocked, though he did what he could to conceal his reaction.

Still, Archmaster Belegra chuckled and leveled a finger at him. "What would you do for me, Icari? Tell me. What would you do?"

Squirming in the chair that now seemed a prison, Icari wanted to flee, but his limbs would not respond. Trying desperately to find words, he found his mouth worked of its own accord. "I would die for you," he said involuntarily.

Tilting his head back, Archmaster Belegra erupted in laughter that held no joy. "Of course you would, my servant. Of course you would."

* * *

It was an unusual awakening as stones fell from Catrin's face and cheeks when she raised her head. Some defied gravity for a moment, clinging to her skin, as if they had become embedded in her flesh. Standing slowly, she brushed off the few tenacious stones that still adhered to her and laughed at the strange patterns left on her skin by the stones. She looked almost reptilian, as if she had scales. The effect did not last long, though, and her skin returned to its normal state.

Wondering how soon the monks would arrive, she climbed free of the basin. When she went for a mug of water, she noticed that the pitchers had been refilled, and she wondered if this were a subtle hint. It became obvious later that the monks would not return for her that day, and she decided to spend her day napping and amusing herself. One of her naps ran into the next morning.

* * *

Oily, black smoke rolled from the lamps that lit the Watering Hole, and Miss Mariss wiped the tears from her eyes. The smoke from the makeshift lamp oil was only part of the reason she cried; what had once been a joyful existence had turned into constant struggle. Everything was in short supply these days, especially good humor. Without decent food and drink, business was slow, and she spent much of her time simply trying to survive.

Scrubbing the soot from the walls, she did what she could to keep her inn clean, but it was a battle she always lost, and she began, once again, to despair.

Many of the people she held dear were in the Chinawpa Valley, beyond the atrocity known as Edling's Wall. Construction of the wall sapped the Pinook of resources when they were needed most. Miss Mariss could not understand how people could spend their time building a barrier between themselves and their countrymen when there was not enough food to go around. Fools they were, the lot of them, she thought.

Looking around, she wondered why she stayed, why she didn't just join those in the Chinawpa Valley, those with good sense. But just like every other time the thought had occurred to her, she realized she could not leave behind her inn--the place that had been her mother's life and her grandmother's before that. No. She would stay and try to make the Masters see that they were wrong to divide the Godfist. Knowing they would never change their minds or their greedy ways, she returned to scrubbing, her tears running anew.

* * *

The first sight Catrin saw when she woke was a hooded figure leaning over her, and she squeaked in surprise. The figure backed off quickly and waved a silent apology while Catrin tried to figure out where she was. Her mind muddled, the stone bath confused her, but somewhere between sleep and wakefulness, it all rushed back. She shook her head to clear the last of the drowsiness then climbed from the basin.

As she stood too quickly, the blood seemed to rush from her head. Dizziness overwhelmed her, and the monk lent support while she regained her balance. Catrin thanked the woman and drank three mugs of water while she waited for the spell to pass. Slowly she began to feel better. Supporting herself again, Catrin gave a nod, and the monk led her back to the hall and opened the third door in. Catrin followed, whimsically wondering how they could top the previous days, and she tried to prepare herself for the unexpected.

Inside stood another stone table next to a bubbling pool of murky brown mud that shifted and moved. Tiny specks of something shiny caught the light as they shifted, giving the pool an even more mystical appearance. Another female monk waited inside, and Catrin marveled at how adept she had become at gender identification; it had become almost effortless.

Once Catrin was supine on the table, the women coated her with a thick layer of the sparkling mud that almost immediately began to dry. When she was thoroughly coated, they left her to dry in silence. The drying mud pulled at her skin as it shriveled and cracked, and in some places it itched terribly, but she endured, not wanting to move. It was not long, though, before the women returned. They peeled the husk from Catrin, and the feeling of cool air on the newly exposed skin was intense. They wiped away the rest of the mud with a damp cloth, and the entire process was repeated, consuming the rest of the day.

* * *

Fierce winds drove the sleet, turning it into stinging projectiles that immediately froze on whatever it struck. Borga Jahn walked with his head down, each step a trial as he had to stomp through the thick layer of ice that coated the snow; to walk on top of the ice was impossible.

"We should turn back," Enit said. "We'll die long before we ever reach Ohmahold."

"You knew what you were getting into when you accepted this assignment. Keep walking." Both knew this was a mission from which they would not return; they also knew they had to succeed. General Dempsy would keep his word, which meant there was no turning back. He did not know what deal Enit struck, and he did not care to know. For Borga, success was the only option. To fail was to send his daughter, Bella, to her death, and that he could not even think about.

Bella was a good girl; too kind and sweet to be in an army. Borga could not blame her for deserting, and with his final act, he was determined to set her free. This task would be completed even if he had to do it alone, and given Enit's whining, that was beginning to seem increasingly likely.

Borga looked around and said, "We need to make shelter for the night, or we'll freeze to death."

"Make a shelter out of what? Snow and ice?"

"Precisely. Now dig. We need to form a pocket of air beneath the snow; that'll keep us warm."

"Warm?"

"Warmer than we would be exposed to this wind. Shut up and dig," Borga said, tempted to just kill Enit now and go on by himself, but he knew that together they had a better chance of succeeding. He would tolerate Enit for Bella's sake.

When they had a shelter large enough to hold them both, they settled in for what would be a long night.

"I thought you said it would be warmer in here."

"Shut up, Enit."

* * *

Catrin woke in a strange room that was moderately furnished, but she did not recall how she had come to be there. It was an uneasy way to start her day, but she still looked forward to whatever adventure it would bring. When the monks arrived, she discerned one male and one female. The male was obvious due to his height and girth, but she confirmed her visual assessment with her other senses.

When the monks selected a door, Catrin was almost certain she had been through that one before, but the room beyond was nearly empty. Lamps hung on the walls, and a thin layer of cloth lined the floor. The cloth was tightly woven and appeared to have been treated with some sort of sealant. When Catrin stepped into the room, the cloth gave way, cushioning her foot. She followed the trail of footprints left by the monks and amused herself by walking in the man's large footprints. By the feel, she guessed that the floor had been covered in a layer of sand before the cloth had been laid. Intrigued, she wondered what its purpose could be.

The male monk approached her and nodded a bow that Catrin respectfully returned. She steeled herself as he moved behind her. Using his hands, he began to manipulate her, stretching her stiff muscles, and she felt like a clay doll in his powerful grip. Some of the stretches and contortions were painful, but others felt wonderful as they released pent-up tension.

Bones occasionally popped and shifted as she stretched, and it felt glorious. She was surprised, though, when the man contorted her body, seemingly for the sole purpose of producing loud pops. The positions were not all that uncomfortable, and the releases felt good, but she couldn't shake the impression she was being attacked by a bear. When he grabbed her head, swiveling it back and forth, she prayed he did not underestimate his strength and twist it right off her neck.

A sudden jerk of his hands was accompanied by an alarmingly loud series of crunches, and for an instant she feared he had snapped her neck. When he removed his hands from her head, she moved her neck tentatively and not only found it still attached, but discovered the knot in her neck was gone, and she hadn't even realized her neck was sore until after the relief of tension.

He gestured for her to lie on the floor, and Catrin wondered what he would do to her next. He rolled her to one side, manipulating her low back in ways she would have never imagined. The pops and cracks were not as loud or as plentiful, but those that occurred felt massive. Rolling her onto her stomach, he placed his hands on her head for a moment then departed.

The female monk approached, and Catrin was a bit shocked when the woman stepped on her, and she was even more surprised when the second foot followed. More loud pops and cracks accompanied the woman's footsteps as she worked Catrin's flesh with her toes. Catrin was glad the female monk was performing this part of the ritual; the man would have crushed her.

When the treatment was completed, she was led back to the room with the stone-filled basin. The energy of the stones beckoned to her, and she rushed to finish drinking her water, anxious to immerse herself in the rainbow of energy textures.

* * *

"Do you think Catrin is purified yet?" Osbourne asked over the evening meal.

"With as much manure as she shoveled over the years, they've got a lot of purifying to do," Strom said, laughing.

"Do you really think they'll make Cat cut her hair?" Chase asked.

"There's a good chance," Benjin said. "I only told you it was a possibility so you would not be surprised. She may not be very happy about it."

"I can't imagine Cat without any hair."

"It'll grow back," Benjin said softly, and he looked around the common room. Tables were beginning to fill up. They had agreed to keep Catrin's activities to themselves, and he did not wish to be overheard. The murmur of many voices filled the air, but still he kept his voice low. "Just keep doing what you are doing, and everything will be fine."

"I know," Osbourne said. "I'm sorry. I just keep thinking about what they might be doing to Cat, and it gives me the crawls."

"This whole place gives me the crawls," Strom added.

"Things here may seem strange," Benjin said, "but if these people journeyed to the Godfist, they would find our ways just as strange. You'll get used to it."

"I just want to see Catrin do whatever it is she's supposed to do, so we can all go home," Chase said.

Benjin looked at the faces around him, knowing none of them would be going home soon, knowing their homes may no longer even exist, but he said nothing. The rest of the meal was eaten in silence.

* * *

The days and nights that followed were variations of the first few days, and Catrin enjoyed herself thoroughly, although she was not overly fond of shaving. Despite the lack of food, she seldom felt pangs of hunger. It was more the desire for taste and spice that gave her cravings than it was the desire for solid food. She lost count of the days and lost track of which doors in the hall led to which rooms. As she approached what she thought to be the final days of the cleansing, she was immensely proud of herself for having gone through with the process. It had been a scary thing to take on alone, and she felt strengthened by the experience.

When four monks, three female and one male, arrived for her one morning, Catrin anticipated the conclusion of the ritual. She followed the figures in respectful silence and did her best to perform her part. Although she had laughed and teased the monks during part of her time with them, she could feel the seriousness in the air. This was a sacred affair, and she was determined to show proper humility and respect. They took her to a narrow room with oddly shaped openings in the walls.

Without instruction, she climbed atop the table. Trying to center herself, she closed her eyes, took slow, deep breaths on the count of seven, and calmly addressed her thoughts. No one touched her, but she could feel the presence of hands above her head, feet, hands, and naval. She felt no pressure, but a warm tingling sensation infused her flesh as the energy shifted and moved.

Her meditation evolved into a deep trance, her body feeling as if it were waving back and forth without moving, and at first, she didn't notice the sound. Rhythmic music created by many voices chanting in harmony started low and soft, but it gradually grew in volume and intensity. There seemed to be no distinct words or meaning, and Catrin immersed herself in the deep bass vibrations. Two distinct chants merged around her: one came from the left, the other from the right. As one intensified, the other would subside, and gradually they reversed, creating a deep, pulsating sensation.

The joy of floating along the energy now swirling around her was magnificent, but it felt self-indulgent; she was here to be cleansed, not pampered. Beginning her meditation again, she concentrated on each thought as it came to her. Some were dark and challenging; others, light and amusing. Each one she processed and accepted before casting it away. Having become more adept at the process, and in the midst of the energy, she found it possible to admit and accept some very difficult things--things that would normally have driven her to tears.

Envisioning a fountain of energy flowing from her forehead to the sky, she poured all the hurt and pain from her soul into the wellspring. She allowed it to be as it would be and embraced the things that made her who she was. It seemed, at first, as if her fountain of anguish would flow forever, but it finally began to abate. As it dwindled, a pure flow of energy took its place. More and more, love and joyfulness washed away the pain. As the flow became pure joy, she cast it out in all directions, to be shared with everyone and everything. The energy poured through her and from her, and it felt as if a worn, dead shell were blasted away before the onslaught.

The next breath was like Catrin's first. Inhaling deeply, she savored every scent in the air, each one a marvel. The air around her body vibrated as if alive, and she kept her eyes closed, afraid to break the spell. As her mind settled, she found the center of her focus. It was a small dot in her consciousness that seemed far away at first, but she applied her will and flowed closer. It grew no larger as she approached; it just felt nearer.

When she could finally touch her center, it was sharp, like the tip of a pine needle. Catrin figured something so important should be larger; then maybe it would not get lost so often. As the energy surrounding her reached a crescendo, she applied it and her will in an attempt to enlarge her center of focus. It grew slowly at first, resisting the change, but the rate of growth became exponential, and on every breath it seemed to double in size.

Letting the energy flow, she experienced the life essence around her. As her energy field grew, it enveloped the monks. Using it, she expressed respect and love to them, and she thought she sensed reciprocation. Her consciousness expanded into the stone and began to encompass the rooms in the hall. She felt the mud baths, the rock basin, and still she flew outward. Feeling the life within the temple, she embraced it.

A nagging absence of life in one part of her awareness tugged at her, but she could not focus on it. As she tried to narrow her perceptions down to that feeling, she sensed ancient life in another part of her consciousness. The chanting began to grow softer, slowly and gracefully dissipating, denying Catrin the opportunity to investigate the strange sensations. She gradually drew her consciousness back in as she lost the ability to maintain her far-reaching center.

When her center shrank to the size of a melon, she grabbed on to it with her mind and solidified it. She imagined it as a large version of the polished onyx from the stone basin. It had weight and texture; it was solid and real. With a deliberate mental effort, she stored it in a very special location: floating atop the night-black stone at the center of the Grove of the Elders, which still existed in Catrin's memory.

Utter silence filled the room in the absence of chanting, and Catrin could no longer feel the monks contributing to her energy flow. Her body tingled and still seemed to vibrate long after the monks departed. Left to revel in the feeling of having been cleansed and remade, her body and consciousness sang. Gradually, the effects wore off, and exhilaration was replaced by weariness. Somewhere in between, she drifted into a deep and dreamless sleep.

Chapter 11

True success is nearly impossible to realize alone. Seek out those who are skilled where you are weak, and together you will prevail.
 --Archer Dickens, scientist

* * *

"The boy has some good ideas here," Gustad said as he looked at Strom's rough sketch.

"You replaced me with a stick?" Osbourne asked.

"A very special stick," Gustad said. "We'll need to grind the notch smooth so it won't bind."

"The real magic is in the strap," Strom said. "We confine it to a narrow channel as it gets wound around the shaft. Every turn, the shaft becomes larger and increases the speed of the pour."

"That just might work," Milo said, a gleam in his eye. "How soon can you have it done?"

The question was like a kick in the stomach, and Strom had no idea what to say. He'd been so excited about his idea, yet he really knew nothing of how to actually make it. Gustad stood mumbling over the drawing then began making his own markings.

"Forty days," he said.

Strom smiled, allowing himself to hope. Maybe he, too, was meant to do something special. He looked back at his friend and the monk who remained in the room before he followed Gustad to the forge.

Osbourne watched as Milo pored over Strom's sketch and Gustad's markings. Seemingly without thinking, he moved the candle away from Milo's robes.

* * *

A gentle nudge brought Catrin from her slumber. A female monk helped her dress in a warm robe and soft, fur-lined boots then led her from the room. Unsure if she would be led to yet another room, she was hesitant to set her expectations differently, not wanting to be disappointed. She was thus pleasantly surprised when they went beyond the last door and into the dark hall beyond.

The hall was unlit through a series gentle bends, and Catrin used her senses as guides. Then a faint light illuminated the base of a spiral stair hewn from the walls of a towering cylindrical shaft. When they reached it,

Catrin stopped to look up. The stairs seem to rise for an impossible distance. High above, sunlight streamed through an archway, illuminating parts of the stair and leaving other parts in shadows and lamplight. The climb was arduous, and Catrin was short of breath when they finally reached the landing.

Beyond the archway waited a stunning view. A valley lay cradled between three mountain ranges. At the center stood an ancient tree, massive in size. Not tall like a greatoak, it sprawled. Its branches thicker than the trunks of most trees, it shaded most of the valley. Covered in deep green moss, the bark had a life of its own, and hanging bunches of silvery threadmoss clung to the mighty leviathan.

At the far end of the valley, Catrin could just barely see a shaded entranceway, and the wonders that lay within beckoned to her. The monk led her onto the snow-covered grass and along a path that led to the tree's trunk. Beneath its bows, snow covered only small patches of ground, and lush grasses emerged in tufts. Gold-colored seedpods dotted the grounds, and Catrin was amazed that something so large could grow from something so small.

Near the massive trunk, several monks sat in a circle, all their heads completely shaved. Catrin recognized Mother Gwendolin and Brother Vaughn, though they both looked much different without hair. Honored by their sacrifice, Catrin felt her eyes well with tears. The others were unfamiliar, but they turned to watch her approach. Though she tried to mimic the graceful stride of the monks, Catrin fell short of creating the gliding effect.

Mother Gwendolin waved with a smile, and Catrin was thrilled that someone might actually speak to her. She had not realized how much she depended on interaction with others until she had been in relative seclusion.

"Greetings, Catrin. I hope the day finds you well," Mother Gwendolin said.

"Thank you, Mother. I feel wonderful."

"Please sit with us," Mother Gwendolin said. "I've asked a few others to join us. You've already met Brother Vaughn, who not only cares for the aviary, but also has great knowledge of the Greatland's geography. To my left is Sister Hanna, who is an accomplished historian and scholar specializing in the time of the Purge. To her left is Brother Jamison, who is responsible for analyzing the political climate and nuances here and abroad. And to my right is Sister Velona, who is somewhat of a historical detective and mystic. For decades she has been studying every available piece of material related to Istran phases."

Catrin greeted each of them warmly and thanked them for taking time to talk with her. Those who had not already met her seemed taken aback by her humility.

Intimidated by the vast amount of knowledge attributed to these people, Catrin hoped she did not appear to be a complete fool. At the same time, she was ecstatic to finally have access to people who might have some real answers.

"You have completed the purification ritual, and you are to be congratulated on your accomplishment," Mother Gwendolin continued. "Many do not complete the ritual on their first attempt. Some elements are simply beyond their level of acceptance, but you persevered. From what I've heard, though, those who administered your ritual shall never forget it. I'm told you were a very unique subject to observe . . . and to be observed by," Mother Gwendolin said with a raised eyebrow, and Catrin blushed, remembering the man who had sensed her probing.

"Completion of the ritual grants you access to the Inner Sanctuary, and from now on you need only go through a brief cleansing to regain entry. Those within this circle agreed that clarity would be crucial during this time and chose to undergo the ritual as well. Many elements of the ritual need not be performed in specific order, and we have done simultaneous purifications in the past, but never have we done this many at one time. It required the efforts of every trained monk in Ohmahold to make it happen, and I'm proud they rose to the challenge."

Catrin's awe at their dedication to what was essentially *her* cause was extreme and left her with a feeling of gratitude toward these people she had just met. "Thank you all for what you've done."

"Everything we discuss will be held in the strictest confidence, but we understand some things should remain clandestine. You will need to decide what must be disclosed, and to whom you trust that knowledge. We realize that you will need to discuss some things with Benjin and perhaps others, and we will not ask you to swear a vow of secrecy, but understand that under any other circumstances, we would."

Catrin nodded her understanding.

Mother Gwendolin continued. "There are many things we wish to discuss, but I know you have come to us in search of answers, and I will let you ask some of your questions first."

After considering carefully for a moment, Catrin decided to reword her reason for seeking out the monks. "I've come seeking knowledge and understanding regarding the power I wield. I don't understand it, and while I have done some amazing things, I have no real control over my power. I don't understand why I was chosen to be the Herald of Istra. What am I supposed to do?"

Mother Gwendolin rocked back on her heels with a whistle. "Not one for simple questions, are you? I must tell you first that we will not be able to tell you what you are supposed to do. None of us know. In order to give what answers we can, you must understand some things. The Cathuran order is devoted to knowledge and understanding of the world around us and the creatures that inhabit it, including ourselves. We have all taken an oath of neutrality, which forbids us to interfere in the affairs of the world under most circumstances.

"We will give you our open and honest opinions as we are able, but you must understand that each of us has our own personal views, and we will only be expressing our individual perceptions of the world. It is our belief that life is the greatest mystery ever conceived and that no one will ever know the true meaning until after they depart this world, perhaps not even then. Do not take our words for absolute truth. Instead, use them to formulate your own perception of truth. Do you understand?" she asked.

Catrin nodded her understanding again, though she was beginning to wonder if she would ever get a straight answer.

"Do you believe in predestination?" Mother Gwendolin asked. Catrin wasn't certain she understood, which must have shown on her face. "In other words, do you believe the course of future events has already been determined?"

"I don't know," Catrin answered hesitantly. "I don't think so."

"Interesting," Mother Gwendolin replied. "It would seem to me that one must believe in predestination in order to believe that prophecies can be real. If the course of events has not been predetermined, then true prophecy could not exist. Prophecies, you see, are paradoxical in nature and can only be proven authentic if they are unknown during the events they portend. Otherwise, knowledge of the prophecies can affect the course of events. Thus, a prophecy can be instrumental in its own fulfillment. Would you have attacked the Zjhon if they had not invaded the Godfist?"

"No. I wouldn't have attacked anyone. I had no reason to destroy the Zjhon. I wasn't even certain they existed, and I still have no desire to destroy anyone. I want only peace," Catrin replied.

"Then I think we must regard the prophecies of the Herald of Istra to be nothing more than self-fulfilling prophecies and glorified predictions. The writer knew Istra's return would surely result in some individuals displaying unusual powers, just as they did during the last Istran phase."

"But why am I the only one to have these mysterious powers?"

"You are not," Mother Gwendolin responded. "Others across the Greatland, and I presume on the Godfist, have experienced changes as well, but most have been subtle. The trauma of your near-death experience shattered barriers within your mind, whereas others have only caught a glimpse of what lies beyond. Healers have seen their treatments become more effective, animal trainers have found their innate ability to communicate with animals strengthened, along with a host of other subtle occurrences.

"One extreme case was reported in the Southland. Witnesses say a young man caused a huge explosion when bandits attacked him. The explosion killed the bandits. Unfortunately, the resulting rockslide killed the young man as well. All these occurrences, in and of themselves, are not that remarkable and can be easily dismissed as exaggerations. You, on the other hand, lived on the Godfist and wielded considerable power. You were not chosen by Istra to be her Herald; you were chosen by the Zjhon. The prophecies created the image of a great destroyer, and you fit the painting."

Catrin swayed as she digested Mother Gwendolin's explanation. Could it be that simple? Could it be a huge coincidence or, as Mother Gwendolin put it, the self-fulfillment of a prophecy that was based on probable predictions? It seemed a cruel and cold explanation, and one that provided no real indication as to how she should handle it. If she was only the Herald because of what the Zjhon believed, then how could she possibly remedy the situation? How could she make the Zjhon believe she was not born to destroy them? She did not voice the questions, fearing she already knew what the answers would be.

"Your survival may be all you can hope to achieve," Mother Gwendolin said, as if reading her thoughts. "The Zjhon are devout in their beliefs, and they will not easily give up their search for you. Perhaps you will be able to create peace among the nations, but it is impossible to say. In my reality, the future is undetermined; therefore, endless possibilities exist. In such a reality, one can achieve incredible things with effort and determination, or they can lose everything by making bad decisions. It is a magical and tenuous existence. It is up to you to decide what is in *your* reality."

Catrin was not sure if she should be encouraged or depressed, and she tried to find her center. The revelations of the day befuddled her, despite the clarity she felt as a result of the purification, and she struggled to focus. She traveled in her mind to the Grove of the Elders and located her visual representation of her center. It was smaller than when she left it, and she took a moment to expand it. This simple exercise in self-control helped her tremendously, and she found her confidence along with her center. "I accept your counsel on the matter of prophecies, and I thank you for the imparted wisdom. I've adjusted my perception of reality and will continue to do so. Can you teach me to control my powers?" she asked.

Mother Gwendolin exchanged a glance with the other monks.

"She's definitely not one for asking easy questions, Mother," Sister Velona said. "I've searched for many years, but I'm afraid I can tell you very little of how to control your powers, as it seems to be different for each individual. I can, however, tell you some things you should avoid at all cost. Are you familiar with the stories of Enoch Giest and the Sleepless Ones?"

"I've heard stories, but I don't remember all the details."

"During the wars between the Zjhon and the Varics, there were many gruesome battles, and both nations lost many men and women. Enoch

Giest was a captain in the Varic army, and he was determined to defeat the Zjhon. During a relatively minor skirmish, he was wounded and lay dying on the battlefield. He'd always thought himself gifted but had never been able to use Istra's power," Sister Velona said.

"As his lifeblood flowed from his body, he knew he was dying. He hoped and prayed he would somehow survive, and then, as the result of some epiphany, he tried to heal himself with Istra's power. He'd never succeeded at anything else with the power, and he had no reason to believe it would work, but given no other options, he applied his will to the task. Somehow, he broke down the barrier between his conscious mind and his subconscious mind.

"It's the subconscious mind that controls the beating of our hearts, our breathing, growth, healing, aging, and more. Under normal circumstances, our conscious minds have very limited control over these functions. For example, you can affect your rate of breathing and even hold your breath, but you cannot kill yourself by deciding to stop breathing. If you hold your breath long enough, you will only pass out, as your subconscious mind takes over.

"We're not certain how, but Enoch took control of his bodily functions. He stopped the bleeding and, afterward, found it easier to continue healing himself. He communicated directly with his formerly subconscious mind, which then became his alter-consciousness. He learned exactly what his body needed to repair itself, and working in concert with his alter-consciousness, he made himself anew," she continued.

"Enoch was so excited about his discovery that he explored ways to pass along his ability to his countrymen. Most could not duplicate the feat; only two others managed to break down their barriers with his guidance and assistance. Discouraged by his failures, he roamed the battlefields, searching for those mortally wounded, and his success rate increased dramatically. Word of his exploits spread, and his appearance on the battlefield drove men to discard their fear. They fought with wild abandon, winning many victories, and Enoch passed his ability to many dying men. But he could not bring back the dead, and hundreds died despite his efforts.

"Within a decade, almost every Varic man still alive had gained the ability to heal themselves. The Varics were not far from conquering the Zjhon, and the Elsics believed they would be next, but that is another story. The Varic nation began to thrive again with the aid of Enoch's imparted healing powers. There were times, it was said, that every Varic woman alive was pregnant. But the next generation of Varics proved to have very little aptitude with the power of Istra, and almost none attained healing powers.

"The passing of traits from one generation to the next is a mysterious process, and it was not until the grandchildren of Enoch's generation were born that the unexpected aftereffects manifested. The second generation since the time of Enoch's discovery was decimated; most did not live past birth. Of those that survived birth, the majority died soon after. They would simply fall asleep and never wake. Enoch watched in horror as his nation's death knell rung, and it was far too late to effect any change.

"By this time, many of the first generation of healers had gone to their graves from either old age or deadly wounds they were unable to heal. Despite the ability to heal themselves, they were unable to heal others. If a self-healer took a wound that rendered them unconscious, they usually perished. Enoch saw the healers dwindling in number and waited in horror for his own grandchild to be born.

"Determined to save the life of his grandchild, even at the cost of his own, he assembled everyone adept with Istra's power and gathered them around his son's wife, Alia, to await the birth. Alia's labors produced a baby boy in apparent good health, but Enoch knew his grandchild would most likely die if he ever fell asleep. He used every conceivable technique to keep the infant from sleep, but it soon became apparent the child would eventually succumb to exhaustion.

"Driven by desperation, he used his powers to reach into the infant's mind and establish a mental link. He smashed the feeble barriers of the impressionable mind and used his alter-consciousness to supplant that of the child. In this way, Enoch was able to control the child's breathing and other body functions, keeping him alive. He hoped to break the link once the child grew stronger, but it was not to be. The boy, Ain, was wholly dependent on Enoch for the maintenance of his bodily functions. The two had to remain together always and could not even go into separate rooms without both becoming violently ill.

"Legends say other Sleepless Ones survived, but those instances were rare. The stories of Enoch and Ain say that, together, they were able to stall the aging process and gain longevity. It was said they committed themselves to preventing the same thing from happening during the next Istran phase, but then the madness set in. Both Enoch and Ain were faced with situations no other mortal would encounter, and their beliefs crumbled around them. The ancient writings say they went mad, but I often wonder if they actually entered a new reality. Either way, they disappeared from the writings of men. I've told this tale so you will clearly understand the gravity of the situation and the seriousness of my warning. Do not try to heal yourself," Sister Velona concluded.

Catrin needed a moment to absorb and store all the details; then she nodded and thanked Sister Velona. "If the Herald prophecy is false, then perhaps I should just go home. I don't need magic or power in my life, and I can just go back to being normal."

"I'm sorry, dear. This has gone too far for you to disappear now. Too many people are focused on finding you and destroying you. Your only choice in this matter is to fight or die. There will be no going back to normal."

Despair was starting to settle on Catrin when Mother Gwendolin interrupted her thoughts. "Perhaps this would be a good time for you to tell us a bit more of your story. It may answer some of our questions and raise new ones in your mind. I know it may be painful, but would you tell us of your mother and the circumstances of her death?"

Catrin did not object to telling what she knew; the pain was old and did not cut as deeply as it once had. She told them of the days preceding her mother's death, or at least what she knew of them. She did not remember much of the events herself, but she remembered very clearly the things she had overheard when she was older--things not intended for her ears. She told of her mother and aunt going to market to get the ingredients for a special meal. Catrin did not know what they had been celebrating. Whatever it was, it no longer mattered.

She told of the glorious meal, some of which she remembered for herself. She recalled how excited her mother had been to let her try a sweet bun, but Catrin had not liked the taste and spat out the only bite she took. She remembered everyone else laughing while they enjoyed their buns; it was a memory that still stung, which surprised Catrin.

When she began to describe the symptoms her aunt and mother developed, Mother Gwendolin went pale and sat with her hand over her mouth, but she let Catrin finish her description. By the time Catrin finished telling the details she had overheard from her father and Benjin over the years, Mother Gwendolin had tears in her eyes and she looked as if she would be ill. The usually serene woman appeared absolutely stricken, and she let out an awful wail. Catrin watched in confusion as she writhed in anguish.

"Oh, Catrin," she sobbed, pounding the soil with her fists. "I'm sorry. I'm so very sorry. I could have saved them; I should have. How could I have been so selfish and blind?"

Chapter 12

In the days beyond her coming, echoes of the past shall peal like thunder.
--Prophet Herodamus as translated by Brother Jamison, Cathuran monk

* * *

"This challenge will be extra difficult," Benjin said. "I told the merchants you would be coming, and I purchased the goods you are going to steal. The purpose is to test your ability to move with stealth. If any of the merchants see you take anything, then I will lose my wager with them. You don't want me to lose my wager, do you?"

"I wouldn't bet on it," Chase said, looking over the list: One red pepper, one loaf of apple bread, and three balls of netted cheese. "No problem. I'll be back soon."

"Good luck," Benjin said.

Though he didn't need stealth to approach the market, Chase kept himself hidden and watched what everyone around was doing. When he saw the vegetable vendor, he settled in for a good look. The vendor was a young man who seemed to be looking everywhere at once. He stood right behind the display of red peppers, ready to fend off a would-be thief.

For a while, Chase just watched. Then he saw an opportunity. Two beautiful girls were walking toward the shop. When the vendor's head was turned, Chase darted across the narrow street and approached from the opposite direction as the girls.

"Good day, ladies," the man said, and that was all the time Chase needed. Quickly and quietly, he reached out and grabbed a single red pepper. When the vendor looked back, Chase was already seeking the next item on his list.

While hiding in a darkened alley, he spotted a young boy playing with a ball and stick. "Ho there, young man," Chase said. "I'll give you a copper to ask the baker a bunch of questions."

"I can do that."

Chase smiled, handed the boy a copper, and slid into the shadows, one step closer to his loaf of apple bread.

* * *

Confused, Catrin moved to Mother Gwendolin's side and tried to console her. From the looks the other monks were exchanging, they were as confused as she was. Mother Gwendolin took several deep breaths and gradually regained her composure. A young monk approached with jars of water, and Mother Gwendolin drank deeply when Catrin offered one to her. Catrin could barely stand the suspense, but she respected Mother Gwendolin and gave her time to calm herself.

"I'm sorry, Catrin," Mother Gwendolin said after another deep breath. "Your mother and aunt were poisoned. They were given a deadly overdose of mother's root, and I believe you were also a target, for mother's root only affects females."

Catrin was stunned. Her father and Benjin had always believed there had been some sort of foul deed involved with her mother's and aunt's deaths, but it had never felt real to Catrin. Now that Mother Gwendolin confirmed their suspicions, Catrin felt a deep, burning anger rise from the depths of her being. She had suppressed it for so long, uncertain it was warranted, but now the justification existed. She balled her hands into fists and wished she had something to punch, wanting very much to vent the searing fury before it consumed her.

"I wasn't certain at first," Mother Gwendolin said, breaking the heavy silence, "but you described every symptom of a mother's root overdose, and the sweet buns would have made a perfect vessel. Mother's root has a sickeningly sweet taste that could be masked with honey or sugar and become almost undetectable. Had you eaten your sweet bun, you would most likely be dead. And were it not for my envy, your mother and aunt would most likely be alive." Catrin was taken aback by the admission and waited silently for an explanation.

"When I met Benjin, he was trying to make his way back to Endland after parting company with your mother and father. He was so handsome, honorable, and in so much pain. I was drawn to him, and I admit I fell in love with him," she continued, looking embarrassed. "Benjin was smitten with your mother, and his heart was broken, but I didn't see it--didn't want to see it. I convinced myself he would fall in love with me and we would be happy together. We both had a love for herb lore, and we spent days discussing various rare plants and roots, but he did not fall in love with me. He didn't even seem to see me as a woman. I was jealous and hurt, which made me most uncharitable.

"During our last days together, Benjin asked me to help him transcribe my notes on several rare herbs of which he had no previous knowledge. I remember it clearly, though I wish I didn't. I was angry and didn't want to help him. I copied the section on mother's root, and I remember omitting the information on the effects of an overdose simply because I didn't feel like doing it. I included the information that warned against overdoses and left it at that. Now I see how high the price of my envy was. I would change it all if I could. I'm so sorry."

Catrin tried to find words to absolve Mother Gwendolin of guilt, but she found none. Instead, she gave her a hug, and they cried together for a while. Mother Gwendolin regained her composure and seemed to realize it was pointless to torture herself.

"I will send Benjin an invitation to meet with us this evening. There is nothing we can do about it now, but he deserves to know the truth," she said.

At that same moment, another young monk approached. "Many pardons, Mother, but Brother Vaughn asked me to come right away if any birds returned. These just came in from Drascha Stone," he said, bowing, and he presented several small, rolled pieces of parchment. She received them with a sad smile, her cheeks still shining with tears.

While Mother Gwendolin read, Brother Vaughn proudly explained their system of using pigeons to send messages between holds. He said several monks from each hold would travel to the other holds during the warm months, and they would carry many birds with them. The birds could then be released at any time to carry messages quickly back to their home hold. It was not a perfect system, he said, and messages were often lost. Important messages were sent with multiple birds, and any urgent messages received by one hold were forwarded to every other hold upon receipt. This, he said, helped to ensure that no Cathuran stronghold would ever be completely isolated from the others.

Mother Gwendolin looked up from the messages and handed one to Brother Vaughn. "I think this will be of most interest to you. It would appear a landslide in southern Faulk has uncovered the skeletal remains of a giant winged beast. The message indicates the beast would have been larger than a warship--incredible," she said. "There is also word of Zjhon troop movements. Several large detachments are converging near the northern tip of the Inland Sea in Lankland. I suspect they will be bound for Ohmahold by the spring melt. It would appear the Zjhon have reason to believe Catrin is here."

The news gave Catrin a cold feeling in her stomach. Now Ohmahold would be subjected to a siege simply because she was there, much as the Godfist suffered because of her. She tried not to castigate herself, knowing, deep in her heart, it was not her fault, but that failed to lessen her anguish. It was difficult to sit near Brother Vaughn, who could barely contain his excitement. The discovery of the winged beast clearly had his imagination running wild, and she tried to draw from his enthusiasm rather than dampen it with her melodrama.

"Do not be overly concerned," Mother Gwendolin said, sensing her thoughts. "Ohmahold is well defended and well provisioned. We can be completely self-sufficient in the event of a siege, and the Zjhon will have to battle the Wastes. When they launched their attack on the Godfist, they sent nearly two-thirds of their strength, and now they are left with insufficient troops to hold lands only recently conquered. I'm told the armies are now conscripting young women into service. These nations have already lost most of their working-age men, and now the Zjhon are sapping them of young women as well. The rural farmers have been the hardest hit. The Zjhon come unexpectedly, and the farmers have been ill prepared to defend themselves. The Zjhon take their young folk and livestock, and they make notes of any small children, so they can return for them later.

"In the meantime, the elderly and the very young are left with all of the work of growing food and caring for what remains of their livestock. The Greatland is on the cusp of famine and a full-scale revolution. I fear there are dark days ahead of us, and there is little we can do to stop it."

"I must accept the things I cannot change and focus on what I can do, I suppose," Catrin said, trying to find some escape from the futility. She glanced at Sister Hanna, who had not said a word since their introduction. "Sister Hanna, perhaps there is something you can help me with. I've been trying to translate a phrase from High Script. Do you know what Om'Sa means?" she asked.

Sister Hanna appeared impressed that Catrin would attempt to translate High Script. "I've seen that phrase only once in all my studies, and that was in one of the oldest texts we have. High Script evolved over the centuries, and the earliest versions are the most difficult to translate. From the context in which I saw the phrase, I interpreted it to mean *departure* or *exodus of the first men*. I cannot be certain my translation is correct, for phrases in early High Script can have many meanings, depending on the order of the words and their context, which makes the translation more art than science. In what context, may I ask, did you see this phrase?"

"Om'Sa is the name of a book that was given to me. It's very old, and I could not translate much of it. It's in my room at the First Inn, perhaps we could ask Benjin to bring it with him this evening," Catrin said, and Sister Hanna seemed genuinely excited about the prospect.

Mother Gwendolin added the request to her missive and sent the young monk to deliver the message.

"I know this has been a trying day for you, Catrin, and for me as well, but I sense events are beginning to accelerate. I'm sorry to bring this up, but I think it will be important for you to understand the nature and properties of noonstone," Mother Gwendolin said, and Catrin wondered what noonstone was.

"From what we know, the fish figurine you found, Imeteri's Fish, was carved from noonstone. Noonstone is very rare, and as you found, it can be used to store a finite amount of Istra's energy. In truth, noonstones are actually crystals that only form under the most rare circumstances. The old texts say they only form during the Istran noon, when thousands of comets can be seen in the skies at any given time. Even then, it is written that they only form under deep salt water and only when the wind is blowing east."

Catrin found it hard to imagine anything could be so rare, and again she felt the sting of having destroyed Imeteri's Fish. "How did the ancients find and retrieve the crystals if they were under deep water?"

"We don't know," Mother Gwendolin admitted. "While that remains a mystery, there are some things I do know. Noonstone is clear and shiny when it is fully charged, and it becomes chalky and porous when its store of energy has been depleted. When energy is drawn from the stone, it grows warm to the touch, and if you draw too much energy too fast, then it will get hot. If you continue to draw upon a depleted stone, it will eventually disintegrate, and the crumbled remains will no longer be viable. The stone will be destroyed."

Catrin nodded in acceptance. Much of what Mother Gwendolin said confirmed what she had deduced on her own--only too late. It was good to have the information confirmed, but Catrin doubted she would ever find another noonstone, which made the discussion seem pointless.

"What is Istra? Is she a goddess or a bunch of rocks in the sky?" Catrin asked, partially in an attempt to change the subject.

Mother Gwendolin laughed and shook her head. "You've a talent for asking questions that are nearly impossible to answer," she said. "Again, understand that this is my opinion. I believe the ancient peoples had no way to explain heavenly bodies, so they made up stories of gods and goddesses to define the unknown. Istra was their personification of the comet storm that lasted for over a hundred and fifty years. And comets are not big rocks in the sky; those are called *asteroids*. We believe comets are made of ice and they radiate their own energy. It is this energy you feel, much like you feel the warmth of the sun.

"If you explore ancient legends and stories of the gods and goddesses, you will find all the major heavenly bodies represented in some way or another. The sun is known as Vestra, the periodic comet storm is known as Istra, and the moon is known as the Dead God, father of the gods and goddesses, who was said to have been killed by his children. Groups of stars were given names and attributed grand deeds. It was even believed that great kings and heroes would become chains of stars upon their deaths. I believe the comet storm is a very natural occurrence, and some of our order have even hypothesized that comets may have been the very source of life itself. If comets are truly made of ice, then it could have been a comet that collided with Godsland and provided her oceans."

Catrin watched as her simple world of gods and goddesses dissolved into a highly complex universe of endless possibilities. If the gods did not really exist, at least in the form of omniscient super-beings, then who decided fate? Could life possibly be nothing more than a series of random occurrences? The evidence pointed toward something even grander than predestination and far more logical than random chaos. Life seemed to consist of many patterns and appeared to follow certain rules. The rules allow for a certain amount of predictability, whereas the complexity of the interacting forces provide entropy, resulting in a constantly changing universe based on orderly precepts--order within chaos.

The thoughts were as confusing to Catrin as they were revealing, and she had a difficult time coming to terms with the multitude of possibilities. She sat quietly for a time, simply allowing her thoughts to flow.

Mother Gwendolin must have sensed that she was overwhelmed because she adjourned their meeting for the day. In addition, the afternoon shadows had grown long, and they needed to get back to the Outer Sanctuary to meet with Benjin. The other monks bade Catrin and Mother Gwendolin a good evening and returned to their own tasks, and Catrin followed Mother Gwendolin back to the Outer Sanctuary.

When they arrived at one of the private dining rooms, they found Benjin already seated and in the middle of a glass of wine. Catrin's waxed leather bookcase sat on the table. Mother Gwendolin left Benjin and Catrin in privacy for a while.

"How are the others faring?" Catrin asked and was relieved to see him smile.

"Better than I would have anticipated, which is a blessing; it could have been a very long winter. Instead, Osbourne has taken up glassmaking and has really shown some promise. Milo seems truly thrilled to have an apprentice. Gustad has taken Strom under his wing, and I think he might be the father figure the boy needed. Strom has already proven himself a capable smith under Gustad's instruction, and I foresee a new future ahead of him. Vertook is in his absolute glory. He's managed to get Brunson to attempt the Arghast method of horse training. Brunson allowed Vertook to select any foal he desired, and then he selected one for himself. Now the two of them are spending every waking moment bonding with the foals. They even sleep in the fields with the animals.

"I've been working with Chase on his swordsmanship. He's quickly becoming a capable fighter, and the exercise is helping his arm heal. We spend a good deal of time discussing strategies and gambits. He's made it quite clear that he's committed to protecting you. He doesn't begrudge the others their pursuits, but he'll have none of it. All his efforts are dedicated to preparation for what may lie ahead." He paused when Mother Gwendolin returned, her face an impassive mask, and Benjin was clearly taken aback by her stark visage. Catrin sat in quiet suspense, trying to decide if she should leave the two in privacy, but she could not make herself move.

"Benjin, I have wronged you, and I am very sorry," Mother Gwendolin began. "I'll put this as kindly as I can, but there is no easy way to tell you. When we first met, I fell in love with you, and I was envious of your feelings for Elsa. You pined after her when I was right there for the taking." She stopped a moment when she saw the look of shock on Benjin's face, which slowly turned to one of comprehension and shame.

"How could I have been so blind?" he said softly, but Mother Gwendolin gave him no time to feel guilty.

"Do you remember when you asked me to help you transcribe my notes?" she asked, and he nodded mutely. "I was angry and my feelings were hurt, and I did a poor job on the pages I transcribed. I copied what I considered the most important things and left out some of the cursory details. My omission cost you dearly, and again, I'm very sorry. I would change it if I could," she said, and she handed him a page from her notes-- the page describing mother's root.

He looked baffled at first as he read over the information he had memorized years ago, but then he came to the part Mother Gwendolin had not transcribed, the part that described the symptoms and treatment of an overdose. His face lost all color, and every muscle in his body seemed to tense as he read the words that could have saved Elsa and Willa. Veins stood out on his neck and forehead, and Catrin thought he might explode. Tears streamed down Mother Gwendolin's cheeks, and her lip quivered.

Benjin set the parchment down slowly then stood. Catrin thought he might leave without another word, but instead he paced slowly around the room, looking like an angry cat about to seek revenge, his lithe movements promising a quick death. After some time, his shoulders hunched as his anger seemed to turn to sadness.

"You must not blame yourself for this, Mother, nor should I be allowed to blame myself," he said in a voice thick with emotion. "We are not responsible for their deaths. We did not murder them. If circumstances had been different, perhaps I would have been able to save them, perhaps not. We would have saved them if we could, but we could not."

Mother Gwendolin nodded and wiped the tears from her cheeks. Then she rushed to hug him. "I'm so sorry," she whispered through fresh tears.

"I'm sorry as well, Gwen. I never meant to hurt you. I just didn't realize," he replied, but Mother Gwendolin silenced him with a finger on his lips.

"You need not explain. You are already forgiven. Now that we better understand the past, let us deal with the present," she said.

Benjin began pacing again, his hostility returning full force.

"When I find Baker Hollis, there will be justice."

Chapter 13

In the absence of drive and purpose, talent can remain forever undiscovered.
--Vitrius Oliver, sculptor

* * *

The reality of her mother's murder settled in slowly, inexorably, like the measured beat of a chisel being driven into her soul. How could anyone be so wicked? What had her mother and aunt done to deserve such hatred? Deep down, though, other questions haunted her. Was it because of her, because of something she did? Was she to blame for their deaths? Perhaps if she had done something differently, her mother and aunt would still be alive.

Nothing could bring them back; she knew that, but the pain was now fresh, as if the loss had been only yesterday. She wept for the hole in her world, the place they should have filled. Then she felt a feeling of peace wash over her, as if they were safe and happy--and with her. She wondered if it was her imagination that conjured the smell of roses, but then she decided it didn't matter; it brought her joy and absolution.

* * *

Covered in sweat and grime, Strom ran the file along the last tooth of the final gear. Finally, they were ready to assemble his machine, and all he could do was hope it would work. Nagging fears of failure made his stomach ache. Hard work helped keep his mind from worry, and he poured himself into the task. If his boiling machine did not pour glass, then it would not be due to a lack of effort.

Milo hovered nearby, always silent but always watching. He knew they were nearing completion, and Strom thought he might not be able to stand the anticipation any longer.

"I think it's ready to go on the shaft," Gustad said. "You've done an excellent job. Now it's time to put your idea to the test. Are you ready?"

"I'm ready," Strom replied after he secured the final gear in place. With dread, he grabbed the handle and started to crank. Slowly the crucible began to turn. After cranking the crucible back to the upright position, Strom filled it with sand and placed a bowl beneath it. Trying to be as smooth as he could, he cranked the handle and simulated the pour.

"Just a little too fast," Milo said. "It accelerates the pour too soon."

"I can't believe it works at all," Osbourne said.

Strom ignored Osbourne's comment, determined to find a way to slow the initial part of the pour. "What if we cut off the first part of the strap and stitch on something thinner; then it won't accelerate much until it reaches the thick strap," he said.

Milo produced a sack made of strong but thin material, and he cut a length from it. After a few more tests pouring sand, Milo calculated the length of strap to be replaced. Stitching the light material and leather proved to be difficult, but Gustad showed Strom how to use an awl to make holes in the leather.

After a few more test pours, Milo declared the pouring machine ready for a test with real glass. They were running out of sand, and Strom felt the pressure.

When Osbourne pulled the crucible from the furnace, he performed his practiced movements and placed the rod on Strom's machine. When he went to secure the strap, though, the heat was too much, despite his thick, leather gloves. By the time the strap was attached, the glass had already cooled too much.

"Don't despair, young Strom. No one designs machines without flaws; the real challenge is to overcome those flaws. We'll just find a way to fix it and try again. Eventually we will succeed."

"How much sand do we have left?" Osbourne asked.

* * *

The modest room Catrin had been provided within the Inner Sanctuary offered little in the way of distraction. She was glad when Mother Gwendolin arrived, if only for something new to think about.

"I hope the morning has greeted you kindly," Mother Gwendolin said as she led Catrin through a maze of corridors.

"I've had a great deal to consider, but I'm feeling a bit better about things. Thank you."

"I'm sorry to burden you further, but time rushes away from us, and there is much we must learn," Mother Gwendolin said, and Catrin nodded. "Much of the information we have regarding ancient times is isolated and without context, which makes it exceedingly difficult to give any of it credence. But there is something I've benefited from personally, and I would like to share it with you. I think, perhaps, it will help you to see more clearly."

"Please, go on," Catrin said, eager for anything that might give her direction. She felt lost in a sea of critical decisions she wasn't prepared to make.

"It's called a viewing ceremony, and I find it helps me focus when I'm unable to resolve a debate or conflict. Would you like to try?"

"What does it involve--I mean, it's not painful, is it?" Catrin asked, feeling silly, and Mother Gwendolin laughed. Her laugh was like the tinkling of fine chimes, and it set Catrin's heart at ease.

"No, child, it's not painful. The viewing chamber is a very special room with two adjoining chambers. A group of specially trained monks will gather in each of the chambers, and they will perform an ancient melody. It's actually quite enchanting."

"Yes, I think I would like that. Thank you," Catrin said, and she wondered what she was getting herself into. The opportunity was certainly too good to pass up, but the Cathurans had already proven full of surprises, and she wondered what the viewing ceremony would reveal.

When they arrived at their destination, a hallway with three elaborately painted doors, they were greeted by a large gathering of robed and hooded monks standing in silence. Catrin smiled, realizing Mother Gwendolin had assumed she would say yes. With a simple nod, Mother Gwendolin sent the monks to their respective chambers. As they filed through the outer doors that bore images of colorful birds, Mother Gwendolin led Catrin through the center door. This door was painted to resemble the night sky, which Catrin noted contained no comets.

Within the chamber stood a large, thronelike chair that was made of a glossy, umber stone streaked with veins of silver and obsidian. Directly across from it, at eye level, was a round hole in the stone wall, beyond which lay open sky. On either side of the chair were twisted orifices that presumably led to the outer chambers where the monks awaited. Mother Gwendolin led her to the seat. Catrin climbed atop the cold, hard stone, doubting she would be able to get comfortable enough to meditate.

"Try to clear your mind of all things. The old writings say, 'Ride the vibrations and you will be free.' I don't think I've ever achieved the desired effect, but it has been helpful nonetheless. When you feel you are finished, just ring this bell," Mother Gwendolin said, and she produced a delicate pewter bell from her robes. It bore the figure of a fairy clinging to the bell, and its ring seemed impossibly loud and clear. Catrin placed the bell on the arm of the throne.

Icy wind gusted through the opening in the wall, and Catrin shivered, wishing she had worn something more substantial than her leather jacket over a homespun top and leggings. Removing the heavy shawl from her shoulders, Mother Gwendolin wrapped it around Catrin with a benevolent smile.

Pulling the shawl tighter, Catrin soaked in its warmth.

"I will leave you now. May you find that which you seek," Mother Gwendolin said, and she left the room, shutting the door behind herself.

The melody drifted to Catrin slowly as she sorted her thoughts and sought her center. A different cadence and tone came from each side, but they merged into seamless harmony--not the disjointed noise of two independent groups, but intentional and purposeful diversification. The two dissimilar parts formed a perfect whole. Drifting on the music, she let it carry her from her burdens.

As she let her spirit float, the drums began. Starting softly, they grew to a pounding crescendo, resonating in a way that seemed impossible, and Catrin could feel them more acutely than she could hear them. The thunder of them rattled the foundation of her being and seemed to shake loose the dust and clutter from her soul. It was as if she were shedding a dead skin, and she experienced herself as a wave of energy rather than her physical form. It was glorious and terrifying.

Despite the exultation of these new feelings, she grew frustrated. Surely some revelation should have come to her by now, some inkling of what path she should take. But the ecstasy was void of insight, and she felt as if she were missing something critical, something just out of reach. Concentrating, she squeezed her eyes shut but still struggled in vain. After numerous attempts, she relented, her will spent.

With a forlorn sigh, she resolved to ring the bell, but as she leaned back, too fast, the back of her head smacked against the unyielding stone with a hollow *thunk*. Her jaw dropped and her eyes flew open with the shock of pain. Her vision focused on the sky beyond the opening in the wall. It was beautiful and inviting, and in her next breath, she was soaring through it.

Her awareness flew among the clouds, and she reveled in the glory of existence for a time, but the strangeness made her wary. She wondered at her lack of form and realized a silvery thread of energy trailed her, like a strand of gossamer leading back to her physical vessel. The confining husk that usually held her awaited in the viewing chamber. She could feel the connection, and she clung to it. Though she enjoyed the invigorating freedom, she knew she would need to return to her prison of flesh; she would be lost without it.

Lost.

Like the sudden realization that one is falling, Catrin snapped to her senses and realized she had no idea where she was. Her consciousness soared across the heavens with alarming speed, the land sliding away beneath her. Pristine snow gave way to a brilliant display of late fall colors. The coastline of what Catrin guessed was the Inland Sea came into view, and she soared closer, changing course by the sheer force of her will. The rocky coast was breathtaking from above. Sunlight danced off the sea, and the land rose in sharp contrast, a myriad of details and textures.

Though she was tempted to orient herself from what she remembered of the maps and where the Inland Sea was, she realized it was too risky; she needed some confirmation. With trepidation, she soared over the waves, hoping she would not get lost over endless seas. Lulled by the monotony of the homogenous waves, Catrin felt herself being drawn into a strange trancelike state, and she fought to keep her concentration.

When rocks jutted from the waters below her, Catrin felt a thrill of expectation, and when a smooth and sandy coastline materialized in the hazy distance, she soared with confidence. Now she was almost certain she was somewhere over Faulk, and she prepared to find her way back to Ohmahold, but a curious sight drew her attention. Like a trail of ants, a line of people snaked along the coast and through the plains, and it was difficult at first to determine which way they moved. South, Catrin decided.

Intrigued by the masses, her curiosity won out over her desire to return to her body, and she flew along, letting the trail of humanity guide her until she came upon a place crawling with activity. Devastation greeted the eye; it looked as if the side of a mountain had fallen onto the plains, and the mass of its rubble could obscure entire towns. Rich, brown soil, newly exposed to the sun, looked like a gaping wound on the land, and as Catrin looked closer, she saw a thin line of people climbing toward an area framed with fallen timber. The obviously man-made fortifications stood out in stark contrast to nature, even in its disorder.

Willing herself closer, she hovered above the odd structure. It was not tall; in fact, it seemed only to form a stable platform. At its center, though, lay the partially exposed skeletal remains of a giant creature. Catrin became excited when she realized this was the beast the monks had reported, and she tried to commit as many details as possible to memory for the sake of Brother Vaughn.

It seemed odd that there were no workers busy uncovering the rest of the beast, and she looked, once again, at the line of people. They continued past the man-made plateau, as if the ancient remains were of no interest. They wound around the mountain to the opposite face. The southern face was nearly whole, with one notable exception. Nearly halfway to its peak, a large section of rock had been torn asunder, leaving a gaping chasm. An eerie glow emanated from the chasm, and it was there the throng congregated, their faces reflecting the ominous light.

Fear and uncertainty crawled across Catrin's consciousness, and she could almost feel the hairs on her physical body rise. A faint urging called her back to her body, but she pulled away, needing to see the source of the bizarre light. She hovered closer to the chasm, past the enraptured faces, until she was directly above it. There, staring back at her was the face of a goddess, larger than a giant and throbbing with inner light. The sight shocked her, and for a few moments, she wondered what it could possibly be. When the realization came, it blotted out all thought and all other possibilities. It left no room for doubt or conjecture; it was as certain as the sunrise.

It was one of the Statues of Terhilian, the bane of humanity.

Cold realization after cold realization slammed into her consciousness, and she reeled in horror, suddenly wishing she had been more attentive during her lessons. Before her was the greatest threat to ever face her world, and it looked as if the Zjhon were determined to exhume it. If what she had been taught was true, the statue would charge in the light of Istra and Vestra; then it would detonate. She did not know what the scale of the explosion would be, but the vision her mind created made her quail. A deceitful weapon, left over from a war long past, once again threatened all life on Godsland.

A strange wrongness floated to Catrin along the thread of energy that led back to her body. It felt of worry, anxiety, and mostly fatigue. With a final glance at the face of Istra and the bones of the beast, she stored as many details as she could then started her retreat. Intent on returning with all due haste, she raced along her thread. It was taut and straight as the path of an arrow, and she let the tension of it guide her.

The resonance of the melody changed suddenly, and her thread of energy wavered and went slack. It was a frightening sensation, but it lasted only a moment before the harmony became strong once again--different, but strong. With renewed vigor, she pulled herself along, the land rushing away beneath her. Once she moved back to the east side of the Inland Sea, she soared north.

Giggle.

Catrin cast about her, trying to locate the source of the strange, disembodied voice when it sounded again.

Giggle.

This time Catrin sensed the direction the noise came from, and she scanned with her senses. A male energy, full of mischief and humor, soared alongside her. She could not see anything to indicate the presence, but she could feel it, taunting her, constantly flitting away from her scrutiny.

Consumed by her desire to return to Ohmahold, Catrin tried to ignore the entity and continued watching the horizon, but the land seemed to crawl past her now, as if she were flying through mud.

The impish presence followed her, and she felt a change come over it: shame, grief, regret, and anger all flowed freely. The feelings struck her, and she felt pity. No one should have to feel so much pain without consolation, and that was the prevailing undercurrent: *No one cares. No one will comfort me. No one loves me. I am no one.*

It was painful, even from the outside, and Catrin changed her approach. She poured love and understanding toward the wayward energy, and it responded to her with disbelief, but she continued to convey kindness and caring.

Confusion, helplessness, and a deep wave of regret slammed into Catrin. She felt as if the entity were resisting someone--not her, it was someone else. She could feel the presence by proxy, through the reactions of the anonymous energy. The reactions were childlike, and Catrin suddenly realized she was dealing with a young energy, one that was being coerced. She decided anonymity was a barrier that hampered communication, but when she asked for a name, she received shame and grief in return--no name.

Catrin tried to understand how it would feel to have no name, and she was overcome with compassion. Everyone deserved a name, and she was determined to name the energy, to give him something to hold on to, something around which he could build his own identity. A name was more than a label or moniker. It was the center of one's perception of one's self. It was indelible and, once given, could never be taken away. All of this, she conveyed while searching for the right name.

Prios. A name of power, of that Catrin was certain. She wasn't certain it had any true meaning, but to her, it meant strong of heart. She conveyed this as best she could, and the response she received was one of great honor, but it was short lived.

Pain. Fear. Regret.

Confusion washed over Catrin, but now it was her own. The world seemed to twist and veer beneath her, and the link to her body went slack. In an instant, it became tangled and knotted, and she tumbled out of control. Panic clutched her, and she could feel the wrongness in her tangled lifeline. Prios battered her with energy, and whenever she seemed to have righted herself, he sent her spinning again. Light and dark fluctuated around her, as if the sun and moon had suddenly sped up, and she was helpless to stop it.

In a desperate attempt to dissuade him, she sent forth the mental image of her mother and, more generally, the feeling of unconditional love--the feeling she got when she delved into her earliest memories: mother, safety, warmth, caring, all wrapped up in single-minded intent.

Searing pain. Loss. Regret.

The feelings pummeled her until she relented, and she realized that Prios had relented as well. He was gone, no trace of his energy remained, but the damage was done. Catrin had no idea where she was or how to find her way back. To make matters worse, she sensed pain from her physical body and suddenly knew she was near death. If she did not get back soon, she would never be able to return. It was not just a feeling she had; she could almost hear someone shouting the words at her, repeatedly, like a mantra.

Scanning the landscape below, she saw no snow, only brownish farmland, and she guessed she was still in the south. A glimpse of the sun gave her a bearing on direction as it set at its normal, inexorable pace. She moved north with all the speed she could muster, but the tangle of energy still connected to her body slowed her even as it grew weaker. Snow appeared on the ground below, and her hope was renewed.

When the northern coast of the Greatland loomed on the horizon, she urgently turned east. Mountains pierced the clouds ahead, and she could almost feel the closeness of her body as it called to her in its final throes of life. She felt herself begin to waver and focused all the energy that remained in her. The vibrations took on new intensity, as if the monks knew she was preparing one final attempt to return.

Soaring toward the mountains, she moved faster, now guided by the pain and tingling of her physical form. She was close, and the closer she drew, the more intensely she felt the discomfort. It was strange to seek out pain when her instinct was to avoid it, but it was preferable to the encroaching numbness. In this case, pain meant life, and she hurtled toward it. Cold stone stood before her, an impenetrable barrier, but she passed through it without the slightest lessening of speed. It granted her passage without complaint.

Solid rock gave way to a labyrinth of corridors and rooms, both natural and man-made. Catrin paid them little mind as she struggled to close the distance separating herself from her dying body. Only when she entered a vacuous hall, filled with relics and tomes from a time long past, did she even notice her surroundings, and the myriad of curious items within the hall impressed themselves upon her mind.

The next instant brought relief as she pierced the walls of the viewing chamber. Her body sat in ashen stillness upon the stone seat, and even as she drew close, it took on a bluish hue. Her consciousness slammed into her physical form with jarring impact, and she struggled to orient herself, questing for the remembrance of her form. Her body no longer seemed to fit, as if it could not contain her, but she forced herself into its confines.

She had expected great amounts of pain, but her limbs were leaden, and she was unable to move. Numbness nearly claimed her, and she made herself draw a deep breath; it became more of a choke, but she did begin to breathe again. Her vision was clouded and dark, and though she noticed shadowy forms moving around her, she could identify no one. Sounds collided with her senses, but she could make sense of none of it. The only thing that mattered in the world, at that moment, was breathing. With each breath, the tingling in her flesh grew, and the pain charged in behind it.

Catrin welcomed the pain; she embraced it. Cramps, burning agony, and sharp pangs were all wonderful and delicious. She felt them acutely and relished them. As her breathing grew to a steady rhythm, her senses returned, her eyes focused, and she was stunned to see Benjin, his head completely shaved. He knelt before her with tears in his eyes. He must have sensed her return to cognizance because he rushed forward to hug her.

"Thank the gods you've come back," he whispered, and Catrin returned his hug with her unwieldy arms. She tried to speak, but her throat was so parched that she feared it would crack apart. Mother Gwendolin appeared with a mug of water. She looked horrible, as if she were afflicted with some ghastly illness. Her eyes were sunken; her skin was nearly as ashen as Catrin's, but a weary smile crossed her face. She handed Catrin the mug and waited for her to drink.

Catrin's hands shook as she tipped the mug, and sweet water dribbled over her lips. There was only a small amount in the mug, but it was like a cup of pure life, and it rejuvenated her as it moistened her dehydrated throat. She handed the drained mug to Mother Gwendolin and wordlessly begged for more. Another mug was handed to her, and it contained little more than the first, but Catrin was glad to have it.

"You must rest now," Mother Gwendolin said, but her voice cracked and sounded raw.

Catrin realized for the first time that she was wrapped in warm blankets. Benjin scooped her up, blankets and all, as if she were little more than a fallen leaf. Mother Gwendolin guided him to a sleeping room, and he gently laid her down on the bedding. Once he was certain she was comfortable, he retrieved another mug of water from Mother Gwendolin, into which he stirred a pinch of brown powder.

"Drink this. It'll help you rest."

"Not yet. I have dire news," Catrin croaked as she sat up, but Benjin forced her back down with only a slight push of his finger. He placed the mug in her hands and crossed his arms over his chest. "Whatever it is, it can wait until morning."

Too weak to argue, Catrin drained the mug for the sake of her thirst as much as anything else. Within moments, she fell into a deep sleep, haunted by visions of a glowing face.

Chapter 14

Fanaticism is a plague. It threatens the fabric of our world and must be stopped regardless of the cost.

--Von of the Elsics

* * *

"You gave us quite a scare, young lady," Mother Gwendolin croaked, wagging her finger at Catrin in a good-natured way. "Please, tell me of your experience. The unknown is driving me to distraction."

"How long was I gone?" Catrin asked, her own voice still rough and grating.

"Fourteen days."

Fourteen days! Catrin was stunned. Her journey had felt like little more than an afternoon jaunt, but then she recalled the cycles of light and dark during Prios's attack, and she surmised that he had somehow affected her perception of time. She didn't hate him for it, convinced he had been coerced, but she also realized she was lucky to have survived. After weeks of fasting, her body had been in no condition to sustain her.

"We had to train every monk available to keep up the ritual chanting, and there's not a clear voice left in the hold. Benjin insisted upon being at your side, and he underwent a condensed version of the purification ritual. He never slept; he just sat with you and held your hand. We were worried beyond reason, and I fear he blames me for endangering you. He sleeps now, though he'll be wroth with me when he wakes. I slipped a bit of sedative into his tea."

Guilt stabbed at Catrin, and she resolved herself to set Benjin straight about a few things when she saw him next, but she was so weary. Her journey had taken its toll, and she wasn't certain she would ever be whole again; she felt disconnected and isolated. She seemed more of a spectator than a participant in life, tucked away in her bed, and she yearned to move about, but her body resisted her attempts.

"The journey was dangerous," Catrin said after a moment's consideration. "But it was made disastrous by means of outside interference. Someone was coerced into interfering with my journey. I know it; I could feel it. You did not place me in danger. My enemies did that. Regardless, I bear momentous news. One of the Statues of Terhilian has been found and is being excavated."

Her words seemed to ring Mother Gwendolin's reality like a bell. She sat in stunned silence, unable to formulate a response.

"I followed a trail of pilgrims to their destination, and there I found the bones of the great beast, but it was the exposed face of Istra, on the opposite side of the mountain, that drew the throng. I looked upon her, and she shone back at me. I cannot say for certain what others saw, only my perception of it."

Tears slid down Mother Gwendolin's tired face, and her breath shuddered when she made to speak. "This is the worst possible news, and it comes on the heels of other ill tidings. General Dempsy has returned from the Godfist with only three of his ships. He's spreading a wild tale of destruction that lays total blame at your feet. He claims you destroyed his armies in cold blood, single-handedly, leaving a trail of gore wherever you trod. He has joined with the forces gathering to assault Ohmahold, and we have word they are constructing monstrous siege engines."

General Dempsy was the man who led the siege on the Godfist. Now she had a name, which granted her power, and Catrin stored the information away.

"The Greatland is on the verge of widespread famine and starvation," Mother Gwendolin continued. "Drought and the lack of capable hands threaten to leave thousands without food. The armies have conscripted the majority of able-bodied persons along with the majority of the livestock, and the seeds of war are all that have been sown. Our civilization is on a path to destruction, and events are moving faster than anyone could have foreseen. And now a Statue of Terhilian enters the fray. It is hard to believe, but I do believe you. If you say you have seen the face of Istra, I believe you. I just have no idea what to do about it."

Catrin could empathize. The news was all very overwhelming, and she could find no suitable course of action to take. Depression settled on her, and she shook herself physically to dislodge it. "I need to get out of this bed."

"I suppose we could walk a bit if you are feeling well enough, but we should not go too far."

Sudden flashes of memory returned, images of tomes and artifacts obfuscated by a thick layer of dust. Catrin recalled her frantic return and the wondrous sight that had caught her attention. "I don't mean to pry, but are you aware of a large hall, within Ohmahold, that is filled with books, swords, and a variety of oddities covered in dust?" she asked.

"I'm not aware of any such hall. How did you come to know of it? There is no place in this hold that is allowed to accumulate so much dust."

"When I was returning from the south, the strange presence confused me and I was lost. I came back into Ohmahold through the stone, and during my journey, I passed through the hall. I think I could find it."

Curiosity seemed to overcome Mother Gwendolin's reluctance to tax Catrin's strength, but not without due consideration. "Are you certain you feel strong enough? Is it far?"

"I want to try. I'm not certain how far it is, but I'll let you know if I get too tired." In truth, she was already weary, but her own curiosity drove her onward. She could sleep when she knew what the mysterious room actually contained. Perhaps some lost volume held the answers to her questions. She let her instincts and her memories guide her to the area she had passed through. The trail led them to the maze that secured the entrance of the Inner Sanctuary. "It's in there."

"Are you certain? We've mapped the entire labyrinth, and only the halls that bear the death symbols remain unexplored. You see, the ancients left us a code that we use to identify the safe passages within the labyrinth, and the defensive halls are marked with specific patterns of symbols."

"It's this way," Catrin said as she grabbed a lantern and led the way into the maze. She followed her instincts, and Mother Gwendolin confirmed the safety of every corridor before they entered it. Letting Mother Gwendolin concentrate on remembering where they were, Catrin concentrated on where they were going.

"I've never walked this part of the maze before. This passage is almost never used to my knowledge, for it leads nowhere. There are only death passages leading from it," Mother Gwendolin said, but Catrin walked in anyway. This was the passage, every bit of instinct and guidance she had pointed just beyond it. When they reached a four-way junction, Catrin stopped, and Mother Gwendolin carefully inspected the markings. Catrin was not certain which of the decorations were significant and which were frivolous.

"All these corridors are death chambers. We can go no farther this way."

Catrin used her senses to peer ahead. The corridor that stood directly across from her was the one; she knew it. "What exactly are the death chambers?" she asked.

"We don't know every variation, but they are filled with traps, many triggered by pressure plates. Some will crush you under a pile of rock, while others impale their victims on sharpened stakes. None has been triggered in my lifetime, and I'm uncertain what exactly lies down that corridor." Driven by an impulse, Catrin strode into the hall, and Mother Gwendolin drew a sharp intake of breath.

Nothing happened.

Catrin's steps did not falter, and she did not hesitate. She let her confidence carry her farther along the hall, and still nothing happened.

Mother Gwendolin conquered her own fears and joined her. She took Catrin's hand and held it in her own. "You are very brave. Are you certain you wish to go deeper? We could both die."

"I'm willing to risk my life. I believe I'm right, but I'll not ask you to risk yours, nor can I ask another to go in my stead. This is mine to do."

"And I have faith in you. I believe in you, and I'll walk beside you in this," Mother Gwendolin said, tightening her grip on Catrin's hand. With a squeeze in return, Catrin strode ahead. A small part of her mind warned against arrogance, but she knew she was safe; this was the way. The two walked, hand in hand, in the lamplight, and when they reached a corner, they each began to breathe again. Resting for a moment, they prepared themselves for what lay ahead. Then they turned the corner together.

Awaiting them was a sight beyond even Catrin's expectations, her memories accounting for only a small fraction of what she saw before her. Row upon row of shelves stood in ranks, lined with hide-bound tomes. Racks of weapons lined the walls, and enormous tapestries hung high above. Fantastically complex devices filled a large corner of the hall, and the sight of them sparked the imagination: Who knew what wondrous purpose they could serve? So much of what she saw was foreign and unidentifiable that it was overwhelming. Mother Gwendolin stood at her side, bereft of words. Her hands were plastered to the sides of her face, and she simply stared in wonder.

The rush of the excitement faded immediately, though, as shouts echoed loudly through the halls and the sound of many booted feet shattered the silence. It was muffled and distorted in the great hall, but its portent was clear: something was very wrong. Mother Gwendolin immediately bolted from the hall and rushed back to the maze. Catrin was close on her heels, her exhaustion banished by fear. When they gained the mighty stair, Mother Gwendolin shouted to those above.

"What is it?"

"Men down in the pastures," someone called back. "Enemy in the hold!"

A chill ran up Catrin's spine, and the words drove her feet. She and Mother Gwendolin pounded up the stair, following a stream of armed men and women. Benjin charged among them, some three turns above her, and still Catrin wondered at his appearance without his hair. He had let it grow for so long, and she felt guilty for getting herself into trouble. Otherwise, she was certain he would not have allowed his head to be shaved.

The effort of the climb and the close quarters, jostling as they climbed, started to wear on Catrin, and she felt light-headed. When they finally reached the upper level, the throng poured onto the plateau and surrounded the highest pasture. In the center of the pasture lay two still forms flanked by two foals that wailed in their mourning.

"Vertook! Brunson!" Catrin shrieked as she ran headlong toward the bodies, her heart pounding. No enemy showed themselves. There was nothing but serenity surrounding the two dead men. When she drew close enough to make out the details, she saw the shafts of arrows protruding from their backs. Bright red fletching caught the light and shone like a beacon of death. The pain in her chest made her wonder if she would die of a broken heart.

The burst of energy she used to get there wore thin, and emotions overwhelmed her. Grief and anger flared high. Deep-seated fears and regrets were merciless in their assault. Leaning to one side, her knees buckled. Mother Gwendolin stepped in front of her and reached out to catch her. Catrin hit the ground hard, and she wondered a moment that Mother Gwendolin had failed to catch her.

Mother Gwendolin stood, frozen, her face locked in a look of extreme shock. The color drained from her face, and a crimson rose bloomed on her smock. She crumbled to the ground in the next instant, and Catrin cried out in horror. A shaft protruded from Mother Gwendolin's back, and the plateau exploded with activity. Two archers had been hidden among high rock formations, but they had revealed themselves to take the shot.

Guards climbed toward them, but one assassin turned and leaped off the cliffs to his death. The other nocked an arrow and drew. Three arrows struck him before he could release, and his shot flew high over Catrin's head. With a scream of agony and frustration, the second assassin fell from the cliff.

Catrin was mired in confusion--everything had happened so fast. Unwilling to believe this was real, she prayed it was all a dream and waited for something to wake her, but nothing did. Rough hands grabbed her and pulled her from the plateau, back into shelter. When her eyes met those of Captain Longarm, tears blurred her vision, and she barely recognized him. He gave her a sad smile.

"I'm sorry for your losses, Lady Catrin, and we'll all grieve Mother Gwendolin, but I must get you to safety. We don't know if there are more men laying in wait, and I'll not take any chances with your life," he said as he guided her to a hall filled with the largest table she'd ever seen. With a highly polished surface, the table looked as if it had been carved in place. Hooded monks already occupied many of the chairs surrounding it, but no one acknowledged Catrin when she arrived.

The mood in the air was appropriately somber, but Catrin found it oppressive. She could not seem to comprehend the day's events. Everything seemed to be happening around her, but she did not feel a part of it. She had no influence on the course of events.

"What was she doing on the plateau?" Sister Velona raged as she entered the hall, her face revealed by her erratic movements, and her tirade broken only by random bouts of sobbing. "How could anyone have been so foolish as to allow her safety to be jeopardized in such a way? Your incompetence has been fatal this time. Boil you all!" News traveled fast around Ohmahold, and those of station soon packed the hall. The gamut of emotions was expressed, shouted, cried, and rehashed.

"To the harpies with the Zjhon and their evil ways! They must be stopped," one man shouted as he pounded his fists on the table.

"Hang those who allowed her to go into harm's way," another demanded, but cooler heads prevailed, and such overreactions were quickly quelled.

Catrin shrank in on herself. The deaths were all because of her. This was all her fault. Ultimately, she could be blamed for much of the problems facing the world--it was a difficult thing to accept. When Benjin arrived, her composure completely fled, and she ran to him. Sobbing into his robes, she let him lead her back to a seat.

When her tears had run their course, she looked up at him; his face was a mask of grim determination. Only the tears that slid down his cheeks gave evidence of his pain and mourning. The meeting came to a sense of order as Brother Vaughn pounded a gavel against the table, and the noise cut off all conversation.

"It is a dark day for us, brethren, but we must maintain our resolve. Two men scaled the cliffs to gain access to Ohmahold. They took the lives of two good men and our beloved Mother. This cannot be changed, and only those who committed the heinous deeds can be held responsible. They stole from us the chance to exact our preferred manner of justice, but in taking their own lives, they did justice. They admitted their guilt and removed themselves from our world."

His words were not joyful, but they kindled reason among those gathered, and some who had been so vocal at first were now abashed and subdued. Catrin leaned on Benjin's shoulder and took whatever comfort he could offer. The pain in her chest had not abated, and the throbbing was impossible to ignore, but she endured as best she could.

"In the event of her passing, Mother Gwendolin requested Sister Velona succeed her. I make the motion to enact the late Mother's wishes. What say you?" Brother Vaughn asked. The response was muted but in unanimous agreement. Sister Velona appeared stunned, as if she had been unaware of Mother Gwendolin's desires, and she was removed from the room to prepare for her ascension. In her absence, Brother Vaughn continued to moderate.

"The Cathuran order has always advocated neutrality in the affairs of the nations, but under these circumstances, we cannot remain indifferent. War is upon us. Lady Catrin's cause is to defeat the Zjhon, and I make the motion that we support her in her quest. What say you?"

Heated debates raged around the table, and Brother Vaughn let the collective sort their opinions and establish their stances before he called them to order.

"What say you?" he asked again, and the motion was approved but with little enthusiasm. Catrin could not blame them. They had suffered a tremendous loss, and none of them had known her for very long. "We all have our own preparations to make for the interment, but I suggest we form committees to handle the basic governing of Ohmahold until after Sister Velona's ascension. What say you?" This was met with almost unanimous agreement, and they proceeded to assign committees and their chairs. Catrin turned to Benjin with uncertainty in her eyes, but he was still unaware of her dire news, and she decided on her own to stand and speak out.

"Brother Vaughn and those of the Cathuran order, I request permission to address the assembly," she said, trying to honor the formalities. She flushed as every eye turned to her; the fact that hoods obscured the eyes and faces made the experience increasingly disconcerting.

"I make the motion to grant Lady Catrin the floor. What say you?" Brother Vaughn intoned, and Catrin was surprised to receive unanimous approval.

"I, too, mourn the loss of Mother Gwendolin. She was kind, and I will always cherish her memory. But I also bear distressing news that I had only just reported before . . ." She trailed off, not wishing to say the words, and she sensed approval. "During my time in the viewing chamber, I found its true purpose. I left my physical body and soared through the heavens." She paused as reactions rippled through the room: disbelief, wonder, distrust, and excitement all within the mixture.

"My journey took me south, where I spotted a line of pilgrims that stretched across the land. When I located their destination, I saw a great landslide and the bones of a mighty beast being excavated. It was not the bones, though, that drew the pilgrims. On the other side of the rockfall, I found a chasm, where the land had been torn apart, and within, I saw the glowing face of Istra. They are exhuming a Statue of Terhilian." Shock and horror radiated through the room, and not a sound was made for some time.

"Von of the Elsics created the statues to trick the Zjhon and the Varics into destroying themselves, and it nearly worked," one hooded figure said, and Catrin thought she recognized the voice of Sister Hanna. "Both nations gathered around what had been described as tokens of peace from the gods. Even after the destruction caused when the statues exploded, the Zjhon continued to believe the statues were truly divine--gifts from the gods themselves. They were convinced the statues weren't responsible for the devastation, rather they blamed it on nonbelievers. They'll parade the most deadly artifact ever created as if it were a trophy, a true sign of their superiority. It seems we find ourselves faced with the same debate that raged nearly three thousand years ago. Are the Statues of Terhilian divine gifts that must be honored and worshipped in order to please god and goddess, or are they gruesome weapons that will release cataclysmic forces once charged?"

Sister Hanna turned to Catrin directly. "You are certain you saw this, are you not? This is not a matter to be taken lightly. You did say the face glowed, did you not?"

Her questions hammered at Catrin's resolve, but she did the best she could to maintain grace in the face of such scrutiny. "I am certain," she said without a trace of doubt. Debate raged in the hall, and Catrin returned to her seat. Benjin cast her a questioning gaze, and she related the tale of her vision journey. He listened intently, and Catrin had to raise her voice above the din.

"Our world has become a very dangerous place indeed," Benjin said when she finished her tale.

"Agreed," Brother Vaughn said as he approached them from behind. "I apologize. I did not mean to impose upon your conversation, but I feel we should meet in private when this meeting has adjourned, which should be shortly. Please remain behind when the others depart." Catrin and Benjin nodded their assent, and Brother Vaughn returned to address the assembly. At the same time, Catrin remembered the hall.

"Brother Vaughn," she said, and he returned to her side. "I nearly forgot in the insanity of this day. I have good news as well."

"Good news would be most welcome on this otherwise lightless day," he said, and Catrin could see how drained he was. She could feel his fatigue and anguish as if it were her own. In many ways, it was. When she told him about a lost hall filled with ancient treasure, a flicker of hope crossed his visage, and he thanked her.

"Brothers and Sisters, a light shines in the darkness; we have been blessed with new hope to face the despair. I've just been informed that Lady Catrin has located a cache of ancient knowledge within Ohmahold. I make the motion that we send a committee to investigate and convene this meeting until the evening meal. What say you?"

Excitement washed over the room but was quickly subdued in the memory of their loss. Nonetheless, it was at least one good omen, and some clung to it. A committee was assigned, and Catrin found herself whisked from the hall. Brother Vaughn led the group, and she spoke to him as they walked, filling him in on the details.

"You walked into a death chamber?" he asked, incredulous.

"It seemed like the right thing to do at the moment," she said under Benjin's accusing glare, but when they reached the hall, she did not hesitate. She marched ahead of the group, despite the many protests. Brother Vaughn and Benjin matched her stride, and she was honored by their display of trust. Only when Brother Vaughn exclaimed, "By the heavens! So much knowledge that has been just beyond our reach," did the rest of the group edge along the hall.

Brother Vaughn visibly resisted the urge to explore and left another monk in charge of the investigation. "Come, let us slip off while the rest are occupied," he said, and Catrin followed him with Benjin on her heels.

Chapter 15

Nothing could be more terrifying than horrors wrought by one's own hand.
--Imeteri, slave

* * *

Brother Vaughn led them to a warm and cozy section of the hold. Thick carpets covered the floors, and lanterns bathed the halls in an inviting glow. Elaborately carved doors were staggered along the halls, and he stopped at one that bore a scene of eagles soaring over a magnificent waterfall. He paid it little mind as he admitted them to his personal apartments, which was an honor, and Catrin recognized it as such.

The walls of his home were covered in paintings and sketches of birds, which were fantastic in their variety and beauty. A partially completed sketch of the violet hummingbird rested on an easel, and Brother Vaughn's talents were obvious; the detail and accuracy was without equal. Shelves and tables were covered in scrolls and sheets of parchment with scribbled notes. Only one of the four chairs around the table was free of scrolls and bound tomes, and Catrin decided to stand rather than disturb the organized clutter. Benjin paced the floor, a fury of emotions plain in his visage. Brother Vaughn seemed to have forgotten they were with him as he searched under various piles of parchment.

"I know they're here somewhere," he said as if he speaking to himself. "Ah, yes, here they are." He held a wooden box that barely filled his palm. It was made of dark, rich wood and had a lustrous finish; gold filigree covered the corners, and the clasp formed the head of a fearsome serpent.

"There are those within our order who spend their entire lives seeking artifacts from antiquity. You have Brother Ramirez to thank for finding, identifying, and preserving these. Though he went to his grave many years ago, I'm sure he would be thrilled to see you have them. Mother Gwendolin planned to give them to you, and she asked me to retrieve them. I deliver them to you now as the fulfillment of one of her final wishes," he said and raised the lid. Light reflected merrily off two fully charged noonstones that lay within. They were much smaller than Imeteri's Fish had been, but now that Catrin knew their value, they seemed large--a treasure.

Catrin accepted the box with trepidation. She did not feel comfortable accepting such a valuable gift, but she did not want to dishonor the wishes of Mother Gwendolin, and she chose to receive the endowment with grace. She would bear the gift along with the memory of Mother Gwendolin, a tribute to her kindness and wisdom.

"It is a precious gift, indeed. I vow to use these only toward the good of the world, and when I have finished my work, I will return them to you. You have my word," Catrin said, and she bound herself to the commitment. Brother Vaughn gave her a smile and a small bow as she tucked the gilded box into her pocket. Just having the stones near her brought comfort and solace, and she would treasure them for as long as she possessed them.

"I'm afraid we must move on to less pleasant subjects," Brother Vaughn said. "I have enough support within our order to help you on your way, but you'll not be allowed to remain at Ohmahold. Please take no insult from this. We Cathurans are not without our own politics, and with our long history, there are long-standing issues at hand. The ascension of Sister Velona will not be a smooth one, and while I fear no attacks from within our order, I don't think you should be here come spring. The armies will be at our doorstep, and there will be no telling what will happen." It was obvious his heart was heavy with sadness and regret.

Catrin reeled. Where would she and her companions go? No refuge awaited them. Nowhere was safe. She couldn't think of any place that would accept her, and a sharp pain pierced her heart. Nowhere was she welcome. Benjin gave her arm a squeeze, and she appreciated his support and calm.

"It would be terribly difficult to remain inconspicuous while traveling with young men," Brother Vaughn continued. "It'll be hard enough to explain why you aren't with the armies. Benjin is old enough that he should be able to appear lame. We do not object, in any way, to Osbourne, Chase, and Strom staying with us. We have no grievances with any of you, and it may be the safest place for them to be," he said.

Catrin was torn and confused. She couldn't imagine them sending her and Benjin out into the snow; it would be as good as sending them to their graves.

"Before you come to any conclusions, there is more," Brother Vaughn said in response to her consternation. "I am violating protocol, but I will do what I feel is right. There are mines that run throughout these mountains, and we recently discovered an ancient complex that stretches for hundreds of miles. It is a perilous journey, but there is one way out that I am familiar with. It's far from pleasant, but I can get you to a place within the virgin forests of Astor. From there, I can try to summon Barabas and hope he sees my signal. It may take some time for him to arrive, but he will guide you through the wilderness."

"Who is Barabas?"

"He's a trusted friend. Otherwise, I find him indescribable. You'll simply have to meet him for yourselves."

"I'll need to speak with my Guardians about this," Catrin said, unsure of what to do, though it seemed she had little choice, having worn out her welcome.

"Yes, of course, I understand. But I'm afraid we have little time. If I am to guide you, we must leave this day. Soon I'll be entrenched in ceremony and ritual. I have but ten days before the rites of ascension begin, and I'll be hard pressed to make it back in time. Please do not delay."

"Thank you. Your kindness and support are greatly appreciated. I'll seek out my Guardians this instant and will return to you as soon as possible."

"I would do more if I could, but I am bound by my duties," he said as Catrin and Benjin departed for the First Inn. Before they closed the door behind themselves, though, he called after them. "Have you any weapons at the guardhouse?"

"Yes. Thank you for reminding me," Catrin replied.

"I'll write you a weapons pass so that you may arm yourselves," he said as he scribbled on a piece of parchment, closing it with his wax seal. "Just give this to the guard, and he will return your weapons. Keep it with you in case any of the guards stop you on your way back."

Catrin and Benjin spoke little during the long walk, but his presence alone was comforting. The uncertainty of her future consumed Catrin's thoughts. She considered Brother Vaughn's words regarding the boys, but she hated the thought of leaving them behind; they had all come so far together. But even if they stayed, at least she would not have to go alone.

Word of the attack preceded them. The streets were empty, and a somber pall hung over the common room at the First Inn. Chase, Strom, and Osbourne sat at a corner table. When Catrin and Benjin entered, they leaped from their chairs and rushed to greet them. Tears flowed freely as they shared their grief along with the joy of seeing one another. Benjin urged them back to the table. They huddled together, and Catrin rattled off the news in a whisper.

"No," Chase said. "I'll not be left behind to hide while you two go off into danger. I'll not hear of it."

"Now, Chase . . ." Benjin said.

"Absolutely not."

Catrin was torn. She didn't want to hurt Chase, but his presence would be a danger to her. A plan began to form in her mind, one that would never work, but at least it was a plan. She left the others to argue while she plotted the path in her mind, and she heard not a word they said. When her mind was set, she interrupted their debate.

"Benjin and I will depart this day. Brother Vaughn will guide us, and we'll make for Faulk. We should be able to blend in with the pilgrims until we reach the statue. I'll destroy the statue, and then we'll continue south to the coast." Chase tried to interrupt her, but she plowed over his efforts. "Chase, your task is most important. You will depart following the ascension ceremonies, when Brother Vaughn is available once again. You will locate us a ship and arrange for it to pick us up on the southern coast of Faulk. Strom and Osbourne will stay here and assist the Cathurans in their ventures until I send word. Agreed?"

"That's the craziest plan I've ever heard," Chase said, and Benjin chastised him with a look. "How are you going to destroy the statue? And once you do, how are you going to escape? And even if you manage to escape, which seems highly unlikely to me, how will you locate the ship along such a large coast?"

"We'll meet you at the most southern and western tip of Faulk, then. The rest I haven't figured out yet, but it is the best plan I have come up with so far."

"You've lost your senses," Chase muttered.

"Actually, I think much of her plan has merit," Benjin countered. "I agree there would be no good way to explain your presence travelling with us. Everyone on the Greatland of your age has already been conscripted. If you walk free, that marks you as either a traitor or deserter. It would seem the task Catrin assigned to you is the most dangerous of them all, but you've trained well for it, and I've faith in you. Catrin and I can travel in disguise. I'll be a lame old man and Catrin my youngest daughter. We can simply tell folks her brothers and sisters were conscripted, and she was left to care for me."

"I still don't like it," Chase said, but he seemed to realize the necessity of their separation.

"Neither do I," Catrin said. "If I had my choice, things would be much different, but they are what they are, and we must do the best we can given the circumstances."

Chase nodded in morose silence. Strom and Osbourne did not object to her forceful requests, and she truly believed they could help the Cathurans in some way. She worried about their safety, but security seemed to have vacated their world, leaving only fear and despair to fill the void.

"It's all so sad," Strom said. "I wish things could go back to the way they were. I don't want you to leave, but I understand. I just hope we really do get word from you someday soon. You do promise to come back for us, don't you?"

"I give you my word. If I'm able, I'll come back for you."

"And I give my word as well," Benjin added.

"You take good care of her," Chase said, his voice heavy with emotion as tears rimmed his eyes. He gave Benjin a tight hug and faced Catrin.

"It's a tough world out there, Cat, and I won't be there to grant your kills a quick death. Be strong, take care, and meet me on the shores of Faulk. I'll await you there." He managed to say it all without his voice cracking.

Catrin embraced him. She kissed him on the forehead and promised she would be there; nothing could keep her away.

After she retrieved her staff and her personal items from her room at the inn, she and Benjin left, waving farewell. It was surreal, walking away from the First Inn, intent upon leaving her companions, her Guardians, her friends. It was a painful parting, and despite her promises, she knew she would probably never see any of them again. Chase had been right; her plan was insane, and she didn't expect it to work, but at least she would leave this world doing the best she could. If there were some way she could avert the disastrous threat the Statue of Terhilian posed, then she would have done a great deal for the world. It was a worthy cause and, she supposed, one worth dying for.

"You mean to go through with your plan?" Benjin asked as they huddled against the icy winds.

"I don't know. I have to at least try to destroy the statue before it detonates, which is most likely suicide, but what other course of action could I take and keep a clear conscience?"

"We will just have to deal with the details along the way. We'll find some way to overcome the obstacles, you and I. We always do." His words offered Catrin a small amount of comfort, and she leaned on him as they walked. So many times he had been there for her; she did not know what she would do without him.

Captain Longarm was not in the guardhouse when they arrived, but another guard retrieved their weapons and returned the parchment to them. Benjin handed Catrin her knives and grabbed his own knife and sword. The rest he asked the guard to return to storage, and with that, they departed for the Inner Sanctuary.

Brother Vaughn looked nothing like himself when they returned. He was dressed in leathers with picks and hammers dangling from his belt. He wore a sturdy leather cap and gloves, and he slung a pack over his shoulder as they entered. Two more packs, near to overflowing, sat in a corner. Catrin and Benjin needed no prompting, and they shouldered the packs. Catrin stood with her staff in hand, trying to be confident, but her knees shook. This was perhaps the most dangerous parting yet.

"There is no time to waste. We must leave at once," Brother Vaughn said, but he stopped to flip through a book that contained charts and drawings of the moon.

"I must beg a favor of you," Catrin said. "I have a mission for Chase that requires him to depart after the ascension. Will you guide him?"

"It won't be easy. The rites of ascension are long and will require much of my time. I cannot abandon my responsibilities at such a crucial time, but I will find a way to accomplish it."

Catrin nodded her thanks, aware she was asking a great deal of him, and also knowing he would keep his word regardless of the cost. She was glad he did not downplay the inconvenience; she valued his honesty, even if it did make her feel guilty. It was preferable to pretty lies.

Brother Vaughn led them to the main stairwell, and they descended to its base, where the air was icy and dank. Lanterns had been left for them, and only the light they shed kept the darkness at bay. From his pocket, Brother Vaughn retrieved a small sand clock, which he turned over and put back in his pocket.

The rough-hewn tunnels beneath Ohmahold often intersected with other tunnels and passages. After only a few turns, Catrin was completely lost. Several times, they passed monks working in the mines, using mules to pull cartloads of salt and ore.

"Much of our livestock is born and bred within the mines," Brother Vaughn said. "It saves us the need to hoist the animals, and it also provides a secure food source in the event of a siege. We've water, salt, ore, and, in some cases, light, all within the mining complexes. But until recently, there has only been one way in or out of the mines for the sake of security. Only when the salt miners tunneled into an existing mine did we realize the ancient complex even existed."

"What about the place where we will exit the mines. Is it well hidden?" Benjin asked.

"Extremely," Brother Vaughn replied as he checked his sand clock. "We need to move faster," he said as he strode ahead of them.

Most of the tunnels looked exactly alike, rough-hewn rock supported by wooden buttresses and joists. The wood was treated with creosote and kept in good condition, but Catrin still felt like the mountain might crush her under its weight.

After what seemed like a day of walking, they reached a rough section of tunnel that ended in an oblong breach.

"This shaft leads to the ancient mines, but it is quite a drop to the floor below. Take care when you enter," Brother Vaughn said as he climbed through the opening. Benjin followed, and Catrin heard his low whistle when he reached the floor. She handed her staff down to him, and she dropped through the orifice. The fall was farther than she anticipated, and she landed hard, knocking the breath from her.

The floor on which she lay was cut into geometric patterns, and though covered with grime, they were still a marvel. The tunnel dwarfed those recently mined. The walls were cut smooth and straight, and the ceiling was lost in the darkness. Evenly spaced arches supported the tunnel, and they were carved with images of trees and flowers. Some bore images of wildlife, but no human forms were present. Catrin dusted herself off and turned in a full circle, taking in the majesty of the place.

Brother Vaughn did not give her long to enjoy the sights, though, as he set off at a brisk pace after once again checking his sand clock. The floors were level and the tunnels free of debris, which made for easy traveling. Intersections came and went, but Brother Vaughn gave them scarcely a glance as he passed them. The only indication that he noticed them at all was his mumbled count incremented at each one. When he reached what Catrin thought was the twelfth nearly identical intersection, he turned right.

The turn made Catrin feel they had made progress, and she fooled herself into thinking the journey was near complete. It seemed impossible that the mines could go on much farther, and the monotony of it played tricks with her mind. When Brother Vaughn called for a rest, Catrin had no idea how long they had been walking. Time seemed to lose meaning beneath the land, and Brother Vaughn's desire to keep track of the hours was starting to seem more reasonable.

They ate in silence, each consumed with his or her own thoughts. The salted beef satiated Catrin's hunger, but her spirit was restless. She missed the sun and stars, and though they had been in the mines only a short time, she felt separated from Istra's energy. The lack of power made her feel vulnerable, and she pulled the noonstones from the gilded box. They felt wonderful in her hands. She rolled them in her palm and let them soothe her, not drawing any of the energy they held in reserve; instead, she just basked in their existence and the security they gave her.

An enormous arch loomed in the distance. Like the gates to a dark dimension, it was guarded by a multiheaded serpent whose fangs dripped with venom. Though carved from stone, it was a fearsome sight, and Catrin was loath to enter such a mystical portal. Brother Vaughn paid it no mind, and the serpent did not strike him as he passed through, but Catrin felt the reptilian stare intensely, and she had a vision of the beast coming to life. It was almost as if the carvings spoke to her: "Your descendents will pay dearly for your trespass," said the vision. Catrin shivered as if it were a premonition rather than the conjuring of her frightened mind. Benjin seemed troubled as well, and he looked over his shoulder frequently, which drove Catrin to do the same. She felt as if she were an intruder, and she half expected an army of ancients to descend upon them.

Beyond the intimidating arch lay a domed room that seemed impossibly large. Every part of the walls, with the exception of periodic archways, was carved to resemble a forest, and the detail boggled the mind. It was as if she stood in the center of a grove of stone, where each leaf, branch, and trunk was a masterpiece. Birds soared through the skies, and butterflies rested on rose petals. Even without motion, the enormous waterfall seemed alive, so clever was the craftsmanship.

"I would speculate these mines were in use for at least a thousand years," Brother Vaughn said, seeing the looks of awe on their faces. "I do not see how such mastery could have been achieved in any shorter span of time."

Catrin felt oddly at home among the still trees, and she almost didn't want to leave the hall, but Brother Vaughn moved steadily toward the fourth archway on their right. She ran her fingers along the magnificent carvings and marveled at smooth lines and lifelike curves. Some of the leaves were so thin, she imagined she could see through them, and she wondered how they could have been created. To see such delicate forms made from rock seemed impossible, yet it stood before her in all its glory.

As they exited the cavernous dome, Catrin glanced back at the archway and saw that it, too, was guarded by a mighty serpent. She could feel its eyes on her back, and she looked over her shoulder twice as often as Benjin. When a loud sound echoed through the halls, they froze. Straining their ears, they tried to figure out where the noise had come from, but the acoustics of the mine made it nearly impossible to pinpoint, and Brother Vaughn grew nervous. He looked over his shoulder as often as Catrin and Benjin, which did not make either of them feel any better, but they left their concerns unspoken.

The halls once again became a monotonous blur, and the dull cadence of their steps, a lullaby. Exhaustion dogged Catrin, and every step was a struggle. She leaned on Benjin, and they shuffled along together. Her vision blurred as she walked in a stupor, kept upright by only Benjin and her staff. Not wanting to complain, she did her best to deal with the fatigue, but it was overpowering. Her eyelids were leaden, her eyes burned, and she let Benjin guide her.

"We have to stop," Benjin said.

Brother Vaughn suddenly became aware of Catrin's condition. "Yes, yes, of course. Please forgive me. I should have realized."

Catrin slid to the floor and curled into a ball as soon as Benjin stopped. The throbbing in her head made it difficult to formulate any coherent thoughts, and she cradled her head in her hands. Benjin offered her food, but she refused. Her appetite had fled, and only pain and misery filled its place. As much as she would have liked to sleep, though, she remained awake and restless. Obscure fears and anxieties nagged at her, and she was helpless against them.

Would the Zjhon capture them? Would Chase survive his quest for a ship? Did Ohmahold stand any chance against the encroaching siege? The uncertainty gnawed at her, and she felt responsible for too many lives--too many futures. Her confidence waned, and she wondered how she could have been so foolish as to act on her ridiculous plan. There was little chance of success and an even smaller chance of survival. Her mind tormented her with all the possible ways she could die. Fires scorched her skin, axes cleaved her, swords severed limbs, and arrows pierced her flesh.

Unable to contain her pain, she wept, and Benjin pulled her close. With his powerful arms around her, she felt almost safe; he would keep the horrors at bay. Still, it took her far too long to find sleep, which she knew she would regret on the morrow.

* * *

Rolling into a tucked position, Chase hesitated only a moment before he sprang. He took three steps then launched himself into the air, tumbling and swinging at the same time. The crack of the impact echoed off the mountains, and Captain Longarm dropped to one knee, clutching his thigh.

"I'm going to feel that in the morning," he said.

"Sorry," Chase said.

"You've gotten better, but I'm getting too old to take that kind of beating, maybe one of your friends will spar with you," Captain Longarm said, pointing to where Strom and Osbourne stood talking to a pair of girls who'd come to watch the spectacle.

"Oh no. Not me. No, sir," Strom said as they approached. "You'll have to find someone else to beat on. My hands are my trade."

"Your trade, huh? I thought you were going to be a stable hand the rest of your life," Chase said.

"You heard me. I'm to be a great smith. Perhaps, if you're nice to me, I'll make you a *real* sword."

"Don't look at me," Osbourne said as Captain Longarm turned a questioning gaze to him. "I'm still sore from last time."

"I suppose you're just going to have to find a real enemy to take your frustrations out on, young man," Captain Longarm said, and he turned to leave.

"Thanks for everything, Burrel. Sorry about the bruises," Chase said, but Captain Longarm just waved his apology off. Still breathing hard, Chase sat on a nearby stump and regained his breath. There was no excuse for his hitting Burrel as hard as he had, but he could not stand waiting any longer. As foolish as he thought Catrin's plans were, he was still determined to do his part, and soon he would leave the shelter of Ohmahold; he needed to be ready. For today, though, all he could do was wait.

"I see you no longer fly like a stone," said a familiar voice from behind him. "Perhaps you could show me how to defend myself against unwanted advances."

"Certainly, Winnette," he said. "First let me show you a proper defensive stance."

Perhaps waiting wouldn't be so terrible after all.

Chapter 16

Beneath the soil lies the heart of the world, and her veins run gold and silver.
--Tobrin Ironspike, miner

* * *

Catrin grew weary of the mines and the walking. They passed various chambers of different sizes along the way, but they stayed within the halls and plodded along in the gloom. Faint echoes teased them, and at times, Catrin thought she heard the slow drip of water.

After what seemed like a month, they reached an intersection, and Brother Vaughn turned. The new hall seemed like all the rest at first, but then Catrin noticed a change: They were ascending. The incline was slight and barely discernable, but Catrin felt it in the backs of her legs. Longing to see the sky, she hoped they were nearing the exit.

The incline continued, and from the shadows, a curve in the hall appeared. It was the first time the tunnels had been anything but straight, and Catrin grew anxious. Beyond the gentle curve, a narrow cavern emerged, and nestled within it was a pond of dark and foreboding water that lay under a haze of steam. Brother Vaughn extinguished his lantern and asked Benjin to douse his as well.

Total darkness crowded around them, and Catrin could see nothing in the pitch, but after a moment, Brother Vaughn rekindled his lantern. The sudden brightness hurt Catrin's eyes, but it was better than the impenetrable darkness.

"I believe it's safe to exit, but if I do not return, wait for half a day before following. There is an opening in the far wall, just below the surface. You must swim under the rock, and when you clear it, you will be outside. Use the wax in your packs to seal them as best as you can. I'll see you on the other side." After one final look at his sand clock, Brother Vaughn handed it to Benjin. Looking doubtful and concerned, he swam to the far end of the pond and disappeared below the surface.

Catrin held her breath. She didn't know what possible dangers could prevent Brother Vaughn from coming back, but icy fear clutched her bowels. She'd lost too many friends already, and she desperately wanted Brother Vaughn to return safely. Bubbles appeared in the water near the far wall, and Catrin jumped when Brother Vaughn's head popped up not far from where she stood.

Benjin assisted her with the sealing of her pack, and they joined Brother Vaughn in the water. It was not a complete surprise to find the water unusually warm--the steam had been a clue--but it still seemed a bizarre phenomenon. Brother Vaughn wasted no time, and he dived below the surface again. Benjin waited a moment then ushered Catrin through next.

With a deep breath, she ducked under the water and pushed off with her feet. It was difficult to swim with her staff in hand, and she hoped she did not have far to go. A flurry of small forms bumped into her along the way, which was uncomfortable and disconcerting, and she struggled to remain oriented. She used the staff to feel for the end of the stone, and as soon as it gave way, she thrust herself to the surface. Icy night air greeted her, and she gasped for breath.

"Stay in the water for now," Brother Vaughn said as he gained the rocky shore. A full moon shed plenty of light to see by, and Catrin watched as Brother Vaughn gathered wood for a fire. She could see the mist of his breath before him, and she knew he must be freezing. With wet and shaking hands, he attempted to kindle a fire, but it refused to catch. Catrin and Benjin wanted to climb free of the water, but they were already soaked to the bone, and the cold air would assault them, just as it sent shudders through Brother Vaughn's form. For the moment, they held their packs high and waited.

A small orange glow gave them hope, and Brother Vaughn blew gently. A wisp of smoke rose into the air, and the crackle of burning pine needles carried across the water. At the first sign of flames, Catrin pulled herself from the water, but she soon regretted it. They would need a sizable bonfire to keep the frigid winds at bay, and she paced around the meager fire, rubbing her hands along her raised flesh, hoping to generate warmth and stave off the numbness.

As she paced along the shore, she tripped on an unexpected obstruction. The fire suddenly leaped higher as Benjin tossed more pine needles on, and Catrin could see the obstacle: it was the skeletal remains of a large animal. Perhaps a horse or bear, she was not certain. In the light of the growing fire, she saw other skeletons of various sizes.

"What danger did you fear when you swam through?" Catrin asked.

"Daggerfish," Brother Vaughn replied, and Catrin was shocked by his words. She had learned of daggerfish many years ago. They were said be capable of removing the flesh from a horse in a matter of moments, which was further evidenced by the bleached remains strewn along the shore. Though small, daggerfish possessed razor-sharp teeth and voracious appetites. They were said to travel in schools, and their attack was likened to a cloud of death.

"You suspected there were daggerfish in these waters?" Catrin asked, incredulous.

"Suspected? No. I knew for a fact these waters are infested with them. I was just uncertain what time of day it was. Had I been wrong, we would not be speaking now," he said with a shrug.

Catrin was too stunned to speak, and she just stared at him in horror.

"It is a little-known fact, you see, that daggerfish will not feed under a full moon. Most folks are warded off by the evidence of their presence, and few are willing to risk their lives to find out such a thing."

Chills ran along Catrin's spine as she realized it was the daggerfish she had bumped into during her swim, and she shivered. She could not imagine what it would be like to be torn apart by razor-sharp teeth, but macabre visions filled her mind.

"I'm truly sorry for not telling you, but many would have balked no matter what I said; thus, I left you in ignorance. Please accept my apologies," Brother Vaughn said, looking sheepish.

"Well. We're still alive, thanks to you," Catrin said, "and I'm grateful for that, but please, if ever we are in a similar situation, apprise me of the danger. I would rather know what death I face," Catrin said, and Brother Vaughn nodded his assent, however unlikely it was they would ever be in similar circumstances.

The heat of the fire seeped into Catrin's clothes, and steam rose from them as they dried. The surrounding land soared at steep angles, with the exception of the north, where it opened into a rolling forest. The trees were not as large as greatoaks, but they were some of the largest oaks, elms, and sycamores in the world.

"Our fire should only be visible in the forest to the north, which is, for the most part, uninhabited. It should signal Barabas of our need, and I hope he'll arrive before long. I don't want to leave before you have become acquainted, but if he does not arrive soon, I will have to leave you," Brother Vaughn said, and they settled around the fire to wait.

Catrin turned her back to the fire so it would dry the rest of her clothes. The chill had mostly left her, but still she shivered.

Benjin wandered nearby as he gathered bits of wood for the fire.

Brother Vaughn rested. "Will you wake me after two turns of the sand clock?"

"Yes," Benjin said, accepting the sand clock. "I'll keep watch until then."

Catrin's thoughts wandered to Vertook. In all the chaos, she hadn't had time to properly grieve his loss. He'd been a good friend to her, and his death was as unfair as anything Catrin had ever experienced. The pointless waste of life filled her with rage, and she longed to lash out at someone--anyone. Benjin seemed to sense her unrest, and he placed his arm around her shoulders. She shared his warmth but found no solace.

Too much had been taken from her in such a short time, and she began to harden to the cares of the world. Why should she even attempt to save the Zjhon from the Statue of Terhilian when they would kill everyone around her to prevent that very thing? Perhaps she should simply let them suffer the consequences of their folly, but the thought rang discordant, and she knew she could never be so callous; it was simply not her nature. She cared deeply about every living thing, and no amount of hardship could change that, she hoped.

Her thoughts turned to the gods and the origins of her world. She'd heard fanciful stories about gods gambling on the outcome of seemingly random events and cheating each other with their subtle influences on the lives of men. Those tales had never rung true for Catrin; it seemed too petty a pastime for beings capable of creating such a beautiful and amazing place.

Considering what she'd heard about ancient peoples making up stories of gods in order to explain the unknown, she wondered if people in the future would look back on her generation and laugh at their misconceptions. Perhaps they will laugh away many of society's current superstitions and beliefs, and yet they will still probably have their own delusions.

She wondered where the religious pomp and ceremony had come from and who had written the sacred writings. As far as she knew, no one in at least a thousand years had written anything considered sacred, and she wondered why the old writings were sanctified. She began to think the sacred texts had been written by ordinary men and were littered with the opinions of those men, who claimed to have been influenced by the gods.

Catrin had seen what society did to those who claimed anything close to divine inspirations. She had seen Nat Dersinger ostracized for that very reason, and she had been a party to it. She'd held tightly to the beliefs taught by ancient prophets and had cast insults at a living prophet. How could one believe prophets existed in ancient times but somehow could not exist now? The realization shamed her, even if it conflicted with Mother Gwendolin's teachings.

It took time to reconcile herself to many of her feelings, and she had more questions than answers. She imagined what life would be like if she had all of the answers, and she decided it would be much easier but excessively boring. If she always knew what was about to happen, then there would never be any excitement or surprises in life, and though she was weary of surprises and excitement, she could not picture life without them.

Brother Vaughn's snores broke the silence, and Catrin steeled herself from sleep. Someone needed to stay alert, and she was unwilling to ask it of Benjin alone. She stood and walked circles around the fire in an effort to keep her blood moving and the lethargy at bay. Benjin saw the wisdom in her actions and joined her. He walked in the opposite direction, and they smiled at each other every time they passed.

Catrin nearly leaped from her skin when a voice like grating stone bellowed from the trees: "Greetings, landfriends."

A great bear of a man strode from the forest. He stood taller than anyone Catrin had ever seen, and his chest was as big around as a barrel. The furs and skins that adorned him accentuated his fearsome appearance. His hair was dark and coarse, like that of a horse's tail, and the curls of his beard covered much of his face. Still, a wide grin was visible beneath it.

"Barabas, my friend," Brother Vaughn said through a stifled yawn. "It's good to see you well. I'm sorry to call on you, but the need is great."

"Have no fear, landfriend. I come freely and will assist you if I can. Strange powers are afoot. I feel danger encroaching, but we'll face this new challenge together. Yes?"

"I'm sorry, old friend, I cannot join this quest, for I must return to Ohmahold. Our dear Mother Gwendolin was laid down by the Zjhon, and I must attend the ascension of her successor," Brother Vaughn said. A frown crossed Barabas's face, carving deep furrows on his brow.

"This is Catrin Volker of the Godfist," Brother Vaughn said, but Barabas interrupted him.

"She's more than that," he said, his eyes full of Catrin, as if she were a treasure. "Greetings, heart of the land. I've awaited you. And your shield, I see. You are her protector. Yes?" Barabas asked, his eyes on Benjin.

"You are correct. I am Benjin Hawk. It is a pleasure to make your acquaintance, Barabas." He stepped forward and offered his hand to the large man, but Barabas surprised them all by lifting Benjin from the ground in a mighty hug.

"You've done well to get her here alive, Guardian Benjin," he said as he lowered Benjin to the ground. "And you, heart of the land, you've done well to survive the perils of your journey. It pleases me to see you both."

"And it pleases us to see you," Catrin said in an attempt to return the compliment. His words were strange, and she wondered what he meant by her being a heart of the land.

Brother Vaughn stood and spoke quietly with Barabas a moment; then he turned to Catrin. "I must leave you now, while it is still dark, but I wish you a safe and blessed journey. May fate be kinder to you than it has been in the past, and may we meet again under brighter skies."

"You have my most sincere thanks, Brother Vaughn," Catrin said. "I'll never forget what you've done for me, and I'll keep my word. We will meet again, and I'll return what you've left in my keeping. Until then . . ." She stepped forward to embrace him, and he hugged her warmly.

Benjin stepped toward the monk, his hand outstretched. "I cannot thank you enough, and I know we've asked more from you yet. I hope our requests don't inconvenience you terribly."

Brother Vaughn took the offered hand. "Do not fret. My journey will be a pleasure compared to what you face. Blessings to you all," Brother Vaughn said as he entered the steaming water, and soon he was lost in the depths.

Catrin was sorry to see him go. He was one of the few pillars of strength left in her world, and she cherished him for that, but she knew he had left her in capable hands. The energy that radiated from Barabas was filled with rightness, as if he lived more like a tree than a man.

After removing a tanned skin from his raiment, Barabas used it to carry water to the fire and extinguish it.

"Come, landfriends, we've dallied too long in the light of your fire. We should be gone from here before others respond to the beacon," he said, and he led them into the night. He bore no torch or lantern, and in the shadows of the mighty trees, they followed him by sound more than sight.

Moonlight streamed through bare branches, and what Catrin did see was a wonder. The life within this forest was as pure as any she had ever encountered. It was mostly untouched by man and lived by its own rules. It was pure and just felt right.

When she reached out with her senses, the land responded. It greeted her and made her feel at home, as if it had been awaiting her return. It was a strange thing to think, given the fact that she had never been there before, but something about it was familiar; it was home. Oddly, she felt even her staff respond to the land, as if it were reaching out to greet its brethren.

Barabas smiled as he watched her, as if he could sense her questing as well as the response. "The land greets you well, does it not, heart of the land?"

"It does, Barabas. But may I ask why you call me that?"

"You truly do not know?" he asked, clearly astonished by her question.

"I fear I do not," Catrin said. "There are many things I do not know."

Barabas laughed from his belly. His laughter was pure and joyous, its deep chorus akin to the sound of stones being poured into a bucket. "So you've chosen forgetfulness in this life. Your spirit knows all there is to know about this world, but the mystery can be fun. Yes?" Barabas said, confusing Catrin even further. "Even if you've chosen to forget, I suppose there is no harm in telling a bit. Your spirit has been here before, and it shall come again. You are a heart of the land because you have lived as every form of life on this blessed planet. You've basked in the sun as a blade of grass, soared in flight as a swallow, and swum the seas. You know the pain of childbirth and death, and you know the joys of rebirth. You and I, we've traveled far and wide together, and I must admit, I'm surprised you do not at least recognize me. I take no offense, mind you. I'm just surprised. There are others like you, but normally only a few are here, in this world, at one time. My kind have been called the souls of the land, and your kind have been called the hearts of the land."

"I don't have the images of those memories," Catrin said," but I feel a kinship to you and this land. It speaks to me. I've touched the land in other places, and I've felt its life, but never has it greeted me as such."

"Ah, then at least you've not left all memory behind. Perhaps our time together will awaken that which lies hidden, hmm?"

"You may be right. It seems your words have already changed me."

"Hmm," he said, his eyes far away. He led them deeper into the forest. "Where are you bound, Catrin?" Her name sounded strange on his lips, and he looked as if he were not sure it was befitting of her.

"We're bound for southern Faulk. The Zjhon have unearthed a Statue of Terhilian," she said, but she stopped when he slowly turned to face her.

His face was crimson, and the veins stood out on his forehead. The cords of his neck strained against his anger, and his clenched fists quivered at his sides. "To the deepest abyss with Von of the Elsics. The land has not yet cleansed itself from the last time his aberrations were unleashed. We should've destroyed them when we had the chance, but the time was too short, and once Istra's power was gone from the world, we were without the means. The land must not be made to pay the price for the madness of men--not again," he said.

Catrin was relieved she was not the target of his rage. He was a fearsome man when he was calm, but in his anger, he was terrifying. "Be not afraid, heart of the land. I've no quarrel with you, but the news you bring darkens my soul. The Statues of Terhilian use the faith of the devoted as a weapon against them. It is death brought about by deceit, and such a thing should never be done. We've still to pay for mistakes made by Von of the Elsics."

"I wish it wasn't true," Catrin said, and Barabas nodded. His steps were firm as he stormed ahead with purpose, and keeping up with him became a challenge. He said no more as he walked, and Catrin suspected he was too angry to be civil. He so closely resembled a charging bear that it almost frightened her, but she could not blame him. If what she had been taught about the statues were true, then the Zjhon were essentially condemning themselves.

"Do you think there is any way to convince the Zjhon the statue is deadly?" Catrin asked.

"Hmm. There is always the possibility, but I think it highly unlikely one could accomplish it in time. The energy shed by Istra does not pass through rock and soil freely, but some does penetrate, and it's possible the statues will detonate during this pass even if they remain buried. Exposed, they are an immediate threat and could discharge at any moment."

Catrin could find no words to respond. She struggled to find some solution, anything that would prevent massive loss of life, but she doubted they would ever be able to get close to the statue ... unless they were in shackles.

The rustling of leaves beneath their feet was the only sound. Some foliage still clung to the trees, but the forest floor was thick with them, and silent movement was nearly impossible. Ahead of them materialized a tree that was larger than most and bore a roughly triangular opening in its trunk. Over the opening hung several skins that had been stitched together, and Barabas pulled them aside.

"Welcome to my abode."

"Beautiful," Catrin said. "It's amazing you found such a tree."

"Amazing? Certainly not. I asked the forest for shelter, and it provided for me--just as it should be," Barabas replied, and her confused look seemed to surprise him. "When I need meat, I ask the herd, and a sacrifice presents itself. If I have need of fire, then the forest provides me wood. Whatever I need of nature, I have but to ask. Too many have forgotten this. They just take what they want from the land without any thought or respect, and they strip her of wealth that cannot be replaced. Surely you remember this at least."

"I'm sorry, Barabas. I've much to learn," she said, and he sighed heavily.

"Truly, heart of the land, you've chosen a trying time to embrace ignorance."

Chapter 17

Each of us is uniquely qualified for some task. We have but to find it.
--unknown philosopher

* * *

The interior of the tree was as remarkable as its outer appearance. The wood within was polished and richly grained, but most astonishing was the formation of shelves and a sleeping crevice large enough for Barabas. A ring of stones formed a small fire circle in the center of the chamber, and in the domed ceiling, a funneled opening bore a layer of soot. Catrin suspected the opening continued to open air and formed a natural chimney. Little else adorned the relatively small living space, and they stood elbow to elbow as Barabas tucked dried fruits and meats into his pack. He allowed Catrin no more time to contemplate his dwelling as he urged them back into the night.

"We've no time to dally. We can travel within the forest to the center of Astor, and from there, we will need to skirt between smaller areas of woodland. We are certainly not the most conspicuous of bands," he said with a chuckle and immediately set off at a pace that was difficult to match. Catrin's legs burned from the exertion, and she tired long before Barabas. He seemed to sense her fatigue, and not long before she would have had to ask for a rest, he simply stopped and lowered himself to recline against a towering elm. Catrin and Benjin joined him, and they ate in the stillness.

The forest was a riot of scarlet and umber, and the quiet murmur of the life within it was like the heartbeat of the world. Tranquility such as this could not be constructed; it could only grow naturally. All of man's attempts at beauty and grace paled in comparison to the architecture of life. Even creatures that were at times frightening and strange had their own unique elegance. A small lizard scurried through the leaves, and its rough, angular hide so closely resembled tree bark that it could become nearly invisible. Catrin admired the function of its form, and she recognized its beauty, even if the thought of touching it made her skin crawl.

When she considered Barabas, she was faced with an enigma, and she struggled to understand his place in her world. It was not that he seemed out of place. On the contrary, he could almost become a part of the scenery--much like the lizard. Taken out of his element, he was remarkable and unusual, but within his world, he was simply a part of nature. Eventually, her curiosity won out over her fear of being uncouth.

"I mean no insult by this question, Barabas, but may I ask what manner of man you are?" she blurted, and the words did not sound at all like what she had intended. "That is... I mean... You're very different from everyone I've ever met, and I'd like to understand you better." Still, she felt clumsy and rude, but Barabas just let his infectious laugh roll from him, as if he had no such inhibitions or insecurities. She envied him.

"You tickle me, heart of the land. Truly you do. You are wise beyond your years, and yet you've not the knowledge most would require to become wise. It amazes me. Your very existence is a paradox," he said, shaking his head. "Do not fear you will offend me with your questions. I'll answer them as best I can. As to what manner of man I am, some would label me druid, others shaman, and still others see me as a madman. I see myself as a part of life, a piece of the whole. Like a thread in a tapestry, I am not important in and of myself, but without me and the rest of the threads--the tapestry--would cease to exist. Do you understand?"

"I think I do, but how did you come to be this way? Did your parents teach you these things?" she asked, and she was unsettled to see a flash of pain in his eyes.

"The land raised me and provided for me. I never met those who brought me into this world, but men and women have helped me, and they have taught me much. They influenced much of what I am, and I've always tried to take with me the best of all the beings I encounter, just as pieces of you will always go with me from now on. The memory of you is a part of me, and the memories of all my teachers, human and otherwise, are parts of me. The land and the animals have taught me as much, if not more, than my human mentors."

Catrin was not sure she understood any more about Barabas than before she asked, and she hoped his words would make more sense in time.

* * *

"We should've brought this thing up in pieces," Strom said through gritted teeth. "We could've assembled it once we got it all up there." Milo and Gustad launched into their usual debate, and Strom was frightened by the fact that he was beginning to understand them. Sometimes he was even tempted to interject his own thoughts, but it just seemed like asking for trouble.

"I'm losing my grip," Osbourne said. "We need to put it down."

"Be careful of the lenses, boys," Gustad said.

"We know. We know," Strom said as they eased the looking glass to the stairs. All of their effort had gone into reconstructing this ancient relic, and though they could see little through the parabolic lenses when in the workshop, Milo remained convinced it would work. He said it had been found atop Limin's Spire, and there it could be used to see the stars.

Looking up, Strom gave up trying to count how many more stairs they had left to climb.

"We must get the looking glass to the spire before nightfall," Milo said, as he had a number of times before.

Strom was tempted to go get some big, strong men to carry the looking glass, but he knew he could not. No one else knew how much work went into repairing this relic, and he could not trust anyone else to handle it. Thinking back to the feeling of success he'd had when they finally produced a workable lens, he smiled. Though they never achieved a perfect pour, Strom was proud to have gotten close. The imperfections in the first lens were few, and there was a perfectly clear area in the center. The second lens was even better, for which Strom was thankful; there was barely enough material left to make even one more pour. Milo was insistent that they not resort to remelting glass, and Strom often wondered what it was he feared.

"I'm ready," Osbourne said.

Grunting, they lifted the looking glass and, once again, began to climb.

"This thing better work."

* * *

After a few days in Barabas's company, Catrin came to see him as a guardian of the land, and that image pleased her. It seemed at times that he spoke to the trees and the soil itself, as if asking directions, and he would move off with confidence. Catrin had her own way of communing with the natural world, but she did not receive coherent thoughts. Instead, vague impressions brushed against her consciousness. She tried to listen in on his conversations with nature, but they were simply beyond her grasp, as if she were listening for something that could only be seen.

On the fifth day of their journey, though, vague impressions became an almost overwhelming expression of emotion. Tears streamed down her face as waves of joy mixed with sadness washed over her. It came from all around her yet felt as if it were her own. When she glanced at Barabas, she saw his eyes welling, and Benjin sniffed.

"You sense it, heart of the land?" he asked, and she nodded, mute. "What of you, Guardian? You sense it as well?"

"I feel joy and sadness all around us, and... I think... a melody," Benjin said.

"Hmm, indeed. The dryads are singing a farewell dirge, which does not bode well for our travels. I know not what danger they anticipate, but I've never heard the virgin forests sing of such an end. It's as if the trees expect to be wiped out almost completely."

"That's horrible! We must save them," Catrin cried, but Barabas laid a hand on her shoulder.

"It's not all sadness, heart of the land. You can sense the joy as well. In death, there is rebirth, the chance to begin anew. The forest prepares for a catharsis rather than extinction. I will miss the trees; they have been good to me, and I love them dearly. But I know they will return someday, and so will I, and then we will once again breathe the same air. Still, in this time of peril, I fear the implications this will have on our journey."

His words created an anxious mood, and they moved in wary silence, alert for any signs of danger to the trees and themselves. It was not until late that night that the first signs of trouble showed themselves. The air had become unseasonably warm--not balmy but well above freezing--and distant thunder told of storms. Occasionally they saw far-off flashes of lightning, but it was the growing orange glow on the northern horizon that alarmed them. Within a short time, the acrid smell of smoke assaulted them. The forest was afire, and Catrin knew they were but kindling before the fury of the inferno. Dried leaves would need little urging to ignite, and the glow became brighter as the night wore on.

"Should we flee the forest now? I don't want to be burned alive," Catrin said, reluctantly revealing her fears.

"The trees will guide us and will warn me if we are endangered. For now, I sense the danger is greater beyond the trees. If we go into the open now, I fear things will not go well."

"I trust you, Barabas, and I trust your instincts, but can you be sure the trees will know when we must leave?"

"Nothing is certain, but I trust them more than I trust myself," he said.

She tried to have faith, but fire struck her with a primal fear.

"The winds are from the west at the moment," Benjin said, "but if they turn to the south, we could be in trouble. Stay aware of the winds, and we will know when the fires will approach."

"Well said, Guardian."

Catrin tried to share their confidence but found it difficult to sleep with the smell of fire in her nostrils. When morning arrived, a haze hung over the land until the winds picked up and clouds of smoke rolled across them. The winds were still mostly out of the west, but they seemed to be taking a southerly turn. By midday, the fires came into view, and the devastation was appalling. Flames climbed high into the sky and became so intense that tornados of fire raced through the hills, leaving nothing but smoldering ash in their wake.

Large embers and bits of ash clogged the air, and the smoke threatened to choke them, but still Barabas kept to the trees. He skirted around the fires and always seemed to find some stretch of land that had not yet been burned until they reached a hillside that was nothing but cinder. Hot embers lay under a blanket of gray powder, and they picked their way through the remains of the fire. The soles of their boots were poor protection from the intense heat, and they moved as quickly as they could to reach an island of trees that lay beyond the hill.

The remaining trees stood as a bastion of hope. Some part of the virgin forest remained unmolested, and yet as they drew closer, the song of the dryads grew stronger. The land resonated with it, and it was clear the danger was not past. When they were nearly halfway across the field of ash, darkness washed over them. Banks of ominous clouds rolled eastward, and they blotted out the light. No lightning brightened the landscape, but a heavy rain began to fall.

Rain seemed like a boon at first, for it doused the embers and cooled their feet, but the steady fall intensified and became a downpour, and the distant trees disappeared in the haze. The group struggled through clinging mud, and Catrin often lost her footing. Unseen stumps and roots were concealed under a blanket of ash, waiting to snag the unwary, and the wet ash was deadly slick in places. As they moved with dreadful slowness, fears blossomed in Catrin's mind. The song of the dryads did nothing to assuage them.

At one point they stopped and huddled together. The winds shrieked and tore at them, and only the support of Benjin and Barabas kept Catrin on her feet. Later the rains abated, and they were left to slog through knee-deep mud. It was excruciatingly slow, and their goal was just beyond their reach. Unburned trees loomed ahead of them, and they drove themselves onward as if that stand of ancient trees would be their salvation.

The rumble began so low that they thought it was the rains, but it grew louder until it became an ear-shattering roar. The ground trembled, and through the mist came a wave of death. It came from high in the mountains where the storm had rapidly melted the snow, and the burned-out landscape offered nothing to slow it. Nothing stood between the flux and them, and the flood gained momentum as it roared across the land.

"To the trees!" Barabas shouted over the clamor, and they tried to run, but the mud clung to them and made their legs and boots heavier and heavier. Each step was a struggle, but fear drove them, and as the massive wave crested the hills above them, they reached the first of the remaining trees. Catrin was about to discard her staff and climb when Barabas grabbed her by the waist and tossed her high into the air, far higher than she would have thought possible. Branches rushed toward her at alarming speed, and she latched onto one as she reached the top of her arch.

Barabas gave Benjin a boost to begin his climb, and Benjin was barely above Barabas's head when the flood reached them. It happened so fast that it didn't seem real. A wave of brown and gray rolled across the land and wiped it clean. It overtook Barabas before he could climb to safety, and Catrin cried out as he was washed away.

"Worry not, heart of the land," she heard him yell as he was carried beyond her sight. The dryads continued to sing their farewell, and many of the trees succumbed to the deluge. The sight of the massive trees being washed away was awful, but the slow tilting of the tree they were in was terrifying. Catrin and Benjin climbed higher, but the mighty tree leaned farther, and the roiling flow grew ever closer. When the tree broke loose from the soil, it moved in a lumbering circle, slowly spinning in the current. Its top remained above water, though, and they huddled in the branches. Other trees and debris battered them, and Catrin used her staff to fend them off.

Cradled by the limbs, she sensed the dryad with her, protecting her in one last dying effort. Catrin sent her thanks into her physical bond with the tree, and she felt she could lend her strength to the dryad. Her energy poured into the bark and into the flesh of the tree. She was not sure if it was due to the effort of the dryad or pure luck, but they dipped into the roiling waters on only two occasions, and each time they were thrust back into the air.

As the flow diminished, the tree became wedged against a tangle of downed trees and vegetation that was knotted between a pair of hillocks. Catrin and Benjin held on to one another and lent each other warmth and strength as they waited out the flood.

When the waters receded, the landscape was nightmarish. What had been lush forest was now a wasteland, and not a single tree remained standing within their sight. Mud and rock clogged the valleys, and large sections of land had been ripped from their moorings, leaving huge gashes in the countryside. Benjin helped Catrin climb from the twisted mass, and they fought to break free of the mud.

Night closed around them, and they shivered in the cold air. No dry wood could be found for a fire, and they kept moving just for the sake of the warmth the activity provided. Catrin feared if they stopped, they would never rise again, and despite her nagging exhaustion, she pushed on, determined to live. She couldn't allow those who had died for her cause to have died for naught. She did not add Barabas to her mental list, for she felt he was still alive. It was not merely a foolish hope; she could sense him. She could not tell the direction in which he lay, though she had some clues about that, but she just got a general sense that he lived, as if he sent reassurance to her across the distance between them.

She and Benjin listened for anyone who might be in need of help, but the night was eerily quiet; only the sound of draining water disturbed the stillness. When morning arrived, it brought bright sunshine that seemed inappropriate in the face of such carnage. It almost seemed the sky should mourn the losses on the land below, but it acted of its own accord and blinded them with its glare. By midday, they found a hill that still bore trees, and they climbed to its top. There they built a small fire and tried to get warm.

Though no longer completely sealed with wax, the packs had kept out most of the water and mud. They shared some dried beef strips from Benjin's supply. Despair washed over Catrin as they ate. Even though they were alive, she felt lost. If Barabas did still live, it was doubtful he would find them, and they were now faced with traveling on their own. Benjin's presence was all that kept her from spiraling into a deep, dark depression, but he seemed to be struggling with demons of his own, and neither of them spoke for the rest of the day. No words seemed suitable for such dire circumstances.

After a brief respite, they descended into the mud once again. Despite traveling along high ground whenever they could, much of their time was spent knee-deep in the quagmire. Near dusk, they reached a broad river that was swelled beyond its banks and clogged with debris. It was there that the flood had reached its end, and Catrin could only hope the banks would hold, for beyond lay perfect rectangles of farmland, though few crops grew in the fields, and not a single soul could be seen.

Following the mighty river south, they looked for a place to cross but found none before darkness surrounded them, and they spent another night huddled in each other's arms. Catrin did not remember falling asleep, but she woke to Benjin's deep snores, and she let him sleep. Leaning her head against him, she enjoyed a few moments of peace.

When Benjin woke, they moved farther south, and not long after, a stonework bridge appeared in the distance. As they drew closer, it became apparent that the bridge was an engineering marvel. The river was not much more narrow there than anywhere else they had passed, and huge supports disappeared into the muddy waters. Catrin could not imagine how such a bridge had been constructed, and she stared at it in wonder. The water was only a few hand widths below the arched bridge in places, and she wondered if the swelled river would simply carry it away.

A crowd of people was gathered near the bridge, and when they saw Catrin and Benjin, they came to help. Fear clutched Catrin and she looked at Benjin, who seemed to be torn, but then he leaned close and took the staff from her hands.

"They've already seen us," he said. "If we flee, they'll most likely alert the local militia . . . that is, if any militia still remains. It's too great a risk, I think. Let me do the talking."

Catrin wanted to argue, every sense told her to flee, but the lure of warmth and food was too great, and her fatigue was too intense for flight. Thus, they moved slowly toward the approaching crowd. Upon closer inspection, she saw that the group was made up of the aged and the very young. Benjin leaned heavily on the staff as they walked, and his affected limp was quite convincing.

Covered in mud and ash, they must have been a remarkable sight. When they arrived, two men helped support Benjin as he walked. A girl of maybe four summers brought Catrin a flask of water that she accepted eagerly if not to quench her great thirst, then to wash the filth from her face.

"Yer lucky to've survived," an elderly man said as he approached. "From where d'ya come?" he asked, and Catrin immediately sensed his distrust. Her clean face made her age easy to guess, and that alone made her suspicious in their eyes. Catrin regretted washing her face, but there was nothing to be done about it now, and she held her tongue.

"We hail from northern Astor, but the fires drove us from our home, and the flood washed us here," Benjin replied in a trembling voice, his accent thick with northern, rural qualities.

"Pardon my insolence, stranger, but why's this one not been conscripted?" the man asked, pointing to Catrin.

"My five sons and two oldest daughters are in the Northern Wastes, and I fear I'll never see them again," Benjin said, his voice cracking and tears welling in his eyes. Catrin would have been impressed by his dramatics, but she knew he had an abundance of real pain to draw upon, and his tears need not be forced. The sight of his tears filled her own eyes, and her lip quivered as he continued. "This's my youngest daughter, and since my lady-wife passed to the grave, she's all I have. Even the armies could not part her from me." He said the words with conviction and stood with his chin high. He did not back down from the stares, and his fierce pride seemed to endear him to them.

"Many pardons, friend. I'm sorry fer yer losses, and yer welcome to join us, though we've little to offer. The armies have taken all we could give, and then they took more. We may be poor hosts, but we welcome you. I'm Rolph Tillerman," he said as he extended his hand to Benjin.

"Well met. I'm Cannergy Axewielder, and my daughter is named Elma," he said, and Catrin did her best not to appear surprised. She hadn't even thought about the danger of using their real names, and she chastised herself for her foolishness.

"Ah, a woodsmen, eh? That'd explain a great deal. Let us be gone from this place, the smell offends me, and ya look like ya could use a warm fire and some food."

Benjin allowed the men to aid him as he walked. The steady flow of water beneath the bridge was unnerving, and Catrin feared the bridge would collapse under their weight. The thought of falling into the frigid water nearly drove her to a run, but she restrained herself and matched the pace set by Benjin and his escorts.

Beyond the fields stood a cluster of homes and barns that seemed like the hub of a great wheel. It seemed odd to Catrin, who was accustomed to each farm existing as an island, whereas these huddled together, and their lands extended like spokes. Despite the strangeness of the configuration, there were many things that reminded her of home, which brought a sharp pain to her chest. The smell of a cook fire, a whiff of horse manure, and the hearty folks who surrounded her all invoked vivid memories, and she failed to hide her anguish.

"Don't cry, dear'n," an elderly lady said as she took Catrin's hand. "You're safe now."

Catrin wished she could believe it.

Chapter 18

Kindness, unlike most things, becomes greater when it is given away.
--Versus Macadilly, healer

* * *

Rolph led them to his home, which was painfully similar to the one Catrin had grown up in, and his wife, Collette, pulled her aside.

"Come with me, Elma. Let's get you cleaned up. Shall we?"

"Thank you, Lady Tillerman. You're very kind," Catrin replied, trying to match Benjin's accent and fearing it came out sounding contrived.

Collette laughed a light, tinkling sort of laugh. Lines spread from the corners of her eyes when she smiled, but the sparkle in her eyes spoke of inner youth. "I'm no lady, that's a'certain. Call me Collette," she said, and Catrin was struck by her kindness and by the similarity between these people and her own. These were good people. They were not filled with malice or spite. They led simple, wholesome lives, and she felt a kinship to them. The realizations made the entire conflict seem even more ludicrous. She had no quarrel with these good folk, and they harbored no ill toward her. Yet it was their blood that was being shed, that of their children. Catrin began to think of these people not as the Zjhon, but as the people of the Greatland. The Zjhon were the ones who desired war, and all others were simply their victims.

Collette led her to a private room that held a large iron tub.

"Take off those filthy clothes, and I'll bring you some bathwater," she said, but Catrin drew a sharp intake of breath when saw a pair of deep-brown eyes peering through a crack in the wall, and Collette turned. "Jessub, you scoundrel, shame on you! That's no way to treat a guest. Off with you! Straight to yer grandpa you go, and tell 'im what you've done. And don't think I won't check with him either," she said, and then she turned to Catrin. "Forgive him, m'dear. He's young and naturally curious, and you're a fetching lass."

Catrin flushed crimson. She certainly didn't consider herself fetching, and she eyed the crack in the wall with trepidation. Collette smiled kindly and covered the crack with a towel.

"He'll bother you n'more. I assure you of that," she said as she left Catrin to her privacy, and Catrin was certain she was correct, for Jessub's cries rang out loudly as he received his punishment. Catrin felt bad for him and wished they wouldn't spank him on her behalf; she'd always hated being punished as a child, and she felt Jessub's shame as if it were her own.

Only the luxury of the steaming tub could pull her thoughts away, and she eased into the water, which soon turned black with mud and soot. Despite her efforts, her skin would not come completely clean, and she settled for mostly clean. As the water began to grow cool, Catrin emerged from the tub, and she toweled off her raised flesh. Collette had left fresh clothes for her, and Catrin shook her head. She seemed to always find herself donning the clothes of others while a stranger washed her garments. She supposed she was growing accustomed to it, for it did not bother her as much as it had in the past. The loaned garments were overlarge and well worn, but they were clean, dry, and not uncomfortable.

An alluring aroma wafted into the room, causing her stomach to grumble, and Catrin was grateful when Collette handed her a bowl of broth. It was a light soup made of potato and onion, but it tasted delightful, and it warmed her soul as much as it did her belly.

"I wish we'd more t'share, m'dear, but times are hard," Collette said with a sad smile.

"It's wonderful, and I'm thankful for your generosity. I only hope I'll be able to repay you in some way."

"Nonsense. It's our duty t'help those in need, and you owe us nothing, but I appreciate the thought," she said as she brought Catrin a small loaf of bread. The crust was dark and hard, but the inside was light and airy, unlike the bread made on the Godfist. Catrin did not mention it for fear of revealing her ignorance. Perhaps this type of bread was common in the Greatland, and she did not want to raise any more suspicions.

Benjin and Rolph joined her in the common room, and Benjin looked much better after his bath. His clothes were strange, but they fit him well. Catrin rummaged through her pack and brought out some dried fruit and cheese that she shared with the rest.

"Good cheese," Rolph said with his mouth full, and Collette scolded him for his manners. A young boy came in meekly, refusing to meet Catrin's eyes. From his shamefaced look and the awkward walk of one with a sore bottom, Catrin guessed this was Jessub. When she offered him some dried fruit, he accepted it with tears in his eyes. Rolph gave him a steely glance, and Jessub raised his red eyes to hers.

"I'm sorry I peeked, Lady Elma," he said with a catch in his voice. He looked to be no more than seven summers, and Catrin could not be angry with him.

"It's a'right, Jessub, 'long as it doesn't happen again. Agreed?" she asked, the flush returning to her skin as all eyes rested on her.

"Yes, ma'am," he said, and he retreated from the stares. With a shove on the door, he was gone.

"Takes after you," Collette said with an accusing glance at Rolph.

"Don't glare at me, woman. I didn't peek. Though I can't say I blame the boy. Yer the prettiest thing to grace this house for some time," he said with a wink at Catrin, and she blushed anew. Benjin nearly choked on his bread, and mirth danced in his eyes, but he said nothing.

"Leave the poor girl alone, you wretched old man," Collette said, and she stood behind Catrin as if guarding her virtue.

"We can put you up in the barn fer a spell," Rolph said, ignoring his wife's glare. "It's not much, but it's dry and there's straw you can bed on. We've some blankets t'spare, so you won't freeze t'death."

"Elma can sleep in my room," came a high voice from outside, and Collette chased Jessub off with a broom.

"Off with you, you naughty child. You've caused enough trouble fer t'day."

"I thank you for your hospitality," Benjin said. "We should leave on the morrow and will not outstay our welcome. I've a brother in the south, and I hope to find work there, for my livelihood left with the fire and flood."

"Tough times fer all, these are. Come, I'll show you to the loft," Rolph said, and they followed him to the barn. All but two of the twenty stalls were empty, and those held swayback mares. At the far end of the barn, a ramp led to the loft, which was not a difficult climb, even for Benjin with his affected limp. Many of the bales were broken, and loose straw lay in mounds. Catrin tossed the blankets Rolph had given her over one mound, and she did what she could to form it into a comfortable bed. The crisp night air frosted their breath, but beneath the warm blankets, she and Benjin quickly dropped into sleep.

* * *

Looking out over the Falcon Isles and the seas beyond, Nat found himself in awe of creation. Blue skies harbored fluffy, white clouds, continually morphed by gentle breezes. Neenya stood at his side, tears streaming down her cheeks, seemingly overwhelmed by the beauty of nature. Slowly, Nat extended his hand until it brushed against her fingers. For a moment, he seemed frozen in time, waiting for her to respond. At first she seemed not to notice, but then a thrill ran through him as Neenya's fingers closed around his. In the next instant, her grip was all that kept him from tumbling over the ledge as his vision clouded and his knees would no longer support him.

Wrapped in a frilly dress, Catrin danced and spun. All around her, dangers lurked, like grisly thorns waiting to snag and entangle her. No reaction registered on her face, as if she were oblivious to the threats, and only sheer luck kept her safe. Slowly the vines encroached, surrounding her and constricting; still, Catrin danced.

Never before had the vision seized Nat so utterly and completely, and never before had the vision been so clear. "May the gods have mercy on her."

* * *

When the morning sun crept through gaps in the walls, Catrin rose to stretch her sore muscles. She and Benjin had slept later than they had in a long time and felt better for the rest. As they climbed down the ramp, Catrin saw a group of men, Rolph included, leaning against the fence. The men faced a large pasture that was occupied by a single, black colt. Catrin was shocked to see a bow at Rolph's side, and she moved in to investigate, Benjin hobbling along at her side. Their stomachs rumbled with hunger, but her curiosity won out over her appetite.

"Ho there, Rolph," Benjin said. "You don't mean to shoot that colt, now do you?"

"Aye, Cannergy. If we can't catch 'im any other way, I'll have to wound 'im. No one's been able to catch 'im so far, and his time's a-runnin' short. He still wears his yearlin' halter, ya see, and if'n we don't get it off soon, he'll be ruined. The armies left us only three horses, and I need 'im for breeding. T'will be a blasted shame if I have to shoot 'im, but what else can I do?"

Catrin could not believe her ears, and she could sense Benjin's inner struggle. He could catch the colt, but it would reveal his deception, for he could not do it while faking his limp.

"May I try?" Catrin asked, and all eyes turned to her.

"She's good with animals," Benjin added.

"We've nothing to lose, lass. But don't get yerself hurt. He's a feisty colt, and you'd not be the first to be injured by 'im. T'be honest, I don't hold out much hope for it. No offense to yer skills, but in a field that big, it's dern near 'mpossible."

Catrin was not offended by his lack of faith, but she did not intend to chase the colt around the pasture; all that would do was wear her out.

"Have you a length of rope and some soft cloth?" she asked, and her question raised more than one eyebrow.

Obviously intrigued, Rolph nodded and went to retrieve the items for her. When he returned, he handed them to her with a curious look, but he did not ask what she would do. He and the others chose, instead, to simply watch in silence.

Catrin walked the fence, inspecting the posts. When she found one that did not wiggle when she pushed on it, she tied one end of the rope around its base. After a few tugs to ensure its stability, she tied a noose and stop-knot on the other end. The blanket she used to pad the noose, and she tested it by looping it over her own head several times. Once she was confident she could quickly secure it over the colt's head, she climbed through the slats of the fence.

The colt watched her enter his pasture, and he raised his tail as he trotted in a wide arc, challenging her to catch him, but she did not even look at him. Ignoring him completely, as if he did not exist, she walked into the pasture and sat on the ground. With the noose in her lap, she picked blades of grass and inspected them as if that were her only reason for being there. The men stood at the fence, and no one spoke a word. A tense silence hung in the air.

For a while, nothing happened, but Catrin was in no hurry; she had all day if that was what it took. After she picked the spot in front of her nearly clean of the coarse grass, though, the colt became curious. He approached her from behind and nipped at her shoulder before charging away. Again, Catrin ignored him. He returned two more times, and each time he stayed longer and became bolder. At one point, he put his head over her shoulder and nudged her with his nose, but an instant later he wheeled and snorted.

Catrin hoped his inquisitive nature would continue to get the best of him, and so it did. On his next return, he stuck his head into her lap and nearly knocked her over, which was the exact moment she had been awaiting. Quick as a striking snake, she looped the noose over his head and rolled away from him as he panicked. She was not quite quick enough in her escape and received a clout on the head for her troubles.

Her goal, though, had been achieved. The colt fought, wide eyed, against the rope that held him fast. The stop-knot prevented him from crushing his own windpipe, and the post remained firmly rooted, much to her relief. She watched and waited as his struggle became wild, and he threw himself against the restraints with abandon, but still the post held, though it did begin to move a bit more with each yank.

In a desperate move, the colt tried to get a running start, but when the rope went taut, it knocked him from his hooves, and in that moment, Catrin sprang, leaping onto him and straddling his neck. With her weight firmly settled just behind his ears, the colt could not get enough leverage to stand. He continued to flail, but Catrin spoke soothingly into his pinned ears. After a few more moments of struggling, the colt surrendered and stopped fighting.

The yearling halter was already cutting into the colt's growing flesh, and Catrin could see that Rolph was right: left on any longer, the flesh would have grown around the overtight halter. As gently as she could, she undid the buckle and pulled the halter from his head.

"Have you a halter?" she shouted, and the stunned men sprang into action. Rolph returned moments later with a much larger halter made of leather and brass. He handed it to her and let her do the honor of placing it on the colt. Careful to avoid the newly exposed flesh, she slipped the halter on. The colt struggled under her weight but was still unable to rise.

"Lead line," Catrin said, and it came out as an order, but Rolph didn't flinch. He just handed her a lead line. Once she had it secured to the halter, she pulled the noose from the colt's head. "Have you a stall ready?"

"Yes'm, and I'll have the aisle cleared," Rolph replied, and Catrin prepared for the most dangerous part of her task. Using her hand to keep weight on his neck, she climbed off and stood. As soon as she took her hands from his neck, the colt stood. He tried to fight her for a time, but she was skilled at avoiding his kicks and strikes, and she refused to let go. They spun in circles, and she slowly edged him toward the gate.

The men backed away and allowed her room to move as they left the pasture and entered the barnyard. Still they spun, and still Catrin moved him toward the barn. When she tried to get him through the open doors, the whites of his eyes showed and his panic increased, but much of the fight was out of him.

"First stall you can get 'im into will be fine," Rolph said, and she made for the first stall on the right. The door was narrow, and the colt balked. He strained against the lead line and halter, which Catrin knew must be painful on his raw flesh, and the pain increased his frenzy.

"Smack 'im on the rear," she shouted, and Rolph rushed to comply. In an instant, the colt went from resistance into a leap. He struck his hip on one side of the doorway and nearly trampled Catrin in the process, but he was in the stall. With a quickness born of skill and fear, she unhooked the lead line and fled the stall. Rolph slammed the gate shut behind her. The colt paced the stall restlessly, still blowing from the workout, and Catrin dropped to the floor, blowing nearly as hard as the colt. Benjin and Rolph reached her side as soon as she hit the ground and checked her for injury.

"I'm fine," she said. "Just winded."

"We owe you a great debt, Elma. You saved that colt, and you've given us back hope. With 'im available for breeding, we can replenish our stable yet. Didn't even have to shoot 'im," Rolph said with a broad smile. "Never seen the likes o' that, I tell ya. Yer a clever girl indeed."

Catrin blushed at his compliment, and her stomach practically roared in hunger.

Rolph heard the rumble and seemed to recall himself. "Ye've not even eaten yet; shame on us. Come, let's feast to yer success," he said, and she gladly followed him inside.

As Rolph entered the cottage, ducking his head under the low door, Collette stepped in behind and cuffed him on the back of his head. "You great oaf, how could ya let that poor girl catch yer colt on an empty stomach." Rolph made no argument, and Collette turned to Catrin. "I saw what ya did out there, Elma. Yer brave and smart as can be. Couldn't be more proud of ya. To celebrate, I pulled out our last cured ham. We'll eat well this day, for ye've given us back our livelihood. Ya don't even know how many times those men tried to catch that rascal, and here you pluck 'im in a single mornin'. Tickles me," she said, and she gave Catrin a warm hug.

"Did ya see that, Gramma?" Jessub asked as he stormed into the house, and rather than wait for an answer, he acted out the entire scene. His antics sent laughter into the air, and it was one of the most joyful moments of Catrin's life; she had truly helped these good folks, and it warmed her heart. Still she felt guilty eating the last of their meat.

"Are you certain you wish to serve the ham? Soup would be fine."

"Nonsense! Ye've earned a good meal, and I'd say the first foal born should be yers as well," Collette said in a tone that left no room for argument.

The meal she served was nothing short of spectacular, given the circumstances, as she broke out the best of their stores: ham, bread, and cheese were accompanied by sugared nuts and apple cider. Very little was said as everyone enjoyed the meal, but it was a merry silence. A weight seemed to have lifted from Rolph's shoulders, and he looked younger than when they had met.

"Ye've got to name that colt now," Collette scolded Rolph. "I don't think 'No-good rotten son of a common hussy' suits him anymore."

Rolph laughed from his belly, and his laughter was contagious. Catrin's full belly soon hurt, and joyful tears ran down her cheeks. "I think I'll call 'im Elmheart. What d'ya think of that, Elma?"

"I think that suits him just fine. I'll take pride in his naming."

"That ya should. That ya should," Collette said, nodding her head.

"As much as I hate to leave your hospitality," Benjin said with a hand on his full belly. "We should be on our way. We've a long way to go."

"I'll not send y'off on foot. No sir, I won't. I may not have a horse to spare, but I've an ox and an old oxcart. If ye'd be willing to help me fix up the cart, I'd say ya more than earned it," Rolph said, and Catrin's jaw dropped open.

"That's far too generous a gift for us to accept," she said, and Benjin nodded his agreement.

"I'll not hear it. No, I won't," Rolph insisted, and Collette added her vote to his.

"Are you sure you can do without?"

"Ah, I must admit our gift is not all it'd seem. Curly's no prize. He's cross-eyed and unp'dictable, but he'll pull a cart. B'sides, in a few weeks, the colt'll be broke, and I can use 'im to pull the plow if'n I needs to. We'll be fine."

* * *

Rocks tumbled into the ravine as Lissa tried to regain her footing, the heels of her sturdy boots finding no purchase amid the brittle layers of shale. Using her gloved hands, she slowed her fall and eventually came to a stop. Before her stood only open air, below a sheer face that raced to meet the river valley far below. Using the skills Morif had taught her, she climbed slowly back to safety.

He'd always been a mentor to her and had listened when no one else would. She wished he were with her now, but she knew even he would make her go back, make her face what everyone seemed to think was her responsibility--her duty. No one could make her face that--no one. Instead, she made the choice for her people. She would rather they perish as free people than survive as slaves to the Zjhon and Kytes.

Better to be free, she thought as she searched for food and shelter. Better to be free.

Chapter 19

If you wish the devout to ingest poison, wrap it in pomp and seal it with ideology.
--Von of the Elsics

* * *

 Catrin, Rolph, and Benjin worked on the oxcart in the afternoon sun. The cart was in poor condition, and one of the wheels was seized. After they removed the wheel and greased the hub, it moved more freely, but was still less than perfect. Catrin was glad to have the cart as it would make their travels much easier, and she hoped it would help them appear more like locals. Collette folded the blankets from the loft and insisted they would make a good cushion for the splintery wooden seat. Their kindness in such a trying time spoke volumes for their generous souls, and Catrin vowed to never forget them and all they had done for her.
 When the cart was deemed ready for travel, Rolph led them to a pasture on the outskirts of the farmstead. On his way, he retrieved a bushel basket of hard corn still on the cob, and he handed an ear to Catrin.
 "Take this out to him. Hold your ground now. He's harmless," Rolph said with a mischievous grin, and Catrin reluctantly slipped through the fence.
 Curly stood at the far end of the field, tall as a horse, half again as long, and twice as big around. His shaggy coat added to his girth, making him look like a barn on legs. As soon as Catrin stood within the fence, he turned and charged, building momentum as he came. Afraid she would be run down, Catrin did as Rolph had instructed: she held her ground, albeit with her eyes closed.
 Heavy breathing and the pounding of his hooves grew closer, but just before she thought Curly would trample her, he stopped. When Catrin opened her eyes, he stood before her, eyeing her with one eye; the other stared off to her right. He snorted and nudged her with his broad head, and only then did she recall the ear of corn she held at her side. As she extended it to him, he grabbed it greedily from her hand. He shoved his ear into her hand as he chewed, nearly knocking her over. She scratched behind his ear, and he leaned into her, groaning with pleasure.
 The ear of corn kept him busy for only a moment, and he nudged her hands for more. As she turned to walk back to the fence, he followed on her heels, occasionally nudging her from behind.
 "I think he likes you," Rolph said with a chuckle, and Catrin stuck her tongue out at him, which set him to laughing from his belly.

"He seems like a friendly beast," Benjin said. "We can't thank you enough for your generosity."

"It's the least we can do."

Catrin slid back through the fence, and they retrieved the oxcart. Rolph brought a yoke and lines from the barn, and Curly paced the fence excitedly, rattling the gate as he passed it. But as Rolph opened the gate, a bell rang out in the distance. Its peal sent a chill down Catrin's spine and raised the hair on her arms.

"Citizens call!" echoed across the distance. "Citizens call!"

Despite Curly's protests, Rolph closed the gate. "Well, let's see what news the crier brings," he said, and Benjin nodded, showing no signs of concern. Catrin followed nervously as they crossed the fields to a small town. The call for citizens continued even after they arrived, giving those in more remote areas the chance to congregate with the rest. A large crowd had gathered around the crier, who stood atop a stage of crates draped with a red cloth.

"Good citizens, I greet you with news both grand and dire," the crier said with a dramatic flourish. "In the south of Faulk has been found the likeness of god and goddess, the very symbol of the Zjhon, with a life its own. It glows from within, proof it is a divine gift from the heavens, and we rejoice!" His words were met with a muted hush, but he continued on, apparently undaunted by the lack of applause.

"The faithful are called to the great city of Adderhold to gaze upon god and goddess, to worship in person. Failure to do so will be considered insult and heresy. Prepare yourselves, pilgrims, for Istra and Vestra call you to them, and only the masses can assuage their thirst for worship."

A louder murmur rushed through the crowd. Few seemed pleased by the prospect. Angry and frightened faces surrounded them, and the air grew foul with tension. The charge of it weighed on Catrin as the masses broadcast their anxiety, and waves of it battered her senses. She breathed in deeply to stave off the nausea, and the crier waved his arms for silence.

"The next is sad beyond reckoning, and I ask that the weak of heart be seated," the crier continued, waiting it seemed more for dramatic pause than anything else. "The armies have returned from the Godfist with only three ships. The rest were lost. The Herald Witch laid waste to the armada, killing our people and her own without discretion. She has betrayed god, goddess, the Greatland, and the Godfist with her actions, and her own people have cast her into exile. The remains of our armies took mercy on the good people of the Godfist and helped in what ways they could before they left in pursuit of the renegade Herald Witch."

Catrin swayed on her feet, along with many of those around her, but for different reasons. She knew it to be false--all of it--and she was appalled by the depth of the Zjhon's deceit. They lied to their own people because they feared the truth. Rolph leaned on Catrin and nearly fell, and she supported his weight. His face was contorted into a mask of pain and grief, and Catrin's fury rose higher. The crier's lies caused him needless pain, and she resented it deeply. She had set the armies free, but the crier's words made it sound as if she had slaughtered everyone.

"Go, citizens. Prepare yourselves for the final triumph of the Zjhon. Together we shall beat back the Herald Witch, and we will prevail. To Adderhold with you, one and all! The divinity shall arrive at Adderhold by spring, and all are required to attend. In their light shall the rifts in the Greatland be healed and the enemy crushed. Until I see you there, I bid you blessings in the light of Istra, Vestra, and the Zjhon Church."

"What do they expect us to do? Eat stones?" someone in the crowd asked. "How can we leave our fields and homes and expect not to starve?" The crier had no answers for them; instead, he just packed his stage cloth and moved on to the next town. The crowd milled in confusion. No one seemed to know what to do, and some seemed on the verge of panic. The false news of the armies' losses had the most devastating effect. Many wept in mourning for family members they presumed dead.

Catrin, Rolph, and Benjin walked back to the farmstead in oppressive silence. Rolph's shoulders occasionally shook with sobs, and Catrin sensed that he dreaded relaying the news to Collette. She stood in the barnyard when they returned, and she dropped to her knees when she saw Rolph's face; she had no need to hear the words from him. He ran to her, and they clung to each other for support. It was a gut-wrenching sight, especially when one knew the news was false. Catrin had an enormously difficult time holding her tongue, but Benjin's pointed stare urged her to do just that. Rolph helped Collette into the house, and he returned a moment later.

"Mother needs a rest," he said, his voice heavy with emotion. "Let's get you settled while I've still the energy to move." They opened the pasture gate, and Curly nearly charged to the oxcart. "Thinks he's going to town. He's well known, and the children always bring him corn. It can make fer a wild ride, but he does no harm," Rolph said, and while Benjin loaded their gear, he pulled Catrin aside. "I've one last gift for you." He led her into the barn and pulled a heavy coat from a hook in the feed stall. "This belonged to one of m'sons, Martik," he said, his lip quivering. "He was studying arch'tecture before the Zjhon came. He used to say he'd one day be the builder of great things. He won't be needin' this jacket anymore, and I want you t'have it. Keep the hood up, and it'll be harder to guess yer age. I hope it helps to ease the troubles of yer journey in some way."

"Will you go to Adderhold?" she asked.

"Not me. Boil the Zjhon fer taking m'boys, and boil the Herald Witch for killing 'em. Boil 'em all," he said, his face going crimson.

His words struck Catrin like a physical blow. Though she understood his reasons for saying them, they stung and shamed her. She longed to tell him the truth, to tell him his sons most likely lived as citizens of the Godfist. Would he even believe her if she told him? Tortured by the sight of his tears, she could take it no longer. "Do you trust me?" she asked, and he appraised her with his eyes.

"Aye, Elma. I trust you," he said, and the use of her pseudonym shamed her; he trusted her despite her deception, and she wondered if she deserved his trust.

"The words you heard today were false. The Herald did not kill all the men who did not return; she freed them. Most of them still live. Though they face a harsh winter with little food, I expect the majority will survive," she said, and she felt as if a vice had been released from her chest; the giving of truth allowed her to breathe again. Still, she knew she had just risked everything. Rolph's face was almost impossible to read as he contemplated her words, and she waited anxiously for some response.

"How do you know this? Tell me true."

"We've not been completely honest with you about our origins, I admit, but I would not deceive you about such a thing. I know these things because I was there. I saw it with my own eyes."

"So you're saying m'boys live?"

His simple question impaled her; she could not have felt his pain more keenly, and it left her rattled. "I cannot say for certain. Some men were killed during the invasion."

"I thank you for your words, Elma. You'd best get going," Rolph said as he noticed Benjin with an angry look on his face, and Catrin wasn't even certain he believed her. Acting as if nothing had happened, she and Benjin left as quickly as they could, which turned out to be faster than Catrin had expected. As soon as Rolph untied Curly, the ox charged toward town. Catrin and Benjin bounced along in the oxcart, barely able to keep themselves from flying off. The charge did not last long, though, and Curly slowed, unable to maintain the pace for a long distance. The jostling became bearable, and Catrin glanced at Benjin, who had not said a word.

"You are your father's daughter, of that there can be no doubt," he said, shaking his head.

"He was in so much pain because of the crier's lies. I couldn't let him believe his sons were all dead at my hand when they most likely live; it would've been too cruel."

Benjin didn't harass her any further about it, and they rode in silence for a while, heading on a westerly course.

"Do you think we should make for Adderhold?" she asked, if for no other reason than to break the uncomfortable silence.

"I suppose we haven't much choice. There's little chance of us getting anywhere near the statue while it's being transported, though I'm not sure we have any chance of getting near it when it arrives at Adderhold either. We'd have to pass through lands held by your family and those held by their rivals, the Kytes. A more dangerous path I cannot imagine. Do you know what you will do when we get there?"

"I have no idea, but I must try. It would be cowardly of me to turn my back on these people. The people of the Greatland would pay the greatest price for the Zjhon's folly, and I cannot allow that to happen. I just hope we're right about the true nature of the statue. I can find no way to prove our beliefs or disprove the beliefs of the Zjhon. I suppose I'll have to act on faith alone."

"Blind faith," Benjin said.

"Blind faith, indeed," Catrin said. She hoped some other solution or some bit of proof that would allow her to believe more firmly would present itself, but none came.

Following a narrow cart path, they passed local farmers on their way. Folks waved as they passed, and they returned the waves, trying to appear as if they belonged there. Benjin urged Curly to pick up the pace. Curly would have none of it, though, and set his own pace, despite Benjin's clucks, chirps, and more than a few smacks on the rear with the lines.

As night fell, they entered more heavily settled lands, and the lights of a distant town shone on the horizon. Reflections of the lights could be seen in the wide river that lay on the far side of town. A copse of oak and elm stood on a nearby hill, and Benjin steered Curly toward it as best he could. Curly resisted his direction, and they nearly rode past the trees, but Benjin managed to get him stopped. At the bottom of the hill, Benjin handed Catrin the lines and climbed from the cart. After retrieving an ear of corn, he lured Curly into the trees.

Curly chewed noisily on the corn while Benjin tied him off to a tree. Once Curly was unhooked and taken care of, they set up a small camp and ate sparingly from their provisions. They lit no fire, for fear of drawing attention to themselves, and they spent a long night huddled together for warmth.

**

The following day was bright and clear, and the morning sun warmed the air enough that they could no longer see their own breath before them. The road into town was congested with wagons, carts, and hundreds on foot. Catrin and Benjin blended into the crowd as best they could and eventually made their way into town. The streets were jammed with pedestrians and roaming vendors. Curly was ill suited for such tight quarters. He stepped on toes and knocked over vendors' carts, leaving behind a trail of angry people wherever they went. Benjin sought out the market proper and spotted a man selling livestock.

"It'd be nice to ride all the way to Adderhold, but I think we should sell Curly while we can. Major bridges in the Greatland bear a toll, and we'll need coin to cross," he said.

Catrin didn't like the idea one bit, but she could think of no other way to get coin short of stealing, which she was unwilling to do. They approached the livestock vendor, and he appraised them as they moved closer. Catrin suspected he saw an easy profit as he moved into the crowd to great them.

"That beast has lived beyond its years, Yusef would say," he said, shaking his head. "Not fit for plow or plate. Don't think he can use that one. No, Yusef doesn't."

"These days there's little to be had," Benjin replied. "Most would be glad to have such a fine beast. P'haps there're others here who'd be more interested," he said, casting his gaze around the market. Catrin searched for other vendors selling livestock, and while she saw a few goats and a handful of chickens, no one else had large animals for sale.

"Try if you'd like, but anyone here'll tell you that Yusef is the man t'see," the vendor said as he spread his arms wide and bowed deeply.

"And what would Yusef offer for this fine beast and cart?"

"Yusef has no need for the cart, but he supposes he could dispose of it without a great deal of trouble. Yusef offers a silver."

"Good luck to you, Yusef," Benjin said, and he chirped to Curly, who completely ignored him.

"Don't be hasty now. A silver for a beast that appears to be deaf as well as blind is a fair offer, but Yusef is a generous man. A silver and two coppers."

"Three silvers."

"Three silvers! Why that's robbery, friend. Surely, Yusef deserves to eat. Two silvers."

"Three," Benjin said, and Yusef appeared wounded by his firm stance. He made no counteroffer; instead he just shook his head as if in deep thought. "Perhaps now is not the time to sell," Benjin continued. "Prices will only go higher as the pilgrimage begins, and we've nothing but time. Perhaps the traders in the next town will be more generous."

"Thieves, they are. Why, you would have to travel all the way to Adderhold to find a better offer, and even then you take your chances. You seem like good people, and Yusef has a soft place in his heart, he does. Three silvers."

Benjin climbed from the cart and shook his hand. "Deal."

As soon as the coins were in Benjin's hands, Yusef seemed to forget that he and Catrin existed, and he began hawking Curly as if he were a prize bull. "Who will give me five silvers for this fine beast? Full of vigor, he is, and Yusef'll even throw in this finely crafted cart," he shouted into the crowd even as they unloaded their packs.

While Catrin stuffed the blankets from the seat into her pack, the wind blew the hood away from her face, and she hastily pulled it back up. She and Benjin shuffled through the crowd, and Benjin continued to affect his limp and lean on the staff. It did him little good in the jostling crowd, and they were nearly knocked off their feet several times within the sea of people. The lack of respect these folks showed one another was remarkable. It was as if they were so great in number that none of them mattered as individuals. Each person was just another body congesting the streets.

A long line snaked away from the base of the bridge, and a dozen guards stood at the height of the span, holding up the mass of people crossing. Fear gripped Catrin at the sight of them, and she cast Benjin a furtive glance, but he seemed unconcerned.

"Toll collectors," he said, and his statement was confirmed as she watched the soldiers accept coins from each person who passed. They waited as patiently as they could in the line, but it moved dreadfully slowly, and Catrin began to see the wisdom in Benjin's decision to sell Curly. It would have been difficult to maneuver him through the crowd, not to mention the coin they needed to pay the toll.

When they reached the highest part of the span, they were packed tightly against the other people waiting to cross. The stone beneath Catrin's feet seemed to move from side to side, and she feared the bridge would collapse from the weight of so many people. Her feet sore from standing so long, she shifted from one to the other to ease the pain, but it provided only a small amount of relief.

The line continued to move inexorably forward, and the scrutiny of the guards drew ever closer. Catrin felt trapped. If the guards somehow realized who she was, she would have no way to escape. The crowd packed tightly on all sides, and panic threatened to relieve her of her sanity.

Benjin must have sensed her distress, for he took her hand and gave it a small squeeze. "Just a little farther, li'l miss. Hold on for a while longer, and this'll all be behind us. Try to imagine yourself in the middle of an open field," he said.

Catrin tried to take his advice, but the mass of energies around her assaulted her even with her eyes closed. She could sense them. She could feel their impatience. Their smell filled her nostrils, and she thought she might be sick. In an effort to stem off the nausea, she concentrated on her breathing, which had become short and rapid. Deep breaths probably would have settled her stomach if it were not for the smell of unwashed bodies.

When they finally reached the guards, Catrin's hair was soaked with sweat, and her hands trembled. Benjin approached a guard, who gave him a bored glance.

"Copper apiece," he said.

Benjin handed him a silver and pointed to himself and Catrin, as if he were mute. The guard was obviously disgusted to have to make change, and he sighed heavily as he dug in his pouch. After a moment, he produced a handful of coppers and shoved them into Benjin's hand.

"Next time bring coppers," he said and turned his attention to the next in line.

The line on the far side of the toll moved rapidly, and within a few short moments, they gained the far shore. Catrin sucked in the cool air as if she had been drowning, and Benjin dragged her off to one side.

"Calm yourself. We're not out of danger yet. There're more soldiers about."

"I'll be fine in a moment," she said, and she felt her panic begin to recede. They were across the bridge, and though she felt she was stepping from one precipice to another, she was almost accustomed to it; it had begun to feel normal.

* * *

Rats scurried at the edge of the torchlight, and the shadowy form of Chase's guide filled most of the dank tunnel they were following. The land surrounding New Moon Bay was riddled with sewers and passages, and this one was supposed to take Chase to a ship. After days of hiding in cellars and crawling through sewers, Chase was looking forward to being back at sea.

Very little had been said during his travels; Brother Vaughn had made most of the arrangements. Chase didn't even know the name of his guide or what ship he was being taken to, but he made himself keep walking despite the uncertainty. Catrin needed him, and he would not fail her.

The air became less foul as they walked and began to smell more of salt than sewage. When they reached the end of the tunnel, his guide simply pointed to a familiar-looking ship in the harbor and turned and walked back into the tunnel.

The water was far below the tunnel exit, and Chase stared down at the waves crashing on the rocks, hoping the water would be deep enough where he landed. Before his courage fled, he took a running leap into the harbor and struck the water hard. As he reached the surface, wiping the water from his eyes, he heard voices.

"Who goes there?" barked a gravelly voice.

Coming toward Chase was a small rowing craft filled with uniformed men. Taking a deep breath, he slipped beneath the dark water.

Chapter 20

Evil exists only in the hearts of men.
--Ain Giest, Sleepless One

* * *

As he climbed back to the chamber atop the mountain, Nat's legs trembled from exertion as well as fear. Only the hope that he would learn something important kept him moving. Within the chamber, his visions became absolute, blotting out his current reality and showing what he thought were vivid glimpses of a likely future. Though they left him feeling nauseated and abused, he kept coming back, drawn by morbid fascination and the quest for knowledge.

Beside him, Neenya climbed, and her presence bolstered his confidence. Never before had someone shown such faith in him. As he slowly learned her language, all barriers between them seemed to fall. To trust someone so completely was a thing Nat had never believed himself capable of, but Neenya's unwavering dedication and loyalty made it impossible for him to feel otherwise.

Concern was clearly visible in her eyes as they reached the final stage of their climb, but there was something else there, something Nat could not easily define. It was acceptance, he finally decided, and he sighed. Though endeared by her devotion, Nat also felt the weight of responsibility. The Gunata, as Nat now knew the villagers called themselves, believed in him. They believed he had been sent to them to do something special, something important. Neenya had given her life over to him, leaving behind whatever it was she had done in the past, and Nat prayed he would not fail them.

When the chamber entrance came into view, Nat quailed. Only the needs of those who were depending on him drove him forward, and he practically fell into the chamber. As he crawled forward, drawing ragged breaths, the power of premonition obliterated all other thought.

Neenya held him in her arms, and when the vision finally released him, he looked into her eyes, tears streaming down his face. No words could express the horrors he'd seen, and as he pulled Neenya closer, he squeezed his eyes shut, praying that, just this once, his visions were untrue. "I'm so sorry," he whispered. His body shook in grief as his mind reconciled what he'd seen. As he wept, Neenya sang softly, rocking him to sleep.

* * *

The days merged into one long, miserable blur. Catrin could not recall how long it had been since they sold Curly, but the blisters on her feet spoke of more days than her memory could reconcile. They trudged along, surrounded by pilgrims who marched in morose silence. It wasn't a joyful journey for any of them; it was more like a death march. Like sheep to the slaughter, they put one foot in front of the other and nothing more. The people seemed to know they were going to their deaths, yet they continued.

Catrin despaired and wondered why they would leave their lives behind to seek out an idol. Even if the archmaster had mandated their presence, he was certainly in no position to enforce his edict, but they seemed not to care. From what Catrin sensed, most simply wished the misery to end.

The roads were churned to mud, at least until the snows came; then they froze, their texture sealed by frost. Ruts and frozen footprints threatened to turn their ankles, and illness began to spread. Catrin could not breathe through her nose, and a cough rattled in her chest. Benjin did what he could to secure dry places to camp and wood for fires, but the landscape was usually picked clean long before they arrived.

Large groups huddled together at night for the protection in their numbers, but Catrin and Benjin kept to themselves. They had no desire for the company, and those around them seemed to have no desire for the fellowship of strangers.

Occasionally they passed an inn, and the rosy glow that came from within beckoned to them, but Benjin insisted they save their coin for food, which was becoming increasingly expensive. Vendors took advantage of the massive migration and inflated their prices. Perhaps the shortage of food could explain away the cost increase, but Catrin resented it. She felt as if they preyed on the poor and hungry, and she detested them for it. Anger and spite were all that kept her going at times, and she used her fury to stay warm.

"You've not lost hope, have you?" Benjin asked at the end of another silent day.

Catrin remained mute for some time before answering. "Hope," she said. "Hope for what? A quick death? An end to the misery? I've no idea what to hope for. I cannot hope to save these people, and they cannot save themselves."

"Such thoughts will get you nowhere. There's always a chance that things will work out, and you're not the only one attempting to stop this madness. Others labor toward the same end, and we can only pray they've not given up," he said, but she continued to spiral into her own personal nightmare.

"Even if the statue is destroyed, what then? There are no crops in the fields. The food supply is already growing scarce, and disease is sure to follow. I begin to wonder if saving these poor wretches from a quick death is the right thing to do. If they'll only suffer slow deaths, then what good will I have done?"

"You act as if all is already lost, but the sun still shines and we still live and breathe. I, for one, plan to do whatever I can. I'll not give up until my last breath leaves my lips."

"Good luck to you, then," she said. "I'm tempted to simply lay down and die. I've no more to give, and this dreadful march will never end."

Benjin stopped and yanked her aside by her arm. His face was crimson, and she had never seen him so angry; he frightened her, and his grip was painful. "How dare you give up! Did your father teach you nothing? Anything worth doing is difficult, and this could not be more worthwhile. How could you expect it to be easy? You shame me." At one time, those words would have stung, but she simply shrugged.

"Who knows if my father is even alive? I doubt it. I'll never see him again, and if he wants to be disappointed, then let him. And that goes for you as well. Perhaps you would rather walk alone."

"It's tempting, but I'll not allow you to give up so easily. If I have to drag you by your ears, you'll fight, and you'll win, if only to spite me," he said, and a crooked smile actually tried to form on his lips.

Catrin couldn't fight him; he was right, and she knew it. That didn't make it any easier, but it did keep her moving. "You're right. I know, but I'm tired. So very tired."

"I know, li'l miss, but I'm here to help you. I'll always be right by your side. You can count on that," he said.

She leaned against him for support. "You amaze me. How can you stay positive amidst this horror?"

"It's not easy, and I'm not saying it is, but it's all in how you look at it. We could've been hung, or drowned, or burned a dozen times now. How did we survive those things? How are we still here to try? Hope, determination, and in some cases, sheer stubbornness."

"Well, that's one thing we have in abundance. If only we could eat it," she said and actually chuckled.

"There, you see? I told you we could do it. Laughter keeps the world alive, you know." And with that, they stepped a little lighter, marched a little faster, and the pain seemed to ease in Catrin's feet, as if it had been imposed by her despair rather than the endless footsteps. When an inn appeared on the horizon, Benjin led her toward it.

"But we should save our coin," she protested.

"One night's lodging won't break us, and I think we've earned a bit of respite. I'd also like to look for signs of the Vestrana." Their hopes were dashed when they arrived, though.

"Full up," the innkeeper said when they inquired about rooms, and the sheer number of folks jammed into the common room gave her statement credence. The rotund woman turned to tend other customers.

"Please miss. A stall in the stables, a bit of floor in the kitchens, we'll take whatever you can offer." The woman looked disgusted, but Benjin pleaded with his eyes.

"Two coppers and you can sleep in the loft with the rest of the fools," she said, and Benjin quickly pulled four coppers from his pouch.

"Might we get a bit of food to go with our lodging?"

"You're a pushy one," she said, but she accepted the coin. "Potato broth is all we have left, but this'll get you two bowls."

A thick layer of grease was congealed on top of the broth, and it tasted little better than laundry water, but it was warm and it felt good in Catrin's belly. They drained their bowls in short order, and the innkeeper had the stable boy show them to the loft. At the top of the ladder, they found mounds of flea-ridden straw, and there was barely a spot to be found that did not harbor a sleeping body. People cursed them as they wandered through the disorganized mass of humanity, but they eventually found a corner in which to lie down. Catrin pulled the blankets from her pack and prepared the best bed she could for them, and they laid themselves down to rest.

"You get some sleep," Benjin said. "I don't trust these folk not to rob us. I'll keep watch for now. I'll wake you later."

She would have argued, but his words were muffled by her wide yawn, and she let sleep claim her. When she woke, sunlight streamed through the cracks in the walls, and Benjin slept beside her, his belt knife still in his hand. When he woke, she saw that his purse and other valuables were beneath him. He was an intimidating figure, knife in hand, and she supposed that had been enough to keep any would-be thieves at bay.

The sun already high in the sky, they left the inn long after most of the others who had shared the loft with them. A small town lay ahead, and in many ways, it looked the same as every other town they had already passed. It made Catrin feel as if they had been walking in circles.

"We're nearing the western border of Astor," Benjin said as they entered the dirty little hamlet. "Soon we'll be in Mundleboro, the lands ruled by your mother's family. We'll have to be extra careful when we get there. Keep your hood up at all times. I've been searching for signs of the Vestrana, but the signals I've seen are conflicting. They are close to correct but include subtle warnings. I'm afraid to seek their aid since it seems they fear they've been infiltrated."

Walking past the smithy and shops, Benjin stopped at a storefront that displayed cured meats. Salted hams, smoked fish, and several strange reddish sausages hung under the watchful eye of the storekeeper.

"What'll you be needing?" the beady-eyed man asked, and it was clear he did not trust them. His look urged them to buy something or move on.

"How much for the pepper sausage?" Benjin asked.

"A silver."

"Why, that's robbery. Surely you cannot expect to get such a price?"

"Already have and will again. Take it or leave it," the man said, and he cleared the sword at his waist from its scabbard, daring them to steal it. They did not intend to stoop so low, but that price would consume most of the coin they had, and they still had a long journey ahead of them.

"Come on, li'l miss. Let us find a more pleasant thief to steal our coin," Benjin said.

The storekeeper spit at them as they left. The argument drew unwanted attention, and several people among the crowd stared at them as they turned away, as if they hoped for a fight to break out, if only to break the monotony.

At that moment, a chance wind gusted through the streets, and the hood was pulled from Catrin's face. As she rushed to pull it back up, she saw a woman who was as wide as she was tall, and she was walking toward them.

"Lady Lissa! What in all the gods' lands are you doing here? You were to be at Ravenhold weeks ago. And what have you done with your hair?" she asked as she approached, and Catrin looked about to see who she addressed, but then the woman stopped abruptly and her eyes went wide. She leaped across the short distance that separated them and grabbed Catrin by the arm.

"If you make a move," she said in a low voice, "I'll shout for the guards and label you thieves. Come with me quietly, and no one gets hurt. Understand?" Only then did Catrin feel the pressure of a cold blade against her back. Benjin stood, frozen, seemingly afraid the woman would run Catrin through. Without a word, they let the strange woman lead them into a nearby inn.

The common room was crowded, but no one paid them any mind except to curse them for pushing through the throng. The knife at her back urged her up the stairs, and they stopped before a sturdy wooden door at the end of the hall. This door was the only one to bear a lock, and the woman produced a key from the folds of her shawl. Within a moment they were inside, the door locked securely behind them.

"Don't think to lie to me. I'd know you even if you were burned from head to toe. You're Mangst as sure as Vestra shines," she said.

Benjin let out a heavy sigh. "Who are you?" he asked, and the woman wheeled on him with her knife.

"The questions are mine to ask. Never you mind who I am. The question is who are you, and what are you doing here?"

"That's a long story and not one easily explained," Benjin began, but the woman cut him short, literally; she sliced the air before him as if to demonstrate her skill with the knife.

"Shut your mouth. I'm not asking you. I ask her. What is your business here?"

"We're bound for Adderhold," Catrin said, unsure of what else to say. She decided a small bit of truth was all she was willing to give. She didn't even know who this woman was or what evil deed she suspected them of committing, but her patience was already worn thin.

"Lies," the woman said, and she punctuated her statement by tapping her slender blade on Catrin's chest. It was a move meant to threaten and cow her, but Catrin had had enough. She and Benjin had done nothing to deserve such treatment. With a quickness she didn't realize she possessed, she clasped the woman's wrist and twisted hard, driving her knee into the woman's groin. By the time the woman hit the floor, Catrin had the blade wedged between the woman's multiple chins.

"Easy now. Easy. Let's not get too excited. Let her up, li'l miss. We mean her no harm, and she means us none. This is all just a misunderstanding," Benjin said, but his words were ignored.

Catrin snarled at the woman, who now became the target of all her anger, all her resentment. Suddenly this woman was the source of all their troubles, and with one twist of her wrist, she would be gone. It would be so easy. The woman's flesh was soft and pale and would part easily before the razor-sharp blade.

Benjin grabbed Catrin's arm and pulled the knife away from the woman's throat, but he got no gratitude. The woman pulled another blade from her belt, and they all stood in suspense, assessing one another.

"Please, both of you. We can solve this peacefully. Put the blades away. Shedding each other's blood will help no one," Benjin said.

His words penetrated the haze of fury that still gripped Catrin. With obvious reluctance, she reversed the blade and handed it back to the woman, who seemed surprised.

"Now let us begin again. I'm Benjin Hawk," he said, and the woman's eyes grew wide again. "And this is Catrin Volker, daughter of Elsa Mangst."

His words might as well have been a physical blow for the effect they had on the woman. She fell back against the far wall, and her breathing became rapid. Catrin was shocked by his honesty.

"By the gods, it's true. Isn't it?" she asked with a hysterical glance at Catrin.

"He speaks the truth," Catrin said, and it was as much an accusation against Benjin as it was an affirmation. The woman sat down heavily and stared at them as if they were beyond explanation.

"You don't mean to kill me," the woman said, making it more a statement than a question, but Catrin felt the need to respond nonetheless.

"We never intended you any harm, but you certainly scared us," she said, and she was surprised to see the woman relax a bit and actually sheathe her blades.

"I am Millicent, maid to the Lady Mangst," the woman said, and now it was Benjin's turn to appear shocked.

"Millie? I didn't even recognize you."

"You need not tell me the years have been unkind; I am aware, but they've touched you as well," Millie said.

"You know each other?" Catrin asked.

"It's been many years," Benjin began before Millie cut him short.

"Since you and that scoundrel, Wendel, stole Elsa away from us."

"After all these years, you are still shortsighted, I see," Benjin said, but Millie ignored him.

"Let us speak no more. This matter should be taken up with the lady, not her lowly servant. I'll arrange for passage to Ravenhold. Be warned, if you try to escape, I'll have you hunted down and killed. Do I make myself clear?"

"You do, but your threats are unnecessary and insulting," Catrin said with an arch look, daring the woman to question her integrity again. Millie gave her a sidelong glance but said no more. Instead, she walked out the door, leaving them alone.

"This is not going to go well," Benjin said almost to himself.

"I assume my family will not be happy to see me?"

"Or me," he said, shaking his head.

"Well, let them be unhappy. I've no intention of staying long. You don't think they'll try to stop me, do you?"

"I don't know, li'l miss. I'd hoped to avoid them completely. They're not fond of me to begin with, and I have no idea how they will react to you, but I doubt they'll welcome you. Your mother's family are not the most forgiving people I've ever met."

Catrin asked him no more questions, knowing he would not have the answers. She supposed she would just have to take it up with the Lady Mangst--whoever that was. It bothered her a great deal that she didn't know, yet she decided not to ask. She would find out soon enough.

The room began to feel very small as she paced back and forth, and the air felt thick and heavy, as if she were breathing water. She did not know how long Millie had been gone, but it seemed like days, and when she finally returned, Catrin's patience was lost to her.

"We must leave at once," Millie said. "I was not to return for three more days, but this'll not wait. I've arranged a carriage for you. It waits in front of the inn. Come."

"Will you be joining us?" Catrin asked, uncertain of what exactly was taking place.

"I'll be traveling in a separate carriage, but they will travel together. So, yes, in a sense. Morif will act as your bodyguard and assure your safety."

In other words, Catrin thought, he would be their jailer, there only to make sure they did not try to escape. The fact bothered her greatly, but she put no voice to her misgivings, for she doubted it would do any good. Without another word, she and Benjin followed Millie from the inn.

As promised, two carriages waited, and they were like no carriages Catrin had ever seen before. Completely enclosed, with small doors in the side and smoky glass windows, their black finish shone in the sun, and even the wheels were spotless. Each one was drawn by a team of four horses, which appeared to be more for show than out of need. The carriages were large but not so large as to require more than one horse. The horses were obviously bred for looks; their coats gleamed, and their manes flowed. Their forelocks were so long that it was a wonder the horses could see anything. These were nothing like the horses her father raised, which were primarily workhorses, bred for power. And these were far showier than the horses of the Arghast tribes. It reminded Catrin of the townies, who used their horses primarily as a display of wealth, and the thought left a foul taste in her mouth.

Morif proved to be an imposing man. He was missing one eye, but his movements spoke of death. His muscles were well defined, and the cords of his tendons stood out in relief. He gave them a baleful stare as they climbed aboard the carriage, and Catrin returned it, which seemed to surprise him. She would show him no fear, and for once, she felt none. Let him try to hurt them, and she would show him just how dangerous she was.

The interior of the carriage was opulently appointed with deeply cushioned seats and smoky glass windows framed by frilly curtains. The journey to Ravenhold took four days, and they spent their nights in the best rooms the inns along the way had to offer. The common rooms were always full when they arrived, but somehow Millie always managed to secure not one, but two rooms each night.

Morif kept watch outside their door, and the tension between him and Catrin grew as time passed. She knew she should leave the man be, but his very presence annoyed her. At every opportunity, she let him know she didn't appreciate his watchfulness, whether it was something as small as stepping on his toes when she passed, or something as overt as spilling her dinner down the front of him. It was clear he struggled to restrain himself, but Catrin didn't care. She almost wished he would provoke her so she could take out her fury on him.

When she was honest with herself, it was not him she loathed. It was the thought that her family was automatically distrustful of her. It went against everything her father had taught her, and she resented the fact that they used his name without any trace of respect. She'd had her fill of people looking down their noses at her, and she thought she might bite the nose off the next person who did it.

Strange sensations crossed her mind, though, as they moved closer to Ravenhold. She was farther from the land of her birth than she had ever dreamed she would be, and yet, in some small way, she felt as if she were coming home.

Chapter 21

The souls of heroes are forged by the gods and tempered with the pain of life.
--Matteo Dersinger, prophet

* * *

Ravenhold proved to be an impressive sight. Larger than the Masterhouse and constructed with far more decorative appeal, it appeared to have been built more for show than strength. The land surrounding it was fancifully landscaped, and even in the dead of winter, there was color everywhere from the scarlet berries on the holly trees to the orange and yellow leaves of the sprawling oaks. Rose bushes lined the roadway, and Catrin knew they must be gorgeous in springtime.

Despite its beauty, the place filled her with dread. She was but a simple farm girl. There was no place for her here. The grand facade included bas-reliefs and statuary, and all of it lent to the air of superiority, as if the people who dwelt there were of a higher race. The closer they drew, the smaller Catrin felt, and it was a feeling she liked not one bit. Benjin tried to start a conversation a number of times, but her irritation would not allow for it. Instead, she brooded in oppressive silence.

No one greeted them at the gate except stable hands, and Millie instructed them to follow her. Morif shadowed them, and Catrin cast him baleful glances, but he ignored her completely. A subtle sidestep nearly tripped him, and she smiled--ignore *that*. He didn't lay a hand on her, but the look in his eye conveyed his thoughts.

As they climbed the wide marble stair that led to a pair of oak doors twice Catrin's height, she forgot about Morif and took in all the details. Carved from the white stone, a pair of roses presided over the entrance. They twined around one another, their thorns curved delicately away from the stems, and the name *Mangst* was engraved in an arc over them. It seemed an arrogant display, but it was overshadowed by what lay within. Thick carpets covered the center of the wide halls, leaving only a couple of hand widths of polished stone visible along the edges.

The walls were adorned with likenesses of those she supposed were her ancestors, for they all bore the family resemblance. Small gold plates at the bottoms of the portraits gave the names of those depicted, and Catrin tried to memorize each name as she passed them. There was a regal-looking man with gray hair only over his ears--Rasmussen Mangst--and a stern-looking woman in her middle years--Marietta Mangst. Their stares seemed to follow her, accusing her of besmirching their name. She was a ragamuffin among nobility, and her leathers and homespun seemed rags amid the glory of these trappings.

Millie led them to a side hall decorated with finely carved tables that bore elegant pottery and dried flowers--mostly roses. When she reached a set of oak doors, Millie ushered them inside.

"Please wait here while I alert the lady to your presence."

"I'll do no such thing," Catrin said, her hands on her hips. "You've dragged me here against my will, and I'll either see the lady now or be on my way."

Morif crossed his arms over his chest as if to bar her path, but Catrin pushed him out of her way. He glanced at Millie, obviously looking for direction, and she sighed.

"Very well," she said. "Suit yourself."

"I believe I'll do just that," Catrin replied with venom.

Millie jogged ahead, but Catrin refused to be rushed. She let Millie gain distance on them as she strode with feigned confidence through the hallowed halls of her ancestral home. She felt no more comfortable, but she refused to let her insecurity show. Morif followed them with a scowl, but she pretended he wasn't there. Instead, she acted as if she were the one who ruled this house.

Benjin walked beside her and matched her step. He didn't appear happy about her outbursts, but he supported her nonetheless. They were in this together for right or wrong, and she appreciated his not chastising her when it was obvious he didn't approve.

A pair of young men in rose-embroidered livery flanked doors no smaller than those at the main entrance. Millie rushed toward them. The men did not stall her, and she scurried inside. When Catrin and Benjin arrived, however, they barred the way. Catrin didn't attempt to force her way past them and instead stood in as regal a manner as she could muster. She listened intently but could hear only muffled conversation at first.

"What?" came a louder voice from inside. "Here? Now? Why did you not leave them in an audience room?" This was followed by more low conversation. The two young men exchanged puzzled glances but remained at attention. "Insisted, did she? Well, bring the whelp in. Let us see what she has to say for herself." Catrin heard the disdain in the lady's voice, and her mood worsened.

Millie was pale and shaken when she reappeared, and she motioned for them to enter. Catrin waited a moment, just for the sake of being contrary, and the two young men wore their shock on their faces.

"Let's not start things off badly, li'l miss. We've been summoned," Benjin said, urging her inside.

"I'll enter when I'm good and ready," Catrin said, and a tense silence hung over the hall. After a very long moment, she strode into the room as if it were her own, and Benjin followed closely.

"So, Benjin Hawk, you darken my doorway once again, after all these years. What do you plan to steal this time?" asked the elderly woman who waited inside. She was petite and her skin hung on her like an overlarge garment, but her eyes bored holes into whatever met her stare.

"Lady Mangst," Benjin said with a slight bow, but he said no more, as if he had not heard her question.

"And who is this waif at your side? Someone posing as my granddaughter?"

"Catrin Volker, Lady. Daughter of Wendel Volker and Elsa Mangst," he replied in a polite tone even as Catrin's anger flamed higher.

"Do not speak that foul name in my presence. That man stole my daughter, and his get is not worthy of my name."

"If you wish to address my Guardian, you will do so with respect. And with regards to my father, you are not fit to speak his name, for you would only foul it with your forked tongue," Catrin said as she stepped between Benjin and her grandmother.

All the color drained from Millie's face, and she eased into the shadows, but the Lady Mangst drew herself up, and a fire to rival Catrin's burned in her eyes.

"Respect is earned, not given."

"Every creature deserves a basic amount of respect. Unless, of course, you consider yourself better than everyone else," Catrin replied.

"Insolent child."

"Self-righteous wench," Catrin parried, and the air between them was charged with hostility.

"Now, ladies, surely we can be civil," Benjin interjected, and both women wheeled on him.

"Stay out of this," they said in unison.

"At least you two can agree on something," he mumbled as he took a step back.

"So what brings you here, sweetling?" the Lady Mangst asked.

"Your serving woman dragged me here on the threat of my life. I had no desire to come here. In fact, I believe I'll be leaving now," Catrin said as she turned to leave, but she was shocked to hear a slap echo through the room. She turned to see Millie with tears in her eyes, holding a hand to her face, and the Lady Mangst turned from Millie to face Catrin once again.

"You expect me to believe that you were not bound here anyway? Where else would you be headed?"

"Adderhold," Catrin replied.

The Lady Mangst spit on the floor. "What would you want in that house of vipers and vermin, to worship idols perhaps?"

"I don't see where that is any of your business."

"I'm your grandmother."

"You certainly don't act like it," Catrin said, and she realized this argument would get them nowhere, but she refused to back down, refused to show weakness in the face of one so pious. And she was surprised to see her antagonist reappraise her.

"So you ask nothing of me? No coin or lands or titles? You do not claim your birthright?"

"As I said before, I wouldn't have come at all if not for your underlings," Catrin replied, and she felt a little ashamed for being obstinate when her grandmother seemed to be warming to her, even if only slightly. "I ask nothing of you but my freedom."

The Lady Mangst said nothing for a few moments as she considered Catrin's words. Benjin and Millie exchanged furtive glances, but Catrin ignored them all. Her thoughts were muddled by her emotions, and she struggled to focus. So much had happened in such a short time, and she felt she was reacting poorly rather than using the situation to her advantage. It was possible her family could aid her in her quest, if only she could prove herself in their eyes.

"You've not told me why you were traveling to Adderhold. May I ask why?" the Lady Mangst asked in an almost conciliatory tone, but Catrin judged it genuine.

"I've no desire to worship the Statue of Terhilian. I wish to destroy it."

Her grandmother's eyes bulged. After a sharp intake of breath, she broke into a fit of coughing that threatened to claim her completely. Millie rushed to prepare her tea, but the spell passed long before the water was heated. Still Millie brought her the tea, and she sipped it with tears in her eyes. Catrin could not tell if the tears were from the coughing or something else entirely, but she waited patiently for a response.

"I truly do not mean to be rude this time, but I must ask. What makes you think you're capable of such a thing? Though, before you answer, I will add that I think it a noble goal and one I wish I could do myself."

Catrin cast Benjin a querying glance, but he only shrugged in return. The decision was hers.

"I'm not only your granddaughter. I am also the one they call the Herald of Istra."

This statement brought on a new fit of coughing, and Millie looked as if she would faint. Benjin gave Catrin no indication as to his feelings on her decision, but it was done now, and she couldn't take the words back. She would simply have to live with the consequences. The Lady Mangst slowly recovered, and after sipping her tea, she met Catrin's gaze.

"You don't really expect me to believe that, do you?" she asked, and Catrin sensed no sarcasm. She decided to take no offense and drew a breath to answer, but Benjin could no longer hold his tongue.

"Please don't ask her to prove her powers. It's far too dangerous, and I don't want to see anyone get hurt."

"It's not a problem, Benjin. I will do this for my grandmother as a sign of respect," Catrin said, and Millie nodded firmly, as if this were how it should be. Catrin closed her eyes and focused her mind on the one thing she shared in common with the lady: her mother.

She focused on memories of her childhood: her mother's scent, the feeling of her gentle caress, the warmth of her embrace, the safety and security she had always felt in her mother's presence. All of these she poured into her meditation, not allowing the startled gasps to disturb her. She added the tinkling laughter and the love her mother had always shown for her and her father. Lastly, she added the sorrow, grief, and loss brought on by her mother's death. It was painful to recall, but she felt it necessary to convey the full truth. With the kindest and gentlest of intentions, she sent her focused thoughts to her grandmother.

When she opened her eyes, she saw Millie kneeling on the floor, her jaw hanging slack. The Lady Mangst had her back to Catrin, but her shoulders shook and her voice trembled with anguish when she finally spoke. "Leave me now, I beg of you."

Catrin was startled by the request, but the trembling of her grandmother's shoulders gave further evidence of the impact of her demonstration. Millie slowly drew herself up and motioned for them to follow her. Catrin and Benjin did so without question, for the lady's distress was plain to see, and they left her to grieve.

"My dear Elsa, why did you leave me?" they heard her wail as the doors closed behind them. Catrin felt no joy at bringing her grandmother pain, and she walked in subdued silence. Millie wobbled as she walked, and it was obvious that the day's revelations had been hard on her as well.

"I want to thank you for the kindness you showed our lady, despite your disagreements, and I apologize for my actions. I have wronged you, and I hope you'll forgive me," she said when she stopped before a set of doors.

"We all make mistakes. And since I have already forgiven you, I must ask you to forgive me for my insolence and rudeness. Had we met under better circumstances, I'm certain we could have been friends."

"It's kind of you to say, Lady Catrin," Millie replied, and Catrin felt she was sincere, though the title still seemed ill fitting.

"Please accept our hospitality. You'll find the apartments within well appointed, and I'll attend to your needs personally."

"Your kindness is appreciated. You have my thanks," Catrin said, and Millie bowed deeply before her.

"I'll send for food and bath water."

Catrin nodded her thanks. Her efforts and emotions had taxed her, and she was grateful for the respite. Benjin joined her as she entered the apartments, and he whistled as he looked about.

"Millie has honored you by bringing us here," he said. "If I am not mistaken, these quarters are reserved for their most respected guests."

Catrin was not surprised by his words, for the apartments were lavishly appointed. Deep carpets cushioned her feet, and beautiful works of art adorned the walls, depicting scenes of nature as only the most talented artists could render them. Elaborately carved chairs bore soft cushions, and a fire burned in the fireplace. Two doors led to private sleeping chambers that were not much smaller than the common room. Within she found a delightfully soft feather mattress shrouded by a canopy of sheer material.

Though the bed was inviting, Catrin could not bear the thought of soiling the linens; she needed a bath desperately. A parade of liveried servants arrived with steaming basins of water and washtubs that required four men apiece to carry. The men placed the tubs within the private rooms, and they filled them with water and rose petals before departing with respectful bows. Others followed with soft towels, robes, and a bounty of exotic foods. Catrin thanked them for their efforts, which seemed to confuse them more than anything, but she was truly grateful for the gifts.

Heat soaked into her bones as she slid into the scented water, and she allowed herself to remain in the tub until the water had gone nearly cold. She dried her wrinkled skin with the plush towels and donned a robe that bore her family sigil.

Sitting by the fire, she sampled the array of delicacies. Deep red wine cleansed her palate as she ate both sweet and salty, and soon her hunger was sated. Benjin joined her, looking completely out of place in his robe, which made her giggle, but he ignored her jibes as he attacked the food with vigor. With surprising speed, they finished every morsel, and they settled into the cushions with their bellies full. The fire lulled Catrin into a deep trance, and she soon forgot about the bed as the chair cradled her like a pair of loving arms.

When Millie returned, Catrin stirred from her stupor, and she was unsure if she had been sleeping or simply in a daze.

"The lady wishes to speak with you now. Will you follow me?" Millie asked.

"I should dress first," Catrin said.

"You're fine as you are. The lady's private apartments are but a short walk from here."

She followed Millie into the hall with Benjin in her shadow. True to her word, Millie led them only a short distance before they arrived at another grand entranceway, flanked by a pair of guards who nodded to Millie and immediately allowed them to enter. The apartments within were not much more grand than those provided to Catrin and Benjin, which only served to confirm the honor that had been granted to them.

"Come, my dear. Please sit beside me, and we'll let the fire warm our bones," the Lady Mangst said. "As I grow older, the cold does pain me so." Catrin moved to the seat beside hers. "Come, Benjin, do not be shy. I promise not to bite--this time."

Benjin sat on the edge of a nearby chair, and Catrin was struck by the changes in her grandmother. She was no longer hostile, and Catrin sensed deep-seated pain, both physical and emotional.

"By the gods," the Lady Mangst said, "I don't know why you wear your hair so short, but you look exactly as your mother did at your age, more one of the boys than one of the girls. You have her look about you, but mostly, it's in your eyes." After wiping away a tear, she turned to Benjin. "Please, tell me how my daughter died."

"I'm very sorry. Elsa was murdered."

"In what manner?"

"As far as we've been able to figure, it was a large dose of mother's root concealed in sweet buns from the local bakery, which was run by Baker Hollis. I know of no reason he'd commit such an atrocity, but I mean to find out."

"The Kyte family put him up to it, of that I can assure you. Catrin's aunt was killed in the same horrible manner. They are a despicable lot," the Lady Mangst said.

"How did you know about my aunt's death?" Catrin asked, confused.

"How would I not? I was by her side during the entire ordeal."

"Wait. I don't understand," Catrin said. "My aunt died on the same day as my mother, on the Godfist. How could you have been there?"

"I'm very sorry, dear, but it seems you've lost two aunts to the Kytes. I assume you speak of your father's sister?"

"His brother's wife. I had another aunt?"

"Your mother's sister, Maritza. She was killed some fifteen years ago. It seems they've taken both my daughters from me, but not before each bore me a granddaughter. You and your cousin, Lissa, are my only living descendents."

"I'm very sorry, Lady," Catrin said, sincere. The pain of her mother's death had faded with time, but it was fresh for her grandmother, like an open wound, and now knowing she had lost another aunt made her heart ache.

"Please, call me Grandma, if you would. That's what Lissa has always called me, and it would please me greatly if you would do the same."

"Thank you, Grandma."

"It must've been difficult for you, growing up without your mother."

"My father and Benjin always cared for me, and I wanted for nothing. Though, I miss her dearly."

Her grandmother raised an eyebrow and seemed to reappraise Benjin.

"It would seem I owe you a debt of gratitude, Benjin Hawk. You and Wendel have raised my granddaughter as a fine and strong young woman."

"Wendel deserves more credit than I, but I did what I could, and I'd do it all again if given the chance," he said, and the lady nodded, tears in her eyes.

"The darkness of these days has soured my disposition, and I was angry with Elsa--so many years she had been gone without a word. Now, of course, I understand the reason, though it makes it no easier to bear. I thank you for coming and for not leaving. You would've been entitled given our treatment of you."

"Let's put that all behind us. I forgive you for any hostility you expressed, and I forgive myself for reacting poorly. I hope you'll do the same," Catrin said as she took her grandmother's hand in hers.

"Yes, dear, of course," she responded, patting Catrin's hands lightly. "Now tell me. How do you plan to destroy the Statues of Terhilian?"

"Statues?" Catrin said, swaying in her chair.

"Oh dear, you didn't know. I'm sorry to give such dire news, but a second statue has been discovered in the Westland."

Catrin sat back heavily in her chair as desperation clutched her, and she found it difficult to breathe. What had started as a nearly impossible quest had just become completely hopeless. There was no way she could destroy two statues; she wasn't sure if she could even disarm one of them. She cradled her head in her hands as a cloud of impending doom threatened to crush her under its weight. "I don't know, Grandma. I honestly don't. When I heard of the first statue, I simply had to try, but now . . . now I see no hope at all."

"Nonsense, child. There is always hope."

Chapter 22

Darkness, no matter how powerful it may seem, can be driven back by the tiniest spark.
--unknown soldier

* * *

"There is perhaps a way you could travel safely to Adderhold, but I doubt very much you will like it. Before I tell you what it is, there are some things you must know."

Catrin wasn't certain she wanted to hear what her grandmother had to say, for fear of more bad news.

"When the Zjhon forces attacked us, I knew we could not resist. If we had, we would've lost far too many of our good subjects. Instead, I negotiated terms that would allow the subjects of Mundleboro to remain mostly unmolested, though under Zjhon rule. In truth, the Zjhon did not wish to depose us; they simply insisted we adopt their religion and support the efforts to spread the teachings of their Church. It wasn't something we wished for, but it was far less disruptive than a full-scale invasion would've been; thus, we surrendered.

"The conditions of our surrender were unpleasant, and we still lost a large number of able-bodied men to conscription, but for the most part, life went on as it had before. This kept the majority of our subjects happy, and they paid the increased taxes with little protest. Things have changed since then, though. Now the Zjhon are demanding higher taxes and something far more sinister. They've demanded a marriage between the Mangst and Kyte families. While they claim the move is intended to strengthen both lands and reduce border conflicts, it'll surely weaken Mundleboro and Lankland alike."

Darkness clouded the periphery of Catrin's vision, and flecks of light danced before her eyes as the words sank in. A less desirable union she could not imagine.

"Your cousin Lissa is to wed the youngest grandson of Arbuckle Kyte, but she has defied me. I've no idea where she is hiding. This is another reason I was so wroth when you arrived. I make no excuses, mind you; I simply need you to understand the dire circumstances that we find ourselves in.

"If Lissa is not within Adderhold by the appointed time, our family will forfeit our hold on these lands. The Zjhon will descend upon us, and there is little we can do to stop them. The only solution I can find is to send you in her stead."

The words were like a blow to Catrin's stomach, and the air left her lungs with a whoosh. She attempted to respond several times, but her tongue refused to form the words. Benjin appeared as dumbstruck as Catrin, his jaw hanging slack.

"You wish me to marry into the family that murdered my mother and both my aunts?" she asked finally.

"I've not asked it of you. I said it was the only solution that I've been able to find. I know you have no reason to love the people of Mundleboro, but it seems their fate lies with you, as your blood right would have dictated anyway. You have the opportunity to make this sacrifice for them, and they would love you for it. But, again, I don't ask it of you. This is something you'll have to take on willingly, for I'll not force your hand."

"If Catrin traveled under the guise of Lissa, we would be granted access to Adderhold, which is our main goal, and that would put us far closer to the statue than we would have been able to achieve on our own. Perhaps this is a boon, li'l miss," Benjin said, appearing thoughtful.

"Have you lost your senses?" Catrin asked, appalled that he would even consider it. She had no wish to be married, let alone to one of her family's mortal enemies. However, while she knew nothing of the people of Mundleboro, she did feel responsible for their safety, if for no other reason than because she felt her mother would have wanted to spare the innocent. She'd been a kind and loving woman, and Catrin could not imagine her leaving thousands to die when it was within her power to save them, but the thought of sacrificing herself made her physically ill.

"Don't feel pressured to make your decision now, dear, but the appointed day is rushing toward us, and by the new moon, we must either comply or prepare for war. I've considered offering myself up, but I have already been married, and they would surely decline. Unless Lissa finds it in her heart to return, I'm afraid we have no other options. Millie, please bring Catrin a calming elixir, she looks as if she's going to faint."

Indeed, Catrin found it difficult to remain upright as she was faced with responsibilities she'd never imagined. She was but a simple farm girl; certainly she had not the makings of a ruler, even a powerless one.

Benjin came to her side and placed a hand on her shoulder. She supposed he was trying to reassure her, but it felt like compulsion, as if he were trying to persuade her to make the sacrifice. She wanted to rebel against him and her grandmother, to lash out and make them regret asking this of her, but a vision of her mother came to her. Strong and proud, she said nothing, but her eyes commanded Catrin to be noble, to take the lives of her subjects in her hands and cradle them, just as she had cradled Catrin those many years ago. And mostly, she seemed to ask Catrin to do that which her mother had failed to do: accept the responsibility of her birthright and protect those who needed her.

It seemed strange to Catrin that being born of noble blood would carry so much weight and onus. She'd always thought the nobility leeched off those who worked the land, but now she saw an equally daunting encumbrance. Perhaps the true role of those with power was to serve those who toiled for the sake of their brethren. No longer did the scales seem tipped in the favor of nobility; now they seemed to almost balance one another. The common people needed the nobility as much as the nobles needed them. Like the cycle of life itself, if one component failed, all would perish.

Ignorance had been so much easier to bear.

"It's my duty to protect those who cannot defend themselves, and if that means I must sacrifice myself for the greater good, then so be it," she said before the courage to utter the words left her. She hadn't known what kind of reaction to expect, and in truth, she hadn't even taken the time to consider how her words would be received, but the sobs that wracked her grandmother's feeble form nearly made her weep.

"You are truly my granddaughter," her grandmother said when her emotions subsided. "I couldn't be more proud of you, and I know your mother would approve."

"You have her strength and the beauty of her heart," Benjin added. "She would, indeed, be proud . . . just as I am."

Their words would have warmed her soul if not for the icy fear that threatened to consume her. She trembled as she imagined herself surrounded by those who'd attempted to kill her when she was only a babe. They must be monsters, these Kytes, and she envisioned herself within their houses, like a lamb surrounded by hungry wolves. The visions terrified her, and she nearly fled. It would be so much easier to disappear into the masses, to become anonymous and unimportant, as she had been when she was just the daughter of a horseman. Perhaps, she thought, that was what Lissa had done.

Deep in her heart, she knew running away would bring her no happiness. Images of those she failed would haunt her, not the least of which would be her father, the man who had taught her right from wrong, who had instilled his values in her, and who had trusted her to do what needed to be done. She could not let them down; her conscience would simply not allow it.

"I don't know if I'll be able to neutralize the statue, but I still plan to try. The marriage is within my power, and despite my misgivings, I will do it. I set out to save as many people as I could, and though this is not how I intended to do it, it serves the same purpose. Perhaps, with the luck of the gods, I'll find a way to achieve both," she said.

"You are a courageous young lady," Millie said as she approached with a lightly steaming mug that she held in trembling hands. "Your bravery makes me proud to serve your family. Here, sip this. It will help to calm you."

"Thank you, Millie, but no. I need my wits about me," Catrin said. Millie nodded and downed the contents of the mug in only a few gulps before she walked away, looking dazed.

"I'll not yet hold you to your word, Catrin, for I feel you should take the rest of the day to consider carefully. You may return to me on the morrow," her grandmother said, and it was obvious that her words were a dismissal. Millie led Catrin and Benjin back to their apartments, and not a word was spoken. It seemed no one would try to influence Catrin one way or another on this matter. Secretly, she prayed Lissa would arrive and relieve her of the burden.

* * *

In the days that followed, Catrin firmed her resolve, and Lissa remained absent. Though she'd never met her cousin, Catrin began to loath her. What kind of person could abandon her responsibilities? The fact that Lissa was said to resemble Catrin in almost every physical way did not sit well with her, and she resented someone else bearing her likeness but not her morals.

Millie had taken to dressing Catrin every morning, and each day brought a new affront. Frilly dresses and lace-trimmed petticoats were anathema to her. She was uncomfortable no matter how hard she tried to get used to the attire she was expected to wear. She knew she could not arrive for the wedding dressed in her leathers and homespun, but in the evenings, she often donned them for the solace they brought her.

It was on one of these occasions that she suddenly grew panicked as she realized the gilded box that held her noonstones was missing. She could not bear to think of Millie as a thief, and she supposed they might have fallen out when her garments had been taken for cleaning. Benjin was nowhere about, and her anxiety increased when she realized her staff was also gone. After a frantic and futile search of the apartments, she sat down and cried. The stress overwhelmed her, and she hugged herself in an effort to stave off a massive wave of depression. Her entire life was in disarray, and she could no longer take it. The fact that she needed to leave for Adderhold in the morning helped not at all. When Benjin and Millie entered, all smiles, she did what she could to hide her distress, but it was of no use; her anxiety was plain to see. "I've lost my staff and my stones," she managed to say.

"I know you're upset, li'l miss, but everything is going to be fine. I promise you," Benjin said. "Right now, I want you to take a deep breath and dry your eyes; we need to visit with your grandmother."

"I need to change back into something more suitable," Catrin said, and her face flushed with embarrassment.

"You look just fine to me," Millie said and, taking Catrin by the arm, led her from the room.

Millie propelled her through a number of halls that Catrin had never walked before, and she began to get a cold feeling in her stomach. She couldn't have been more surprised, or more mortified, to be led into a cavernous hall, filled to capacity with well-dressed strangers. At the far end of the hall, behind a table laden with fine foods and colorful pitchers, sat her grandmother; beside her waited a single, vacant chair. Unerringly, Millie's course led to that chair.

Every eye upon her, Catrin felt vulnerable, and she wished for Benjin to sit beside her. Instead, he stood directly behind her in the ceremonial role of her Guardian. His presence was one of the few things that kept her from crawling under the table to hide; her grandmother's warm and welcoming smile was another.

"Why did you let me come dressed like this?" she asked Millie with an accusing look.

"It'll be good to let them see you as you are. These are good people. They'll not judge you poorly. Most are simple folk, and your attire may very well endear you to them even more. Don't be embarrassed. You're beautiful no matter how you dress, and these people owe you a great debt. They've come this day to honor you."

"Citizens," the Lady Mangst said in a bold voice that carried across the hall, and a hush fell over the assemblage. "I present to you my granddaughter, Catrin Volker-Mangst, daughter of the late Elsa Mangst."

The crowd raised a cheer, and Catrin was honored by the use of the Mangst name, though it sounded foreign to her ear. At the same time, she was honored that her grandmother had chosen to use the Volker name as well--a show of respect for her father. She blushed furiously as the crowd erupted in a cheer, and some even called out her name.

"The Lady Catrin has offered herself for service to her land and her people, and she will depart on the morrow for Adderhold." This statement was met with less enthusiasm, and Catrin assumed the people knew she was to wed a Kyte. "But this day bears another significance; one that I think Catrin has forgotten under the weight of her responsibilities. On this day, the Lady Catrin reaches her majority, and I ask you to celebrate with us."

A deafening roar erupted in the hall, and Catrin's knees nearly buckled. She'd forgotten, and the sudden remembrance nearly overcame her. She had dreamed of this day for years, but all of her visions had included her father. He was supposed to be there to accompany her as she left childhood behind and entered the world of adulthood. His absence brought her physical pain, and only the reassurance of Benjin's hands on her shoulders prevented her from breaking down completely.

"One and all, raise your glasses and join me. Drink to the honor of this brave and glorious child as she begins her new journey."

A great clatter followed as all the people in the room held their goblets aloft.

"To Catrin," they shouted on her grandmother's cue, and Catrin could no longer contain her tears. Never before had she been given such an honor, and the significance of it was not lost on her. Quietly, in the shelter of her mind and soul, she thanked her mother and father for bringing her into this world, and in that moment, she felt them with her. The vision of them raising a glass to her brought her strength, and she stood on shaking knees.

"I thank you, one and all," she said, and the room shook as the crowd chanted her name.

Her grandmother stood by her side and gave her a smile. "Let us feast," she said, and the room was soon filled with the sounds of revelry.

Food and drink were served to Catrin first, and she declared it the finest feast she had ever attended, which was not an embellishment. Roasted duck was served alongside glazed ham and sugared beets. The finest wine filled her goblet, and it gave her a heady rush as she drank it too quickly. No one was denied their fill, and liveried servants rushed to fulfill the whims of every guest. Amid the din, Catrin turned to Benjin, tears welling in her eyes. "Thank you," she said.

"I'd not forget such a day, and I know your father would give anything to be here. I can only hope that I can fill the void in some way," he said, and she took his hand in hers.

"I'm so glad you're here. Thank you for always being there for me," she said as she squeezed his hand softly.

After the sweets were served, musicians played merry tunes, and every member of the crowd lined up to greet Catrin. Many approached with trepidation, but Catrin decided to discard all propriety, and she embraced each of them as if they were family. She hugged, kissed, laughed, and cried with them, and in doing so, she won their hearts completely. They lavished her with gifts of flowers and gems, and Millie stood behind her, taking each gift and treating it as if it were the most valuable treasure. The table became a monument of their gratitude, and Catrin could hardly believe their generosity. Behind her was amassed more wealth than she had ever expected to see in a lifetime.

It was a young boy who gifted her with the finest thing of all, though, and his gift came in the form of a request. "Will you dance with me?" he asked, his cheeks flushed with excitement, and his mother appeared mortified by his bold request. She grabbed him by the arm and scolded him, but Catrin smiled and spread her arms wide.

"I would be honored," she said, which brought a shocked look from the boy's mother and a beaming grin from the boy. "What is your name, sir?"

"I'm Carrod Winsiker, Lady Catrin. You honor me," he said as seriously as if he were courting her, which brought a prideful smile to his mother's face, and the crowd erupted as Catrin allowed him to whirl her around the center of the hall. The musicians played a joyous tune with a fast tempo, and soon everyone in the hall danced. It was the most wonderful night in Catrin's life, and she wished it would never end.

When Carrod was exhausted, he bowed to Catrin and thanked her for the dance, but before he could walk away, she kissed him on the cheek. He blushed and held his hand over the spot where she kissed him, and as he ran to his mother, she beamed at Catrin. Benjin remained at his place behind her seat, and Catrin led him to the dance floor. He surprised her completely; he danced wonderfully.

"You never told me you could dance."

"It's a closely guarded family secret," he replied as he whirled her through the crowd of dancers.

Like all good things, the celebration had to end, and as the night grew long, the crowd began to disperse. When all the revelers were gone, Catrin rubbed her aching feet and stifled a yawn. The servants cleared the remnants of the meal, and only Catrin, her grandmother, Benjin, and Millie remained in the hall.

"You're an amazing woman, Catrin," her grandmother said, and the title did not escape her notice. "I was afraid our subjects would reject you, but in a single night, you made them your own. I believe they'd follow you anywhere."

With that, she bade them a good night and retired to her chambers, obviously taxed by all the excitement. Benjin and Catrin followed Millie back to their apartments, and she closed the door behind herself as she left. Catrin was about to seek her bed when Benjin emerged from the other room looking like the cat that caught the bird. He carried her staff behind his back and approached her.

"Before you go off to sleep, there is one more gift for you. This is from your grandmother and I," he said as he presented the staff to her. She was uncertain why he would gift her with her own staff, but then she saw the noonstones gleaming in the eyes of the serpent. "I hope you don't mind. I knew you needed some way to have the stones accessible, and this seemed fitting."

Indeed, it was as if the staff had been waiting for the stones, and together, they completed the whole.

"It's perfect," she said.

Chapter 23

To persevere when all seems lost is the most courageous act.
--Wendel Volker

* * *

Dressed as a peasant, Lissa watched as the parade of carriages prepared to leave Ravenhold, and she could barely contain the growl that threatened to escape her throat. An imposter, a usurper, and worse was riding in *her* place to Adderhold. Only days before, Lissa had returned to overhear tales of Catrin, the savior of Mundleboro. Unable to bear the taste, she spit.

How could her grandmother betray her in such a way? She had run away to prevent the marriage between the Mangst and Kyte families. Why would her grandmother send a stranger in her place?

"Pure madness," she muttered through clenched teeth. Torn, she tried to decide what to do next. If she let this Catrin go in her stead, all she had gone through would be for naught. Yet if she tried to stop it, she would reveal herself, and Morif would probably take her to Adderhold in chains.

Lissa did not relish the thought of their next meeting, certain he was furious with her for leaving. He was always going on about how her actions hurt Millie. Lissa didn't care about Millie at that moment, though, as the carriages began to roll. Her last chance to act was at hand and she stood, frozen. Unable to move or speak, she simply watched until the carriages disappeared from view.

* * *

The journey to Adderhold was only slightly less miserable than it would've been on foot. The carriage jostled constantly over the uneven roads, or it sat waiting for the crowds of people clogging the roads to disperse. Catrin was struck by the resentment her passing brought about. People cursed them, rotten vegetables were thrown at the carriages, and murderous looks followed them. These people had not been at the celebration, and they had no reason to love her. The dozen guards assigned by Catrin's grandmother did what they could to control the situation, and Catrin insisted none of them harm any of the people, but it was difficult for them to comply as many altercations broke out.

Her people's despair brought Catrin physical pain, and she found the yoke of responsibility terribly difficult to bear. She had almost grown accustomed to feeling responsible for the people of the Godfist. It was a natural role that any citizen would feel compelled to fill, but her responsibility for the people of the Greatland was suffocating. The entire known world's future depended on her actions, and it appeared many would die no matter what she did.

Shifting in her seat, she adjusted the folds and layers of her skirt, which seemed to bunch under her no matter how she sat.

Benjin scowled, as he had been wont to do of late.

"What are you thinking?" Catrin asked.

"Hmm. Well, I was just trying to understand the relative disappearance of Vestrana agents across the Greatland. Of the inns we have encountered, only two offered any indication of the Vestrana, and even those signals were mixed. I suppose the times are much more dangerous these days, and it may be that they have become more secretive because of infiltration. It's mostly unimportant now since we've secured our entrance to Adderhold."

Adderhold. Catrin imagined a place crawling with snakes and scorpions, a dark and evil place that waited to consume her. She knew it was foolish to let her imagination run wild, and the visions were probably far worse than what actually awaited her, but a contagious dour mood blanketed those around her. Millie rode in a carriage with two other serving women, but each time they were together, she seemed more nervous and fretful than the last. She feared everything from an ambush to poisoned food, and the fact that her fears were plausible put their entire party on edge.

Along the Inland Sea, the lands were clogged with ragged campsites, and a foul stench hung in the air. The roads impossibly jammed, their caravan was forced to move overland through a maze of disarray. The twined roses on the doors of their carriages became a liability as angry mobs, made up of those from Mundleboro and Lankland alike, left their bonfires to express their displeasure to the exposed nobility. Scuffles broke out between the mobs and her guards, but mostly cold iron kept the peace. As they neared the docks, though, the mass of people became denser, and the spaces between campsites were not wide enough to admit them passage.

A writhing mass of humanity stood between them and the road, which was as impassable as the clogged meadows, for it was jammed with people. They were only a short distance from the dock, but reaching it seemed impossible. One brave guard rode ahead to seek the officials at the docks; he was hard pressed, but he rode aggressively. Most moved out of his way; those who moved too slowly he pushed out of the way.

An uproar rolled across the meadows, and many shook their fists in the air as a mounted detachment plowed through campsites on their way to the carriages. Men became bold and rocked the carriages back and forth, and one man was fatally kicked by one of the horses drawing Catrin's carriage. Visions of assassins closing in around her gave Catrin the chills, and she clutched her staff, ready to defend herself. Within the confines of the carriage, though, there was no room to maneuver. Catrin felt trapped. Benjin's short sword was cleared from its scabbard, and he'd already reached for the door at least a dozen times, but he remained within the carriage.

Surrounded by guards and dock officials, they began a painfully slow procession through scattered remains of campsites, and Catrin doubted these people would love her as those at her majority banquet had. How could she blame them? She'd always disliked those who thought themselves more important than she. Her passage was a necessity, though, and this affront was simply unavoidable. The gathered crowd booed loudly as Catrin and her guards were escorted onto a waiting ferry. No one else was allowed to board with them, and hundreds were forced to wait for the next ferry.

Glad to be gone from the unruly crowd, Catrin relaxed a bit. Through the overcast skies, she could feel the energy of the comets above her, and she knew the next time the night skies were clear, she would see them. The energy bolstered her strength, and she let it calm her stomach as the carriage rocked along with the ship. It was a strange feeling, to sit in a carriage while aboard a ship. The horses had been unhooked for safety's sake, and the carriage's tongue was firmly secured, yet she felt as if she were perched on a branch in high wind, as if the carriage would slide from the deck and into the sea.

"Can we take a walk on deck?" she asked, but Benjin shook his head.

"Can't risk an ambush. Nearby ships could harbor assassins, and given the family history, I'd be surprised if they didn't. Best to stay in here until we reach Adderhold."

"Lovely."

Benjin tried to make the time pass more quickly by quizzing Catrin on her etiquette and ceremonial duties. While it took her mind from the motion of the ferry, it also reminded her of what lay ahead. Her role in this wedding was small. She need only show up and say a few words. Under no circumstances was she to look a man, especially a Zjhon holy man, in the eye. The restrictions on her behavior were ridiculous and triggered deep-seated resentment. Even as a member of a royal family, she was forced to endure the rules of others. The thought of kissing the archmaster's ring made her want to retch; she hadn't forgotten about his letter:

"... My emissaries will remain on the Godfist until you have presented yourself to me personally. This matter must be settled between you and me. It would be a pity if your countrymen and mine suffered needlessly as a result of your selfishness. I beg you to put away your ego and do what you know is right . . ."

Even after so much time, his words rang in her memory and raised her fury. Belegra had caused hundreds to die then laid the blame at her feet. Trying to contain her rage was like standing before a flash flood, and despite her efforts, it threatened to consume her. Only the reason in

Benjin's voice kept her from succumbing. His logic and planning gave her something to hold on to, something to believe in.

"After the exchange of names," he said, "you'll each carry a torch to a pile of kindling. You'll kneel and then light it with your torches. I'm guessing they'll place the kindling near the base of the statue for effect. That'll probably be your best chance to reach it," Benjin said.

"When I stand from the fire, toss me the staff. I still have no idea what I will do then, but I'll think of something . . . I hope."

Benjin seemed unable to formulate a proper response to that statement, and they spoke little more during the crossing. A tailwind drove the ferry toward the island that cradled Adderhold. The citadel rose on the horizon, and the closer they got, the more intimidating it became. The island was not small, yet Adderhold dominated it as if the man-made structure were larger than the land that held it.

Parapets reached so high into the sky that their tops were lost in the clouds, and the wall that snaked around the hold seemed impossibly thick. The buildings within were oddly shaped; nothing seemed squared or even at right angles. Instead, the city seemed to writhe, all curves and gentle sweeps. As they neared land, she saw that the structures, in many cases, were shaped like serpents, their fanged jaws forming entranceways and windows. The beaches resembled the far shores in many ways except that there was nowhere for the pilgrims to go. The island constricted them.

Alerted of their coming, Adderhold's guards created a narrow avenue through the knot of pilgrims. Those on the island were more subdued than those on the far banks; here there was no place to hide, and cross words could get them killed. Still they cast venomous glances toward the lace curtains that were pulled over the windows of the carriage. Fear was not all-powerful, though, and one man had the courage to throw a rock at them. His aim was uncanny, and the window shattered, the rock landing on Catrin's lap. The residue of the angry energy still clung to the rock, and she flung it to the floor. After brushing the reddish slivers of broken glass from her dress, she sat in a state of readiness, prepared for whatever assault might come next.

Amazingly lifelike carvings of serpent heads protruded from the walls that surrounded Adderhold, and the largest ones guarded a towering archway. No gates barred the entrance. A large structure stood atop the arch, looming above the massive tunnel. Darkness enshrouded the carriage as they entered, and a deep chill set into Catrin's bones before they emerged from the other side.

Adderhold was a bizarre mixture of the hideous and exquisite. Lush gardens were inhabited by ghoulish statuary and serpentine themes. The way they were crafted made them appear as if they would reach out and strike anyone foolish enough to come close. The buildings were constructed of a grainy, white, stonelike material that Catrin had never seen before. It sparkled even in the dim light, and it had allowed the architects to create wonderfully flowing lines.

Beyond the shops and homes that ringed the city stood the keep. Carved from the side of a mountain, it looked as if it would consume the city, so aggressive was its stance. Coiled and focused, the keep was formed to resemble a single serpent of such stature and ferocity that most could not enter without fear of being devoured. Elite guards lined the cobbled boulevard that led to the keep, and their embossed plate gleamed. Their helmets were fashioned in the likeness of pit vipers, giving them an inhuman appearance.

No one spoke, and no trumpets blared. Catrin's party entered the gaping maw with no welcome waiting within. Stables stood to their left, and they moved in that direction. Benjin disembarked first, checking for danger, then helped Catrin from the carriage. As her feet touched the reed-covered flagstone, a hooded man approached in a steady, measured pace. He seemed to be trying for the gliding effect mastered by the Cathuran monks, but he could not complete the illusion.

He said nothing when he stood before them. He just nodded and turned back the way he came, departing with the same unvarying gait. Catrin and her attendants followed him, and it seemed to her that the mood was more suited to a funeral than a wedding; anxious tension thickened the air. Atop a grand stairway stood another facade with bas-reliefs in the form of Istra and Vestra. The archway was unguarded, and the halls were empty. Their boots echoed loudly, and she felt as if the oppressive stone would close in upon her and grind her to dust.

Slender windows filled with multicolored glass provided meager light, which was supplemented by firepots that hung from ornate chains. The polished flagstone ended at a recessed stair, which was guarded by the most fearsome serpent carving yet. This one struck a primal fear in Catrin, for this was no glorified snake. Furrowed ridges protruded over the eyes and emerged from flesh as horns, which gave it an air of intelligence, and one other feature distinguished this beast: wings.

So cleverly had the carving been created that the feral stare seemed to follow Catrin, stalking her every move. Recalling the skeletal remains found near the statue, she needed little more evidence to believe the old tales. Dragons had once roamed the land and flown the skies. Atop all her other problems, it seemed a bad omen, and dread filled her as they moved deeper within the keep. The place seemed designed to take the spirit from all who entered, and the builders had done their job well. Each step seemed to take her closer to her death.

The robed man abruptly stopped in front of an archway that opened into what appeared to be a temple since it contained nothing but rows of bare benches. More colorful windows adorned the far wall, and one window in particular drew Catrin's eye. Beyond it was the glowing silhouette of Istra, Goddess of the Night. Only part of her visage was visible through the slender opening, but it was exactly as she had seen it during her astral travels; only now, it glowed more brightly.

The somber procession filed into the room. They tried to make themselves comfortable on the unforgiving benches, but it was impossible.

"These accommodations are an insult," Millie said with her hands on her hips, but their guide simply turned and left the room.

"This will be fine, Millie," Catrin said, hoping to lessen the tension. "I've no desire to stay here long. We'll do what we came here to do, and then we'll leave. Until then, we'll just have to accept whatever hospitality is offered."

Benjin nodded his agreement, and Millie mumbled something unintelligible that Catrin doubted was complimentary toward the Zjhon. As evening came, the skies were afire with color, and the eerie, greenish light of the statue grew brighter yet. Sleep was impossible, and Catrin ignored Millie's protests that she couldn't be married with sagging eyes. The wedding was a farce, and everyone knew it, bride and groom included.

For two days, they were left with little more than broth to sustain them. Millie paced the floors, casting furious glances at anyone who crossed her path. The waiting was dreadful, and no matter how hard she tried, Catrin could not make the days fly by any faster than they would. Even Benjin became snappish.

* * *

Atop Limin's Spire, the winds gusted, and even within the shelter of the stone walls, it was painfully cold. The structure's lack of a roof helped not at all. But the skies were clear, and Milo was convinced he had the focusing mechanism working properly.

"I have only a few more parts left to assemble," Milo said. "Then we will see things no one has seen in thousands of years."

Strom and Osbourne watched, waited, and shivered.

"I just want to get this done and get down from here. Heights make my head spin," Strom said.

"The view is incredible, don't you think?"

"I try not to look at it."

"That's it," Milo said. "We're ready."

Strom and Osbourne wasted no time. After wrapping the looking glass in leather, they picked it up and began climbing to the top of the pedestal. There was no railing; nothing stood between them and a terrifying drop. Tears streamed down Strom's cheeks from more than the wind stinging his eyes; he feared that same wind would blow him from the spiral stairway.

Not long after they passed what Strom considered the halfway point, his arms began to quiver from the exertion, but he was determined to keep going, and he gritted his teeth.

"I'm not going to make it," Osbourne said. "I need to put it down now."

Frustrated, Strom eased his end of the looking glass down. Leaning against the pedestal, he closed his eyes and waited for his arms to stop tingling. Osbourne moved around him, walking up and down stairs. It made Strom want to scream. How could he not realize how close they were to falling into an abyss? Milo, at least, had the sense to remain still.

When Osbourne announced he was ready, Strom stood, planted his feet, and opened his eyes. After a deep breath, he bent down and picked up his end of the looking glass. As they neared the top, the climb seemed a bit easier, and they soon reached the mounting bracket. With one final effort, they lifted the looking glass and gently set it in the bracket. Milo slid the pins into place, and finally Strom and Osbourne could relax.

"This thing better work," Strom said.

"That's what you said last time," Osbourne said.

"Yeah, I know."

Milo aimed the looking glass away from the morning sun and began turning the large ring he said would focus the lenses, but his arms weren't long enough to reach the ring while looking in the eyepiece. "Osbourne, my boy, I need you to turn the adjuster while I look through the glass."

With slow and tentative movements, Osbourne turned the adjuster and, by the look on his face, feared the whole thing would come apart in his hands.

"Wait. Stop," Milo said. "Go back. Stop! That's it!"

"It really works?" Strom asked, unable to believe what he was hearing.

"Strom, come here. You're eyes are better than mine. Help Osbourne adjust it."

His excitement finally overcoming his fears, Strom gazed into the eyepiece, but all he saw was the blue of the midmorning sky, and there was nothing to focus on.

"It will be easier at night, but do the best you can. This is important," Milo said as Gustad arrived with a leather satchel. "I'll be back." Both Gustad and Milo climbed down, wanting to look at their books and calculations somewhere more sheltered from the wind.

"Turn it some," Strom said, and the image grew fuzzy. "Go back the other way." This time the image became clearer, but then it grew fuzzy again. "Go back just a bit. There. Stop. That's the best I can do without something to look at. Let's swing this around and see if we can find anything."

"I don't think that's a good idea."

"Come on, Osbo. We did most of the work on this thing. I think we've earned the right to take a look around. Besides, Milo and Gustad are hiding something. Look at them down there. Did either of them tell you what this was all about?"

"No."

"Then let's find out. We just push here, and it should swing right around."

"Don't look at the sun!" Osbourne yelled.

Strom aimed lower, closer to the horizon, looking for something and not knowing what. But then he saw something strange and stopped. "Turn the ring," he said. "Back the other way. Stop!" Unable to believe what he saw, Strom just stared in silent awe for a moment. "By the gods. What *is* that?"

"What is what?" Osbourne asked as Milo and Gustad started climbing back to the top of the pedestal. Strom stepped back and let Osbourne look for himself. He didn't need to look again, the image was imprinted in his memory.

". . . should be visible by now," Gustad said as they reached the top, but then he looked Strom in the eyes and ran to the looking glass. Osbourne stepped away, bereft of speech.

"The charts we found in the lost library are real," Gustad said as he stepped away from the looking glass. Milo rushed in for his chance to see. "Istra has arrived."

* * *

Catrin and all the others stood when a soldier entered the hall. Millie blocked his path and looked him in the eye.

"Be ready by midday," he said, casting a cold and disinterested glance around the room.

Millie controlled her anger enough to nod and only turned her back on the man. She fussed over Catrin's hair for an impossible amount of time, most of which Catrin spent staring out the rose and chartreuse windowpanes. The sky beyond was clear, but she could feel the comets coming; they were close. She felt as if she could reach out and touch them. Though there was little evidence to support her feelings, a cloudbank on the eastern horizon seemed strange to her--unnatural.

She was to wed this day, and she'd never even seen the face of the man who would be her husband. When she turned her thoughts to the wedding, her anxieties brought their full weight to bear. She didn't even know if she'd be able to gain access to the statue, let alone destroy it. Feeling like a prisoner, she doubted she'd be free to do anything beyond take the vows. As her mind went in circles, she resigned herself to the uncertainty. She'd know what to do when the time came--she hoped.

As the sun moved toward its zenith, when Vestra was at the height of his power, a dozen robed men arrived to escort the bride. Benjin took his place behind Catrin as she followed her guards from their cell, as she had come to think of it. Like a funeral procession, they walked in silence, and a pall of sadness hung over them, one and all. Tears were shed, but none were tears of joy. Catrin missed her father dearly on this day, a day he should have shared with her, and she wiped her eyes with the sleeves of her flowing dress. Millie cast her a sideways glance but said nothing.

At the turn of a corner, the sound of a large crowd carried through the halls, and a sunlit field became visible in the distance. At its center stood the Statue of Terhilian. Though only its base was visible from their current vantage point, there was no doubt as to what they saw. The land surrounding the level field angled upward in all directions, like a giant bowl, and ascending rows of stone seats had been carved from the mountainside. In only a few places was the stone still visible; most seats were already taken, and the rest were filling quickly.

Primal fear struck Catrin's heart. Not only must she face her new husband and the Statue of Terhilian, she must do it in front of the largest assemblage she'd ever witnessed. Only one thing consoled her, and that was the location of the altar, which was scant paces from the base of the statue. Her guts twisted into knots when she saw another procession coming from the opposite direction. In the lead came a proud young man who walked with his chest out and his head tilted slightly back.

It was not his physical features that intrigued her, though; it was the nimbus that surrounded him. Unlike the auras described in the old tales, it had no color and was only clearly visible when she squinted. But when she did, she could see an area around him that distorted whatever was behind him, like the heat of a fire only less fluid.

He ignored Catrin completely, and she felt her face flush. Surely he must be curious about his new bride. How could he not even try to see what she looked like? Perhaps, she thought, he had already decided she was a monster, a hideous and undesirable wretch not worthy of his blood.

In a moment of sudden clarity, she realized she had done the same to him. No matter how kind or polite he was, he'd always be a Kyte, one of the people responsible for the deaths of her mother and aunts, and who knew how many others. She made herself look anywhere but at him, knowing he would sense her stare. She looked beyond the statue to the towering archway that dominated the eastern end of the arena. It was twice as large as the one at the main entrance, and Catrin guessed it was the only opening large enough to admit the statue.

In the skies beyond, the strange thunderhead grew larger and uncharacteristically bright, as if illuminated from within. But Catrin soon reached the raised dais, and the statue blotted out the rest of her world. The energy radiating from it felt unclean, nothing like the waves of energy that descended from the skies. Like a kernel of hard corn held over a fire, its inside boiled, and at any moment, it could release all its energy in a single, devastating flash. Standing before it took much of her willpower, and her knees felt untrustworthy, as if they would buckle in the slightest breeze.

When the groom stood directly across from her, she looked skyward once again, and the heavens were aglow. The storm was no storm. It was a comet scudding across the skies. Grinding against the air, it erupted into a conflagration the likes of which had not been seen in thousands of years. Its energy slammed into Catrin, and combined with the noxious charge from the statue, it was more than she could handle. She swayed on her feet, and Benjin supported her from behind. As he held her, her staff pressed against her bare forearm. The feel of the polished wood was comforting, and she took solace from it.

"Behold, the eye of Istra," a voice boomed, startling Catrin. She had no doubt it was Archmaster Belegra who spoke, but she could not make herself look at him, afraid of what she might see. "This day she has come to witness the union of Lankland and Mundleboro under her light and likeness. Vestra joins her, high in the skies, and we ask for their blessings. Give us a sign, and we'll rejoice!"

Catrin waited along with everyone else for some sign, and none were disappointed when red lightning spanned the eastern horizon, cast out in all directions from the raging comet. The distant rumbling did not fade like natural thunder; instead it grew steadily, intensifying, but no one was prepared for the blast that knocked them from their feet and seats alike. A wave of fetid air roared from the west, and the ground shook.

The western horizon took on its own eerie glow, one that matched the light of the statue. And Catrin knew, in that instant, without any doubt, the Statue of Terhilian that had been found in the west had just detonated, and she shrank away from the realization that tens of thousands had just perished in an instant. A new cataclysm had begun, and the next component of destruction stood within throwing distance of her. Zjhon guards formed a ring around the dais and effectively barred her path.

Most people had regained their feet, though the moans of the injured could still be heard, and angry voices protested from the crowd.

"The other statue has exploded!" someone shouted, and many looked about to see who it was, but no one laid claim to the statement.

"The Herald Witch has attacked the Westland," a woman shrieked, and Archmaster Belegra jumped on the opportunity.

"Friends, we are besieged. The Herald Witch has brought war to the Greatland, and we are all in dire peril. We must stand together and face our common foe as one unified nation. If we remain separate, surely we will perish," he bellowed, and the acoustics of the arena carried his words to even those in the highest rows. Ragged cheers broke out, but many within the crowd seemed unsure, as if their faith had been something of little consequence in the past but was now coming to haunt them. They would need to quickly decide what they believed, for now their lives depended on it.

"Can the Herald travel a third of the Greatland in the span of just one breath?" a familiar voice asked, and Catrin searched for the speaker without success.

"Of course not," Archmaster Belegra replied, seemingly outraged by the notion. "No one can do such a thing. The Herald Witch is powerful, but she's not unstoppable. We have but to join with one another, and we can defeat her. We must do this before she brings any more evil into our world." He seemed pleased with his words.

"Could the Herald cause such destruction in the Westland if she was here, within Adderhold?" the same voice shouted from the crowd, and the speaker became easy to locate, as just about everyone in his vicinity moved away. He stood proud and defiant, and Catrin could hardly believe the cruelty of fate when she recognized him: Rolph Tillerman, one of the few people in the Greatland who might guess her identity. She cursed herself for her own stupidity. She should never have let her tongue slip, but the damage was already done, and all she could do was wait to see how dire the consequences would be.

"There's no way the Herald Witch could cause such damage from a great distance. We are safe here," Archmaster Belegra replied.

"Then the attack on the Westland could not have been committed by the Herald," Rolph bellowed triumphantly.

"How could you know such a thing?" Archmaster Belegra asked, clearly confident that Rolph would only prove himself witless, but Rolph's response stirred the frightened crowd into frenzy.

"I know this for certain, since the Herald of Istra stands before you," he said, and Catrin leaned heavily on Benjin as Rolph's eyes turned to her. "In a wedding dress."

Chapter 24

Death, like life, is part of the natural cycle. To fear one is to devalue the other.
--Manul Praska, shaman

* * *

Time slowed and Catrin swung her head in a wide arc, taking in every detail as she spun. All eyes were on her, and she felt every stare acutely, especially those from within the hoods of the men surrounding Archmaster Belegra. Hostile energies gathered there, making ready the attack, and Catrin was jolted by the recognition of one.

Prios.

The pattern of his energy was unmistakable, and she sensed his recognition of her even without being able to see his face. He gave no outward sign save a small twitch of his hood. But then her gaze moved to the very close face of her betrothed. His eyes were filled with rage, and his aura reached out for her like fingers of flame. For a moment, time accelerated; then he was leaping for her throat with deadly quickness.

Instinct drove her, and the heady abundance of energy she'd been absorbing made her off-balance parry a massive blow that sent him tumbling through the air. Even as he spiraled into a crowd of those attempting to flee, she wondered at the fact that she didn't even know his name, this Kyte whelp, and she wondered if it wouldn't soon be a name she'd wish to forget. For the moment, though, he'd pose no more threat; his limp form was dragged from the field by his guards. The flesh of her neck and throat stung, and when she ran her hand over it, it came away covered with blood. Had he raked her flesh without ever touching her? She wondered at that, but her attention was required to stay alive, and the world rushed around her again.

Her momentum carried her, and she found herself facing Benjin, who tossed her staff into the air between them. Catrin leaped to meet it halfway and caught it deftly. She rolled over it and sprang into a fighting stance only to find no one between her and the statue. One man moved to bar her path, but his eyes bulged, affixed to the heel of her staff, and he fled. She risked a quick glance at her staff. The serpent head stood out in bold relief, outlined by pulses of liquid energy, and, for the first time, the true nature of the serpent was revealed. Tendrils of liquid fire clearly showed the outlines of wings, but Catrin could look upon it no more. The noonstone eyes shone bright white, and blue spheres obscured her vision long after she looked away from the blinding glare.

The comet above seemed likely to destroy them all as it moved in front of the sun and was spectacularly backlit during the eclipse. Deep shades of purple and amber rolled away from the massive sphere of ice, and a towering cloud of vapor trailed behind it. The air sang like an anvil rung by a thousand hammers, accompanied by the monotonous thundering that threatened to vibrate everything into oblivion.

So quickly did Catrin propel herself to the statue that she had to let her body catch up. The thrumming air seemed to suspend her flesh, and her spirit barely clung to it. Her hands fumbled as they gripped the staff and prepared for impact. With all the force she could muster, she struck the glowing base of the statue. The energy trapped within pealed and flowed through the staff, through Catrin, and into the land itself. She could do nothing to stop it. Every muscle in her body contracted, and her face contorted in a twisted rictus.

Immediately she realized her mistake. The statue contained a small but highly charged core of noonstone opposite some other type of stone she did not recognize, one that stored a massive negative charge. Only a thin layer of dense metal separated the two charges. If that insulating barrier broke down, the resulting chain reaction would be monstrous, just as the one in the Westland had been. The explosion would be felt all the way in Endland, which seemed almost unfathomable to Catrin, having struggled to cross the massive expanse.

The men rushing toward her and those with bows drawn compounded her problems. Missiles were already on their way to meet her when she flung energy about her for protection. An angry sphere of red and lightning formed a shield around her. Arrows and spears burst into flames as they struck the wall of plasma, falling away harmlessly. But Catrin's resolve nearly faltered when men dived upon her sphere, hurling themselves against her energy flow. She felt their energy clash with hers and their spirits released by the impact. Each one was like a knife to her heart, and she wept.

"Please stop! I cannot keep you safe if you attack me. The energy has me trapped. Please stop! Please," she wailed, but Belegra urged more men to assault her defenses. He showed no regard for human life as he chided those who would preserve themselves. Those who stood around him, those hidden within the depths of their robes, seemed compelled into action. Each had access to Istra's power, but they were bound by Archmaster Belegra's will--slaves. As the archmaster moved his arms in wild and rigid gestures, the robed figures attacked without moving.

Hot, fetid rays of adulterated power emanated from them. Each of the energies merged with the others and was orchestrated by Archmaster Belegra. Somehow, he exerted nearly total control over these men, with the exception of Prios, who was clever. His energy separated itself once beyond Archmaster Belegra's field of influence and only brushed across the surface of Catrin's sphere, whispering to her, over and over again.

"You gave me a name. You gave me power."

Archmaster Belegra was completely consumed in his machinations and seemed unaware of the communication between Prios and Catrin. The remaining mixture of energies, however, slammed into her sphere, and she reeled. The impact was worse than the time she had been kicked in the chest by a plow horse, and she wondered if her ribs were broken. Archmaster Belegra continued to pummel her with the twisted energies, but it became obvious he would not be able to do so much longer. His breathing was ragged, and beads of sweat raced down his mottled flesh.

Without so much as a twitch, Catrin sensed Prios separate himself from the twisted flow completely, and he lashed out at Archmaster Belegra. Like a striking snake, a thread of energy arced between them, and they both collapsed. The others swayed on their feet as the compulsion ended abruptly, and two fell to their knees, leaving only two standing.

Catrin took advantage of the respite and desperately reached into the statue, casting her senses over the deadly charges. There seemed an impossible amount of energy still trapped within, considering what had already been released, and she despaired. At the rate it was draining, it would take days if not weeks to deplete, and the insulating barrier was rapidly breaking down. It writhed and bubbled, boiling. Desperate, she tried to draw the scorching heat out of the core. Slowly the barrier cooled to a near-solid state, though the ground around Catrin's feet caught fire.

With the insulator stabilized, she returned her efforts to draining the excessive energy stored in the noonstone core. After the initial shock, she became desensitized to the massive energy flow, and though she felt as if she were slowly melting away, she could control herself and the flow of energy much better.

"Good people of the Greatland, flee!" she shouted. "I fear the statue will explode no matter what I do, get as far away as you can. I'll hold it as long as I am able."

"Don't listen to her," Archmaster Belegra shouted as he pulled himself from the ground. "Attack! Avenge your brethren! The Herald Witch is the true cause of these evils. Destroy her! Any who flee are traitors, and their lives will be forfeit."

His words rang discordant over those who still milled about the arena, and only a few fought to reach Catrin. The majority continued to flee, but some rallied together and advanced on Archmaster Belegra and his supporters. With his time undoubtedly short, Archmaster Belegra launched a desperate attack. He tore the energy from those who surrounded him and thrust at the Statue of Terhilian itself.

In one motion, he undid all that Catrin had accomplished. The barrier began to vaporize, and she knew it would soon break down completely. She attempted to divert his continued onslaught, but the mass of wild energy was beyond her control. As she tried to influence its course, it leaped out in all directions and struck down men and women without discretion. Even as she pulled away from it, lesser bolts of energy blasted Benjin and several of her guards. Their smoking forms lay frighteningly still where they landed, and Catrin nearly lost consciousness.

Breathing became almost impossible in the overheated air, and she drew ragged gasps. The arena spun before her as her vision clouded. The world was collapsing around her, and there was nothing more she could do. She'd given all she could give, and it hadn't been enough. Doomed to failure, she wondered why she even bothered to continue struggling. It would be so much easier to just give up, to lie down and die, but some inner fire still burned, and while any chance existed, she would fight.

After sucking in the deepest breath she could manage, she prepared to launch her final assault on Archmaster Belegra. Her skin grew taut and her fingernails peeled back as she gripped the staff, drawing more energy than she'd ever tried to contain before. She drew not only from the statue, but also from the staff, the noonstones, and the air itself. The natural energy helped to balance the wild forces trapped within the statue, but her exhaustion threatened to claim her. She walked a knife's edge between delivering a mighty blow and succumbing to it.

The polished surface of the staff bubbled, and her fingers bit into its flesh. Blistering sap raised welts on her hands, and she could draw no more. Fear gripped her as the reality of her situation set in. She was about to die, and so was everyone nearby. She could not hope to deliver this much energy and still remain standing; the statue would run its course, and with the comet still grazing the atmosphere, it wouldn't be long before it was all over.

Resigned to her death, she peeled her hands from the staff, and for a moment marveled at the imprints of her fingers carved deep into the wood. Turning to face Archmaster Belegra, she drew herself up. He was not unprepared, though, and launched an attack of his own. Green and yellow flames roared from his fingers as he drew upon the remaining members of his cadre, which included Prios, who seemed to have no more fight left in him. His form slumped forward as his life's energy was drained.

Enraged, Catrin delivered her blow, hurtling a rope of fire and lightning at Archmaster Belegra's head. He ducked under the assault, but the heat took his hair and blistered his flesh. With a terrible cry, he fled, and Catrin wobbled. She spun and reached about her, searching for something to hold on to, and her hands landed on the staff, still protruding from the statue's base. Her fingers settled precisely in the same place that bore their recessed imprints, and the energy surged through her again.

Without even understanding exactly what she was doing, she tugged on the energy and pulled it to her, embracing it. Her body thrummed, and she felt her spirit becoming free. She watched with a sense of indifferent attachment as she hung in the air above her physical form.

Before her, the statue glowed so brightly that it was blinding, and beyond it, the remnants of the crowd parted like the sea before the hull of a fast ship. Catrin barely heard the howling that split the air, but she saw an enraged bull of a man charging the statue.

"Do not despair, heart of the land! I've come for you," he bellowed, and Catrin recognized him at last.

Barabas.

"Abomination, be gone!" he roared as he closed the gap, and Catrin drifted closer to her body, intrigued.

Barabas struck the statue at a full run, and the arena was rocked with the concussion. The Statue of Terhilian trembled on its base, and Catrin felt Barabas as he was freed from his body. His spirit sang as it blasted free, knowing his sacrifice had not been in vain.

Some force moved Catrin's ephemeral spirit, and she slammed back into her body. Though she felt as if a part of her were lost, she became, once again, constrained by her physical form just as it hit the ground, and her breath whooshed from her lungs.

The statue was no longer a viable weapon. Barabas had done that which Catrin had not thought to do. Rather than deplete the positive charge, he had neutralized the negative charge by hitting it with his own positive energy. The noonstone core still stored a tremendous charge, but the reactive agent was gone.

An ear-shattering crack brought her out of her stupor. The Statue of Terhilian split down its center. Istra and Vestra were parted from their eternal embrace and sent crashing to the ground. Large pieces fractured into smaller sections, and it rained stone. Rough hands grabbed Catrin by the back of her dress and dragged her away from the disintegrating leviathan. She floundered, her limbs leaden and unwilling to respond to her command, and she let the darkness claim her.

Before she drifted into oblivion, a warm and bright spirit visited her, and Barabas spoke one last time before he departed the world of the living.

"Be strong, heart of the land. Your work is not yet done."

Epilogue

Hunching his shoulders over the massive crystal he carried, Prios struggled to keep his grip. Heavy and slick, the ebony stone's sharp edges bit into his hands, but he made no complaint. He'd spoken out once, when he was younger, and Archmaster Belegra had ordered his tongue cut out. Even deprived of speech, he could communicate well enough with those sensitive to Istra's power. Archmaster Belegra and the others of the cadre had little difficulty understanding the mental images he sent them, and Catrin had understood him even when their bodies had been leagues apart. It was the memory of her that kept him going.

She gave me a name. She gave me power.

It was his mantra, and he repeated it to himself over and over. Prios. She had named him Prios. The name gave him pride, and he built his identity around it. He was no longer a nameless slave child, powerless and weak. He was Prios, and he was the master of his own destiny.

After the destruction of the statue, he had expected to be killed for his betrayals, but the archmaster acted as if he were unaware. Prios still couldn't believe it, though, and he dreaded the moment when Archmaster Belegra unleashed his fury. Surely he was not so blind that he hadn't noticed. Even if he were truly ignorant, what of the other members of the cadre? How long until one of them revealed his deceit? They had no reason to love him, yet they, too, had reason to hate Belegra. He had enslaved them all and used them without mercy. Prios could not know if the others were aware of his actions or if they would remain silent, and his life hung from the thinnest thread. All he could do was move on and hope for the day he would be reunited with Catrin. His dreams were full of her, and the thought of joining her was like a beacon in the darkness. It guided him forward and kept him from despairing.

Nearly losing his footing on the slippery gangplank, he thought a moment about letting himself fall into the dark waters, taking the precious crystal with him. It was so tempting. He would be free of his bonds at last, freed from the cruelty of his existence. Again, a vision of Catrin came to his mind. She glowed so brightly, and she lured him, just as the scent of roses draws the honeybee. She was brave and powerful, beautiful yet humble. He drew strength from her and climbed aboard the ship determined to find her. He would join her, and together they would be free.

She gave me a name. She gave me power. And, one day, I will be free.

BRIAN RATHBONE

DRAGON ORE

Prologue

Fields of aquatic vegetation shimmered under clear, blue waters, patches of white sand standing out in bold contrast. The *Stealthy Shark* sliced through calm seas as silent as her name would imply. Standing at the bow, Chase and Fasha watched Istra's eye set the skies afire, and neither dared give voice to their thoughts.

The longer Catrin had been gone, the less Chase liked her plan. Brother Vaughn had been true to his word and, in getting a message to Fasha, had done more than his share to help Chase achieve his goal, but that goal still seemed unattainable. The southern shores of the Greatland stretched on endlessly, and unlike on maps, there were no markings to show where Faulk ended and the Westland began.

"The southern coast of the Westland is less inhabited than that of Faulk," Fasha said. "There are places we can wait for her."

Chase just nodded, silent, unable to maintain much hope. The Greatland was so vast, a person could easily disappear into it, and he feared Catrin and Benjin would do just that.

During their journey, skirting the coastline, they had stopped at small and hidden docks along the way, getting news and supplies. Reports were clear. The Statue of Terhilian found in southern Faulk had been moved to Adderhold by barge, and more recently, another had been found in the Westland. Catrin would have to go to Adderhold. And if she survived that, would she go next to the Westland? Indecision gnawed at Chase. Should he stay with the original plan when his gut told him to go find her? He weighed every possibility in his mind as the coastline slid by.

News of revolts and unrest throughout the Greatland made him wonder if Catrin would ever even get within sight of the statue. It seemed unlikely. Trying to be strong, he committed himself to waiting, just as Catrin had asked him to do. Any other course was just too risky.

In an instant, though, the world changed. A blinding flash of green light backlit the coast, and moments later, a thunderous blast rocked the ship, followed by low, rumbling echoes in the distance.

"May the gods be gentle," Fasha said, her hand over her mouth. Chase swayed on his feet and braced himself on the railing.

"That came from the Westland, didn't it? It was over that way," Chase said, motioning ahead and to the left of their position.

"It did."

"Then the one Catrin set out to destroy?" he asked.

"Will be next."

"I need to get to Adderhold."

Scowling fiercely, Fasha concentrated, and there was a long pause before she nodded firmly and spoke, "I will take you to Madra. Perhaps her wisdom will show us a way."

Chapter 1

The wise old wolf is not wise because he's a wolf, but because he's old.
--Javid Frederick, farmer

* * *

Floating in a haze of semiconsciousness, Catrin wondered if she were dead. Death had claimed her; she knew it had. Her body had failed, unable to cope with the stresses applied by so much power. Yet it did not feel like death; something of life remained. Unable to define it, she searched for what seemed an eternity. Beyond the haze of sleep, something called to her, demanding her attention. It would not be denied, and it found her.

It was an itch.

Refusing to allow rest, it demanded she notice and, at the very least, scratch. Driven by the nagging irritation, she tried to move, and the sensations of her body slowly returned. The painful tingling of flesh left too long without blood ravaged her, and her leaden limbs failed to respond, refused to answer her desperate call for motion. Unable to lift her arms, she struggled to see what bound her and held her fast.

Her eyelids were crusted shut as if they were glued in place. Unwilling to relent, she forced them open. Soft light was like a furious blaze, daring her to see. Still she insisted, and the clouds in her eyes faded enough for her to see the face of an unfamiliar man hovering over her. Fear impaled her.

"Benjin," she tried to say through parched lips, needing his strength more than ever before. But her ears heard only an incoherent mumble, as even her voice refused to do her bidding.

"A moment, m'lady," the stranger said. "Only a moment and he'll be here. He's been by your side for days, but exhaustion overcame him." Another figure darted from the shadows and out of the room before Catrin could see who it was.

Her efforts drained the little energy she possessed, but she would not allow herself to succumb, afraid that, if she let herself sleep, she might never wake again. Holding her eyes open by the sheer force of her will, she endured pain with every involuntary blink, but her vision grew clearer, and the fog began to lift from her mind. When Benjin arrived, the concern on his face made her wonder how horrible she must look.

"It's good to see you awake, li'l miss," he said, obviously trying to be cheerful despite her condition.

When Catrin tried to reply, her parched throat ached and she could only cough.

"Get her some water," Benjin said to Morif, who waited in the shadows. He filled a small cup and handed it to Benjin, who held it to Catrin's mouth. She let it pour over her lips, and she rolled it over her tongue before swallowing. Water slid down the back of her throat and tickled, resulting in another fit of coughing, but at least her throat was now moist. She wanted to drain the entire cup, but Benjin gave her only a small amount more before he set the cup aside. "Can you talk?"

"I think," she said, but she had to stop and swallow. "I think I can." Even as she spoke, though, the itching overpowered her. Feeling began to return to her limbs. Her arm moved, unwieldy and slow, and her fingers curled to scratch her side.

Benjin gently took her hand. "You must not scratch no matter how bad it itches."

Catrin looked at her hand. Layers of dead skin, peeled and cracked, encased her like a dried husk, and her blackened fingernails curled back away from the nail beds. Despair shadowed her soul. How could she go on like this? Who had done this to her?

Barabas.

The name was like a sledge landing between her ears. He had done this to her. She had been ready to depart this world, but Barabas somehow sent her back. This was his fault, and she hated him for it. Tears stung her eyes and tickled the sides of her face. She wanted to reach up and soothe it, but she could not. Even if she'd had the will to raise her arm and scratch with her wasted nails, Benjin would stop her, and she hated him for that. "Go away. All of you. Get out."

Benjin frowned, and she thought he would resist, but he nodded slowly. "Rest some more for now, li'l miss. Things'll be better when you next wake."

"Leave me alone," she said, hating herself for it.

* * *

Weeks passed as Catrin recovered. Her fingernails fell off, and eventually she was allowed to rub away the dead skin. Still she itched. Her skin appeared whole, but it was as if the air itself offended the new skin, leaving it blotchy and irritated. Slowly, her strength returned, and when Benjin arrived for one of his daily visits, she actually smiled.

"Would you like to walk?" he asked, and her soul soared. The thought of getting out of bed, standing upright, and walking in the sunlight thrilled her. She was ready--more than ready. Benjin moved to her side and helped her sit up, but her confidence faltered. The world moved unpredictably, swaying from side to side, and her stomach protested.

"Deep breaths. Be calm. Close your eyes if it helps."

It didn't help. Instead she focused on the doorway. Concentrating on the angles, knowing what they should look like, she willed her mind to see it the way it truly was. Gradually it stopped moving, and it felt like a victory when Catrin saw clean, right angles. After a few more deep breaths, she nodded to Benjin; she was ready. He eased her legs over the side, and the cold stone felt good under her feet. She wobbled as she stood, and she leaned on Benjin heavily at times, but she was standing--another victory. They did not walk in the sunlight as she had hoped, but even darkened halls were far better than being confined to bed.

After he'd helped her back into bed, Benjin handed her a small mirror. "Don't be alarmed," he said.

When she mustered the courage to look, she saw a stranger. Her skin was reddish and looked as if it would crack into a thousand pieces if she moved too quickly, but it was her hair that brought tears to her eyes. Still short, the tips looked as her hair always had, but the roots were as white as goose down.

"I look like an old woman."

"It's not so bad," he said, "and it may wear off. You're already looking better. Do you want me to cut it for you?"

"No," Catrin said. The part of her hair that retained its color was a part of her old self, and she refused to let go of it. So many things about her and her world had changed, and she clung to anything that reminded her of her old life; precious little remained, and she cried herself to sleep.

* * *

Each day brought new challenges and new accomplishments. Training herself as she would a horse, Catrin walked a little farther every day, slowly rebuilding her strength and endurance. During this time, she learned of things that happened after the destruction of the statue. Barabas's body had not been found, as if he had disappeared into the statue. Morif and Millie had dragged Catrin and Benjin away from the arena, searching for a place to hide.

People began to rise up against the Zjhon, and most within Adderhold sought to flee, but one man came looking for Catrin: Samda, a Zjhon Master and former servant of Archmaster Belegra.

"He's shown nothing but compassion for you," Millie said. "He's kept us hidden and safe. You can trust him."

Catrin didn't believe a word of it. How could a Zjhon Master want anything other than her death? Yet he could have had them killed or imprisoned and had not. He could have left her to die but had not.

"Why did you come to our aid?" she asked him one day.

"I did what I believed was right, m'lady."

"And when the Zjhon invaded the Godfist, did you believe that was right?"

"At the time, m'lady, I did," Samda replied, his eyes downcast.

"But you no longer believe that?" she asked, and he only shook his head in response. "What changed your mind?"

"Many things, m'lady: the explosion of the statue in the Westland, Archmaster Belegra's disregard for human life, and his refusal to admit he'd been wrong. He chose, instead, to make up lies about you, and that I could not abide. But mostly, m'lady, it was you," Samda said, meeting her eyes. She saw no guile there, no deception, only deep regret.

"What about me?"

"At first, it was your presence here when the other statue exploded. I could find no way to explain it. There was only one logical conclusion: we, the Zjhon, had been wrong. We had interpreted the holy writings to say what we wanted them to say. I suspected it many years ago, but I could not discard my beliefs so easily. Can you imagine suddenly realizing that everything your family ever taught you was false? It wasn't easy, but you and Archmaster Belegra convinced me. He threw away lives as if they were of no value, and even as men sought to end your life, you wept for them." Tears filled his eyes.

"I didn't want to believe, even then," Samda continued, "but how could I deny it? I considered fleeing with the rest, but where would I have gone? What would I have done? How could I have lived with myself, knowing so many lives had been lost because of my folly? I could not. I had to find some way to right my wrongs and those committed by the Zjhon empire. I had to help you, and I made my decision. I stopped thinking and started acting. I brought you here so you could heal in safety."

Here turned out to be a complex of caves and tunnels, deep beneath Adderhold.

"There were only a few within Adderhold that know this level of catacombs exist, and of those, I am the only one remaining," Samda said. "The rest have either fled with Belegra and his elite guards or have disappeared."

"What of Belegra? Where do you think he has gone?"

"I believe he seeks the Firstland, m'lady," Samda said. "I was not privy to all his plans, and we did not often discuss the possibility of defeat; it seemed unlikely. But I do know that he'd been studying ancient texts, searching for sources of power. I suppose that is the greatest irony. He speaks of your powers as abominations, yet he seeks those very same powers with relentless ambition, and it seems he has talents of his own--as you have seen for yourself."

"The power to coerce and enslave?" Catrin asked, a fury rising within her. "Yes. I've witnessed it." It was that power that held Prios in thrall and prevented his freedom. The connection between her and Prios was difficult to understand, but she was connected to him nonetheless, and she detested Archmaster Belegra's mistreatment of him. "Who are the robed figures he used to attack me?"

"His cadre, as he calls them. They are from all over the Greatland, ranging from highborn to slave. Before the appointed time of Istra's return, Belegra gave orders: Anyone who manifested powers of any kind was to be brought to him, in shackles if need be. I know not how he learned to coerce them and use their powers, but I fear he seeks even greater and more dangerous arcana within the halls of the ancients."

Catrin wanted to ask about Prios, but she did not yet fully trust Samda, and she decided to keep their connection a secret. "Is the location of the Firstland known?"

"Not to me, m'lady, and if Belegra knew, he'd have kept the knowledge hidden. It's a long-standing Zjhon practice--keep secrets close and only ever reveal part of the truth. This is how the Godfist was taken by surprise, you see. Hundreds of years ago, when the Zjhon held the only copies of many ancient texts, new copies were created and filled with false information. Rather than remove the sections that told when Istra would return, our ancestors changed the dates--among other things--while preserving the original texts in sacred vaults."

Catrin swayed as the past began to make sense. Benjin had once said that the Vestrana's calculations had been wrong, and now she knew why. Things could have been much different had they known the truth.

"I know not what Belegra will find, if anything. He goes in search of legends and myths, believing he will find Enoch and Ain Giest still alive . . . or maybe even dragons."

"Dragons?"

"Indeed, m'lady, dragons," Samda replied, and he drew a deep breath. "Legends say they were a source of incredible power. Unfortunately, there are very few details in the texts. It seems dragon lore was such common knowledge in those times that it was either not written down or not preserved. We've found vague references but nothing to indicate exactly what kind of power they possessed or how it came to be harnessed by men. The only thing I can say for certain is that, at one point in our history, man and dragon worked together."

Catrin's imagination conjured skies filled with mighty wizards on the backs of dragons. It was both thrilling and terrifying.

"Belegra also seeks knowledge, which is power in itself. In particular, I believe he searches for the locations of the other Statues of Terhilian."

"What?" Catrin asked, agape. "How many statues *are* there?"

"I cannot be sure, but I believe four--possibly five--were buried before they exploded. Of those, two have been found. That would leave the possibility of three unaccounted for."

Three statues--they could be buried just about anywhere, and they could explode at any time, even if left underground. There seemed no way to evade the impending disaster. Frustrated, Catrin changed the subject. "What about the Zjhon armies? Where are they now?"

"I can't say for certain. The siege on Ohmahold has most likely been called off since you are obviously no longer there, and I assume Belegra will join his forces with those of General Dempsy. With the ships that returned from the Godfist, they could sail with a sizable army."

"Still, there would be a considerable force left behind, and they may be coming to retake Adderhold," Benjin added.

"Indeed, and we should not be here when they arrive, but where will we go?" Samda asked, and silence hung in the air.

Catrin was torn. Part of her wanted to go south to meet Chase, as they had planned, but another part wanted to return to Ravenhold, and yet another part wanted to return to Ohmahold. In the back of her mind, though, when she put aside her responsibilities, she wanted most to return to the Godfist. Any road she chose would be perilous; every choice would leave her vulnerable in some way. "South," she said, her mind made up; she would not abandon Chase.

"With an army possibly coming from the north, I'd say that's a wise choice," Benjin said. "With any luck, your cousin will already have transport to Ohmahold arranged."

Samda raised an eyebrow but said nothing.

Millie, though, stood in the corner with her hands on her hips. "You would leave your grandmother to suffer the wrath of the Kytes alone?"

"I can only be in one place at a time. I promised Chase I would meet him. I made no such promise to my grandmother. She'll have to wait for now, but I'll return to Ravenhold when I can," Catrin replied, and Millie pursed her lips.

Morif chuckled.

"What are you laughing at?" Millie asked.

"The girl's got fire. You must grant her that," he replied, smiling. "I like a girl with fire."

Millie just crossed her arms and cast angry glances around the room.

"The more immediate problem is how to get out of Adderhold," Benjin said. "I'd rather not be seen if possible."

"There is a way, but we should leave soon," Samda said.

"Do you feel strong enough to travel, li'l miss?"

"I'm ready," she lied.

Through darkened halls, Samda led them, only the light of his lamp guiding the way. Catrin leaned on her staff, her fingers resting in the impressions left by her grip during the destruction of the statue--a silent reminder. Though the staff had been dull and ashen when Benjin returned it to her, its sheen was beginning to return, and the torchlight danced across its surface.

After a meandering trek through the underbelly of Adderhold, Samda stopped at a corner that looked no different from the rest, ran his hands along the wall, and pushed open a hidden door. Inside, a narrow flight of rough-hewn stairs descended into the darkness. A cool breeze carried the smell of the sea, and around a bend in the stair, yellowish moonlight danced across dark water. A small landing jutted into the water, and moored there was a sailing vessel large enough to carry roughly a dozen people.

"Very few know this place exists. I doubt anyone is watching the outlet, but we must be as quiet as possible."

They boarded the boat, retrieved the lines, and using the four rows of oars, paddled toward the moonlight. The opening in the cavern wall was tall and slender. Beyond it stood a ring of towering stones, seemingly barring their path, but as they approached, a narrow channel became visible between two rows of massive stones. There was little room for mistakes, and despite their efforts, they grazed the rocks twice before gaining open water.

A haze blurred the stars and gave the moon a brownish tint, as if the skies were tainted. Still, the light of distant comets bolstered Catrin's strength; energy soaked into her bones and warmed her against the chill wind that descended from the west. The sails snapped taut as they were raised, and with Benjin's help, Samda guided the ship into deep water, far from either shore.

"It's dangerous for us to go out this far in such a small craft, but I think we should get south of Waxenboro, where the lands are much less populated, before we go near shore. We can't go too far, though. South of Mahabrel the Inland Sea becomes much more dangerous and unpredictable. I wouldn't advocate crossing in this boat," Samda said. As if to prove his point, the growing waves tossed them about, nearly capsizing the small craft.

Weakness still caused Catrin to tremble, but she felt much better breathing the salty air. Her body might never be able to do things it had once done, but she was determined to try. Barabas had said her work was not yet done, and she tried to prepare herself for whatever might come next.

After taking a deep breath, Catrin reflexively raised her hand to her hair. She could not feel where the translucent whiteness ended and the remaining color began, but she knew it was there--a crutch. Using her knife, she hacked away the color, shearing the ties to her childhood and embracing the future. No longer could she afford to be a frightened little girl, holding on to relics of the past for the comfort they brought. She needed to face her future with confidence and purpose. As an offering to the sea, she cast her hair into the waves, and with it went one of the shadows that had been haunting her soul. She felt freed and renewed, but these feelings were accompanied by a great weariness. Knowing she needed sleep in order to heal, Catrin calmed her mind and meditated herself to sleep.

* * *

Moving through the darkness, Chase cursed every branch that snapped beneath his boots. Fasha had given him no reason to believe the people here would be hostile, but she hadn't given him any indication that they would be friendly either. All he knew was approximately where to find this woman named Madra and that he could trust her. Fasha had given him directions and even drawn him a map, but he feared he was hopelessly lost, and the thought of finding someone to ask made him feel ill. These people had more reason to fear him than to trust him, and he decided he would keep searching, even if he had to retrace his steps back to the shoreline and begin his journey again.

Just as the thought entered his mind, Chase caught a flash of light through the trees and his hopes soared. Fasha had said that Madra's farm was isolated from the others, like an island within a sea of trees, but he had not thought it could possibly be this deep in the forest. As he cleared the last of the trees and entered a field of tall grass, he stood bathed in pale, yellowish light. Ahead lay lands that seemed to have once been manicured but now were being reclaimed by weeds. Pastures were fenced only in spirit; lines of posts held an occasional slat between them but would keep in no horses or livestock. A feeling of sadness overcame him as he used the tree line for cover, seeing visions of his own homeland, abandoned and neglected. Tears filled his eyes.

When he reached the nearest barn, he was again dismayed by the state of disrepair. Most of the roof had collapsed, and much of what had once been in the hayloft now clogged the aisle as it seemed the ceiling, too, had succumbed to neglect. Staying to the shadows, Chase moved ever closer to the dim light that danced around the edges of a doorframe. Like a distant ray of hope, it drew him forward and banished his fear. When he reached the door, he knocked softly. No answer came. After a moment of trepidation, he pushed open the door. His eyes were met by a contradiction. Inside, sitting alone at a table with nothing but a jar of whiskey and a glass, waited Madra.

A fierce and strong spirit huddled within an aging body. Eyes that spoke of a stone will were rimmed with tears, and a powerful jaw trembled as it tried to hold back the pain. At first, she did not even acknowledge his presence. Instead, she poured another drink. "And who might you be?" she finally asked without looking up.

"My name is Chase," he said when she raised her eyes and met his gaze. He tried to say more, but his knees suddenly felt weak, and his hands began to tremble. He could feel Madra's pain and could think of no words that would be meaningful in the face of such despair.

"I've no patience for halfwits, boy. Go on. Talk. Who sent you?"

"Fasha," he managed to say.

"Let me guess: You came looking for help?"

"Yes, ma'am."

Madra just nodded, bit her lip, and poured her last drink. For a time she simply sat and stared at it. After a few moments, though, she picked it up, stood, and walked outside. Chase followed. Beneath the moon, stars, and comets, Madra stood silent for some time, tears falling to the dusty soil beside her tattered boots. In the end, she raised her glass to the gods: "I beg for help, and you send me those in need. I ask for mercy, and you further test my will. Fine. Have your joke, you thankless jackals. I'll just have to clean up this mess myself!" she said just before she downed her last drink. "Come on, pup. We've work to do."

As he followed Madra back into her home, Chase wondered what he'd gotten himself into.

* * *

When the sun rose, casting a glow across the water, neither shore was visible; only the location of the sun guided them. The winds had taken a southerly turn and grown fierce; their boat cut the waves under full sail, riding the growing swells. With no point of reference, it looked to Catrin as if they were moving slowly, but occasional flotsam appeared in the water and was soon lost in the distance.

"We must get closer to shore before the sea claims us," Benjin shouted to Samda, and they set a westerly course.

By midday, the western coast came into view. The land was mostly forested, and only occasional farmsteads and mills gave any indication of inhabitation. But as the day wore on, the smell of smoke grew heavy on the air, and the setting sun backlit columns of smoke, red and orange, making it appear as if the sky were on fire.

"Perhaps we should move back into deeper water," Benjin said as they neared the coast. The columns of smoke were now close, and acrid clouds rolled over the water. As they passed an isolated farmstead, a band of mounted men appeared, raiding and setting the buildings afire.

"Bandits and thugs," Morif said. "The Zjhon weakened all the lands, and now that they've been routed, anarchy reigns." Samda flushed and kept his eyes downcast. "I mean you no insult, Samda. You've been good to us, but the Zjhon have set the Greatland on a path to destruction." Millie stood, tight-lipped, and cast scathing glances at Morif, but he seemed not to notice as he watched the raiders move on. "There's little food to be had, and too many young folk are dead, with the Zjhon armies, or on the Godfist. If order is not restored, there'll be nothing left to raid by spring."

Catrin watched the razing of the farmstead in horror, seeing visions of her own home destroyed, but she stifled her tears. "Turn back east," she said. "I don't want to land near here." Benjin nodded at her statement.

"The southern waters are far too dangerous," Samda said. "Storms and massive waves strike without warning. It'd be wiser to skirt the western coast and look for a safer place to land," Samda said.

Catrin got a cold feeling in her stomach when she looked at the burning farmstead, and she decided to trust her instincts. "No," she said. "We will risk the crossing."

Chapter 2

Oversight begets disaster.
--Omar Zichter, architect

* * *

An unnatural mist obscured the landscape, green and yellow like a plague, but Catrin recognized her homeland nonetheless. How she had come to be back on the Godfist was lost to her. A part of her seemed to know that she dreamed, but that knowing was overshadowed by fear and foreboding.

Harborton appeared deserted. Not a soul could be found, no birds sang in the trees beyond, and even the leaves were still. As she neared the family farm, though, dark shapes milled about, distorted by the foul mist.

In the barnyard she found her father, Benjin, Uncle Jensen, and even Chase, though she wondered how he had found his way home. Everyone she cared about from her homeland was there, yet no one spoke or even seemed to notice her. Their faces were contorted into masks of fear and rage lit by a feral glow. As one, they moved toward the pasture from which the glow originated, and there, Catrin saw what drew them. The face of Istra stared up from the depths of a gaping wound in the land, and the glow became brighter with every step she took.

She tried to warn them, to tell them to run away, but her voice made no sound, no matter how loudly she tried to scream. Frustration set her soul ablaze as she fought to alert them of the danger, but they would not see--could not hear. Moving inexorably closer, they walked to their deaths, and Catrin was helpless, unable to stop them. Clawing her throat, trying to find her voice, she moved through the cloying mist. With an effort born of love and terror, her scream finally split the air, and every face turned toward her, but before she could warn them, the haze wrapped them in its fetid embrace.

In a flash of ill light, they were gone.

* * *

Gentle hands shook Catrin awake. Her eyes burned, and she wiped the sweat from her brow, her mouth tasting of blood.

"It's all right, li'l miss," Benjin said. "I'm here. It was just a dream."

Even in the bright morning light, she could not shake the visions from her mind, and she trembled as she stood. Sucking in a deep breath, she let the damp and salty air drive away the horrors of her dreams. Shading her eyes with her hand, she could see the eastern coast beneath the rising sun.

Prevailing winds continued to drive them, and she estimated they would reach land before noon. Samda brought her a mug of water laced with herbs. "This will help clear your mind," he said.

"Thank you," Catrin said, but she spilled the drink when she spotted a dark and menacing ship approaching. "There's a ship behind us."

"Looks like a mercenary ship," Benjin said, "and I doubt they're friendly. I don't think we can outrun them, even at full sail, but let's raise all we have. Maybe we can make it to shallow water before they catch us." He and Samda moved with purpose to get as much speed as they could. Catrin and the others secured themselves as speed drove the boat into the waves.

After tossing everything that was not precious or essential, the mercenary ship still gained on them, and Catrin knew it would overtake them well before they made land. Benjin and the others seemed to come to the same conclusion and prepared themselves to fight.

Catrin tried to decide what to do. She hadn't used her powers since the destruction of the statue, and she was terrified that they would no longer work or, worse yet, that they would unintentionally hurt those she loved. As her breathing became rapid, she tried to exert control over herself, and she drew deep, steady breaths. It was much like the first time she climbed back onto a horse after having been thrown. Tentatively, she reached for Istra's power. Like breathing, the act of opening herself to the energy felt natural, only, in this case, it felt as if she had spent most of her life holding her breath. The power came reluctantly at first, but then it surged, coming to her in a rush and nearly sweeping her away.

Something within her had changed. It was as if the power she'd felt before had been flowing through a pinhole, and now the dam had burst. With deliberate effort, she pulled herself away from the energy flow. It tempted her with its sweet caress, but she knew she could not give in to its lure or she would be lost. The sudden deprivation of power after such a heady flow made her dizzy, and she swayed where she sat.

As the mercenary ship drew closer, her crew gathered at the bow and hurled insults and jeers across the water. They promised death in a myriad of fashions, and though Catrin knew it was a tactic, she had difficulty avoiding its effects. Her mind invented visions of her death, and she began to sweat. Benjin and the others remained silent, conserving their energy, knowing they would need every reserve to survive.

"They're going to catch us, but they don't want to sink us. They want to rob us. All we have to do is keep them off of us long enough to get to the shallows," Benjin finally said into the silence. "Have no mercy, and don't hesitate. If they drop their guard, take full advantage."

Catrin trembled as the ship drew closer, almost within bow range. The shoreline was so close, she could almost feel the sand beneath her toes, but the water looked plenty deep almost all the way to the white beach, an underwater cliff dropping off into oblivion not far from shore.

Knowing she had to act, Catrin stood on trembling knees and braced herself against the mast. Her staff in hand, she tried to figure out what to do next.

"What are you doing?" Benjin asked. "Get back down. You'll make a good target up there."

"I have to stop them."

"But you aren't fully healed yet. It may not be safe . . ." He trailed off.

"I have to try," Catrin said as she closed her eyes and concentrated. In the past she had used her power to trigger much larger sources of potential energy, but now there was no storm to draw upon, no lightning to call. She would have to rely on Istra's energy alone to assault the ship.

Slowly she opened herself to the source, allowing only a trickle of energy to escape through the mental barrier she maintained between herself and the unmoderated flow of power. A plan began to form in her mind, and though the energy pounded on her barrier, she remained in control.

The air itself carried and conducted energy. As she expanded her senses beyond the bounds of her physical form, she found that she could see, smell, and taste the air around her. Heavy with moisture and teeming with static charge, it became like clay molded by ethereal hands. Pulling the air closer, Catrin gathered it in her cupped palms and packed a continuous flow into a sphere of energy. The air came to her easily, but putting it in the sphere and containing the pressure became increasingly difficult. Drawing more heavily on the energy flow, she reached into her staff and let its comforting energy bolster her.

When she opened her eyes, a translucent ball floated above her palm, its surface always shifting and changing. Raising her palm to her lips, she blew, and the ball of air floated toward the encroaching ship. The farther away it got, the more difficult it was to control and maintain. It was not quite over the bow of the other ship when she had to release it.

A sound like a thunderclap cleaved the air accompanied by a blast of icy wind. At first the mercenaries were stunned, but then arguments broke out. Catrin's attack had been mostly ineffective, but it had convinced some of the mercenaries that this prey was too dangerous to pursue. While they argued, though, the ship moved ever closer.

"Are you all right, li'l miss?"

"I'm fine," she said, putting more of her weight on the mast and trying to steady her quivering knees. "If they do not heed my warning, I'll attack."

Benjin shifted in his seat and looked torn, but he said nothing. The shadow of the mercenary ship was about to close over them, and Catrin drew a deep breath. Just as she began to open herself to the power, men appeared on the mercenary ship with bows. As one, five men drew and aimed at Catrin. In an instant, she drew deeply and let the power flow around her, still drawing more. Her body began to sway from side to side, her arms moving with the rhythm of the power. Arcs of energy trailed behind her staff as it moved, and her hair stood on end. The bowmen did not release, and their arms began to shake from the strain. Slowly, one by one, they lowered their bows.

A shrill cry echoed across the water, and two bodies were thrown over the side of the mercenary ship. Just as the ship moved close enough for the men above to make the jump, it veered away. Catrin released the flow and slumped to the belly of the boat. Though she hated to see anyone die, she had difficulty feeling compassion for the dead captain, and she hoped those who committed the mutiny would remember this day and change their ways.

Just as she began to relax, Millie drew a sharp intake of breath and Benjin cursed. Across the sands came two riders at a full gallop.

"We need to get back to deep water and find another place to land," Benjin said as an army wound its way down a nearby ridge. As the men worked, Catrin watched the riders approach. Wind caught the sails, and the boat began moving away. One of the riders stood in the stirrups and waved his arms, yelling. At first Catrin could not hear what he said, but then the wind shifted and his words drifted to her: "Catrin, wait!"

Benjin heard Chase's call as well, and he smiled broadly as he brought the boat about. Chase reined in his horse, jumped off, and waded to meet them. He looked different--older. The beginnings of a beard darkened his visage, and Catrin wasn't certain she liked it.

"You look awful," he said as the boat reached shore.

Catrin lowered herself to the sand. "Thanks. You're looking rough yourself. Have you considered shaving?"

"I like it and I'm keeping it."

Catrin laughed and her burdens felt lighter knowing Chase was safe. They walked from the water with their arms around each other. Benjin and Samda rigged the sails on the boat, and they pushed it back out to sea. "I don't want to leave any evidence that we landed here," Benjin said. "Greetings, Chase. You've done well. I look forward to hearing your tale."

"It can't be as good as yours," Chase said with a wink.

A woman with graying hair and eyes like ice stood nearby, holding the two horses. Lines around her eyes gave her a hawkish appearance. Despite all her power, Catrin could get no sense of what the woman was thinking or feeling; she was like a stone.

"Catrin, Benjin, this is Madra. She's the leader of the army you see," Chase said.

"This is the mighty Herald of Istra?" Madra asked. "From the tales I've heard, I expected someone as tall as a bear with eyes of fire."

"Tales are often exaggerated," Catrin responded.

Madra smiled then laughed. "I suppose they are."

Catrin introduced Samda, and she did her best to make him sound like a friend, but Madra and Chase both eyed him with anger and distrust.

Chase pulled Catrin aside while Benjin made the rest of the introductions. "What really happened?"

"To make it all very brief," she said, "I met a druid, who led us through the forests, but the forests caught fire, and then there was a flood. And then I caught a farmer's horse, and he gave us his cross-eyed ox. We sold the ox, and then Millie recognized me and took me to Ravenhold, where I met my grandmother. I can't even tell you the next part. You won't understand."

"Tell me."

"Do you promise not to hate me?"

"Tell me."

"I know who killed our mothers, and I agreed to marry one of their family."

"What?" he said, but their conversation was drawing attention.

"We should discuss this in a more secure location," Madra said. "Let's move inland and make camp."

"Take the other horse, Cat," Chase said. "You look like you could use a rest."

Despite her pride, Catrin did not have the energy to decline. She did, however, turn away his offer to give her a boost. She was not that weak.

Lines of soldiers snaked across the sand, and as they drew closer, Catrin saw that they were mostly old men, women, and children--only those the Zjhon armies had left behind. Madra rode ahead to find a suitable place to make camp, and Catrin let Chase lead her horse at a walk while she filled him in on the rest of the details.

"We nearly passed each other," Chase said. "If not for that thunderclap, I would never have known to look for you here. We were heading north, to Adderhold. After the statue exploded, I thought you might not be able to get to me, so I came looking for you."

"I'm grateful fate allowed you to find me. Tell me about Madra and her army. How did you come to travel with them?"

"Fasha brought me to Madra."

"You met Fasha?"

"Yes," Chase said. "She is among the most spirited and brightest people I've ever met. I hope to sail with her again someday. Brother Vaughn took me to the Vestrana in Endland, and they took me to Fasha. We sailed the *Stealthy Shark* to Faulk, but I knew something was wrong when the statue in the Westland exploded, and that's when Fasha took me to Madra. At that time, I don't think even Madra would have guessed that she would be leading an army, but after the statue exploded, the people had had enough. It was Madra who organized them and began the march to Adderhold. I joined them and came in search of you. There were fewer of us in the beginning, but everywhere we go, people join us. In every town it's the same: people are afraid when we arrive, but once we tell them what we are doing, they support us and many join our ranks. But now I don't know what to do. This is not our war, but I'm not sure I can abandon them."

"What does Madra want?" Catrin asked.

"Peace," Chase replied. "The problem is that none of us know how exactly to achieve it."

Catrin understood the problem, having faced the same dilemma herself, but she was no wiser than anyone else. "I wish I knew."

"There is something else I have to tell you. Fasha brought word from the Godfist. I'm sorry, Cat, but someone tried to kill your dad. He was still alive when Fasha left the Godfist, but no one could say if he would survive. Uncle Wendel is strong, though, and I know he still lives. I thought you should know."

Catrin rode in silence, terrified by the thought of someone trying to kill her father and frustrated by not knowing if he still lived. Chase told her more of what happened after she left the Godfist, but she could barely listen. It was just too painful to hear how wrong her plan for peace had gone. She had hoped to unite the people of the Greatland and the Godfist, but her actions had only divided them further.

Beyond a series of steep dunes, the grasslands rolled toward a distant mountain range. Madra and another rider had already staked their horses, and they were pitching tents as Catrin and the others joined with the rest of the army. Walking beside these people, she could hardly consider them an army, and she wondered what good they hoped to accomplish. It was the same question she asked of herself, a question for which she had no answer.

When they arrived at the campsite, Catrin dismounted and began to unsaddle the horse. A woman approached with a currycomb and a bucket of water. "I can care for him, m'lady."

"I'm Catrin. What's your name?"

"Grelda, m'lady."

"You don't need to call me 'm'lady.' I'd enjoy caring for him if it's not an imposition."

"I'll hold 'im for you, m'lady. He likes to kick."

Catrin shook her head and started brushing the gelding's roan coat. Watching his every move, Catrin was ready when he kicked, and she deftly stepped aside. When his coat was brushed, she let him drink. Watching his ears move on each swallow, she pulled the bucket away before he drank too much. The routine gave her peace as it took her back to a simpler time in her life. "Thank you," she said as Grelda led the gelding to the pickets, where only two other horses were tied.

"Madra kept four sound horses hidden from the Zjhon," Chase said. "One went lame on the way here. We don't have enough to do much good except for scouting and occasionally carrying those who need rest. The army moves at a terribly slow pace. Only when Madra has gotten us passage on barges have we made any real progress."

Considering her new circumstances, Catrin began to weigh every option in her mind, but there was no clear choice.

Her thoughts were interrupted, though, when Madra approached. "Now would be a good time to tell us your tale," she said and sat, cross-legged, across from where Catrin stood.

Others gathered, and soon Catrin faced much of the army, who sat silently, waiting for her to speak. Her staff in hand, she spread her arms and opened herself up to a mere trickle of energy to amplify her voice, but the power seemed to have ideas of its own. Inadvertently, she took a step backward, nearly overwhelmed by the rush of raw energy that threatened to wash her away. With a deep breath, she prepared to tell her tale, but before she even spoke, someone in the crowd gasped, and Catrin opened her eyes.

No one moved or spoke up, and Catrin opened herself to the power once again; this time ready for the onslaught. "I am Catrin Volker, daughter of a horse farmer, and the one declared the Herald of Istra," she said, and she recounted her journey, leaving out no details. Gone was the time for secrecy.

For the first time, no one questioned her tale, and no one scoffed at her claims. These people had seen enough already. They believed. It was not from the silence she learned this, but from powerful waves of anxiety that could not be concealed. "I have no desire for conquest. I want only peace, but there are grave dangers facing our world, and I must do what I can to prevent more people from dying. There are more statues to be found, and Archmaster Belegra's search for weapons of power threatens us all. I do not ask you to join my quest or forward my cause. I ask only that you strive for order and peace, even if you must fight to achieve it. I cannot tell you yet what I will do next, as I've not yet had time to consider all that has changed. I ask you to consider my words and allow me some time."

"You have given us a great deal to consider, and we, too, will need time to evaluate this new information. Until we gather again, please consider yourselves honored guests," Madra said.

Catrin released the stream of power reluctantly, despite her struggle to control it, and it left her yearning for more. Taking a deep breath, she steadied herself, letting the cool evening air caress her. It lulled her and soon she yawned. "I need to rest."

"We don't have any extra tents, but you can sleep in mine," Chase said.

"Thank you, but I think I'd like to sleep under the sky tonight."

"If that's what makes you happy, but if it starts raining, don't come in my tent all wet."

Staring up at the sky from her bedroll, Catrin reveled in the light of the moon, stars, and comets, her fatigue suddenly abated. She counted four comets in the sky, and their energy rejuvenated her.

Within moments, though, the stillness of the night sky was disturbed as what looked like tiny comets streaked across the sky before disappearing. Several people who were looking at the show gasped and exclaimed. Chase came from his tent when he heard the commotion.

"What is it, Cat?"

"I'm not sure. Look to the sky," she said. "It seems harmless, and it's actually quite beautiful."

Chase watched with her for some time as the firestorm raged, but then he stood and stretched. "I should be sleeping," he said as he left for his tent.

Catrin watched longer than she should have, but she was mesmerized and knew she might never witness such an event again. Eventually, she made herself close her eyes. In the quiet of her mind, she heard the faint melody of life, and it lulled her to sleep.

* * *

Madra watched the skies with a mixture of fascination and dread. The world she had known was gone, and in its place was a world where nothing was certain, where entire nations feared a girl who looked as if she might be afraid of her own shadow. Though Madra sensed strength in Catrin, she doubted it would be enough. She, too, had been a gentle flower in her youth, full of hope and optimism, but the world had hardened her. It had taken her optimism and tempered it with cold fear and bitter futility. At times, she thought she might shatter from the stress of it.

Looking across the grass to where Catrin lay, Madra drew a deep breath and did her best to find some shred of hope. For Catrin's sake and her own, she tilted her head back and gazed to the skies. With all her might, she sent her prayers to the gods, hoping that maybe this time they would hear.

Chapter 3

Our eyes are most critical of those who are reflections of ourselves.
--Elinda Wumrick, mother of three

* * *

Distorted echoes of string instruments and cymbals filled the halls of Ravenhold. There was no tune or melody, as if those who played could not hear the notes. Banquet tables were laden with rotting food. Faceless men and women danced without rhythm, as if some unseen force drove them.

Catrin stood at the center of it all in her wedding dress. But when she looked down, it was soiled and torn. Her grandmother beckoned from the head table, but Catrin could not break free from those who danced. Her every step was blocked, and it seemed she was getting farther away. Lissa, looking as Catrin imagined her: like herself but with eyes of ice and fire, stood at her grandmother's side, her slender hand extended to point at Catrin, a silent accusation.

Hands grabbed Catrin's waist and propelled her around the floor, twirling her until she was dizzy. Her legs could no longer hold her, and she fell and fell and fell. When at last she struck cold stone, she looked up to see Carrod Winsiker staring down at her, his lips curled into a sneer. He laughed and the room spun. Every face she saw was twisted in contempt, mocking her. Lissa threw a piece of moldy bread at her, and her grandmother laughed.

Shame and grief overwhelmed Catrin, and she begged for mercy, but they surrounded her, accusing her of abandoning them. Her grandmother came to the fore and opened her mouth to speak, but no sound emerged. Instead, a crimson rose bloomed on her chest, and she dropped to the floor, an arrow protruding from her back. On the balcony stood Catrin's betrothed, engulfed in a nimbus of power. He reached out with fingers of flame and raked the soft flesh of her throat. Crying out in pain, she looked down to see blood soaking her already fouled dress.

When she raised her head again, robed figures threw ropes of fire into the crowd, and those who danced burst into flame, but still they danced. Wicked laughter pounded in her ears, and as a haze of blood clouded her vision, they were gone.

* * *

"No!" Catrin shouted, grappling with hands that restrained her. She lashed out, desperate with fear.

Benjin frowned down at her. "It was a bad dream. Wake up, li'l miss. You're safe."

Slowly, reality supplanted the image of her dream, and she relaxed.

"I'm sorry."

"You've nothing to be ashamed of," he said. "Fate has been unkind to you, and you've not even had time to grieve. Allow yourself to do that, and then, perhaps, the dreams will not be as bad."

"Thank you." People milled about, and several cast Catrin questioning glances.

Madra approached. Everyone in the camp showed deference to her, yet she had a kind word, a pat on the shoulder, or an embrace for each of them. The harsh persona dissolved in those moments, and Catrin saw the real Madra.

"Our dreams bring messages," she said when she reached Catrin. "But they are rarely understood. Give them credence, but do not rely on them for council."

"Thank you, Madra."

"When you've eaten, please join me," Madra said as she walked back to her tent.

Chase brought a half loaf of bread, some smoked fish, and a flask of water. "What do we do from here?" he asked.

Catrin had known this time would come, but she was still not ready to answer. Haunted by her dreams, she tried to find reason, tried to find a course that would not lead to disaster. In a moment of clarity, she firmed her resolve and made a choice. "We go to Ohmahold," she said, but she turned her head when Millie made an annoyed sound in her throat. "On the way, we'll stop at Ravenhold, but we'll only remain there a short time." Millie looked smug but seemed satisfied.

"And after Ohmahold? What then?" Chase asked.

"I'll not remain long in Ohmahold either. I'll fulfill my commitments, and then I'll find a way to get to the Firstland. Belegra poses a serious threat, and I cannot allow him to enslave anyone else. I would go in search of the other statues, but I've no idea how to find them. At least with Belegra I know where he has most likely gone, even if I don't know how to get there."

"Wherever *we* go," Chase said, with a pointed look at Catrin, "*we* are going to need a ship. Fasha was headed for New Moon Bay. Madra knows ways to contact her, as does Brother Vaughn. I guess *we* just need to find a map."

Catrin simply nodded her acknowledgment.

"I think Belegra may have a map, but I doubt you'll find another," Samda said. "I believe it was among his most closely guarded treasures."

"We'll find a way," Chase said with a firm nod. "Let's go. Madra awaits."

On their way to Madra's tent, Catrin saw fear in the eyes of many she passed. Making the mistake of looking one woman in the eye, Catrin felt a wave of terror pour out. Some may seek out the ability to inspire fear in others, but Catrin detested it. It made her feel like a monster.

Madra, at least, showed no signs of fear when they approached. She sat next to the remains of a small fire and motioned for Catrin to sit. Chase and Benjin seemed unsure if they were welcome, but Madra smiled. "Please, all of you, sit with me and let's discuss what lies ahead."

"Thank you, Madra."

"We set out to confront the Zjhon armies and reclaim what is rightfully ours. You're welcome to join us, if you choose. What you've already done has aided us. We're indebted to you for that, but we'll not kneel to you."

"I don't want anyone to kneel to me," Catrin said. "I seek no power or authority. I only want peace. And while I support your goals, I, too, have things I must achieve. I must return to Ravenhold and Ohmahold to fulfill my commitments, but if our paths remain the same for some time, I would welcome a place in your camp."

"Fair enough."

* * *

Driven by a strong wind, the *Stealthy Shark* knifed through the waves, sending sea spray high into the air. Feeling the cool mist on her cheeks was one of the things Fasha loved most about the sea, and most times, it brought a smile to her face, but on this day, it brought only fear and sadness. Watching Chase as he had waded from the surf, departing her world and entering the world of the land-bound, something inside of her had changed. She could not define what had changed, but nothing in her life had been the same since. Not even the rush of dodging patrol ships brought her any real joy. It was as if all the things that had been important to her suddenly lost their meaning.

Chase's desperate--almost primal--need to save his cousin had affected Fasha more than she had originally realized. Though she knew she belonged at sea, she found herself wanting to meddle in the affairs of the land-bound, something her mother often cautioned against, saying it was a certain path to trouble. Still the thoughts lingered, and Fasha continued to question herself. When sails appeared on the horizon, she had no choice but to concentrate on survival. Her conscience would have to wait.

***

Weeks of traveling with Madra's army proved to Catrin that she never wanted to become a soldier. Half of every morning was spent breaking camp, and half the evening was spent making camp. She had to admit that this specific army had problems that no other would. Children ran through the tents in packs, playing and roughhousing. Other, smaller children cried late into the night, every night, making sleep difficult to find. Tempers were short, and patience was in shorter supply than food. When Catrin could take no more, she joined Madra and Benjin by one of the many campfires.

"Soon we'll turn west, toward Adderhold," Madra said.

"We'll go east to Ravenhold," Catrin said. "Thank you for everything you've done for us, and may you find what you seek."

"May the gods be with us all, and may you make your peace--if not for the world, at least for yourself."

"Thank you, Madra. You are kind. I've a favor I must ask of you," Catrin said, and Madra raised an eyebrow. "May I use one of your horses and ride ahead? There're some things I need that may be hard to come by with an army in the area."

"You ask a great deal. We've only three horses, and I cannot afford to lose any of them. I'm sorry. I cannot grant this request. All of them need to be shod, and Hedron says his back hurts too much to do it now."

"Benjin and I can shoe them for you," Catrin said. "I ask nothing in return. It's a small thing we can do to repay the kindness you've shown Chase and the rest of us."

"If you have the skills," Madra said, "I can get you the tools. I'm certain Hedron will appreciate it, as I do."

Catrin and Benjin followed Madra to Hedron's tent. He struggled to stand when they arrived. "Ah, Madra. I'm of no use to you at all now, am I?"

"Nonsense. You'll heal, and then you'll work twice as hard," she said, and they both smiled. "Catrin and Benjin have offered to shoe the horses."

Hedron smiled and shook Benjin's hand. "Well, come then. There's a shoeing kit in the saddlebags. Poor animals are sore in need. Bless you for your kindness."

The shoes were indeed wearing thin, and some were pulling away from the hoof, the nails loose or missing. Catrin held each horse as Benjin did what he could. Some shoes were near to wearing all the way through, and he shook his head. "I'm not sure how long this will last, but they're on better than they were. The filly's shoes are pretty far gone."

"Far better. Far better, indeed," Hedron said. "I'd give her new shoes if we had 'em, but everything is scarce these days."

"Which horse has the best shoes?" Madra asked.

"The chestnut gelding," Benjin said. "Only one of his shoes is wearing thin."

"Take him," Madra said. "Meet us within four days. Don't make me regret this decision," she said. Then she turned her attention to other matters within the camp.

Catrin sought out Millie. "I need gold. Do you have any you would loan me against the gifts I've received?"

"The gold is yours, m'lady. I merely keep it safe. Spend it wisely," she said as she handed Catrin a small but fat purse.

Despite his protests, Catrin persuaded Chase to stay. Leaving her staff in his care, she and Benjin saddled up the chestnut and mounted. "We'll meet you in four days," Benjin said, and Catrin felt the stares on her back as they rode away. The sensation was overwhelmed, though, by the freedom of being on horseback, even if only as a passenger. Synchronizing her movements with the horse, they became almost as one, and she breathed in deeply, enjoying the serenity of the moment.

"What are we after?" Benjin asked.

"I need new clothes, and I'd like to get whatever food we can."

"Clothes?"

"No matter how much power I may have, people look at me and see a peasant and a child. I need clothes that will create a much different impression."

"I suppose you're right," Benjin said, "but this is a dangerous foray. We've no idea what the political climate is in these lands or how people will greet us. They may accept your gold and then slip a knife between your ribs."

Catrin didn't have a response for that. She felt it was a chance she had to take.

They rode through silent wilderness for much of the day, but then more settled lands came into view. Few people worked the fields, but some stood from their labors and stared as Catrin and Benjin rode by. More stares followed as they entered a small town, and Benjin slowed their mount to a walk.

Shop owners hawked wares silently by holding up their finest products and displaying others on outdoor shelves and racks. An elderly woman held up a pair of leather leggings as they passed, and Catrin whispered to Benjin to stop. He reined in and tied the horse off to a nearby post.

The shop owner nodded to Catrin, and only when they were inside the shop did she speak. "Welcome, lady. What have you need of?"

"I need three pairs of leggings, a coat, and shirts," Catrin said while admiring the different designs on display within the shop while Benjin stood at the door, watching the shop and their horse at the same time. "I like this design," Catrin said, looking at a jacket of supple leather with reinforced rawhide patches on the elbows and shoulders, the inside lined with soft cloth. "Can you make the leggings to match this?"

"That I can. Just let me get you measured," the shopkeeper said as she retrieved a long piece of string. With deft and quick movements, she made small knots in the string after each measurement. "I can have those ready in ten or twelve days."

"I need them sooner," Catrin said. "Can you have them done in two days?"

"Impossible. I have work to finish for other customers, and I'd have to work day and night, even if I wasn't already behind. I'm sorry. No."

Catrin nodded and fingered her purse. Pulling out two gold coins, she placed them on the counter. "I need them in two days."

"Yes. Yes. Certainly, m'lady," the shopkeeper said, her eyes going wide. "I'll have them ready. Is there anything else you need?"

"Where might I find a cobbler?"

"My husband's the best in the land, m'lady. Let me get 'im for you," she said and disappeared into the back of the shop. A moment later, a bearded man appeared, looking half asleep, but his wife urged him from behind.

"Mala says you need shoes?"

"Boots. I need a pair of sturdy but comfortable boots. And I need them in two days."

"Can't be done," he said, but Mala cuffed him in the back of the head and whispered in his ear. "Two days, then," he said, rubbing his head. After he measured her feet in equally efficient fashion, Catrin handed him a gold coin.

"Two days."

* * *

"I wish you'd been less generous with the gold," Benjin said as they rode from town. "We're conspicuous enough as it is."

"We don't have time to wait. I did what I had to do."

"I know, li'l miss. I just have a bad feeling."

"Let's ride to the next town and see if we can find a cooperative food merchant," Catrin said, having bad feelings of her own.

As the sun set, Benjin began looking for suitable campsites, and eventually they settled beneath a grove of oaks. Compared to the chaos of the army encampments, the song of the tree frogs was like a lullaby, and Catrin slept better than she had in weeks.

* * *

In the light of Madra's fire, Chase wondered what would happen next. Here he sat in a strange land, far from his home, yet he found himself tied to these people by bonds of brotherhood and friendship. Their cause was not his, but he felt guilty knowing he would only leave them to their fates. In other circumstances, he would stay with them and help them reclaim their lives, but he knew he could not. It seemed hopeless.

The challenges ahead of Catrin seemed just as insurmountable, and he quailed in the face of them. Once he had felt strong, even powerful. In his sheltered world, back on the Godfist, he had always been certain he would succeed, but now his world seemed impossibly large and equally dangerous, which left him feeling insignificant and powerless. Thinking of his friends and family, he suddenly missed them more than he had ever thought possible. Across the fire, he noticed Madra watching him. Their eyes met, and he could not look away.

"You're a good boy," she said, and Chase could not hide his surprise. "When the gods first sent you to me, I thought you were just another test, but you've proven yourself to me. You're brave, honest, and hard working. No matter what path you choose, you've as good a chance as any to succeed."

Chase was dumbstruck. He'd never expected to hear such words from Madra. She'd always been gruff yet fair and harsh without being caustic. He'd always thought himself a burden to her and that his efforts had barely made his presence tolerable. Now, looking in her eyes, he saw something entirely different. The rough exterior had been hiding what lay beneath, and through the cracks that she allowed to show, she revealed a bit of herself to him.

"You remind me of my youngest, Medrin. He's a good boy too," she said and her voice cracked.

Chase moved closer and squeezed her hand. "You'll get them back," he said. In the next moment, his perceptions of the world changed once again as one of the strongest people he'd ever met laid her head on his shoulder and cried.

* * *

The sun brought a cheerful summer day to life, and it seemed to

Catrin almost as if everything were right in the world. Honey farms and wheat fields dotted the countryside, and soon a larger town came into view. The streets were congested with merchants and beggars alike, both ready to part the unwary from their coin.

Benjin kept to the main thoroughfare and dismounted only when they reached the market proper. Here, guards patrolled and no beggars could be seen. Despite the added measure of safety they brought, Catrin feared the sight of them. Benjin tied their mount to a post in front of a place that sold wagons, not far from a shop that smelled of baking bread.

"Let me have the gold. I'll do the talking," Benjin said, and Catrin handed him the purse. "Good day to you, sir," he said to the wagon merchant.

"That it is," the man replied as Benjin wandered around the lot, inspecting the available wagons. "What can I help you find?"

"I'm not certain I see anything that would suit my needs."

"Most of the good ones have gone, and no new ones are being built, friend. You won't find a better selection in all the Greatland during these trying times. Perhaps this fine, single-horse cart would make your burdens lighter?"

"How much?"

"Four silvers."

"Two," Benjin countered.

"Three."

"Three and you include the harness."

"Deal."

Catrin was amazed at how quickly the deal was made. And she saw a look of suspicion cross the merchant's face as Benjin handed him a gold coin, not having anything smaller. The merchant handed Benjin his change in silvers as if each one were an insult. Benjin apologized and slipped the man another silver for his trouble. This brightened the man's expression considerably, but Catrin still sensed distrust.

After unsaddling their mount, Benjin put the harness on him and hooked it to the wagon. When he was done putting the saddle in the wagon, he walked to the baker's shop. Inside, all manner of bread, cake, and biscuit were on display, and bakers were busy taking fresh loaves from massive stone ovens.

"Greetings, friends. What can Amul do for you today?" asked a rotund and flour-covered man from behind the counter.

"I need as many loaves of bread and hard biscuits as you can sell me."

"Well, I certainly couldn't sell you everything since I've my regular customers to think of, and that would take a lot of coin, friend. Have you an army to feed?" the baker asked with a hint of his own suspicion.

"Sometimes it seems that way, friend Amul, but no. How much can you spare?" Benjin asked, and the baker visibly appraised Benjin and Catrin.

"Twenty loaves of bread and twice as many biscuits," the baker said after a moment's contemplation. Benjin paid him handsomely, and they loaded their wagon with haste.

Their purchases were starting to draw attention, and they rushed to escape the scrutiny. Before they left town, though, Benjin made a hurried bargain with a meat merchant, who sold them ten cured hams, and a blacksmith, who sold them a gross of horseshoes and nails. They had spent most of the gold Millie had given Catrin, but she was happy with what they had been able to get.

Fearing they would be followed, Catrin spent most of the ride looking over her shoulder, but no one came. Pulling the wagon was slower than riding, and their horse occasionally struggled with the additional weight, but it was overall a pleasant way to travel. When night arrived, they made camp in a grassy clearing, tied the gelding off to a nearby tree, and took turns sleeping under the stars.

* * *

Watching the night sky, Nat considered his fortune. He'd wasted a lifetime on the Godfist, fighting the preconceived notions of others, always having to prove himself sane. Now, after coming to the Falcon Isles, he found himself transformed from madman to teacher, pariah to mentor, outcast to leader.

The Gunata tribe had been wary of him at first, probably due to bad experiences with others of fewer morals than he. They were a primitive tribe that only in recent decades had come into contact with civilized people. *Civilized*--the word rang falsely in Nat's mind. Civilized: to be civil, benevolent. The term seemed more fitting to describe the unsophisticated Gunata than anyone from the Godfist or the Greatland.

The Gunata did not seem to judge one another or cast aspersions. They lived a simple existence where the tribe mattered more than any individual, yet every person was valued. Nat found it truly refreshing. Still, he had tried to avoid developing feelings for Neenya, but it was a battle he lost. As he had learned bits of her language, and she his, they had become closer, speaking a language only they understood.

During his trips to the mountain, Neenya was always by his side, helping and protecting him. When she told the Gunata of his visions, the elders seemed relieved, as if Nat were filling some crucial role. Nat wasn't certain he understood their reasoning, but they had taken him in, and they treated him as an elder. When Neenya offered herself to him as a wife, the elders approved. Despite the warnings in his head, Nat could not resist.

With the full moon at its zenith, Nat and Neenya stood before the elders.

"Zagut," Chief Umitiri said, and Nat knew that was his signal to kneel. Neenya knelt at his side, her hand in his. Each elder came to them and kissed each of them on the forehead. Chief Umitiri came last. He grasped Nat's head between his thick-fingered hands and looked Nat in the eye. When he kissed Nat's forehead, it felt like a hammer blow, and Nat was thrust into a violent fit as visions overtook him-- visions of Catrin standing before a charging bull with hooves of fire.

Chapter 4

In times of rapid change, those who do not adapt, perish.
--Emrold Barnes, historian

* * *

As Catrin approached the leather shop, staying hidden in the shadows, the hair on the back of her neck stood, and a bead of sweat slid down her face. Instincts warned of a trap. Trying to decide if she could trust Mala, she looked at her tattered garments and decided to take the risk. Benjin waited outside town with the wagon, and if she did not return soon, he would come looking for her.

With a deep breath, she entered, and Mala gave a start, her eyes flitting to the back of the shop. "Welcome, m'lady," she said loudly. "I'm just putting a few stitches in the last pair of leggings. Only a moment I'll be. You can try those on for size while you wait."

Catrin pulled the jacket on, and it was a good fit. From the corner of her vision, she saw a figure dart out the back of the shop--the cobbler, she presumed. The boots were ready for her on the counter, and she quickly put them on. The fit was remarkably good, and she complimented his work.

"The man has a gift," Mala said without a hint of a smile, and again she glanced at the back of the shop.

"I cannot wait any longer. I must be going. I'll take those as they are," Catrin said, and she jumped as the cobbler returned. The shopkeeper just continued to sew. The two exchanged a glance, and Catrin nearly bolted.

"Ah, yes. 'Boots. Two days.' I see you've tried 'em on. How do they fit?" the cobbler asked.

"They fit just fine. Thank you. I really must be going now. You can keep that pair if they are not yet finished," Catrin said, grabbing what was ready and turning to leave.

"No. That won't do. Here. These are finished now," the woman said, and she gave Catrin a sack to carry everything in. Catrin thanked her as she backed toward the door. Though there was no visible sign of danger, she ran all the way back to where Benjin waited.

"I'm not certain, but I think someone is coming after us."

"Let's go," Benjin said, and they were soon moving as fast as they could, given their burdens. Heading north and west, they hoped to intercept Madra, but as the sun was sinking low on the horizon, there was no sign of the army.

With a growing gap between themselves and town, Catrin began to feel safer, but she did not relax completely. The snap of a branch in the distance brought her to full attention, and she scanned the nearby trees. Nothing moved.

"I'll watch what lies ahead," Benjin said. "You keep your eyes on the road behind us and the trees. If we're attacked, let the horse go and follow me to the trees. Got it?"

"Got it," she replied, holding on as he urged their horse for more speed.

Just as shadows covered the land, they came, swift as the wind, as if sprung from the abyss. One moment Catrin was watching the trees, the next she was ducking under a whistling blade. Benjin was not as quick, and he cried out. Two shadowy silhouettes passed them and spun around, preparing to make another charge. Catrin quickly turned to Benjin. He was holding his side, and there was blood on his shirt, but his other hand was steady and gripping a sword. He made no move toward the trees. Wishing she'd brought her staff, Catrin opened herself to the power and prepared to fight.

When the riders approached again, Catrin was ready. Using all her senses, she cast out about her, searching for energy sources. The air was filled with raw energy, but most of it was disorganized; positively charged particles simply canceled out nearby negatively charged particles. Catrin knew, though, that she could extend her field of influence and gather like particles to build up a massive charge. Then, just as she could blow out a candle by expelling air from her lungs, she could use the air to conduct her gathered charge. With her hands held high, she hurtled a bolt of energy at one rider. Like lightning, it arced from her fingers and struck with a crack. The charging horse leaped sideways, crashing into Catrin and knocking her from the cart. She hit the ground only a breath before her attacker. He remained mostly still, his leather armor blistered and smoking.

As she pulled herself up, she heard Benjin grunt as he, too, was thrown from the cart. The man she'd unhorsed was getting up, and her use of power had left her trembling. Unsure if she could deliver another blow without passing out, she ran toward him and, doing as she'd seen Benjin teach Chase, delivered a powerful kick to the startled man's jaw. His head jerked sideways, and he crumpled to the ground.

Behind her, Catrin heard hooves approaching at high speed, and she turned to see the other rider bearing back down on Benjin. After dropping his sword, Benjin drew his belt knife and threw. It sailed, end over end, and the handle struck the rider in the face with a solid *thunk*. Benjin unhorsed him as he passed, and he hit the ground with a thud and a sickening crunch. He was dead when Catrin and Benjin reached him. Catrin's kick had left the other man unconscious and bleeding.

"How badly are you hurt?" Catrin asked.

"He nicked me a couple of times, but I'll be fine. I just have to keep my right arm down to stop the bleeding. Can you catch the horses?"

"I think so," Catrin said, her legs still trembling. "What do we do with him?"

"Leave him," Benjin said, wincing. "Catch the horses and get me to the camp. I need stitches, and I can't do this one myself."

The three horses were surprisingly easy to catch, and the two the men had been riding--both fillies--seemed very familiar with one another, giving Catrin no trouble. After tying them to a tree, she gathered what had fallen from the wagon and reloaded it; then she helped Benjin into the seat. With his free hand, he held a lead line that Catrin hooked to the fillies' halters, and Catrin drove the wagon, trying to avoid the many ruts and obstacles along the way.

Eventually, the light of the campfires led them to the army, and they were greeted by the sentries' swords.

"Hold!"

"It's Benjin and Catrin returned and wounded," Benjin barked, and a host of people rushed to assist them. Madra insisted on stitching Benjin's side herself, saying it was worse than he'd made it out to be. Meanwhile, Catrin told their tale to the crowd of expectant faces around her.

The addition of two fine horses to their stock and the wagon full of food were received with wonder, and this act seemed to finally break down the barrier of fear between these people and Catrin. Those who had shied away from her glance some weeks ago now gathered around her.

* * *

"This is taking too long," Jensen said as he watched the second new building take shape. "Half of us are going to freeze t'death if we don't do something."

"That's exactly what the Masters are hoping for, I think," Wendel said. Still weak from his wounds, he was overwhelmed by frustration. If he were fit to walk, he would have already found the underground lake. Now he had to look to Jensen and the others to do most everything for him. He felt of no use at all.

The men from the Greatland proved to be quite skilled; Martik, in particular, had an excellent mind for practical building techniques. His skills were useless, though, without materials. Wendel and many others despised the idea of clear-cutting forestlands; they were simply too precious. Individual trees were being selected and cut down in a way that left the forest intact, but the process consumed equally precious time.

"We may be able to use rock," Martik said.

"Might be able to quarry it," Jensen said, "but moving it'll be tough."

"We have seven horses?" Martik asked.

"Six that are sound," Wendel said.

"I have some ideas about ways to move very heavy things," Martik said. "I could get the rock moved. Perhaps we should settle near a good quarry site?"

"How much weight do you reckon you could move?" Wendel asked.

"With six horses and ten men, I could drag a warship up here."

"Come with me," Wendel said. "I have an idea."

* * *

As dawn cast long shadows across the camp, most were just rising, but the sound of pounding hooves brought many to attention. Madra and another rider had been out scouting, and they were racing back. A crowd gathered, and people scrambled to secure Madra's mount as she dismounted before the filly even stopped.

"Mounted troops coming. Northeast. Prepare yourselves," Madra said, and her words spawned a flurry of activity. What had been a sluggish and awakening camp turned to a determined rush. "They looked like the Kytes' men, but I'm not certain."

Not long after, fifty mounted men poured onto the field at a leisurely pace. At their head rode the youngest grandson of Arbuckle Kyte, Catrin's betrothed, and she still didn't know his name. Millie was not far away, and Catrin went to her side. "What's his name?" she whispered into the suspense-filled air.

"You don't know his name? Shame on me. Shame on you. His name is Jharmin Olif Kyte, and he doesn't look happy."

Catrin turned back to him, and when he saw her, a nimbus of power appeared around him, outlining his form in undulating waves of light, like flames. Madra came to Catrin. "We must go meet with him."

"Perhaps it would be better if you went alone," Catrin replied. "He's not fond of me."

"Be that as it may, you must come, unarmed. He knows you're here, and he'll undoubtedly demand an audience with you."

Leaving her staff and knife with Benjin, Catrin walked beside Madra, a sour feeling in her stomach. All the mounted men behind Jharmin were intimidating, but it was Jharmin who posed the greatest threat, despite the fact that he, too, was unarmed. The skin on Catrin's throat itched, as if remembering his fiery touch.

"I had reports of an army on my lands, and now I find the Herald Witch leading a travesty that soils our fields. What makes you think you can cross Lankland without my permission?"

Despite his insults, Catrin chose to remain cordial. "I don't lead this army, and they do not follow me. Our paths are merely the same at the moment."

Jharmin made a noise in his throat and rolled his eyes. "So who *does* lead this mockery of an army?"

"I do. I am Madra of Far Rossing, one of your *former* subjects," Madra said without a hint of courtesy.

"Former?"

"Quite. At one time, your family protected the land and our people, but then you surrendered to the Zjhon. You've been little more than puppets since."

"How dare you speak to me that way, peasant! I should send you back to the hovel you came from," he said, the nimbus around him expanding.

"Please," Catrin said. "There has been enough bloodshed. Now is not the time for fighting. What this land needs is peace and leadership so that it can be rebuilt. A battle today will do nothing but reduce the number of able-bodied people available to do that rebuilding. Would you send your homeland into ruin?"

"Silence, witch. Your evil tongue cannot poison our minds."

"You call her a witch, yet if it were not for her, you would be dead," Madra said.

"Lies and tricks. The Herald Witch makes people believe she's come to save them when all she's done is kill the good people of the Greatland. I don't know exactly how she caused the other statue to explode, but I was in no more danger within Adderhold than I am right now," Jharmin said, looking smug.

"You're an arrogant fool," Madra said as she turned to walk away.

"I want you off my lands by nightfall, and you're never to return-- any of you," Jharmin said, his face growing redder as the conflict wore on.

"You'll have to kill us all, then," Madra said. "You can kill your own subjects. I won't stop you. I can only imagine, though, how all those young people in the Zjhon armies will feel when they find out you killed their parents and children."

"Don't mock me, woman. I'm the protector of my people. It is you that poses a threat, and it's my responsibility to protect Lankland from *you*."

Madra tilted her head back and laughed a harsh, barking laugh. "Kill us, and there'll be fewer left to protect, m'lord. But have it your way. My army goes where I lead it, and I'll leave your lands when I am good and ready. If you wish to fight, then let us be done with it and fight now. What do you say?"

"I say you travel with the Herald Witch, and that makes you my enemy."

"What did I ever do to you?" Catrin asked, no longer able to contain her anger.

"Beside the fact that your family has been killing my family and people for over a hundred years? How about pretending you would marry me just so you could attack Archmaster Belegra."

"I went to Adderhold willing to marry you if that was what it took to save people's lives. You can believe what you want about me and about the statues; I'll not try to change your mind. But do remember that your family has been killing my family for just as long. I know since you killed my mother and both my aunts in a most cowardly fashion," Catrin said, becoming more incensed with each word.

Jharmin appeared genuinely surprised by the accusations and simply stood with his mouth open for a moment. "I don't know what you are talking about."

"That's just how his grandfather wants it," Madra said.

"Silence!" Jharmin said, glaring.

"Jharmin, please," Catrin said, trying desperately to avoid violence. "If you say you knew nothing of their deaths, then I believe you, but you must also understand that I've had no knowledge or involvement in what my family has done here in the Greatland. I grew up on the Godfist. This is all new to me, and I don't know how to fix it, but I'm certain fighting isn't the answer."

Jharmin stood silent, apparently considering her words, but just when he was about to speak, there was a shout from his men. Catrin turned to look where a man pointed. Above the rolling hills, a waving pennant rose, showing Istra and Vestra in their immortal embrace. Soon the standard bearer then the body of the Zjhon army came into view. Row upon row of mounted riders approached, followed by orderly columns of foot soldiers. In the distance the supply wagons were barely visible.

Catrin and Madra looked at Jharmin. "You two had best go prepare yourselves," he said; then he went back to his men.

"What are we going to do?" Catrin asked as she and Madra walked back to camp and the awaiting sea of worried faces. Only the underlying determination on those faces kept Catrin from despairing. These people would die fighting if they had to. Catrin hoped it didn't come to that.

"This is what we came for," Madra said. "Although having the Kytes here makes things more interesting, we'll do what must be done," she said, and she turned to her soldiers. "Stand at attention. Show no fear. If I say attack, attack, but until then, do *nothing.*"

The next few moments passed slowly, like the mire of dreams, and Catrin watched events unfold with detached indifference, as if it were not real. It was too strange to be real. She and Madra walked together but apart, Jharmin came from another direction, and a swaggering, older man came from yet another. "State your intentions," he said, his arms crossed over his chest.

"Jharmin Kyte, grandson of Arbuckle--"

"I know who you are. State your intentions."

Jharmin looked shaken, and Catrin was amazed no one else could see the flames that leaped higher around him as his fury grew, but it was obvious they could not.

"I came to investigate reports of an army on my lands," Jharmin said, "and a report that two local guards had been killed," he said, glaring at Catrin. She considered responding but decided to keep her mouth shut.

"I have orders to bring in the Herald Witch," the man said. "We have no need for your services. You're dismissed."

Jharmin's flames soared and danced around him, and his face flushed. "I must insist that you not do battle on these lands. I will remain to see that the people of Lankland are not made to suffer."

"So be it, pup. Stay if you want, but stay out of my way or you might accidentally fall on my sword." Not waiting for a response, he turned to Catrin. "*You* will surrender immediately, otherwise we'll kill you all. *You*," he said, turning to Madra, "will go away."

Madra wasn't looking at him, though, and she did not react to his statement. Instead, she scanned the Zjhon lines. Suddenly she gave a start. "Medrin, Chelby, attend me!" she shouted across the distance. The Zjhon commander turned slowly, and he flushed as two horses separated from his lines.

"Shoot anyone that deserts!" the commander shouted. The two riders continued forward, and Catrin gasped at the twang of a bowstring. One rider ducked under the arrow, and a scuffle broke out in the Zjhon lines. One of the men in Jharmin's army stepped forward and called out another name then another. Behind Catrin, men and women called to their children.

Soon nothing could be heard over the din. More and more riders and those on foot began to leave the Zjhon lines, their loyalty to their families far stronger than their fear of death. The Zjhon commander, who'd not even been courteous enough to give his name, now found himself faced with a flood of defectors. Those still loyal fought to join together and rally, but that number was shrinking rapidly. When the dust settled, Madra's army was by far the largest, with Jharmin's not far behind. The Zjhon commander suddenly found himself faced with superior force.

Jharmin made no move and said nothing; he just stood with his arms crossed over his chest and stared at the Zjhon commander. Catrin knew the danger was not yet averted. A battle between Jharmin's and Madra's armies would lead to horrific casualties, and she had not yet counted the Zjhon out of the equation. When she made up her mind, she could only hope that her actions would not lead to a bloodbath.

Chapter 5

To forget the past is to jeopardize the future.
--Meriaca Jocephus, historian

* * *

"Samda!" Catrin shouted, and everyone turned toward Madra's army, which now looked like a real army. "Approach!"

Samda came swiftly, but his measured stride spoke of confidence. "Lady Catrin," he said when he arrived.

"Traitor," the Zjhon commander spit. Jharmin stared at Samda with distrust.

"I am a traitor to a failed faith. We were wrong, Grevan. Archmaster Belegra is wrong."

"Bah! Lies," Grevan said.

"She has coerced him. He can't be trusted," Jharmin added.

"Mind yourself," Samda said. "Do not forget who presided over your right-to-inherit confirmation." Jharmin flushed and looked at the ground. "And you, Grevan. Who was it that granted you the crest and mark?"

"You'll not intimidate me," Grevan said. "You may have granted me the crest and mark, but it was by Archmaster Belegra's authority. I could execute you now for treason. The Herald Witch will come with me."

"Yes. Yes," Samda said. "You have your orders, Mark Grevan. You can execute me now and take the Herald Witch into custody. What is there to hinder you?" Samda asked with a feral smile. "I can still smell the burning flesh of the last men who attacked her."

"If you feel it is right to follow Archmaster Belegra," Madra said, "then I suggest you follow him into whatever hole he's chosen to hide in."

A tense silence hung in the air. Mark Grevan made no move. "What of you, Jharmin? Where do you stand?"

Jharmin took a moment to consider before he replied. Looking each of the assembled in the eye, he seemed to struggle. "I stand with the people of Lankland," he finally said, "and I believe they have just spoken. You are to remove yourself from my lands and never return."

Mark Grevan said no more. Turning on his heel, he strode away. When he reached what remained of his army, he gave no orders. Instead he mounted, wheeled his horse, and rode back the way he had come. A handful of men followed him, but more chose to go their own way, and they scattered, some alone, some in small bands.

"There will be more," Samda said. "That was but a fraction of the Zjhon's number."

"Thank you, Samda," Catrin said, and Samda bowed before returning to Madra's army. "So, Jharmin, what will it be? Shall we rip each other to ribbons? Or will we rise above this cursed feud?"

It took a moment for Jharmin to respond. The mantle of flames that only Catrin's eyes seemed to be able to perceive dwindled as he seemed to find his calm. When he spoke, his voice conveyed more sadness than anger. "I agree the feud between our families has brought no good to our peoples or us. I declare no peace with you, though, for I've no authority to do so. I will, however, grant you passage across my lands."

"I'll no longer be traveling with Madra and her army, will you grant them passage as well?"

"Madra and her army represent the people of Lankland. I'll not stand in the way of their revenge on the Zjhon. My men will escort them wherever it is they wish to go, and I will escort you personally from my lands."

"Are we in agreement?" Catrin asked, looking at Madra.

"We are," she said.

"We are," Jharmin added.

"Then let it be so," Catrin said. "I must make the arrangements for my party's departure. Lord Kyte, if you would excuse me."

"I'll await you on the hill," he said as he turned to walk away. Catrin and Madra walked back to the waiting army.

"I can now provide horses for you and your companions, so you can ride to Ravenhold," Madra said. "I have my children back, but there are many more sons and daughters out there. This army will go on until all those that live have been returned to their families."

"I wish you blessings and the speed of the gods on your quest, Madra, and I thank you for your generosity. You are a great hero."

When Madra laughed, the humor reached her eyes. She smiled and shook her head. "Look at us. Two great heroes, neither willing to admit it."

* * *

"I insist we stop in the very next town and procure a carriage or a wagon," Millie said. "I'm not built for horseback." Her complaining had started the instant she was told she would ride, and since then it had only grown worse.

Morif rode alongside Catrin and kept his voice low. "If you make her ride all the way to Ravenhold, she'll waddle like a duck for the next moon." Millie shot him a narrow-eyed glance, and he pulled back, chuckling.

"As soon as we can, Millie. As soon as we can," Catrin said, trying not to smile. In truth, much of the terrain they had to cover was not fit for a carriage and would make for a rough wagon ride, but Catrin hoped, for Millie's sake, that they could soon travel by road.

Jharmin and his squad of guards rode at a distance, camping within sight but out of earshot. When they came to a large town, Jharmin rode out to meet Catrin. "On the other side of Mickenton, we can pick up the trade road. I will get us passage down the main thoroughfare, and I don't want anyone wandering off."

"There're things we need from the market," Catrin said.

Jharmin frowned. "What do you need?"

"A carriage and harness."

"I'll have one of my men purchase it for you and deliver it tonight. You may camp here," he said and rode away.

"You'll have your carriage this night," Catrin said to Millie when she returned. "We'll make camp here, and tomorrow we'll be escorted through Mickenton. From there, we travel by road." Her statement brought about many smiles and sighs of relief, not to mention a chuckle from Morif. Millie turned her nose up and walked away.

Jharmin was true to his word, and two of his guards arrived, one with a fine carriage, the other on horseback, carrying an extra saddle. After unhooking his mount, the guard cleaned everything meticulously, and he presented the harness and carriage to Catrin. "Lord Jharmin sends this as a gift."

"Please tell Lord Jharmin that his gift is appreciated," Catrin said. "But I can pay for the carriage."

"I assure you there is no need, m'lady. Lord Jharmin was quite clear on this."

"Thank you, sir."

The guard nodded a stiff bow then returned to his companion, who was tightening saddle straps. As they rode away, Catrin pondered the meaning of Jharmin's gift. She supposed it would be worth it to him if it helped to speed their journey off his lands.

Beyond Mickenton, travel became easier. The trade road was wide and level, and there were many inns along the way. Somehow, Jharmin got word ahead of them, and each night they would come to an empty inn, waiting for them alone. Again, Catrin wondered if this generosity was more insult than gift. If he wanted to keep her company isolated from his people, so be it.

"The day I leave the Greatland will be a joyous day," she said to Benjin one afternoon.

"I understand," he said. "I had hoped never to return, and I'll be happy to leave it behind as well. Under other circumstances, I would say there is great beauty here, but when I look around, I see only conflict and misery, and I tire of it."

By the time they reached the border of Mundleboro, the tension was unbearable. When a rider wearing the Kyte family sigil, the head of a bull, came at speed, everyone in both camps waited expectantly. The foamy sweat around the girth of his saddle spoke of a hard ride, and Catrin feared bad news. She watched, holding her breath, as he dismounted and reported to Jharmin. The change in Jharmin's posture was enough to confirm Catrin's fears; his shoulders slumped, and his head dropped forward. Even from a distance, Catrin could feel his pain.

Moments later one of Jharmin's guards approached. "Lord Arbuckle Kyte has succumbed to age," he said. "Lord Jharmin asks that you leave Lankland on the morrow. He is needed at Wolfhold and will leave this night. Two guards will be left to assure your safe passage back to Mundleboro."

Pain seared Catrin's heart. Compassion for Jharmin overwhelmed her. "Does Jharmin's father live?" Catrin asked Millie.

"No," she said. "He died many years ago in a hunting accident."

"Did my family have anything to do with that *accident?*"

"No. I don't believe so. Your grandfather had his grandfather killed, and then Jharmin's father killed your grandfather. To my knowledge, that was the last killing your family committed."

Catrin was shamed by the tale, and she vowed to put an end to the killing. With her head bowed, she walked toward Jharmin's camp. He was nowhere in sight, but she moved with purpose and intent.

"Hold," a guard said as she neared.

"I request an audience with Lord Kyte."

"A moment, m'lady."

Jharmin emerged from his tent, his eyes red and swollen. "Say what you have to say."

"I came to express my sincere condolences."

His head snapped toward her, and his face flushed, but then he seemed to sense her sincerity. "Thank you for your concern. I doubt your grandmother will feel the same."

"Jharmin," Catrin said, taking his hand in hers. She was surprised when he didn't pull away. "Our families have been horrible to each other, but the time has come to heal this age-old wound. No more can we afford petty squabbles. Let our generation be the one that puts things to right."

Jharmin pulled his hand free slowly and walked toward the horse lines. He walked to his horse, which was kept separate from all the rest, and ran his hands over the glossy coat.

Catrin moved with him, and she scratched at the base of the horse's mane. The colt stretched out his neck and groaned, wiggling his top lip back and forth.

"You know animals," Jharmin said, and Catrin nodded. "Then you understand that it can be difficult to undo a lifetime of training."

"I understand, but I also know our families stand to lose everything in the coming months. I may have grown up on the Godfist, but I really do have the best interest of the Greatland in my heart."

"Go back to your camp," he said with a long sigh. "I'll send word that I will be delayed, and I'll travel to Ravenhold with you. We'll finish this feud one way or another."

His words were clearly a dismissal, but Catrin felt there was a victory in them, a victory for the people of the Greatland.

Millie and Morif left in the carriage with the dawn, hoping to give the Lady Mangst time to prepare for guests. Catrin could only hope her grandmother would understand.

* * *

"Enjoying the wine, Beron?" Master Edling asked.

"Yes," Master Beron replied. "It's quite good."

"And the ham? It's to your liking?"

"Indeed."

"Then you'd best listen to me," Master Edling said. "If Wendel Volker and his Greatlanders have their way, our days of ruling here are over. Gone will be the days of fine eating and drinking. Can you picture yourself working the fields or gutting fish?"

"You've made your point. What is it you want?"

Master Edling smiled. With Beron on his side, he was closer to having a majority vote on the council. Endless deliberation and inconsistent alliances had already proven costly. If he'd had his way, Wendel Volker would already be dead, but others hadn't seen it that way, and his use of Premon Dalls had lost him favor. That would all end now. He was one step closer to regaining his power.

"I want you to talk to Jarvis and Humbry. See if you can get them to listen to reason."

Master Beron snorted. "You expect them to listen to me? They don't trust either of us, and they are terrified the Herald will return."

"I'll attend to the Volker girl. You talk to Jarvis and Humbry. I don't care what they believe; I expect you to convince them. Understand?"

"I understand."

* * *

Trying to think of what to say to her grandmother, Catrin clenched her jaw. While she hoped this day would be a new day for Lankland and Mundleboro alike, she knew it had the potential for disaster and ruin, and she could only pray those involved would recognize the uselessness of continued fighting.

Jharmin and his men broke camp and waited for Catrin and her party in a meadow. His guards unfurled his standard, and Catrin got a chill thinking about riding into Ravenhold under the Kyte sigil.

"Your mother would be proud," Benjin said as he helped load her packs and secure them behind her saddle.

"I'm doing my best, but I fear it won't be enough. The hatred between the Mangst and Kyte families has lasted for ages, how can I hope to undo it in a day?"

"You can't," Benjin said. "But you can take the first step. That's often the most difficult one. From there, momentum will carry you along."

In her new clothes, Catrin felt even more out of place. She had hoped to present an imposing image, but she feared she only made herself stand out. The leggings were comfortable but still needed to be broken in. Tossing her leg over her mount proved more difficult than she anticipated, and she suffered the embarrassment of having to try three times before she gained the saddle. With her staff resting in the heel Benjin attached to her stirrup, she rode comfortably.

No one spoke as they approached Ravenhold, but the view of her ancestral home was awe inspiring. Jharmin's face bore no expression, but Chase was clearly stunned by what he saw. He'd seen buildings that physically dominated the land, but Ravenhold seemed to be part of the surroundings, and the landscaping lent to the effect.

Lining the roadway that led to the imposing main entrance, guards stood at attention. Still as stones, they kept their eyes straight ahead, seemingly focused on nothing. Unnerved by the effect, Catrin would almost have preferred leers and catcalls. Atop the central stair, the Lady Mangst emerged, followed by a slip of a girl with fire in her eyes. In the moment Catrin saw her, she resented anyone who had said they looked alike. Lissa had a hard and self-righteous air about her, and the slanted sneer on her face appeared all too natural. Catrin's gut twisted when their eyes met; fury seared the air between them. Her grandmother stood serene and patient, apparently oblivious to the open hostility

Lissa radiated.

Jharmin approached with his head high and his chest puffed out, but he managed not to look pompous or arrogant. It was a skill Catrin had to admire. He bowed to the Lady Mangst and Lissa. Catrin bowed as well, and Lissa's fury polluted the air; it washed over Catrin in waves as she straightened, and she tried not to snarl. So much raw emotion was difficult to suppress.

"Lord Kyte," the Lady Mangst said formally. "You are welcome in my home. I am grieved to hear of your grandfather's passing. You have my most sincere condolences."

In Jharmin's eyes and the heady mixture of emotions radiating from him, Catrin sensed a struggle. She assumed he was trying not to let his distrust of the Mangst name despoil this opportunity.

"Lady Mangst, I humbly accept your hospitality and your sentiment," Jharmin said, and he seemed almost sincere.

"Come. Let us feast."

Catrin walked alongside Jharmin. "Thank you," she said.

"It is not for you that I do this," he replied.

"Whatever the reason, I thank you," she said, and though he made no response, she sensed his guard drop just for a moment. It was a short walk to the banquet hall, and Catrin was amazed by what had been done in such a short time. Arrangements of fresh flowers adorned each table, and liveried servants stood ready with covered trays. Lissa was seated to her grandmother's right, and Jharmin sat to her left. Catrin took the seat next to him, and felt, once again, like an outsider within Ravenhold.

"It has been many years since this house hosted a member of the Kyte family," said the Lady Mangst. "It has been far too long. I welcome you, Jharmin Olif Kyte, and I thank you for the kindness you've shown my granddaughter." Catrin felt Lissa's glare. "You have shown great courage and humility in coming here. I commend you."

"I've postponed my journey home so that we might discuss the future. As Catrin has said, the time for fighting is past."

"Agreed."

"How, Lady Mangst, would you suggest we resolve the differences between our families?"

"Perhaps the Zjhon were right about one thing," the Lady Mangst replied. "Perhaps a marriage between our families is for the best." Lissa's face flushed, and she glared at anyone who met her gaze. "My granddaughter Lissa has reconsidered her refusal to marry. When it was the will of the Zjhon, she found this difficult to accept. Now she sees that it is simply the best thing for our people."

Lissa showed no enthusiasm for the prospect, but she did not voice any objections.

"Ah. So that is why you sent Catrin in her stead?"

"It is."

"Lady Lissa, I've not heard you say this is what you desire. Do you wish to see this marriage through?" he asked, and the Lady Mangst nodded to Lissa.

"Lord Kyte, it would be an honor to join your house," Lissa replied formally.

"I suppose you have no reason to desire me as a husband, but a bitter marriage is not something I seek. If you will not come to me of your own free will, then I suggest we look for some other way to resolve this conflict. Perhaps Catrin would have less aversion to marrying me?"

Catrin opened her mouth, but she could find no words. Lissa, though, did not give her the opportunity. "Forgive me, Lord Kyte. It has been a trying time."

"I understand, Lady Lissa. Catrin tells me you believe my family was responsible for the death of your mother. I cannot guarantee that my family was not involved, but I can tell you that I had no knowledge of such cowardly acts. On behalf of my family, I apologize. I realize this may not mean much to one who had to grow up without a mother, but it is the best I can offer at this time. Perhaps, if you would allow me, I can do more over time."

Lissa was bereft of words.

"Our family owes you apologies as well," said the Lady Mangst. "We've not been innocent of senseless and cowardly deeds. I can assure you that Lissa and Catrin had no knowledge of these doings. I take responsibility for the actions of my late husband and his father. I know they did not treat your family well."

"All this suffering over a feud whose origins are long since forgotten," Jharmin said, shaking his head.

"Not completely forgotten," said the Lady Mangst. "It was the death of your great-great-great-grandmother that started the feud. She was riding with Catrin's great-great-great-grandfather when she was thrown from her horse. She landed on an outcropping of jagged shale, and a sharp edge slit her throat. His explanations were never accepted, and so began the senseless acts of violence. Perhaps now we can leave it in the past."

"Can we do this, Lady Lissa? Will you join with me to right the wrongs of our forefathers?"

A long moment of silence hung between them, but then Lissa drew a deep breath. "Yes, Lord Kyte. I will."

Chapter 6

Beneath the waves exists a bizarre world, full of life.
--Gorksi Veraga, fisherman

* * *

Departure from Ravenhold was bittersweet for Catrin. Despite meeting under less than friendly circumstances, Millie and Morif had been loyal companions, and they had saved her life more than once. Millie dabbed tears from the corners of her eyes as Catrin's party prepared to depart for Ohmahold. Just before Catrin mounted, Millie discreetly pressed a fat purse into her hands. "It's yours, m'lady. May it lessen the burdens of your journey."

"Thank you, Millie. You are a good friend. I'll never forget you."

"You will come back and visit. I insist. If not for me, for your grandmother."

"I make no promises, but I assure you I will try," Catrin said. Lissa avoided her as best she could, but Catrin pulled her aside. "I know you don't like me, but I hope you'll find it in your heart to forgive me. You're my cousin, and I don't want bad feelings between us. Even if you disagree with my actions, or I disagree with yours, we are family."

"You need not remind me of the blood that bonds us. I've spent my life trying to protect the people of Mundleboro, and you walk in as if these lands are rightfully yours. Where were you during the droughts . . . or during the Zjhon invasion? You've no idea what our people have been through, and you had no right to take my place. Go back to your homeland and never return," Lissa said, and she walked away.

"She'll come to understand over time," Jharmin said, seemingly embarrassed by Lissa's behavior.

Catrin's grandmother trembled as she embraced Catrin, and she whispered in her ear. "I am so very proud of you. You deserve the Mangst name more than any of us, and I thank you for what you've done. Come back to us. You'll always have a home here."

"Thank you, Grandma."

As the sun reached its zenith, Benjin mounted and called for the rest to do the same. Samda climbed awkwardly atop his mount with Chase's help, and Catrin cast one final glance at her ancestral home, not knowing if she would ever see it again. In her pocket was a rolled parchment, a writ of passage bearing her grandmother's seal impressed in wax. Within Mundleboro, at least, they would have no reason to fear the local authorities. In the lands beyond, however, the writ would be little more than a piece of parchment, a keepsake.

Following a familiar trail, they rode back toward Ohmahold. A creeping fear gripped Catrin when the toll bridge came into view. Beyond that bridge she no longer had the protection of her homeland. When they reached the top of the span, the toll collectors viewed them with suspicion, but one look at the writ of passage, and they were more than accommodating. The captain of the guard even offered to provide them with an escort through town.

"Thank you, friend," Benjin said. "But that won't be necessary. It's kind of you to offer, though."

When they passed the market, Catrin saw Yusef hawking his livestock, and she wondered what had come of Curly. It had been necessary to sell him, but still she felt guilty.

A few days later, they came to the farmstead where the Tillermans lived, and Catrin asked that they make camp on the outskirts. "There's someone here I need to speak with."

"Are you certain that's wise?" Benjin asked.

"Wise or not. I'm going."

"I'm coming with you."

They rode slowly, trying to not to alarm the locals. Those who saw them went indoors and closed up tight. When they reached the Tillerman farm, it was Jessub who saw them first. "Gramma, Grampa, Cannergy and Elma are back! Look at Elma's clothes and hair and--"

Collette appeared at the cottage door, and she pulled Jessub inside. Rolph emerged from the barn, and he drew a deep breath when he saw them. "I want no harm t'come to my family. If yer angry, punish me. Leave them out of it."

"Be at ease, Rolph. I've not come for revenge. I just had to know why," Catrin said, and Rolph looked relieved but tired. His shoulders seemed to sag under an enormous weight.

"I am sorry. I truly didn't mean ya harm, but I couldn't take Belegra's lies. I couldn't let 'im put other parents through what he put Mother 'n' me through. This came only days after ya left," he said, handing her a wrinkled and worn piece of parchment. On it was a badly faded message, but between the lines was a newer message, a message from Rolph's son Martik.

Father and Mother,

Artus and I are both in good health. I'm so sorry. I tried to keep Fenny safe, but he fell ill during the long voyage to the Godfist. He died before we got here.

The Herald of Istra gave us a choice between freedom and death, and we chose freedom. The Herald gave us time to get to land before she destroyed the Zjhon ships. She could have killed us all but didn't. Her father has granted amnesty to all those who defected, even when his own government would not. Wendel Volker is a good and just man, and I suspect his daughter is no different. She has left the Godfist and is presumed to be traveling to the Greatland. Her name is Catrin Volker, and she is a granddaughter to the Lady Mangst.

Artus and I will come home to you when we can. Until then, know we are safe. Please tell Jessub I miss him, as does Uncle Artus.

All my love,
Martik

"Two o' my sons still live 'cause o' you. I owe ya a great debt. I know I've repaid that debt poorly, and I'm sorry fer that. Ya have my gratitude."

"You need not thank me," Catrin said. "I did what I did because it was the least horrible way I could find to save myself and my homeland. People died as a result of my actions, and that is something I will lament until the end of my days, but it is done. All I want now is for the people of the Greatland and the Godfist alike to be free and safe."

Rolph looked over Catrin's shoulder, and he motioned for Collette and Jessub to come out. "Everything's as it should be," he said as they approached.

"I told ya t'would be," Collette said with a smile. "That man nearly worried 'imself into a sickbed."

"Did ya really get married 'n' fight the Zjhon 'n' destroy the statue 'n'--"

"Jessub, hush," Collette said, but Catrin knelt down in front of the boy.

"I did some very scary and foolish things because I had little choice. I would much rather have spent my time on the farm."

"Not me! I'm gonna be an adventurer when I grow up, 'n' I'm gonna fight bandits 'n' find treasure. You'll see!" Jessub said; then he ran across the barnyard, fighting imaginary foes.

Collette looked at Catrin with tears in her eyes. "I knew I liked ya, soon as we met. I knew ya were a good girl. I can never thank ya enough for sparin' our sons and the other young men. They were only doin' what they were told, and they're such good boys. Ya saved 'em, and yer father's protectin' 'em. Ya'll always be welcome here."

"Thank you--both of you. I must go now. When you get news of my deeds, always know that I'm doing the best I can."

"May the gods bless ya!" Collette called as they rode away, and Catrin actually felt safer knowing she could always go to the Tillerman farm.

"Wait! Elma, *wait!*" Jessub called as they left, and Catrin turned her mount. "I made this for ya," he said, breathing hard.

Catrin opened the folded piece of parchment carefully, for it was worn and tattered around the edges. On it was a faded message, but painted over it in bold strokes was a striking image of a winged woman hovering over a man.

"That's you and my daddy," he said, and the sincerity in his big, brown eyes was like a knife into Catrin's soul.

Climbing down from her horse, she gave Jessub a hug and a kiss on the forehead. "You're a good boy, Jessub."

"Gramma said ya saved my daddy and Uncle Artus. I wish ya coulda saved Uncle Fenny too," he said.

"I'm sorry,"

"Ya did the best ya could," he said with a firm nod. "Good-bye, Elma. Good-bye, Cannergy."

"You did the best you could," Benjin echoed as they rode away.

Catrin tried to hide her tears.

* * *

Wendel watched in amazement as Martik orchestrated a monumental operation. Six horses, ropes, and a dozen men hauled on the massive section of greatoak. At first it had seemed like sacrilege, but the trunks would only lie and rot. Why not make use of them?

Using the trees that were downed to make a trail between the valley and the grove, Martik assembled a rolling monster. Logs were placed in the path before the greatoak, and then they were soaked with water to make them slick. With three horses on each side, they pulled, and amazingly, the leviathan moved.

Now at a place where they had to make a sharp, uphill turn, things were getting tense.

"Keep 'em ropes taut!" Martik shouted, despite the fact that he knew the men were trying to do just that, but the horses had reached a place where the incline was too steep. "Boil me. What made me think I could do this?"

"You're doing just fine," Wendel said. "Breathe deeply for a moment and relax yourself."

Martik stood for a moment, trembling with anxiety, but then he relaxed noticeably.

"Now you're ready to conquer this thing," Wendel said. "Come at it with a clear mind."

Martik nodded and looked thoughtful. "Thank ya," he said.

"If it were me," Wendel said, scratching his chin, "I'd unwind the rope around the trunk one time, and that would be enough extra rope to get the horses past the incline."

Martik made an annoyed sound. "Why didn't I think o' that?"

"Sometimes you just have to look at things from a different viewpoint."

* * *

As Catrin, Benjin, and Chase skirted the farmlands, they came to the stone bridge. It now stood well above the swift-running water, which was no longer clogged with debris. Beyond, though, the flood damage was still evident, even if the grass was already beginning to cover it.

As they crossed over a series of hills, Catrin was surprised to recognize parts of the landscape, even as nightmarish as it had been during the flood. If she remembered correctly, they were nearing the area where she and Benjin had climbed the tree, the place where they had lost Barabas. Thinking of him was painful, and she pushed him from her thoughts.

Around a bend, flashes of red and orange were visible. As they crested a rise, a field of flowers awaited. Two hills formed a small valley, and it was covered with vibrant life, the flowers making it look as if it were still afire.

"Pyre-orchids," Benjin said in a whisper. "They're extremely rare and only grow after forest fires, and then only under certain conditions. We must harvest them."

"We don't have time," Catrin said.

"Difficult times are ahead, li'l miss. In those kinds of times, disease can wipe out entire cities. Pyre-orchids can be used to treat almost every known plague. We cannot afford to miss this opportunity."

"Then let's do what needs doing and move on."

Harvesting the orchids proved as easy as removing the flower from the stem, and they soon had the flowers bundled together and divided up between them. Beyond the burned-out forests of Astor were lands that Catrin dreaded. She doubted she could find the place they had exited the ancient mines, and even if she could, they would have to wait for the full moon to get past the daggerfish, which left them little choice but to travel through populated lands.

At the first town they reached, Benjin spotted signs of the Vestrana at a local inn. "I'm going to go in and talk to the innkeeper," he said. "I'd like to get rooms for the night but only if we can remain discreet. Stay here and try not to draw attention to yourselves." He slipped into the inn.

Waiting for him to return, Catrin held her breath. Despite signs of the Vestrana, she feared a trap. When Benjin appeared at the back corner of the inn, she drew a deep breath. With a wave, he told them to join him, and they led the horses to the back of the inn, where two stable boys waited. Benjin gave each stable boy a copper and asked that they stack the bales of orchids somewhere dry. They looked at him strangely, but he tossed them each another copper and they were eager to help.

The innkeeper was an older, bearded man with a broad, vein-streaked nose. His name was Orman, and his smile was infectious. "Welcome to the Brendton Inn, friends. The food's hot and the beds clean. If you'll follow me, there's a private room this way. I'll bring your dinner there."

"Does he know who we are?" Catrin asked when Orman left.

"I think he suspects, but he gave all the right signs. We should be safe in his care," Benjin said.

But Catrin still had doubts. Too many things were no longer certain or safe. When Orman returned with food, she wondered if it might be poisoned but decided she could not live the rest of her life in fear. With trembling hands, she grabbed a stuffed pepper. It was delicious.

Orman returned to clear the plates and brought a tray of mugs and a jug of dandelion wine. "Secret family recipe," he said. He poured wine for each of them and handed out the mugs. When he handed Catrin her mug, their eyes locked. His brief stare commanded her attention without being overt. Wrapping her hand around the mug, she realized there was a piece of parchment cleverly wrapped around half the mug so it was concealed in her grip. Toward the top, she felt a wax seal.

Uncertainty festered in Catrin's belly, but she just thanked Orman for the wine. He left as if nothing had occurred, closing the door behind himself. The secrecy employed in delivering the message demanded she read it in private, but her curiosity would not be quelled. With a quick glance, she saw the image of a hummingbird impressed into the wax. Excitement charged through her. "I need to collect my thoughts," she said. "I'm going to meditate for a while."

The others spoke softly as Catrin settled herself into a corner with her back to them. The seal broke away easily, and she opened the parchment with a mixture of hope and dread.

Birds roost where dandelions hide.

Frustrated, Catrin tried to understand what the message meant. The hummingbird seal would almost certainly belong to Brother Vaughn, and the mention of birds solidified that deduction. The taste of dandelion wine was still on her tongue, and Orman had said it was a secret recipe, but she struggled to find meaning in *Birds roost*.

The message was a warning, of that she was certain, and she guessed it wasn't safe to go to Ohmahold. Birds. Messages. The realization slammed into her consciousness. Orman would send a message by bird. Could it really be so simple? "I think Brother Vaughn wants us to wait here for him," she said when she returned to the table.

"Did you get that from your meditation or did you just decide you like this place?" Chase asked.

"A cryptic message was delivered to me, and I'm not certain, but I think it's a warning," she said, still feeling compelled to keep the message secret. Sharing it would reveal Orman as the messenger, and she sensed that would be against his wishes. Perhaps he feared Samda. "I think Brother Vaughn wants to meet us here."

"Would you care to share the message?" Chase asked. "Maybe we could help interpret it."

"No. The message was intended for me alone, and I cannot share it. I'm sorry."

Chase raised an eyebrow but did not press her further. Benjin looked her in the eye and seemed satisfied by what he saw.

"I don't think it's safe to stay here long. There are more people looking for you than just Brother Vaughn. There may be other messages being exchanged this very moment," Samda said.

"I agree," Chase added, and when he met her eyes, Catrin saw his determination and knew he was going to fight her.

"Come with me," she said, and he walked to the corner with her. She could feel the stares on her back, but she could think of no other way to convince her companions without offending Samda and still respect Orman's privacy.

When she showed Chase the message, he looked uncertain at first, but then he seemed to see the hidden meanings. "I think Cat's right. I say we wait here, at least for a few days," he said when they returned to the table.

"We need to get a better understanding of the layout of the inn and its surroundings," Benjin said. "I don't want to be trapped here. We'll pair up and keep watch on the streets. If someone is trying to trap us, we'll need as much warning as possible."

* * *

Despite what were mostly pleasant days in a comfortable setting, Catrin paced the floor, unable to stem her anxiety. Every horse or wagon that passed was suspect, and even when in her room, she could not stifle her worry. Having stayed abed longer than the others, she tried to calm her mind. When the door to her room suddenly flew open, she nearly leaped from her skin. No one entered, but then two grinning faces peeked in. Only her happiness to see them could overcome the overwhelming desire to wring their necks.

"Strom! Osbourne! How did you get here?"

"We came with Brother Vaughn." At the mention of his name, he came to the door, grinning as wide as the rest.

"Greetings, Catrin. I was confident you would understand my message, but I must admit it's a relief to find you here. There are many things we need to discuss."

Chase charged up the stairs from the common room, having heard the commotion. "Who goes there?" he challenged. "By the gods, how'd you get in here? Forget it. I don't care." He ran to embrace Strom, Osbourne, and Brother Vaughn. "I'll go get Benjin and Samda."

"Who?" Brother Vaughn asked, his visage going stony.

"Samda was a Zjhon Master, but his beliefs have changed. He's been helping us," Catrin said.

"I know who he is. A detestable man if I ever met one. We can get you out of here without him ever knowing. Chase, can you try to get Benjin to come alone?"

"Wait," Catrin said. "I don't want to leave Samda. He saved my life, just as you did. I could no more leave him behind in such a way than I could you."

Brother Vaughn seemed torn, but then he tightened his jaw and nodded. "Let us talk where we can be comfortable and drink a bit of Orman's dandelion wine, then."

In his excitement, Chase darted ahead to apprise Benjin, taking the stairs two at a time. Catrin walked beside Brother Vaughn. "I respect your opinion, and I'm sorry for disagreeing with you."

"People *can* change, but they rarely do. I will trust your judgment, but it will take some time before I will trust his."

"I can ask no more than that," she said as they entered the private dining hall. Food and wine were waiting when they arrived, which made Catrin slightly uncomfortable, not liking when others anticipated her moves.

Benjin still wore a shocked expression when he arrived.

Chase followed. Then came Samda, who wore a mixture of guilt and pride like a cloak. Catrin watched the looks exchanged between Brother Vaughn and Samda. There was no kindness between them, but they both managed to remain civil.

"How did you get in here?" Benjin asked. "We've been watching every entrance."

"Orman's a crafty fellow," Brother Vaughn said. "Full of surprises, he is. I'll not spoil his fun by revealing his methods." Strom and Osbourne nodded in agreement.

"I suppose the important question is: What do you plan to do next?" Brother Vaughn asked.

"I'm going after Belegra," Catrin said. "I believe he goes in search of the Firstland."

"I've gotten reports that give your suspicion credence, but I must ask how you plan to find the Firstland."

"I don't know, but I must find a way."

Brother Vaughn paced the floor in deep thought but stopped suddenly in front of Samda. Their noses almost touching, he growled. "You know why I loathe you. You know what you did. Catrin has accepted you, and I have chosen to honor her decision, but if you reveal any of what I say to anyone or if you betray her, I'll find you, and you will die slowly."

Catrin held her breath, shocked by the venom that poured from Brother Vaughn.

"What the Zjhon did was wrong--I know--but nothing can bring those shepherds back, no matter how much I will it to be so. I'll not betray you or Catrin."

"Be true to your word, and you have nothing to fear," Brother Vaughn said, and he turned back to the group, his visage once again peaceful. "There has been great change in the Cathuran order since the Zjhon killed Mother Gwendolin." He paused to glare at Samda, who seemed truly surprised and confused. "Long-standing beliefs are being challenged, and the order is divided. I could not remain while they squabble amongst themselves. I made my choice, and I started searching for you. When the bird came, Strom, Osbourne, and I made good our escape before the balance of power shifted."

"You left the order?" Catrin asked, shocked.

"In a sense, yes. There have been times in the past when the order dispersed to find truth, and I am on such a quest. The library you found contains thousands of volumes, and it'll take generations to glean all that we can from them, but I did make some discoveries before I departed Ohmahold. You were correct when you translated *Om'Sa* to mean *men leave*. The book you found chronicles the departure of the first men from the Firstland.

"They fled the Gholgi, who we now know were large, reptilian creatures that somehow betrayed the first men. The picture is still very cloudy, as I have only tapped the smallest part of the knowledge that was hidden. If only we had more time," he said with a sigh. "I found no maps to indicate where the Firstland is, but I did find something rather intriguing: a reference to a powerful staff known as the Staff of Life, and your staff matches the description, except yours has no stones in the eyes of the serpent, if I recall correctly."

"Your memory is correct," Catrin said. "But Benjin had the noonstones mounted in the eyes. The serpent, I believe, is a dragon. If I draw heavily on the staff, the eyes shine and the wings become visible." After retrieving the staff from her room, Catrin showed him.

"Amazing. The wings were not described, but perhaps they were unknown at the time. Otherwise, thanks to Benjin's uncanny intuition, the staff looks exactly as it was described." He drew a sharp intake of breath when he saw the handprints embedded in the staff's flesh. "By the gods! How did that happen?"

Catrin told the tale, and those who hadn't heard it stood in shock. Samda seemed confused. "Those are not noonstones," he said, pointing to the eyes of the serpent.

"What?" Catrin asked.

"I've seen noonstone; it's as black as night. Those, I believe, are something even more rare--dragon ore. I thought you knew."

"Where did you see this black stone?" Brother Vaughn asked.

"It was one of Belegra's treasures. He showed it to me once as a way to convince me he was right, to show he had the favor of the gods," Samda replied, looking haunted. "He said that once he uncovered its secrets, he would be able to save the world. I believed him then."

No one spoke for a moment, and even Brother Vaughn seemed to recognize Samda's pain. An idea began to form in Catrin's mind, but she kept it to herself. For the moment, it really didn't matter; she understood how to use the stones she had, whatever they were called.

Samda suddenly cocked his head to one side, "Do you hear that?"

Chase hurried to the window and pulled the shutter slowly open. "We've got to go. Now! Zjhon riders, coming fast."

A moment later Orman charged through the door, his face bright red. "Get your things and get upstairs."

Chapter 7

Beyond the civilized lands exist wild places, inhabited by creatures both curious and deadly.
--Rianna Goresh, trapper

* * *

It didn't take long for the group to gather their belongings since none of them had allowed themselves to get comfortable. At the end of the upstairs hall, Orman waited. He took them through a door that led to another stairwell. "Watch your heads," he said as he climbed.

The roof sloped down on both sides, and the attic ceiling was not high enough for even Catrin to stand straight. Orman opened a massive wooden chest that sat in a corner and took out the old blankets that filled it. After fighting with it for a tense moment, he removed the bottom of the chest, revealing a hidden shaft with a ladder descending in to the darkness.

"Down ya go," he said.

Strom went down first since he knew the way, and he lit a torch that waited below.

"I need you to send a message," Brother Vaughn said to Orman before he left. "I need a ship where foxes roost. You know who to contact."

Orman nodded.

Catrin waited until only she, Benjin, and Orman remained in the attic. "Thank you for all you've done. Good-bye, Orman," she said as Benjin urged her into the shaft.

The tunnel below was dark and cold and smelled like nothing else. Walls of rough stone and dirt cut a meandering course, but the tunnel was relatively short. At the end, another ladder led to a hatch that was already open. Looking down were the faces of the two stable boys, and their visible anxiety demanded haste.

"Thanks, Wilmer, Jidan; you've done well," Brother Vaughn said as he climbed from the tunnel.

Catrin followed and emerged in the feed room behind the stables. In the pasturelands beyond, their horses waited, saddled and loaded.

"By the gods, are those pyre-orchids?" Brother Vaughn asked.

"Yes," Catrin said. "We found them on our way, and Benjin insisted we harvest them."

"Bless him, but we won't have the time to dry them properly. They'll surely mold, and I cannot let such a treasure go to waste. Is Mirta still the healer in these parts?" he asked Wilmer, who nodded, mute. "Take these to her. It's very important. She'll know what to do. Understand?"

The boys nodded and quickly unloaded the pyre-orchids. Brother Vaughn went to one of the bundles and removed a single orchid. After marveling at its beauty for a brief moment, he carefully tore the delicate petals off, one by one, and pressed them into a book he retrieved from his pack.

After reaching into her purse, Catrin tossed each boy a gold coin then waved good-bye. The boys talked excitedly about how they would spend their new fortune.

Whether by design or luck, the evergreen trees lining the pasture gave them perfect cover during their escape; Catrin suspected it was by design. Riding double, they had to move more slowly, but they still managed to cover a lot of ground before nightfall. No pursuers revealed themselves, but that didn't mean they weren't there, waiting for an opportunity to strike. Constantly alert, Catrin scanned the trees around her as they moved through lightly forested foothills.

"We'll be heading north and west through the forest for most of the way," Brother Vaughn said.

"Where are we going?" Chase asked.

"To my ancestral home. It was abandoned generations ago, but I know the way."

The northern forests were untouched by fire, and Catrin reveled in the glory of the undisturbed land. Concentrating as hard as she could, she tried to hear the dryads. The song she heard was so soft, she wondered if she were imagining it, but its incredible beauty and complexity argued otherwise.

When they camped for the night, she went to her bedroll early and spent hours listening to the song of nature. The next day brought warm, gentle breezes that stirred the turning leaves. Many succumbed to the call of the wind and drifted to the forest floor below, and the group rode through a rain of color.

With all the movement, it was difficult to remain watchful, but Catrin spotted a dark shape moving through the trees ahead, and she held up her fist to call a halt. In a moment, she knew it was already too late for stealth. The dark shape stopped, and a low whistle split the air.

"They've seen us," Benjin said, and the pounding of hooves gave additional proof. "There's no time to run. Arm yourselves."

Catrin pulled her staff from the stirrup. Mounted men, in gear similar to that of the elite troops they had encountered in the past, charged through the trees. Benjin and the others formed a protective ring around Catrin. Chase, Strom, and Osbourne dismounted, so passengers would not hinder those who rode.

Chase made first contact with the enemy when he stepped from behind a tree and used a fallen branch to unhorse one of the Zjhon. Torn from the sight by a rider bearing down on those who surrounded her, Catrin wished she had a bow. Instead, she drew her belt knife and threw. It struck the soldier's helmet but did little besides distract him. The distraction was enough for Benjin, though, and he landed a killing strike.

More riders circled and scored hits of their own. Samda was pulled from his horse, and only Osbourne's intervention kept him from being killed. In saving Samda, though, Osbourne turned his back on another rider. Samda's shout warned him, and he ducked just in time, getting only a slice across his face.

Samda grabbed a handful of dirt and threw it into the eyes of the rider's mount as he charged past. Blinded, the horse fought his rider, and they went down when the horse tripped on a rotting stump. Chase appeared a moment later on a Zjhon horse, which matched strides with the horse beside him. Shouting a battle cry, he leaped from the saddle and grappled with the other man, pulling him to the ground, but the soldier's boot caught in the stirrup, and his mount dragged him. Chase held on for a moment but then let the panicking horse finish off the soldier.

Riders passed so quickly and in so many directions, Catrin could not keep track of where all the attackers were. Three men rode in close and occupied Benjin, Chase, and Brother Vaughn. Catrin winced at every blow they took. Unwilling to sit idly by while her companions fought, she opened herself to the power. Like drawing a deep breath before diving into the water, she inhaled the energy and held it within herself until she felt she might explode. The sound of hoofbeats from behind said she would have her chance to fight.

Turning just as the soldier closed the gap, Catrin held her staff high and prepared to unleash her stored energy. He pulled his sword back for a mighty swing, and time seemed to slow as it arced back toward her, slicing the air and singing the song of death. Before it reached her, though, Samda shouted her name, and time seemed to accelerate. Catrin opened her mouth to shout, but she had not even formed the words when Samda jumped between her and the blade.

He crumpled to the ground soundlessly, the soldier's sword protruding from his chest, and Catrin was so shocked that she failed to deliver her own attack. Deprived of his sword, the soldier punched Catrin in the face as he rode by and unhorsed her. She tried to brace herself but still hit the ground hard. Her horse pranced around her, and she had to roll to keep from being trampled.

Chase pulled her from the ground. "We're in trouble," he said, but then he had to defend himself as the attack raged on.

In a desperate attempt to protect her party, Catrin drew, once again, on the energy around her but could not focus, and the energy refused to do her bidding. After a desperate effort, the floodgates opened, and the river of power washed over her, unchecked. Sucking in deep breaths, she struggled to keep her footing lest she be swept away.

Three riders wheeled in unison and weaved through the trees as they charged. One flew from his saddle when Strom released the branch he'd been holding back; it struck the soldier across his nose with a crunch. Osbourne released the branch he'd been holding but to little effect; the leaves just raked against his target's face.

When Brother Vaughn ran with astonishing speed toward the momentarily stunned soldier's charging mount, Catrin shouted, but he did not hear. The thought of seeing him run down tore at her heart, but to her surprise, he sprang at the horse's head and latched onto the bridle. Using his weight, he brought the animal's head down until he touched the ground; then he rolled clear. The horse, carried by its momentum, flipped forward and sent its rider crashing into a nearby tree. The horse pulled itself from the ground and disappeared into the trees.

The last soldier continued forward, and Benjin rode to meet him. Overwhelmed with power, Catrin tried desperately to find a way to release it. The song of the dryads grew stronger in her mind, and she could feel their presence as they bolstered and guided her. With a terrified shriek, she cast out her energy, trying to connect it with the soldier. Just as his sword arced toward Benjin, a visible tendril of energy reached out to him. With a blinding light and a sharp crack, her energy connected with him and flowed violently between them.

The soldier was thrown from his horse and landed, smoking, on the ground. Benjin moved in to finish him off. Catrin, though, felt as if she had been the one struck, and she crumpled to the ground. Chase arrived at her side. "Are you hurt?" he asked.

"No. I don't think so. Samda?"

"I'm sorry, Cat. He's gone."

Lowering her head to cry, Catrin vented her impotent rage and sorrow. Nothing she could do would bring him back, but that didn't lessen her anguish, guilt, or her poignant sense of loss, which had become all too familiar. Only the need to tend to the wounded kept depression from claiming her.

Benjin had several deep wounds, and Catrin helped Brother Vaughn close and bandage them as best he could. Chase walked with a limp, and Osbourne's face was covered in drying blood, but at least the bleeding had stopped. Using a damp cloth, Catrin wiped the blood from his eyes.

"I tried to save him, Cat. I tried so hard. I'm sorry I failed."

"You did the best you could do, and you helped save all of us that live. Samda gave his life for me, and there was nothing any of us could've done to stop him," she said.

"He kept his word," Brother Vaughn said as he pulled a blanket over Samda. "It may not make up for everything he did, but Samda died an honorable death. People can indeed change. I underestimated him."

Still wary, they gathered the Zjhon horses still in the area, giving each of them their own mount. Making better time, they rode in somber silence. Samda's body, tied to the saddle of a Zjhon horse, was a painful reminder of the dangers they faced and the losses they had suffered.

When they reached a field dotted with small mounds that were laid out in an orderly fashion, Brother Vaughn stopped, motioned for everyone else to remain where they were, and walked into the field. For a few moments, he stood silent, but then he turned back to them, "Here lie my ancestors. Samda has earned the right to lie with them."

Though he had once been an enemy, he had also been a friend and protector. With hearts encumbered by grief, sadness, and regret, they laid Samda to rest. Before they left the burial mounds behind, Catrin found an acorn and planted it near where Samda lay, so that, from his death, new life could spring.

* * *

Mirta bent over little Becka, wiping the sweat from her forehead. Becka breathed shallow, ragged breaths, and Mirta could do nothing to help her. Becka was among the first, but it would spread, and Mirta began to cry, certain what she saw was the beginning of a plague.

As she wiped her tears, the bell rang, and she moved to the front of her shop, most of which was serving as a temporary sick house. When she saw two young boys, her heart sank. Would they, too, succumb?

"Miss Mirta?" one boy said meekly. "We have something for you, but it's kind of big. Where d'ya want it?"

"I don't have time for tricks today, boys," Mirta said. "I'm not expecting anything, and I don't have any room. If you're not sick, then run along."

"But, Miss Mirta, won't you at least look? The man said you'd want it. I can't remember what he called it. Fire lily? No, that wasn't it."

"Pyre-orchid?" Mirta asked, astonished, but her feet were already taking her through the door. There, on a simple wood cart, sat enough pyre-orchids to treat half the Greatland, but they were starting to rot. "Thank the gods! You must help me get this inside right now. You're Orman's boys, aren't ya?"

"Yes, ma'am. I'm Wilmer and this is my brother, Jidan."

"Good," Mirta said. "Your father won't mind me borrowing you for the day. Once we have them unloaded, I'll send one of you back with a message for him."

"Yes, ma'am," Wilmer said.

* * *

"There isn't much left," Brother Vaughn said as they rode into a secluded valley clogged with underbrush. Here and there, though, evidence of what had once been a glorious home could still be found. Fluted columns and crumbling walls struggled for existence as the land reclaimed them. "Be watchful. There are unmarked wells and other dangers beneath the growth."

Beyond the valley waited the sea, and the waves called to Catrin like an old friend. Her time aboard the *Slippery Eel* had been an experience she would never forget, and though she would never have called herself a sailor, a part of her was at home on the seas.

"A ship should meet us here soon," Brother Vaughn said. "Until then, we wait." When they reached an area relatively free of underbrush, he led them to a rough archway at the base of the mountains. Beyond the archway was a natural chamber large enough to hold them and their mounts. "This cavern was once used for storage, but it should serve us well. There is a river nearby where we can fish."

His mention of fish reminded everyone of their hunger. Brother Vaughn led Catrin, Chase, and Strom to a likely fishing hole. They did their best to fish without the proper gear, but their efforts yielded only two small fish before nightfall. On the walk back, though, Brother Vaughn gathered tubers and roots he said would make for a fine stew. It was not the best meal any of them had ever eaten, but it greatly improved the mood.

Chase constructed a wall of branches to cover the archway, and they huddled around a low fire as the evening chill set in.

"I must thank you again, Catrin," Brother Vaughn said, "for having the courage to locate the library at Ohmahold. The treasures within have provided inspiration for every member of the order, and I look forward to sharing much of what I've learned with the farmers and craftsmen of the world. Gustad has examined some of the weapons and armor and claims to have learned more about metalworking in one day than he had his whole life."

"You should see the swords, Cat," Strom said. "The metal shimmers and Gustad said one sword had been folded more than a thousand times. Milo let us look at it with his lenses, and you could actually see it!" Strom said.

"Yeah, and those new lenses came from things Milo found in the library," Osbourne added.

"I'm glad," Catrin said. "Did you find anything to help me?"

"I assembled a team of trusted colleagues," Brother Vaughn said. "We found as much as we could. It was distressingly little, and much of it was difficult to understand, but I'll do my best to help you. We found a text written in the oldest form of High Script, and then we found a more recent copy that had been translated. Using this text, we have been able to translate much more of *Om'Sa*.

"As I told you before, the first men fled the Firstland because they were losing the war against the Gholgi. Before the war, we believe man used the Gholgi much as we use horses for transportation. The references we've found indicate that they were intelligent creatures, and they learned fast. When they had gained a certain level of understanding, they revolted. The tales of the carnage are horrifying."

"You don't think the Gholgi are still there, do you? I mean, if they are, won't they just kill Belegra and his men?" Osbourne asked.

"We don't know. I'd never heard of them before translating *Om'Sa*, but I must assume they still exist."

"Hopefully, if any are still there when we get there, they will have forgotten what the first men taught them. Maybe they'll be afraid of us," Osbourne said.

"I'm not sure what to hope for," Catrin said.

"Many of the things we learned are of no consequence here," Brother Vaughn continued. "But Sister Annora found some things that might be helpful. Though I'm not certain I'll get it right, I'll try one with you," Brother Vaughn said, looking at Catrin.

"What do you need me to do?"

"If everyone else could remain quiet for a few moments, please. Catrin, I want you to stare straight ahead and remember exactly what you see, every detail. Then I want you to close your eyes and picture exactly what you saw."

"I see it."

"Now open your eyes. Does it look any different?"

"No. Is it supposed to look different?" she asked, but he did not answer.

"I want you to close your eyes again, and picture exactly what you saw. Do you see it?"

"I do."

"Now I want you to keep your eyes closed, and open *this one*," he said, and he smacked her hard on the forehead. Catrin sat back from the surprise and the impact, her eyes still squeezed shut, but it was as if someone had thrown open the shutters; a world of energy was revealed to her. She could see everything around her with her eyes shut, but it all looked very different. Rather than seeing colors or texture, she saw ever-moving patterns of energy both intricate and beautiful.

Around each person's wounds, she saw disturbances in the energy fields and areas where nothing moved at all. Oddly she saw a subtle but similar disturbance around Brother Vaughn's ears and head.

"Do you have trouble hearing?"

"Yes. Sometimes I do. At times I get a terrible ringing in my ears. How can you tell?"

"I see disturbances in your energy field."

"It worked?"

"Yes. It worked," Catrin said, and as she opened her eyes, her new vision overlaid what her eyes saw. Though initially disorienting, the combined senses gave her a much clearer picture of her companions' health. When Benjin turned, she saw the injury in his shoulder that pained him so much, old as it was. The more she looked with her new senses, the more natural they became, until she could no longer imagine life without them. Colors were richer and more vivid. Scents on the breeze told stories, and even the caress of that wind felt more personal.

"I'm so very happy," Brother Vaughn said, beaming. "I didn't think it was going to do anything, and then I would've looked quite the fool, smacking you in the forehead and all. Do you see anything else? Is there anything else you can do with your new sight?"

"I can see the disturbances caused by all of your wounds, and I can sense your overall well-being much more acutely now, but I'm not certain there is anything I can do with it besides maybe identify illnesses."

"Give it time," Benjin said. "Some use will present itself."

"Well said," Brother Vaughn added.

"Is there anything else you could teach her?" Osbourne asked, excited by their success.

"There were two more things we could try. Do you feel up to trying something else?"

"I do."

"Are you gonna smack her again?" Strom asked. "I'd like to see that again."

Catrin stuck her tongue out at him and closed her eyes.

"I want you to put your ear to the ground and tell me what you hear. Cover your other ear if that helps."

Catrin did as he instructed. "I think I hear my own heartbeat and a hollow echo."

"Now I want you to listen for words," Brother Vaughn said. "Do you hear a song or melody?"

"I have heard songs of nature, but I don't hear anything like that now. No."

"Try asking a question."

"Ask the ground a question?" Strom snorted, but Chase shushed him.

"Will a ship come for us?" Catrin asked. There was no response, nothing at all. "I don't hear anything."

"Ah well, I suppose it was worth a try," Brother Vaughn said, clearly disappointed.

"What else can you try?" Osbourne asked, his enthusiasm unabated. "C'mon, Cat, you're good at this kind of thing. You can do it."

"The last exercise was said to be the one least often achieved, but I am willing to try if Catrin is."

"I can try one more."

"We have to go outside for this one. Pick any tree that calls out to you."

"Trees call out to people?" Strom asked; Osbourne elbowed him in the ribs.

Catrin ignored him and walked through the trees, listening for the slightest contact. With her new vision, she saw energy fields around the trees and just about everything else. A nearby tree showed signs of disease, its leaves riddled with spots; most had already fallen off. "This one."

"Put your arms around it and pull yourself close. Don't turn your head to the side; look straight into the tree and press your nose and lips against the bark."

"You want her to hug and kiss a tree?"

"Shut up, Strom!" everyone else said in unison.

Catrin didn't let it bother her, she would do almost anything to increase her powers, and that realization was exhilarating as well as frightening. Approaching the tree, she reached out her arms and embraced it. Pressing her face against the jagged bark, she waited. Nothing happened.

"I don't feel anything," she said, her voice muffled against the bark of the tree. Disappointment coursed through her.

"I'm sorry. That's all the ancient druid text said to do. I don't know anything else to try."

"This, too, was worth trying," she said, still hugging the tree. "Thank you, Brother Vaughn. Thank you, tree." Just as she was about to pull away, she heard a faint melody. Pressing her face harder against the tree, it grew louder and clearer. Harder she pressed and louder it grew.

"Catrin?" she heard someone ask, but she ignored him and everything else her ears heard; she listened, instead, with her heart. The melody grew louder and took on more intensity. The bark her face was pressed against began to feel warm and soft, and slowly her face slid forward, into the tree. It was a bizarre sensation, but she did not feel threatened; instead she felt like an honored guest.

Before her third eye, a figure materialized. Childlike in build, the figure had a beautiful face, full of wisdom and the serenity of ages. "Greetings, heart of the land."

"Greetings, tree mother," Catrin replied, unsure where the words had come from. Like the echoes of a distant past, she felt as if she had done this before; it felt natural and right.

"It has been so long since your kind has spoken to us. I suppose we stopped listening."

"The knowledge was lost," Catrin said. "It was only recently rediscovered."

"Speaking to you makes me weary. I am so very tired."

"I see a disturbance in your energy. Can I help you?"

"Thank you, heart of the land. You are kind, but it has been so long, I don't remember how. I've forgotten the old songs. But I'll try."

Wrapping Catrin in a warm embrace, the dryad began to sing. Her energy flowed against Catrin's, and slowly they began to merge. From deep in Catrin's mind, a new melody came, playing harmony to that of the dryad. Together they sang until their energy vibrated and undulated. Like dark spots in the dryad's aura, the disturbances swirled and coalesced, but the melody seemed to vibrate them apart, and Catrin began to focus on them. Some she took into herself, trying to make order from chaos. A feeling of nausea and weariness overwhelmed her, and she thought she might lose consciousness.

"You are tired, heart of the land. You must go now, but I thank you. I send you away with a gift. Live well, heart of the land. Live well."

In the next moment, Catrin was back in her body and the bark was biting into her flesh. She pulled away and steadied herself; her legs wobbled and shook. "I don't know your name. Please, tell me your name," she said, and in the back of her mind she heard a voice whisper: *Shirlafawna.*

"Are you well? Catrin! Talk to me!" Chase said.

"I'm fine. I'm just tired," she said, but then she gasped. From behind each tree peeked a dryad in their physical forms, and they greeted Catrin as friends. Shirlafawna had given her a glorious gift indeed. Looking at Shirlafawna's tree, Catrin sensed the energy field recovering even if her eyes still saw disease; her senses showed a return to health; the physical would follow. Somehow, *that* she knew. Despite her exhilaration, she was truly weary, and she returned to the cavern to rest.

Chapter 8

Without forgetfulness, forgiveness is incomplete.
--Amelia Kudara, maidservant

* * *

"Do you see that?" Brother Vaughn asked as they walked back from the river.

"I see it," Catrin said as a strange shape flew overhead; it was unlike any bird she'd ever seen.

"The winged foxes are found only here. My uncle brought me here when I was a boy, knowing how much I loved anything that flew, and these were his gift to me. A marvel unlike any other, unique to my homeland."

"They're beautiful," Chase said as another fox leaped an impossible distance between two trees, using its winglike membranes to sail through the air. It was then that Catrin recalled what Brother Vaughn had said about needing a ship where foxes roost, and now she understood his meaning.

Nearby, a violet hummingbird floated around some bushes, looking for one last drink before his migration. Catrin watched him with all her vision, mesmerized by his beauty. He seemed to sense her scrutiny and boldly flew in front of her, weaving back and forth before her face. For a moment she was connected to him, and she lent him energy for the long journey. Extending her hand, she offered a perch, and to everyone's surprise, he landed on her finger, chirped, and momentarily stuck out his translucent, strawlike tongue.

After a brief rest, the bird chirped and seemed to wish them farewell before leaping into the air. He turned and flew straight as an arrow, and Catrin could still sense him long after he was lost from sight, the sensation growing fainter as the distance between them grew.

"That was one of the most remarkable things I've ever seen," Brother Vaughn said. "I've coaxed them with sugar water, but never have I seen one land on a person."

"He sensed me watching him, I think," Catrin said. "When he came to look at me, I offered him a place to rest, and then I lent him energy for his journey."

"Truly astounding," Brother Vaughn said.

When they returned to the cavern, Catrin no longer had to wonder who the intended recipient of Brother Vaughn's message was, for Nora,

Kenward, and Fasha Trell waited within, already talking with Benjin. Though Catrin had never met Fasha before, there was no question who she was; the family resemblance was remarkable.

"Good. You've returned," Nora said with a nod. "We've no time to waste. There're still soldiers in these parts, and I want no part of fighting on land."

The greetings were made in haste as everyone scrambled to gather the gear. Catrin felt as if a strong wind were sweeping her away as they marched toward the coast. At the bottom of a rocky ridge, two ships waited in a small cove: the *Slippery Eel* and the *Stealthy Shark*.

"When I got Brother Vaughn's message, I knew it was time we did something more," Nora said. "Duty calls us to help in the name of the Vestrana. For many lifetimes the Vestrana has been a useful tool--a convenience--but now it must serve its true purpose. We must help the Herald achieve victory over the madness. I don't need a seer to tell me it's so."

"Thank you, Captain Trell. All of you have my thanks," Catrin said.

"Are you joking?" Kenward said. "Do you think I'd miss the greatest adventure of all? Not me."

Nora smacked him on the back of the head. "You'll behave yourself and follow orders, fool boy."

"Yes, Mother," he said, but then he glanced at Fasha and they grinned at each other.

Nora rolled her eyes. "They'll be the death of me yet," she said. "The real question is how to get to the Firstland. We could spend a lifetime wandering the seas and not find it. What do we know?"

"I've never found anything to prove it," Brother Vaughn said, "but I've always believed the Firstland lies to the south. If we could find the Keys of Terhilian, we would have a much better idea. The old texts say in the great carving of the Terhilian Lovers, the man points to the Firstland and the woman to the Greatland."

"I've always thought the Firstland was to the east," Kenward said. "Past the mountain island and the great shallows."

Fasha scoffed and rolled her eyes.

Nora just shook her head. "I was thinking north, beyond the ice seas. Anyone want to offer up west?" she asked, throwing her hands up in frustration, but an idea began to form in Catrin's mind.

"When hummingbirds migrate, do they make stops along the way?" she asked Brother Vaughn, and Kenward cast her a curious glance.

"If I'm correct, they make the journey in a single flight, as hard as that is to believe. Why do you ask?"

"When we first met, you said you thought the violet hummingbirds migrated to the Godfist, but I'm certain they do not. If they do not migrate to the Godfist, then perhaps they travel to the Firstland."

"How can you be certain? You've not been to every part of the Godfist. Maybe they all go to the eastern or southern coasts," Chase said.

"I'm nearly certain. I can still sense the hummingbird that landed on my finger," Catrin said, and now Nora and Fasha gave her astonished looks. "He grows faint as he gets farther away, but he's that way," she said, pointing, her eyes closed.

"East!" Kenward said, and he did a happy dance that clearly disgusted Fasha.

"I'd say southeast," she said, her arms crossed over her chest.

"Maybe a little south," Kenward conceded, but his grin did not fade.

"I've nothing better to go by. South and east it is," Nora said as they reached the shoreline.

* * *

In a wagon loaded with jars of powdered pyre-orchid, Mirta rode through town, trying to avoid the roadways that were still clogged with snow. On the main thoroughfare, the snow was mostly cleared, and she had to guide her mare around only occasional patches of ice. Along the way, she stopped to see Becka, who was now fully recovered. The spread of illness had been staunched, here at least, but Mirta knew many others throughout the Greatland were at risk. Orman wouldn't tell her who had sent the precious flowers, but Mirta had her suspicions. Wilmer and Jidan weren't talking, and Mirta had to admire their ability to keep a secret. She supposed it was a family trait.

What really mattered was that the gift not be wasted. It had taken time to dry and prepare the powder, then months making sure that the sick were truly cured. Now she knew she could wait no more. In the harshness of winter, there would be many in need. For them, Mirta was leaving her home, her loved ones, what seemed her entire life. Suisa could tend to those she left behind; she was a skilled woman with a kindly manner. Still, Mirta's heart ached as she released herself from responsibility to home and opened herself to responsibility to everyone.

With a wave to the crowd that had gathered to see her off, despite the cold, Mirta chirruped and slapped the leather lines across her mare's rump.

***

As the seasons passed, a new sort of normality set in, Rolph Tillerman did as he and his ancestors always had: he worked the land. His efforts provided food for his family and for others around him, but lately his labors seemed almost a waste of time, a poor attempt at keeping starvation at bay. Jessub was a growing boy, but he was not ready to take his place as the man of the farm, and Rolph began to question how much longer he would be able to hold up under the physical strains of his labors. His father had always said that farming was the work of a young man; teaching that young man to farm was the job of his father. Martik. If only he were here to raise Jessub, to teach him all the lessons he would need to survive, then things would be better.

"I'm just too old," Rolph said to himself as the pain in his back escalated from a dull ache to a sharp, stabbing pain. Forced to admit he could no more, Rolph held a hand to his back and walked slowly to the cottage where Collette waited, her hands on her hips.

"Didn' I tell ya no' to work yerself t'death?" she asked. "Better to git a little done each day, I says, an' then a little more the next. That's what I says, an' look at ya. Come on now. Git in here and let me git a look at ya. Foolish old man."

As Rolph settled himself in the most comfortable position he could, he stayed quiet while his wife lovingly massaged his aching muscles and lectured him about being more careful and listening to her. Rolph closed his eyes and let himself relax. At least some things in his world remained the same. That realization gave him hope. Somehow he would find a way to make things right.

A moment later, though, Jessub charged into the cottage, the door slamming behind him, which was something he'd been scolded about far too many times. Covered in mud, cuts, and scrapes, he looked the part of a scamp, especially with the broad grin on his face. "Gramma, Grampa," he said, "look what I caught!" He held up a small, lizardlike animal that still squirmed in his hand.

"I don't care what it is," Collette said, immediately shuffling the boy back outside. "I want it out o' my house, and yer not t'come back in 'til yer stripped and washed. Understood?"

"Yes, Gramma," he said, and though his eyes were cast downward for a moment, in the next he was running back to the mud hole, presumably in search of more salamanders. "That boy'll be the death o' me yet."

Rolph just shook his head and sighed.

***

Staring at the endless waves, Catrin wondered if she would ever see land again. Having long since lost contact with the hummingbird, she was no longer so certain of their course, and they had seen nothing for months--no fish, no birds, nothing but deep water.

Kenward stood nearby watching the *Stealthy Shark* as she slowed and turned. "What is that woman up to this time?" he said, but then came the mirror flashes, and he cursed. "Prepare to board the *Shark*. She's wounded and we must capture the crew."

Catrin sighed. Nora never stopped. Rather than simply sail, the entire trip was transformed into a training exercise. Each drill brought new challenges, and Catrin was certain this one would as well. The races and some of the maneuvers had been exciting and even fun, but boardings were brutal. Only practice weapons were used, but they left everyone bruised and welted, not to mention exhausted.

"They've beaten us back twice already," Kenward said. "And they've taken us twice. No mistakes. No mercy. If my mother or sister leave an opening, take it, or they will humiliate you. Trust me on this. Leave them welted and bruised at the end of this day, and there'll be more racing than boarding for the next week."

The crew readied themselves, rallied by his words. Catrin felt her heart pounding, and she gathered her will, wanting to avenge Kenward's losses and her own. His eye was still blackened from a punch his own mother had landed. Strom had already "killed" Catrin by sneaking up on her and hitting her across the back with the flat of his sword. Benjin had forced her to submit twice without ever hitting her. Holding her corner of the boarding net, she waited for Kenward's command, ready to fight.

At ramming speed, he sailed without wavering.

***

"What's that boilin' maniac doing?" Fasha shouted. "Raise the--"

"Hold!" Nora said. "Not yet. Stand ready to be boarded. Take no prisoners," she added with a pointed glance at Benjin.

"He's gonna sink both of us," Fasha said but remained at her post. The *Slippery Eel* charged through the waves as Kenward used every trick he knew to get speed. The crew moved without hesitation, despite what were obviously ludicrous orders. "How does he get his crew to go along with his crazy ideas?"

"They believe in him," Nora said. "Fools and dreamers they may be, but somehow they make it work."

"Kenward will come for mother and me," Fasha said. "He'll be seeking revenge. I'm certain of it."

"Chase and Catrin will come for me . . . together I think," Benjin said.

"Do you think our plan is gonna work?" Strom asked.

"They'll never see it coming," Fasha said. Nora remained silent, anxiously watching the *Slippery Eel*'s daring approach. "Stand ready to repel!" she said as the *Eel* executed a turn that left it coming toward the *Shark* sideways, driving a wall of water before it. "Brace yourselves!"

Atop the *Eel*'s wake, the *Shark* heaved and rolled, her decks thrown far from the *Eel*'s.

"Hold!" Kenward's shout carried above the roaring water. As the *Shark* rolled on the receding wave, it came back closer to the *Eel*. Sliding down in the water, her decks dropped below the *Eel*'s. "Now!" came Kenward's command.

Howling like animals, his crew attacked. Catrin and Chase moved toward Benjin, who looked up to see if Osbourne and Strom were in place. Taking a deep breath, he bent his knees. Fasha bounced lightly on the balls of her feet, swaying back and forth like a panther waiting to strike. She gave him a nod. The bait was ready, the trap set.

* * *

Catrin gained the *Shark*'s deck before anyone else and ran, growling, at Benjin. His eyes met hers, daring her to take him. Chase caught up to her and charged alongside. Kenward roared like a madman as he charged Fasha and Nora. "Now!" he yelled only an instant before Benjin did the same.

Using all the quickness and agility she possessed, Catrin turned sharply and rolled. Rising up, she used her momentum to hurl her sword at Strom. Chase executed a similar maneuver, though all Catrin saw was a blur of limbs beside her. With a loud crack, Catrin's sword landed across the backs of Strom's hands, making him lose his grip on the net he held. Chase's sword struck Osbourne so violently, he fell from the rigging, cursing. Their net fell harmlessly to the deck, their trap sprung.

Kenward caught Benjin off his guard and smacked him across the chest with the flat of his blade. Fasha went down in a heap under Bryn, who dropped from the rigging. "Dead!" he yelled. Nora watched it all with an air of detachment, but that changed when Catrin slid across the deck into the backs of her knees. Grabbing Chase's sword as she passed it, Catrin rolled herself in position to stab Nora. "Dead!" she shouted.

"Dead!"

"Dead!" came the call across the deck, and nearly two-thirds of the *Shark*'s crew was down.

"Advantage Kenward," Nora said as Catrin helped her rise. Kenward smiled as he helped his sister from the deck.

"Good fight, Sis."

"Good fight."

"You're a madman, Kenward," Nora said, "but somehow you inspire those around you to equal madness. I'd never have expected Catrin to take me down, nor Bryn Fasha, but you gave them heart and courage. I'm proud of you and your crew. Now get your ship away from the *Shark* before you sink us all."

Fasha made a disgusted sound in her throat and rolled her eyes.

"Aw, now don't be sore because you lost, Sis."

"Next time," she said. "No mercy. No prisoners."

"Next time," he said, grinning. "Thanks, Mom. See you soon!"

"Fool boy."

* * *

Victory greatly improved the mood aboard the *Slippery Eel*, and Kenward gathered everyone at the prow. "The words my mother said today were neither trivial nor easily earned. Today you made my mother proud of me, and I thank you for that," he said, a catch in his voice and a tear in his eye. "You made me proud, and you gave Fasha and my mother reason to respect and fear you. You're actually starting to frighten me a little."

Laughter helped ease the tension, and Catrin began to see the wisdom of Nora's drills. Rather than letting the crews consider the unlikelihood of finding the Firstland or worry over the shortage of food, she kept them busy, honing their skills, while developing teamwork and camaraderie.

Everyone turned when, across the water, sounds of celebration came from the *Stealthy Shark*. "Seafloor ahead!" the lookout called an instant later. "Land ho!"

Still distant on the horizon, a dark smudge rose above the waterline. Like a bastion of hope, it drew them on. Ahead, dark water suddenly changed to azure, and sandy, white bottom came into view. Mirror flashes flew between the ships, and Kenward paced impatiently. "Drop anchor."

"What?" Chase asked. "Why are we stopping?"

"Mother fears the shallows. She says we'll run aground if we enter now. These are tidal waters, and she wants to wait for the full moon."

"That'll be weeks from now," Chase said, dismayed.

"True, but there should be an abundance of sea life along the shelf. We'll fish and eat whatever we can catch. We can't load our holds; that would only put us lower in the water and increase the risk of running aground. We'll have to do that when we reach the other side."

"How far across is it?" Catrin asked.

"I wish I knew; that would make convincing Mother to move on much easier, but not knowing, I can't argue her logic. Waiting for the full moon will give us the greatest chance of survival. If we were to get caught by receding tides, we could get stuck, at the very least, but more likely, we'd be sunk. For now, we wait."

"I bet we can catch more fish than they can," Chase said, grinning. Kenward grinned back and used his mirror to issue the challenge.

"We'll eat good tonight," Chase whispered to Catrin with a wink.

* * *

In the darkness, Prios climbed. With no light to guide him, he could rely only on the senses his power provided. Climbing without sight, that most primal sense, was disorienting and more terrifying than anything he had ever imagined. The only consolation was that he could not perceive the heights from which he perilously hung.

On his back was an empty pack, meant only to secure his goal. He had no food or water to sustain him, and Prios knew that he could waste no time. Each moment his death became more likely, and he bit his lip as he continued to climb.

When at last he reached an opening in the face of the mountain, Prios was overcome by a sense of foreboding. The hairs on his arms and neck stood straight, and sweat began to seep into his eyes. Within the mountain, he sensed massive life, both vibrant and deadly. His life now hung on an assumption. If these beasts were not truly dormant at night, then he would most likely be dead within moments.

Before he lost his courage, he took a step into the massive stone chamber. Though he could not see its vastness, he could *feel* it. Pockets of life could be felt all around, but one in particular drew Prios closer. No attack came, but he wondered if he was simply being toyed with, being made to believe he could succeed in such an audacious theft only to be torn to shreds before he could make good his escape.

When he reached an area where the life force around him was divided into many smaller entities, he tried to ignore the fact that he sensed one massive entity behind all the smaller ones. Prios froze and remained as still as a stone, his hair, once again, standing on end. Overwhelmed by the sensation that something was watching him, waiting for him to make his fatal mistake, he waited and prayed.

Unable to bear the suspense any longer, he reached out and laid his hands on a warm and smooth shell. Perhaps it was his imagination that caused the shadows to shift and swirl, but it caused him to pause for a moment, and as he did, his senses perceived something. Amid all the small life forces around him, one stood out. Though it emitted no light, Prios could feel the power. A smile formed on his lips, as he realized that this was his opportunity to give Archmaster Belegra exactly what he had asked for and, at the same time, give him something that may be beyond his ability to control.

As soon as his hands touched the shell, he felt the shadows move again, and he could no longer deny his fear. With the speed of desperation, he put the egg in his pack and secured it on his back before running back to the cavern entrance. Without his sight, he was unprepared for such speed, and a protruding piece of rock sent him sprawling, nearly sending him tumbling into the open air. With only a hand's width of stone ledge behind him, Prios checked to be certain the egg was still whole. It could have been a freak wind, but he thought he felt hot breath on his neck, and he needed no urging to begin his descent. With his eyes squeezed shut, he lowered himself over the ledge and waited for powerful jaws to close around him.

Pressed against his back, the egg in his pack shifted, and Prios sensed awareness. As he moved to the next toehold, a name floated into his mind like something from a dream: Kyrien.

* * *

Having eaten more types of seafood than she had ever imagined existed, from armored skate to monstrous crabs--they seemed to catch some of everything--Catrin longed for a steak or a piece of bacon. Grubb identified some fish that were unsafe to eat and a few more he wasn't certain about; those were thrown back. It seemed a harmless practice at first, but staying in one place surrounded by bleeding fish turned out to be a mistake.

Dorsal fins the size of mainsails jutted from the water and circled the ship. Catrin and Chase stood at the gunwales, watching the terrifying display. Deep booms reverberated through the ships as the massive predators inspected them by bumping into them. Jarred by the impacts, Catrin watched in horror as dark shadows glided through the water with amazing speed and grace. She prayed they would go away.

Seabirds, also drawn by the chance for an easy meal, gathered around what remained of the discarded fish. In a moment that would forever be burned into Catrin's memory, one of the giant sharks leaped from the water, jaws agape, and took a mouthful of seabirds with it before crashing back into the water with a mighty impact. Seeing the agility of such large and dangerous creatures made Catrin feel small and vulnerable, yet she could not look away, held in thrall by their terrifying beauty.

With such danger in the waters, fishing efforts were curtailed. After moving to deeper water, both crews spent time simply resting and hoping the sharks did not return.

* * *

Along with the full moon came more than a dozen comets, their combined light creating a dreamlike landscape. Uncertainty gnawed at both crews as they entered the shallows, not knowing if they would ever escape.

Even when she was not on duty, Catrin kept watch; underwater hills and barely submerged islands threatened them at every moment. When the way ahead became too difficult to gauge, men were sent out in boats to check the depth and find safe passage. Using a weight tied to a long length of rope, they quickly made measurements. Markings on the rope indicated the safe level, and too many times that marker was near the surface.

Despite the danger, they had to concentrate on their task, for wondrous sights abounded, threatening to draw the attention of those on watch. During Catrin's off-duty watches, she occasionally let herself become absorbed in the beauty of the strange place. Colorful fish darted around equally colorful reefs. Flights of manta rays, each wider than the ships were long, glided through the water, looking as if they were flying.

As they moved farther into the shallows, small islands dotted the horizon, providing additional navigational challenges. The mountain was still distant, but it became ever more intimidating as it grew closer.

It was shocking to see life take hold in such a bizarre place, but there were islands covered with trees and bushes, and the waters around them teemed with creatures. The trees' branches harbored birds, snakes, frogs, and even crabs. Snakes moved from island to island, skimming the surface with their serpentine movements.

Beyond a cluster of islands, they reached a place where no land broke the surface and the waters became a bit deeper. Here grew trees like nothing any of them had ever seen before. Stiltlike root systems extended to the seafloor and kept the trunks above water. Encased in delicate crystals, the bark and leaves danced in the light. Given the robust green color of the leaves and their strong energy fields, Catrin guessed this was a normal condition rather than some bizarre ailment.

"Are those what I think they are?" Brother Vaughn asked Kenward.

"I'm not sure what kind of trees they are, but they certainly are remarkable."

Fasha brought the *Stealthy Shark* in close, and Benjin shouted across the distance, "Could those really be saltbark trees I see?"

"I think you're right," Brother Vaughn shouted back. "Saltbark is a precious remedy told of only in legend," he said to Kenward. "Can we send a boat in to investigate?"

"We can't afford to waste any time," Kenward said. "If you go, you must not fall behind. Any delay could cost us our lives. Are you certain a few leaves are worth the risk?"

"It was said to cure ailments with no other known remedy. It can cure blindness in some cases; it can be used to treat poisonous snakebites, jellyfish and ray stings, and I'm certain there are other things I've forgotten."

"It's your skin you'll be risking. I'll not stand in your way."

After a brief discussion with Benjin, Brother Vaughn asked that they lower a boat. "We can pick up Benjin since he is most interested in the trees, and we'll harvest what we can as quickly as we can. You'll not have to wait on us," he promised. Kenward assigned crewmembers to man the oars, and Catrin stepped in front of him.

"I'm going," she said.

"Too dangerous."

"I'm going." He tried to speak a couple of times, but then seemed to reconsider, and he stepped aside, allowing her to climb down. Brother Vaughn came next, loaded with empty sacks. Bryn and Farsy manned the oars. Catrin released her oars from the locks and tried to match their strokes. Soon they skimmed across the relatively still waters. Benjin boarded with excitement in his eyes, and they worked together to get out in front of both ships.

"We can harvest until the *Eel* reaches us, and then we'll need to get back. No sense taking unnecessary chances," Benjin said.

Feeling as if she were in another world, Catrin watched the surreal landscape slide by. Saltbark trees, most widely spaced, seemed to prefer isolation, but not far in the distance stood a cluster of trees separated by only narrow channels.

Benjin guided them toward it. "Be careful. We've no idea what might be hiding within the branches. All we need are the leaves. Try not to pick any area bare."

When they reached the first tree, Catrin could hardly believe her eyes. Each deep green leaf was encased in a delicate frosting of nearly identical crystals. Reaching out, she pinched a stem, and the leaf came off easily in her hand. Holding it up to the light, it cast rainbows across her palm. Knowing they had only a limited time to harvest, she got busy picking leaves.

Despite Benjin's warnings, she became careless in her haste and yanked her hand back with a sudden intake of breath when a coiled snake hissed from behind the foliage. Their wariness renewed, they moved from tree to tree, crabs scattering as they approached. A small lizard fell into the boat, and Catrin climbed as far atop the gunwales as she could. Benjin used a gloved hand to return it to the trees, and only then did Catrin return to her seat.

Casting a sidelong glance at the ships, Benjin declared it time they return.

"Wait," Catrin said, seeing a flash of movement within the trees. "Did you see that?"

"I didn't see anything," Benjin said, and everyone else shook their heads. Still Catrin watched the trees and jumped when a green-haired dryad peeked around her tree. Coated in the same sparkling crystals, her hair gleamed. Her eyes shone with life and curiosity. Longingly, the dryad stretched her hands out toward Catrin, who wished she could ask them to turn back.

"Is something wrong, li'l miss?"

"No," she said, unsure why she was reluctant to share what she had seen. It just seemed too private, and she would respect the dryad she longed to embrace.

Chapter 9

On the final day, a scourge of wind and fire shall descend from the skies, and all creation shall be laid low.
--Fisidecles, the Mad Prophet

* * *

Watching the increasingly shallow waters that surrounded them, Catrin's eyes were drawn to the mountain that now dominated the horizon. Clouds filled the air around it, and its energy seemed almost threatening. As it drew ever closer, the scenery began to change. Evidence of a long-forgotten civilization surrounded them. Rectangular forms, clearly the remains of buildings, dotted the area, and jars littered the seafloor, some of which were whole.

The crews watched in silence, awed by the sights. A monolithic hand reached from the sand, the sword it held broken and worn. Nearby were the remains of a ship. Only the skeleton remained, laid out neatly and standing out in stark contrast to the white sand. The forefoot and stem were well preserved, however, and were fashioned to resemble a dragon in flight. The sight of the dragon, seemingly flying underwater, thrilled Catrin, despite the dangers the ancient shipwreck warned of.

A large island came into view. It was covered with trees that were laden with color, flowers weighing down their branches. Here Catrin saw a beautiful but distressing sight: violet hummingbirds by the hundreds, forming clouds of iridescent light that danced through the trees. If the birds ended their migration here, that meant Catrin's idea of following them to the Firstland had been founded on a mistake. She had gambled and lost. Now they were months from the Greatland and faced with the possibility of getting stuck there.

Twice the *Slippery Eel* dragged along the seafloor, dangerously close to running aground, but Kenward did not want to completely empty the hold yet, not knowing how much farther the shallows continued. The *Stealthy Shark* rode higher in the water, but they, too, had come close to disaster, caught between shallow water and the ruins of an ancient fortress, but her crew managed to avoid the dangers.

"Have mercy!" the lookout called. "Look at that!"

A ring of stone pillars, each the size of a greatoak, stood in a circle. There would be twenty-four in all, if not for the two that had fallen and now lay across the shallows ahead, creating a formidable barrier. Each column had a face carved on it, and they were visages of madness and despair.

"We're gonna have to sail around it," Kenward said.

"Zjhon warship grounded to the south, sir. Looks like it's been abandoned," Bryn called out from the rigging.

"They didn't make it," Kenward said. "I hope we have better luck than they did."

The sight of the ship gave Catrin heart; this was no ancient shipwreck. Perhaps they were going the right way after all. Still, there would be no way to tell which way to go beyond the shallows. Kenward had once told her that ships leave no footprints, and now she understood the hard truth of his words.

After furious debate between the ships, they split up to survey the area, hoping to find a safe channel to sail through. Kenward turned the *Eel* north, sailing perpendicular to the fallen columns. Pieces of other columns, which had obviously been much taller at one time, littered the area, and they had to move slowly. The farther north they sailed, though, the fouler the air became, filled with a noxious odor.

Beyond the fallen columns were luminous rifts in the seafloor; the gas they spewed churned the waters violently, and a foul haze hung over the water.

"It's not safe to sail over gas bubbles," Kenward said. "Ships have sunk in water filled with bubbles. When there is so much gas in the water, it disturbs the buoyancy that keeps us afloat. If even part of the ship enters those waters, she could be torn apart. We'll have to go back."

Not long after they turned around came a dreadful series of flashes--a distress call. The *Stealthy Shark* was grounded.

"They made it past the Zjhon warship, but the currents pulled them into sand. They are trying to pull themselves free using the anchor and windlass, but it doesn't look good. The only blessing is that they are on a sand bar. If we can pull her free, she shouldn't take much damage. We just have to get to the other side. Mother wants me to come south now and tow them backwards, but I disagree. We're going to try and make the other side, and then we'll pull them forward."

"Are you sure you want to disobey your mother?" Catrin asked, imagining the fight it would cause.

"My mother knows that sometimes you must follow your instincts to survive. My instincts are telling me to get through first. Besides, if I fail, she'll have a long swim before she can scold me."

Setting a course for the columns that still stood, Kenward scanned the water along with everyone else. They found several gaps between fallen chunks of column, but they led nowhere.

"There!" Bryn called. "Look, sir, to the north. See the gap?"

"Send a boat to check the depth, and see if the water beyond is deep enough as well."

Men scrambled to comply, knowing that time was running out for the *Shark*.

The gap proved wide enough for the *Eel* to slip through unscathed, which was obviously not the case for the Zjhon ships that had preceded them. Rub marks and even bits of wood clung to the columns.

"They came this way. That's for certain," Bryn said, and Kenward nodded his agreement, clearly deep in thought.

As they sailed within the columns, Catrin was overwhelmed by the similarities to the Grove of the Elders, and even though it was covered in water, she could feel the power of the land beneath her. Here, too, she guessed, was a place where the power of the land was most concentrated. Drinking it in, she let the natural energy flow around her and bolster her.

The seafloor rose in a gentle dome that crested at the center of the columns. Unable to cut straight through, Kenward guided the ship in an arc, following the columns as guides. Once past the fallen columns, he turned north. As they passed through two of the tallest columns that remained standing, Catrin felt as if she were leaving one world and entering another. Departure from the intense energy field left her swaying on her feet.

Cutting a meandering course, they reached waters not far from where the *Stealthy Shark* waited, eerily still in the water. Gathered at the stern, the crew were taking turns at the windlass. As soon as they spotted the *Eel*, a flurry of flashes came.

"She's not happy," Kenward said with a grin. "We'll see what song she sings when I pull them out. Fasha might just walk the plank on her own." When they had gotten as close to the *Shark* as they safely could, he turned to his crew. "Get a boat dropped and take a heavy line to the *Shark*."

Once the rope was firmly secured to each ship, Kenward raised the sails. For a time, nothing happened, but then both ships began to slide forward a finger's width at a time until the *Shark* slipped free.

The waters ahead were deeper, and the level of tension decreased greatly, but still they were wary of unforeseen obstacles. In the shadow of the giant mountain, which was now so close that Catrin felt she could reach out and touch it, the foul smell they had experienced earlier became strong once again, and pockets of bubbles suddenly erupted in the waters around them. Careful to avoid the roiling waters, they lost time finding a clear path.

Cheers rose from both ships, though, when the lookouts spotted the end of the shallows, and Catrin climbed the rigging to see the dark waters for herself. Beyond a ragged line of white sand, it beckoned and threatened. Unexplored waters awaited.

When the ships gained deep water, the order to fish immediately followed. Knowing they might need more food than the ships could hold to survive the voyage, they made use of every bit of space and packed it with food. Both ships sat low in the water by nightfall.

"I must admit," Kenward said. "I feel as if I have survived the dragon's claws only to land in his teeth. Do you have any idea of what way we should go now?"

"I don't," Catrin said, wishing she could do something. Then a desperate idea came to her, and she wondered if it could work. "Brother Vaughn, may I discuss something that happened in the Inner Sanctuary with violating confidence?"

"These circumstances warrant flexibility. Speak freely."

"Were you one of those who chanted during my time in the viewing chamber?"

"Yes. I was."

"Do you know both sides of the harmony?"

"Actually, I do. I learned only one part at first, but when you did not return, we had to be creative, and I ended up learning the other part as well. What are you thinking?"

"Could you teach the crew how to perform the chant?"

"I suppose I could," Brother Vaughn said, thoughtful. "I don't know if it will work without the stone chair . . . or the special chambers. I don't know."

"We could try," Catrin said firmly.

"We could try," he conceded. "But I'm still not certain it will be safe."

After gathering the off-duty members of both crews, Brother Vaughn instructed them on the chants. He taught them both parts as a precaution. Catrin, though, did not attend the sessions, afraid knowing the individual parts too well would somehow affect her ability to perceive it as a whole rather than the sum of its parts.

"Are you certain you want to try this, li'l miss? We almost lost you under the best of conditions. Trying from out here could be deadly."

"I can think of no other way to find the Firstland. We could sail for the rest of our lives and not find it. I will at least make an attempt."

"I suppose you're right."

* * *

Rolph Tillerman packed the last few items into the wagon that would take him away from his home, away from the place where he, his father, and his grandfather had been born and raised. Most of the items packed were for practical reasons, but a few were purely for sentimental purposes--he simply could not leave his entire past behind. Collette did what she could to hide her tears, but he could feel her pain as if it were his own. She had married him here and raised their children here.

Only Jessub seemed excited about the prospect of their journey, and at times, it seemed only his enthusiasm kept Rolph and Collette moving. Under any other circumstances, they would have stayed, but the choice had been taken from them. Hampered by injuries and his advancing age, Rolph had been unable to plant enough crops to keep them fed, and when it looked as if most of what he planted would succumb to pests and disease, he knew what he had to do. Others, too, could no longer afford to remain, and what had once been a thriving community now looked to be in its final days. Rolph knew that the others would help him if they could, but no one was in a position to do anything beyond survive, and it seemed they would need a great deal of luck to do that. Luck seemed one of the many things that were in short supply, and Rolph would not risk Collette's or Jessub's life on it. Instead, he would take an equally daunting risk, and he wondered if he were making a mistake.

Jessub appeared from behind the barn, dirty and scraped as usual.

"Come on, Jessub," Collette said. "We've got to go now, an' look at ya. Yer a boilin' mess, and you've torn yer last good pair o' breeches. Git up here this instant!"

"I'm comin', Gramma," Jessub said, his smile never wavering. "I just had to git my knife from the loft."

Rolph shook his head. He'd been hesitant to give the boy a knife for fear that he'd lop off his own thumbs just to see what it felt like. In all his years, he'd never seen a boy as inquisitive and rambunctious as Jessub, save maybe himself at that age. With one final look at his home and a squeeze on the shoulder from Collette, he chirruped and smacked the lines on Elmheart's rump. A new journey had begun.

***

In the deckhouse, they gathered. Hastily constructed partitions divided the room only in spirit. Facing the open door, Catrin looked out at the blue sky; clouds like salmon scales forecasted wind, but she was determined. Three times already Brother Vaughn had found reasons not to proceed, but she could wait no more.

"Now is the time. Please begin," she pleaded.

"Are you certain, li'l miss?"

"I am."

At first, the disjointed chanting seemed nothing like what she had experienced at Ohmahold, but then the two groups found synchronicity, and the harmony meshed. Wooden containers used as drums provided the bass. The vibrations were not as deep, but they resonated within the deckhouse.

Closing her eyes, Catrin rode the vibration and drew a trickle of energy, when she opened her eyes, she flew into the blue sky, free of her mortal shroud. In a moment of sheer bliss, she rolled and danced on the wind, lighter than a feather.

Determined not to waste the opportunity, she flew across the water, faster than the wind, casting her senses in every direction, drawing more and more power as a result. In a trancelike state, she flew, searching for land with all her senses. Then, in a moment of clarity, she realized that all she had to do was search for life and she would most likely find land.

At first, all she found were large, fast-moving sea creatures, but then she began to sense rivers of life flowing toward one place. When she moved over one of these shimmering rivers, she saw schools of migrating fish. Farther ahead, she found land. Tiny at first, it grew so quickly that Catrin could hardly believe her speed. What had first appeared to be one landmass was really a series of many small islands. On one, carved into the face of a massive cliff, was a familiar but foreign image: a man and a woman sharing an embrace. Except these figures were nothing like Istra and Vestra; they had large, round eyes and broad noses. They wore strange clothing and even stranger headdresses.

Despite the embrace, one of the man's arms was extended, pointing . . . to the Firstland; the woman pointed back to the Greatland. Exhilarated, Catrin prepared to return, but when she turned around, she made a terrifying discovery. Unlike her trip from the viewing chamber, no trail of energy extended back to her body.

Trying to gauge the direction from which she had come, she

realized how dire her situation really was. If she was off by even the slightest amount, given the distance she had covered, she would have very little chance of finding the ships.

Desperation gripped her as she made her best guess and applied her will to speed. Only the chance of spotting the giant mountain or the shallows kept her from losing all hope. Homogenous waves slid past, only occasional whitecaps breaking the monotony. Unable to accurately judge her speed, she had to be ever watchful, lest she fly right past them.

Weariness set in, and she could no longer extend her senses because it took all her energy just to continue moving. The waves moved ever slower past until she moved no faster than a ship, and she began to lose hope.

You must come.

The intense feeling brought Catrin from her stupor. Rather than words in her mind, this was more like overwhelming emotion, pouring into her, bolstering her, and she began moving a little faster. Still, she struggled to remain focused, feeling as if she were diffusing, like a drop of extract in water.

Do not despair.

Again, Catrin realized she was losing concentration. It would be so easy to just fall asleep, to let herself dissolve away, to become one with all creation.

I need you. You must free me. You must.

The emotional intrusions annoyed her, disturbing her rest. She was so tired and wanted only to sleep a while longer. A wave of desperate need washed over her, overwhelming her, and she was flooded with the hope that someone *would* come. Someone *would* end the agony and despair. *Someone.*

Catrin. Catrin. Catrin.

When her eyes opened, it was a shock. Her body demanded breath, and she sucked in air. Her limbs would not respond, and when she saw Benjin take her hand, it did not look like her own; her skin was ashen with a bluish tint. For the moment, breathing was paramount.

* * *

"This is crazy," Gustad said as Milo stood his shoulders, scraping bat droppings from the walls of a massive shaft that was filled with bats. Nearly fifty miles south of Ohmahold, they had covered the entire distance underground, never leaving the ancient mine complex. Several times Gustad had feared they were hopelessly lost, but they did manage to find the place indicated on their map.

"The ancient text says this stuff is what we need," Milo said. "This is the only way I know how to get it. You wouldn't consider keeping a bat as a pet, would you?"

"Not a chance," Gustad said, the very thought giving him a chill. "Hurry up. You're not light on the shoulders, you know." With his hands holding Milo's legs, Gustad stood with his knees slightly bent, trying to hold on to Milo's constantly shifting weight without hurting his back.

"I'm almost done," Milo said. "I need more light."

"I can't hold you and the torch," Gustad said.

"Let go of my leg and hand me the torch. I'll only be a moment more."

Gustad squatted down and grabbed the torch from where he had propped it. Standing back up was slow and difficult, but Milo used a toehold to support much of his weight. Still, Gustad was breathing hard when he handed Milo the torch.

Bits of rock and bat dung fell from the air as Milo worked, and Gustad wiped his face with one hand, holding Milo steady with the other. Pain seared his shoulder as Milo stood on his toes to reach something.

"There's a great big spot . . . just out of reach," Milo said, his effort to stretch clear in his voice. Shifting his weight, he slipped, sending sparks and bits of still-burning torch all around. Blowing and using his free hand, Gustad wiped the embers away from his face. An ember on Milo's robe started to smolder, but he could not reach it. He opened his mouth to say something, but a shout of pain was all the came out as Milo put most of his weight on one foot, creating tremendous pressure on Gustad's shoulder.

A moment later, Milo must have realized he was on fire, for he leaped from Gustad's shoulders and stamped out his robes, at times only a hand's width from the ledge, beyond which lay the gaping shaft that dropped an unknowable distance into the darkness.

"These droppings had better be worth it," Gustad said, rubbing his sore shoulders.

* * *

Leaning on the gunwale, Catrin pointed. "That way," she said. "There we will find the Keys of Terhilian, and the Terhilian Lovers will show us the way. But if I remember correctly, the man pointed . . . that way."

Kenward looked to where she pointed. "South and then southwest. I don't suppose we should risk trying to cut straight to the Firstland.

Better to sail to the keys and then let the Terhilian Lovers point the way. If we knew how far the keys were from the Firstland, we could chance it, but since we don't know, I suppose we'll have to go the long way."

After a series of mirror flashes, it seemed Nora and Fasha agreed. Orders were given to fish. "We'll fill the holds again if we can. The winds are growing stronger, which'll make that more difficult, but you know your jobs. Let's fish."

Catrin attacked her tasks and helped others finish theirs. Once the trawl tubs, nets, and pots were dropped, there was little to do except wait.

"I'm glad we'll be leaving here soon," Kenward said as he joined Catrin, both staring at the shallows behind them. "That mountain gives me the crawls."

Catrin wondered if he might be more sensitive to energy patterns than he knew, for, to her, the mountain's angry energy field raged like an inferno. Like a pot of boiling water with the lid left on, its intensity grew. "I agree," she said.

"Let's see if we've caught anything. The sooner we're done, the sooner we leave." Kenward issued orders and demanded speed from his crew. Everyone moved with determination and purpose, knowing that following orders was the surest way to stay alive. The wind continued to hinder their efforts; the fish just seemed to stop biting, but still they caught a host of crabs. Catrin joined those who boiled and cleaned the crabs, trying to get them into some preserved form.

The *Stealthy Shark* had better luck in the deeper water and loaded their hold with tuna and small sharks. The big sharks did not show themselves on this side of the shallows, which made Catrin feel a great deal safer.

The crew retrieved their gear and made for the waters near the *Shark*. Kenward was stubborn, but he was not foolish enough to deny that Fasha had found the better fishing ground. Fasha's messages indicated that her hold was full, but they would continue fishing until the *Eel*'s hold was filled. Kenward swallowed his pride and gratefully accepted what was sent from the *Shark*. The combined effort filled the hold in a relatively short time, and there seemed a collective sigh of relief when they set sail for the Keys of Terhilian.

"I can't say exactly how far the keys are," Catrin said later that day. "It's difficult to gauge, but I would say three months."

"At least we're not sailing blind," Kenward said. "Your abilities amaze me. It's a pity they're so dangerous to use. I feared you would never return from your journey. How do you do it? Is it like flying?"

"It's hard to explain, but I'd say it's better than flying because you don't have to worry about falling. I just make up my mind which way to go, and the world moves beneath me, as if I'm not moving at all. Tell me. What do you see when you look at the mountain?"

He raised an eyebrow but then concentrated on the mountain for a long time. "Pressure," he said finally. "Inevitability. I can't explain it."

"I think, Kenward, you've more talent than you know. I, too, see the 'pressure,' as you put it. I wonder if you don't have some abilities with Istra's power."

Kenward stood, stunned, his mouth hanging open. "You really think so?"

"Let's find out. Say nothing," she said. "Chase, would you come here a moment?"

"Let me finish this first," Chase said, helping Farsy load pine boxes back into the hold. He came over when they were done. "What do you need?"

"Look at the mountain, and tell me what you see."

"I see a mountain. It's big. What's this all about?"

"Do you see anything unusual about it?"

"C'mon, Cat," he said, but then he saw how serious she was; with her eyes she pleaded. Sighing, he turned and looked again. Catrin watched him intently and jumped when he gave a start.

"Gods have mercy," he said. "I thought you were nuts, but the mountain is breathing--flexing. It just moved!" His shout got everyone's attention, and both crews watched in horror as the colossal and seemingly permanent mountain jumped and split. With the ferocity of the gods, the top blew apart and a column of fire leaped into the sky. Nearly half of what remained slid sideways and dropped into the sea with an inconceivably violent impact. Black clouds filled the air and rolled across the sea as if the world were ending. No one moved at first, but then the reality of the situation set in.

"Turn us about!" Kenward barked. "Set a course back for the mountain!" For a moment, the crew hesitated, unsure they had heard correctly. "Now!" he shouted, and no one argued. Too many times he had proven his wisdom and skill, which was needed now more than ever before. Frantically, he signaled the *Shark* then started cursing when the response came. "They'll run before the wave and clouds, but I don't think we have enough time. The wave will overwhelm us. Have I judged wrongly?"

"What wave?" Catrin asked, and Kenward pointed. In fascinated horror, Catrin watched the seas rise to an impossible height, nearly as tall as the mountain had been, and the wall of water raced toward them like the shadow of death.

"I trust your instincts," Catrin said. "Do what you think is best."

Anguish was clear on Kenward's face as the *Stealthy Shark* disappeared in the diminishing light, heading in the opposite direction. Before the wave reached them, dense ash began to fall from the sky, coating everything. Unlike the ashes from a fire, it was heavy and gritty. Like black snow, it fell and accumulated, weighing them down.

"Keep the decks clear of ash," Kenward demanded. "If we take on too much, it'll either sink or capsize us." His words inspired haste, and despite the encroaching darkness, the crew struggled against an irrepressible tide of ash.

The pressure in the air suddenly changed, and Catrin drew a deep breath through the cloth she had wrapped around her face. Kenward howled like a madman as the wave overtook them. Sailing straight into it at full speed, they began to climb, and soon they were pointing straight into the sky, staring at a roiling mass of ash and fire streaked with red lightning.

Groaning as she flexed against the tremendous forces, the ship slowed. Holding on, Catrin cried out as Farsy and another man tumbled from the rigging and into the dark waters below. Finally cresting the wave, the *Slippery Eel* seemed to drop from the sky.

* * *

Benjin watched, helpless, as the *Slippery Eel* was lost from sight. Death would come no matter which course they chose, he thought. He would have preferred to stay together, but Nora and Fasha stood firm and stayed their course, away from the eruption. Powerless and impotent, he cursed fate and waited for the inevitable.

Rising up to blot out the sky, the wave came, roaring as it displaced the wind. Tying himself to a cleat that protruded from the deck, Benjin stood facing the stern, staring up at the roiling sky, only rope and harness keeping him from falling into the water below. Feeling more as if he were on the face of a cliff than the deck of a ship, he closed his eyes and held on as tight as he could.

Overwhelmed by the speed and height of the wave, the *Stealthy Shark* rolled forward, tumbling end over end along the crest like a piece of driftwood in the surf. Above the roar could be heard the snapping of wood. The rigging was torn away first along with the masts, but then the seas claimed the deckhouse, steerage, and most of the gunwales, tearing them away is if they were made of parchment.

When Benjin once again felt air on his face, he sucked a deep breath and prepared to be plunged beneath the water again, but what remained of the *Shark* stayed upright and raced down the trailing edge of the swell. Looking around, he saw Fasha still moored to a cleat. Like him, she had chosen to tie herself off to a part of the deck itself. The choice had saved their lives, but they were alone; no one else remained.

Fasha looked up after untying herself. "I've lost the *Shark*."

Chapter 10

Life is fragile and can be quelled in uncountable ways.
--Brachias Pall, assassin

* * *

Momentarily weightless, Catrin hung, suspended in air, until her feet touched the deck once again. The *Slippery Eel* slammed into the trailing edge of the wave and raced back toward the relatively calm waters behind it. More waves came but none as big as the first.

"Men overboard!" Catrin shouted. Not far away, she spotted someone in the water. Determined to help, she tied an oar from one of the boats to the end of a rope and cast it toward him. For several tense moments, Catrin watched Farsy try to reach the oar, fighting the waves. Kenward slowed the ship, and Farsy grasped Catrin's line.

Chase came to her aid, and they pulled him in, wrapping him in blankets once he was on deck. The crew searched the water for the other man, but he was lost. After a headcount, they found it was Nimsy, a man who'd always been kind to Catrin, and she wept in mourning, tears streaking her soot-stained face as she continued to shovel ash from the deck.

"Have mercy! The finger of the gods!" someone shouted, and Catrin looked to the rigging, following the stares. There she saw a terrifying sight. Orange and red flames licked the rigging without consuming or even scorching it. Fingers of liquid light crawled over the mast and crow's nest, reaching toward the sky. Sheets of translucent flame enveloped the sails and danced over them, seemingly without touching them, as if it were only the specter of fire. It was almost like what she had seen in the Pinook harbor but visible to all.

The energy of the ash storm intensified, reaching out to them, and Catrin feared they would be struck by ghastly red lightning. When the crew began praying and casting offerings into the sea, she joined them by offering a lock of her hair. Perhaps if she gave something of herself, she thought, the gods would show mercy.

Shouts on the other side of the deck got her attention, and a crowd gathered there as Nimsy was miraculously pulled from the water. Could the gods have heard their prayers? Unsure what to believe, Catrin cut a much larger lock of her hair and cast it into the waves, knowing it could do no harm.

Turning slowly, the *Slippery Eel* came about and made for the waters where the *Stealthy Shark* had last been seen. The ash cloud blotted out the sky from above, and more ash rolled steadily across the water toward them.

"Take cover in the deckhouse!" Kenward ordered, and the crew rushed to comply, seeing what looked like the breath of a demon bearing down on them. "Hold your breath and cover yourselves," he shouted just before the remains of the pyroclastic cloud washed over the *Slippery Eel*, engulfing her in a rolling maelstrom of ash and fire. When it passed, shouts and coughing were all that could be heard. Covered in ash and burns, the crew put out the fires and gave every effort, but the ash accumulated faster than they could remove it, slowly pulling them under.

Like a blessing from the gods, a strong wind descended from the north and drove the ash before it, dispersing it. While it made the problem worse for a while, eventually the air began to clear and the sun was visible behind a foul and gauzy haze. Ash still fell, but the intensity was greatly dissipated as the wind diffused the ash and spread it over a larger area. Fire still belched from what remained of the mountain, but even that began to subside.

Tears filled Catrin's eyes as the first of the debris appeared. Seeing only small bits at the start, she prayed the *Stealthy Shark* had survived, but then large chunks began to appear, scattered across the waves. Kenward watched with his jaw clenched, and Catrin could almost see his heart breaking. She held her breath, waiting for something to wake her from this nightmare.

"Survivors to port!" the lookout shouted, and Catrin ran to see who it was. On a floating section of sail and rigging were Strom, Osbourne, Nora, and three of Fasha's crewman. Elated, Catrin help lower the boarding net while men cast out lines for them to grab on to.

Osbourne reached the deck first and asked for help preparing a litter. "Nora's hurt bad," he said. "We're gonna need help getting her aboard."

Kenward and his crew moved with determination that bordered on panic. Soon, though, the crewman secured Nora to the litter and she was raised to the deck. Barely conscious, she apprised Kenward on her condition and how her wounds were to be treated. Even as they set broken bones and closed gaping wounds, she continued to give orders through clenched teeth.

"Find Fasha," she said before her eyes closed. Kenward stood over her, willing her chest to rise and fall.

"Do what you can to find the rest," Catrin said. "I'll come for you if her condition changes."

"Bless you," he said as he turned back to his crew. "Get boats in the water! I want everyone found. Now!" As soon as the boats were in the water, he moved the *Eel* away, looking for anyone in the distance.

Nora was taken to Kenward's cabin and made as comfortable as possible. She drifted in and out of consciousness, mumbling incoherently. Catrin sat at her side, trying to remember what she had learned from past attempts at healing. Perhaps she was fooling herself, she thought, but her efforts seemed to calm Nora and sent her into a peaceful sleep. After a time, Catrin felt she had done what she could do, and she went in search of Kenward to apprise him of her condition. He stood at the wheel, his eyes filled with tears. They had found more debris but no more survivors. As daylight began to fade, he turned the *Eel* back to retrieve the boats.

Cheers carried across the water as three more of Fasha's crew were pulled into the boats. Catrin and Kenward stood side by side, trying to deny the harsh reality. Benjin, Fasha, and most of her crew were lost. The *Stealthy Shark* was no more.

"I'm so sorry," Kenward said as his shoulders began to shake. His poignant anguish washed over Catrin, mixed with her own, and drove a wedge into her soul. Impotent rage gnawed at her very being, and she felt as if she would erupt, just as the mountain had.

Kenward continued the search for three days, but it was Nora who demanded they move on. "If they were going to be found, it would've happened by now. We must accept it, Son. They're gone."

* * *

Nat waited on a mossy rock near the spring where Neenya swam. This place was special to her, and she brought him here only when she was feeling especially happy. Her smile drew him closer, and he marveled at the way the light danced in her eyes.

It had been a long time since he last visited the mountaintop; he always seemed to be busy with one task or another. Life was pleasant here, and he could easily forget his worries. Trips to the mountain brought only pain and grief. Most of the time, he didn't even understand his visions. What good came from them? Secretly, he'd been working on mental exercises that he hoped would suppress the visions. It shamed him, but a peaceful life with Neenya seemed worth it.

As he bent down to kiss her, though, he felt a warm sensation on his lips, and he wiped them with the back of his hand, which came away covered in blood. Neenya's scream faded as the world shifted.

Atop an unbelievably tall wave ran a white panther; on its back rode Catrin, her colorless hair pulled back by the wind. The staff she held came alive, its eyes gleaming as it spread its wings and flew. The white cat reared, but the water pulled at his legs, and he tumbled into the leading edge of the crashing wave. In an instant Catrin and her cat were gone.

Still the water came, and Nat, standing on the highest mount, watched the seas rise until the water lapped at his feet.

"Neenya," Nat said when the vision released him. "We must hurry."

* * *

Pulling hard on the too light load, Mark Vedregon cursed the monsters that continually ruined his nets. They had caught enough fish to feed his men for a week, but as had happened so many times before, *something* cut the nets before they reached the surface. More of the reptile beasts, he suspected--Gholgi, Belegra had called them. Powerful and crafty, they were proving to be capable foes. Hindering their fishing efforts was only one of the ways the beasts harried Mark Vedregon and his men, slowly wearing them down.

"Nets were cut again, sir. Shall we repair 'em?"

"Not now. We can do that when we get back to shore. Drop the trawl tubs. Maybe we'll get lucky and hook some of those boiling beasts in the process."

"Aye, sir."

"Even if we could catch enough to feed us," Second Richt said, "Archmaster Belegra will take it to feed his pet." His moody gaze scanned the seas, but then he stopped. Pointing out to sea, he stood mute and trembling, unable to make himself speak. Mark Vedregon gave frantic orders, and the crew moved with haste, despite knowing it was already too late. The sea would claim them.

* * *

Miss Mariss walked the avenues, passing faces both familiar and strange. So many things had changed, and yet many were still the same. When she reached the docks, Amnar greeted her with his usual toothless grin.

"Hallo, missus," he said. "I set a nice mackerel aside fer ya and a few toadfish. The currents run strange these days; I'd have more for ya if I could."

"I appreciate what you have, Amnar. We make do with what we can get these days," she said, moving on to where Lendra and her new mate, Bavil, waited.

"The pots were heavy today, Miss Mariss. We've blue crab, shedders, and wall-climbers for you."

"Thank you," she said, dropping a silver into Lendra's palm. Looking beyond the docks, Miss Mariss wondered how Strom, Catrin, and the others fared, but a curious sight drew her attention. Children playing on the beach ran out to grab stranded fish and crabs as the bay began to rapidly recede. Faster that the swiftest tide, the water rushed away from land, as if there were a great hole in the seafloor.

For a time she was mesmerized by the sight, as were others, but then the realization set in and her mind could conceive only one explanation. "Get away from the water! Make for high ground," she shouted. "The seas are coming! The seas are coming!"

* * *

At the helm of the *Slippery Eel*, Kenward gripped the wheel as if it were his only link to sanity. Sadness, more powerful than anything he'd ever imagined, threatened to cripple his mind and body. Tears sprang to his eyes without warning, as feelings of loss manifested as physical pain. He felt as if his heart were truly broken.

Using a short staff as a cane, Nora limped to his side, but he said nothing; he just continued to stare out at the endless horizon.

"I miss her too," she said.

Those words were more than Kenward could bear, and he began to cry. "I'm so sorry," he said, and he gave the wheel over to Bryn. Unable to even lift his eyes to meet hers, he walked to his mother and wrapped her in a tight hug as he wept.

"It wasn't your doing, Son. You are not to blame."

"I was supposed to save her," he said, feeling as if his chest might explode. "Why couldn't I save her?"

"I don't know. I'm sorry, Son. I miss her too," Nora said. Together they cried. In a rare display, they stood, holding each other. Crewmen came, one by one, each with a kind word or a pat on the shoulder. Silently and together, the ship mourned.

To Kenward, the loss seemed surreal, and he kept expecting to wake up, for all this to have been but a dream. Nothing seemed as it should. Colors were dull, and sounds that might once have been beautiful were now harsh and somehow disrespectful. The world without Fasha seemed a poorer place. She had been a second half of him, always there to counter him, a constant challenge to his wits. His mother had intended to hand the *Trader's Wind* down to Fasha; he was certain of it. That thought led him to another crushing realization: His pain was but a small fraction of what his mother must be experiencing. "I know I can never take Fasha's place," he said, "but I'll try harder."

"Nonsense," Nora said. "You're doing just fine. Fasha is my

daughter, and nothing could ever replace her, but I would be just as lost without you."

Kenward raised his eyes, surprised by what he heard.

Nora laughed. "A fool boy you may be, but you're *my* fool boy."

* * *

By the dim light of her lamp, Nora lay in her hammock, caressing the walls of Kenward's ship with her fingertips, her mind elsewhere. She was proud of Kenward for allowing himself to grieve, and she was proud of herself. She'd been taught to conceal her feelings from the crew, to always present a confident front. While the tactic had worked well during her career, Kenward had taught her something. His crew exuded something that surpassed loyalty. They followed him not because he commanded them, but because they *cared* about him; some might say they loved him.

It explained the one thing that Fasha had always questioned: How did he get his crew to obey his reckless orders? Nora could see Fasha as she had been in those moments, her arms crossed over her chest and fire in her eyes. From her pocket, she pulled a gold locket that filled her palm. Inside were things that would be valuable to only a mother: the dried, crumbling remains of a sea daisy and a tiny coral fan. Kenward had given her the sea daisy when he was five summers, and the coral had come from a small, unnamed island they had found when avoiding a massive storm. After the storm had passed, Fasha, who was ten at the time, spent an afternoon swimming around the colorful reefs. When she came back to the ship, she was so excited to show Nora what she'd found. Fasha's smile and laughter were forever ingrained in her memory.

Flipping the locket closed, Nora sighed. Somehow, she would keep Kenward safe.

* * *

When the Keys of Terhilian finally came into view, they looked little like what Catrin recalled. What had been white beaches lined by thick forest were now fields of mud and debris as far as could be seen. She sighed in relief when they came to the Terhilian Lovers, which had withstood the fury of the sea.

Kenward set a course, following the megalithic statue's pointing finger. "Let's get there and be done with this," he said. "I've no more taste for adventure. I'll happily take a quiet life of trading."

"It took you long enough to figure that out, fool boy," Nora said, leaning on her short staff. Her bones were still knitting, but she insisted on watching over the crew. Catrin agreed with Kenward, wanting nothing more to do with adventure. What she would have once thought of as glorious and exciting now tasted of death and despair. Too many had died, and Catrin could find no justification, no end worth those means.

The possibility of any of them surviving this journey grew smaller with every day, and Catrin knew she would probably never leave the Firstland, assuming they found it. If she did, though, she promised herself she would go home. Dead or alive, that was where her father was, and she was determined to find her way back to him.

From the beginning, her journey had been costly, but the loss of Benjin was more than she could bear. Only the love she had for those still around her kept her from throwing herself into the sea. Chase stood by her side and put his arm around her. "Do you want to talk about it?"

"No."

"You can't keep it all inside, Cat; it'll eat its way out eventually."

"Then let it," she said, feeling foolish. "Talking won't bring them back, and I doubt it'll make me feel any better. Why bother?"

"I miss him too," Chase said, and his simple admission uncorked the wellspring of emotion she could no longer keep inside.

Her jaw quivered and her shoulders shook, but she did not want to cry. To cry was to be a victim, to lament her losses and accept them, but she didn't want to accept them; that was simply too painful. She wanted someone to blame, someone to *punish*.

"I need exercise," she said. "Will you spar with me?"

"Will you talk to me afterward and tell me how you are really feeling?" Chase asked.

"If I must."

"You must," he said, getting practice swords from storage. He tossed one to Catrin but was unprepared for her sudden attack.

"So that's how you want it?" he asked, lying on his back and rubbing the lump that was growing on the back of his head. Rolling backward, he got back to his feet and readied himself for her next attack.

Pent-up rage drove Catrin. In front of her, she saw not Chase, but the source of all her problems, and she attacked without thought or mercy. Moving by sheer instinct, she fought as she had never fought before, and Chase fell before her attacks.

"That's enough for me," he said, limping and rubbing his bruises. "Find someone else to beat up." He walked away, looking hurt.

Catrin was not yet done venting her anger, but no one else would spar with her, having seen how poorly Chase had fared against her raging attacks.

Unwilling to keep her anger inside any longer, she searched the dry hold and found a sack of dried reeds. After hanging it from the rigging, she attacked, her practice sword slicing the air, pounding the sack mercilessly. Even after reducing the sack to shreds, though, she did not feel any better.

Her heart pounding, she climbed atop the bowsprit. "Why do you hate me so much?" she screamed at the sky, challenging the gods themselves. "What have I done to deserve such evil and malice?"

Crew members stopped what they were doing, and Bryn readied a harness in case she fell from her dangerous perch, but Catrin barely noticed them. "Come, Istra. Come, Vestra. Right here . . . right now. Let us end this. If you wish me to suffer, then come down here and fight me yourselves. Cowards! I don't fear you, and I spit on your names. I cast your own hate back at you. What do you say to that?"

As if to answer her, lightning split the air and thunder rolled across the water. Gusting winds threatened to knock her from the bowsprit, but she remained there, challenging the gods to a duel. Only when Chase grabbed her ankles did she see the world around her again. Dark clouds moved in swiftly from the west, and stinging rain began to fall.

"Cowards!" she shouted one last time, shaking her fist in the air, before she let Chase guide her back to the deck.

"Cripes, Cat. You're scaring the crew. Calm down."

Shaking, Catrin took deep breaths and tried to do as he said. When the rage passed, though, exhaustion took its place, and she let Chase carry her to her cabin.

"It'll all work out somehow, Cat. Even if we have to take on the gods themselves, somehow we'll make it right. I promise," he said as he pulled a blanket over her, and she fell into a dreamless sleep.

* * *

"Not too much now," Milo said as he leaned in over Gustad's shoulder.

"I know. I know," Gustad said as he mixed water with the materials listed in the ancient text. Since Milo had found a recipe for what had been called *fire powder*, he had focused on nothing else. Gustad had tried to talk him out of experimenting with the formula a dozen times, fearing it was too dangerous, but Milo would not be dissuaded. His hands more steady than Milo's, Gustad gently rolled the mixture and kneaded it until it was uniform.

"That looks about right to me," Milo said. "Let's take it outside and test it."

"Just a moment," Gustad said. "Let me clean up all this mess." Despite his efforts, a mixture of different ingredients covered the worktable, and a fine dust hung in the air. "Could you get me some water?"

"You and your cleanliness," Milo said. "We can clean up when we get back from testing this. Now let's go." Reaching his hand out to the metal bowl that held the snakelike pieces of fire powder clay, a tiny blue arc of static leaped between his finger and the bowl. It was enough to ignite the dust in the air and produced a mighty thump. The initial explosion threw Milo and Gustad back, which was a blessing since the ignited dust engulfed the fire powder snakes. Two larger explosions followed, creating a mighty cloud of noxious smoke.

From beneath the remains of a crumbled worktable, Gustad crawled. His hair smoking and his face blackened, he glared at Milo.

"I told you it would work," Milo said, grinning, and Gustad just shook his head.

* * *

"Birds ahead, sir," Bryn called from the crow's nest.

"Land can't be too far," Kenward said. "Double the watch. Keep your eyes open for outcroppings and reefs. I want no surprises."

Catrin, her gaze focused on the waves, looking for any sign of obstacles, was terrified to see a huge, dark shape dart beneath the ship and emerge on the other side, its movements graceful and serpentine. More came, seemingly drawn by curiosity if not hunger. None broke the surface, leaving Catrin and the crew to guess at their true nature.

"Never seen the likes of that," Kenward said. "They haven't attacked yet, but remain watchful nonetheless. Bring out the spears from the hold; we may need to fend them off yet." His words inspired fear in the crew as they watched the dark shapes moving beneath them, taunting them, staying just deep enough to remain ambiguous.

"Rocks to port," Bryn called, and Kenward guided the ship clear of the danger. "Land, sir! I see land!"

Excitement ran through the crew as a large landmass came into view, but for Catrin it was a moment of dread. Here she was, the Firstland, a place of legend and the place where some said the first men and women were born. It was a place abandoned--surrendered--by her ancestors. As it stretched across the horizon, Catrin was overwhelmed by anxiety, suddenly convinced she would die on the Firstland. In the past she had believed, deep down, that she would survive, that someday she and her loved ones would all get home safely, but Benjin was gone. Too many others were already dead. What reason did she have to believe she wouldn't be next? She found no reassurance, and her guts churned.

The shores had been devastated far worse than the Keys of Terhilian. High into the mountainous terrain, the twisted mass of mud and severed life dominated the landscape. Birds clouded the skies over the mass of rotted vegetation. Though most of the carcasses had been picked clean, leaving only bleached bones as evidence of their existence, land-based scavengers searched for an easy meal. Even from afar, the smell was overpowering, and Kenward ordered more sail.

"We'll need to find a part of the coast that was not affected by the wave. The waters here are far too clogged with debris to be safe, and no one wants to travel through that mess," he said. For nearly half a day, they saw nothing but destruction, but then they reached an area dominated by towering rock formations that jutted from the sea and sheltered a large bay.

"Look!" Chase called, pointing. Two peaks, close together, cradled what remained of a Zjhon warship. Seeing the ship high above them was disconcerting, and Catrin was filled with a mixture of hope and dread. Surely no one had survived, she thought. Maybe Archmaster Belegra was already dead, and they could just go home. No matter how much she wanted to believe it, she knew it wasn't true. Her death awaited. Like a looming premonition, the feeling had grown stronger every day that Benjin was gone. Even bright skies could not chase away the cloud of darkness that followed her, surrounding her. Despite the nagging despair, she drew a deep breath and turned to face the wind, determined to do the best she could.

Beyond a gap in the wall, pristine, unmolested shoreline was visible. Black beaches skirted heavily forested and mountainous terrain. Along the shores, creatures both varied and bizarre covered the landscape. Huge animals that looked like bloated seals crowded together on jutting rock formations. Others like wild boars, only with skin like marbled leather and the size of horses, roamed in packs. Saltwater crocodiles as long as the *Slippery Eel* rested in shallow waters, often with only their eyes above water.

In a horrifying display, a whale, black as night, thrust itself from the water and onto a rocky outcropping, grabbing one of the bloated seals and tossing it into the air. Others of its ilk moved in and assisted with the kill, giving Catrin her first glimpse of predators working as a team. Her father and Benjin had told her about wolves hunting in packs, but it was shocking to witness such calculated and communal brutality, something she had thought only humans were capable of.

Painfully aware of her own carnal nature, inherent and blood given, she wondered if it could be overcome or if, deep down, they were all just predators waiting for their next kill. Thinking of Barabas and Mother Gwendolin along with other kind-hearted folks she had met on her journey, she knew it could suppressed, and she gained even more respect for those who did it so well, seemingly without effort.

Across the bay, jagged peaks rose on either side of a wide river valley, and even from the distance the sights there were awe inspiring.

"The Valley of Victors," Brother Vaughn said in little more than a whisper. "I had always thought the old tales exaggerated, but here it is before me. The old tales failed to express its true majesty. I am humbled."

"Looks like a good way to get inland," Kenward said.

"That should be the Perintong River," Brother Vaughn said. "Beyond the Valley of Victors and the Eternal Guardians should be the ancient city of Ri. That's where Belegra would go. I'm nearly certain of it."

Catrin nodded, filled with dread. "Take me as far upriver as you can, please," she said, and Kenward gave the orders.

Trembling, Catrin gripped her staff, trying to master her fears. Even the landscape challenged her courage. Steep walls lined the river valley, and every inch was covered with some kind of carving, but it was the carvings of armed men, monstrous and proud, that demanded Catrin's attention. Even worn by the ravages of time, enough detail remained to convey the ferocity of these men, for men they all were. Not a single female image was to be found, which Catrin found even more disturbing.

Winds, funneled by the massive valley, drove the *Slippery Eel* upriver, against the sluggish current. Around a bend came the most imposing sight yet. Crouched down, one on either side of the river, waited a pair of megalithic stone warriors, each with one arm in the water and the other held in the air, gripping swords that crossed overhead.

The features of one were nearly indistinguishable, but the other delivered an imposing glare. Half his face was missing, yet he seemed to stare into Catrin's soul and find her wanting.

"The Eternal Guardians," Brother Vaughn said, and Catrin knew their image would haunt her dreams.

Chapter 11

To enslave that which is free is to invite your own betrayal.
--Barabas, druid

* * *

Beyond the guardians, the valley walls closed in. The river narrowed, and the current became swift and turbulent. Ahead, fallen monuments obstructed the river, evidenced by the mighty but broken hand that jutted from the swirling water.

"Can't go around that," Kenward said. "What will you do, Catrin? Now that we are here, what will you do?"

"I must find Belegra, even if that means searching the Firstland from end to end," she said. She could not turn back, not after having come so far and having lost so many. She had to complete this journey in honor of those who had given their lives toward that end.

Dark shapes moved within the trees along the shores, and strange, raucous calls rose above the roar of the water. Eyes appeared in the water near the ship, and the crew jumped when an impact left the ship thrumming.

"I can't keep the *Eel* here," Kenward said. "I'm going to have to keep much of the crew aboard and return to the harbor, but that leaves only a handful of people to accompany you. I don't know what to do."

"You know exactly what to do, fool boy. You just don't *want* to do it, so you refuse accept it. Do what must be done."

"Thank you, Mother. You are correct; I know. If you are to reach Ri, Catrin, I suggest you take a landing party to shore a short ways back downriver, where the waters are calmer. We'll sail back to the harbor and prepare for the long journey home. When you've achieved your goal, come back to your boat. Light a signal fire--the more smoke, the better--and we'll come for you. There are mirrors in your packs; use those if you can't get a fire lit. I'm sorry I can offer no more."

"Well said, my son."

Uncertainty festered in Catrin's belly. Daunted by the thought of exploring the Firstland with only five people, she set her jaw, her determination bolstered by the commitment of those who stood around her: Chase, Strom, Osbourne, and Brother Vaughn. All stood ready to disembark, and Catrin sensed no fear from them, only the drive to do what must be done.

The land slid by quickly, and Kenward selected what he considered an ideal place for them to disembark. The current was sluggish, and reddish, gritty sand formed a bare shoreline. Beyond, the forest claimed every scrap of land in its emerald grip. When faced with the question of which bank to land on, Catrin let her instincts decide: east. She wasn't certain why. She had no visions or overpowering emotion; it just felt right.

"May the gods bless you on your journey," Kenward said. "We'll wait sixty days. If you do not return, we must sail."

"If you've seen no signal in thirty days, leave. Don't wait for us if it puts your lives in danger," Catrin said, a tear in her eye and a catch in her voice.

"You'll be back in less than thirty, but we'll wait sixty," Nora said with a sharp nod, and Kenward smiled. Catrin wished she shared Nora's confidence. "Your packs are loaded, and we're ready to drop your boat. Travel well and return safe."

Catrin and the others climbed into the suspended boat, and the crew lowered them to the water. The parting was surreal; she found it difficult to believe that she was about to step onto fabled soil abandoned by man more than three thousand years past. Only lightly armed, she doubted her party was prepared for the trials ahead. This place harbored creatures they had never seen before and knew nothing about. Anything that moved was suspect.

Once ashore, they dragged their boat to some nearby trees and covered it with branches, aware that even this task could be deadly if carried out carelessly. Picking through the branches, they found snakes, frogs, and colorful lizards in abundance. Even with great care, there were a few tense moments.

Moving deeper into the forest seemed suicide from what Catrin had already seen; her mind imagined every creature as a deadly and poisonous foe. Given that she had no way to tell which were dangerous and which were benign, it was a healthy outlook, even if unpleasant.

Sailing with the current, the *Slippery Eel* was soon lost from sight. Any feeling of security Catrin had fled with the *Eel*, but she led the group as best she could, slowly picking their way into a foreign and unknown land. Using short swords, they cut through obstacles at a crawling pace, but sunlight could be seen on the forest floor ahead, and the group moved with determination.

When they broke free of the tangled mass of vines and thorns, they entered a strange twilight, where the vegetation took on surprising shapes. Despite the dense growth, the outlines of ancient structures could still be seen, and occasional walls still stood, covered completely in growth and looking as if they had occurred naturally.

Chase pulled the vines back from a column, revealing the fine detail that was previously hidden. Gracefully fluted and tapered, they were a marvelous testament to the ancients' stonework and building skills. Farther on, they discovered a field of man-shaped growths that harbored ancient sculptures of men with ideal physiques, their muscle definition conveyed with tremendous detail.

No one spoke as they moved among the eerie shapes, and Catrin couldn't shake the fear that they would all suddenly spring to life and attack. When they reached the far end of the field, they found a low, stone wall. Beyond it was a relatively clear space and another, similar wall. Between, the land was flat and, for a short distance, unobstructed: a road.

"If this is a road, it should lead to Ri, shouldn't it?" Chase asked.

"Your reasoning is sound. We should follow the road," Brother Vaughn said.

Catrin could give no reason for her fear of the road, only that she felt sick whenever she looked at it. Perhaps, she thought, it was because of what she would find at its end. Knowing it made sense to follow the road, she reluctantly agreed.

The rest of the day was spent picking through the less dense foliage that was reclaiming the ancient roadway, but their progress was significantly faster than when traveling through the forest. In some places, larger structures remained mostly standing, and in one case, an elaborate entrance decorated the side of a mountain. Catrin was tempted to explore it, but her gut told her she had not yet reached her destination and she resisted the urge.

"How do you know Belegra isn't in there?" Chase asked.

"It just doesn't feel right," was the only answer Catrin could provide, but it seemed to satisfy him. Crowded between the river and the valley walls were a continuous supply of distractions, enticing places that could hold treasures beyond their reckoning, and only the will to achieve their goal kept them from straying.

When they came to a place where the road was blocked with massive stones and the trees and vines that covered them, they found evidence of a fight, and it looked as if many Zjhon soldiers had died. Pieces of armor and torn bits of uniforms littered the ground, but a nearby mound told of survivors; someone had buried the dead.

Evidence of those Catrin sought should have been welcome, but it only increased her uneasiness; the knowledge of another, unknown foe had everyone on edge, and they moved slowly, scanning the trees for danger.

When darkness claimed the land, they had to stop. They made a hasty camp with a small fire. Beyond the meager light of their fire, Catrin could see little in the darkness. The leaves above blocked the small amount of light the night sky gave through thick clouds.

Shadows moved around them, detectable by only the minute change in the shade of darkness. It was the smell that brought Catrin to full alert. Musky and overpowering, the odor suddenly filled the air. Before she could even open her mouth to give warning, the trees exploded with activity. Even though the attackers had the element of surprise, they did not find the camp sleeping. Wary and afraid, most had been lying awake in their bedrolls, and they sprang to action.

Gathering around Catrin, her Guardians sought to defend her from a foe they had not yet clearly seen. Catrin reached to the sky, searching for distant comets by feeling for their energy. Pale blue light washed over the camp as ropes of liquid lightning arced between her fingers, reaching toward the sky. In that light, the Gholgi were made even more terrifying, looking otherworldly.

With skin like moving granite, they resembled bears with long, feral jaws lined with gleaming teeth. Most of the time moving on all fours, they stood nearly as tall as Catrin, but when confronted, they stood on their hind legs and towered over her and her Guardians.

Their movements were not of a full-on attack, though; instead they charged through the group, splitting them up, trying to separate their intended prey from the pack. Strom and Osbourne took to the trees when they were nearly run down, and one of the Gholgi went down when Strom swung from the branches and kicked it hard in the face. The beast's head snapped to one side, and it crumpled to the ground.

Brother Vaughn rolled away from a charging Gholgi, but when he stood, another swept his legs out from under him.

Issuing her own roar, Catrin unleashed her attack. Streaks of energy struck multiple Gholgi, stunning some and knocking others down, but one still came. Only Chase remained by Catrin's side as she swayed on her feet, and he stepped forward to meet the approaching Gholgi. The beast roared--a sound like distant thunder--and stood on its hind legs. Chase charged in, his sword leveled at the beast's abdomen, even as Catrin drew on every power source available to her. The Gholgi used its height to level a massive blow at Chase's head before Catrin could react. Chase ducked away from the blow but was sent spinning and landed in a heap.

Three Gholgi got between Catrin and her Guardians, and they changed their tactics. Now they had her separated, and they drove her into the forest. Osbourne swung down from a branch, trying to reproduce Strom's kick, and did succeed in blinding one of the Gholgi with his heels before he fell from the tree. Brother Vaughn and Chase tried to reach Catrin, but the Gholgi repelled them.

Followed by two of the beasts, Catrin fled as fast as she could through the dense foliage. Like a sentient being, the forest hindered her every movement, tangling her in its web, trying to devour her. Growing louder as they came, the Gholgi gained on her, and she knew she could not outrun them; she had to turn and fight.

Trying to draw more energy while at a full run proved to be impossible, and she searched for the best place to make her stand. Ahead, where the land rose steeply, two Gholgi stepped into her path, making the choice for her. Moving together, they tried to herd Catrin back into the trees, but as soon as she stopped, she drew deeply and lashed out. Twin beams of energy split the air, and Catrin clenched her teeth, ready for the backlash of her attack. When it came, it was less than she'd expected, and she hoped that just being prepared for the repercussion could somehow lessen it. The Gholgi were momentarily stunned, and Catrin ran for higher ground, away from the forest.

She had taken only three good strides before the Gholgi resumed their hunt with what seemed a renewed sense of urgency. Grunts and growls passed between them, sounding to Catrin as if they were speaking a guttural language. Driven by fear, she climbed, hoping the Gholgi were not skilled climbers. Ahead lay a rocky vale, and if only she could reach it, she would be safe. It was an irrational thought, but it inspired her to even greater speed. Exhaustion threatened to overcome her; her vision blurred and the world took on a yellow haze, but she drew a deep breath and climbed.

Beyond one last boulder waited rich grasses that promised a soft bed. Littered with chunks of granite and bathed in moonlight, the vale looked as if some god had split a mountain into bits and sprinkled them along the valley floor. Reaching up to grab the top of the boulder, Catrin cried out as a Gholgi clutched her leg, pulling her backward, its claws biting through her leggings and into her flesh.

In the moment before she knew she would succumb, the attack suddenly stopped; the Gholgi released its grip and was gone. Exhausted and losing blood, Catrin could make no sense of what had just happened, and she concentrated on simply reaching the vale. In a dreamlike state, she crawled across the grasses to one of the boulders.

Leaning against the rock was more comfortable than she had expected, and she was grateful for a place to rest; she felt safe. Cutting her leggings away from the wounds on her leg, she winced. From deep gashes, some nearly to the bone, seeped her precious blood. If she did not stop the bleeding, she would die, but her meager efforts did not staunch the flow.

Weariness began to overtake her and she thought it might be nice to lie down on the grass and sleep, but a nagging voice in the back of her mind reminded her that sleep meant death. She was not ready to die yet; her work was not yet done.

Pulling her eyes open, she realized she was already lying down, the grass pressing against her face. After pushing herself back into a sitting position, she drew a deep breath, and her head spun.

Draw on the life around you.

She didn't know from where the message came, but it was a welcome one, full of hope and compassion. Opening herself up, she allowed the life around her to flow into her, and she was surprised by the power of it. Looking down, she saw blood still running from her wounds, and she knew the additional energy would not be enough to save her. She had to find a way to stop the bleeding.

Despite the warnings, she thought of Enoch Giest and how he had healed himself. The lines of all those he taught to heal themselves had been doomed. Knowing the effects, Catrin concluded it was worth the risk as long as she did not have children or teach anyone else how to do it. Of course, that was assuming she could figure it out herself in the limited time she had left.

Using the last of her strength, she reached out to the comets and drew a trickle of power. Combined with the life energy she still felt flowing around her, she attained clear thought. She knew what her body had to do to heal itself. All she had to do was get a message through the barrier between her conscious and subconscious minds without shattering it in the process.

Somehow, instinctively, she knew where to find the barrier, and she visualized it as a wall of stone and mortar in her mind. Not wanting to take down the entire wall, she chipped away at the mortar around a single stone. With her trusty, old belt knife, which still existed in her memory, she broke away the mortar, and light began to stream through from the other side, blindingly bright and filled with colors Catrin had never before seen.

Determined, she wiggled the stone until it started moving a little more with each swing. Then it broke free with a suddenness that left her reeling. Radiant light poured through the hole, and Catrin approached it with apprehension. Beyond lay an unknown reality, the part of her that truly understood how her body worked yet was somehow blind to her immediate need. She knew her body could create a clot to stop the bleeding and fill the wounds with scar tissue, but it did not seem to realize the imminent need, for her blood still flowed.

Applying her will, she pressed her face to the wall and shouted into the hole, "Stop the bleeding. Heal my leg." She sensed something akin to acknowledgment and pulled her face away. With the stone still in her hand, she brought it back up to the hole, but before she could slide it into place, she looked through and saw a stunningly beautiful face staring back with an equally awestruck expression.

Thrilled and terrified, Catrin stared for a moment, memorizing every detail, every curve and highlight, but then from somewhere came a warning, little more than a sense of danger. Closing her eyes, Catrin shoved the stone back into place. Only then did she realize the damage she had done: None of the mortar remained. Light streamed around the stone. Then the stone wiggled.

It had never occurred to Catrin that her subconscious might want to communicate with her just as badly, but when the stone suddenly fell from its hole, she scrambled to replace it, trying to remember how mortar was made. Perhaps, she thought, if she could think of how to make mortar, she could conjure up some to fill in around the brick. It seemed strange to think of making mortar in her mind for what was only her visual representation of something, but it felt very real to her.

Stuffing the stone back into the hole, she tried her best to imagine up some mortar, and she cheered when she finally succeeded. Just as she reached up to apply her mortar, though, her heart leaped; the stone slowly moved away from her and fell through to the other side.

Light poured through, and Catrin's curiosity soared, but the warnings returned, and she slammed her hands, full of mortar, over the hole. In her mind, she stayed there, guarding her meager barrier and hoping her mental wall would not come tumbling down. Sleep overcame her, and her dreams were filled with visions of Enoch and Ain Giest laughing at her.

* * *

Stretching himself between a branch and a rock outcropping, Chase prayed he didn't slip. Keeping himself from looking down was difficult; it was an almost morbid fascination, wondering if the fall below would kill him or just leave him broken and wounded.

With a grunt, he thrust himself across the divide and dug his fingers into the first impression he could find. Slamming his body against the stone, he used his knees and toes to keep his grip. When he gained the top of the outcropping, he leaned against the cliff wall behind him, regaining his breath, and looked down.

Losing himself in the vertigo, he let his mind go where it would. Visions of the Gholgi attack were etched in his memory. Osbourne and Brother Vaughn had both been hurt, and he'd sent Strom back to the ship with them, for protection. It had seemed like a good idea at the time, but now he was alone and had no idea of how to find Catrin, if she still lived. Unwilling to believe her dead, he pressed on, staying to the higher reaches to avoid most of the wildlife, though he wondered if the climbing was any less dangerous than what waited below.

Nightfall brought overwhelming despair since it meant he would not find Catrin this day; she was lost to him. Tears dripped from his nose, and he wiped them away angrily. They were not defeated yet. Catrin still lived, he told himself, and he made himself believe it.

Chapter 12

In the deepest shadows, fire, both terrible and magnificent, can spring to life.
--Casicus Mod, coal miner

* * *

Encumbered by the basket of fish he carried, Prios climbed the loose rocks with great care. Belegra had ordered everything he caught saved, but Prios filled his stomach while away from the archmaster's watchful eyes. These days they seemed to see only what they wanted to see, and Prios was determined to take every advantage.

Catrin was near; he could feel her presence. Despite Belegra's madness, he could not risk reaching out to her. The last time he had, Belegra had fallen on him, demanding to know what he'd been doing, full of suspicion and rage. Prios had endured the beating and stuck to his original tale: he'd been searching for their foes, keeping watch for danger. Belegra had not believed him, but other matters distracted him, and Prios lived in fear of the moment Belegra remembered his treachery.

Staring up at the heights, he prepared himself to play the role of faithful slave, though it sickened him more each time. Soon he would be free, all this but a memory. Reaching the ancient stone stair, which provided sure footing, Prios barely looked where he was going.

Waiting inside the gaping cavern, Belegra paced, impatience clear in his posture. "Is that all you've brought back? That is barely enough for half a day. When Vedregon returns, I'll have you flogged for your failure!"

Prios did not bother to tell him that Mark Vedregon was dead, along with all the other soldiers and the rest of the cadre. Those who had not been killed by the Gholgi or disease where taken by the sea. Prios had tried to tell Belegra the truth, but he refused to hear; instead, Belegra always claimed he would have Prios beaten or tortured when the soldiers returned.

Taking the basket of fish to the hole in the cavern wall, Prios prepared to feed Kyrien.

"He's too weak to come to you. Get in there and feed him," Belegra said. His eyes wild with fervor, he licked his lips.

Prios could not help feeling that Belegra wanted Kyrien to eat him instead of the fish. Leaving the basket right under the hole, he straddled it and pulled himself into the foul-smelling chamber. The hole was barely large enough to admit the basket, but he yanked it through. Kyrien cowered in the back of the chamber, his green-flecked gold eyes fixed on Prios, following his every movement.

Dumping the basket not far from Kyrien's head, Prios backed away. Kyrien sniffed the fish and snorted, then smacked Prios with his tail.

"Clean up while you're in there," Belegra said.

Prios did as he was told, despite every instinct telling him to flee the crowded cell. Kyrien hated him, and Prios feared the beast would rip him to shreds if he ever overcame his fear of Belegra. For now, Kyrien simply cowered in the back of his cell, and when the sun was high, he wailed.

* * *

Filled with horror, Catrin awoke, still leaning against the mass of granite. When she tried to rise, her body was sluggish. Slowly, she felt the blood returning to her limbs, and she stood. Echoing through the vale was a haunting call; like the cries of a wounded animal, it was filled with despair and, at times, an odd glimmer of hope. Hearing it made Catrin want to cry.

In a sudden rush, memories of the previous day overwhelmed her, and she looked down at her leg. Her leggings were tattered and missing the section she had cut away. Beneath were scabbed gashes where her open wounds had been. The flesh around them was pink and smooth, but she could move without a great deal of pain, and she wondered if her memories could be real. Had she truly healed herself?

Closing her eyes, she located her center then the wall that stood between her conscious and subconscious minds. No matter how hard she tried, she could not make the wall whole again. Always one stone was missing, and the mortar that filled the hole was riddled with cracks and fissures that allowed the brilliant light to pour through. With a deep breath, she made herself open her eyes. She was still alive, and she chose to treat every new moment as a gift. She should be dead--she knew it, and now she needed to make the best of what she had.

The keening wails continued, and Catrin firmed her resolve. She would find the poor creature and ends its misery. Even as the thought entered her mind, Catrin sensed a shift in the energy around her, and the vale was transformed. No more were the grasses littered with boulders; in their places stood dragons. Tall and proud, they surrounded her.

In awestruck fascination, Catrin watched the only remaining boulder, the one she had slept against, unfold itself. Granite-colored skin shifted and moved and began to take on a greenish hue, as if reflecting the grasses around it. A massive head on a serpentine neck moved in front of Catrin's face and oscillated back and forth in a hypnotic motion.

Free him.

Overwhelming compulsion came with the raw emotion of the message. It was not like the way Belegra controlled his cadre, it was more like a melding of intentions. The strength of the desire blended with Catrin's own desire, and her will to accomplish the task became one with the dragon she faced.

Raising itself up to its full height, standing on its two powerful legs, the majestic dragon spread its wings and moved its head back down to Catrin. With a touch more gentle than she would have imagined possible, it pushed her with its rock-hard maw.

Go.

The command was palpable, but Catrin refused to leave just yet. She remembered the sensations she had felt the night before and the messages she had perceived. Looking the dragon in the eye, Catrin drew herself up with all the courage she could muster. "Thank you," she said. "All of you."

The dragons all raised a keening wail to match that of the one she heard from above, and Catrin left them behind, determined to succeed. Following the sound proved difficult in a place where the echoes had a life of their own, but she moved with purpose, using her staff to provide stability in rough places.

As she drew nearer, sound overwhelmed her other senses, and for a time, she moved without seeing, only the call guiding her. Looking up, she saw the side of a mountain covered with winding stairs and crumbling roadways. At seemingly random intervals, grand entranceways dotted the rock face. The wails came from one such entranceway, high above where she stood. Squinting, she followed the stair with her eyes. From the high entranceways down to the winding terrace where all the stairways originated, she traced it. When she reached what she thought was the correct stair, it showed no evidence of recent use, and Catrin climbed with little confidence, not knowing if she were taking the right path.

Despite places where the stair was nearly perfectly preserved, there were places it barely existed. In one such place, Catrin came to a gap. Below was a sheer drop to the vale floor. Driven beyond reason by her desire to end this quest, she leaped across the divide. As she soared through the air, her arms windmilled. The heel of her staff struck rock before she landed. The impact sent her spinning, and she nearly lost her grip on the staff. Off balance, she struck the rock hard, driving the wind from her lungs. Her legs still hanging over the ledge, gravity began to pull at her, and she scrambled to find a handhold. With her left hand, she found a small crack and dug her fingers in, crying out from the pain. With her other hand, she drove the tip of her staff into another nearby crack. Using all her strength, she pulled herself up. When she finally gained the relative safety of the stair, she allowed herself only a moment of rest before resuming her climb.

Higher up, in a place where two sets of stairs came close together, Catrin saw parts of the other stair that were new and hastily constructed. That was the stair Belegra and his men used.

Trying to decide between stealth and a clear path, Catrin finally decided on a safe climb; she would have to face Belegra one way or another, and she doubted surprise would give her any substantial advantage. Climbing between the two stairs was dangerous, but she hoped the rest of the climb would be easier. Movement and shouting from above gave her a start, and she flattened herself against the rock, hoping not to be seen.

Whoever it was went back inside, and Catrin completed the climb to the newly repaired stair. Following it up, she was constantly alert for signs of movement, and she thought she saw something moving through the trees below. Perhaps, she thought, it was Belegra's men. Knowing she might have only a short time before the soldiers returned, she climbed with haste, throwing caution aside.

When she reached the top of the stair, the wails were like a physical assault, but as soon as she stepped toward the entrance, it stopped. With the light behind her and relative darkness within, Catrin stood momentarily blinded.

"So, the Herald Witch has come to witness my triumph!" Archmaster Belegra said, his voice grating and raw.

Stepping into the chamber, Catrin barely noticed the exquisite carvings that adorned the entranceway or the ancient sculptures that lined the walls. It was the object in Archmaster Belegra's hands that drew her attention: a chunk of dragon ore the size of a melon that sparkled even in the dimness of the mountain hall.

A foul smell filled the air, and Catrin turned to a place where a doorway had recently been walled in and reinforced. Only a small hole let her see what was within. Pinkish and sickly, the dragon looked very unlike those she had seen in the vale, but there was little doubt as to his true nature. As soon as she looked at him, she knew his name: *Kyrien*. It came to her like a song filled with joy and life, despite what her eyes told her. His eyes locked with hers, and in that moment, she knew what she had to do. With a deep breath, she drew power from the air and from her staff.

Quietly and humbly, another reason for her presence emerged from the shadows, his head down and his face concealed within the hood of his robe, Prios came. She knew him the instant he moved, and she turned back to face the one foe she had in the room. "You will enslave and corrupt no more, Belegra. Stand down now or I will attack."

Hysterical laughter threw him into a brief fit of coughing, but he regained his composure and faced Catrin with sudden clarity in his eyes, which narrowed as they beheld her. Disturbances in his energy field were so intense that it looked to Catrin as if his energy would collapse in on itself. "Burn," he said in a low and unfamiliar voice, as if he were a completely different person. His hands, gripping the dragon ore, sent ropes of fire and lightning sailing through the air toward Catrin, but she was not unprepared and created a shielding sphere around herself.

His attack struck her barrier with a violent impact that sent her reeling, nearly pushing her over the nearby ledge. Maintaining the protective sphere sapped her strength, and Catrin knew she needed to launch an attack of her own. Momentarily dropping her defenses, she hurled blue lightning at Archmaster Belegra, sending it with all the rage she possessed. Howling, she lashed out again and again, but he brushed her attacks aside as if they were little more than annoyances.

His laughter started as a deep rumble in his chest, but then he began to cackle, and in another moment of transformation, he spun and attacked. Balls of fire raced before bolts of fetid lightning, and a wave of nausea poured over Catrin as they approached. She hastily cast her defenses about her, but the onslaught threw her aside and pinned her to the chamber wall. Helplessly she watched as Prios joined the attack, his movements synchronized with Belegra's.

Inexorably, her sphere began to shrink under the pressure, and she could feel the heat on her face. Hot air burned her lungs as she sucked in desperate breaths, and still the attacks continued. Dizziness began to overtake her, and the world grew dark despite the flames that surrounded her.

* * *

The wailing drew Chase on, and he found himself in a rocky vale. When he saw grass stained with blood and a piece of the leather from Catrin's leggings, he was as frightened as he was relieved. There was too much blood, and he wondered how she could have walked away.

Turning to the mountain where the wails originated, Chase saw the stairways. He covered his eyes as he thought he saw a form moving up the rock face. Moments later, the wailing stopped, and Chase knew it must be Catrin. Taking off at a run, he climbed with abandon. Seeing flashes of light and hearing thunderous booms from above, he could only pray he got there in time.

*　*　*

Relent.

The command came just when the pain had reached its height, and Catrin was tempted to obey, tempted to just give up. It would be so much easier to let someone else be in control. She was so very tired. In the corner of her sight stood Prios, deep in the throes of compulsion, coerced to do that which was not his will. Kyrien, trapped in a tomb of stone, did not deserve such a horrid fate; she could not relent. They should suffer no more.

The pain began to fade, and her sphere slowly grew. Belegra looked spent, drenched with sweat and breathing hard, a wild look in his eyes. Prios looked worse, and Catrin knew Belegra would run him dry without another thought. Watching as a nimbus of power began to form around Belegra, who seemed to have found his strength, Catrin prepared a hasty attack. Prios lay, unmoving on the floor.

The nimbus grew brighter and more intense as Belegra drew an enormous amount of energy. The stone around his feet grew red hot, and he stepped back. Catrin launched her attack not on Belegra, but on the rock around him. Meanwhile, he cast a massive wave of raw energy at her, flames leaping out and forming the tortured faces of those she had lost, and they howled at her as they came. At the last moment, she cast up a sphere to protect herself, but it was insufficient, and she was thrown, tumbling, to the back of the hall.

Belegra howled in glee as Catrin fell before his attack, but he also took two steps away from the super-heated stone. As he raised his arms for the killing blow, his aura glowing like the sun, Kyrien struck like a massive viper. His head and neck shattered the wood and plaster that filled the doorway to his prison. Before the wood and stone hit the floor, he snapped Belegra up in his jaws and bit down hard. It was over in an instant, and Catrin could hardly believe what she had just seen. Consumed from within by blue flames, Belegra began to burn.

With only his head and neck freed, Kyrien gave Belegra's body one last shake then cast it aside. An instant later, Chase ran into the cavern. Seeing Catrin on the ground, smoking, he charged in, looking for someone to fight. His eyes landed on Prios, who was trying to stand, and Chase descended on him, howling. Even Catrin's screams could not pierce his blinding rage; only Kyrien's fierce visage kept him from killing Prios. Kyrien moved his head between Chase and Prios and locked eyes with Chase.

The sword dropped from Chase's hand, and he turned away from the dragon. Then he ran to Catrin. She was trying to stand as he approached, and he helped her to her feet.

"Anything broken? Are you hurt?"

"I'm bruised and burned and scraped, but I think I'll make it. Prios?"

He moved from behind Kyrien slowly. His face was still concealed, and he approached with his head down.

"Who is this?" Chase asked.

"Prios was one of Belegra's cadre. He was enslaved and compelled to attack me, but now he is free," Catrin said, and the hooded face snapped up at her words. Reaching up, Catrin pulled the hood back and looked on the face of Prios for the first time. He was only slightly younger than she, and to her, he looked beautiful.

I am free?

"You are free."

"Why doesn't he say anything?" Chase asked, suspicious.

"He speaks in my mind," Catrin said. "He has helped me in the past, despite the risks, and I trust him. He comes with us."

"What about the . . . uh . . . dragon?"

"We need to find a way get him out of there."

"The walls are really thick, Cat. It would take days to chip him out even if we had the right tools, which we don't."

"We're getting him out," she said in her most commanding tone, but then she remembered the others. "Where are Strom and Osbourne and Brother Vaughn?"

"I sent them back to the ship after the Gholgi attacked. Osbourne hurt his knee, and Brother Vaughn broke a few ribs, I think. Strom went with them so they would not be helpless in a fight. I came looking for you."

"I knew you would," Catrin said with tears in her eyes as she hugged him. "Thank you. You've always protected me."

"Who knows what kind of trouble you'd get yourself into if I wasn't around? I'm just saving myself the hassle. So how are we going to get this dragon out?"

There is water nearby, and I have a bucket, and this might be of use to you.

Prios approached, holding Belegra's dragon ore, and he handed it to Catrin. Even before it touched her skin, she could feel its power, far greater than anything she'd ever experienced before, as if the greater size allowed it to contain exponentially more energy. Even after the massive amount Belegra had drawn from the stone, it still held an enormous charge. Yet there seemed to be flaws. Something was simply not as it should be, and she was hesitant to use the stone.

Desperate for a way to free Kyrien, her mind reeled with possibilities, but then she remembered what Prios had said: *There is water nearby.* "Fill everything you can with water and bring it back here," Catrin said.

"What?" Chase asked. "What good is water going to do? We need tools, Cat."

"The water will be all we need. Please help Prios," Catrin said as Prios was already moving to obey her command. In that moment she made a vow to talk to Prios, to help him understand that he had to do what she asked only if he believed it was the right thing to do. He was free.

Chase looked smug when he and Prios returned, each with a large container of water. "Are we going to scrub the stone away?"

"Stand back and be ready to throw the water at the rock on my command," Catrin said. Chase still looked unconvinced. Using the same technique she had used against Belegra, she heated the rock until it glowed like a hot ember. "Now!"

Chase and Prios moved in unison, and a wall of water rushed toward the rock. It struck with a hiss and a series of loud cracks, and several chunks of rock fell away. "We need more water," Catrin said, and Chase did not hesitate. Kyrien huddled at the back of his cell, but Catrin sensed he knew what she was doing, and he occasionally bugled in what sounded like an expectant call.

Chase and Prios returned just as the rock began to glow almost white. "Again," Catrin said. More chunks erupted this time as the structural integrity of the wall began to break down. With each successive time they threw water on the glowing rocks, more of the wall fell, but the process took time.

Kyrien lost patience and roared as he charged from the back his prison and threw himself against the wall with percussive force. Brittle stone fell before his desperate need, and the chamber walls exploded. Catrin, Chase, and Prios fled before the dragon as he charged to the entranceway, seeing the sunlit sky for the first time in his life. Before Catrin could even say good-bye, he gave a triumphant roar, leaped over the edge, and disappeared from view.

Running to the ledge, Catrin looked down to see Kyrien falling like a stone. He struggled to fully extend his wings, and even when he did, he still fell at tremendous speed. Suddenly, the air below was filled with activity. Other dragons, most larger than Kyrien, flocked around him. One of the largest, who Catrin thought she recognized as the one she had slept against, positioned himself directly beneath Kyrien, straining his wings to hold his own weight and that of Kyrien. Perilously close to the treetops below, the dragons halted their fall and began to gain altitude.

Crying out to his brethren, Kyrien wobbled in the air as they left him to soar the winds on his own. Twice other dragons kept him from crashing to the ground, but he seemed to be gaining confidence as he got the feel for flight. Flexing his wings, he soared high into the sky. He gave one last cry before disappearing into the clouds.

Chapter 13

Procrastination robs the world of countless treasures.
--Massimo Arturo, scribe

* * *

For a moment, Catrin simply stood, motionless. So much had happened in such a short time that she found herself in a state of shock. Only when Chase moved to her side and took her by the arm did she return to her senses.

"Come over here and sit down," he said, and she let him lead her. On a huge chunk of what had once been part of Kyrien's prison, she sat. "How bad is your leg?" Chase asked, looking over her wound. "I don't understand. You took this wound yesterday, yet it looks like it happened weeks ago."

"I'm not sure," Catrin said, not wanting to admit what she had done, and very much wanting to keep the struggle with her subconscious a secret. No matter how ashamed she was of healing herself, despite the potential consequences, she was alive. Her heart broke a little when she silently vowed to bear no children, but she would not repeat the mistakes made by Enoch Giest. If she had no children, then there was no way Catrin could pass along any deadly traits. Still, tears slid down her face.

"Whatever the reason," Chase finally said, "it's a blessing. Are you in pain?"

"Only a little, but I'll be fine."

"Is Prios hurt?"

I am uninjured, but I need to rest.

His voice was timid in Catrin's mind, and he approached her slowly, his eyes downcast. When he reached the chunk of rock, he climbed up next to Catrin, curled into a ball, and slept.

Chase finished his inspection of Catrin's wounds. "Looks like you'll live. I think we should stay up here for the night. I'm going to try and find some wood for a fire and some food."

Prios did not move or even open his eyes, but his voice whispered in Catrin's mind: *Both can be found in the chambers at the back of the hall.*

"There is food and wood back there," Catrin said, pointing.

"How do you know that?" Chase asked.

"Prios told me."

"I thought he was asleep."

"Not quite yet."

Chase left to explore the back of the hall but not before casting a suspicious glance at Prios, who still appeared to be asleep. When Chase returned, his arms were laden with wood, and he placed it within the existing fire ring. With plenty of kindling, he soon had a small fire going. On his next trip, he returned with salted fish and some hard cheese.

"Not much left after this," Chase said as he and Catrin ate. "Not sure how Belegra expected to survive up here."

In a moment of panic, both Chase and Catrin realized that there might still be Zjhon soldiers about. They could be out hunting and could return at any time. Chase quickly stood, and Catrin drew a sharp intake of breath.

They are all dead. I, alone, survived.

"I thought you were sleeping," Catrin said.

I would, if you would stop flooding me with anxiety. When you worry, your thoughts boom in my head like thunder.

"I'm sorry," she said, embarrassed.

"You have to tell me what he's saying," Chase said, "or this is going to make me crazy."

"He says the rest of the Zjhon soldiers are dead. He's all that's left. I'll tell you the rest, Chase. I promise. But first I need rest."

"You two sleep. I'll keep watch."

*　*　*

Standing at the gunwales, Strom tried to relax, but his hands seemed to constantly clench into fists of their own volition. Osbourne and Brother Vaughn were recovering from their wounds and Strom was torn.

"You can't go back in there alone," Kenward said. "It's just too dangerous."

"Yet that is exactly what Catrin and Chase are doing. I'd be in no more danger than them. I can't just stay here and wait while they struggle to survive. I've already seen the dangers they face, and I don't know how they could survive it alone."

In a moment that brought Strom to tears, three of Kenward's crew came forward: Farsy, Bryn, and Nimsy. "We'll go with him," Farsy said. "Others volunteered as well, but we know we can't all go."

Kenward seemed torn, and he paced the deck while he considered. Nora stood nearby, watching him, and she tapped the toe of her boot on the deck. "I'm sorry," Kenward said, "I can't let any of you go. If you were lost, then chances are none of us would ever see our homes again. We simply can't afford to lose--by the gods!"

Everyone turned to see what had frightened Kenward, and Strom saw a terrifying sight. Like a wave of death, a black tide raced toward them. Like a single, huge organism, it moved faster than the swiftest horse. Strom braced himself and offered a hasty prayer, knowing they would need every bit of help they could get. No longer could he hope to find Catrin and Chase; now he could only hope to survive.

* * *

"Get up," Chase said. "He's gone."

"What? Who's gone?" Catrin asked, still trying to clear her mind of sleep. Outside, it was still nearly dark, only the blush of the false dawn gave any light.

"Prios."

With a wide yawn, Catrin sat up, her body stiff and sore. "He'll be back."

"How can you be sure it's not a trap? He could be going for help. I know he said the rest were dead, but I don't trust him."

"Prios and I are connected," Catrin said. "There is a bond between us that I cannot explain, but I know it's there. We can trust him. I assure you of that." As if to prove her point, Prios returned to the hall in that moment, carrying a basket of freshly caught fish.

Breakfast.

"Thank you," Chase said after Catrin relayed Prios's words. "I'm sorry I didn't trust you."

Trust should be given only to those who have earned it. Maybe, someday, he and I will trust each other. Maybe today.

Catrin relayed his words, but Chase made no response; instead, he helped clean the fish while Catrin sliced the fresh roots Prios had found. Using Belegra's cook pot and a jar of fresh water from his stores, they made a bland but filling stew, and knowing they would need all the energy they could get, they ate all of what they had.

When they finished the meal, Prios took Catrin by the hand and silently led her to the back of the hall. Beyond the rooms used for storage and what had been sleeping quarters for the soldiers was the room Belegra had used. Inside were two rough stone slabs. One he'd used for a bed and the other as a table. On the table, next to the remains of a burned-out candle, was a stack of leather-bound books, and Catrin looked upon them with undisguised fear.

The books are not evil. They are just books. Perhaps you can do some good with them.

Despite his words, Catrin reached out for the books with

trepidation, haunted by the fear that Belegra had left a trap for her. When she lifted the books from the table, though, nothing happened, and she felt foolish. Taking those and a few other items that could be useful, she loaded them into her pack. Chase and Prios rummaged through the stores and filled packs for themselves.

As they reached the entrance of the hall, Catrin looked out over the mountains, down the river valleys, and to the sea. There, the *Slippery Eel* waited. "Let's go home," she said.

* * *

"Prepare to fend 'em off," Kenward said as the tide of dark shapes gathered near his ship, hiding beneath the waves, waiting to strike. This was not an act of curiosity; Kenward could feel the hostility. Unwilling to leave Catrin and Chase behind, he kept the *Slippery Eel* moving, but the dark shapes followed them wherever they sailed. With great speed and endurance, they moved faster and farther than the wind could drive the *Eel*. "We can't outrun them--whatever they are."

"Not sure we can fight 'em either," Nora said. "If they are Gholgi, as Brother Vaughn has guessed, then they have tough, armorlike skin that we are unlikely to penetrate with spears. If they try to board us, we must repel them as we would any other foe, but if they attack the underside of the ship--"

"We're helpless," Kenward finished the thought for her. "Put us under full sail. Let's just see how long these things can keep swimming."

* * *

Finding the way back to their boat proved to be more difficult than Catrin had imagined. Surrounded by dense forest, it was easy to lose their way, and each time Chase had to climb above the canopy to gauge their course, they lost precious time. As daylight began to fail, chilling fear nearly paralyzed Catrin, who knew the Gholgi would come. If only she knew when.

Climbing and cutting their way through the underbrush while trying to remain alert for danger was exhausting, and Catrin swayed on her feet, taken by a spell of dizziness. The world seemed to shift and move, and only the tree trunk she found herself clinging to kept her from falling.

Chase cursed and stopped. "I know you're tired, Cat, but we can't keep stopping," he said. "If we don't make it back to the ship before dark, we could be in big trouble."

"I know. I'm sorry," Catrin said, ashamed of her own weakness.

"You've been through a lot. I suppose it's to be expected, but you're going to have to push yourself. Rest for now. I'm going to climb up and make sure we're going the right way."

Catrin lost track of how many times they had stopped and how many times Chase had changed their direction after one of his climbs. The jungle looked the same no matter how far they went, and she started to fear they would never get out.

"We're getting closer. I promise you," Chase said as he climbed back down, but Catrin lacked the energy to respond. Prios moved without complaint. When Catrin rested, he rested, and when she walked, he walked with her. Like a second shadow, he always seemed to be right behind her, and she took comfort from his presence. He was living evidence that she had done something worthwhile, and that knowledge helped to keep her moving. Somewhere, up in the clouds, Catrin imagined Kyrien soaring on the wind, and the image made her smile. That made two good things, and she moved ahead with newfound energy.

It was Chase who called the next break, and Catrin dropped to the ground, suddenly weary once again. The sun was beginning to sink, and their journey took on a new sense of urgency. Though Chase said they were nearing the boat, Catrin wondered if he was saying that just to keep her moving. At the moment, she no longer cared which it was; all she wanted was to be free of the jungle. The longer she stayed under the canopy of green, the more she felt she would never leave.

As they cut through a thicket of bramble, though, the landscape changed. Ahead, huge granite boulders, only their tops free of lichen and moss, rose from the jungle floor and blocked the way ahead. Chase climbed up first; struggling to get a solid grip on the slippery surface. He clawed through the soft moss and dug his fingers into hidden cracks. When he reached the top, he secured a rope to a nearby tree and tossed the other end down to Catrin. Even with the rope, the climb was treacherous, and Catrin cried out when she lost her footing. With only the rope holding her, she crashed into side of the rock, slamming her wounded leg into a sharp corner. When she finally reached the top, her leg was soaked in blood; her scabs had been ripped open.

Prios made the climb without difficulty while Chase bandaged Catrin's leg. She was tempted to heal herself again but feared the consequences. Already the barrier between her conscious and subconscious minds was breaking down, and she did not want to risk damaging it further. Despite her vows, she feared other, unforeseen ramifications. Still, every painful step tempted her.

Beyond the stones lay a narrow valley that sloped gracefully downward.

"Now we just need to keep moving lower. Eventually we should find water, and from there we just follow the shore until we find the boat."

Bolstered by Chase's confidence, Catrin moved as fast as she could, and they started to make what seemed like real progress. The land continued to slope downward, and when the wind shifted, the sound of running water drifted to them. Ahead, the small valley they followed opened into a much larger valley. Beyond one last hill, they found a sheer drop. A few tenacious trees grew from the side of the mountain, but they were widely spaced.

"I'm going to look for the best way down," Chase said. "Wait here."

Catrin and Prios found a shady spot and leaned against the spongy moss.

"I think I see where we left the boat," Chase said when he returned. "There looks to be a way down, but it won't be easy."

"Let's not waste any time," Catrin said as she stood. "I just want this to be over."

Chase led them along a meandering path, where they followed a ledge that was, at times, only a hand's width across. Using his knife to create handholds in the soft limestone, Chase did what he could to make the climb easier. There came times, though, when they had no choice but to jump between large rocks and boulders. Chase led the way, and some of the rocks moved when he landed. Catrin could only hope they would stay in place long enough for her and Prios to cross. Each landing brought new levels of pain. Blood seeped through Catrin's bandages, and at times dizziness nearly overcame her. Her vision became cloudy and blurred. Chase allowed her to rest, but the breaks were kept short. Even when they did stop, Catrin found it impossible to relax in such precarious positions.

When they finally reached the shore, her will was nearly spent. Soaked with sweat, her hair hung down into her eyes, causing them to sting and burn. Her legs trembled with every step, and her breathing was labored.

Be strong.

Having Prios behind her, enduring the same trials yet never complaining, helped Catrin to remain focused. She could not fail him now, not when they had come so far.

"There it is!" Chase shouted, triumphant. Catrin made it to the boat before she collapsed to the ground. Prios helped Chase gather wood for the signal fire. Unable to find much dry kindling, Chase shaved bits of bark into a pile. Prios struck the flint, and each spark was like a ray of hope. When one finally caught and the air filled with smoke, Catrin began to believe they might actually make it.

As the fire established itself, flames leaped high into the sky, but Chase said it still was not enough. He and Prios gathered as many pine branches as they could find, creating a pile near the fire. When they had what they considered to be enough, they threw it all on top the fire at once. For a moment, it looked as if they had extinguished the fire, but then great billows of smoke began to pour around the pine needles. In a blinding flash, the fire erupted with its full strength. Popping and hissing, it sent flames and burning embers high into the twilight skies.

"And now," Chase said, "we wait."

* * *

"Damage report!" Kenward shouted with the slightest hint of panic in his voice, his knuckles white from clutching the wheel.

"The hull's not been breached, but they beat joints loose in places. We've got a thousand small leaks," Bryn replied.

"You're making too much speed for the shape we're in," Nora said. "The *Eel* will come apart if we keep this up."

With the wind at his back, Kenward could not resist the speed. He needed to get away from the boiling Gholgi to give his crew time to make repairs. Though none of the beasts had shown themselves, Kenward was now convinced it was the Gholgi they faced. These creatures were clever and strong and, if nothing else, determined.

"Maintain current speed. Make repairs as best as you can. Keep in mind that we'll most likely get attacked again."

"Yes, sir," Bryn said before spinning on his heel and running belowdecks.

"It's your ship," Nora said. "I'm going to supervise the repairs. Send someone for me if you need any advice to ignore."

Drawing a deep breath, Kenward hoped he was right. All of their lives were at stake, and he had never felt more vulnerable. In all of his close encounters, he had always been confident he would somehow survive, but now he had a sick feeling in his stomach.

"Smoke, sir! The signal fire's been lit!"

"Boil me," Kenward said, knowing he needed to make repairs before going back into shallow waters; that was where the Gholgi wanted him. "What am I supposed to do now?"

"I just saw a bright flash, sir, as if something exploded," the lookout yelled, and an instant later, what sounded like a thunderclap reached them.

"Set a course for the signal fire!" Kenward yelled, his mind made up. As his gut continued to churn, he wondered if he was taking his final risk.

***

The attack came swiftly and nearly silently. No smell announced the presence of the Gholgi since the attack came from the water. Charging to shore, nearly a dozen Gholgi attacked. Chase jumped to his feet and ran to meet them, howling. The first Gholgi raised its mighty clawed hand to strike Chase down, and Catrin reacted quicker than she ever had before. In the span of a breath, she drew on the power around her and unleashed it in a single action. A bolt of electric light slammed into the Gholgi, scattering them and leaving some stunned, but others were quick to mount another attack.

After Catrin's instinctive release of power, she noticed it had very little backlash. Feeling only slightly drained, she used the new technique to fire off bolts of energy at every approaching Gholgi. Each strike stunned its target, but it was not enough to stop the attack, and more Gholgi were emerging from the water. One terrified glance at the water revealed hundreds of dark shapes moving toward the shallows.

Concentrating on the two Gholgi that were bearing down on Chase, Catrin pulled Belegra's chunk of dragon ore from her pocket. Drawing on it, her staff, and the air, she prepared to deliver a more powerful blow, but before she released her attack, Prios's voice thundered in her mind: *You are not strong enough alone. Use me.*

Like a flash flood, he gave himself to her completely and utterly, and she was overwhelmed by the very essence of him. It took only an instant, but it seemed much longer to Catrin. Praying her momentary hesitation had not cost Chase his life, she attacked. Ropes of fire and lightning raced across the shore and struck thunderous impacts. The shoreline was suddenly littered with smoking Gholgi forms; others had been tossed back into the water.

Limping, Chase retreated. All was still for a moment, and over Chase's shoulder, Catrin saw the *Slippery Eel* as she rounded the bend. In the next instant, though, her hopes were dashed. Undaunted, the Gholgi resumed their attack, and now they came in even larger numbers.

"Stay behind me!" Catrin shouted and no one argued. With Prios still open to her, Catrin allowed both of them to draw from her staff and the oddly disjointed energy of Belegra's dragon ore. As soon as she opened the energy to him, Prios pulled deeply, and she could sense his shock and wonder.

It's so beautiful.

Almost drawn in by his fascination, Catrin had to pull herself back to the fight. Gholgi were advancing toward her, and to her horror, the

Slippery Eel also seemed to be under attack. With a cry of anguish, she attacked. Again the Gholgi fell before her fury, and again it was not enough. It seemed an endless supply of Gholgi waited for their own chance to attack. When she looked out to the *Slippery Eel*, her last glimmer of hope began to fade.

* * *

Kenward watched as his ship was overwhelmed. Gholgi clung to the *Slippery Eel*, pulling her lower in the water. Some tried to board the ship, but most seemed content to simply pull the ship under with their sheer weight. One of those bold enough to make the deck had his mother cornered, and he rushed to her aid. The beast turned as he came, screaming, and Kenward thrust his spear into its reptilian eye. Issuing a shrill scream, the Gholgi dropped back over the railing.

"Go for their eyes!" Kenward shouted, but he knew it would not be enough; there were simply too many.

* * *

Swaying on her feet, Catrin prepared to deliver another blast of power. Prios was nearly drained, and she could ask no more of him. Using her energy alone, she cast out a desperate attack. In the momentary pause it created, she watched as the *Slippery Eel* was slowly and inexorably pulled under water. Gholgi clung to the ship like a writhing mass of ants. The attack on land began again, just as the *Slippery Eel*'s prow dipped below the water.

Above the roar of the attack, a keening wail could be heard that made every Gholgi take pause. Looking up, Catrin saw a circling cloud of dragons. Calling out in unison, the mighty serpents folded their wings and dived. Many struck the water, full speed, and others pulled up to skim over the shore. In the next instant, the air was filled with activity and the screams of the Gholgi.

Catrin watched in awe as Kyrien swept down in front of her and cast the Gholgi aside. Using his head and tail, he sent them flying through the air. His brethren continued to strike the water, looking like giant seabirds.

"Now's our chance," Chase shouted above the din. Prios and Catrin raced to his aid as he began sliding the small boat to the water.

Kyrien stayed near Catrin and snapped up any Gholgi that came too close. Once they were in the water, though, the situation became even more dire. Dragons continued to crash into the river, only to launch back into the skies a moment later. Tossed by growing waves, Catrin and the others barely held on. When she looked around, Kyrien was nowhere to be found.

Though progress was slow, the *Slippery Eel* grew ever closer. The ship was now riding higher in the water, as most of the Gholgi were now fighting for their lives. Catrin, Chase, and Prios rowed as hard as they could and approached the *Slippery Eel*. Apparently not wanting to waste time retrieving the boat, the crew dropped a boarding net over the side. Catrin leaped to the net first; the others followed. But her leg no longer wanted to hold her weight, and she had difficulty climbing. When Chase reached the deck, he leaned over the gunwale and extended his hand to her. "Grab on, Cat. I'll pull you up!"

Exhausted, she reached out to him, but before their hands met, a reptilian claw reached from the water and grabbed her legs. Desperate, Chase extended himself further, kept on the ship only by Prios, who grabbed him by the ankles. His hand connected with Catrin's, and she clung to it. With all her strength, she tried to hold on, but slowly she began to slip.

"No!" Chase screamed. "Don't you dare let go!"

There was nothing more she could do; she had no strength left, and she felt her fingertips sliding over his, as the Gholgi's grip grew ever tighter. Just as she thought she would succumb, the Gholgi released her and screamed, its lower half engulfed in Kyrien's jaws. After tossing the Gholgi away, Kyrien nudged Catrin from behind, and she let Chase pull her onto the deck. The last thing she saw before she passed out was Kyrien, wheeling in the sky, circling over the ship.

Chapter 14

Our weather is controlled by the ocean currents. Should they ever falter, all will lament.
--Sister Meigan, Cathuran monk

* * *

Coming awake with a start, Catrin sat up in her hammock. Her head spinning, she wiped the sweat-soaked hair away from her face. The door opened, and daylight streamed in.

"It's good to see you awake," Osbourne said as he closed the door. "I brought you some broth."

"Thank you. How long did I sleep?"

"Not that long. Since last night. You look horrible."

"Thanks," Catrin said before sipping the broth.

"Brother Vaughn wanted me to report back on your condition. You rest."

The broth was weak, almost tasteless, but it warmed Catrin's belly. After a yawn and stretch, she climbed from the hammock. Her legs were unsteady, and she leaned on the door for a moment before opening it. Cool sea air greeted her, and she breathed in deeply, taking strength from it. The decks were near empty; by the sound of things, most were belowdecks making repairs. Brother Vaughn and Osbourne emerged from the hold and walked toward Catrin as soon as they saw her.

"Back to bed with you," Brother Vaughn said, holding his ribs and sounding like a scolding father. Osbourne walked with a severe limp.

"The ship needs repairs, and everyone is needed," Catrin said.

"You'll be no use to us if you drop from exhaustion, not to mention the loss of blood. Your wounds are healing exceedingly well, but you still need to rest."

"I will, but first I need to know what dangers we still face."

"Things have improved a great deal," Brother Vaughn said. "The dragons have driven off the Gholgi, and the crew has been able to make many of the needed repairs. There are men on shore now gathering materials to make additional repairs."

"The dragons are still here?" Catrin asked.

"Only your dragon remains," Brother Vaughn said. "He's kept a vigilant watch, and there have been no more attacks."

"Kyrien? Where is he?" Catrin asked, and Brother Vaughn pointed.

High above, resting on an outcropping of rock, Kyrien sunned himself. Somehow sensing Catrin's gaze, he extended his serpentine neck and looked back at her. Then he gave a triumphant call. Moments later he leaped from the rocks and soared above the *Slippery Eel*.

"You see?" Brother Vaughn said. "We are well protected. Now back in you go."

Captivated by the sight of Kyrien soaring majestically on the thermals, Catrin was held in thrall, but she allowed Brother Vaughn to escort her back to her cabin. Once inside, she realized he was correct about her condition. The short walk left her winded, and she collapsed back into the hammock, her dreams filled with wings and green-flecked, golden eyes.

* * *

Master Beron walked in silence, his mind consumed with the dilemma he faced. Master Edling wanted him to convince the others to declare everyone north of the Wall a traitor, but Master Beron disagreed. Only the threat of poison in his food or a knife in the ribs kept him from siding with the others.

Through the halls of the Masterhouse, he walked, taking corridors he rarely used just to delay his audience with Master Edling. When his legs began to ache and he had still come up with no solutions, he gave up hope. As he walked into Master Edling's apartments, he was a beaten man. "I'm sorry, sir," he said. "I cannot convince the others. They still care for their countrymen, and they fear the wrath of the Herald."

"I *told* you I would attend to the Herald myself!"

"I believe you, but they don't believe me. They cannot understand that you have the power to protect us from her."

"Come, then," Master Edling said, his robes gliding across the floor as he led Master Beron from his apartments. "I'll show how I will defeat the Herald. Then you can convince the others. If you don't do it, I will. I'm certain it would be better for them if you made them believe. My methods might be slightly less gentle."

Master Beron cringed. Master Jarvis had always been a good friend to him. He was kind and honest. The same could not be said for Master Edling, but still Beron struggled against his own fears. Should he flee? Should he, too, go north of the Wall? Would they even accept him there? His thoughts were interrupted when Master Edling made an unfamiliar turn. "Isn't this a servant passage?"

"Keep quiet, or I'll silence you myself."

Master Beron closed his mouth and allowed Master Edling to lead.

After three more turns, which Beron committed to memory, Master Edling stopped. He turned his back to Beron and, in some unseen way, triggered a doorway to open. "Get in there."

Beron walked into the darkness, not knowing what to expect. Master Edling closed the door before lighting his lamp. Beyond two short halls, they came to a room filled with treasures of all varieties. Master Edling walked straight to an oddly shaped, metallic rock, which rested on a supple piece of red cloth.

"A gift from the gods," Master Edling said, his eyes full of fervor. "Dropped from the sky, it was delivered to us hundreds of years ago. The gods have blessed us. We will prevail over the Herald. I'll show you the scriptures."

Master Beron looked at the strange stone, wondering if a weapon from the gods would be so formless, but as he looked at it, he saw magical symmetry and graceful lines all over it. What had first looked like big holes, under a careful eye, were each a work of art. It looked as if the winds of a billion years had scoured the rock's surface into patterns. Then he read the scripture.

In the hands of the righteous, the sky stone will capture the power of the mighty one.

"I'll take her power and use it as my own. I'll bring true power back to the Masterhood," Master Edling said.

* * *

"We've made the best repairs possible with the materials available to us, sir," Bryn said. "There's not much more we can do. We've stopped all the leaks, and we have additional pitch ready should we need to patch any new leaks."

"Your crew has done well," Nora said with a firm nod.

"Thank you, Mother," Kenward said. "A better crew I could not ask for."

"On that we agree," she said.

Bryn flushed, embarrassed by the compliment. Catrin stood at the gunwales, her strength returning. Given her leisure while she recovered, she spent most of her time watching Kyrien and his kin. Though Kyrien kept constant vigil, other dragons occasionally joined him, and their synchronized acrobatics drew more than just Catrin's eyes.

"Such fearsome beauty," Nora said as she joined Catrin.

"I can't make myself look away."

"You've an attachment with Kyrien; that much is clear. He seems a noble and loyal beast to protect us in such a way. I would never have guessed such a thing would happen."

"They are more intelligent than I would have thought possible," Catrin said. "Kyrien and another spoke in my mind; they spoke not in words, but in images and emotion. They asked me to save Kyrien from Belegra, and I suppose they are repaying the debt."

"Whatever the reason," Brother Vaughn said, "they have saved us all. I've always loved flying creatures, but these dragons are beyond my wildest expectations. None are as large as the skeleton found in Faulk, but they are undeniably beautiful. Their ability to communicate makes them even more remarkable."

For a while they simply watched as Kyrien and two other dragons danced in the skies. Much of the crew stopped to watch as others joined the dance. Like a flock of birds, the dragons moved in unison, as if of a single mind, changing directions so dramatically that it was a wonder none collided.

"We're ready to raise our anchors and set sail," Kenward said. "We've only to fill the hold with fish before we are ready to leave this place. I assume we are to travel back to the Godfist?"

"Yes," Catrin said. "I'm ready to go home."

"I suppose the safest route will be to go back the way we came. There may be a shorter route to the Godfist, but we've no way of knowing."

Belegra had a map.

Turning at the sound of Prios's voice in her mind, Catrin looked for him. It took a moment before she found him reclining in the shadows. Remembering Belegra's books, Catrin turned back to Kenward. "I think we have a map."

"What?" he asked, clearly excited. Few things seemed to excite sailors more than maps and charts.

"Before we left the mountain hall," Catrin said, "we took some books from Belegra's quarters. I had completely forgotten, but I think we should look there first." After retrieving her pack, she rummaged through and found the leather-bound tomes. Holding the first in her hand, she was loath to open it, but she remembered Prios's words: *The books are not evil.* Running her fingers over the unadorned leather binding, she made herself open it.

The pages were of finer quality than any Catrin had ever seen before, and the text had been meticulously scribed. Much of what she saw seemed to be equations and formulas, and after leafing through the pages, she set it aside. When she opened the second volume, she immediately found what she was looking for. Kenward, Nora, and the others stood by, waiting with undisguised anticipation. Folded in half was a finely woven canvas with a colorful map painted on it. The crease down the center had damaged parts of the map, but it was otherwise whole. Kenward drew a sharp intake of breath when she handed it to him.

"By the gods!" he said. "It's all here. The Firstland, the Greatland, the Godfist--all of it. And look here, there are at least three chains of islands I've never seen or heard of. What a treasure!"

"Taking this route," Nora said, "we can make it back in half the time."

Catrin looked at the map, trying to figure out why the thought of taking a different route made her stomach hurt. The map gave no indications of any danger save a large expanse of open water, but something told her emphatically not to go that way, and she was torn. "Can you think of any dangers that we would face taking the direct route?"

"There are always dangers," Nora said, and she pointed to a place on the map. "Most of these waters are unfamiliar to me, but there are some parts I have traveled. The biggest danger I think we would face are storms, and we could run into those anywhere."

Still, Catrin could not shake the feeling, and she decided to give her instincts credence. "Something is telling me not to go that way. I cannot explain it, and can find no reason to support it, yet I feel compelled to heed it."

"Sometimes we must listen to our instincts," Kenward said, "especially when they contradict the most likely course. Given your magic, I would be inclined to follow your gut. In my younger days, I would have taken the shortest course no matter what you said, but now I have seen too much, and I find myself given to caution."

"It's certainly taken long enough to beat some caution into you, fool boy," Nora said, but her eyes shone with pride.

"Are you certain about this?" Chase asked as he forced himself into the cramped cabin, trying to get a better look at the map. "I don't want to spend another year at sea if we don't have to."

"I can't tell you why, Chase, but I feel very strongly about this. I've no desire to prolong the journey home, but the thought of going back any way but the way we came makes me ill."

"It's decided, then," Kenward said with a sigh. "I'll have to save exploring those waters for another journey."

Under Kyrien's watchful eye, they fished until the *Slippery Eel* sat heavy in the water. As Kenward set a course for the Keys of Terhilian, Catrin stood at the stern watching Kyrien. As the Firstland faded in the distance, two other dragons joined Kyrien. They escorted the ship to deep water, but as the sun began to sink below the horizon, the other two dragons refused to go any farther. Circling, they called out to Kyrien, and he seemed torn. After several long and tense moments, the other dragons turned on their wingtips and soared back to the Firstland. Catrin watched, also torn. Part of her wanted Kyrien to come with her, to be a part of her life, but she wondered what kind of life he could have without other dragons. In the end, she knew she needed to do what was best for Kyrien. Opening herself to a trickle of power, she did her best to communicate with him using only her mind: *Go. Be free. Live well!*

His only response was a mournful call; then, after diving down and soaring low over the deck, he flew after his brethren, back to his home. Catrin watched with tears in her eyes, hoping he would live a happy life. Though she had known him only a short time, she left the Firstland with what felt like a gaping hole in her heart. Prios joined her and seemed to share her sadness.

I will miss him too. I was responsible for delivering him to Belegra, which is something I may never be able to forgive myself for, yet somehow he found it in his heart to do just that. I always thought he hated me. He could have let Chase kill me, or he could have killed me himself, but he did not. I cannot say I understand it, but I will forever be in his debt.

"Perhaps, someday, you will get a chance to repay that debt," Catrin said.

I don't see how I ever could, but I suppose it's possible. No one can say what the future will hold.

* * *

In the following weeks, Catrin spent much of her time with Brother Vaughn. Together they learned everything they could from Belegra's books. One volume was about the physical laws of her world; it was this tome that was filled with equations--most of which only made Catrin's head hurt, and she doubted she would ever find any of it useful. Brother Vaughn had little more success, and they set that book aside.

The second seemed of little use at first since it contained descriptions of mythical creatures, from harpies to bearbulls, most of which neither Catrin nor Brother Vaughn believed existed. When Brother Vaughn flipped to the section that described dryads, though, Catrin became intrigued, especially since much of what it said rang of truth. "I thought of those other creatures as mere fairy tales, but I know dryads exist. Could these other creatures really have once existed?"

"I suppose it's possible," Brother Vaughn said. "Let's see what other creatures are described." Turning the pages carefully, he passed a section describing giant birds called phirlons and another on glowing sea serpents known as godhairs. It was when he reached the section on dragons that he drew a sharp breath. He read aloud: "Of dragons there are three types: *verdent, feral,* and *regent. Verdents* are most common and are by far the largest dragon species. Despite their size and power, they are docile and easily tamed. All *verdent* dragons have mottled bluish-gray coloring.

"*Feral* dragons, as black as night, are as ferocious as their name would imply. Generally, *ferals* are solitary creatures that only congregate during mating season, but there have been incidents recorded where groups of *ferals* have attacked *verdents* who intruded on their territory.

"*Regent* dragons are the most rare and intriguing species. *Regents* seem to live more like ants than dragons. That is to say that they live in colonies and have specialized roles. Each colony has but one female-- the queen. There are many types of *regent* males: warrior, protector, hunter, and nurturer are but a few."

"So Kyrien is a regent dragon?" Catrin asked.

"I would say he fits the description, and the skeleton found in Faulk would have to have been a verdent."

Seeing a vision of skies filled with all three types of dragons, Catrin felt a chill run down her spine. The thought was thrilling and terrifying.

"*Regent* dragons have other remarkable qualities," Brother Vaughn continued. "The ability to change the color of their skin to blend in with their surroundings is among the most formidable trait. Regents are so skilled in camouflage that they can become nearly invisible in almost any environment. It is their innate ability to transform noonstone into dragon ore, though, that makes these creatures the most highly sought after."

Pulling Belegra's dragon ore from her pocket, Catrin held it up. It caught the light and cast it about in disorganized fashion, which detracted from its beauty. "So that was why Belegra wanted Kyrien," she said. "For this."

"It would appear to be so."

Nothing could be worth the torture Belegra inflicted upon Kyrien. She was tempted to cast the stone into the sea, but Catrin came to see that even though the way the stone was created was evil, the stone itself was not. When she began to view it as a gift from Kyrien, a piece of him that she could take with her, it became a cherished treasure.

The book gave few more details, and they set it aside. The third volume gave Catrin chills, for it told of ways to enslave the mind of another. Chilled by the gruesome and cruel techniques described in painful detail, Catrin decided that this book truly was evil. "This is knowledge that no one should have. I think we should burn it."

Brother Vaughn seemed appalled by the idea of burning a book at first, but as he looked through the rest of the book, he came to agree. There was no joy in the act, but Catrin felt a little safer knowing it was gone. With any luck, those skills would be lost forever.

Catrin's thoughts turned to all that had been lost, and tears gathered in her eyes. When one fell to the floor, Brother Vaughn looked up. "Will you tell me what's bothering you?" he asked.

"I just feel so alone," she said. "It's not that you and everyone on the ship are . . . It's just . . ."

"I miss them too," Brother Vaughn said, and Catrin let her emotion flow. "May I share something with you?"

"Please do," Catrin said with a sniffle.

"What is there between us? Right now. What's separating you and me?"

"Nothing, I guess," Catrin said.

"Nothing? Really."

In the silence that followed, Catrin tried to understand his meaning, but then something occurred to her. "Air?"

"Air. Indeed," Brother Vaughn said. "Now I want you to step away from everything for a moment, including the air."

Catrin smiled, knowing it was impossible. "I suppose I could submerge myself in water."

"Not for long. But the point is that you and I are parts of the same system. We are parts of the world, and we cannot separate ourselves from it. Everything I do influences you, and everything you do influences everyone and everything else. Do you understand?"

"I think so," Catrin said.

"Since we are part of this enormous system, we are always connected and can never truly be alone. And even when we seem to depart from this world, our energy remains. In this sense, we are one and we are eternal."

His words gave Catrin solace, and she turned her thoughts back to anything that could help her in the future. Again she looked at the dragon ore she held. So precious and so very rare, she was afraid she would drop it and shatter it into tiny pieces. Oddly shaped, it felt clumsy in her hands. The stones in her staff had been masterfully cut, their symmetry somehow balancing them. Then she remembered Imeteri's Fish; it had been such a simple carving, yet it, too, had symmetry and balance. "Do you think the shape of the dragon ore could enhance its effects?" she asked.

"The thought never occurred to me," Brother Vaughn said, "but I suppose it's possible. Do you have reason to believe it could?"

"The stones Mother Gwendolin gave me have been carefully cut, where Imeteri's Fish was just a simple carving. The one thing they have in common is that one side seems to balance the other. When I hold Belegra's stone, it feels unstable, out of balance."

"Perhaps you should have a gem-cutter cut it for you? Or you could carve it yourself. You did say that Imeteri's Fish was only a rough carving. Surely you could do just as well," Brother Vaughn said.

Catrin turned the translucent stone in her hands, and as she looked at it, a simple but elegant shape became apparent to her--the shape the stone wanted to become. It was as if all she had to do was peel away the husk that shrouded the stone's true form. "Could I be so bold as to try to carve it myself? I've no skill for art or carving. I might destroy it."

"I suppose you must follow your heart."

* * *

Cradled by her hammock, Catrin closed her eyes. As had become a bit of a ritual, Prios chose this time to spend with her. Though walls separated them, it was as if he were sitting beside her.

"Is it not difficult for you to talk to me without touching me?" she asked aloud, despite the fact that she had only to think of saying it to him for him to hear. "You could come in here while we talk if you'd like."

There is a bond between us that I do not understand. I believe I could speak with you over almost any distance without the slightest strain. It is something I share with no one else. Perhaps it is your abilities, but I wonder if it isn't something else . . .

Catrin let his unspoken question go unanswered, afraid of things she was not yet prepared to face. Grateful that he could not read her thoughts unless they were directed to him, she changed the subject. "Do you think I should try to carve the dragon ore? I'm afraid I'll only destroy it."

I know nothing of the properties of dragon ore, but I, too, sense its flaws despite its purity. When I look at nature, I see varied shapes and forms of life, yet those forms are not chaotic or random, as the shape of Belegra's dragon ore seems to be. My instincts tell me that giving it orderly shape and form will give it new life. I cannot be certain, and there is the risk that you will destroy it, so I am hesitant to give council.

"It would be so much easier if someone would just tell me what I am supposed to do."

I've lived my life doing what others have told me to do. While not being responsible for my own destiny may have been easier, I certainly would not say it was better.

"You make a good point," Catrin conceded. "I suppose I'll just have to stop my whining and get on with it." She could almost hear Prios chuckle.

*   *   *

As the sun rose over the sea, the lookout called out: "Land!" His call drew everyone to the deck. Having seen nothing but waves for months, it was a thrill to see land, even if they would only pass it by. When they neared the Terhilian Lovers, the sun cast a ruddy glow, and there, perched upon the man's outstretched arm, waited Kyrien. Glimmering like a jewel, he spread his wings and extended his tail. Dropping his head down, he wove back and forth hypnotically. No one spoke, and Catrin was held in thrall, not wanting to move or speak for fear he would fly away, but he just watched them as they slid past. Not long before he would have been lost from sight, he slipped from his perch, spread his wings only part of the way, and slammed into the water.

Watching for him to emerge, Catrin waited at the gunwales for most of the day, but he did not show himself. She was left to wonder if his presence was but a final farewell.

"He's a remarkable beast, your Kyrien," Nora said as she walked to Catrin's side.

"I had hoped to see him again, but I think he's gone."

"With such a rare and mystical creature, I don't suppose you'll ever know what to expect."

*   *   *

In the light of her cabin, Catrin prepared herself. Before her was the dragon ore and the sharpest knife she could find. To the side sat a leather bag she would use to collect the chips and shards, each one precious. Taking a deep breath, she picked up the knife before she lost her nerve. Using only light pressure, she pulled the knife against the stone. Not even a scratch was made in the glossy surface. Trying again, she used greater force but achieved no greater effect.

Brother Vaughn watched with anticipation. "Apply your will," he said.

Opening herself to a trickle of energy, she tried to keep the torrent from pulling her away. Despite greater understanding, her power remained difficult to moderate, and a bead of sweat formed on her brow. Directing her energy along the fine edge of the knife, she pulled it toward her, and blade parted stone. A tiny shard separated from the dragon ore and sat, perched, atop the gleaming knife.

"Well done," Brother Vaughn said. "Now do it again."

* * *

"When we get back," Osbourne said, "I'm gonna eat for a week. Ham, bacon, sausage--anything but fish."

"Bread and apple butter," Strom said.

"A big, juicy steak with potatoes," Chase added.

"Slices of pepper sausage with chunks of smoked cheese," Kenward said from behind them, and they all turned. "Aye, a seafarer I may be, but I've a love for land food."

"Do you think we'll ever make it back home?" Osbourne asked.

"We'll make it," Kenward said. "And when we do, the first meal is on me."

"I'm going to hold you to that," Strom said.

"You've all earned it. I've spent most of my life at sea, and I can think of no passengers I'd rather have on my ship. Hopefully you'll find some reason to take to the seas again someday."

"So there's no chance you'll stay on the Godfist?" Strom asked.

"Not for long," Kenward said. "I tried it once, but life on land didn't suit me. All those invisible lines that divide one man's space from another's were beyond my understanding. The sea is the sea. No one can claim it or take it away from me."

In a way, Osbourne could see his point, but it did nothing to dampen his longing for home. To feel the grass between his toes or to run through the forest would be glorious indeed. Things that had seemed mundane, even boring, in his old life now had new meaning, new significance. If ever they make it home, he thought, his life would be forever changed, and he would no longer take for granted the things he now knew he loved the most.

After finishing their meal in silence, they dispersed, each having tasks waiting. It seemed on a ship, the work was never done.

* * *

"If we run full sail," Kenward said, "we could make to the shallows just before the full moon."

"We need to fish while still on this side of the shallows," Nora said. "Or have you forgotten the sharks? Your ship is in no condition to face any foe, let alone make full speed. It would be wisest to take it slowly and fish while we wait out the cycle of the moon."

Pacing the deck, Kenward struggled. Why must his instincts always push him to do the exact opposite of what his mother suggested? He valued her council, no matter what she thought, but he had learned to follow his gut. "We can't sail the shallows with a full hold, and we'll have to fish on the other side either way. Raise full sail," he said. Nora made an annoyed sound in her throat and walked away.

"She doesn't look happy," Chase said as he approached.

Kenward just shrugged. "I have that effect on her."

* * *

Wiping the sweat from her eyes, Catrin squinted, trying to figure out the best way to make the final cut. Before her was the physical manifestation of the image she had seen in her mind. Despite her rudimentary carving skills, it was, in its own way, beautiful. Turning the tip of her blade carefully under a delicate section, she trimmed away a tiny sliver, though she nearly cut herself when someone shouted: "Shallows ahead!"

After carefully placing the sliver in her now nearly full bag, Catrin went to the gunwales, secretly hoping to find Kyrien waiting for her.

"Get the gear ready. We fish," Kenward said, and the crew scrambled. Despite their efforts, the fish simply weren't biting, and they caught only a few small sharks. As the light began to fade, the frustration was palpable. "We need to catch enough fish to feed us for a while. I didn't want to fill the hold, but I didn't want to starve either. If we don't catch something soon, we are going to have to wait another moon before we cross the shallows."

"Aye," Nora said. "Nothing to be done for it but to keep trying."

"Fins to port, sir!" called the lookout.

Glossy fins parted the water, tossing a wake on each side as they came. Then, as if they understood the fear it would instill, they slipped beneath the dark water. Catrin tried to prepare herself for an impact, but not knowing exactly when it would come made it nearly impossible. When the sharks did hit the ship, it felt as if all of them hit at once, and the *Slippery Eel* rolled to one side before slowly righting herself.

"Pull in the trawl tubs!" Kenward ordered. "As soon as they are in, we raise full sail and make for the shallows. Prepare yourselves!"

In a frenzy of activity, the crew readied the ship to come about, but the men retrieving the trawl tubs cursed. They had caught something, and whatever it was, it was big.

"*Now* the fish decide to bite," Strom said as he helped the men struggling to turn the windlass.

"Sir, some of our repairs have been knocked loose. We're taking on water," Bryn reported.

"Lock the windlass," Kenward said then, with a single stroke of his belt knife across the tensioned rope, cut the trawl away. "Full sail.

Now!"

The *Slippery Eel* thrummed as the sharks slammed against the hull again, and the crew needed little urging to make speed. Catrin clung to the railing, a sick feeling in her stomach. The sharks seemed determined to sink them, and she knew that, in the water, they would make an easy meal. Though the moon was nearly full, a thick covering of clouds blanketed the skies, and the shallows were barely visible. Sailing full speed into those waters seemed in itself suicide, and that was assuming the sharks didn't get them first.

"There's someone in the shallows, sir! Light ahead!"

Chapter 15

To depend solely on a single food source is to risk starvation.
--Ruder Dunn, farmer

* * *

Near complete darkness hindered the crew's efforts to find a clear path when entering the shallows. Though the firelight was still distant, it cast dancing reflections across the water, making it even more difficult to find obstacles. In a bold spectacle, the sharks pursued the ship into the shallows. At times it seemed they would surely become trapped in the sand, yet they remained a threat.

"Bring out the spears!" Kenward ordered. "There's no place for them to hide in the shallows, and I want them to feel our sting!"

Catrin watched as crewmen leveled long spears at the sharks. Some simply stabbed at those that drew too close, others threw their spears with all their strength into the sharks that circled the ship. Most had little effect or simply missed their mark, but one landed a mortal blow. The badly injured shark thrashed wildly, churning the water, and its brethren turned on it, quickly tearing it apart. The grisly display made Catrin's stomach churn as she imagined what it would feel like to be pulled apart. Deeply disturbed, she kept her eyes toward the firelight.

The closer they came, the larger the fire grew, as if feeding off their very energy. Occasionally, a dark silhouette blocked out parts of the fire, but little more could be seen. When finally the sharks were left behind, Kenward slowed the ship. "It would be risky to go any farther in these conditions," he said. "We could do it if that fire wasn't ruining our night vision. I want to know who started it."

"You're starting to show the wisdom of a seasoned captain," Nora said.

"If you call being scared out of my shorts wisdom, then I guess it's so."

"Fool boy."

"Drop the boats," Kenward said. "Arm yourselves and be ready for a fight. I've no doubt they know we're here, and they may be laying in wait."

Despite the fact that whoever it was probably already knew they were coming, the crew did their best to remain silent. After the boats had been lowered, Catrin stood next to Chase, waiting her turn to climb down. "You stay here," he said. "We'll go find out what's going on."

"Not a chance," Catrin said, and she grabbed the railing and jumped over. Scrambling down the boarding net, she gave no one else the opportunity to dissuade her. Waiting on the ship would have been pure torture; better to see for herself.

Farsy climbed into the boat with her, handed her an oar, and dipped his own. Soon they glided through the relatively calm waters. The fire could be seen through the withered remains of saltbark trees, many of which appeared to have been smothered in volcanic ash. An oily film coated the water and at times was so thick that it clung to their oars. As they moved past a small island, their view of the fire was finally unobstructed, though there seemed to be no one about.

"Do you see anyone?" Farsy asked in a whisper.

"No," Catrin said. The fire was built on a wooden platform that extended between the roots of a saltbark tree and a nearby rock outcropping. Looking back to the other boats waiting in the distance, she saw Chase slip into the dark water.

* * *

"Looks like a trap," Chase said. "Hold back." He and Bryn used their oars to slow the boat, keeping it in relative darkness. "Wait here." Flexing the muscles of his arms and shoulders, Chase silently lowered himself into the water. With his belt knife between his teeth, he slipped beneath the surface.

Swimming as far as he could on a single breath, Chase moved to the other side of the fire, and there he slowly broke the surface. Not far away, someone else watched from the water. Giving them no time to escape him, Chase moved closer. With one swift motion, he brought his knife up to the man's throat. "One move and I give my knife a good yank."

Behind him the water stirred, and Chase had no time to react before the tip of a crude spear was driven under his chin, slamming his mouth shut.

"One move and you'll be a head on a stick."

* * *

Trying to locate Chase again, having lost sight of him when he went underwater, Catrin looked about, cursing the darkness and the light. A commotion on the far side of the platform got her attention, and she leaned out far, trying to get a better look.

"By the gods! Is it you?" came Chase's voice over the water. "Benjin! Fasha!"

Still overextended, Catrin's knees buckled, and she nearly fell face-first into the water, but Farsy grabbed her and pulled her back into the boat. Their boat swayed, nearly capsizing, but Catrin looked up in time to see Benjin climb from the water.

Standing on the platform, the flames casting a rosy glow over him; he looked nothing like the man Catrin remembered. Long, mostly gray hair was plastered to his face and fell to his shoulders. His beard, which he had always kept trimmed, was now long and straggly. Thinner, but still well muscled, he wore only a loincloth.

A moment later, Fasha and Chase joined him. She wore little more than Benjin, and her skin shone like gold. Catrin could form no words and began to sob. A wave of relief crashed over her, and she tumbled in the surf. Only Farsy's strong hands kept her from falling over, and she clung to him, overwhelmed by emotion.

"I'm here, li'l miss!" Benjin said, his voice rough and gravelly. Catrin could take no more. Standing, she jumped into the water and swam as fast as she could to meet Benjin, who immediately swam to meet her. When at last they touched, Catrin latched on to him and would not let go. Still sobbing, she clung to him all the way back to the *Slippery Eel*.

"I thought you were dead," she said haltingly. "We searched--"

"I know you did, li'l miss. I know. The currents carried us away, and though we saw you, you could not see us. You never made it close enough to hear us, but we know you tried."

As the water slipped by, Catrin looked up the see a dryad peeking around her saltbark tree. With a silent thank you, Catrin closed her eyes and cried.

* * *

Shaved, washed, and clothed, Benjin looked more like the man Catrin remembered, but the gray dominating his hair and beard made him look much older. As he raised a mug of water, his hand trembled, and she tried to hide her concern.

"A few planks of my deck held together," Fasha said. "Benjin and I used it as a raft and paddled our way back to the shallows. We nearly lost the raft when the cloud of fire came. We both ducked underwater and held our breath for as long as we could. When we came back up, the raft was far away."

"Fasha is a strong swimmer," Benjin said, pride in his eyes. "She caught up to it and brought it back to me."

"You could've caught it yourself," Fasha said, "if you hadn't already begun to take a chill. Thought I was going to lose him for a while there, but the saltbark leaf seemed to help a great deal--that and being dry and warm."

"Wood was hard to find," Benjin said, "and neither of us wanted to be without a fire. When I was strong enough, we swam to the Zjhon ship and, each day, we brought back more wood. The Zjhon had fairly well stripped the ship of anything else of use, but we were happy to burn what was left."

"I wanted to build a boat and sail back into trade waters, but Benjin insisted you would come back. Thank the gods he was right. Otherwise, I might've had to feed him to the sharks."

Catrin told the tale of their adventures. Benjin and Fasha listened, obviously having a difficult time believing all they heard. As if he knew when his name was being spoken, Prios joined them, keeping his eyes downcast.

"Do not fear us," Benjin said. "You helped save Catrin, and for that I'll always be grateful."

Prios bowed his head to Benjin and Fasha then slipped into the shadows, seemingly reluctant to be the focus of attention. When Catrin began to tell more of Kyrien, a hush fell over the room, and Benjin looked thoughtful. "You're attached to this dragon in some way?" he asked.

"I won't claim to understand it," Catrin said, "but yes. I think so. He was waiting for us when we reached the Keys of Terhilian, and part of me hopes to see him again, but I don't know if I ever will. He's so regal and beautiful, I find it difficult to describe. Belegra was willing to torture and destroy him ... for this." Holding out her hand, she revealed the dragon ore carving.

Even in the dim lamplight, Catrin's panther gleamed, its simplicity making it all the more striking. Smooth lines and subtle curves showed the mighty cat, alert and ready to pounce. So aggressive was its stance that it was uncomfortable to view the carving from the front, yet there was playfulness about it.

"Where did you get that?" Benjin asked, reaching his hand out slowly, seemingly almost afraid to touch it.

"Belegra used Kyrien to create dragon ore. I brought his chunk of ore back with me, but it seemed unbalanced, as if it needed to be in a different form. So I carved it."

"How did you come up with the cat shape?" Osbourne asked.

"It's a panther, I think. I just looked into the stone before I started carving, and I could see the shape of the panther already inside it, waiting."

Waiting for you to set it free.

Catrin gave a start and looked up to meet eyes with Prios.

You set the panther free. Just as you did for me and for Kyrien. You freed the panther from a prison of stone, but you have forgotten something, something special, something important.

"Is something wrong, li'l miss?"

"I'm fine," Catrin said. "Sorry. Prios can speak in my mind, and he was reminding me that I've overlooked something." Looking into the eyes of the carving, Catrin opened herself to it, seeking its name.

Koe.

More a thought than a voice in her mind, the name came to her and she spoke it aloud. It felt powerful and right, and though the panther looked no different than it had before, Catrin found she saw Koe in a new way. The name felt right.

It's a good name, Prios said in her mind.

"Seems quite fitting," Benjin said at almost the same time, and others nodded in agreement.

"I saved all the chunks and slivers of stone that I cut away, and I plan to experiment with them. My gut tells me there is a great deal I can learn from them."

"You must use caution," Benjin said. "You know the power of dragon ore and how devastating a mistake could be."

"I know," Catrin said as she carefully slid Koe back into her pocket.

"Can Prios speak in others' minds?" Fasha asked suddenly. "I mean, other than yours, Catrin?"

I could speak to Belegra and the others in the cadre. I never tried with anyone else except you. It is more difficult over distance. I find it easiest if I can touch the person I wish to speak to.

Catrin relayed his words, and Fasha seemed disappointed, but Benjin looked thoughtful.

"If someone can hear Prios," he said, "then that would mean they almost certainly have access to Istra's power."

Yes, Prios answered in Catrin's mind, and she relayed his answer.

"Prios," Benjin said. "Would you mind trying to talk to those of us on this ship? If we know someone has access to the power, then maybe Catrin can help them develop their abilities."

"I'm not so sure how much help I'll be," Catrin said.

I want to do this. You can free these people too. I want to help you free them all.

His words were an inspiration, but they also brought tremendous responsibility, the weight of which was nearly crushing. It made her feel as if she alone were responsible for the fate of the world. The feeling passed, and she told the rest what Prios said. His words brought tears to Fasha's eyes, and Benjin shook his hand. Prios seemed unsure of how to respond, but then he reached out and laid his hand on Benjin's shoulder. Benjin's eyes showed disappointment when Prios simply shook his head.

Chase and Osbourne were the next to be disappointed, but then Prios laid his hand on Strom's shoulder.

"I heard him! He said, 'Be free'!" Strom cried out and Prios nodded his head. Catrin and the others were stunned, and no one said a word. Prios continued around the room, and when he laid his hand on Fasha, she gasped. In the next moment, she underwent a transformation. First her face flushed, then she smiled, then she cried. Prios simply nodded when Kenward, too, heard his words.

Brother Vaughn and Grubb were the only others among those left on the ship who could hear Prios. Grubb seemed more confused than excited. In contrast, the rest seemed to have nothing but questions, and Catrin sighed, knowing answers were far too rare.

* * *

As the hammock cradled Catrin, the motions of the ship lulled her, and she let her mind wander. So much of her world had changed, and she couldn't imagine what would come next. With the help of Prios, she had attempted to teach the others how to access Istra's power, but they had no success. The others simply seemed incapable of connecting themselves with the flow. Maybe someday she would find a way to teach others, but for the moment, she made herself think about other things.

Images of her father and uncle and her home flooded her mind. Tears coursed down tracks that Catrin thought might carve valleys in her flesh if she cried any more, but still the tears came.

You will see your home again. And you will set them all free.

Prios's voice was like a whisper in her mind, and Catrin wondered if she had only dreamed it, but sleep claimed her in the next breath. His voice whispered in her dreams, caressing her, and she wrapped herself in his energy like a warm embrace.

Sleep well.

* * *

In the morning light, the lookouts scoured the waters for a safe course. Retracing their route back through the massive fallen columns, they moved into slightly deeper water, and for a while Catrin felt almost safe. With Benjin by her side, the world seemed a brighter place. Sadness still clung to her for the loss of so many others, but at least he had been returned to her, as if the gods had truly shown mercy. Fasha never seemed to be far away, and Catrin wondered at the change in both of them. The looks they exchanged often spoke of more than friendship.

Even in calm waters, there was much work to be done, and most of their time was spent assisting the crew. Weakened repairs were mended, and the *Slippery Eel* was once again watertight. When the end of the shallows finally came into view, Catrin felt a stirring in her stomach. She was another step closer to home, but no one could know what awaited them in deep water.

"Get the fishing gear ready," Kenward ordered, and the crew began making preparations, all the while watching the seas for any signs of sharks. After the trawls had been dropped, everyone waited in tense anticipation. Knowing they must fish or starve, the threat of sharks had them all on edge. Kenward took no chances, though.

"Pull in the trawls!" he commanded. "If we caught anything, there'll be blood in the water. I want to be well away from here before we drop the tubs again."

Though the fish were biting, what they caught was small, and Kenward's precautions made the process of filling the hold painfully slow. Big sharks were sighted on several occasions, but Kenward did his best to use the wind and currents to his advantage, and they filled the hold without any attacks. Exhausted, the crew finally allowed themselves to relax.

Catrin stood at the stern and watched the water slip away, silently hoping to see Kyrien flying on the winds. Prios stood by her side but said nothing, comforting her with his presence alone.

* * *

By the light of a small lamp, Chase looked at his companions and smiled. He and Strom and Osbourne had been through a great deal together, and now Prios was quickly becoming a part of their group. Chase found that he had sorely misjudged Prios. His quiet and reserved demeanor was unnerving. The fact that he had no tongue made it almost difficult to look upon him for the images it brought to mind, but Chase was beginning to see beyond those things. Slowly, Prios revealed himself as a vibrant personality with both a mischievous streak and a sense of humor.

Though there was always work to be done on a ship, Chase liked to make certain that they all spent some time together, and their late-night talks often lasted until the sunrise. Most times Catrin would join them, but on this night she had complained of a headache and gone to her hammock earlier than usual.

Strom began telling tales, and Prios seemed enthralled by his dramatic reenactments of events. After hearing stories of how Chase had trained at being stealthy, Prios made eye contact with Chase. Using his amazing ability of expressing himself with only his facial expressions and body language, he sized Chase up, smiled, and issued an unspoken challenge. Though Chase could not hear Prios speak in his mind, he had no trouble deciphering the challenge: If you are such a mighty sneak, then prove it!

"What would be the hardest thing to steal on this ship?" Strom asked with a knowing grin.

"Catrin's staff?" Osbourne asked.

Prios turned his nose up, and Strom snorted. "Too easy."

"She never takes Koe out of her pocket. I bet she sleeps with him under her pillow."

Prios gave a firm nod.

"Koe it is," Strom said.

Chase smiled, put his hands behind his head, and yawned. "Is that all?"

A sly look crossed Prios's face, and he waved for Strom to lean closer. Reaching out, he laid his hand on Strom's shoulder.

"Ha!" Strom barked. "He says to make it a real challenge, I will stand guard at the prow and Osbo will stand guard at the stern. If either of us sees you, then you've failed."

"And if I succeed?"

Prios shrugged, seeming to think it was unlikely, and that just made Chase even more determined.

"If you succeed," Strom said, "we'll all bow down and show due respect for the master sneak."

"Good enough for me," Chase said.

* * *

Osbourne strained his eyes and ears, trying his best to catch Chase in the act. Though a part of him wanted Chase to succeed, it would be a true victory only if they did their best to stop him. At the slightest sound, Osbourne whipped around and ran to the gunwales. Had he heard a splash? Watching the dark water slide by, he saw nothing beyond the usual wake left by the *Eel*. Convinced he'd been hearing things, he returned to his post.

No more sounds, save the snapping of sails, the creak of rigging, and the sound of the water rushing by, broke the silence. Even the crew was silent, as if they knew what was transpiring, and Osbourne found the stillness unnerving. When Strom walked around the corner, he nearly leaped from his skin.

"Did you see anything?"

"No," Osbourne said. "I thought I heard something, but I didn't see anything."

Strom just shook his head, "I didn't either, but Prios came to get me, and Chase is all smiles. How do you think he got by us?"

"I don't know," Osbourne said. "I think he may have tricked me."

"Let's go find out."

As they entered Chase's cabin, Osbourne was surprised to see Chase as dry as tinder. "I was certain you'd gone over the side."

"That's what I wanted you to think," Chase said with a triumphant grin.

"So let's see it," Strom said, his arms crossed over his chest.

Chase just grinned and reached for his pocket, but then the color drained from his face, and his victorious bravado suddenly changed to anxious desperation. For a moment, he searched his pockets, and then he searched the cabin. "She's going to kill me."

"You never actually stole it, did you?" Strom asked, seeming almost hopeful.

"I swear to you: I took it, and now it's gone."

Tense silence hung over the group, and Osbourne thought Chase might actually cry. When Prios's shoulders began to shake, the others turned to him, thinking he was overcome with remorse, but he surprised them all when he made the first sound any of them had ever heard from him. Though the gift of speech had been taken from him, he proved that Belegra had not taken the life from him when he laughed. So pure and joyous was his laughter, that the others simply waited in silence to find out what could possibly have tickled him so.

With a look of apology, he ended Chase's torment as he produced Koe from a concealed pocket in his shirt.

"How did you--? When did--? Oh, for the love of everything good and right in this world, forget it. I don't want to know," Chase said, and without saying any more, he stormed into the night.

Osbourne looked at Strom, and for the first time in a long time, they laughed.

* * *

"That really wasn't very nice," Catrin said when Prios told her about how he had tricked Chase. A sly smile crept across his face, yet a hint of blush shaded his cheeks. "And I would appreciate it if you would challenge him to steal someone else's things next time." Again, Prios simply smiled in response. Every day they spent together seemed to bring them closer. With increasing frequency, he showed that, in many cases, he could communicate without the need to speak in her mind. It seemed he had a talent for expressing himself without speech or words. Others, too, had made note of this talent, and Catrin was grateful for it, as it seemed to make his life aboard the ship much easier. Knowing he could communicate in other ways just made the times when he did speak even more special.

Though I look forward to seeing you reunited with your family and your homeland, I must admit that I am afraid.

"Afraid? What are you afraid of?"

What if your people do not accept me? What if your family does not like me? I'm not certain my story will give them reason to trust me, and I fear I will only make things worse for you.

With his shoulders hunched and his eyes cast down, Catrin could feel his pain and anxiety. Though she tried to put herself in his position, to understand how he must be feeling, she found it impossible. The circumstances of his life were just too far from anything she had ever experienced, and though she could sympathize, she knew she would never completely understand. "Once they come to see your true nature, they will come to feel as I do."

And how, exactly, do you feel about me?

Though he did not truly speak, it was as if Catrin could hear the tremble in his voice. Something in his emotion was betrayed to her, and she sensed his fear and anxiety. In that moment, she realized the courage it had taken for him to ask. "I think . . ." she hesitated, and he raised his eyes to meet hers. In them, she saw not only fear, but hope as well. "I think I love you."

* * *

When land was finally sighted again, Catrin could barely contain her excitement. All of them had known the *Slippery Eel* was too small to make the journey to the Falcon Isles safely, but they had unanimously chosen expedience over caution. Storms had chased them and rogue waves appeared without warning, but somehow they had survived. The Falcon Isles were the last stop Catrin planned to make before she returned to the Godfist, and she did not intend to stay long. Nora insisted they take a week to make proper repairs, but Catrin hoped the job could be done in less time. Each day seemed longer than the last, and she wasn't certain how much longer she could stand the anticipation.

As the smaller islands slid by, Catrin moved to Nora's side. Fasha and Benjin stood not far away, and they turned when Catrin addressed Nora. "Will you leave from the Falcon Isles to go back to the *Trader's Wind?*"

"A big part of me wishes to do just that, but I know I would only spend my days worrying over your fate. I've come too far to leave you just now. I must see this to the finish. I wish to see you reunited with your family, and only when you are safe will I return to my ship," Nora said with a firm nod.

"Thank you," Catrin said. "I owe you and your family a great debt. I only hope I can find a way to repay you someday."

"Nonsense," Nora said. "We've only done what was right. You owe us nothing. Given the chance, I'd do it all again."

"Trade vessel ahead," the lookout called, and the crew gathered at the gunwales, anxious to see another human face. It was thrilling to see someone besides her shipmates, and excitement ran through her as the ship slid by. The crew of the trade ship eyed them with suspicion, but a few were brave enough to offer a wave. There was the chance that hostile ships would also be in the area, and most kept their eyes to the seas, but there was still an air of celebration aboard the ship. Grubb prepared a special meal using spices and stores normally kept under strict ration, and many a tale was told. Catrin smiled and laughed more than she had for a very long time, and when some of the crewmembers began to sing, she danced.

* * *

Straining under the weight of the planks she carried, Catrin asked Benjin to stop so they could rest. The walk from the lumber mill to the docks was not long, but the way was crowded and it took effort to weave their way through. When a man passed by whom Catrin thought she recognized, she assumed she must be mistaken.

"Things have changed," Benjin said, reading her face. "That was Kenmar Wills. You know him because he used to live in Harborton. It would seem there are many people here from the Godfist. This entire town has grown up in the time we've been gone. I can only imagine what we'll find when we return to the Godfist."

Catrin tried not to let his words dampen her excitement, but beneath her desire to get home was a petrifying fear that things had changed too much, that her home no longer existed. With a grunt, she lifted her end of the planks, and they began walking back to the *Eel*.

"That's the last of it," Benjin said when they finally reached the deck.

"Take the rest of the day off," Kenward said. "We've got the materials we need now."

"I need to go look for someone," Catrin said after retrieving her staff.

Benjin frowned. "Nat Dersinger?"

"Yes."

"If you must," Benjin said with a sigh. "I don't want you going alone, though. Take Chase with you."

Though she wanted to go alone, Catrin didn't argue. She'd considered asking Prios to come along, but what she truly needed was time to talk to Nat--alone. Chase seemed to agree with Benjin and followed her down the gangplank. "It'll be good to have my feet on solid ground for a while," he said, and despite his casual tone, Catrin knew he would come whether she wished it or not.

Though solid, the land itself created feelings of uncertainty, as there were still signs of devastation everywhere. It seemed unfathomable that an eruption so very far away could cause so much destruction. A distinct line stretched from coast to coast, showing how high the water had gotten. It was a wonder anyone survived. The docks and the buildings that stood were apparently new construction using materials recovered after the water receded.

Most of the people they passed were busy with their own tasks and paid no attention to Catrin and Chase. A few cast suspicious glances; others hawked their wares. Catrin stopped to look at some sausages, knowing how Benjin loved them. She bought three varieties, and after she'd paid, she asked the man if he knew of Nat Dersinger. The man's face turned from friendly to sour, and he just pointed to a place at the end of the docks, where civilization ended and the forest began. Catrin thanked him, but he seemed eager to have her away from him, and she and Chase began walking toward the end of the docks.

When she saw birds take flight from behind a nearby building, Catrin wondered if word of her coming were already on its way to the Godfist. If it were, there was nothing she could do about it, and she just kept walking.

"We're not going to be able to find anyone out there," Chase said, but then he stopped short when a tall man stepped into their path. A skirt of reeds covered his loins, but the rest of his body was covered in red paint, with white and black markings painted strategically to make him look better muscled than he actually was. Atop his head was a crown of vines, and the black paint around his eyes gave him an angry appearance. He leaned on a simple wooden staff, but only when he spoke did Catrin recognize him.

"Greetings, Catrin."

Chapter 16

Evil often hides beneath a veil of righteousness.
--Fetter Bains, agnostic

* * *

"Come," Nat said, and he led them to a narrow but well-worn trail that wove through the rotting mass and into the forest. "It's not far."

"Why are you dressed like that?" Chase asked.

"I have joined the Gunata, a tribe native to the islands. I married the daughter of a chieftain, and I have become a leader within the tribe."

"You're married?" Catrin asked, and Nat smiled. Despite the paint he wore, it was the warmest smile she'd ever seen from him. There was a light in his eyes, and the fear fled from her; all that remained was the desire to meet the one who made Nat so cheerful. "That's wonderful. I'm so happy for you!" Charging forward, she hugged him, getting his paint all over her clothing.

"Come. I must bring you to the elders. They've been waiting for you."

"Waiting? How did you know we were coming," Chase asked, suspicious.

"I had a vision," Nat said without hesitation. Chase rolled his eyes but said no more. Beyond a turn, they came to a place where the trail emptied into a lush meadow. The land rolled gently and was blanketed in thick grasses. In the middle was a large fire surrounded by the silhouettes of people, most of which stopped and turned to watch them approach.

Speaking in a tongue Catrin did not understand, Nat announced them. None of the Gunata spoke or approached; they simply watched as Catrin and Chase followed Nat to a massive log. Here he sat and gestured for everyone else to be seated. Catrin sat next to Nat and Chase beside her. From the crowd of Gunata, one woman approached. Dressed in a wrap of woven palm adorned with flowers of every description, she came straight to Catrin. Going to one knee, she kissed Catrin's hand. "Thank you," she said in a thick accent, but the look in her eyes effectively conveyed her message.

"Catrin, Chase, this is my wife, Neenya," Nat said. Neenya wore a warm smile, but her eyes were timid. Catrin returned her smile. Neenya sat on the other side of Nat, and now the entire group was seated in a circle around the fire. "When I arrived here, the Gunata seemed to be waiting for me, just as they have waited for you. I tried to communicate with them, but they only pointed to the mountain. Neenya took me there. The way was difficult, but what I found there was worth it. Atop the mountain is a sacred place, a place where the visions are much stronger and clearer. I must take you there. That is what they are waiting for."

"You and your visions," Chase said, clearly disgusted. "We're finally ready to go home, and you want to drag Catrin into the jungle because of a daydream."

"The visions are far from daydreams," Nat said in a level voice. The Gunata seemed unsettled by the tone of Chase's words. "I don't know how to convince you, but I will try. Things are seldom specific in my visions, but as I said, they are stronger atop the mount. In a vision, I saw Catrin riding a wave."

"That's it?" Chase asked.

"Let him finish," Catrin said.

"Catrin rode atop a white cat--a panther, I believe," Nat said.

Chase's eyes went wide and he choked, which set him into a fit of coughing. Catrin simply reached into her pocket and pulled out Koe. When the Gunata saw the shining cat, they all began to talk at once. Nat just nodded. "Will you come?" he asked, looking Catrin in the eye.

"I will."

* * *

"I don't like it," Benjin said.

"I agree," Chase added.

"I'm going," Catrin said. "You can choose to believe whatever you wish, but I believe Nat's visions deserve credence. After all, he's been right before. Kenward said he'd wait for us, and Prios can contact me if there is trouble, so let's just go and get it done. Then we can go home."

Benjin and Chase seemed to realize that arguing would get them nowhere. After grabbing their packs, they followed Catrin down the gangplank. Waiting below, dressed for hiking, Nat seemed annoyed that Benjin chose to come along, but he said nothing; instead he just led them back onto the trail. As they walked past where the Gunata were gathered, Neenya joined them and took the lead. She, too, was dressed in leathers.

Nat dropped back to walk beside Catrin. "There was something else puzzling about my vision," he said in a low voice meant for only Catrin's ears. "I see the stones you have mounted in the staff, and I suppose that explains the dragon with gleaming eyes, but the dragon in my vision flew."

"Then it was another dragon you saw. His name is Kyrien."

Nat stopped and stared at Catrin a moment but said nothing as Chase and Benjin stood waiting. It was a while before he spoke again. "You've seen a real dragon?"

"Yes. More than one."

Shaking his head and muttering under his breath, Nat walked in what seemed a daze. "I had hoped you would prove my visions false, but you have not. There have been other visions since, each more terrifying than the last. There are troubled times ahead for our world, Catrin. We must prepare."

"What did you see?" she asked.

"I cannot even describe the horrors I've seen, but I can tell you this: There will be a time of great prosperity that will lull most into complacency, but you must be vigilant. You must remind them of the danger that lurks just beyond the horizon. You must learn to live beneath the soil, and you must learn to grow food there, or you and yours will perish."

"What dangers do you foresee? What foe do we face?"

"It's impossible for me to say. I've seen death flow from the skies and the seas. I've seen the land itself coil up and strike you. In my dreams, though, you have stood before the coming fury. You, alone, have the power to save us all; you have but to find it, and find it you must, for you do not yet possess the strength you'll need."

"Strength she'll need for what?" Chase asked, and Nat made an annoyed sound.

"Nat's visions bring dire warnings of a peril we have yet to face," Catrin said. "For that, I will need strength."

Chase seemed to want to say something more, but he bit his lip and remained silent. The forest grew thick around the trail until the trail itself disappeared. Following Neenya, they meandered through lush greenery and vicious needle-vines. Neenya did her best to choose a clear path, but still they had to remain always watchful for danger. Nat explained that Neenya's sharp hiss was a warning when danger was near, and Catrin jumped every time she heard it. Sometimes she failed to even see what danger Neenya warned of, but other times she saw snakes, dangerous plants, and once, a bright red scorpion.

"The blood scorpion is said to have a sting like fire," Benjin said as he avoided the small but deadly creature.

Neenya seldom stopped, but when she did, she generally collected edible fruits, berries, nuts, and roots. On one occasion, though, she stopped in a thicket of tall, stalklike plants with green stems as thick as a man's fist. Using her long knife, Neenya cut down one of the stalks, carefully cutting along one of the many brown rings that divided the stalks into sections. After handing each member of the party a section, she showed them how to cut the top open and drink from the strange plant. The milky juice was sticky and sweet with a tangy aftertaste, but it left Catrin feeling refreshed.

As darkness began to fall, Neenya immediately chose a place to make camp and set about building a fire. The place she chose to camp looked as if it had been used recently; Neenya built her fire on the remains of another.

"It is not safe in the jungle at night," Nat said. "Only fire will keep the predators at a distance, and even then you must be cautious. There are snakes here that can swallow a person whole."

"Was this your camp?"

"Yes. Neenya and I have camped here before. There are several campsites along the way that we may be able to find. Others have already been reclaimed by the jungle."

Catrin pulled a fallen log closer to the fire, and after checking it thoroughly for scorpions, she sat.

While everyone was busy setting up camp, Nat pulled Catrin to the side. "The visions I had were of challenges that await, but I know there are more immediate dangers you need to be aware of. I'm as certain as the sun."

"And you think I will learn something from seeing this place?"

"I can only say what I feel," Nat said. "All my instincts say you must go there."

Catrin said no more, and when Benjin approached, Nat seemed to suddenly realize he had some task waiting for him.

"What did he have to say?" Benjin asked.

"He thinks it's important that I go to the mountain," Catrin said. "I think he believes I will have a vision."

"What do you think?"

"I'm not sure. I should be excited about a place that might give me some insight, but I have a sour feeling in my stomach. Either way, I have to do this for Nat. I hope you can understand that."

"I suppose I do, li'l miss," Benjin said, and he patted Catrin on the shoulder as he rose to look for food. "The world always looks brighter on a full stomach."

* * *

With one arm holding a cloth over her face, Catrin climbed, trying to keep the sand out of her eyes, nose, and mouth, but it was impossible. The wind played tricks, growing calm only to suddenly return full force, driving sand and dirt before it.

"We should wait until the wind dies down," Benjin yelled through the cloth he held over his face. Catrin barely heard him as the wind screamed and growled around them.

"It will not get better any time soon," Nat said. "And then it will rain."

Careful not to lean too heavily into the wind, Catrin tried to be ready for when it died down without warning. Already she had stumbled twice and nearly fallen, only Benjin's firm grip on her jacket had kept her upright. Choosing her steps with greater care, she tried not to look down, for every step took them higher.

When they finally reached the chamber atop the mountain, Nat led Catrin in. Within, the wind still howled at her, but it no longer touched her, and Catrin instantly felt safer. Much of the floor was covered in a layer of dirt, but what was exposed was a marvel. Intricate patterns and circular drawings coexisted in orderly chaos, and rods of colorful metal were inset in the floor, bisecting it at regular angles. In the ceiling of the chamber were three precisely sized and spaced holes that let in sunlight. To her right stood a large opening that looked out over the world below. Amazed by how far she could see, Catrin was overwhelmed by the sense of height the view gave her, and her guts constricted.

"Come here and look out to the seas," Nat said.

"I can't," Catrin said, suddenly terrified.

"It'll be fine, li'l miss. I'll be right here holding on to ya."

Slowly, deliberately, Catrin moved toward the opening. Then she stuck her head outside until she could no longer see the chamber walls in her periphery, her face exposed to raging currents. For a moment she simply stared out across the landscape, but then her vision began to swim. Only the feeling of Benjin's grip kept her from screaming. Slowly he began to pull her back, but something was happening. "No," she said. "Just hold me."

Benjin did as she asked, and she watched as the landscape morphed.

A crowd gathered outside the Masterhouse. With their arms in the air, they chanted. Above, on a raised dais, stood her father, his hands tied behind his back.

"Treason," said a thundering voice, and Catrin shuddered as its deep vibrations assaulted her being. "The penalty is death!" His words hammered Catrin's chest like a physical blow. Howling, she ran forward as the headsman raised his axe. The crowd parted before her, but a single figure rose up to dominate her sight. The glowing face of Istra stood between Catrin and her father, and she screamed, howling in frustration.

Gasping for breath, Catrin fell back into Benjin's arms, but only a moment did she allow herself to recover. A tickling around her nostrils and a warm sensation brought her hand to her nose, and it came away covered in blood.

"We've got to get her down from here," Benjin said with a scathing glance at Nat.

"We have to hurry," Catrin said. "Have to get home."

* * *

"Is she hurt," a voice called, and Catrin stirred.

"She just needs rest," Benjin said, his deep voice close to her ear.

Only then did Catrin realize she was being carried, and she pulled her head away from Benjin's neck. "How did you get me down?"

"Chase and I took turns carrying you."

Unable to imagine how difficult it must have been to carry her down the mountain, Catrin just closed her eyes and let Benjin carry her to her cabin.

"We have to get back to the Godfist, or they're going to kill my father," she managed to say before sleep claimed her again, and she saw the shock in Benjin's eyes, though she never heard his response.

* * *

"How close is the *Eel* to being fully repaired?" Benjin asked.

"There are one or two places where we may need to reinforce a cracked beam or the like," Kenward said, "but she's seaworthy."

"Is there any way we can make extra speed for this trip? We have good reason to believe that Wendel is in mortal danger."

"There's not much we can do but run light," Kenward said. "Problem with that is you can get awfully hungry before the fish start biting."

"Is it a chance you'd be willing to take?" Benjin asked, locking eyes with Kenward. Both knew the stakes.

"I'd be willing to take that chance, and perhaps one more," Kenward said with a sly wink. "I had some new sails made and some extra rigging hung. Mother thinks I've lost my senses, but I know the *Eel* can take the speed, and more speed means less time spent hungry."

"That's your problem, fool boy," Nora said. "Always thinking with your stomach."

"Aye," Kenward said. "Keeps me well fed. We've no more time to waste, I suppose. I'll just make sure the crew is done loading, and then we'll be under sail."

*   *   *

Standing at the prow, Catrin held onto the railing as the *Slippery Eel* knifed through the water, her extra sails filled with wind and driving her forward with tremendous force. Even so, no amount of sail could make the journey from the Falcon Isles to the Godfist short, and Catrin was made to wait. Most of her time was spent pacing the decks like an angry cat, her hand caressing the carving in her pocket. At those times she thought she might be more comfortable in the form of a panther than anything else, and she wondered about something Barabas had once said. She wondered if she had ever truly lived as a panther, or a butterfly, or even a whale. It seemed too strange to be true, yet she felt an affinity to each of those creatures, and she was left to wonder.

The others tried to keep her company, but they, too, were anxious, and their anxiety poured over Catrin like a wave. Eventually she found herself alone, driven to near madness by the waiting. Unwilling to do nothing, she began to experiment with ways to make ship move faster. At first, she tried pushing more air into the sails, but her efforts were both ineffective and extremely draining, thus she abandoned that approach.

In a moment of sudden clarity, Catrin wondered of she'd ever lived as a bird. The thought gave her an idea. After a lot of thought and experimentation--moving her hand up and down in the wind and feeling the way the air currents changed--Catrin decided to try using a narrow band of energy, like a wing, to slice the air. Her first attempts had no noticeable effect, but as she formed her wing of energy into different shapes, holding it at varying angles, she suddenly felt tremendous drag applied to the ship. It was not the desired effect, but it was a significant effect with relatively little effort. Reversing the curve of her energy wing produced an equally significant increase in the ship's speed; it was as if she were lifting the ship, causing it to ride higher in the water.

Before she went any further, she searched for Kenward, who was arguing with Bryn over the ship's suddenly erratic performance.

". . . can't find anything wrong, sir," Bryn was saying as she approached.

"Then look again," Kenward snapped.

"Bryn, wait," Catrin said, and though he turned his head, he kept moving.

Kenward met Catrin's eyes and called Bryn back. "What's this about?"

"I wanted to see if I could make the ship go faster," Catrin said, and

Kenward's eyes bulged. Of all the things he'd seen her do with the power, the thought of her propelling *his* ship seemed to disturb him greatly. "At first I only managed to slow us down, but I reversed my technique and the ship seemed to speed up."

"By the gods," Bryn said. "*That's* what that was?"

"I've never felt anything like it before," Kenward said, and Nora, who had been inspecting the ship for problems, now stood at his side. "It was as if we'd emptied the hold and lightened the ship. Can you do it again?"

"We have no idea how this will affect the ship," Nora said. "It would a dangerous thing to try, and knowing you, that's all the incentive you'll need to try it, but you've been warned." After wagging her finger in Kenward's face, she walked away.

"Do you think it's safe for me to try?" Catrin asked, now unsure of herself.

"I'll put the men in the hold on guard, and they can tell us if there are any problems developing. I'm anxious to reach the Godfist on your father's behalf and yours. Nothing would make me happier than a way to shorten this particular voyage."

"Then I'll try," Catrin said. "I'll use only a small wing at first."

"A wing?" Kenward asked, but then he shook his head. "Forget I asked. I'm not certain I want to know yet. Maybe you can tell me afterward."

The conversation had drawn attention, and most of the crew stopped what they were doing long enough to at least steal a glance at Catrin. She stood at the prow, her arms cast wide, her staff in one hand and Koe in the other. It took her a moment to find the correct angle and curvature again, but when she did, she felt the ship surge ahead.

"You're doing it!" Kenward shouted, his face a mixture of horror and fascination, which turned more and more to excitement. "Damage report!"

"The hull is showing no signs of stress, sir," Bryn said. "If anything, I'd say there seems to be less stress."

"Catrin, you may use a larger wing," Kenward said with a firm nod.

Bending her will to the task, Catrin opened herself to more power, and she expanded the size of her wing. As she applied her will, she could almost see her diaphanous formation of energy take shape. The ship rose higher in the water, and the crew stood in shock as the ship moved faster than ever before, but there was a sudden lurch when Catrin lost her concentration.

I'm sorry I surprised you.

Prios's voice in her mind and the energy he lent her gave Catrin the power to test larger wing formations and even multiple wings on each side. When she used two large wings, level with the deck, and a pair of wings from the top of every mast, everything changed. The ship moved at unbelievable speed.

"May the gods have mercy!" Nora said. "We're flying!"

Chapter 17

The greatest gifts are those not expected.
--Missa Banks, healer and mother

* * *

The wind blowing in her face, Catrin let the salt air refresh her and keep her alert. With Prios to bolster her, she kept the ship sailing on the winds. Others had tried to help--those who had heard Prios in their minds--but Catrin was unable to connect with them. Their energy was inaccessible to her, and she decided it would be best if it remained that way.

Only during storms and times when Kenward thought there might be fish did she and Prios rest. Although, some of Kenward's recent requests for time to fish seemed contrived, and Catrin suspected Benjin convinced him to lie for the sake of getting her to rest. In truth, she scolded herself for abusing Prios. How she used her own energy was her choice, but she had no right to choose for Prios. Seeking him out, she sat beside him and apologized.

You have not coerced me. What I've done, I've done of my own free will. I am free, and no one will ever enslave me again. For now, I must rest, and so should you.

Though she left feeling silly, it made Catrin feel better to know that she was not misusing her relationship with Prios. His dedication to her cause bolstered her will, and she went to her hammock smiling. Soon she would be home.

* * *

"She's coming," Master Jarvis said as he tucked away the message.

"Yes," Humbry said. "I heard. Wendel has not always been my favorite person, but he always seemed to have good sense. It would be good to see him reunited with his daughter. You had Catrin as a student. Didn't you?"

"I did. She was an average student. If I remember correctly, she was easily bored, but she was a good girl overall. I don't think she would hurt any of us. Well, except for maybe Edling."

Humbry chuckled. "Has Beron been at you to side with Edling again?"

"He never stops."

"I thought he might follow me here," Humbry said. "I don't care what they say, Jarvis. I think we should try to make peace with Wendel and his followers."

"They disobeyed a council edict," Master Jarvis said. "Though it was an edict I was tempted to go against myself. I just don't see how we can convince Beron or Baker Hollis."

"I'll do what I can," Humbry said. "A day doesn't go by that one of them doesn't show up at the farm and talk until my ears hurt. Maybe, this time, I'll do all the talking."

* * *

"No one's ever going to believe this," Kenward said as the *Slippery Eel* skimmed across the water.

"Perhaps it's a tale best not told," Nora said.

"The best ones always are."

"On *that* we agree," Nora said.

"I worry about them, though," Kenward said. "They've been at this for weeks, and Catrin is becoming more and more reluctant to take time for rest. It will do no good to reach the Godfist in time if she has no energy left. The physical exhaustion alone would be enough to put most men abed."

"Women are tougher than men," Fasha said.

"Prios doesn't seem to be faring poorly," Kenward countered, but Fasha just rolled her eyes and walked away. "Hopefully he'll not have to endure much longer. It's impossible to say how much time we've saved, but I think we should be getting close."

"I agree," Nora said.

Walking to where Catrin and Prios stood, in what looked like a deep meditative state, Kenward cleared his throat and spoke softly, hoping not to startle Catrin. The thought of his ship suddenly dropping from the air made his stomach hurt. "Can I talk to you while you work?"

"Yes," Catrin responded, her eyes still closed. "It's more difficult when I divide my attention, but I can do it for a short time."

"We should be nearing the Godfist," Kenward said, and he would have sworn the ship surged ahead with his words. "Normally we would only dock at the cove or along the southern coast, but I can't say what things are like on the Godfist these days, and I want your opinion."

"It would take too long for us to travel around the desert, but I also agree that we should probably avoid the harbor."

"Besides going to the harbor," Benjin said as he approached, "landing on the northern tip of the Godfist, where the Zjhon built their lift system, may be the shortest and safest route."

"I agree," Catrin said.

"It's settled, then," Kenward said.

* * *

With their destination set, Catrin felt a renewed sense of urgency. The duration of their voyage and the additional burden of propelling the ship had dulled her panic, despite knowing her father was in no less danger. There was simply no more she could do, and she made herself accept it.

Beside her, Prios made no complaint, but she could sense his exhaustion as poignantly as her own. Cold weather made their task even more difficult. Still, Catrin could not relent--not yet. Every moment brought her closer to the Godfist, closer to her father and her home, and she doubted she could sleep even if she tried.

"Sails to port, sir!"

The lookout's call sent a thrill through Catrin as she realized they must be getting very close. The vessel on the horizon had the look of a fishing boat, and it seemed unlikely that they would be more than a day from shore.

"Catrin," Kenward said. "I don't think we should let anyone see us sailing like this; it might cause a panic. We should make the rest of the trip under sail alone."

Though she agreed with his sentiment, Catrin was loath to release the energy that flowed through her, and when she did, her exhaustion became acute. Still, she refused to leave the deck, despite the icy winds that drove in heavy cloud cover. She didn't want to miss the first sighting of the Godfist, and she remained at the prow, straining her tired eyes. Prios showed that he had better sense and went to his cabin to rest.

* * *

"You can't be thinking of going?" Jensen asked. Wendel unrolled the message and read it once again.

Wendel,

The people have suffered enough. Let us put an end to this struggle. Come to the Masterhouse immediately so that we might settle this matter peacefully.

This letter will serve as notice to all guards. Wendel Volker is to be assisted on his journey to the Masterhouse, and he is to be treated with respect.

I will await you.

Master Edling

"It's obviously a trap," Jensen said.

"We must at least make an attempt at peace," Wendel said. "I owe that much to Catrin."

Jensen looked angry and frustrated. "You'll go alone? Into the hands of those who've already tried to have you killed?"

"I know who we're dealing with," Wendel said. "Edling is not all powerful. There are others who remain that have good sense. I'm sure if I could talk to Jarvis or Humbry, I could convince them to truly make peace."

"This entire meeting is on their terms. I don't like it. We should request neutral ground."

"I don't like it either, but I'm saving my energy to fight for peace instead of territory."

"I suppose you have a point, but I still don't like it," Jensen said.

* * *

"Land!" Catrin called out, proud to have been the first to see her homeland in the distance, and the sight of it was agonizingly sweet. She longed to raise the ship up and fly, but she honored Kenward's wishes. Chase and Prios came to stand by her, just as she caught a whiff of cold but stale air.

"We're almost there," Chase said, but there was something else in his voice and stance. Looking to the sky, he sniffed. "Do you smell that?"

"I smell something foul," Catrin said. "It smells like the shallows did before the mountain exploded."

Chase stayed a moment longer then went in search of those he wanted to thank for all they had done for him, which left Catrin and Prios alone.

"We're nearing my home," Catrin said, "but I doubt I'll be welcomed. There are more dangers ahead, and I'll not ask you to take any more risks. You've done enough. You deserve to live the rest of your life happy and free."

I go where you go. No matter what dangers we face.

"Thank you," she said, unable to find words that would express what she truly felt.

Clouds gathered and darkened the late afternoon, and the foul smell grew stronger, as if the clouds themselves were rank. Cold wind descended and drove the *Slippery Eel* through choppy surf. Catrin went to her cabin in search of warmer clothing. In her pack she found the jacket that Rolph Tillerman had given her, and she pulled it on for the sake of sentiment as much as warmth.

Benjin entered the cabin. "Chase, Strom, and Osbourne are waiting in the galley. I think we all need to sit down and plan out our next moves. We're not out of danger yet."

"Let's go."

The heat of the galley was a welcome change from the frigid air on deck. Catrin sat next to Chase and made eye contact with Strom and Osbourne, but no one spoke a word as they were faced with fears they could no longer deny. Catrin wondered if her father and uncle were alive, or if Strom and Osbourne had family left to go home to. Fear knotted her stomach, and she began to sweat.

Benjin must have sensed the mood as he entered the galley. "Whether good or bad, the time has come to get the answers to the questions we've had. Though I hope we can all be reunited with our loved ones, we must prepare for the possibility that we may have suffered losses as well." No one else spoke. A pall of sadness hung in the air. "Do not mourn what might not be lost. Be strong for a short time more, and then we'll know. Get your packs ready. Kenward has given me coin and some supplies in case we have need."

As if summoned, Kenward entered. "Sorry I'm late. We're not far from what looks to be the new northern harbor. There're plenty of lights. We can come in, quietly, at the very last dock and probably not be seen, but it's doubtful. Most likely they'll know you're coming. We can go farther east, but not under darkness. The reefs are simply too dangerous to approach after dark."

"What do you think?" Catrin asked everyone gathered.

"This is our homeland," Chase said. "I say we land tonight at the new harbor."

"We need to be careful," Benjin said.

"I agree with Chase," Strom said. "I say we land now."

"Me too," Osbourne said, and everyone turned to Catrin, waiting for her vote.

"We land now," she said.

"Gather your things," Kenward said with an enthusiastic smile. "You will be home soon."

* * *

Only a few lights remained as the *Slippery Eel* glided into the harbor. Catrin had already bade farewell to Kenward, Fasha, Nora, Brother Vaughn, and the rest of the crew, and already she missed them. Three fishermen watched the *Eel* with fear and suspicion as she glided into a slip. The crew scrambled to secure the ship and drop the gangplank.

Tears filled Catrin's eyes as she waved a final farewell; then she walked down the plank. Not liking the way the narrow walkways along the docks moved as she walked, she held her breath until, once again, she placed her feet on the firm soil of the Godfist. Ahead, the three fishermen stood at a long table cleaning fish by torchlight. Even in the darkness, seabirds gathered around to fight over the scraps. The men stopped and watched as Benjin, Catrin, Chase, Strom, Osbourne, and Prios walked by. All three had the look of the Greatland about them, and none chose to speak.

"Good evening," Catrin said as she passed. The men just stared back, seemingly frozen in fear. "How do we get up there?" she asked, pointing to the lights that still illuminated the lift. One of the men pointed to a wide path that led to the lift, and she supposed she would just have to find out when she got there. Her heart raced at the sight of shadowy forms moving at the base of the lift and voices that floated from the shadows.

When they reached the torchlight, the area was clear, and a man was extinguishing the remaining torches. The other people were packed into one of the large wooden boxes that were attached to massive lift ropes. Like oversized crates, the lift boxes could transport people and goods to the tops of the steep cliffs.

"Wait," Benjin said as the man approached the last torch. "We need to get to the top."

"Not tonight you won't," the man said. "This's the last trip up for the day, and we're full up. You'll have to come back in the morning."

"Who goes there?" a voice called from inside the box, and the door flew open. Catrin recognized Cattleman Gerard before he managed to squeeze out of the crowded box. "Benjin? Is that really you?"

"Greetings, Gerard, it's good to see a familiar face," Benjin said. "Where's Wendel?"

"He's gone south of the Wall for the peace treaty. Won't be back for days."

"How about Jensen?"

"He's in Lowerton."

"Where?" Chase asked.

"Ah, yes. Sorry," Gerard said. "I forgot. Lowerton is the new settlement, south of here but north of the Wall." He turned back to the people in the box. "Hey! You all get out of there. These people need to get up top right now. Hurry up!"

A debate raged briefly within the box; then Catrin heard someone say her name. A moment later, people poured out. Watching Catrin and her companions as they boarded the now empty crate, no one said a word. Cattleman Gerard entered the giant crate, which could easily hold forty people, and closed the door behind himself. Catrin watched through the cracks as one of the men yanked on a long rope that hung down from above. Slowly, the crate began to rise into the air, swaying gently at first, but sudden movements often sent it swinging into the timber framework, which groaned in response. Catrin and the others held on tightly to loops of rope that hung on the walls at regular intervals.

A platform came into view, and the crate stopped above it, making them step down as they disembarked, but Catrin didn't care; she was another step closer to her father. The others could go to Lowerton and search for their families, but not her. She was heading south. "What is the Wall you mentioned?" she asked.

"Edling's Wall is what they call it," Gerard said, and already Catrin didn't like it. "They built it after we fled the cold caves. They hit us while we were vulnerable and drove us as far north as they could, and since then, they've held us here. They've been building the Wall to divide north from south ever since. But now there are talks of peace. Your father's gone to the Masterhouse to end the fighting."

Determined, Catrin grabbed a nearby torch and began marching south. The others scrambled to catch up.

"Have you seen my mother or Miss Mariss?" she heard Strom ask, and she slowed a bit so she could hear the answer.

"They're in Lowerton, 'long with Jensen and Osbourne's parents. They've had no end of worry over you, and it'll be an honor to escort you to them."

Catrin nodded, her heart lightened to know no one else stood to lose a parent. Quickening her step, she challenged the rest to keep up.

Chase reached her side and cast her a sidelong glance. "You're going to the Masterhouse."

"I can't risk losing him," Catrin said. "I have to go."

"I'm going with you," Chase said as he grabbed her by the arm, making her stop.

"I coming too," Strom said. Benjin crossed his arms over his chest, and Osbourne did the same.

"I can't protect all of you. I can only protect myself. I must go alone."

"No," Benjin said. His stance and that of the others told Catrin that none of them would back down, and she relented. Somehow, she would have to keep them all safe.

Gerard led them along a well-trodden roadway, and after a series of sweeping bends, they gained the shelter of the valley. Ahead waited a bizarre town. "Welcome to Upperton," Gerard said.

Along the dirt roadway stood cylindrical, wooden buildings, and Catrin gasped. The others turned as she stopped, her hands covering her mouth. There stood what remained of the mighty greatoaks, and Catrin was filled with gratitude that they would live on as shelter from those in need. It seemed a fitting tribute. "Why did you use the greatoaks?"

"It was cold," Gerard said. "We needed housing. Your dad suggested we use the fallen greatoaks. It was a lot of work getting them here, but we used the ships we had to tow them to the lift. Took all our ingenuity to get them up here, but a couple of Greatlanders came up with a way to do it. Heck, they dragged a bunch of 'em to Lowerton as well."

Men and women gathered in the streets despite the cold, and Catrin guessed news of their coming had preceded them. No one spoke as she and her companions walked into town. Just as Catrin could make out faces of the townspeople, a cold wind gusted, bringing with it the foul smell. Everyone watched in horrified amazement as snow began to fall, for it was no ordinary snow. As if dipped in blood, each walnut-sized flake was a deep crimson.

The people of Upperton moved back into their homes, driven by fear. Surely this was a bad omen, and Catrin felt a wave of futility wash over her. What could be worse than having the darkest possible portent coincide with her return to the Godfist? The storm intensified, casting a filter of red over the entire landscape. Soon snow began to accumulate, making it look as if the land were bleeding.

The sound of wings caught Catrin's ear, and she turned to see three birds flying south. Everywhere she went, it seemed, someone was watching and waiting.

"We can't make the journey to Lowerton in this," Gerard said, "whatever it is."

"I doubt we'll be welcomed into anyone's home now," Strom said.

"I don't know how you do the things you do, Catrin," Gerard said, "but I don't believe this has anything to do with you. I was there when you were born. You're no threat to me or any other right-minded person. You can stay with me tonight, and we'll set out for Lowerton with the sunrise. By then the snow should've stopped."

The insides of the greatoak buildings were remarkable. Much of the furniture was carved directly from the walls, and the furniture that was freestanding was obviously made from the same wood. With the exception of the stone hearth and chimney, the mighty trees provided all the needed materials.

"There's not much food these days," Gerard said as he brought out a wooden platter covered with nuts and dried berries. "Next year'll be better. When the terraces are complete, we'll have all the food we need. The Greatlanders have it all figured out. Until then, we just have to squeeze by."

"I thank you for sharing what you have," Benjin said. "It was a long journey, and it's good to be home and with friends."

"That's prob'ly where ya should stay," Gerard said.

"Catrin believes her father is in danger."

"That he is," Gerard said, "and he went there knowin' it. He went 'cause he believes there's a chance to end the fighting. If you go south of the Wall, you might just ruin our best chance for peace."

Catrin sat, staring at the fire, conflicted. How could she be certain her vision would come true? How could she put everyone else at risk on the basis of something she did not understand? In her gut she knew. She had to go south; every instinct agreed. "I'm sorry, Gerard. I mean no disrespect, but I must go. I know my father is in trouble, and if he's in trouble, I doubt peace will follow."

"Sometimes, we must follow our feelings," Gerard said, thoughtful. "If you're goin', the best place to get over the Wall would be the eastern guardhouse; there're no breaks in the wall near there, but the wall is not very high. We keep a close watch on the guards, and the two fellows stationed there are terrified of you: Carter Bessin and Chad Macub. Their only job is to make sure no one comes over the wall, and they seem to be getting a bit complacent."

The names slammed into Catrin, and sudden memory overwhelmed her. Once again, in her mind, she entered the clearing where Peten, Carter, and Chad were attacking Osbourne. In her mind she saw Peten charging down on her then the world flying away.

"I'd wager they are scared," Strom said. "I would be too."

Catrin came back to herself, and in a moment that seemed to prove she would someday heal, she laughed. "We're going to scare the wind out of 'em."

"First," Benjin said, "we have to get there. I suggest we get some sleep. It's going to be an early start."

* * *

Knee-deep, crimson snow blanketed the landscape, giving everything a surreal appearance, which made Catrin feel as if she were walking in a dream. She pulled her hood closer as the wind blew, and drifting snow clung to everything. Beyond a large rock overhang, though, the wind died, blocked by natural rock formations.

Not far ahead roared a swollen, red waterfall, and Catrin recognized the plateau from afar, suddenly realizing that she was now approaching it from the same direction as the Zjhon army had, so long ago. Most of them had died here.

Looking around, Catrin noticed large mounds on the valley floor, and she no longer had to wonder where those she killed were laid. A great sadness welled up in her as they passed the gaping wound in the plateau, though it was already partly overgrown by bushes and trees that poked out of the snow.

Beyond, Catrin saw the terraces for the first time. Like giant snakes, one on top of another, following the contours of the land, the low, stone walls made for a mind-bending view. As soon as she saw them, their design made perfect sense; by creating narrow but level platforms down the slopes, they gained much valuable land for planting.

The roadway ahead was obstructed as a crowd of men worked with hammers and picks to finish the construction of a terrace. Two men argued in the middle of the road, and they seemed oblivious to the group as they approached. Then one of them looked up and saw them. "Whoa! You folks stay as far to the right as possible. Look out for falling rock." He shook his head and started to turn back to the other man, but when his eyes passed over Catrin, he stopped and watched her walk by. "Hey! Wait!"

Catrin was tempted to simply keep walking; she had no time for interruptions, but something in his voice made her stop.

"Where'd ya get that coat?" he asked. "I had one just like that. It even had the same tear on the shoulder."

"Rolph Tillerman gave it to me," Catrin said. "Are you Martik?"

"Yes!" he said, his eyes going wide, and he grabbed Catrin by the arms. "You saw my father? How was he? And my mother? And Jessub?"

"Yes," Catrin said. "I spent time with all of them. They're fine, though they miss you dearly. Wait. I have something for you." Catrin reached into the coat pocket and pulled out the drawing Jessub had given her. It showed Martik with Catrin hovering over him, protecting him.

Martik received it with wonder, and when he opened it, he was stunned. He stood for a moment with the look of a man whose thoughts were far away.

"I promise I'll tell you more when I return," Catrin said, "but I really must be--"

A loud cracking sound filled the valley, followed by shouting. As Catrin turned to look, she saw a large section of rock dislodge itself and roll forward until it crashed to the ground.

"Need help over here!" someone shouted, and everyone scrambled to help. Catrin watched as people lifted rocks away from where a man was trapped, but her eyes were drawn away, lured by a far more ghastly sight. Revealed by the fallen rock were flowing lines and graceful curves lit by an inner glow. Catrin recognized it immediately from the image that was burned into her mind. It was a Statue of Terhilian.

Chapter 18

There is permanence in every action and inaction; each is a choice and cannot be undone.
--Enoch Giest

* * *

"We were just working at the base there," a man said. "Then the whole rock face got unstable and collapsed on us."

A crowd gathered after all the men were pulled from the rubble. Women and young people, who had been nearby preparing lunch for the workers, now tended the wounded. All other eyes were drawn to the glowing curves of Istra's dress.

Catrin moved to stand before it, and she turned to face the crowd, pulling her hood down as she did. "Many of you know me; others may only know of me," she said. "I'm Catrin Volker, and this land is my home. I mean no one any harm. I only want us all to be safe. Right now we are not. What you see is part of a Statue of Terhilian, and it's an immediate threat."

"What can we do?" someone shouted from the crowd.

"I believe I know a way to neutralize the statue," Catrin said. "It will be dangerous to everyone nearby. Please take the children back to Lowerton. I wouldn't want them to be endangered or frightened." Women gathered the children, and soon only adults remained. Catrin wondered a moment that she, Chase, and the others were now adults, but that thought was driven out by what lay ahead. "I'm going to attempt to drain the negative core, but I need more rock cleared away. Here. We need to expose the base."

Despite the danger of another rockslide, men worked feverishly to clear the stone away from the statue, and Catrin waited, drowning in frustration. She couldn't leave the statue behind. She could get killed south of the Wall; then there would be no one left to destroy the statue. It was too dangerous to use her powers to remove the rock since she might set off the statue in the process. With tears in her eyes, she knew she had to choose the needs of her people over her desperate desire to save her father; she had to wait.

When a large, squared corner became exposed, Catrin rushed in to run her senses over it. Her staff in one hand and Koe in the other, she opened herself to the flow, and energy surged through her. With effort, she moderated the flow and kept her balance. Like the others, this statue had positive and negative cores kept apart by a thin layer of insulating material. Remembering how the positive charge had overwhelmed her with its energy, Catrin quailed. Barabas had attacked the negative charge, and she decided to do the same.

Using her staff to establish physical contact with the statue, her fingers resting in the grooves created the last time she attempted to destroy one of these statues, she reached out to the negative core. Slowly her flow of energy penetrated the crystal-like stone that made up the statue and, as it drew close, there was an enormous pop and a flash of light. In the next instant, Catrin was drawn to the statue like nails to a lodestone. Irresistible force pulled her closer until her flesh pressed painfully against stone, and she thought she might be crushed.

The negative core ravaged her with its insatiable appetite for energy, and she felt herself slowly being drained of life. Drawing from her staff and Koe alike, she did what she could to satisfy the core, but still it demanded more. It all happened so fast, Catrin could hardly catch up. Prios reached her side and latched on to her, trying to pull her away. Then, in what must have been an effort to help, he sent his own energy surging through her. Just as it had done with her, the negative core greedily pulled him closer.

With Prios now pressing against her, also trapped, Catrin felt certain she would die. Slowly, though, something was happening to the negative core. The outer edges were beginning to break down, and the deterioration began to take place more rapidly. Drawing a ragged breath, Catrin used every energy source around her, and some in the crowd were shocked to find themselves suddenly hurtling toward the statue. With the last of her will, Catrin flooded the negative core with a positive charge, and the chain reaction reached a white-hot zenith before it vanished without a sound.

Those drawn from the crowd caught themselves before they collided with Catrin and Prios, and everything grew very silent. Catrin did her best to remain standing, but Prios fell backward, still gripping her, and she fell. Prios grunted as she landed on him, and she rolled away. For a moment she rested. Her body had been drained, and it quivered with weakness. Standing was impossible, and speech was difficult, but she managed to grunt Benjin's name.

"I'm here, li'l miss. I'm here."

"Carry me. South."

* * *

Between a pair of oversized guards, Wendel sat, waiting for his fate to be decided. As soon as the red snow had begun to fall, fear spread. Edling had pounced on the opportunity, and Wendel went from peacemaker to traitor in a matter of moments. They said Catrin was back on the Godfist, but he didn't believe them. It was all just a ploy to be rid of him. Jensen had been right.

"In an act of cowardice and indifferent malice," Master Edling said, addressing the other members of the council, "Wendel Volker and his daughter, Catrin, have inflicted our home with a blood scourge. We had hoped the memory of its creation had been lost to time, but the Herald has found a way. You see it all around you. What further proof could you require?"

Master Edling sat, looking smug. Wendel looked at the other council members, but none of them would meet his eyes, and he knew he'd already lost.

* * *

A blurred, red and brown landscape slid by, and Catrin tried to get her eyes to focus. After some squinting and eye rubbing, she saw that she was on a sled, Prios beside her. Four large men pulled the sled, and Catrin sat up too quickly, causing her vision to swim and her head to ache. Then she saw Benjin and Chase, who both called for a halt when they saw she was awake.

"How're you feeling?" Benjin asked.

"Better," she said, but she feared the truth was obvious: her body was drained and needed rest.

"We're nearly to Lowerton."

Propping herself up with the blankets and pillows loaded on the sled, Catrin watched as Lowerton came into view. Again word had preceded them, and the roadway was lined with people, only this time there was no fear. Here were the people who knew her best, and they waited in silent tribute, each holding a candle. Catrin wiped her tears as the first few faces slid by. Some she knew, others she didn't, but she finally felt she was home. Around the gentle bend awaited a sight Catrin could not have expected. There, standing taller and wider than any other building she'd seen and constructed out of six huge shafts of greatoak, stood a building with a weathered and chipped sign hanging above its double doors. Even through her tears, Catrin could read it: *The Watering Hole.*

From the double doors charged two women, their hair flying in the wind as they hoisted their dresses and ran. "Miss Mariss, Miss Bryson," Catrin said as she tried to stand, but her legs refused to support her. Seeing Strom rush to his mother's arms made Catrin's heart ache; it was a sweet ache, but it made her yearn for her own reunion. A moment later, Osbourne's parents arrived at a run. His mother lifted him from the ground and refused to let go. "Stay," Catrin said to Strom as his eyes met hers. "You and Osbourne belong here. I couldn't take you from your parents now. Please. Stay. Live happy lives."

Both Strom and Osbourne seemed torn, but they came to see her truth, and they waved a long good-bye as the sled began moving once again. "Come back to us," Strom shouted.

Farther along, a man stood in the middle of the roadway, his hands on his hips. Chase shouted as soon as he saw his father. He ran ahead and embraced Jensen.

Catrin watched with joy and envy. "Hello, Uncle Jensen!"

"There's my girl," he said as he crouched down by the now stopped sled. "I've missed you."

"I've missed you too, but I have to find my father. He's in danger."

Jensen put his arm around Chase, who now knelt by his side. "I'm sorry, Cat. I didn't want him to go. He thought he'd be safe, but I've been so worried. Can you be certain he's in danger?"

"I'm as certain in this as I've ever been in anything. I have to save him."

"That's good enough for me," Jensen said. "I'll gather those trained to fight, and we'll go get your dad."

"No," Catrin said. "I need to take Edling by surprise. Benjin, Prios, and I will make our way there by stealth. You, Chase, and everyone else stay here. If we don't return, it'll be up to you to keep these people safe."

Jensen took Chase by the arm and led him away, but Chase stopped and turned. "I can't stay here. Not now. Not after everything we've been through. I'd never forgive myself."

Catrin wanted to protest, but the look of pride on Uncle Jensen's face kept her from saying anything more. She hoped she could keep him safe.

* * *

Cruel light poured into the cell, and Wendel shielded his eyes with his hand. Silhouetted in the doorway, his guards waited, and he knew better than to keep them waiting long. Already his bruises and injuries made it difficult for him to walk.

Into the council room they led him, and he was brought to the seat of the accused, a place he'd never thought he would find himself, especially not accused of the highest crime. It seemed a horrible dream. None of this could be real. If only he could wake.

"On the charge of treason, how do you find Wendel Volker?" asked Constable Fredin.

"Guilty," Master Edling said.

"Innocent," Master Jarvis said, despite the glares he received.

"Innocent," Humbry Milson said.

Master Edling looked as if he would explode, but then a guard burst into the room, breathing hard.

He came to Master Edling and went one knee. "An urgent message, sir."

Master Edling's eyes went wide with feigned surprise and fear. He passed the message to the other members of the council and waited.

"I request a new vote," Humbry said, his voice trembling.

"No!" Wendel cried out.

"On the charge of treason, how do you find Wendel Volker?"

"Guilty," Master Edling said.

"Guilty," Humbry said.

"Innocent," Master Jarvis said. One more guilty vote would condemn Wendel to death, and he waited without wanting to hear. He wanted so much to wake.

"Guilty," Baker Hollis said.

On the floor lay the discarded message.

The Herald is coming for you.

* * *

Crouched in the snow behind a mighty elm, Catrin waited. Downhill stood a rudimentary guardhouse, and smoke poured from the small hole in the roof that served as a chimney. Occasional conversation drifted on the wind, and Catrin felt some remorse. Despite their differences, Carter and Chad were her countrymen, and she truly meant them no harm. Scaring them was simply the easiest way she could think of to get to her father. Nothing would stand in her way.

From the far side of the guardhouse, where Benjin, Chase, and Prios crouched, Benjin gave the signal. With a deep breath, Catrin prepared herself. Still feeling drained, she relied heavily of her staff and Koe as she drew a trickle of energy. "I know you're in there," she said, her voice amplified just enough to give it a chilling effect.

Shuffling could be heard from within. "Who's out there," Carter asked, his high-pitched voice laced with fear.

"You knew I would come for you," Catrin said. "Both of you."

"You best just be gone," Chad said, "or we'll come out there after you."

"A threat?" Catrin asked as she drew more power and stepped out from behind the tree. Wisps of blue lightning rolled across her fingers, and she moved her hands in elaborate patterns, trails of light streaming from her fingertips. Speaking words she remembered from books in High Script, she did her best to sound like a wizard of legend, incanting some horrific spell.

"I'm not afraid of you!" Chad challenged, but his aura reeked of fear, and Catrin gave the signal.

"Then you will die!" she shouted, throwing her hands back. Both Chad's and Carter's eyes flew wide as her energy began to reach out for them like fingers of death. Horrified, they watched and never saw Benjin, Chase, and Prios coming. In an instant, it was over. Both Carter and Chad were tied, gagged, and left to sit by their fire.

Benjin even tossed a bit more wood on the fire. "Someone should find them before they freeze t'death." Before he left, though, he removed the short sword and scabbard from Chad's belt. Chase took Carter's sword then helped Catrin over the Wall. Benjin helped ease her down the other side. Even that slight exertion taxed her body and her will. Each step was a challenge, and she weaved as they hiked through the trees.

"We need to rest," Chase said.

"I'm fine," Catrin said. "We need to keep moving."

"Passed out or dead, you'll be of no use to anyone, Cat," Chase said. "Take a short nap at the very least. Please."

He's right.

Catrin cast Prios a scathing glance, but then she let herself admit that they were right. No matter how much she wanted to move forward, she was in no condition to travel, let alone fight. Prios was in nearly the same condition, and she could sense his own inner struggle. "Carry us," Catrin begged.

Benjin nodded in submission.

Chase shook his head. "Better than nothing, I suppose." Chase lifted Catrin easily, and she settled herself so her weight was balanced across his shoulders. It was far from comfortable, but sleep claimed her before Chase had taken three steps.

* * *

As her head leaned back, resting against the snow, Catrin's eyes flew open. Not far away, she heard a distinct and undeniable sound: a feed bucket being slammed against barn walls. In an instant her senses collided. Sound, smell, and even the shadows told her the same thing: she was home. She was not just on the Godfist; this was her farm, her home, and the light streaming from around the barn doors told of a new occupant. Suppressed rage, kept sealed away for so long, suddenly burst forth with its fullest fury. Her breath coming in ragged gasps, she sat up. Benjin, Chase, and Prios crouched nearby, listening and watching.

Crawling at first, Catrin pulled herself forward; then she stood. Slowly and unsteadily, she walked to where they were hiding.

"I'm going in there," she said as she swayed on her feet.

"Get down," Benjin whispered through his teeth. "He's just about done pickin' hooves. We wait until he puts the horse in a stall. Then we go in."

Catrin waited, but she remained standing, certain that if she sat down, she'd not rise again. Through the crack between the doors, she could see only the man's legs as he walked the horse into a stall. Benjin leaped up and Chase matched his stride. Quickly but quietly, they rushed to the barn doors. While the man was still in the stall, they slipped inside. Catrin walked a meandering course behind them, dizzy but more determined than ever. Prios guided her to the barn door, and she slipped inside.

"Just come out real slow," Benjin said, wielding only his belt knife. The man slowly stuck his head out of the stall, and his eyes grew wide when he saw Benjin. When his eyes reached Catrin, he took a step back. She recognized him.

"Easy, Gunder," Benjin said as he sheathed his knife.

"They said you were coming," Gunder said as he trembled. "I didn't believe them."

"We're your friends," Benjin said.

"Yes," Gunder said, still looking terrified. "Yes, we *are* friends. I . . . caught your mare for you. And . . . and . . . you saved my pig that time it got caught in the fence! You remember, don't you?"

"Yes, Gunder, I remember. We're friends."

"Oh, thank you," Gunder said. "Thank you for understanding."

"Why are you here?" Catrin asked, her fury unabated.

"The Masters keep horses here," Gunder said, his eyes cast low. "I'm to care for 'em."

Catrin's anger could find no target. This man was her friend. Once again she made herself stuff the rage down inside, deep in her gut where she could contain it.

"What's the news on the treaties?" Benjin asked.

Gunder looked from Benjin to Catrin. "I'm so sorry," he said.

"There'll be no treaty. The blood scourge, as they're calling it, has everyone scared out of their wits. It gives the Masters power since only they know the will of the gods."

"What about Wendel?"

"Charged with treason," Gunder said in a low voice. "I'm so sorry. He's to be executed tomorrow. I thought he had a chance. The council argued for days, but when they heard you were comin', fear won again."

His words were like a punch in the stomach, and Catrin reeled. Could it be that she was bringing about her vision by her very attempts to stop it?

"Where?" Benjin growled.

"The Masterhouse."

"Boil Edling in grease," Benjin said. "We'll never even get close. They know we're coming."

"They do," Gunder said, "but they won't be expectin' you to look like a wine barrel."

* * *

In the darkness, Catrin tried to anticipate the next bump; already she was covered in bruises. It seemed like days since they left the cold caves, bound for the Masterhouse. Gunder would make his delivery of wine, cheese, and meat as scheduled, and Catrin could only hope his wagon would not be thoroughly searched. The hole, through which she had her only access to fresh air, seemed terribly small from inside the barrel, but she could see through it. When she wasn't gulping for air, she watched the landscape slide by.

The sound of hooves and wagon wheels on wood echoed around her, and Catrin watched as they crossed over one of the many small streams that ran through the lowlands. As the wagon turned, Catrin got a clear view of the countryside. Seeing the Masterhouse in the distance knotted her guts, though she was struck by how much smaller it was than she remembered it. Somehow, her travels across such vast distances had forever changed her perception of the world. Life had been so much easier when her world had extended only as far as the top of the lake. Now everything was different.

As Gunder drove the wagon into the line at the guardhouse, Catrin began to tremble and sweat. Time moved slowly, and she thought she might never get out of the barrel. The wood slats seemed to move ever closer, constricting her like a giant snake. Her face pressed against the wood, she sucked air through the hole and tried to calm herself.

"Delivery for the banquet," she heard Gunder say.

Closing her eyes, she held her breath. Only when the wagon began rolling did she draw another breath. Gunder angled toward the kitchen service entrance, and Catrin watched as a flurry of servants prepared for a gathering, even as crowds of people were already arriving. The Masters would treat her father's execution as a banquet, a reason for celebration! Barely able to contain her anger, Catrin ran her fingers over Koe, the feel of him giving her comfort. Outside the barrel, hidden in the straw, her staff awaited, and she missed the feel of it in her hands. Afraid someone might recognize it, she had covered the heel and much of the shaft with mud. It was a poor disguise, but it was the best that she could do.

When the wagon stopped, Catrin waited, her inner tension mounting. Servants unloaded the cheese and other supplies, and she knew they would come for the wine soon. A gentle knock was her cue, and she carefully pushed the lid open and to the side before crawling out. Benjin emerged from his barrel a moment later, his face a mask of pain, but he made no sound. Bruised and cramped, Catrin understood his pain, and she stood as quickly as she could. Chase and Prios soon joined them.

Moving with increasing haste, she pulled her staff from the straw. Benjin and Chase were ready with their borrowed swords.

"That's all I can do," Gunder said. "They'll know you're here soon-- one way or 'nother. You'd best do whatever ya can now. I need to be away from here before I'm found out. I'll see you north o' the Wall." Without another word, Gunder walked away, looking as if nothing were amiss.

Catrin envied his ability to mask emotion. She jumped at the sound of servants returning, but then there was big uproar from the great covered terrace that stood as the Masterhouse's main entrance. There, a crowd gathered. This was not an expectant crowd, ready for feast and revelry. There was sadness in the air, and something far more horrible in Catrin's perception: acceptance. These people did not want to see her father put to death, but none would stand up to stop it, perhaps believing themselves powerless.

Before the servants could return, Catrin pulled her hood up and walked hunched over, as if in need of the staff to support her. Benjin kept his eyes low, and they did their best to blend in with the crowd. Chase and Prios stayed separate but nearby. When finally Catrin got a glimpse of those on the terrace, she saw a pair of meaty guards holding her father, who hung between them, a haunted look in his eyes. He looked so much older than Catrin remembered, and her rage returned. He could not defend himself, and these cowards would take him from her.

Fate left her no more time to contemplate, for she saw a servant rush up to Master Edling. After the servant whispered in his ear, Master Edling ran his eyes over the crowd, searching for her. Despite nagging fears, Catrin knew she had no more time to waste. This was her last chance for salvation. As she cast back her hood, she threw her arms wide. Holding her staff high, she opened herself to the flow. In her weakened state, the flood of energy nearly washed her away, but she bit her lip and made herself endure. Benjin raised his head and drew his sword, a look of pessimistic determination on his face, as if he fought a battle he knew he would lose.

Angry, red plasma crawled over Catrin's hands and arms, and the crowd parted, rolling away like rippling water from around a tossed stone. Before her, Catrin saw her father, his guards, the Masters, and the members of the council. For a moment the sight of Baker Hollis, the man who had killed her mother and aunt, distracted her. He had stolen from her the most precious things, and now he stood in accusation of her father. A growl escaped her throat as she approached.

Master Edling watched and smiled. "Come, Miss Volker. Join your father!"

For an instant, Catrin hesitated. She sensed no fear from Master Edling, and her instincts shouted in warning. Fear poured from every other soul present but not Edling; he was like a stone. Step after step, Catrin drew closer to him and to her father.

When Wendel heard her name, he raised his tired eyes and screamed. "No! Get away from here, Cat. I don't want you to see this!"

Catrin longed to embrace him, but she turned her gaze to Edling as if she could bore holes in him with her eyes.

"Go ahead. Run away," Master Edling said, standing behind a lectern of stone. "Spend the rest of your life trying to picture it in your mind, all the while knowing you left him to die."

"Lies!" Wendel shouted, and one of the guards cuffed him on the back of the head. Catrin lashed out at the guard; a rope of lightning and fire sent him flying backward, and he landed in a smoking heap. Again Edling smiled, and Catrin gathered all her fury and rage. Determined to incinerate him, she launched her attack. Quicker than she would have thought him capable of, Master Edling ducked down, picked something up, and thrust it in front of him. The object was like nothing Catrin had ever seen. The size of a melon but with a pocked surface, it looked metallic, and it drew Catrin's energy just as the statue's negative core had done.

With a thunderous crack, her energy exploded over the stone yet was utterly absorbed, and the stone demanded more. Her energy rushed out of her body like a draining flood, and she knew there would soon be none left; she would die.

Use my energy.

At her side, Prios waited, but Catrin knew it would not be enough. He would only become a slave to the stone, and Catrin could not allow that. "Attack the building," she said through gritted teeth. "Don't get close to Edling's stone."

Rolling forward, Prios surprised everyone as he leaped into the air. Spinning as he flew, he unleashed a rapid series of short energy bursts. Looking like balls of pure fire, they slammed into the tops of the columns that supported the terrace roof with concussive force. Chunks of the roof began to fall even as the flagstone shook.

"Kill the prisoner!" Master Edling shouted above the din.

"No!" Catrin wailed, driven to her knees by sadness and weariness.

I'm coming.

More like an expression of emotion than exact words, Catrin felt the message.

In a moment that would forever remain clear in her memory, one of the guards surrounding her father drew his sword. Reaching back, he gritted his teeth as he prepared to thrust, but then he was suddenly cast into shadow, twisters of dust and dirt rolling through the air. With a triumphant cry, Kyrien grabbed Wendel in one claw and used the other to send Master Edling tumbling over backward. Like rolling thunder, each flap of his wings sent people sprawling. Grabbing a shocked Benjin in his free claw, Kyrien turned on his wingtip and soared back into the sky.

"No!" Wendel screamed as he disappeared into the clouds. "Catrin!"

Chapter 19

Though the years may change us, we see each other as we were.
--Ort Sisteva, wanderer

* * *

With the connection between her and Edling's stone broken, Catrin reeled. Prios reached her before she hit the ground, and he lent her energy; her head swam with it. All around, people panicked. Many sought to flee, others seemed frozen by fear. The guards pulled Master Edling back to his feet, and he wiped the blood away from his nose. Before Catrin could compose herself enough to stand, he stooped to retrieve his stone. Prios lashed out, again using only short bursts of energy. Edling deflected each one with his stone, but he was losing ground.

Do not connect yourself to him. Disconnect from the energy before it reaches him.

It had never occurred to Catrin before, but even in her muddled state, it made sense. Struggling to stand on her own, she let Prios bolster her strength, and they attacked in unison. Edling could not block every attack, and he was sent spinning. At the same moment, a brief buzzing filled Catrin's hearing, as if a bumblebee had flown past her ear; then there was another. Looking up, she saw arrows raining from the sky; archers lined the trembling roof.

Before she could draw enough energy to protect herself, the sky went dark as Kyrien intercepted the hail of arrows; some bounced harmlessly across the flagstone, but Kyrien cried out as he soared away. Using his wing, he took a parting swipe at the archers, knocking three from the roof and sending the others sprawling. With another cry, he wheeled and swooped, plucking Chase and Prios from the crowd, like pulling grapes from the vine. His thoughts flooded Catrin's mind as he gained the clouds: *Your flock is safe, my queen.*

On the terrace, only Master Edling and two of his guards remained, all others had fled. Demanding all her body had left to give, Catrin charged Master Edling, howling as she came. He held up his stone and she laughed. Then, using short bursts of energy, she attacked the flagstone, sending a shower of fist-sized rocks and debris into his face. Both guards went down, and neither tried to rise. Only their breathing gave any indication of life. Master Edling teetered and looked as if he would fall, blood trickling down the side of his face.

Catrin took advantage of the opening. Rapid bursts flew toward

Edling and he screamed. Energy slammed into him and sent him spinning. As Catrin stopped her attack, Master Edling stood facing her on wobbling knees. With finality, she issued one last attack, sending a ball of lightning and fire soaring into Master Edling's chest. Tumbling over backward, he landed in a sprawl of arms and legs. Catrin knew she could easily finish him, but she'd had enough of killing.

For a moment she stood, swaying on her feet and breathing deeply. Then, from the corner of her vision, she spotted movement. There, someone crouched behind a collapsed bench, but he could no longer hide from Catrin, and he must have known it, for he stood.

"*You,*" Catrin said, a haze of blood clouding her vision.

"Please," Baker Hollis said. "Let me explain."

"*Explain?* You want me to let you *explain?* Did you let my mother or my aunt explain? Did you?" she demanded, and he cowered before her wrath, but she was denied retribution. A blast of wind cast Baker Hollis's hair away from his face, and Catrin drank in his fear. She wanted him to suffer for what he'd done, but quick as a snake, Kyrien snapped her up in his jaws, somehow keeping her secure without impaling her on his daggerlike, back-turned teeth. In the next moment, she was soaring through the skies, and the beauty of it was almost enough for her to forgive Kyrien. He'd deprived her of revenge, but he had saved all that was truly precious to her, and she let her anger slip away.

Her father was safe.

* * *

In a clearing north of the Wall, Kyrien landed and gently lowered Catrin to the ground. Benjin and her father approached with concern on their faces. Only when Catrin stood did either of them visibly relax. Kyrien craned his neck and brought his eyes level with Catrin's. She saw his pain, felt it as her own. Slowly he extended his wing, and Catrin ran her hands along the smooth skin that covered his wing structures. At the second joint, she found a broken shaft protruding from his flesh, blood seeping slowly from the wound.

No one spoke; all were seemingly mesmerized by Kyrien, who watched Catrin as she worked, making low noises in his throat. Using both hands to get a grip on the slippery and splintered shaft, she pulled. With a wiggle and a jerk, the shaft and point came free, and Catrin stepped away from Kyrien's wing. In the next breath, he turned and flapped his mighty wings and, using his powerful legs, thrust himself into the air.

"Wait!" Catrin shouted. "We should clean your wound!" Kyrien trumpeted in response and sent her a vision of him swimming in the seas, letting the salt water cleanse him. As she turned, though, nothing mattered more than reaching her father, and she collapsed into his arms, sobbing.

"Oh my dear Cat. You've come home to me. I'm so sorry. I let you down."

"No you didn't," Catrin said. After wiping her nose, she wrapped her arms around him and held on tight. "You're here. That's all that matters."

* * *

Inside the new Watering Hole, a fire burned in the hearth, and the aroma of food drifted from the kitchens. Catrin thought it was perhaps the happiest moment of her life. Sitting in the same room with her father, her uncle, Chase, Strom and his mother, Osbourne flanked by his parents, and Prios by her side, she could hardly believe it. Laughter filled the hall as exaggerated tales were told, and Catrin raised her mug. "I want to thank you all for being here. Without the people in this room, I would certainly be lost."

Those gathered cheered and raised their mugs. Miss Mariss emerged from the kitchen with a roast over potatoes and onions. For the first time that any of them had ever seen, Miss Mariss sat down to eat with her guests. "We're all family here," she said, smiling. "You all can help yourselves." A moment later, the door opened. Kenward entered, followed by Nora and Fasha, all grinning like fools. "Here comes the rest of the family now."

"You're not giving away our greatest secret, are you?" Nora asked as she walked up behind Catrin and kissed her on the top of her head. "It's good to see you didn't get yourself into too much trouble. I had a hard time keeping Kenward from running off to save you." Kenward actually blushed.

"So what's this well-kept secret?" Catrin asked.

"Ah, the fish is off the hook now, Sis," Nora said with a wink at Miss Mariss.

"'Sis'?" Chase asked. "You two are sisters?"

"That is to say we were fathered by the same man," Miss Mariss said, "but sisters we are. I inherited the good sense to stay on land."

"And I got the good looks," Nora said. Kenward laughed, and she smacked him in the back of the head. "Fool boy."

The door opened again, and Brother Vaughn entered. "Many pardons for my tardiness. I saw the most fascinating variation of finch on my walk, and I simply had to find its nest."

"Please sit," Miss Mariss said, not completely out of her role as hostess, and she handed him a plate. As they ate, a silence fell over the hall, conducive to quiet introspection.

"There is something I don't understand," Osbourne's father, Johen, said. "What is this 'blood scourge'? Does anyone know? Will it really poison the crops?"

"I have a theory," Brother Vaughn said. "In the great shallows, far from here, we passed an enormous mountain. It exploded from within and sent a cloud of fire and ash high into the sky. This was also the source of the giant wave that assaulted your harbor, the Falcon Isles, and other places in the world. The red snow had the same smell I remember from the shallows, just before the mountain exploded."

"But how could something so far away cause red snow here?"

"Just as the oceans carried the great wave," Brother Vaughn said. "The winds must have carried some of the fouled air here. I don't think there'll be any long-term effects, save perhaps fear."

Johen looked doubtful, but Catrin felt a great relief. The red snow was a frightening anomaly, and it made her feel better to have a more practical explanation.

Looking at her father, she marveled at his strength. His hair had gone gray, and he walked with a limp, but his eyes still held the same steely strength. Even when he smiled at her, his face at its softest, there was strength of conviction.

Benjin looked older too--all of them did--but his relationship with Fasha seemed to be bringing out a much younger personality. Catrin watched them as they laughed; there was excitement in their eyes as they discussed plans for the future. Catrin lacked their enthusiasm; ahead she saw a long and difficult road, and she wasn't certain she would ever be truly happy again.

Peace had not been made, and she doubted her attack on Master Edling would endear her to those who already considered her the enemy. Despite having forgiven Kyrien for pulling her away, she had a burning in her stomach, and she knew it could only be quelled by resolving her anger toward Baker Hollis. He had said he could explain, but there was no explanation that could be sufficient; no circumstances could have warranted such a cowardly act. If he'd had his way, Catrin, too, would be dead. Trying to recall the image of her mother and aunt became frustrating, as all she could form was a vague and gauzy image. Memory was fading, and she could no longer picture their faces in her mind.

"I have men looking for Baker Hollis," her father had said, but it came as a shock when a man arrived with an urgent message. "Catrin, Jensen, Benjin, Chase," Wendel said, his voice a harsh baritone that sounded only barely in control. "Come with me." All conversation stopped, and anxiety poured from everyone in the room. Catrin urged Benjin forward, wanting to escape the confined emotion. Her father led them to one of the buildings not built from a greatoak, made instead of pine with a thatch roof. Reddish water dripped onto the dirt floor as the snow inexorably melted. On a crate, with his hands tied, sat Baker Hollis. A well-muscled guard stood behind him, alert and seemingly ready for any threat.

"Untie him," Wendel growled. Baker Hollis rubbed his wrists and began to cry. Everyone who was crowded into the small room had reason to want him dead. By the look of him, trembling and crying, he seemed poignantly aware.

Chase stood with his hands balled into fists, and Catrin had never seen Uncle Jensen so enraged. The pain that radiated from them was nauseating, and Catrin nearly fled, but she had to know. If she did not witness this, no matter how painful, she would never forgive herself.

"Why?" her father demanded.

"I'm so sorry," Baker Hollis said. "I didn't know it would kill them. They made me do it."

"Who?"

"The Greatlanders," Baker Hollis said.

"How did they *make* you?"

"They took my little Trinda. What those monsters did to her, I'll never know, but she's never been the same. I should have killed her, freed her from the horrors, and let them kill me, but I couldn't do it. It wouldn't have saved Willa and Elsa, even if I had. The Greatlanders would've found another way. Please forgive me."

Wendel stood, hovering over Baker Hollis, seemingly on the verge of exploding, but then he seemed to deflate. "The people responsible still hide in the Greatland?" he asked in a voice just above a whisper.

Catrin thought it the most frightening voice she'd ever heard. "The person responsible is dead," she said, only then releasing her anger. She had been ready to rip Baker Hollis to pieces, but now she could find no target for her fury. She remembered the look that haunted Trinda's eyes; she remembered the pain she had plainly seen for so many years. How could she blame Baker Hollis for wanting to protect his daughter? "Arbuckle Kyte ordered their deaths, and mine, but now he's dead. It's over. There's nothing more we can do."

Uncle Jensen wheeled in frustration and kicked the door, which fell before his fury.

Chase bent down and looked Baker Hollis in the eye. "If you ever endanger my family again, I'll hunt down you, your daughter, and everyone you ever loved. If you get threatened into hurting us again, I suggest you come to me first."

Baker Hollis nodded, sweat dripping from his nose.

Chase followed his father into the night, also venting his rage on what remained of the door.

Benjin left Catrin and Wendel alone with Baker Hollis. Catrin sat in silence, trying to reconcile her feelings; her father seemed frozen in time. "I'm sorry about Trinda," Catrin finally said, and Baker Hollis looked up in surprise. Confusion radiated from him, as if he suspected a trap. "I'm sorry about her pain and yours. I'll never get my mother or my aunt back, and you'll never be able to fix what happened to Trinda. For those things, I am truly sorry. I don't like you, and I'm still angry, but I won't kill you." Her words fell like rolling thunder, and there was finality in them.

"Release him," Wendel said, and he turned to leave. Catrin followed him and rushed to catch up when she saw his shoulders begin to shake. For a moment he allowed himself to cry, to once again mourn the loss of his true love, but then he drew a deep breath. "You're stronger than I," he said without looking up. "I couldn't be more proud of you, Catrin. You've grown to be the woman I always knew you could be."

"I draw my strength from you."

"I would've killed him if it weren't for you," Wendel said, still staring at the ground. "I wanted so badly to hurt him, to make him feel my pain." Wendel raised his eyes to Catrin's. What she saw there was not weakness; it was vulnerability presented as a gift to one he knew would not hurt him.

"I love you, Daddy," she said, and he held her tightly as they cried.

"I love you too, my little Cat."

* * *

Warmer weather banished the blood scourge, and the memory began to fade. No longer did people instantly react in fear, and Catrin felt she was making progress at winning back her own people, but it still felt good to be out in the wilderness with only Chase and Prios, searching for the underground lake.

"I'm tellin' ya," Chase said, "it's this way. I recognize that outcropping of trees." Already he'd been convinced three times, and all three times they were disappointed. Catrin found it hard to believe that someplace where they had spent so much time would be so difficult to find, but those memories, too, had begun to fade. Prios just shrugged and followed Chase. He'd become more open lately, using the chalk and slate Uncle Jensen had given him to communicate with those who could not hear him in their minds. In some cases, he used the slate simply because hearing his voice was something not everyone was prepared for, and some people did not seem to understand his gestures and body language. The slate and chalk appeared to remove a barrier of fear that seemed to keep many from becoming close to him. Now he seemed to enjoy using it for fun, as if it had become a game for him.

Chase stopped and turned when Prios tapped him on the shoulder. Prios held up his slate. *Hungry*, it read, and Chase laughed. Prios had written the word hours ago, and at regular intervals tapped him on the shoulder, showing him the same word. From his pack, Chase produced three of the pepper sausages he knew Prios wanted. Since the first time he'd tried one, he'd wanted little else. Prios smiled and accepted the sausage. Chase shook his head and put the other two back. He tossed Catrin an apple, and he nibbled on some cheese, saving the sausages for the next time Prios held up his slate.

Satisfied, they continued their search, and Catrin started looking higher, trying to find the peaks she remembered to orient herself by them. It was not something she was skilled at, but the direction she guessed was the same as the path Chase chose next, and she moved with renewed confidence. "Look!" she said as they moved past a pile of large rocks overgrown with bushes.

Up above rested the rotting remains of the screen Chase had once made to hide the light of their fire. Seeing the place brought back feelings of fear and anxiety, but there were also good memories. Catrin climbed without regret and felt the same sense of awe when she entered the man-made passage. Piles of walnuts still lay where they had been left. Much of the food was gone, and the shelves were overturned, most likely raided by scavengers.

Chase found a salted perch that was nearly whole. "I wonder if it's still good," he mused, holding it up as if he were about to eat it. Prios wrinkled his nose and shook his head; then he smiled and pointed at Chase's pack. Chase laughed and produced another pepper sausage.

Catrin looked beyond the remains of their camp and used her imagination. She pictured all the openings cleared and repaired and boats floating across the hidden lake.

"Now that we've found it again," Chase said, "what will you do?"

"I'll prepare for the future," Catrin said. "I believe what Nat said, and even if he is wrong, what do we stand to lose? If we don't prepare, we stand to lose everything."

"You know I'll help in any way I can," Chase said, and Prios moved to her side.

He smiled and nodded. *I will help.*

"The first thing we need to do," Catrin said, "is make sure we can find this place again. Then we'll go back and talk to my dad and Uncle

Jensen. We'll figure something out."

* * *

As they walked back into Lowerton, Catrin saw a young boy running down the middle of the roadway, and she was struck by recognition.

"Elma!" he shouted as he ran, and Catrin laughed.

Prios squeezed her hand. *Elma?*

"It's a long story," she said.

"I tol' you I was gonna be a great adventurer some day, didn't I?" Jessub Tillerman said. "I sailed all the way to the Falcon Isles and then on t' the Godfist. Just like my dad!"

"Did your gramma and grampa come with you?" Catrin asked. Jessub was bigger and older than when she'd seen him last, and he seemed offended by her question.

"Yeah," he said. "A whole shipload o' people came from the Greatland. Most came t' see you, but I came t' see my dad!"

"Your father is a fine man," she said.

Jessub seemed to forget all about being insulted. "D'ya really have a dragon? What's 'is name? Where is he? Can I see him? Did he really pick ya up in his teeth? How come you didn't die?"

Catrin tried to answer his questions, but each answer spawned a dozen new questions, and she was exhausted by the time she reached the Watering Hole. Her father and a room full of people, some she recognized, some she didn't, waited within. Seeing Milo and Gustad made her smile, and she ran to embrace them.

Rolph and Collette Tillerman moved through the crowd to greet her. "When Martik said his skills were needed here, I knew we had t' come," Rolph said.

"I'm so glad t' see ya," Collette said, and she hugged Catrin.

A moment later, Brother Vaughn approached with a beautiful woman on his arm; they both smiled. "Catrin, this is Mirta Greenroot. You've never met her, but she received a gift from you. It was to Mirta that I sent the pyre-orchids you harvested."

"Thank you, Lady Catrin," Mirta said. Her genuine smile and the twinkle in her eyes endeared her to Catrin instantly. "So much sickness has been stopped because of your gift. I dried it and ground it to powder. Whenever sickness began to spread, I was able to save people and prevent further spreading. I sent powder to healers across the Greatland. Your efforts saved hundreds if not thousands. Now I bring pyre-orchid to your people, as a gift."

Tears filled Catrin's eyes, overjoyed to know that she may have actually saved more lives than she had taken away. It did not banish her remorse, but it did make her feel much better about herself. "Thank you, Mirta. It would seem you and Benjin deserve more credit than I. He insisted we harvest the flowers, and you made certain they did not go to waste. You have a generous heart. I thank you for coming so far to deliver your gift."

"I think I'd like to stay here," Mirta said, suddenly shy, and she looked up at Brother Vaughn.

"Be welcome, Mirta," Catrin said, and Brother Vaughn smiled. Wendel approached. "We found the cavern," she said to him.

"I knew you would," Wendel said. "Before you returned, I wasn't well enough to search for it myself, and no one could find it armed with only my description. With a lot of work, it could be a good, safe place. Many of these people have come here to help you. All you need to do is ask."

"You're right," Catrin said, overwhelmed by the responsibility and expectation. So much had happened in so short a time, she had difficulty gathering her thoughts. Remembering how Mother Gwendolin had used the viewing ceremony as a way to find clarity, Catrin wondered if she couldn't create her own ceremony.

She stood up on a chair to address the crowd. "I want to thank you all for coming . . . and for everything you've done along the way. A new day has come, and we must prepare for what lies ahead. I feel I have a purpose I must fulfill, but I must first grasp the true nature of that purpose. When I return, I will enlist the aid of all who are willing."

Chapter 20

The sum of our lives can be judged only by what we leave behind--our legacy.
--Fedicus Illiani, historian

* * *

Hiking along the wide trail that had been created to get the greatoaks to Lowerton, Catrin prepared herself for meditation. Pulling her layers of clothing tighter, she tried to clear her mind as much as she could, but she was easily distracted. Knowing Chase was following her didn't help. He'd made no mistakes, and she had no reason to believe he was really there except a strong feeling, but that was enough for her. The feeling of his presence was so strong, she kept expecting him to walk out of the trees.

When the trail opened into the meadow, Catrin was transformed, transported back to the first time she'd entered the hallowed grove. She saw the trees as they were then, and she could still feel their energy and that of the stone. Perhaps she had not utterly destroyed the grove after all; perhaps some energy remained, dormant . . . waiting.

As she approached the stumps and grisly remains, she winced, but the energy drew her on. A few mighty trunks still lay where they had fallen, as if waiting for some use to present itself. When she reached the center of the black stone, she realized it did not look as terrible as when she had seen it last. Wind and rain had cleaned away the powdery grit, and now the black stone, though pocked, had begun to regain some of its luster.

Sitting with a crater between her crossed legs, she dug the tip of her staff into the stone. Holding her staff in one hand and Koe in the other, she closed her eyes and relaxed. In her mind, she traveled to the grove of the past and located the visual representation of her center amid the mighty greatoaks. Suffused by the energy around her, Catrin could feel the trees. She could see them and touch them. To her, they were still real, still alive. As she leaned forward, she had the strange sensation of moving downward, as if her staff were sinking into the stone. She kept her eyes closed, not wanting to leave her state of consciousness.

Dryads peeked around each of the trees in her mind, and they sang to her. There were no words, only melodies, but they were rich and delicate, like the tinkling of a fine bell over the sound of pounding surf, backed by the whisper of the wind through leaves. Birds sang their varied songs, somehow in harmony with the dryads, as if nature itself were playing her a chorus.

A feeling of security enveloped her, and she was washed with the relief of tension she hadn't even known she'd been holding on to. No one could touch her here; no one could harm her. She was safe. It was not something she could tell herself; her body had to believe it before she could truly relax. The physical world vanished from her senses, supplanted by the world of energy and possibilities. For a time, Catrin simply bathed herself in its warmth. No concerns pulled at her focus, no worries drained her energy. Here, she was perfect.

Slowly she began to process her thoughts. As always, some were painful, others whimsical. She dealt with her feelings and emotions and was left with only questions of practicality. How would she convince people they needed to learn to live underground? History and Nat's visions agreed. There had already been times when man had to retreat within the land, and Catrin knew she must succeed.

Though she thought she had cleared her mind and dealt with all her worries, an ugly, gnawing fear rose to the surface: *Prios*. Already she had feelings for him, and she suspected he felt much the same, but she had promised herself. After using her powers to heal herself, she'd sworn she would never have children. How could she take away from Prios the ability to pass on his line? How could she ever explain to him? Would he understand?

Suddenly, her calm and relaxing place became a maelstrom of anxiety. Then something, which felt like being tucked in by one you love, washed over her and brought calm. Everything would be as it should. She now knew what she must do.

With a course charted, she felt the anxiety drain away as if it had never been. The decision put her in a receptive frame of mind, and images began to spring forth, seemingly from the nothingness.

She saw a great hall and an underground complex capable of supporting thousands. Instead of a spooky and forbidding place, she began to see it as a thriving microcosm, a miniature ecosystem tucked inside the safety of a mountain. No longer was the hidden lake little more than a curiosity to her; it was a place where they could stock fish. She pictured underground farms fed water and fertilizer from the lake. The vision of her new home gave her great pride, though she had yet to do the work. She would; she knew she would. Seeing it here, in this world of energy, was as good as it being, and it brought tears to her eyes.

Resolved, she felt herself relax even further, and it felt as if, once again, her staff sank lower into the stone. Deep, rhythmic breathing propelled her from one moment to the next, and finally her mind was quiet, free of conflict. The song of nature took on new layers of beauty as it rose to a thrilling crescendo, and Catrin let herself ride the enchanting melody.

The feeling she was being watched made her look about, and not far away, she saw the mental wall that separated her conscious and subconscious minds. Light streamed through the hole, which was now significantly larger, and for a moment Catrin became alarmed. Then from behind a mighty greatoak stepped what looked like a goddess in the flesh. She came, and Catrin gazed upon her own subconscious with awe.

"You are ready now."

"Who are you?" Catrin asked, terrified because she already knew the answer.

"I am you. I am Catrin. Perhaps, to avoid confusion, you would like to call me Elma?" her alternate self asked with a knowing smile.

Catrin's fear was overcome, finding humor and ease in its place. "All right, Elma. I have been afraid of you because I don't want to go insane or hurt anyone. And . . . there is something else . . ."

"I know," Elma said. "I cannot tell you what mysteries lie ahead, for I do not know, but I can assure you that I will do no harm. History does not always repeat its mistakes. If you do not trust life, then your line is condemned either way. Whether you choose to have children whose own children might die terrible deaths or if you decide the risk of passing on a deadly trait is too great, the result will be the same. Only if you give life an opportunity will there be a chance."

Elma's cold but practical logic penetrated Catrin's mind, and she came to see truth in it.

"You are ready now."

"Ready for what?"

"Shirlafawna gave you a gift. It was left in my keeping, and now I present it to you. You are ready."

"I remember Shirlafawna's gift," Catrin said, confused. "After I talked with her, I could see the other dryads."

Elma laughed. "That gift you gave yourself. You took a great risk when you chose to believe. Seeing the dryads was a reward you made for yourself."

Catrin sat in wonder, waiting with unbridled anticipation, as Elma approached. In her hands she held a globe of orange light that pulsed from within. Holding it to Catrin's forehead, Elma pressed with her delicate fingers, and the globe began to slide forward. Warmth and understanding flowed through Catrin. The globe entered her and became a part of her, albeit a part she was yet to comprehend. Her staff thrummed under her fingers, and a wave of power washed over her.

Invigorated and charged, Catrin felt as if she'd been made anew.

"We must prepare now," Elma said, and Catrin did not have to ask for what. Visions filled her mind, images of death and destruction for all mankind. "We cannot allow this to happen."

Catrin nodded, and as she did, Elma walked between the greatoaks and gradually faded until she could be seen no more. Slowly, Catrin's awareness of her physical body returned, and she opened her eyes only to find near complete darkness. Only the blush of the false dawn gave any hint of shape or form, but then the sun peeked above the mountains. Fingers of light caressed the land, and Catrin felt the warmth on her face. Around her the world sang of a new day, a new chance for life. When she focused closer, finally seeing the staff before her and a serpentine tail wrapped around her, she gasped.

Kyrien met her eyes as she craned her neck to see. His eyes sparkled with inner light and excitement, and he nudged her back to the staff. There, she found a treasure beyond any reckoning or expectation. Shirlafawna's gift was in the form of life. From the staff sprouted fresh, green growth, and under each voluminous leaf, was a tiny, golden acorn. Twenty-four in all, there were enough to replant the entire grove. Catrin's heart sang. The fates had been kind to her, allowing her the chance to undo one of her greatest mistakes.

In that moment she thought of Barabas. His last action had been to prevent her death. He had sacrificed his life so she could live, so she could behold the beauty of a new day. She remembered all her fallen friends, all those who had helped her despite the dangers and had paid the ultimate price. She remembered what they all had done, and she loved them for it.

Epilogue

At the center of the new grove, Nat stood, stupefied. Never had he imagined such a thing. In the center of the stone, Catrin's staff--the staff his family had guarded for generations--stood, embedded in the rock itself, and it bloomed. It produced no more acorns, only flowering buds of purple and blue, but it lived and grew! Shrouded by branches, leaves, and flowers, the shaft was barely visible. Nat had to get down on his knees and peer under the growth to see the shaft, and the steely gaze of the dragon met him, its gemmed eyes pulsing with an inner glow. Protruding from the heel, the wooden shaft looked more lustrous than ever, though it seemed no larger than he remembered it.

Evenly spaced, the new greatoaks grew, lean and straight. It would take thousands of years for the mighty leviathans to gain their predecessors' majesty, but the process had begun, and now it was a task only time could achieve. To know that some future generation would come here and see greatoaks that had sprung from the staff his father had given into his care all those years ago gave Nat an immense feeling of accomplishment along with gratitude to Catrin.

Neenya stood in awe of everything she witnessed on the Godfist. Nat had wanted to protect her from the rest of the world, to allow her to live her simpler life among the Gunata, but civilization encroached on the lands held by native peoples, and no longer were the Gunata innocent or ignorant. It was Neenya who convinced him to come back to the Godfist because she feared for his life. Now they were here, and he wondered what he could do. How next would unexpected events overturn his world?

* * *

"She's ready," Fasha said.

Benjin wasn't certain if she was referring to the *Dragon's Wing* or Gwen. At five years old, his daughter was a roaring terror wrapped in innocence. One look from her big, blue eyes melted his heart. He was helpless. Running his hands over the polished wood, he looked for imperfections, trying to decide if they needed another coat of sealer and a few more weeks of polishing before making their sea trials.

"She's ready," Fasha insisted.

Still, Benjin made one final inspection of the *Dragon's Wing*. Carved from a single greatoak, it was like no other ship on all of Godsland. While Fasha and Catrin had been pregnant, Benjin and Prios had worked, carving the masthead, which extended back along the sides of the ship. Modeled after Kyrien, the ship looked as if it were flying, even as it sat in dry dock.

For a moment, Benjin stopped to revel in his new life. Letting go of Catrin had been difficult, but he knew Prios would take good care of her. It was on their wedding day that Benjin's life forever changed. With tears in her eyes, Fasha had asked him to marry her. *She* asked *him*. He still couldn't believe it. For weeks, he'd been trying to find the words to ask her, all the while helping organize Prios and Catrin's wedding. He'd been afraid of somehow making Catrin's day less special and never found the right moment to ask. Fasha had chosen the moment, and he loved her for it.

Catrin's wedding day was filled with tears of joy, and the ceremony touched everyone who attended. Later, when Benjin was asked to speak, he could no longer contain his news, and though he was terrified, he announced his engagement to Fasha. The celebration that followed was one he would never forget.

The familiar sound of bare feet running across the deck alerted Benjin to a coming storm.

"Are we ready, Daddy? Can we go now? Momma says I'm going to love the sea. Can we go now, Daddy? Can we? *Please?*" The last question was punctuated by one of Gwen's most practiced and effective looks.

"Yes. We can go now." Benjin gave the order, and horses were brought in. Hooked to thick lines that ran through a massive pulley, the horses pulled.

Unlike ships built from many small pieces, the *Dragon* was a whole. She didn't creak or moan as she slipped along the guide planks. She entered the water with what sounded like a sigh of relief. In the water, she looked much different than Benjin had imagined. Her wingtips, though close and tight to the ship, soared just above the water line, making the ship look vulnerable where Benjin knew it was strong.

Using Brother Vaughn as his voice, Prios often joked that the carving they did made the wood stronger. As if they were peeling away the bits that were hiding its true form. Looking at it now, Benjin couldn't believe he'd been a part of creating it.

"Fasha, my wife," Benjin said as he wrapped her in his arms, "I love you, and I think you should be captain of this ship."

"I'll need a cook," she said, and they both laughed.

Gwen charged by at full speed. "Can we *leave* now?" she asked without slowing.

Together, Benjin and Fasha raised the sails and let the wind drive the *Dragon's Wing* for the first time. Without a sound, save for the flap of canvas, she sliced through the water.

"Wait!" a voice carried across the water. "Hey! Wait for me!"

A loud splash followed, and Benjin turned to look. Then he just shook his head and laughed. He'd forgotten that he promised Jessub he could come on the maiden voyage. Every few days, the boy would show up and check on their progress, and he must have known they were getting close. Now he swam toward them. Fasha slowed the ship as they waited for Jessub.

Benjin dropped the boarding net over the side, never having expected to use it so soon. "Up you go," he said as he pulled a soaked and exhausted Jessub aboard.

"You were gonna leave without me," Jessub accused.

"It's my fault," Fasha said as she threw Jessub a towel. "I convinced him to sail today. I should have told him to wait for you."

"Yes, ma'am," he said, and Benjin barely contained his laughter. For all his energy and bravado, Jessub feared Fasha's wrath more than anything, which, Benjin supposed, only showed that the boy had good sense.

"Come on, Jessub!" Gwen demanded as she led him to the prow. "Look! I'm flying," she said as she stuck her arms out to the sides. A moment later, she was bathed in shadow. Kyrien soared low over the prow, just above Gwen and Jessub.

"Wow," Jessub said, his jaw hanging slack.

"We're flying!" Gwen said.

Benjin watched in amazement, hoping the likeness would not offend Kyrien. Unlike the tales of dragon riders, Catrin had no control over Kyrien. He was a free creature, and he went only where he chose. It was a fact that Benjin knew bothered Catrin and terrified others, but there seemed no way to change the dragon. In truth, Benjin liked him just as he was.

As if to show his approval, Kyrien rested his chin on the carved image of his head and flew with his eyes closed, letting the motion of the ship guide him. Benjin watched in amazement. A moment later Kyrien trumpeted and tipped his wings. Soaring high into the sky, he disappeared from sight.

In deep water, Fasha raised more sail, and the *Dragon's Wing* flew across the water--free.

* * *

The Watering Hole bustled with activity, and Miss Mariss carried platters laden with food between the many crowded tables. Warm weather had blessed them with record crops, and finally their livestock were plentiful again. Children were born, and the towns of Lowerton and Upperton grew faster than anyone could have imagined. Martik's marvels of engineering made farming possible in otherwise impossible places, and it seemed starvation was no longer a threat.

One of the guests yelled for Miss Mariss and she turned. Prios stood near the doorway, his slate in hand. "Sinjin?" it said.

"That boy best not be in my kitchens again. He'll eat us all back into starvation," Miss Mariss said before she stormed into the kitchen. From behind a cutting block, a small hand reached up and grabbed three pieces of bacon. "You'd best get outta my kitchen, boy!"

With a guilty smile, he darted from the kitchen. Miss Mariss chased him out with a broom, but she was not fast enough to catch him. Prios stood shaking his head as Sinjin darted out the doors and ran down the streets, eating his bacon without slowing.

* * *

"Do you really think we're going to discover anything?" Strom asked Osbourne as they hauled more sand through the halls.

"Who knows?" Osbourne said. "Milo says if we look hard enough, we're bound to find something."

"All I know is we've been through at least fifty bags of sand already, and I'm getting tired of carrying them."

"Me too."

As they returned to the mighty hall where Catrin conducted her experiments, Milo pulled a crucible from the furnace and began to pour it into the mold. Strom watched as Catrin waited for the exact right moment to insert the sliver of dragon ore. She looked older, as if the weight of her responsibilities had aged her more quickly than the rest. Still there was strength about her . . . and determination. She never gave up on one of her ideas; at most one might be set aside for further contemplation.

Strom wondered what it was that made her so sure things were going to go badly in the future. Things were going so well, he thought perhaps they should all take some time to enjoy themselves. Instead he was hauling sand to the furnace. Osbourne gasped beside him and Strom watched. Each time she had tried, Catrin had produced a brilliant light that lasted only a few breaths, but this time, as the molten glass captured the charged sliver in its embrace, a warm, steady glow radiated from it. Even as it cooled, the light continued to shine. No one spoke for a long time until the glass was cool enough to touch.

Catrin picked it up in her hand and smiled. "Sometimes the smallest things can make the biggest difference."

The story continues in the *Balance of Power* trilogy.

About the Author

Born in Salem, New Jersey, Brian spent much of his childhood on the family farm, where his family raised and trained Standardbred racehorses. Brian lives with his wife, Tracey, in the foothills of the Blue Ridge Mountains. After years in the world of Internet technology, the writing of this trilogy has been a dream come true for Brian and what feels like a return to his roots.

More information at BrianRathbone.com

Printed in Great Britain
by Amazon